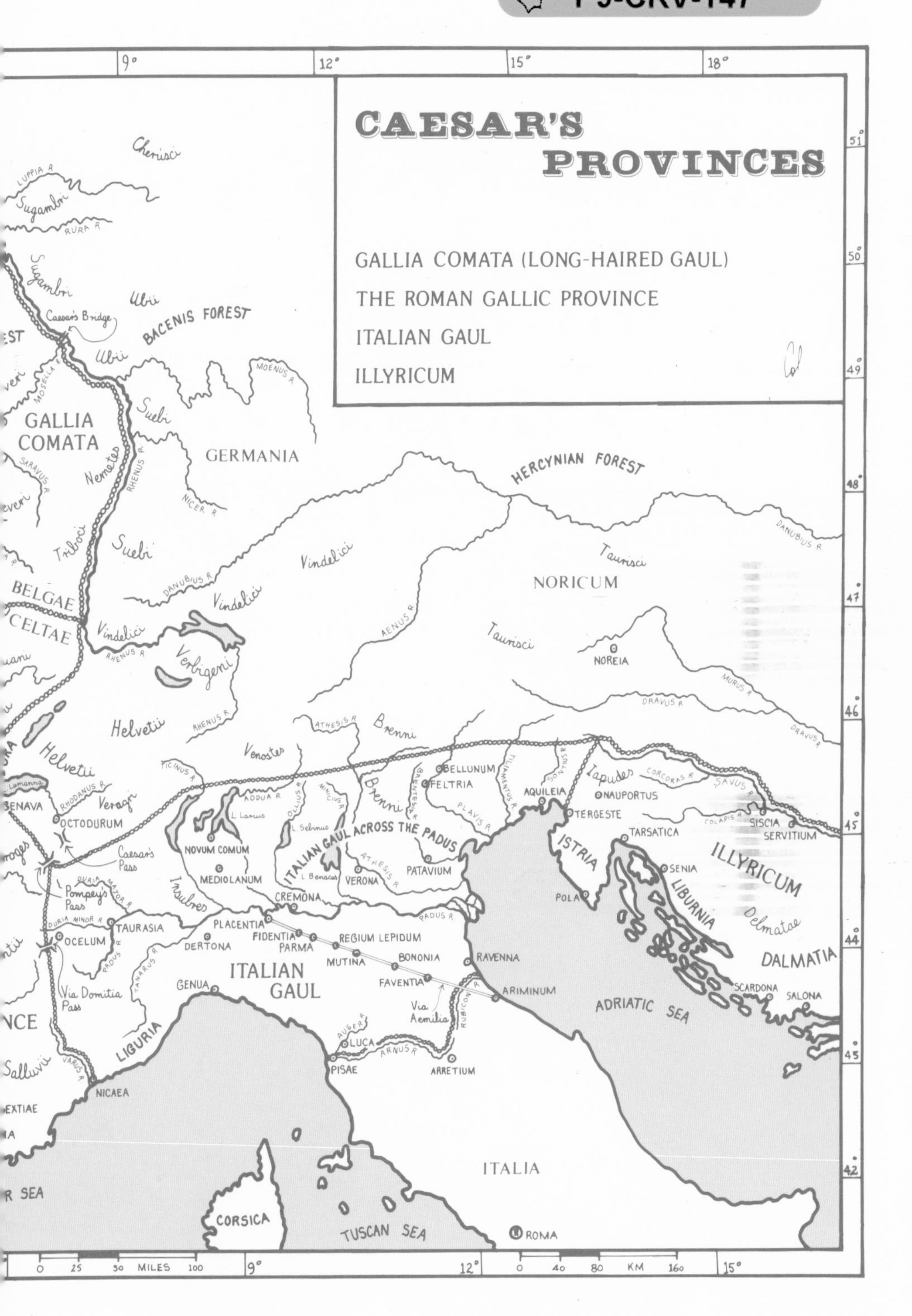
CAESAR'S
PROVINCES
GALLIA COMATA (LONG-HAIRED GAUL)
THE ROMAN GALLIC PROVINCE
ITALIAN GAUL
ILLYRICUM
9°
12°
15°
18°
51°
50°
49°
48°
47°
46°
45°
44°
43°
42°
Cherusci
LUPPIA R.
Sugambri
RURA R.
Sugambri
Ubii
Caesar's Bridge
BACENIS FOREST
Ubii
MOSELLA R.
MOENUS R.
GALLIA
COMATA
Suebi
GERMANIA
SARAVUS R.
Nemetes
RHENUS R.
NICER R.
HERCYNIAN FOREST
DANUBIUS R.
Triboci
Suebi
Vindelici
Taurisci
NORICUM
BELGAE
CELTAE
DANUBIUS R.
Vindelici
AENUS R.
Vindelici
RHENUS R.
Verbigeni
Taurisci
NOREIA
MURUS R.
DRAVUS R.
Helvetii
RHENUS R.
ATHESIS R.
Brenni
DRAVUS R.
Helvetii
Venostes
Lemanna
RHODANUS R.
Veragri
TICINUS R.
ADDUA R.
L. Larius
OLLIUS R.
MINCIUS R.
Brenni
BELLUNUM
FELTRIA
PLAVIS R.
TILIAMENTUS R.
SONTIUS R.
AQUILEIA
Iapudes
CORCORAS R.
NAUPORTUS
SAVUS R.
GENAVA
OCTODURUM
L. Sebinus
ITALIAN GAUL ACROSS THE PADUS
TERGESTE
COLAPIS R.
SISCIA
SERVITIUM
Caesar's Pass
NOVUM COMUM
L. Benacus
ATHESIS R.
PATAVIUM
ISTRIA
TARSATICA
ILLYRICUM
MEDIOLANUM
VERONA
SENIA
DURIA MAJOR R.
Pompey's Pass
Insubres
CREMONA
POLA
LIBURNIA
DURIA MINOR R.
TAURASIA
PLACENTIA
PADUS R.
Delmatae
OCELUM
FIDENTIA
PARMA
REGIUM LEPIDUM
DERTONA
PADUS R.
TANARUS R.
MUTINA
BONONIA
RAVENNA
DALMATIA
ITALIAN
GAUL
FAVENTIA
GENUA
Via Domitia Pass
ARIMINUM
Via Aemilia
RUBICON R.
ADRIATIC SEA
SCARDONA
SALONA
LIGURIA
AUSER R.
LUCA
ARNUS R.
Sallluvii
VARUS R.
PISAE
ARRETIUM
NICAEA
EXTIAE
ITALIA
R SEA
CORSICA
TUSCAN SEA
ROMA
0
25
50
MILES
100
9°
12°
0
40
80
KM
160
15°

CAESAR

Other books by Colleen McCullough

Tim
The Thorn Birds
An Indecent Obsession
A Creed for the Third Millennium
The Ladies of Missalonghi
The First Man in Rome
The Grass Crown
Fortune's Favorites
Caesar's Women

CAESAR

LET THE DICE FLY

Colleen McCullough

William Morrow and Company, Inc.
New York

It is the policy of William Morrow and Company, Inc., and its imprints and affiliates, recognizing the importance of preserving what has been written, to print the books we publish on acid-free paper, and we exert our best efforts to that end.

Library of Congress Cataloging-in-Publication Data

McCullough, Colleen, 1937–
Caesar : let the dice fly / Colleen McCullough.—1st ed.
p. cm.
ISBN 0-688-09372-8 (alk. paper)
1. Rome—History—Republic, 265–30 B.C.—Fiction. 2. Caesar, Julius—Fiction. I. Title.
PR9619.3.M32C27 1997 97-24391
823—dc21 CIP

Printed in the United States of America

First Edition

1 2 3 4 5 6 7 8 9 10

www.williammorrow.com

For Joseph Merlino.
Kind, wise, perceptive, ethical and moral.
A truly good man.

LIST OF MAPS AND ILLUSTRATIONS

MAPS

Caesar's Provinces *front endpapers*
Caesar in Britannia, 54 B.C., and in Belgic Gaul, 53 B.C. 35
Forum Romanum 145
Crassus in the East 187
Route of Caesar and the Fifteenth Legion 223
Caesar and Vercingetorix: The Campaigns of 52 B.C. 238
Alesia 268
Italia in Respect to the Campaigns of 49 B.C. 442
Caesar in Spain, 49 B.C. 499
Macedonia, Epirus, Greece, Via Egnatia, Asia Province 529
Egypt 597
The Known East *back endpapers*

ILLUSTRATIONS

Gaius Julius Caesar 2
Quintus Tullius Cicero 32
Metellus Scipio 112
Vercingetorix 184
Avaricum 242
Titus Labienus 302
Gaius Scribonius Curio 340
Lucius Domitius Ahenobarbus 422
Pompey 492
Roman Magistrates 642

BRITANNIA

NOVEMBER of 54 B.C.

GAIUS JULIUS CAESAR

The orders were that while Caesar and the major part of his army were in Britannia, none but the most urgent communications were to be sent to him; even directives from the Senate had to wait in Portus Itius on the Gallic mainland until Caesar returned from his second expedition to the island at the western end of the world, a place almost as mysterious as Serica.

But this was a letter from Pompey the Great, who was the First Man in Rome—and Caesar's son-in-law. So when Gaius Trebatius in Caesar's office of Roman communications took delivery of the little red leather cylinder bearing Pompey's seal, he did not post it in one of the pigeonholes to wait for that return from Britannia. Instead he sighed and got to his feet, plump and taut like his ankles because he spent the vastest part of his life sitting or eating. He went through the door and out into the settlement which had been thrown up upon the bones of last year's army camp, a smaller compound. Not a pretty place! Rows and rows and rows of wooden houses, well-packed earthen streets, even the occasional shop or two. Treeless, straight, regimented.

Now if this were only Rome, he thought, commencing the long traipse of the Via Principalis, I could hail me a sedan chair and be carried in comfort. But there were no sedan chairs in Caesar's camps, so Gaius Trebatius, hugely promising young lawyer, walked. Hating it and the system which said that he could do more for his burgeoning career by working for a soldier in the field than he could by strolling—or sedan-chairing—around the Forum Romanum. He didn't even dare depute a more junior someone else to do this errand. Caesar was a stickler for a man's doing his own dirty work if there was the remotest chance that delegation might lead to a stuff-up, to use crude army vernacular.

Oh, bother! Bother, bother! Almost Trebatius turned to go back, then tucked his left hand among the folds of toga arranged on his left shoulder, looked important, and waddled on. Titus Labienus, the reins of a patient horse looped through the crook of one elbow, lounged up against the wall of his house, talking to some hulking Gaul hung with gold and blazing colors. Litaviccus, the recently appointed leader of the Aedui cavalry. The pair of them were probably still deploring the fate of the last leader of the Aedui cavalry, who had fled rather than be dragged across those heaving waters to Britannia. And had been cut down by Titus Labienus for his pains. Some weird and wonderful name—what was it? Dumnorix. Dumnorix . . . Why did he think that name was connected with a scandal involving Caesar and a woman? He hadn't been in Gaul long enough to get it all sorted out in his mind, that was the trouble.

Typical Labienus, to prefer talking to a Gaul. What a true barbarian the man was! No Roman he. Tight, curly black hair. Dark skin with big, oily pores. Fierce yet cold black eyes. And a nose like a Semite's, hooked, with nostrils that looked as if someone had enlarged them with a knife. An eagle. Labienus was an eagle. He belonged under the standards.

"Walking some of the fat off, Trebatius?" the barbarian Roman asked, grinning to show teeth as big as his horse's.

"Down to the dock," said Trebatius with dignity.

"Why?"

Trebatius itched to inform Labienus that it was none of his business, but he gave a sick smile and answered; Labienus was, after all, the general in the absence of the General. "I'm hoping to catch the nail pinnace. A letter for Caesar."

"Who from?"

The Gaul Litaviccus was following the conversation, bright-eyed. He spoke Latin, then. Not unusual among the Aedui. They'd been under Rome for generations.

"Gnaeus Pompeius Magnus."

"Ah!" Labienus hawked and spat, a habit he'd picked up from too many years hobnobbing with Gauls. Disgusting.

But he lost interest the moment Pompey's name was said, turned back to Litaviccus with a shrug. Oh, of course! It had been Labienus who trifled with Pompey's then wife, Mucia Tertia. Or so Cicero swore, giggling. But she hadn't married Labienus after the divorce. Not good enough. She'd married young Scaurus. At least he had been young at the time.

Breathing hard, Trebatius walked on until he emerged from the camp gate at the far end of the Via Principalis and entered the village of Portus Itius. A grand name for a fishing village. Who knew what name it had among the Morini, the Gauls in whose territory it lay? Caesar had simply entered it in the army's books as Journey's End—or Journey's Beginning. Take your pick.

The sweat was rolling down his back, soaking into the fine wool of his tunic; he had been told that the weather in Further Gaul of the Longhairs was cool and clement, but not this year! Extremely hot, the air laden with moisture. So Portus Itius stank of fish. And Gauls. He hated them. He hated this work. And if he didn't quite hate Caesar, he had come very close to hating Cicero, who had used his influence to obtain this hotly contested posting for his dear friend, the hugely promising young lawyer Gaius Trebatius Testa.

Portus Itius didn't look like any of those delightful little fishing villages along the shores of the Tuscan Sea, with their shady vines outside the wine shops, and an air of having been there since King Aeneas had leaped down from his Trojan ship a millennium before. The songs, the laughter, the *intimacy.* Whereas here was all wind and blowing sand, strappy grasses plastered against the dunes, the thin wild keening of a thousand thousand gulls.

But there, still tied up, was the sleek oared pinnace he had hoped to catch before it put out, its Roman crew busy loading the last of a dozen kegs of nails, all it was carrying—or, at its size, could hope to carry.

When it came to Britannia, Caesar's fabled luck seemed permanently out; for the second year in a row his ships had been wrecked in a gale more terrible than any gale which blew down the length and breadth of Our Sea. Oh, and this time Caesar had been so sure he had positioned those eight hundred ships in complete safety! But the winds and the tides—what could one do with alien phenomena like *tides*?—had come along and picked them up and thrown them about like toys. Broken. Still, they belonged to Caesar. Who didn't rant and rave and call down curses on all winds and tides. Instead, he proceeded to gather up the pieces and put the ships back together again. Hence the nails. Millions of them. No time or personnel for sophisticated shipwrights' work; the army had to be back in Gaul before winter.

"Nail 'em!" said Caesar. "All they have to do is make it across thirty-odd miles of Oceanus Atlanticus. Then they can sink, for all I care."

Handy for the office of Roman communications, the pinnace which rowed back and forth between Portus Itius and Britannia with a dozen kegs of nails going out and messages going in.

And to think I might have been over there! said Trebatius to himself, shivering despite the heat, the humidity, and the weight of a toga. Needing a good paper man, Caesar had put him down for the expedition. But at the last moment Aulus Hirtius had taken a fancy to go, all the Gods look after him forever! Portus Itius might be Journey's End for Gaius Trebatius, but better that than Journey's Beginning.

Today they had a passenger; as he and Trogus had organized it (in the colossal hurry Caesar always demanded), Trebatius knew who the Gaul was—or Briton, rather. Mandubracius, King of the Britannic Trinobantes, whom Caesar was returning to his people in return for their assistance. A blue Belgic, quite horrific. His gear was checked in mossy greens and shadowy blues, into which his skin, painted in a complex pattern with rich blue woad, seemed to merge. They did it in Britannia, so Caesar said, to blend into their interminable forests; you could be scant feet from one and never see him. And to frighten each other in battle.

Trebatius handed the little red cylinder to the—captain? was that the correct term?—and turned to walk back to the office. Thinking, with a sudden rush of saliva, of the roast goose he was going to have for his dinner. There wasn't much one could say in favor of the Morini, except that their geese were the best in the whole wide world. Not only did the Morini stuff snails, slugs and bread down their throats, they made the poor creatures walk—oh, walking!—until their flesh was so tender it melted in the mouth.

The pinnace oarsmen, eight to a side, rowed tirelessly in a perfect unison, though no *hortator* gave them the stroke. Each hour they rested and took a drink of water, then bent their backs again, feet propped against ridges in the boat's sloshing bottom. Their captain sat in the stern with the rudder oar and a bailing bucket, his attention expertly divided between the two.

As the soaring, striking white cliffs of Britannia came closer, King Mandubracius, stiffly and proudly sitting in the bow, grew stiffer and prouder. He was going home, though he had been no further from it than the Belgic citadel of Samarobriva, where, like many other hostages, he had been detained until Caesar decided where to send him for safekeeping.

The Roman expeditionary force to Britannia had taken over a very long, sandy beach which at its back dwindled into the Cantii marshes; the battered ships—so *many*!—lay behind the sand, propped up on struts and surrounded by all the incredible defenses of a Roman field camp. Ditches, walls, palisades, breastworks, towers, redoubts that seemed to go on for miles.

The camp commander, Quintus Atrius, was waiting to take charge of the nails, the little red cylinder from Pompey, and King Mandubracius. There were still several hours of daylight left; the chariot of the sun was much slower in this part of the world than in Italia. Some Trinobantes were waiting, overjoyed to see their king, slapping him on the back and kissing him on the mouth, as was their custom. He and the little red cylinder from Pompey would start out at once, for it would take several days to reach Caesar. The horses were brought; the Trinobantes and a Roman prefect of cavalry mounted and rode off through the north gate, where five hundred Aeduan horse troopers swung to enclose them in the midst of a column five horses wide and a hundred long. The prefect kicked his mount to the column's front, leaving the King and his noblemen free to talk among themselves.

"You can't be sure they don't speak something close enough to our tongue to understand," said Mandubracius, sniffing the hot damp air with relish. It smelled of *home.*

"Caesar and Trogus do, but surely not the others," said his cousin Trinobellunus.

"You can't be sure," the King repeated. "They've been in Gaul now for almost five years, and for most of that among the Belgae. They have women."

"Whores! Camp followers!"

"Women are women. They talk endlessly, and the words sink in."

The great forest of oak and beech which lay to the north of the Cantii marshes closed in until the rutted track over which the cavalry column rode grew dim in the distance; the Aedui troopers tensed, cocked their lances, patted their sabers, swung their small circular shields around. But then came a great clearing stubbled with the relics of wheat, the charred black bones of two or three houses standing stark against that tawny background.

"Did the Romans get the grain?" Mandubracius asked.

"In the lands of the Cantii, all of it."

"And Cassivellaunus?"

"He burned what he couldn't gather in. The Romans have been hungry north of the Tamesa."

"How have we fared?"

"We have enough. What the Romans took, they've paid for."

"Then we'd better see it's what Cassivellaunus has in store that they eat next."

Trinobellunus turned his head; in the long gold light of the clearing, the whorls and spirals of blue paint on his face and bare torso glowed eerily. "We gave our word that we'd help Caesar when we asked him to bring you back, but there is no honor in helping an enemy. We agreed among ourselves that it would be your decision, Mandubracius."

The King of the Trinobantes laughed. "We help Caesar, of course! There's a lot of Cassi land and Cassi cattle will come our way when Cassivellaunus goes down. We'll turn the Romans to good use."

The Roman prefect came back, horse dancing a little because the pace was easy and it was mettlesome. "Caesar left a good camp not far ahead," he said in slow Atrebatan Belgic.

Mandubracius raised his brows at his cousin. "What did I tell you?" he asked. And to the Roman, "Is it intact?"

"All intact between here and the Tamesa."

The Tamesa was the great river of Britannia, deep and wide and strong, but there was one place at the end of the tidal reaches where it could be forded. On its northern bank the lands of the Cassi began, but there were no Cassi to contest either the ford or the blackened fields beyond. Having crossed the Tamesa at dawn, the column rode on through rolling countryside where the hills were still tufted with groves of trees, but the lower land was either put to the plough or used for grazing. The column now bore east of north, and so, some forty miles from the river, came to the lands of the Trinobantes. Atop a good broad hill on the border between the Cassi and the Trinobantes stood Caesar's camp, the last bastion of Rome in an alien land.

Mandubracius had never seen the Great Man; he had been sent as hostage at Caesar's demand, but when he arrived at Samarobriva found that Caesar was in Italian Gaul across the Alps, an eternity away. Then Caesar had gone straight to Portus Itius, intending to sail at once. The summer had promised to be an unusually hot one, a good omen for crossing that treacherous strait. But things had not gone according to plan. The Treveri were making overtures to the Germans across the Rhenus, and the two Treveri magistrates, called vergobrets, were at loggerheads with each other. One, Cingetorix, thought it better to knuckle under to the dictates of Rome, whereas Indutiomarus thought a German-aided revolt just the solution with Caesar away in Britannia. Then Caesar himself had turned up with four legions in light marching order, moving as always faster than any Gaul could credit. The revolt never happened; the vergobrets were made to shake hands with each other; Caesar took more hostages, including the son of Indutiomarus, and then marched off back to Portus Itius and a minor gale out of the northwest that blew for twenty-five days without let. Dumnorix of the Aedui made trouble—and died for it—so, all in all, the Great Man was very crusty when his fleet finally set sail two months later than he had scheduled.

He was still crusty, as his legates well knew, but when he came to greet Mandubracius no one would have suspected it who did not come into contact with Caesar every day. Very tall for a Roman, he looked Mandubracius in the eye from the same height. But more slender, a very graceful man with the massive calf musculature all Romans seemed to own—it came of so much walking and marching, as the Romans always said. He wore a workmanlike leather cuirass and kilt of dangling leather straps, and was girt not with sword and dagger but with the scarlet sash of his high imperium ritually knotted and looped across the front of his cuirass. As fair as any Gaul! His pale gold hair was thin and combed forward from the crown, his brows equally pale, his skin weathered and creased to the color of old parchment. The mouth was full, sensuous and humorous, the nose long and bumpy. But all that one needed to know about Caesar, thought Mandubracius, was in his eyes: very pale blue ringed round with a thin band of jet, piercing. Not so much cold as omniscient. He knew, the King decided, exactly why aid would be forthcoming from the Trinobantes.

"I won't welcome you to your own country, Mandubracius," he said in good Atrebatan, "but I hope you will welcome me."

"Gladly, Gaius Julius."

At which the Great Man laughed, displaying good teeth. "No, just Caesar," he said. "Everyone knows me as Caesar."

And there was Commius suddenly at his side, grinning at Mandubracius, coming forward to whack him between the shoulder blades. But when Commius would have kissed his lips, Mandubracius turned his head just enough to deflect the salutation. Worm! Roman puppet! Caesar's pet dog. King of the Atrebates but traitor to Gaul. Busy rushing round doing Caesar's bidding: it had been Commius who recommended him as a suitable hostage, Commius who worked on all the Britannic kings to sow dissension and give Caesar his precious foothold.

The prefect of cavalry was there, holding out the little red leather cylinder which the captain of the pinnace had handled as reverently as if it had been a gift from the Roman Gods. "From Gaius Trebatius," he said, saluted and stepped back, never taking his eyes from Caesar's face.

By Dagda, how they love him! thought Mandubracius. It is true, what they say in Samarobriva. They would die for him. And he knows it, and he uses it. For he smiled at the prefect alone, and answered with the man's name. The prefect would treasure the memory, and tell his grandchildren if he lived to see them. But Commius didn't love Caesar, because no long-haired Gaul could love Caesar. The only man Commius loved was himself. What exactly was Commius after? A high kingship in Gaul the moment Caesar went back to Rome for good?

"We'll meet later to dine and talk, Mandubracius," said Caesar, lifted the little red cylinder in a farewell gesture, and walked away toward the stout leather tent standing on an artificial knoll within the camp, where the scarlet flag of the General fluttered at full mast.

The amenities inside the tent were little different from those to be found in a junior military tribune's quarters: some folding stools, several folding tables, a rack of pigeonholes for scrolls which could be disassembled in moments. At one table sat the General's private secretary, Gaius Faberius, head bent over a codex; Caesar had grown tired of having to occupy both his hands or a couple of paperweights to keep a scroll unfurled, and had taken to using single sheets of Fannian paper which he then directed be sewn along the left-hand side so that one flipped through the completed work, turning one sheet at a time. This he called a codex, swearing that more men would read what it contained than if it were unrolled. Then to make each sheet easier still to read, he divided it into three columns instead of writing clear across it. He had conceived it for his dispatches to the Senate, apostrophizing that body as a nest of semiliterate slugs, but slowly the convenient codex was coming to dominate all Caesar's paperwork. However, it had a grave disadvantage which negated its potential to replace the scroll: upon hard use the sheets tore free of the stitching and were easily lost.

At another table sat his loyalest client, Aulus Hirtius. Of humble birth but considerable ability, Hirtius had pinned himself firmly to Caesar's star. A small spry man, he combined a love for wading through mountains of paper with an equal love for combat and the exigencies of war. He ran Caesar's office of Roman communications, made sure that the General knew everything going on in Rome even when he was forty miles north of the Tamesa River at the far western end of the world.

Both men looked up when the General entered, though neither essayed a smile. The General was very crusty. Though not, it seemed, at this moment, for he smiled at both of them and brandished the little red leather cylinder.

"A letter from Pompeius," he said, going to the only truly beautiful piece of furniture in the room, the ivory curule chair of his high estate.

"You'll know everything in it," said Hirtius, smiling now.

"True," said Caesar, breaking the seal and prising the lid off, "but Pompeius has his own style, I enjoy his letters. He's not as brash and untutored as he used to be before he married my daughter, yet his style is still his own." He inserted two fingers into the cylinder and brought forth Pompey's scroll. "Ye Gods, it's long!" he exclaimed, then bent to pick up a tube of paper from the wooden floor. "No, there are two letters." He studied the outermost edges of both, grunted. "One written in Sextilis, one in September."

Down went September on the table next to his curule chair, but he didn't unroll Sextilis and begin to read; instead he lifted his chin and looked blindly through the tent flap, wide apart to admit plenty of light.

What am I doing here, contesting the possession of a few fields of wheat and some shaggy cattle with a blue-painted relic out of the verses of Homer? Who still rides into battle driven in a chariot with his mastiff dogs baying and his harper singing his praises?

Well, I know that. Because my *dignitas* dictated it, because last year this benighted place and its benighted people thought that they had driven Gaius Julius Caesar from their shores forever. Thought that they had beaten Caesar. I came back for no other reason than to show them that no one beats Caesar. And once I have wrung a submission and a treaty out of Cassivellaunus, I will quit this benighted place never to return. But they will remember me. I've given Cassivellaunus's harper something new to carol. The coming of Rome, the vanishing of the chariots into the fabled Druidic west. Just as I will remain in Gaul of the Long-hairs until every man in it acknowledges me—and Rome—as his master. For I *am* Rome. And that is something my son-in-law, who is six years older than I, will never be. Guard your gates well, good Pompeius Magnus. You won't be the First Man in Rome for much longer. Caesar is coming.

He sat, spine absolutely straight, right foot forward and left foot tucked beneath the X of the curule chair, and opened Pompey the Great's letter marked Sextilis.

> I hate to say it, Caesar, but there is still no sign of a curule election. Oh, Rome will continue to exist and even have a government of sorts, since we did manage to elect some tribunes of the plebs. What a circus that was! Cato got into the act. First he used his standing as a praetor member of the Plebs to block the plebeian elections, then he issued a stern warning in that braying voice of his that he was going to be scrutinizing every tablet a voter tossed into the baskets—and that if he found one candidate fiddling the results, he'd be prosecuting. Terrified the life out of the candidates!
>
> Of course all of this stemmed out of the pact my idiotic nevvy Memmius made with Ahenobarbus. Never in the bribery-ridden history of our consular elections have so many bribes been given and taken by so many people! Cicero jokes that the amount of money which has changed hands is so staggering that it's sent the interest rate soaring from four to eight percent. He's not far wrong, joke

though it is. I think Ahenobarbus, who is the consul supervising the elections—well, Appius Claudius can't; he's a patrician—thought that he could do as he liked. And what he likes is the idea of my nevvy Memmius and Domitius Calvinus as next year's consuls. All that lot—Ahenobarbus, Cato, Bibulus—are still snuffling round like dogs in a field of turds trying to find a reason why they can prosecute you and take your provinces and command off you. Easier if they own the consuls as well as some militant tribunes of the plebs.

Best to finish the Cato story off first, I suppose. Well, as time went on and it began to look more and more as if we'll have no consuls or praetors next year, it also became vital that at least we have the tribunes of the plebs. I mean, Rome can suffer through without the senior magistrates. As long as the Senate is there to control the purse strings and there are tribunes of the plebs to push the necessary laws through, who misses the consuls and praetors? Except when the consuls are you or me. *That* goes without saying.

In the end the candidates for the tribunate of the plebs went as a body to see Cato and begged that he withdraw his opposition. Honestly, Caesar, how does Cato get away with it? But they went further than mere begging. They made Cato an offer: each candidate would put up half a million sesterces (to be given to Cato to hold) if Cato would not only consent to the election's being held, but personally supervise it! If Cato found a man guilty of tampering with the electoral process, then he would fine that man the half-million. Very pleased with himself, Cato agreed. Though he was too clever to take their money. He made them give him legally precise promissory notes so they couldn't accuse him of embezzlement. Cunning, eh?

Polling day came at last, a mere three *nundinae* late, and there was Cato watching the activity like a hawk. You have to admit he has the nose to deserve that simile! He found one candidate at fault, ordered him to step down and pay up. Probably thinking that all of Rome would fall over in a swoon at the sight of so much incorruptibility. It didn't happen that way. The leaders of the Plebs are livid. They're saying it's both unconstitutional and intolerable that a praetor should set himself up not as the judge in his own court, but as an undesignated electoral officer.

Those stalwarts of the business world, the knights, hate the very mention of Cato's name, while Rome's seething hordes deem him crazy, between his semi-nudity and his perpetual hangover. After all, he's praetor in the *extortion* court! He's trying people senior enough to have governed a province—people like Scaurus, the present husband of my ex-wife! A patrician of the oldest stock! But what does Cato do? Drags Scaurus's trial out and out and out, too drunk to preside if the truth is known, and when he does turn up he has no shoes on, no tunic under his toga, and his eyeballs down on his cheeks. I understand that at the dawn of the Republic men didn't wear shoes or tunics, but it's news to me that those paragons of virtue pursued their Forum careers hung over.

I asked Publius Clodius to make Cato's life a misery, and Clodius did try. But in the end he gave up, came and told me that if I really wanted to get under Cato's skin, I'd have to bring Caesar back from Gaul.

Last April, shortly after Publius Clodius came home from his debt-collecting trip to Galatia, he bought Scaurus's house for *fourteen and a half million*! Real estate prices are as fanciful as a Vestal wondering what it would be like to do it. You can get half a million for a cupboard with a chamber pot. But Scaurus needed the money desperately. He's been poor ever since the games he threw when he was aedile—and when he tried to pop a bit in his purse from his province last year, he wound up in Cato's court. Where he is likely to be until Cato goes out of office, things go so slow in Cato's court.

On the other hand, Publius Clodius is oozing money. Of course he had to find another house, I do see that. When Cicero rebuilt, he built so tall that Publius Clodius lost his view. Some sort of revenge, eh? Mind you, Cicero's palace is a monument to bad taste. And to think he had the gall to liken the nice little villa I tacked onto the back of my theater complex to a dinghy behind a yacht!

What it does show is that Publius Clodius got his money out of Prince Brogitarus. Nothing beats collecting in person. It is such a relief these days not to be Clodius's target. I never thought I'd survive those years just after you left for Gaul, when Clodius and his street gangs ran me ragged. I hardly dared go out of my house. Though it was a mistake to employ Milo to run street gangs in opposition to Clodius. It gave Milo big ideas. Oh, I know he's an Annius—by adoption, anyway—but he's like his name, a burly oaf fit to lift anvils and not much else.

Do you know what he did? Came and asked me to back him when he runs for consul! "My dear Milo," I said, "I can't do that! It would be admitting that you and your street gangs worked for *me*!" He said he and his street gangs had worked for me, and what was the matter with that? I had to get quite gruff with him before he'd go away.

I'm glad Cicero got your man Vatinius off—how Cato as court president must have hated that! I do believe that Cato would go to Hades and lop off one of Cerberus's heads if he thought that would put you in the boiling soup. The odd thing about Vatinius's trial is that Cicero used to loathe him—oh, you should have heard the Great Advocate complain about owing you millions and having to defend your creatures! But as they huddled together during the trial, something happened. They ended up like two little girls who've just met at school and can't live without each other. A strange couple, but it's really rather nice to see them giggling together. They're both brilliantly witty, so they hone each other.

We're having the hottest summer here that anyone can remember, and no rain either. The farmers are in a bad way. And those selfish bastards at Interamna decided they'd dig a channel to drain the Veline lake into the river Nar and have the water to irrigate their fields. The trouble is that the Rosea Rura dried out the moment the Veline lake emptied—can you imagine it? Italia's richest grazing land utterly devastated! Old Axius of Reate came to see me and demanded that the Senate order the Interamnans to fill the channel up, so I'm going to take it to the House, and if necessary I'll have one of my tribunes of the plebs push it into law. I mean, you and I are both military men, so we understand the importance of the Rosea Rura to Rome's armies. What other place can breed such perfect mules—or so many of them? Drought's one thing, but the Rosea Rura is quite another. Rome needs mules. But Interamna is full of asses.

Now I come to a very peculiar thing. Catullus has just died.

Caesar emitted a muffled exclamation; Hirtius and Faberius both glanced at him, but when they saw the expression on his face their heads went back to their work immediately. When the mist cleared from before his eyes, he went back to the letter.

There's probably word of it from his father waiting for you back in Portus Itius, but I thought you'd like to know. I don't think Catullus was the same after Clodia threw him over—what did Cicero call her at Caelius's trial? "The Medea of the Palatine." Not bad. Yet I like "the Bargain-Priced Clytemnestra" better. I wonder did she kill Celer in his bath? That's what they all say.

I know you were furious when Catullus began writing those wickedly apt lampoons about you after you appointed Mamurra as your new *praefectus fabrum*—even Julia allowed herself a giggle or two when she read them, and you have no loyaler adherent than Julia. She said that what Catullus couldn't forgive you was that you had elevated a very bad poet above his station. And that Catullus's term as a sort of a legate with my nevvy Memmius when he went out to govern Bithynia left his purse emptier than it had been before he set out dreaming of vast riches. Catullus ought to have asked me. I would have told him Memmius is tighter than a fish's anus. Whereas your most junior military tribunes are rewarded lavishly.

I know you dealt with the situation—when do you not? Lucky that his *tata* is such a good friend of yours, eh? He sent for Catullus,

Catullus came to Verona, *tata* said be nice to my friend Caesar, Catullus apologized, and then you charmed the toga off the poor young fellow. I don't know how you do that. Julia says it's inborn. Anyway, Catullus came back to Rome, and there were no more lampoons about Caesar. But Catullus had changed. I saw it for myself because Julia surrounds herself with all these poet and playwright people, and I must say they're good company. Had no fire left, seemed so tired and sad. He didn't commit suicide. He just went out like a lamp that's drunk all its oil.

Like a lamp that's drunk all its oil . . . The words on the paper were blurred again; Caesar had to wait until his unshed tears went away.

I ought not to have done it. He was so vulnerable, and I traded on that fact. He loved his father, and he was a good son. He obeyed. I thought I'd smoothed balm on the wound by having him to dinner and demonstrating not only the breadth of my knowledge of his work, but the depth of my literary appreciation for it. We had such a pleasant dinner. He was so formidably intelligent, and I love that. Yet I ought not to have done it. I killed his *animus,* his reason for being. Only how could I not? He left me no choice. Caesar can't be held up to ridicule, even by the finest poet in the history of Rome. He diminished my *dignitas,* my personal share of Roman glory. Because his work will last. Better he should never have mentioned me at all than to hold me up to public ridicule. And all for the sake of carrion like Mamurra. A shocking poet and a bad man. But he will make an excellent purveyor of supplies for my army, and Ventidius the muleteer will keep an eye on him.

The tears had gone; reason had asserted itself. He could resume his reading.

I wish I could say that Julia is well, but the truth is that she's poorly. I told her there was no need to have children—I have two fine sons by Mucia, and my girl by her is thriving married to Faustus Sulla. He's just entered the Senate—good young fellow. Doesn't remind me in the least of Sulla, though. That's probably a good thing.

But women do get these gnats in their minds about babies. So Julia's well on the way, about six months. Never been right since that awful miscarriage she had when I was running for consul. The dearest girl, my Julia! What a treasure you gave me, Caesar. I'll never cease to be grateful. And of course her health was really why I switched provinces with Crassus. I'd have had to go to Syria myself, whereas I can govern the Spains from Rome and Julia's side through legates. Afranius and Petreius are absolutely reliable, don't fart unless I tell them they can.

Speaking of my estimable consular colleague (though I do admit I got on a lot better with him during our second than our first consulship together), I wonder how Crassus is doing out there in Syria. I have heard that he pinched two thousand talents of gold from the great temple of the Jews in Hierosolyma. Oh, what can you do with a man whose nose can actually *smell* gold? I was in that great temple once. It terrified me. Not if it had held all the gold in the world would I have pinched as much as one sow of it.

The Jews have formally cursed him. *And* he was formally cursed right in the middle of the Capena Gate when he left Rome on the Ides of last November. By Ateius Capito, the tribune of the plebs. Capito sat down in Crassus's path and refused to move, chanting these hair-raising curses. I had to get my lictors to shift him. All I can say is that Crassus is storing up a mighty load of ill will. Nor am I convinced that he has any idea how much trouble a foe like the Parthians will give him. He still thinks a Parthian cataphract is the same as an Armenian cataphract. Though he's only ever seen a drawing of a cataphract. Man and horse both clad in chain mail from head to heels. Brrrr!

I saw your mother the other day. She came to dinner. What a wonderful woman! Not least because she's so sensible. Still ravishingly beautiful, though she told me she's past seventy now. Doesn't look a day over forty-five. Easy to tell where Julia gets her beauty from. Aurelia's worried about Julia too, and your mama's not usually the clucking kind. As you know.

Suddenly Caesar began to laugh. Hirtius and Faberius jumped, startled; it had been a long time since they'd heard their crusty General laugh so joyously.

"Oh, listen to this!" he cried, looking up from the scroll. "No one's sent you this item in a dispatch, Hirtius!"

He bent his head and began to read aloud, a minor miracle to his listeners, for Caesar was the only man either of them knew who could read the continuous squiggles on a piece of paper at first glance.

" 'And now,' " he said, voice trembling with mirth, " 'I have to tell you about Cato and Hortensius. Well, Hortensius isn't as young as he used to be, and he's gone a bit the way Lucullus did before he died. Too much exotic food, unwatered vintage wine and peculiar substances like Anatolian poppies and African mushrooms. Oh, we still put up with him in the courts, but he's a long way past his prime as an advocate. What would he be now? Pushing seventy? He came late to his praetorship and consulship by quite a few years, as I remember. Never forgave my postponing his consulship by yet another year when I became consul at the age of thirty-six.

" 'Anyway, he thought Cato's performance at the tribunician election was the greatest victory for the *mos maiorum* since Lucius Junius Brutus—why do we always forget Valerius?—had the honor of founding the Republic. So Hortensius toddled around to see Cato and asked to marry his daughter, Porcia. Lutatia had been dead for several years, he said, and he hadn't thought to marry again until he saw Cato dealing with the Plebs. That night after the election he had a dream, he said, in which Jupiter Optimus Maximus appeared to him and told him that he must ally himself with Marcus Cato through a marriage.

" 'Naturally Cato couldn't say yes, not after the fuss he created when I married Julia, aged seventeen. Porcia's not even that old. Besides which, Cato's always wanted his nevvy Brutus for her. I mean, Hortensius is rolling in wealth, but it can't compare to Brutus's fortune, now can it? So Cato said no, Hortensius couldn't marry Porcia. Hortensius then asked if he could marry one of the Domitias—how many ugly freckledy girls with hair like bonfires have Ahenobarbus and Cato's sister had? Two? Three? Four? Doesn't matter, because Cato said not a chance of that either.' "

Caesar looked up, eyes dancing.

"I don't know where this story is going, but I'm riveted," said Hirtius, grinning broadly.

"Nor do I yet," said Caesar, and went back to reading. " 'Hortensius tottered away supported by his slaves, a broken man. But the next day he was back, with a brilliant idea. Since he couldn't marry Porcia or one of the Domitias, he said, could he marry Cato's wife?' "

Hirtius gasped. "*Marcia?* Philippus's daughter?"

"That is who Cato's married to," said Caesar solemnly.

"Your niece is married to Philippus, isn't she? Atia?"

"Yes. Philippus was great friends with Atia's first husband, Gaius Octavius. So after the mourning period was over, he married her. Since she came with a stepdaughter as well as a daughter and a son of her own, I imagine Philippus was happy to part with Marcia. He said he gave her to Cato so he'd have a foot in both my camp and the camp of the *boni*," said Caesar, wiping his eyes.

"Read on," said Hirtius. "I can't wait."

Caesar read on. " 'And Cato said YES! Honestly, Caesar, Cato said yes! He agreed to divorce Marcia and allow her to marry Hortensius—provided, that is, that Philippus said yes too. Off the pair of them went to Philippus's house to ask him if he'd consent to Cato's divorcing his daughter so she could marry Quintus Hortensius and make an old man happy. Philippus scratched his chin and said YES! Provided, that is, that Cato was willing personally to give the bride away! It was all done as quick as you can say a phrase like "many millions of sesterces." Cato divorced Marcia and personally gave her to Hortensius at the wedding ceremony. The whole of Rome is flat on the floor! I mean, things happen every day that are so bizarre you know they have to be true, but the Cato-Marcia-Hortensius-Philippus affair is unique in the annals of Roman scandal, you have to admit that. Everybody—including me!—thinks Hortensius paid Cato and Philippus half of his fortune, though Cato and Philippus are denying it vigorously.' "

Caesar put the scroll on his lap and wiped his eyes again, shaking his head.

"Poor Marcia," said Faberius softly.

The other two looked at him, astonished.

"I never thought of that," said Caesar.

"She might be a shrew," said Hirtius.

"No, I don't think she is," Caesar said, frowning. "I've seen her, though not since she came of age. Near enough to it, thirteen or fourteen. Very dark, like all that family, but very pretty. A sweet little thing, according to Julia and my mother. Quite besotted with Cato—and he with her, so Philippus wrote at the time. Around about the moment I was sitting in Luca with Pompeius and Marcus Crassus, organizing the preservation of my command and my provinces. She'd been betrothed to a Cornelius Lentulus, but the fellow died. Then Cato came back from annexing Cyprus with two thousand chests of gold and silver, and Philippus—who was consul that year—had him to dinner. Marcia and Cato took one look at each other and that was that. Cato asked for her, which caused a bit of a family ruction. Atia was horrified at the idea, but Philippus thought it might be smart to sit on the fence—married to my niece, father-in-law of my greatest enemy." Caesar shrugged. "Philippus won."

"Cato and Marcia went sour, then," said Hirtius.

"No, apparently not. That's why all of Rome is flat on the floor, to use Pompeius's phrase."

"Then *why*?" asked Faberius.

Caesar grinned, but it was not a pleasant thing to see. "If I know my Cato—and I think I do—I'd say he couldn't bear to be happy, and deemed his passion for Marcia a weakness."

"Poor Cato!" said Faberius.

"Humph!" said Caesar, and returned to Sextilis.

> And that, Caesar, is all for the moment. I was very sorry to hear that Quintus Laberius Durus was killed almost as soon as he landed in Britannia. What superb dispatches you send us!

He put Sextilis on the table and picked up September, a smaller scroll. Opening it, he frowned; some of the words were smeared and stained, as if water had been spilled on them before the ink had settled comfortably into the papyrus.

The atmosphere in the room changed, as if the late sun, still shining brilliantly outside, had suddenly gone in. Hirtius looked up, his flesh crawling; Faberius began to shiver.

Caesar's head was still bent over Pompey's second letter, but all of him was immensely still, frozen; the eyes, which neither man could see, were frozen too—they would both have sworn to it.

"Leave me," said Caesar in a normal voice.

Without a word Hirtius and Faberius got up and slipped out of the tent, their pens, dribbling ink, abandoned on their papers.

> Oh, Caesar, how can I bear it? Julia is dead. My wonderful, beautiful, sweet little girl is dead. Dead at the age of twenty-two. I closed her eyes and put the coins on them; I put the gold denarius between her lips to make sure she had the best seat in Charon's ferry.
>
> She died trying to bear me a son. Just seven months gone, and no warning of what was to come. Except that she had been poorly. Never complained, but I could tell. Then she went into labor and produced the child. A boy who lived for two days, so he outlived his mother. She bled to death. Nothing stopped that flood. An awful way to go! Conscious almost until the last, just growing weaker and whiter, and she so fair to start with. Talking to me and to Aurelia, always talking. Remembering she hadn't done this, and making me promise I'd do that. Silly things, like hanging the fleabane up to dry, though that is still months away. Telling me over and over again how much she loved me, had loved me since she was a little girl. How happy I had made her. Not one moment of pain, she said. How could she say that, Caesar? I'd made the pain that killed her, that scrawny skinned-looking *thing*. But I'm glad he died. The world would never be ready for a man with your blood and mine in him. He would have crushed it like a cockroach.
>
> She haunts me. I weep, and weep, and still there are more tears. The last part of her to let go of life was her eyes, so huge and *blue*. Full of love. Oh, Caesar, how can I bear it? Six little years. I'm fifty-two in a few days, yet all I had of her was six little years. I'd planned that she'd let go of me. I didn't dream it would be the other way around, and so soon. Oh, it would have been too soon if we'd been married for twenty-six years! Oh, Caesar, the pain of it! I wish it had been me, but she made me swear a solemn oath that I'd not follow her. I'm doomed to live. But how? How can I live? I *remember* her! How she looked, how she sounded, how she smelled, how she felt, how she tasted. She rings inside me like a lyre.
>
> But this is no good. I can't see to write, and it's my place to tell you everything. I know they'll send this on to you in Britannia. I got your middle Cotta uncle's son, Marcus—he's a praetor this year—to call the Senate into session, and I asked the Conscript Fathers to vote my dead girl a State funeral. But that *mentula*, that *cunnus* Ahenobarbus wouldn't hear of it. With Cato neighing nays behind him on the curule dais. Women didn't have State funerals; to grant my Julia one would be to desecrate the State. They had to hold me back, I would

have killed that *verpa* Ahenobarbus with my bare hands if I could have laid them on him. They still twitch at the thought of wrapping themselves around his throat. It's said that the House never goes against the will of the senior consul, but the House did. The vote was almost unanimously for a State funeral.

She had the best of everything, Caesar. The undertakers did their job with love. Well, she was so beautiful, even drained to the color of chalk. So they tinted her skin and did those great masses of silvery hair in the high style she liked, with the jeweled comb I gave her on her twenty-second birthday. By the time she sat at her ease amid the black and gold cushions on her bier, she looked like a goddess. No need with my girl to shove her in the secret compartment below and put a dummy on display. I had her dressed in her favorite lavender blue, the same color she was wearing the first time I ever set eyes on her and thought she was Diana of the Night.

The parade of her ancestors was more imposing than any Roman man's. I had Corinna the mime in the leading chariot, wearing a mask of Julia's face—I had Venus in my temple of Venus Victrix at the top of my theater done with Julia's face. Corinna wore Venus's golden dress too. They were all there, from the first Julian consul to Quintus Marcius Rex and Cinna. Forty ancestral chariots, every horse as black as obsidian.

I was there, even though I'm not supposed to cross the *pomerium* into the city. I informed the lictors of the thirty Curiae that for this day I was assuming the special imperium of my grain duties, which did permit me to cross the sacred boundary before I accepted my provinces. I think Ahenobarbus was a frightened man. He didn't put any obstacle in my way.

What frightened him? The size of the crowds in the Forum. Caesar, I've never seen anything like it. Not for a funeral, even Sulla's. They came to gape at Sulla. But they came to weep for my Julia. Thousands upon thousands of them. Just ordinary people. Aurelia says it's because Julia grew up in the Subura, among them. They adored her then. And they still do. So many Jews! I didn't know Rome had them in such numbers. Unmistakable, with their long curled hair and their long curled beards. Of course you were good to them when you were consul. You grew up among them too, I know. Though Aurelia insists that they came to mourn Julia for her own sake.

I ended in asking Servius Sulpicius Rufus to give the eulogy from the rostra. I didn't know whom you would have preferred, but I wanted a really great speaker. Yet somehow I couldn't, when it came down to it, nerve myself to ask Cicero. Oh, he would have done it! For me if not for you. But I didn't think his heart would have been in it. He can never resist the chance to act. Whereas Servius is a sincere man, a patrician, and a better orator than Cicero when the subject's not politics or perfidy.

Not that it mattered. The eulogy was never given. Everything went exactly according to schedule from our house on the Carinae down into the Forum. The forty ancestral chariots were greeted with absolute awe; all you could hear was the sound of thousands weeping. Then when Julia on her bier came past the Regia into the open space of the lower Forum, everyone gasped, choked, began to *scream*. I've been less frightened at barbarian ululations on a battlefield than I was at those bloodcurdling screams. The crowd surged, rushed at the bier. No one could stop them. Ahenobarbus and some of the tribunes of the plebs tried, but they were shoved aside like leaves in a flood. The next thing, the people had carried the bier to the very center of the open space. They began piling up all kinds of things onto a pyre—their shoes, papers, bits of wood. The stuff kept coming from the back of the crowd overhead—I don't even know where they got it from.

They burned her right there in the Forum Romanum, with Ahenobarbus having an apoplectic fit on the Senate steps and Servius aghast on the rostra, where the actors had fled to huddle like barbarian women when they know that the legions are going to cut them down. There were empty chariots and bolting horses all over Rome, and the chief mourners had gotten no further than Vesta, where we stood helpless.

But that wasn't the end of it by any means. There were leaders of the Plebs in the crowd too, and they went to beard Ahenobarbus on the Senate steps. Julia, they said, was to have her ashes placed in a tomb on the Campus Martius, among the heroes. Cato was with Ahenobarbus. They defied this deputation. No, no! Women were never interred on the Campus Martius! Over their dead bodies would it happen! I really did think Ahenobarbus would have a stroke. But the crowd kept gathering until finally Ahenobarbus and Cato realized that it would be their dead bodies unless they yielded. They had to swear an oath.

So my dear little girl is to have a tomb on the sward of the Campus Martius among the heroes. I haven't been able to control my grief enough to set it in train, but I will. The most magnificent tomb there, you have my word on it. The worst of it is that the Senate has forbidden funeral games in her honor. No one trusts the crowd to behave.

I have done my duty. I have told it all. Your mother took it very hard, Caesar. I remember I said she didn't look a day over forty-five. But now she looks her full seventy years. The Vestal Virgins are caring for her—your little wife Calpurnia is too. She'll miss Julia.

They were good friends. Oh, here are the tears again. I have wept an ocean. My girl is gone forever. How can I bear it?

How can I bear it? The sheer shock left Caesar dry-eyed. *Julia?* How can I bear it?

How *can* I bear it? My one chick, my perfect pearl. I am not long turned forty-six, and my daughter is dead in childbirth. That was how her mother died, trying to bear me a son. What circles the world goes in! Oh, Mater, how can I face you when the time comes for me to return to Rome? How can I face the condolences, the trial of strength which must come after the death of a beloved child? They will all want to commiserate, and they will all be sincere. But how can I bear it? To turn upon them a gaze wounded to the quick, show them my pain—I cannot do it. My pain is *mine*. It belongs to no one else. No one else should see it. I haven't set eyes on my child for five years, and now I will never set eyes on her again. I can hardly remember what she looked like. Except that she never gave me the slightest pain or heartache. Well, that's what they say. Only the good die young. Only the perfect are never marred by age or soured by a long life. Oh, Julia! How *can* I bear it?

He got up from the curule chair, though he didn't feel the movement in his legs. Sextilis still lay on the table. September still lay in his hand. Through the flap of the tent, out into the disciplined busyness of a camp on the edge of nowhere at the end of all things. His face was serene, and his eyes when they met those belonging to Aulus Hirtius, loitering purposefully just beyond the flagpole, were Caesar's eyes. Cool rather than cold. Omniscient, as Mandubracius had observed.

"Everything all right, Caesar?" Hirtius asked, straightening.

Caesar smiled pleasantly. "Yes, Hirtius, everything is all right." He put his left hand up to shade his brow and looked toward the setting sun. "It's past dinnertime, and there's King Mandubracius to fete. We can't have these Britons thinking we're churlish hosts. Especially when we're serving them their food. Would you get things started? I'll be there soon."

He turned left to the open space of the camp forum adjoining his command tent, and there found a young legionary, obviously on punishment detail, raking the smoldering remains of a fire. When the soldier saw the General approaching he raked harder, vowed that never again would he be found at fault on parade. But he had never seen Caesar close up, so when the tall figure bore down on him, he paused for a moment to take a good look. Whereupon the General *smiled*!

"Don't put it out completely, lad; I need one live coal," Caesar said in the broad, slangy Latin of the ranker soldiers. "What did you do to earn this job in such stinking hot weather?"

"Didn't get the strap on my helmet fixed, General."

Caesar bent, a little scroll in his right hand, and held its corner against a smoking chunk of wood still faintly glowing. It caught; Caesar straightened and kept his fingers on the paper until the flames licked round them. Only when it disintegrated to airy black flakes did he let it go.

"Never neglect your gear, soldier; it's all that stands between you and a Cassi spear." He turned to walk back to the command tent, but threw over his shoulder, laughing, "No, not quite all, soldier! There are your valor and your Roman mind. They're what really win for you. However, a helmet firmly on your noddle does keep that Roman mind intact!"

Fire forgotten, the young legionary stared after the General with his jaw dropped. What a man! He'd talked as if to a *person*! So soft-spoken. And had all the jargon right. But he'd never served in the ranks, surely! How did he know? Grinning, the soldier finished raking furiously, then stamped on the ashes. The General knew, just as he knew the name of every centurion in his army. He was Caesar.

To a Briton, the main stronghold of Cassivellaunus and his tribe of Cassi was impregnable; it stood on a steep but gently rounded hill, and was encircled by great bulwarks of earth reinforced with logs. The Romans hadn't been able to find it because it stood in the midst of many miles of dense forest, but with Mandubracius and Trinobellunus as guides, Caesar's march to it was direct and swift.

He was clever, Cassivellaunus. After that first pitched battle—lost when the Aedui cavalry overcame their terror of the chariots and discovered they were easier to deal with than German horsemen—the King of the Cassi had adopted true Fabian tactics. He had dismissed his infantry and shadowed the Roman column with four thousand chariots, striking suddenly during some forest leg of the Roman march, chariots erupting from between the trees through spaces barely wide enough to permit their passage, and always attacking Caesar's foot soldiers, who hadn't been able to come to terms with their fear of these archaic weapons of war.

They were frightening, that was inarguable. The warrior stood to the right of his driver, one spear at the ready in his right hand and several more clenched in his left hand, his sword in a scabbard fixed to the short wicker wall by his right side, and he fought almost naked, curlicued from bare head to bare feet with woad. When his spears were gone he drew his sword and ran forward, nimble and fast as a tumbler, on the pole between the pair of little horses which drew the car, while the driver lashed the team into the midst of the Roman soldiers. The warrior then leaped from his superior height on the pole in among the flailing hooves, laying about him with impunity as the soldiers backed away to avoid the plunging horses.

But by the time Caesar took that last march to the Cassi stronghold, his dour and stoic troops were utterly fed up with Britannia, chariots and short rations. Not to mention the terrible heat. They were used to heat; they could march fifteen hundred miles in heat with no more than an occasional day off to rest, each man carrying his thirty-pound load on a forked stick balanced across his left shoulder, and under the weight of his knee-length chain mail shirt, which he cinched on his hips with his sword and dagger belt to ease its twenty pounds off his shoulders. What they were not used to was the saturation-point humidity; it had snailed them during this second expedition, so much so that Caesar had needed to revise his estimates of how far the men could go during a day's foot slogging. In ordinary Italian or Spanish heat, upward of thirty miles a day. In Britannic heat, twenty-five miles a day.

This day, however, was easier. With the Trinobantes and a small detachment of foot left behind to hold his field camp, his men could march free of impedimenta, helmets on their heads, *pila* in their own hands instead of on each octet's mule. As they entered the forest, they were ready. Caesar's orders had been specific: don't give an inch of ground, take the horses on your shields and have your *pila* aimed to plug the drivers straight through their blue-painted chests, then go for the warriors with your swords, boys.

To keep their spirits up, Caesar marched in the middle of the column himself. Mostly he could be found walking, preferring to mount his charger with the toes only when he required additional height to scan the distance. But he usually walked surrounded by his staff of legates and tribunes. Not today. Today he strode along beside Asicius, a junior centurion of the Tenth, joking with those ahead and behind who could hear.

The chariot attack, when it came, was upon the rear of the four-mile-long Roman column, just far enough in front of the Aedui rearguard to make it impossible for the cavalry to go forward; the road was narrow, the chariots everywhere. But this time the legionaries charged forward with their shields deflecting the horses, launched a volley of javelins at the drivers, then went for the warriors. They were fed up with Britannia, but they were not prepared to go back to Gaul without cutting down a few Cassi charioteers. And a Gallic longsword was no match for the short, upward-thrusting *gladius* of a Roman legionary when the enemy was at close quarters. The chariots drew off between the trees in disorder and did not appear again.

After that, the stronghold was easy.

"Like snitching a rattle off a baby!" said Asicius cheerfully to his general before they went into action.

Caesar mounted an attack simultaneously on opposite sides of the ramparts, which the legionaries took in their stride while the Aedui, whooping, rode up and over. The Cassi scattered in all directions, though many of them died. Caesar owned their citadel. Together with a great deal of food, enough to pay the Trinobantes back and feed his own men until they quit Britannia forever. But perhaps the greatest Cassi loss was their chariots, gathered inside unharnessed. The elated legionaries chopped them into small pieces and burned them on a great bonfire, while the Trinobantes who had come along made off joyously with the horses. Of other booty there was practically none; Britannia was not rich in gold or silver, and there were certainly no pearls. The plate was Arvernian pottery and the drinking vessels were made of horn.

Time to return to Gaul of the Long-hairs. The equinox was drawing near (the seasons were, as usual, well behind the calendar) and the battered Roman ships would not sustain the onslaught of those frightful equinoctial gales. Food supply secured, the Trinobantes left behind in possession of most of the Cassi lands and animals, Caesar put two of his four legions in front of the miles-long baggage train and two behind, then marched for his beach.

"What do you intend to do about Cassivellaunus?" asked Gaius Trebonius, plodding alongside the General; if the General walked, even his chief legate couldn't ride, worse luck.

"He'll be back to try again," said Caesar tranquilly. "I'll leave on time, but not without his submission and that treaty."

"You mean he'll try again on the march?"

"I doubt that. He lost too many men when his stronghold fell. Including a thousand chariot warriors. Plus all his chariots."

"The Trinobantes were quick to make off with the horses. They've profited mightily."

"That's why they helped us. Down today, up tomorrow."

He seemed the same, thought Trebonius, who loved him and worried about him. But he wasn't. What *had* that letter contained, the one he burned? They had all noticed a subtle difference; then Hirtius had told them of Pompey's letters. No one would have dared to read any correspondence Caesar elected not to hand over to Hirtius or Faberius, yet Caesar had gone to the trouble of burning Pompey's letter. As if burning his boats. Why?

Nor was that all. Caesar hadn't shaved. Highly significant in a man whose horror of body lice was so great that he plucked every hair of armpits, chest and groin, a man who would shave in the midst of total turmoil. You could see the scant hair on his head rise at the mere mention of vermin; he drove his servants mad by demanding that everything he wore be freshly laundered, no matter what the circumstances were. He wouldn't spend one night on an earthen floor because so often the earth contained fleas, for which reason in his personal baggage there were always sections of wooden flooring for his command tent. What fun his enemies in Rome had had with that item of information! The plain unvarnished wood had become marble and mosaic on some of those destructive tongues. Yet he would pick up a huge spider and laugh at its antics as it ran around his hand, something the most decorated centurion in the Tenth would have fainted at the thought of doing. They were, he would explain, *clean* creatures, respectable housekeepers. Cockroaches, on the other hand, would see him on top of a table, nor could he bear to soil the sole of his boot by crushing one. They were filthy creatures, he would say, shuddering.

Yet here he was, three days on the road, eleven days since that letter, and he had not shaved. Someone close to him was dead. He was in mourning. *Who?* Yes, they'd find out when they got back to Portus Itius, but what his silence said was that he would have no conversation about it, nor have it mentioned in his presence even after it became general knowledge. He and Hirtius both thought it must be Julia. Trebonius reminded himself to take that idiot Sabinus to one side and threaten him with circumcision if he offered the General his condolences—what had ever possessed the man to ask Caesar why he wasn't shaving?

"Quintus Laberius," Caesar had answered briefly.

No, it wasn't Quintus Laberius. It had to be Julia. Or perhaps his legendary mother, Aurelia. Though why would Pompey have been the one to write the news of that?

Quintus Cicero—who was, much to everyone's relief, a far less irksome fellow than his puffed-up-with-importance brother, the Great Advocate—thought it was Julia too.

"Only how is he going to hold Pompeius Magnus if it is?" Quintus Cicero had asked in the legates' mess tent over yet one more dinner to which Caesar hadn't come.

Trebonius (whose forebears were not even as illustrious as Quintus Cicero's) was a member of the Senate and therefore well acquainted with political alliances—including those cemented by a marriage—so he had understood Quintus Cicero's question at once. Caesar needed Pompey the Great, who was the First Man in Rome. The war in Gaul was far from over; Caesar thought that it might even take the full five years of his second command to finish the job. But there were so many senatorial wolves howling for his carcass that he perpetually walked a tightrope above a pit of fire. Trebonius, who loved him and worried about him, found it difficult to believe that any man could inspire the kind of hatred Caesar seemed to generate. That sanctimonious fart Cato had made a whole career out of trying to bring Caesar down, not to mention Caesar's colleague in his consulship, Marcus Calpurnius Bibulus, and that boar Lucius Domitius Ahenobarbus, and the great aristocrat Metellus Scipio, thick as a wooden temple beam.

They slavered after Pompey's hide too, but not with the strange and obsessive passion only Caesar seemed to fan in them. *Why?* Oh, they ought to go on campaign with the man, that would show them! You didn't doubt even in the darkest corner of your thoughts that things might go crashing when Caesar was in command. No matter how wrong they went, he could always find a way to go on. And a way to win.

"*Why* do they pick on him?" Trebonius had asked angrily.

"Simple," Hirtius had answered, grinning. "He's the Alexandrian lighthouse to their little oakum wick poking out of the end of Priapus's *mentula.* They pick on Pompeius Magnus because he's the First Man in Rome, and they don't believe there ought to be one. But Pompeius is a Picentine descended from a woodpecker. Whereas Caesar is a Roman descended from Venus and Romulus. All Romans worship their aristocrats, but some Romans prefer 'em to be like Metellus Scipio. Every time Cato and Bibulus and the rest of that lot look at Caesar, they see someone who's better than they are in every possible way. Just like Sulla. Caesar's got the birth and the ability to swat them like flies. They just want to get in first and swat him."

"He needs Pompeius," Trebonius had said thoughtfully.

"If he's to retain his imperium and his provinces," said Quintus Cicero, dipping his boring campaign bread into a dish of third-rate oil. "Ye Gods, I'll be glad to have some roast goose in Portus Itius!" he said then, closing the subject.

The roast goose looked imminent when the army reached its main camp behind that long, sandy beach. Unfortunately Cassivellaunus had other ideas. With what he had left of his own Cassi, he went the rounds of the Cantii and the Regni, the two tribes who lived south of the Tamesa, and marshaled another army. But attacking this camp was to break the Briton hand against a stone wall. The Briton horde, all on foot, bared naked chests to the defenders atop the fortifications and were picked off by javelins like so many targets lined up on a drill field. Nor had the Britons yet learned the lesson the Gauls had: when Caesar led his men out of the camp to fight hand to hand, the Britons stayed to be cut down. For they still adhered to their ancient traditions, which said that a man who left a field of defeat alive was an outcast. That tradition had cost the Belgae on the mainland fifty thousand wasted lives in one battle. Now the Belgae abandoned the field the moment defeat was imminent, and lived to fight again another day.

Cassivellaunus sued for peace, submitted, and signed the treaty Caesar demanded. Then handed over hostages. It was the end of November by the calendar, the beginning of autumn by the seasons.

The evacuation began, but after a personal inspection of each of some seven hundred ships, Caesar decided it would have to be in two parts.

"Something over half the fleet is in good condition," he said to Hirtius, Trebonius, Sabinus, Quintus Cicero and Atrius. "We'll put all the cavalry, all the baggage animals save for the century mules, and two of the legions on board that half, and send it to Portus Itius first. Then the ships can come back empty and pick up me and the last three legions."

With him he kept Trebonius and Atrius; the other legates were ordered to sail with the first fleet.

"I'm pleased and flattered to be asked to stay," Trebonius said, watching those three hundred and fifty ships pushed down into the water.

These were the vessels Caesar had ordered specially built along the Liger River and then sent out into the open ocean to do battle with the two hundred and twenty solid-oak sailing ships of the Veneti, who thought the Roman vessels ludicrous with their oars and their flimsy pine hulls, their low prows and poops. Toy boats for sailing on a bathtub sea, easy meat. But it hadn't worked out that way at all.

While Caesar and his land army picnicked atop the towering cliffs to the north of the mouth of the Liger and watched the action like spectators in the Circus Maximus, Caesar's ships produced the fangs Decimus Brutus and his engineers had grown during that frantic winter building the fleet. The leather sails of the Veneti vessels were so heavy and stout that the main shrouds were chain rather than rope; knowing this, Decimus Brutus had equipped each of his more than three hundred ships with a long pole to which were fixed a barbed hook and a set of grapples. A Roman ship would row in close to a Veneti ship and maneuver alongside, whereupon its crew would tilt their pole, tangle it among the Veneti shrouds, then sprint away under oar power. Down came the Veneti sails and masts, leaving the vessel helpless in the water. Three Roman ships would then surround it like terriers a deer, board it, kill the crew and set fire to it. When the wind fell, Decimus Brutus's victory became complete. Only twenty Veneti ships had escaped.

Now the specially low sides with which these ships had been built came in very handy. It wasn't possible to load animals as skittish as horses aboard before the ships were pushed into the water, but once they were afloat and held still in the water, long broad gangplanks connected each ship's side with the beach, and the horses were run up so quickly they had no time to take fright.

"Not bad without a dock," said Caesar, satisfied. "They'll be back tomorrow, then the rest of us can leave."

But tomorrow dawned in the teeth of a northwesterly gale which didn't disturb the waters off the beach very much, but did prevent the return of those three hundred and fifty sound ships.

"Oh, Trebonius, this land holds no luck for me!" cried the General on the fifth day of the gale, scratching the stubble on his face fiercely.

"We're the Greeks on the beach at Ilium," said Trebonius.

Which remark seemed to make up the General's mind; he turned cold pale eyes upon his legate. "I am no Agamemnon," he said through his teeth, "nor will I stay here for ten years!" He turned and shouted. "Atrius!"

Up ran his camp prefect, startled. "Yes, Caesar?"

"Will the nails hold in what we have left here?"

"Probably, in all except about forty."

"Then we'll use this northwest wind. Sound the bugles, Atrius. I want everyone and everything on board all but the about forty."

"They won't fit!" squeaked Atrius, aghast.

"We'll pack 'em in like salt fish in a barrel. If they puke all over each other, too bad. They can all go for a swim in full armor once we reach Portus Itius. We'll sail the moment the last man and the last ballista are aboard."

Atrius swallowed. "We may have to leave some of the heavy equipment behind," he said in a small voice.

Caesar raised his brows. "I am not leaving my artillery or my rams behind, nor am I leaving my tools behind, nor am I leaving one soldier behind, nor am I leaving one noncombatant behind, nor am I leaving one slave behind. If you can't fit them all in, Atrius, I will."

They were not hollow words, and Atrius knew it. He also knew that his career depended upon his doing something the General could and would do with complete efficiency and astonishing speed. Quintus Atrius protested no more, but went off instead to sound the bugles.

Trebonius was laughing.

"What's so funny?" asked Caesar coldly.

No, not the time to share this joke! Trebonius sobered in an instant. "Nothing, Caesar! Nothing at all."

The decision had been made about an hour after the sun came up; all day the troops and noncombatants labored, loading the stoutest ships with Caesar's precious artillery, tools, wagons and mules on the beach. The men waited until the ships were pushed into the choppy sea, doing the pushing themselves, then scrambled aboard up rope ladders. The normal load for one ship was a piece of artillery or some engineer's device, four mules, one wagon, forty soldiers and twenty oarsmen; but with eighteen thousand soldiers and noncombatants as well as four thousand assorted slaves and sailors, today's loads were much heavier.

"Isn't it amazing?" asked Trebonius of Atrius as the sun went down.

"What?" asked the camp prefect, knees trembling.

"He's happy. Oh, whatever grief he bears is still there, but he's happy. He's got something impossible to do."

"I wish he'd let them go as soon as they're loaded!"

"Not he! He came as a fleet and he'll go as a fleet. When all those highborn Gauls in Portus Itius see him sail in, they'll see a man in absolute command. Let the bulk of his army limp in a few ships at a time? Not he! And he's right, Atrius. We have to show the Gauls that we're better at *everything*." Trebonius looked up at the pinkening sky. "We'll have three-quarters of a waning moon tonight. He'll leave when he's ready, no matter what the hour."

A good prediction. At midnight Caesar's ship put out into the heaving blackness of a following sea, the lamps on its stern and mast twinkling beacons for the other ships to follow as they swung into a swelling teardrop behind him.

Caesar leaned on the stern rail atop the poop between the two professionals who guided the rudder oars, and watched the myriad firefly lights spreading across the impenetrable darkness of the ocean. *Vale* Britannia. I will not miss you. But what lies out there in the great beyond, where no man has ever sailed? This is no little sea; this is a mighty ocean. This where the great Neptune lives, not within the bowl of Our Sea. Maybe when I am old and I have done all that my blood and power demand, I shall take one of those solid-oak Veneti ships, hoist its leather sails and go into the West to follow the path of the sun. Romulus was lost in the ignobility of the Goat Swamps on the Campus Martius, yet when he didn't come home, they thought he had been taken into the realm of the Gods. But I will sail into the mists of forever, and they will know I have been taken into the realm of the Gods. My Julia is there. The people knew. They burned her in the Forum and placed her tomb among the heroes. But first I must do all that my blood and power demand.

Clouds scudded, but the moon shone well enough and the ships stayed together, so shoved along that the single linen-canvas sails were as swollen as a woman near her time, and the oars were hardly needed. The crossing took six hours; Caesar's ship sailed into Portus Itius with the dawn, the fleet still in formation behind him. His luck was back. Not one man, animal or piece of artillery became a sacrifice to Neptune.

GAUL OF THE LONG-HAIRS (GALLIA COMATA)

from DECEMBER of 54 B.C. until NOVEMBER of 53 B.C.

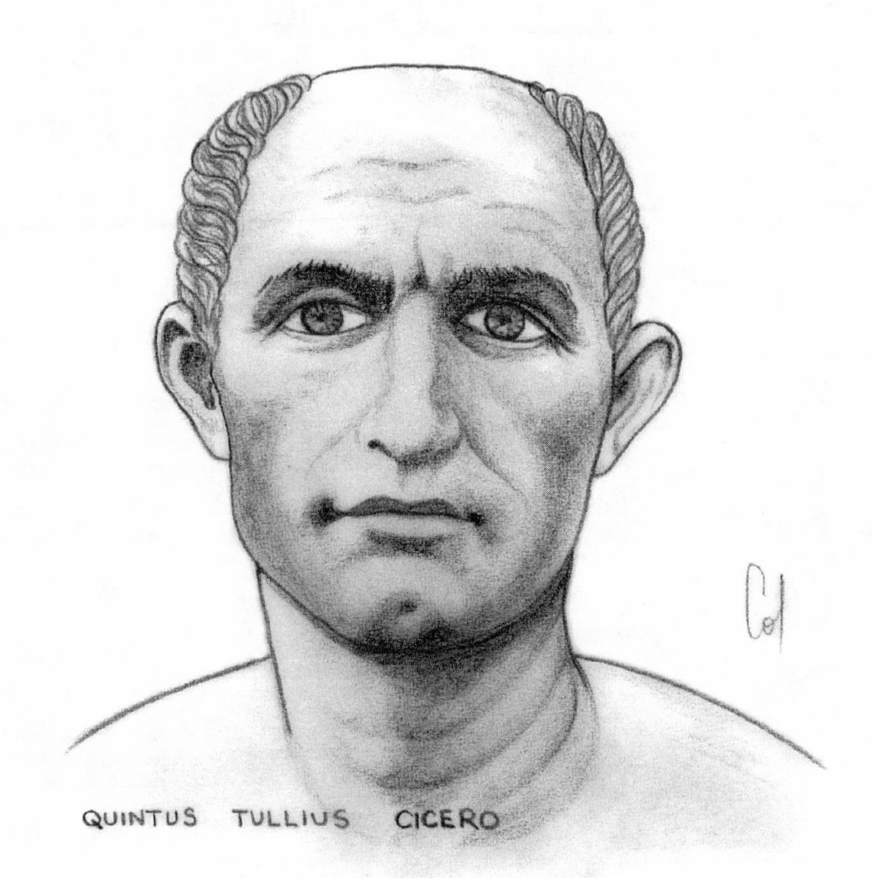
QUINTUS TULLIUS CICERO

"With all eight legions in Portus Itius, we'll run out of grain before the year is over," said Titus Labienus. "The commissioners haven't had much success finding it. There's plenty of salt pork, bacon, oil, sweet beet syrup and dried fruit, but the ground crops from wheat to chickpea are very scarce."

"Nor can we expect the troops to fight without bread." Caesar sighed. "The trouble with drought is that it tends to strike everywhere at once. I can't buy in grain or pulses from the Spains or Italian Gaul; they're suffering too." He shrugged. "Well, that leaves only one solution. Spread the legions out for the winter and offer to the Gods for a good harvest next year."

"Such a pity the fleet didn't stay in one piece," said Quintus Titurius Sabinus tactlessly. "I know we sweltered there, but Britannia had a bountiful harvest. We could have brought a lot of wheat back with us if only we'd had all the ships."

The rest of the legates shrank; keeping the fleet safe from harm was Caesar's responsibility, and though it had been wind, sea and tide which foiled him, it was not politic to make statements in council which Caesar might interpret as reproach or criticism. But Sabinus was lucky, probably because Caesar had deemed him a prating fool from the moment he had reported for duty. He received a glance of contempt, nothing more.

"One legion to garrison one area," the General went on.

"Except in the lands of the Atrebates," Commius volunteered eagerly. "We haven't been hit as hard as most places; we can feed two legions if you'll lend us some of your noncombatants to help us plough and sow in the spring."

"If," Sabinus butted in, voice loaded with irony, "you Gauls above the status of a serf didn't deem it beneath your dignity to man a plough, you wouldn't find large-scale farming so difficult. Why not put some of those hordes of useless Druids to it?"

"I haven't noticed the Roman First Class behind a plough in quite some time, Sabinus," the General said placidly, then smiled at Commius. "Good! That means Samarobriva can serve as our winter headquarters this year. But I won't give you Sabinus for company. I think . . . that . . . Sabinus can go to the lands of the Eburones—and take Cotta with him as exactly equal co-commander. He can have the Thirteenth, and set up house inside Atuatuca. It's a little the worse for wear, but Sabinus can fix it up, I'm sure."

Every head bent suddenly, every hand leaped to hide a smile; Caesar had just banished Sabinus to the worst billet in Gaul, in the company of a man he detested, and in "exactly equal" co-command of a legion of raw recruits which just happened to bear a calamitously unlucky number. A bit hard on poor Cotta (an Aurunculeius, not an Aurelius), but someone had to inherit Sabinus, and everyone save poor Cotta was relieved that Caesar hadn't chosen him.

The presence of King Commius offended men like Sabinus, of course; he couldn't understand why Caesar invited any Gaul, no matter how obsequious or trustworthy, to a council. Even if it was only about food and billets. Perhaps had Commius been a more likable or attractive person he might have been better tolerated; alas, he was neither likable nor attractive. In height he was short for a Belgic Gaul, sharp-featured of face, and oddly furtive in his manner. His sandy hair, stiff as a broom because (like all Gallic warriors) he washed it with lime dissolved in water, was drawn into a kind of horse's tail which stuck straight up in the air, and clashed with the vivid scarlet of his gaudily checkered shawl. Caesar's legates dismissed him as the kind of sycophant who always popped up where the important men were, without stopping to relate what they saw to the fact that he was the King of a very powerful and warlike Belgic people. The Belgae of the northwest had not abandoned their kings to elect annual vergobrets, yet Belgic kings could be challenged by any aristocrat among their people; it was a status decided by strength, not heredity. And Commius had been King of the Atrebates for a long time.

"Trebonius," said Caesar, "you'll winter with the Tenth and Twelfth in Samarobriva, and have custody of the baggage. Marcus Crassus, you'll camp fairly close to Samarobriva—about twenty-five miles away, on the border between the Bellovaci and the Ambiani. Take the Eighth. Fabius, you'll stay here in Portus Itius with the Seventh. Quintus Cicero, you and the Ninth will go to the Nervii. Roscius, you can enjoy some peace and quiet—I'm sending you and the Fifth Alauda down among the Esubii, just to let the Celtae know that I haven't forgotten they exist."

"You're expecting trouble among the Belgae," said Labienus, frowning. "I agree they've been too quiet. Do you want me to go to the Treveri as usual?"

"Not quite so far away as Treves. Among the Treveri but adjacent to the Remi. Take the cavalry as well as the Eleventh."

"Then I'll sit myself down on the Mosa near Virodunum. If the snow isn't ten feet deep, there'll be plenty of grazing."

Caesar rose to his feet, the signal for dismissal. He had called his legates together the moment he came ashore, which meant he wanted the eight legions at present encamped at Portus Itius shifted to their permanent winter quarters immediately. Even so, all the legates were now aware that it had been Julia who died. The news had been contained in many letters to those like Labienus who had not gone to Britannia. But no one said a word.

"You'll be nice and cozy," said Labienus to Trebonius as they walked away. The big horse's teeth showed. "Sabinus's stupidity staggers me! If he'd kept his mouth shut, *he'd* be cozy. Fancy spending the winter up there not so far from the mouth of the Mosa, with the wind shrieking, the sea flooding in, the hills rocks, the flat ground salt fen or peat marsh,

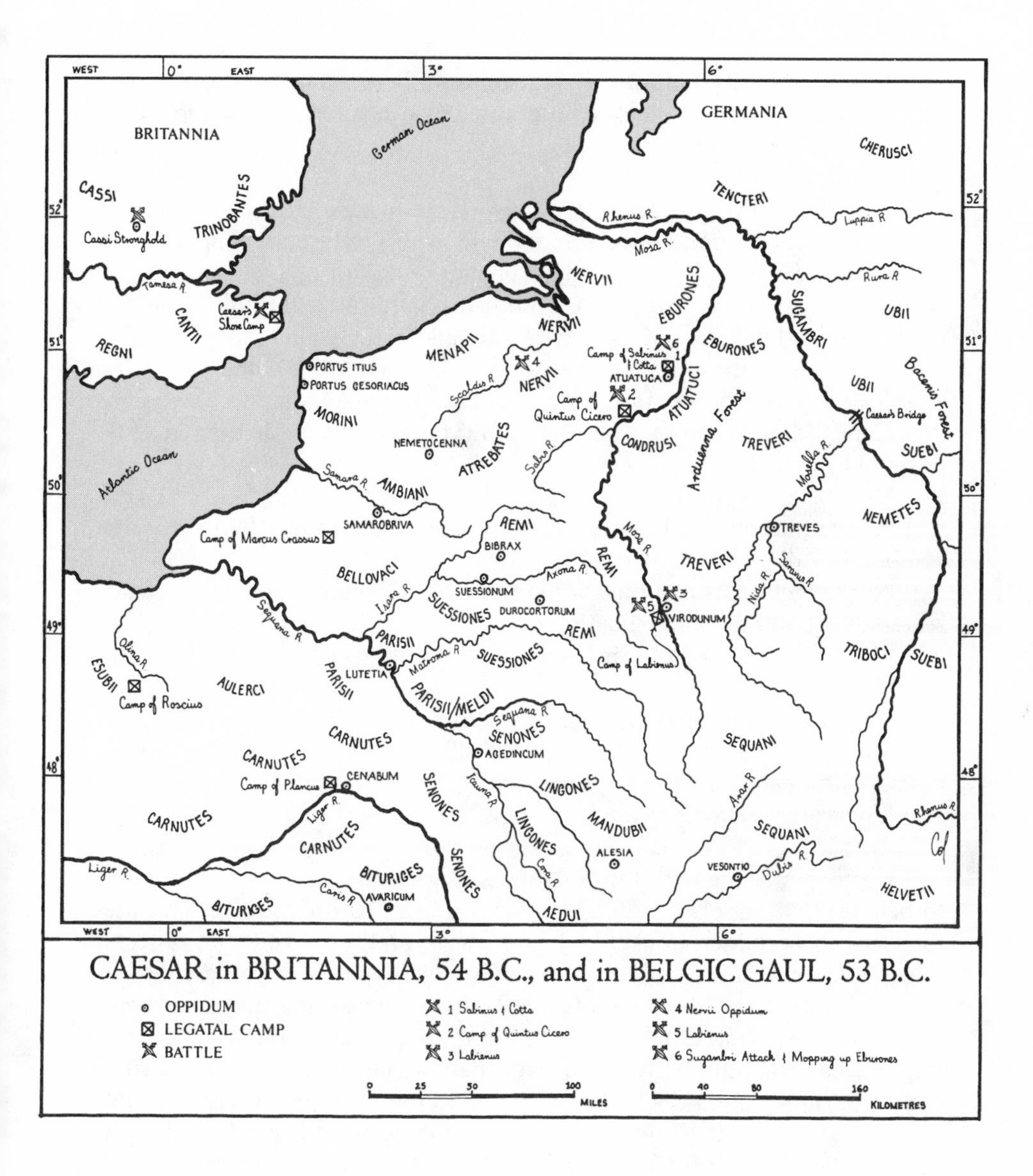

CAESAR in BRITANNIA, 54 B.C., and in BELGIC GAUL, 53 B.C.

and the Germans sniffing up your arse when the Eburones and Nervii aren't."

"They can get to the sea for fish, eels and sea-bird eggs," said Trebonius.

"Thank you, I'm happy with freshwater fish, and my servants can keep chickens."

"Caesar definitely thinks there's going to be trouble."

"Either that, or he's cultivating an excuse not to have to return to Italian Gaul for the winter."

"Eh?"

"Oh, Trebonius, he doesn't want to have to face all those Romans! He'd be accepting condolences from Salona to Ocelum, and spend the whole winter terrified that he might break down."

Trebonius stopped, his rather mournful grey eyes startled. "I didn't know you understood him so well, Labienus."

"I've been with him since he came among the Long-hairs."

"But Romans don't consider it unmanly to weep!"

"Nor did he when he was young. But he wasn't Caesar then in anything but name."

"Eh?"

"It's not a name anymore," said Labienus with rare patience. "It's a symbol."

"Oh!" Trebonius resumed walking. "I miss Decimus Brutus!" he said suddenly. "Sabinus is no substitute."

"He'll be back. You all itch for Rome occasionally."

"Except you."

Caesar's senior legate grunted. "I know when I'm well off."

"So do I. Samarobriva! Imagine, Labienus! I'll be living in a real house with heated floors and a bathtub."

"Sybarite," said Labienus.

Correspondence with the Senate was copious and had to be attended to before anything else, which kept Caesar busy for three days. Outside the General's wooden house the legions were on the move, not a process which created a great deal of fuss or noise; the paperwork could proceed in tranquillity. Even the torpid Gaius Trebatius was flung into the whirlpool, for Caesar had a habit of dictating to three secretaries at once, pacing between the figures hunched over their waxed tablets, giving each a couple of rapid sentences before going on to the next one, never tangling subjects or thoughts. It was his awesome capacity for work had won Trebatius's heart. Difficult to hate a man who could keep so many pots on the boil at one and the same time.

But finally the personal letters had to be dealt with, for more communications from Rome kept coming in every day. It was eight hundred miles from Portus Itius to Rome along roads which were often rivers in

Gaul of the Long-hairs until, way down in the Province, the highways of Via Domitia and Via Aemilia took over. Caesar kept a group of couriers perpetually riding or boating between Rome and wherever he was, and expected a minimum of fifty miles a day from them. Thus he received the latest news from Rome in less than two *nundinae,* and ensured that his isolation did not negate his influence. Which grew and grew in direct proportion to his ever-increasing wealth. Britannia may not have provided much, but Gaul of the Long-hairs had yielded mountains.

Caesar had a German freedman, Burgundus, whom he had inherited from Gaius Marius when Marius had died in Caesar's fifteenth year of life. A happy bequest; Burgundus had fitted into adolescence and manhood indispensably. Until as recently as a year ago he had still been with Caesar, who, seeing his age, had retired him to Rome, where he cared for Caesar's lands, Caesar's mother and Caesar's wife. His tribe had been the Cimbri, and though he had been a boy when Marius had annihilated the Cimbri and the Teutones, he knew the story of his people. According to Burgundus, the tribal treasures of the Cimbri and the Teutones had been left for safekeeping among their relatives the Atuatuci, with whom they had stayed over the winter before embarking on their invasion of Italia. Only six thousand of them had made it back to the lands of the Atuatuci out of a horde numbering over three-quarters of a million men, women and children, and there the survivors of Marius's massacre had settled down, become Atuatuci rather than Cimbri. And there the tribal treasures of the Cimbri and Teutones had remained.

In his second year in Gaul of the Long-hairs Caesar had gone into the lands of the Nervii, who fought on foot and lived along the Mosa below the lands of the Eburones, to which a dismayed and unhappy Sabinus was at present conveying the Thirteenth Legion and an even more dismayed and unhappy Lucius Aurunculeius Cotta. A battle had been fought, the famous one during which the Nervii stayed on the field to die rather than live as defeated men; but Caesar had been merciful and allowed their women, children and old ones to return unmolested to their undamaged homes.

The Atuatuci were the next people upstream of the Nervii on the Mosa. Even though Caesar himself had sustained heavy losses, he was able to continue campaigning, and moved next on the Atuatuci. Who retreated inside their *oppidum,* Atuatuca, a fortress upon a hill overlooking the mighty forest of the Arduenna. Caesar had besieged and taken Atuatuca, but the Atuatuci did not fare as well as the Nervii had. Because they had lied to him and tried to trick him, Caesar massed the whole tribe in a field near the razed *oppidum,* summoned the slavers who always lurked among the Roman baggage train, and sold the entire tribe in one unculled lot to the highest bidder. Fifty-three thousand Atuatuci had gone on the auction block, a seemingly endless crocodile of bewildered, weeping and dispossessed people who had been driven through the lands of the other tribes all the way to the great slave market of Massilia, where they were divided, culled, and sold again.

It had been a shrewd move. Those other tribes had all been on the verge of revolt, unable to believe that the Nervii and the Atuatuci in their many thousands would not annihilate the Romans. But the crocodile of captives told a different story; the revolt never happened. Gaul of the Long-hairs began to wonder just who these Romans were, with their tiny little armies of splendidly equipped troops who behaved as if they were one man, didn't just fall on the enemy in a screaming, undisciplined mass, nor work themselves into a battle frenzy capable of carrying them through anything. They had been feared for generations, but not with realism; until Caesar, they were bogeys to terrify children.

Inside the Atuatuci *oppidum* Caesar found the tribal treasures of the Cimbri and Teutones, the masses of gold artifacts and bullion they had brought with them centuries before when they emigrated from the lands of the Scythians, rich in gold, emeralds, sapphires, then left behind in Atuatuca. It was the General's right to take all the profits from the sale of slaves, but spoils belonged to the Treasury and every echelon of the army from its commander-in-chief to the ranker soldiers. Even so, by the time that the inventories had been done and the great wagon train bearing the booty was on its way under heavy guard to Rome for storage against the day the General triumphed, Caesar knew that his money worries were over for life. Sale of the Atuatuci tribe into slavery had netted him two thousand talents, and his share of the booty would net him more than that. His ranker soldiers would be rich men, his legates able to buy their way to the consulship.

Which had been only the start. The Gauls mined silver and panned and sluiced for alluvial gold in the rivers which came down from the Cebenna massif. They were consummate artisans and clever steel-smiths; even a confiscated pile of iron-tired wheels or properly cooped barrels represented money. And every sestertius Caesar sent to Rome increased his personal share of public worth and standing—his *dignitas*.

The pain of losing Julia would never go away, and Caesar was no Crassus. Money to him was not an end in itself; it was merely a means to the end of enhancing his *dignitas,* a lifeless commodity which those years of frightful debt as he climbed the magisterial ladder had taught him was of paramount importance in the scheme of things. Whatever enhanced his *dignitas* would contribute to the *dignitas* of his dead daughter. A consolation. His efforts and her own instinct to inspire love would ensure that she was remembered for herself, not remembered because she had been the daughter of Caesar and the wife of Pompey the Great. And when he returned to Rome in triumph, he would celebrate the funeral games which the Senate had denied her. Even if, as he had once said to the assembled Conscript Fathers of the Senate on another subject, he had to crush their genitals with his boot to achieve his purpose.

* * *

There were many letters. Some were mainly devoted to business, as was true of those from his most faithful adherent, Balbus the Spanish banker from Gades, and Gaius Oppius the Roman banker. His present wealth had also caught an even shrewder financial magician in his net: Gaius Rabirius Postumus, whose thanks for reorganizing the shambles of the Egyptian public accounting system had been to be stripped naked by King Ptolemy Auletes and his Alexandrian minions, and shoved penniless on a ship bound for Rome. It had been Caesar who lent him the money to get started again. And Caesar who made a vow that one day he would collect the money Egypt owed Rabirius Postumus—in person.

There were letters from Cicero, squawking and clucking about the welfare of his younger brother, Quintus. Warm with sympathy for Caesar's loss, for Cicero was, despite all that vainglorious posturing and conceit, a genuinely kind and loving sort of man.

Ah! A scroll from Brutus! Turning thirty this coming year, and therefore about to enter the Senate as a quaestor. Caesar had written to him just before leaving for Britannia, asking him to join the staff as his personally requested quaestor. Crassus's older son, Publius, had quaestored for him through several years, and this year he had Publius's younger brother, Marcus Crassus, as quaestor. A wonderful pair of fellows, but the main duties of a quaestor were to run the finances; Caesar had assumed that sons of Crassus were bound to have accounting talents, but it hadn't worked out that way. Terrific leading legions, but couldn't add X and X. Whereas Brutus was a plutocrat in senatorial clothing, had a genius for making money and managing money. At the moment fat Trebatius was doing the figure-work, but, strictly speaking, it was not his job.

Brutus . . . Even after so long, Caesar still experienced a twinge of guilt every time he thought of that name. Brutus had loved Julia so much, patiently waited through more than ten years of betrothal for her to grow up to proper marriageable age. But then a veritable gift from the Gods had landed in Caesar's lap: Julia had fallen madly in love with Pompey the Great, and he with her. Which meant that Caesar could bind Pompey to his cause with the most delicate and silken of ropes, his own daughter. He broke her engagement to Brutus (who had been known by his adopted name of Servilius Caepio in those days) and married her to Pompey. Not an easy situation, quite above and beyond Brutus's shattered heart. Brutus's mother, Servilia, had been Caesar's mistress for years. To keep her sweet after that insult had cost him a pearl worth six million sesterces.

> I thank you for your offer, Caesar. Very kind of you to think of me and remember that I am due for election as a quaestor this year. Unfortunately I am not yet sure that I have my quaestorship, as the elections are still pending. We hope to know in December, when they

say the People in their tribes *will* elect the quaestors and the tribunes of the soldiers. But I doubt we will see any elections for the senior magistrates. Memmius refuses to step down as a candidate for the consulship, and Uncle Cato has sworn that until Memmius does step down, he will allow no curule elections. Do not, by the way, take any notice of those scurrilous rumors going around about Uncle Cato's divorce from Marcia. Uncle Cato *cannot* be bought.

I am going to Cilicia as the personally requested quaestor of the new governor for next year, Appius Claudius Pulcher. He is now my father-in-law. I married his oldest daughter, Claudia, a month ago. A very nice girl.

Once again, thank you for your kind offer. My mother is well. She is, I understand, writing to you herself.

Take that! Caesar put the curled single sheet of paper down, blinking not with tears but with shock.

For six long years Brutus never married. Then my daughter dies, and he is married within *nundinae* of it. He cherished hope, it seems. Waited for her, sure she would grow very tired of being married to an old man without anything to recommend him beyond his military fame and his money. No birth, no ancestors worth naming. How long would Brutus have waited? I wonder. But she had found her true mate in Pompeius Magnus, nor would he have tired of her. I've always disliked myself for hurting Brutus, though I didn't know how much Julia meant to him until after I had done the deed. Yet it had to be done, no matter who was hurt or how badly. Lady Fortuna gifted me with a daughter beautiful and sprightly enough to enchant the one man I needed desperately. But how can I hold Pompeius Magnus now?

Like Brutus, Servilia had written only once to, for example, Cicero's fourteen separate epics. Not a long letter, either. Odd, however, the feeling he experienced when he touched the paper she had touched. As if it had been soaked in some poison designed to be drunk through the fingertips. He closed his eyes and tried to remember her, the sight and the taste, that destructive, intelligent, fierce passion. What would he feel when he saw her again? Almost five years. She would be fifty now to his forty-six. But probably still extremely attractive; she took care of herself, kept her hair as darkly moonless as her heart. For it was not Caesar responsible for the disaster who was Brutus; the blame for Brutus had to be laid squarely at his mother's door.

I imagine you've already seen Brutus's refusal. Everything always in order, that's you, so men first. At least I have a patrician daughter-in-law, though it isn't easy sharing my house with another woman who is not my own blood daughter and therefore unused to my authority, my way of doing things. Luckily for domestic peace,

Claudia is a mouse. I do not imagine Julia would have been, for all her air of fragility. A pity she lacked your steel. That's why she died, of course.

Brutus picked Claudia for his wife for one reason. That Picentine upstart Pompeius *Magnus* was dickering with Appius Claudius to get the girl for his own son, Gnaeus. Who might be half Mucius Scaevola, but doesn't show it in either his face or his nature. He's Pompeius Magnus without the mind. Probably pulls the wings off flies. It appealed to Brutus to steal a bride off the man who had stolen his bride from him. He did it too. Appius Claudius not being Caesar. A shoddy consul and no doubt next year a particularly venal governor for poor Cilicia. He weighed the size of my Brutus's fortune and his impeccable ancestry against Pompeius Magnus's clout and the fact that Pompeius's younger boy, Sextus, is the one who's likely to go farthest, and the scales came down in Brutus's favor. Whereupon Pompeius Magnus had one of those famous temper tantrums. How *did* Julia deal with them? You could hear the bellows and screeches all over Rome. Appius then did a very clever thing. He offered Pompeius Magnus his next girl, Claudilla, for Gnaeus. Not yet seventeen, but the Pompeii have never been averse to cradle-snatching. So everybody wound up happy. Appius got two sons-in-law worth as much as the Treasury, two horribly plain and colorless girls got eminent husbands, and Brutus won his little war against the First Man in Rome.

He's off to Cilicia with his father-in-law, this year they hope, though the Senate is being sticky about granting Appius Claudius leave to go to his province early. Appius responded by informing the Conscript Fathers that he'd go without a *lex curiata* if he had to, but go he would. The final decision has not yet been made, though my revolting half brother Cato is yammering about special privileges being extended to patricians. You did me no good turn there, Caesar, when you took Julia off my son. He's been as thick as syrup with Uncle Cato ever since. I can't bear the way Cato *gloats* over me because my son listens more to him these days than he does to me.

He's such a hypocrite, Cato. Always prating about the Republic and the *mos maiorum* and the degeneracy of the old ruling class, yet he can always find a reason why what he wants is a Right Act. The most beautiful thing about having a philosophy, it seems to me, is that it enables its owner to find extenuating circumstances for his own conduct in all situations. Look at his divorcing Marcia. They say every man has a price. I believe that. I also believe that senile old Hortensius coughed up Cato's price. As for Philippus—well, he's an Epicure, and the price of infinite pleasure comes high.

Speaking of Philippus, I had dinner there a few afternoons ago. It's just as well your niece, Atia, is not a loose woman. Her stepson, young Philippus—a very handsome and well-set-up fellow!—gazed at her all through dinner the way a bull gazes at the cow on the other side of the fence. Oh, she noticed, but she pretended she didn't. The young man will get no encouragement from her. I just hope Philippus doesn't notice. Otherwise the cozy nest Atia has found herself will go up in flames. She produced the only occupant of her affections for my inspection after the meal was over. Her son, Gaius Octavius. Your great-nephew, he must be. Aged exactly nine—it was his birthday. An amazing child, I have to admit it. Oh, if my Brutus had looked like that, Julia would never have consented to marry Pompeius Magnus! The boy's beauty quite took my breath away. And so *Julian*! If you said he was your son, everybody would believe it. Not that he's very like you, feature by feature, just that he has—I really don't know how to describe it. There is something of you about him. On his inside rather than his outside. I was pleased to see, however, that little Gaius Octavius is not utterly perfect. His ears stick out. I told Atia to keep his hair a trifle on the long side.

And that is all. I do not intend to offer you my condolences for the death of Julia. You can't make good babies with inferior men. Two tries, neither successful, and the second one cost her life. You gave her to that oaf from Picenum instead of to a man whose breeding was the equal of her own. So be it on your own head.

Maybe it was the sum of all those years of vitriol armored Caesar now; he put Servilia's letter down and did no more than rise to wash the touch of it off his hands.

I think I hate her more than I do her loathsome half brother Cato. The most remorseless, cruel and bitter woman I have ever known. Yet if I saw her tomorrow, our love affair would probably resume. Julia called her a snake; I remember that day well. It was a valid description. That poor, pathetic, spineless boy of hers is now a poor, pathetic, spineless man. Face ruined by festering sores, spirit ruined by one enormous festering sore, Servilia. Brutus didn't decline a quaestorship with me because of principles or Julia or Uncle Cato's opposition; he likes money too much, and my legates make a great deal of it. No, Brutus declined because he didn't want to go to a province wracked by war. To do so might expose him to a battle. Cilicia is at peace. He can potter around it, illegally lending money to provincials, without a flying spear or arrow any closer to him than the Euphrates.

Two more letters, then he would finish for the day and order his servants to pack up. Time to move to Samarobriva.

Get it over and done with, Caesar! Read the one from your wife and the one from your mother. They'll hurt far more with their loving words than Servilia's savagery ever could.

So he sat down again in the silence of his private room, no eyes upon him, put the letter from his mother on the table and opened the one from his wife, Calpurnia. Whom he hardly knew. Just a few months in Rome with an immature, rather shy girl who had prized the orange kitten he had given her as much as Servilia prized her six-million-sestertius pearl.

Caesar, they all say it is my place to write and give you this news. Oh, I wish it were not. I have neither the wisdom nor the years to divine how best to go about it, so please forgive me if, in my ignorance, I make things even harder for you to bear than I know they will be anyway.

When Julia died, your mama's heart broke. Aurelia was so much Julia's mother. She brought her up. And Aurelia was so delighted at her marriage, how happy she was, how lovely her life.

We here in the Domus Publica live a very sheltered existence, as is fitting in the house of the Vestal Virgins. Though we dwell in the midst of the Forum, excitement and events touch us lightly. We have preferred it that way, Aurelia and I: a sweet and peaceful enclave of women free from scandal, suspicion or reproach. But Julia, who visited us often when she was in Rome, brought a breath of the wide world with her. Gossip, laughter, small jokes.

When she died, your mama's heart broke. I was there near Julia's bedside, and I watched your mama being so strong, for Pompeius's sake as well as for Julia's. So kind! So sensible in everything she said. Smiling when she felt it called for. Holding one of Julia's hands while Pompeius held the other. It was she who banished the doctors when she saw that nothing and no one could save Julia. It was she who gave us peace and privacy for the hours that remained. And after Julia was gone, she yielded her place to Pompeius, left him alone with Julia. She bundled me out of the room and took me home, back to the Domus Publica.

It isn't a very long walk, as you know. She said not one word. Then when we got inside our own door, she uttered a terrible cry and began to howl. I couldn't say she wept. She howled, down on her knees with the tears pouring out in floods, and beat her breast, and pulled her hair. Howling. Scratching her face and neck to bleeding ribbons. The adult Vestals all came running, and there were all of us weeping, trying to get Aurelia to her feet, trying to calm her down, but not able to stop weeping ourselves. I think in the end we all got down on the floor with her, and put our arms about her and about ourselves, and stayed there for most of the night. While Aurelia howled in the most terrible, awful despair.

But it ended. In the morning she was able to dress and go back to Pompeius's house, help him attend to all the things which had to be done. And then the poor little baby died, but Pompeius refused to see him or kiss him, so it was Aurelia who made the arrangements for his tiny funeral. He was buried that same day, and she and I and the adult Vestals were his only mourners. He didn't have a name, and none of us knew what the third *praenomen* among that branch of the Pompeii is. We knew only Gnaeus and Sextus, both taken. So we decided on Quintus; it sounded right. His tomb will say Quintus Pompeius Magnus. Until then, I have his ashes. My father is attending to the tomb, for Pompeius will not.

There is no need to say anything about Julia's funeral, for I know that Pompeius has written it.

But your mama's heart was broken. She wasn't with us anymore, just drifted—you know what she was like, so brisk and martial in her step, but now she just drifted. Oh, it was awful! No matter which one of us she saw—the laundry maid, Eutychus, Burgundus, Cardixa, a Vestal—or me—she would stop and look at us and ask, "Why couldn't it have been me? Why did it have to be her? I'm no use to anyone! Why couldn't it have been me?" And what could we say in reply? How could we not weep? Then she would howl, and ask all over again, "Why couldn't it have been me?"

That went on for two months, but only in front of us. When people came to pay condolence visits, she pulled herself together and behaved as they expected she would. Though her appearance shocked everyone.

Then she shut herself in her room and sat upon the floor, rocking back and forth, and humming. With sometimes a huge cry, and the howling would begin again. We had to wash her and change her clothes, and we tried so hard to persuade her to get into her bed, but she would not. She wouldn't eat. Burgundus pinched her nose while Cardixa poured watered wine down her throat, but that was as far as any of us felt we could go. The very thought of holding her down and forcibly feeding her made all of us sick. We had a conference, Burgundus, Cardixa, Eutychus and the Vestals, and we decided that you would not want her fed by force. If we have erred, please, we beg you, forgive us. What we did was done with the very best of intentions.

This morning she died. It was not difficult, nor a great agony for her. Popillia the Chief Vestal says it is a mercy. It had been many days since she had any sensible congress with us, yet just before the end she came to her senses and spoke lucidly. Mostly about Julia. She asked all of us—the adult Vestals were there too—to offer sacrifices for Julia to Magna Mater, Juno Sospita and the Bona Dea. Bona Dea seemed to worry her dreadfully; she insisted that we promise to remember Bona Dea. I had to swear that I would give Bona Dea's snakes eggs and milk all year round, every year. Otherwise Aurelia seemed to think that some terrible disaster would befall you. She didn't speak your name until just before she died. The last thing she said was "Tell Caesar all of this will go to his greater glory." Then she closed her eyes and ceased to breathe.

There is nothing more. My father is dealing with her funeral, and he is writing, of course. But he insisted that I should be the one to tell you. I am so sorry. I will miss Aurelia with every beat of my heart.

Please take care of yourself, Caesar. I know what a blow this will be, following so closely upon Julia. I wish I understood why these things happen, but I do not. Though somehow I know what her last message to you meant. The Gods torture those they love the best. It will all go to your greater glory.

There were no tears at this news either.

Perhaps I already knew that this was how it must finish. Mater, to live on without Julia? Not possible. Oh, why do women have to suffer such unbearable pain? They do not run the world, they are not to blame. Therefore why should they suffer?

Their lives are so enclosed, so centered upon the hearth. Their children, their home and their men, in that order. Such is their nature. And nothing is crueler for them than to outlive their children. That part of my life is closed forever. I will not open that door again. I have no one left who loves me as a woman loves her son or her father, and my poor little wife is a stranger who loves her cats more than she does me. For why should she not? They have kept her company, they have given her some semblance of love. Whereas I am never there. I know nothing about love, except that it has to be earned. And though I am completely empty, I can feel the strength in me grow. This will not defeat me. It has freed me. Whatever I have to do, I *will* do. There is no one left to tell me I cannot.

He gathered up three scrolls: Servilia's, Calpurnia's, Aurelia's.

The detritus of so many men pulling up their roots and moving on meant many fires, for which Caesar was glad. The last live coal he had needed had been found by chance; fires were rare in hot weather. There was always the eternal flame, but it belonged to Vesta and to take flame from it to use for ordinary purposes required ritual and prayers. Caesar was the Pontifex Maximus; he would not profane that mystery.

But, as with Pompey's letter, he had fire to hand. He fed Servilia to it, and watched her burn sardonically. Then Calpurnia, his face impassive. The last to go was Aurelia, unopened, but he didn't hesitate. Whatever she had said, whenever she had written it, no longer mattered. Surrounded by flakes dancing in the air, Caesar pulled the folds of his purple-bordered toga over his head and said the words of purification.

It was eighty miles of easy marching from Portus Itius to Samarobriva: the first day on a rutted track through mighty forests of oak, the second day amid vast clearings wherein the soil had been turned for cropping or rich grasses fed naked Gallic sheep and hairy Gallic cattle. Trebonius had gone with the Twelfth much earlier than Caesar, who was the last to go. Left behind with the Seventh, Fabius had already stripped the defenses of a camp big enough to contain eight legions and re-erected them around a camp which could be comfortably held by one legion. Satisfied that this outpost was in good condition to resist attack, Caesar took the Tenth and headed for Samarobriva.

The Tenth was his favorite legion, the one he liked to work with personally, and though its number was not the lowest, it was the original legion of Further Gaul. When he had raced headlong from Rome in that March of nearly five years ago—covering the seven hundred miles in eight days and fighting his way along a goat-track pass through the high Alps—it was the Tenth he had found with Pomptinus at Genava. By the time the Fifth Alauda and the Seventh had arrived, going the long way under Labienus, Caesar and the Tenth had got to know each other. Typically, not through battle. The army's most quoted joke about Caesar was that for every action you fought, Caesar would have made you shovel ten thousand wagon-loads of earth and rock. As had been the case at Genava, where the Tenth (later joined by the Fifth Alauda and the Seventh) had dug a sixteen-foot-high wall nineteen miles long to keep the emigrating Helvetii out of the Province. Battles, said the army, were Caesar's rewards for all that shoveling, building, logging and slogging. Of which none had done more than the Tenth, nor fought more bravely and intelligently in those fairly infrequent battles. Caesar never fought unless he had to.

There was even evidence of the army's work as the long and disciplined column of the Tenth swung their feet in unison and sang their marching songs through the lands of the Morini around Portus Itius. For the rutted road through the oak forests was already fortified; on either side of it a hundred paces back loomed a great wall of fallen oaks, and those hundred paces were spider-moled with their stumps.

Two years before, Caesar had led a few cohorts more than three legions against the Morini to pave his way for the expedition he planned to Britannia. He needed a port on the Morini coast, very near the mysterious island. But though he sent out heralds to ask for a treaty, the Morini hadn't sent ambassadors.

They caught him in the midst of building a camp, and Caesar almost went down. Had they been better generaled, the war in Gaul of the Longhairs might have finished there and then with Caesar and his troops dead. But before they administered that final blow (as Caesar certainly would have), the Morini withdrew into their oak forests. And by the time that

Caesar had picked up the pieces and burned his slain, he was furiously angry in the cold and passionless way he had made his own. How to teach the Morini that Caesar *would* win? That every life he had lost would be paid for with terrible suffering?

He decided not to retreat. Instead he would go forward, all the way to the salt marshes of the Morini coastline. But not along a narrow track with the ancient oaks overhanging it, perfect shelter for a Belgic horde. No, he would lead his troops upon a broad highway in bright, safe sunlight.

"The Morini are Druids, boys!" he shouted to his soldiers in assembly. "They believe that every tree has *animus*—a spirit, a soul! And which tree's spirit is the most sacred? *Nemer!* The oak! Which tree forms their temple groves, the *nemeton*? *Nemer!* The oak! Which tree does the Druid high priest climb clad in white and under the moon to harvest the mistletoe with his golden sickle? *Nemer!* The oak! From the branches of which tree do the skeletons hang clacking in the breeze as sacrifices to Esus, their god of war? *Nemer!* The oak! Under which tree does the Druid set up his altar with his human victim lying face down, and cleave his backbone with a sword to interpret the future through his struggles? *Nemer!* The oak! Which tree is witness when the Druids build their wicker cages, stuff them with men taken prisoner and burn them to honor Taranis, their thunder god? *Nemer!* The oak!"

He paused, seated upon his warhorse with the toes, the vivid scarlet of his general's cloak lying in ordered folds across its haunches, and he smiled brilliantly. His exhausted troops smiled back, feeling the vigor begin to steal through their sinews.

"Do we Romans believe that trees have spirits? Do we?"

"NO!" roared the soldiers.

"Do we believe in oak knowledge and oak magic?"

"NO!" roared the soldiers.

"Do we believe in human sacrifice?"

"NO!" roared the soldiers.

"Do we like these people?"

"NO!" roared the soldiers.

"Then we will kill their minds and their will to live by showing them that Rome is mightier than the mightiest oak! That Rome is eternal but the oak is not! We will liberate the spirits of their oaks and send them to haunt the Morini until time and men have ended!"

"YES!" roared the soldiers.

"Then to your axes!"

Mile after mile through the oak forest Caesar and his men pushed the Morini backward to their fens, felling the oaks as they went in a swath a thousand feet wide, piling the raw lopped trunks and branches into a great wall on either flank, and counting the tally as each majestic old tree groaned to marry the earth. Almost demented with horror and grief, the

Morini could not fight back. They retreated keening until they were swallowed up in their fens, where they huddled and mourned desolately.

The skies mourned too. On the edge of the salt marshes it began to rain, and it rained until the Roman tents were soaked, the soldiers wet and shivering. Still, what had been done was enough. Satisfied, Caesar had withdrawn to put his men into a comfortable winter camp. But the tale spread; the Belgae and the Celtae rocked in grief, and wondered what sort of men could murder trees yet sleep at night and laugh by day.

Only their Roman Gods had substance, nor did the Roman soldiers feel the brush of alien wings inside their minds. So on the march from Portus Itius to Samarobriva they swung their legs and sang their songs through the miles of silent, fallen giants, unperturbed.

And Caesar, striding out with them, looked at the wall of murdered oaks and smiled. He was learning new ways to make war, fascinated with the idea of taking war inside the enemy's mind. His faith in himself and his soldiers was limitless, but better by far that conquest came inside the enemy mind. That way, the yoke could never be thrown off. Gaul of the Long-hairs would have to bend; Caesar could not.

The Greeks had a famous joke: that nothing in the world was uglier than a Gallic *oppidum,* and it was true of Samarobriva, alas. The stronghold lay on the Samara River in the midst of a lush valley, very burned and dry at the moment, yet still more productive than most places. It was the chief *oppidum* of a Belgic tribe, the Ambiani, who were closely tied to Commius and the Atrebates, their neighbors and kinsmen to the north. To the south and east they bordered the lands of the Bellovaci, a fierce and warlike people who had submitted but stirred ominously.

Beauty, however, was not high on Caesar's list of priorities when he campaigned; Samarobriva suited him extremely well. Though Gaul of the Belgae was not rich in stone and the Gauls were poor quarrymen at the best of times, the walls were made of stone, were high, and had not been difficult to fortify further in the Roman manner. They bristled now with towers from which an enemy force could be seen miles away, the several gates were now behind additional ramparts, and an army camp formidably equipped with defenses lay behind the stronghold.

Inside the stone walls was spacious but not inspiring. No people normally lived there; it was a place for the storage of food and tribal treasures. No proper streets, just windowless warehouses and tall granaries dotted randomly about. It did contain a large wooden house two storeys high; in time of war the chief thane and his nobles lived in it, and at all times it served as a meeting hall for the tribe. Here upstairs Caesar was domiciled in far less comfort than Trebonius enjoyed; during a previous tenancy Trebonius had built himself a stone house above a steamy furnace of coals which heated the floor and the large bath he had installed, together with an Ambiani mistress.

Neither dwelling possessed a proper latrine situated above a stream of running water which carried the excrement away into a sewer or a river. In that respect the troops were better off; no winter camp of Caesar's was without such amenities. Latrine pits were acceptable for campaign camps, provided they were dug deep enough and their bottoms covered daily with a thin layer of soil and lime, but even in winter long-term latrine pits bred disease, for they polluted the groundwater. Soldiers had to be fit, not sick. This wasn't a problem the Gauls understood, for they never congregated in towns, preferring to live in small villages or single homesteads across the countryside. They went to war for a few days at a time, and took their women and slaves with them to deal with all the bodily functions. Only the serfs stayed at home and the Druids in their forest retreats.

The wooden plank stairs to the meeting hall's upper storey were on the outside of the building, protected a little from the elements by an overhanging eave. Beneath the stairs Caesar had constructed a latrine so deep it was more a well, digging down until he found an underground stream which he had mined through a tunnel so long it entered the Samara River. Not entirely satisfactory, but the best he could do. This facility Trebonius used as well. A fair trade, said Caesar, for the use of Trebonius's bath.

The roof had been thatched, this being the usual Gallic roof on a building of any size, but Caesar had all a Roman's horror of fire as well as his private horror of rats and bird lice, both of which thought thatch had been invented for their enjoyment. So the thatch had come off, replaced with slate tiles he had brought from the foothills of the Pyrenees. His house was therefore cold, damp and airless, as its small windows were protected by shutters of solid wood instead of fretted Italian shutters permitting an exchange of air. He made do because it was not his custom to remain in Gaul of the Long-hairs for the duration of the six-month furlough the seasons gave his troops. Under normal circumstances he stayed in whatever *oppidum* he had chosen for winter headquarters for a few days only before setting out for Italian Gaul and Illyricum, where he ministered to those absolutely Roman provinces in the exquisite degree of comfort provided by the richest man in whatever town he was visiting.

This winter would be different. He would not be going to Italian Gaul and Illyricum; Samarobriva was home for the next six months. No condolences, especially now that he knew his mother was also dead. Who would be the third? Though, come to think of it, in his life the deaths happened in twos, not threes. Gaius Marius and his father. Cinnilla and Aunt Julia. Now Julia and Mater. Yes, twos. And who besides was left?

His freedman Gaius Julius Thrasyllus was waiting in the doorway at the top of the stairs, smiling and bowing.

"I'm here for the whole winter, Thrasyllus. What can we do to make this place more habitable?" he asked, handing over his scarlet cloak.

There were two servants waiting to unbuckle his leather cuirass and the outer skirt of straps, but first he had to divest himself of the scarlet sash of his high imperium; he and he alone could touch it, and when it was unknotted he folded it carefully and placed it in the jeweled box Thrasyllus held out. His under-dress was scarlet linen cushioned with a stuffing of wool between diamond-shaped stitching, thick enough to soak up the sweat of marching (there were many generals who preferred to wear a tunic on the march, even if they traveled in a gig, but the soldiers had to march in twenty pounds of chain mail, so Caesar wore his cuirass) and thick enough now to be warm. The servants removed his boots and put slippers of Ligurian felt upon his feet, then whisked the military impedimenta away for storage.

"I suggest you build a proper house like Gaius Trebonius's, Caesar," said Thrasyllus.

"You're right, I will. I'll look for a site tomorrow."

A smile, then he was gone into the big room wherein couches and other Roman furnishings were scattered.

She wasn't there, but he could hear her talking to Orgetorix next door. Best find her when she was occupied, couldn't overwhelm him with affection. There were times when he liked that, but not this evening. He was bruised in spirit.

There. Over by the cot, her fabulous mane of fiery hair falling forward so that he couldn't see much more of his son than a pair of woolly purple socks. Why did she persist in clothing the child in purple? He had voiced his displeasure many times, but she failed to understand, as she was the daughter of a king. To her, the child was the future King of the Helvetii; therefore, purple was his color.

She sensed him rather than saw him and straightened at once, face all eyes and teeth, so great was her pleasure. Then she frowned at the beard.

"*Tata!*" crowed the little boy, holding out his arms.

He had a look more of Aunt Julia than of Caesar himself, and that alone was enough to melt Caesar's heart. The same big grey eyes, the same shape to his face, and luckily the same creamy skin instead of a pinkly pallid, freckled Gallic integument. But his hair was entirely his own, much the same color as Sulla's had been, neither red nor gold. And it promised to deserve the cognomen Caesar, which meant a fine thick head of hair. How Caesar's enemies had used his thinning hair to ridicule him! A pity then that this little boy would never bear the name Caesar. She had named him after her father, who had been King of the Helvetii: Orgetorix.

She had been the principal wife of Dumnorix in the days when he had skulked in the background hating his brother, chief vergobret of the Aedui.

After the survivors of the attempted Helvetian migration had been returned to their alpine lands and Caesar had also dealt with King Ariovistus of the Suebic Germans, he had toured the lands of the Aedui to familiarize himself with the people, for their importance in his scheme of things had grown. They were Celtae, but Romanized, and were the most populous as well as the richest people in all of Further Gaul; the nobility spoke Latin, and they had earned the title Friend and Ally of the Roman People. They also provided Rome with cavalry.

Caesar's original intention when he had galloped to Genava had been to put an end to the Helvetian migration and to Germanic incursions across the river Rhenus. As soon as it was done, he would commence his conquest of the river Danubius all the way from its sources to its outflow. But by the time that first campaign in Gaul of the Long-hairs was finished, his plans had changed. The Danubius could wait. First he would ensure Italia's safety on the west by pacifying the whole of Further Gaul, turning it into a completely loyal buffer between Our Sea and the Germans. It had been Ariovistus the German who worked this radical change; unless Rome conquered and fully Romanized all the tribes of Gaul, it would fall to the Germans. Then the next to go would be Italia.

Dumnorix had plotted to replace his brother as the most influential man among the Aedui, but after the defeat of his Helvetian allies (he had cemented this alliance with a marriage) he retired to his own manor near Matisco to lick his wounds; it was here that Caesar found him as he returned to Italian Gaul to reorganize his thinking and his army. He had been welcomed by the steward, shown to a suite of rooms, left to himself until he wished to join Dumnorix in the reception room.

But he had walked into Dumnorix's reception room at the worst possible moment, the moment in which a big woman, spitting curses, drew back her powerful white arm and punched Dumnorix on the jaw so hard Caesar heard his teeth rattle. Flat on the floor he went, while the woman, a fantastic cloud of red hair swirling about her like a general's cloak, began to kick him. He came up swinging, was knocked down a second time and kicked again, no force spared. Another equally large but younger woman erupted into the room; she fared no better dealing with Red Hair, who blocked her crosscut and landed an uppercut which sent the newcomer sprawling senseless.

Enjoying himself hugely, Caesar leaned on the wall to watch.

Dumnorix wriggled out of the reach of those deadly feet, got to one knee with murder in his eyes, and saw his visitor.

"Don't mind me," said Caesar.

But that signaled the end of the round, if not the bout. Red Hair planted a vicious kick on the inanimate body of her second victim, then retreated, magnificent breasts heaving, dark blue eyes flashing, to stand staring at the incongruous sight of a Roman in the purple-bordered toga of high estate.

"I didn't—expect you—so soon!" panted Dumnorix.

"So I gather. The lady boxes much better than the athletes at the games. However, if you like I'll go back to my rooms and let you contend with your domestic crisis in peace. If peace is the right word."

"No, no!" Dumnorix straightened his shirt, picked up his shawl, and discovered that it had been wrenched off so violently that the brooch which held it on his left shoulder had torn the sleeve from its armhole. He glared at Red Hair and lifted one fist. "I'll kill you, woman!"

She curled her top lip in contempt but said nothing.

"May I adjudicate?" asked Caesar, removing himself from the wall and strolling to place himself in a strategic position between Dumnorix and Red Hair.

"Thank you but no, Caesar. I've just divorced the she-wolf."

"She-wolf. Romulus and Remus were fostered by a she-wolf. I suggest you put her in the field. She'd have no trouble beating the Germans."

Her eyes had widened at the name; she strode forward until she was scant inches from Caesar and thrust her chin out. "I am a wronged wife!" she cried. "My people are no use to him now that they are defeated and returned to their own lands, so he has divorced me! For no reason except his own convenience! I am not unfaithful, I am not poor, I am not a serf! He has divorced me for no valid reason! I am a wronged wife!"

"Is that the competition?" Caesar asked her, pointing at the girl on the floor.

Up went the top lip again. "Pah!" she spat.

"Do you have children by this woman, Dumnorix?"

"No, she's barren!" cried Dumnorix, seizing on it.

"I am not barren! What do you believe, that babies pop out of nothing on a Druid altar? Between the whores and the wine, Dumnorix, you're not man enough to quicken any of your wives!" Up came her fist.

Dumnorix backed away. "Touch me, woman, and I'll cut your throat from ear to ear!" Out came his knife.

"Now, now," said Caesar reprovingly. "Murder is murder, and better done somewhere else than in front of a proconsul of Rome. However, if you want to box on, I'm willing to act as judge. Equal weapons, Dumnorix. Unless the lady would like a knife?"

"Yes!" she hissed.

What might have been said or done then was not, for the girl on the floor began to moan; Dumnorix, clearly besotted with her, rushed to kneel by her side.

Red Hair turned to watch, while Caesar watched her. Oh, she was something else again! Tall and strapping, yet slender and feminine; her waist, cinched with a golden belt, was tiny between large breasts and hips; and her legs, he thought, lent her most of that imposing height. But it was her hair enraptured him. It poured in rivers of fire over her shoulders and down her back to well below her knees, so thick and rich it had a life of its own. Most Gallic women had wonderful hair, but never so much or so brilliant as this woman's.

"You're of the Helvetii," he said.

She swung round to face him, seeming suddenly to see more than a purple-bordered toga. "You are Caesar?" she asked.

"I am. But you haven't answered my question."

"My father was King Orgetorix."

"Ah, yes. He killed himself before the migration."

"They forced him to it."

"Does this mean you will return to your people?"

"I cannot."

"Why?"

"I have been divorced. No one will have me."

"Yes, that's worth a punch or two."

"He wronged me! I have not deserved it!"

Dumnorix had managed to get the girl to her feet, and stood with one arm about her waist. "Get out of my house!" he roared at Red Hair.

"Not until you return my dowry!"

"I've divorced you, I'm entitled to keep it!"

"Oh, come, Dumnorix," said Caesar pleasantly. "You're a rich man, you don't need her dowry. The lady says she cannot return to her people; therefore the least you can do is enable her to live somewhere in comfort." He turned to Red Hair. "How much does he owe you?" he asked her.

"Two hundred cows, two bulls, five hundred sheep, my bed and bedding, my table, my chair, my jewels, my horse, my servants and a thousand gold pieces," she recited.

"Give her back her dowry, Dumnorix," said Caesar in a tone brooking no argument. "I'll escort her off your lands into the Province and settle her somewhere far from the Aedui."

Dumnorix writhed. "Caesar, I couldn't put you to the trouble!"

"No trouble, I assure you. It's on my way."

And so it had been arranged. When Caesar departed from the lands of the Aedui he went accompanied by two hundred cows, two bulls, five hundred sheep, a wagon full of furniture and chests, a small crowd of slaves and Red Hair on her high-stepping Italian horse.

What Caesar's own entourage thought of this circus they kept to themselves, thankful that for once the General wasn't sitting in a pitching gig, dictating to two of them at full gallop. Instead he rode beside the lady at a leisurely pace and talked to her all the way from Matisco to Arausio, where he supervised the purchase of a property large enough to graze two hundred cows, two bulls and five hundred sheep, and installed Red Hair and her team of servants in the commodious house upon it.

"But I have no husband, no protector!" she said.

"Rubbish!" said he, laughing. "This is the Province; it belongs to Rome. Do you think the whole district of Arausio isn't aware who settled you here? I'm the governor. No one will touch you. On the contrary, everyone will bend over backward to assist you. You'll be inundated with offers of help."

"I belong to you."

"That's what they'll think, certainly."

She had done a great deal more fulminating during the journey than she had smiling, but now she smiled, her wide mouth showing all its splendid teeth. "And what do you think?" she asked.

"I think I'd like to use your hair as a toga."

"I'll comb it."

"No," he said, climbing upon his road horse, which had normal hooves. "Wash it. That's why I made sure your house has a proper bathtub. Learn to use it every day. I'll see you in the spring, Rhiannon."

She frowned. "Rhiannon? That's not my name, Caesar. You know my name."

"Too many *x*'s for linguistic pleasure. Rhiannon."

"It means—"

"Wronged wife. Quite so."

He kicked his horse and cantered away, but back he came in the spring, as he had promised.

What Dumnorix thought when his wronged wife returned to the lands of the Aedui in Caesar's train he didn't say, but it rankled. Especially when it became a delicious joke among the Aedui; the Wronged Wife fell pregnant very quickly, and bore Caesar a son the following winter in her house near Arausio. Which didn't stop her traveling in the baggage train the next spring and summer. Wherever headquarters were established, there she and her baby made themselves at home and waited for Caesar. It was an arrangement which worked well; Caesar saw just enough of her to keep him fascinated, and she had taken his hint, kept herself and the baby so washed they shone.

He scooped the child out of the cot and kissed him, held the little flowerlike face against his own scratchy one, then lifted a small hand to kiss its dimpled knuckles.

"He knew me despite the beard."

"I think he'd know you if you turned a different color."

"My daughter and my mother are dead."

"Yes. Trebonius told me."

"We won't discuss it."

"Trebonius said he thought you'd stay here for the winter."

"Would you prefer to go back to the Province? I can send you, though I won't take you."

"No."

"We'll build a better house before the snow comes."

"I'd like that."

As they continued to talk quietly, he walked up and down the room holding the child in the crook of his arm, stroking the red-gold curls, the flawless skin, the fan of lashes drooping on a rosy cheek.

"He's asleep, Caesar."

"Then I suppose I must put him down."

Into the cot well wrapped in soft purple wool, head upon a purple pillow; Caesar remained gazing for a moment, then put his arm about Rhiannon and walked with her from the room.

"It's late, but I have dinner ready if you're hungry."

He lifted a tress of hair. "Always, when I see you."

"Dinner first. You're not very enthusiastic about food, so I have to get as much of it into you as I can. Roast venison and roast pork with bubbled skin. Crusty bread still hot from the oven, and six different vegetables from my garden."

She was a wonderful housekeeper in a way very different from a Roman woman; of the blood royal, yet down on her knees in her vegetable garden, or making the cheese herself, or turning the mattress on her bed, which always came with her, as did her table and her chair.

The room was warm from several braziers glowing amid the shadows, and the walls were hung with bear skins and wolf pelts wherever the boards had shrunk and the wind whistled through, and it was, besides, not yet winter. They ate entwined on the same couch, a contact more friendly than fleshly, and then she took her harp, put it upon her knee and played.

Perhaps, he thought, that was another reason why she still delighted him. They made such wonderful music, the long-haired Gauls, fingers plucking at many more strings than a lyre possessed, music at once wild and delicate, passionate and stirring. And oh, how they could sing! As she began to sing now, some soft and plaintive air as much sound as words, sheer emotion. Italian music was more melodic, yet lacked the untamed improvisation; Greek music was more mathematically perfect, yet lacked the power and the tears. This was music in which words didn't matter but the voice did. And Caesar, who loved music even more than literature or the visual arts, listened rapt.

After which making love to her was like an extension of the music. He was the wind roaring through the sky, he was the voyager on an ocean of stars—and found his healing in the song of her body.

At first it looked as if the breaking Gallic storm would be Celtic after all. Caesar had been snugly ensconced in his new stone house for a month when word came that the Carnute elders, egged on by the Druids, had killed Tasgetius, their king. Not usually something of concern, but in this case very worrying; it had been Caesar's influence had elevated Tasgetius to the kingship. The Carnutes were peculiarly important over and above their numbers and their wealth, for the center of the Druidic web spread throughout Gaul of the Long-hairs was located in the lands of the Carnutes at a place called Carnutum, the navel of the Druidic earth. It was neither *oppidum* nor town, more a carefully oriented collection of oak, rowan and hazel groves interspersed with small villages of Druid dwellings.

Druidic opposition to Rome was implacable. Rome represented a new, different, alluring apostasy bound to collide with and destroy the Druidic ethos. Not because of the coming of Caesar. The feeling and the attitude were well entrenched by this time, the result of almost two hundred years of watching the Gallic tribes of the south succumb to Romanization. The Greeks had been in the Province far longer, but had remained in the hinterland around Massilia and preferred to be indifferent to barbarians. Whereas the Romans were incurably busy people, had the knack of setting the standard and style of living wherever they settled, and had the habit of extending their highly prized citizenship to those who co-operated with them and rendered good service. They fought crisp wars to eliminate undesirable characteristics like taking heads—a favorite pastime among the Salluvii, who lived between Massilia and Liguria—and would always be back to fight another war if they hadn't done too well in the last one. It had been the Greeks who brought the vine and the olive to the south, but the Romans who had transformed the native peoples of the Province into Roman thinkers: people who no longer honored the Druids, who sent their wellborn sons to study in Rome instead of in Carnutum.

Thus Caesar's advent was a culmination rather than a root cause. Because he was Pontifex Maximus and therefore head of the Roman religion, the Chief Druid had asked for an interview with him during his visit to the lands of the Carnutes in that first year Rhiannon had journeyed with him.

"If Arvernian is acceptable you can send the interpreter away," said Caesar.

"I had heard that you speak several of our tongues, but why Arvernian?" the Chief Druid asked.

"My mother had a servant, Cardixa, from the Arverni."

A faint anger showed. "A slave."

"Originally, but not for many years."

Caesar looked the Chief Druid up and down: a handsome, yellow-haired man in his late forties, dressed simply in a long white linen tunic; he was clean-shaven and devoid of ornament.

"Do you have a name, Chief Druid?"

"Cathbad."

"I expected you to be older, Cathbad."

"I might say the same, Caesar." It was Caesar's turn to be looked up and down. "You're Gallic fair. Is that unusual?"

"Not very. It's actually more unusual to be very dark. You can tell from our third names, which often refer to some physical characteristic. Rufus, which indicates red hair, is a common cognomen. Flavus and Albinus indicate blond hair. A man with truly black hair and eyes is Niger."

"And you are the high priest."

"Yes."

"You inherited the position?"

"No, I was elected Pontifex Maximus. The tenure is for life, as with all our priests and augurs, who are all elected. Whereas our magistrates are elected for the term of one year only."

Cathbad blinked, slowly. "So was I elected. Do you really conduct the rituals of your people?"

"When I'm in Rome."

"Which puzzles me. You've been the chief magistrate of your people and now you lead armies. Yet you are the high priest. To us, a contradiction."

"The two are not irreconcilable to the Senate and People of Rome," said Caesar genially. "On the other hand, I gather that the Druids constitute an exclusive group within the tribe. What one might call the intellectuals."

"We're the priests, the doctors, the lawyers and the poets," said Cathbad, striving to be genial.

"Ah, the professionals! Do you specialize?"

"A little, particularly those who love to doctor. But all of us know the law, the rituals, the history and the lays of our people. Otherwise we are not Druids. It takes twenty years to make one."

They were talking in the main hall of the public building in Cenabum, and quite alone now that the interpreter had been sent away. Caesar had chosen to wear the toga and tunic of the Pontifex Maximus, magnificent-looking garments broadly striped in scarlet and purple.

"I hear," said Caesar, "that you write nothing down—that if all the Druids in Gaul were to be killed on the same day, knowledge would also die. But surely you've preserved your lore on bronze or stone or paper! Writing isn't unknown here."

"Among the Druids it is, though we can all read and write. But we do not write down anything which pertains to our calling. That we memorize. It takes twenty years."

"Very clever!" said Caesar appreciatively.

Cathbad frowned. "Clever?"

"It's an excellent way to preserve life and limb. No one would dare to harm you. Little wonder a Druid can walk fearlessly onto a field of battle and stop the fighting."

"That is not why we do it!" Cathbad cried.

"I realize that. But it's still clever." Caesar switched to another touchy subject. "Druids pay no taxes of any kind, is that right?"

"We pay no taxes, it is true," said Cathbad, pose subtly stiffer, face stubbornly impassive.

"Nor serve in the army?"

"Nor serve as warriors."

"Nor put your hands to any menial task."

"It's you who are clever, Caesar. Your words put us in the wrong. We serve, we earn our rewards. I've already told you, we are the priests, the doctors, the lawyers and the poets."

"You marry?"

"Yes, we marry."

"And are supported by the working people."

Cathbad hung on to his temper. "In return for our services, which are irreplaceable."

"Yes, I understand that. Very clever!"

"I had assumed you would be more tactful, Caesar. Why should you go out of your way to insult us?"

"I don't insult you, Cathbad. I'm after the facts. We of Rome know very little of the living structure within the Gallic tribes who have not come in contact with us until now. Polybius has written a little about you Druids, and some other lesser men of history mention you. But it is my duty to report on these things to the Senate, and the best way to find out is to ask," said Caesar, smiling, but not with charm. Cathbad was impervious to it. "Tell me about women."

"Women?"

"Yes. I note that women, like slaves, can be tortured. Whereas no free man, however low his status, can be tortured. I also note that polygamy is permitted."

Cathbad drew himself up. "We have ten different degrees of marriage, Caesar," he said with dignity. "This permits a certain latitude about the number of wives a man may acquire. We Gauls are warlike. Men die in battle. In turn, this means that there are more women among our people than men. Our laws and customs were designed for us, not for Romans."

"Quite so."

Cathbad drew a breath audibly. "Women have their place. Like men, they have souls, they change places between this world and the other world. And there are priestesses."

"Druids?"

"No, not Druids."

"For every difference, there is a similarity," said Caesar, the smile reaching his eyes. "We elect our priests, a similarity. We do not permit women to hold priesthoods which are important to men, a similarity. The differences are in our status as men—military service, public office, the payment of taxes." The smile disappeared. "Cathbad, it isn't Roman policy to disturb the Gods and worshiping practices of other peoples. You and yours stand in no danger from me or from Rome. Except in one single respect. Human sacrifice must cease. Men kill each other everywhere and in every people. But no people around the margins of Our Sea kills men—or women—to please the Gods. The Gods do not demand human sacrifice, and the priests who believe they do are deluded."

"The men we sacrifice are either prisoners of war or slaves bought for the specific purpose!" Cathbad snapped.

"Nevertheless it must stop."

"You lie, Caesar! You and Rome do threaten the Gallic way of life! You threaten the souls of our people!"

"No human sacrifice," said Caesar, unmoved and immovable.

Thus it went for several hours more, each man learning about the mind of the other. But when the meeting ended, Cathbad left a worried man. If Rome continued to infiltrate Gaul of the Long-hairs, everything would change; Druidism would dwindle and vanish. Therefore Rome must be driven out.

Caesar's response had been to begin negotiating for the elevation of Tasgetius to the Carnute kingship, by chance vacant. Among the Belgae combat would have decided the issue, but among the Celtae—including the Carnutes—the elders decided in council, with the Druids very carefully watching—and lobbying. The verdict had favored Tasgetius by a very narrow margin, and had depended on his undeniable blood claim. Caesar wanted him because he had spent four years in Rome as a child hostage and understood the perils of leading his people into outright war.

Now all of that was gone. Tasgetius was dead and Cathbad the Chief Druid was running the councils.

"So," said Caesar to his legate Lucius Munatius Plancus, "we'll try a deterrent. The Carnutes are a fairly sophisticated lot, and the murder of Tasgetius may not have been a design for war. They may have killed him for tribal reasons. Take the Twelfth and march for their capital, Cenabum. Go into winter camp outside its walls on the closest dry ground you can find, and *watch*. Luckily there's not much forest, so they shouldn't be able to surprise you. Be ready to deal with trouble, Plancus."

Plancus was another of Caesar's protégés, a man who, like Trebonius and Hirtius, relied heavily upon Caesar to advance his career. "What about the Druids?" he asked.

"Leave them and Carnutum severely alone, Plancus. I want no religious aspect to this war; that stiffens resistance. Privately I detest the Druids, but it is not my policy to antagonize them any more than I have to."

Off went Plancus and the Twelfth, which left Caesar and the Tenth to garrison Samarobriva. For a moment Caesar toyed with the idea of bringing Marcus Crassus and the Eighth into camp with the Tenth, as they were only twenty-five miles away, then decided to leave them where they were. His bones still insisted that the brewing revolt would be among the Belgae, not among the Celtae.

His bones were right. A formidable adversary has a habit of throwing up men capable of opposing him, and one such capable man was emerging. His name was Ambiorix and he was co-ruler of the Belgic Eburones, the selfsame tribe in whose lands the Thirteenth Legion of raw recruits was wintering inside the fortress of Atuatuca under the "exactly equal" joint command of Sabinus and Cotta.

Gaul of the Long-hairs was far from united, particularly when it came to congress between the part-German, part-Celtic Belgae of the north and northwest, and the pure Celtic tribes to their south. This lack of congress had benefited Caesar greatly, and was to do so again during the coming war-torn year. For Ambiorix didn't seek any allies among the Celtae; he went to his fellow Belgae. Which let Caesar fight peoples rather than one united people.

The Atuatuci were reduced to a handful—no allies there since Caesar had sold the bulk of the tribe into slavery. Nor could Ambiorix hope for co-operation from the Atrebates, with their Roman puppet king, Commius, plotting to use the Romans as a lever to create a new title, High King of the Belgae. The Nervii had gone down badly several years before, but it was a very large and populous tribe which could still field a terrifying number of warriors. Unfortunately the Nervii fought on foot, and Ambiorix was a horseman. Worth seeing what mischief he could brew there, but they wouldn't follow a horse leader. Ambiorix needed the Treveri, in whose ranks horse soldiers reigned supreme; the Treveri were also the most numerous and powerful people among the Belgae.

Ambiorix was a subtle man, unusual in the Belgae, with an imposing presence. As tall as a full-blooded German, he had lime-stiffened, flax-fair hair that stood out like the rays around the head of the sun god Helios, his great blond moustache drooped almost to his shoulders, and his face with its fierce blue eyes was nobly handsome. His narrow trousers and long shirt were black, but the big rectangular shawl which he draped around his body and pinned upon his left shoulder bore the Eburone pattern of checks, black and scarlet on a vivid saffron-yellow background. Just above his elbows were twin golden torcs as thick as snakes, just above his wrists were twin golden cuffs studded with lustrous amber, around his neck gleamed a huge golden torc with a horse's head at either end, the brooch securing his shawl was a great cabochon of amber set in gold, and his belt and baldric were made of gold plates hinged together and set with amber, as were the scabbards of his longsword and dagger. He looked every inch a king.

But before he could acquire the power to persuade other tribes to join his Eburones, Ambiorix needed a victory. And why look further afield than his own lands to find it? There sat Sabinus, Cotta and the Thirteenth Legion like a guest-gift. The problem was their camp; bitter experience had taught the Gauls that it was virtually impossible to storm and take a properly fortified winter camp. Especially when, as in this case, it was built upon the corpse of a formidable Gallic *oppidum* which Roman expertise had rendered impregnable. Nor would surrounding Atuatuca and starving it out work; the Romans counted on the enemy's being clever enough to do that. A Roman winter camp was furnished with good fresh water aplenty, food aplenty and sanitary arrangements which ensured disease was held at bay. What Ambiorix had to do was to lure the Romans out of Atuatuca. His way to secure his end was to attack Atuatuca, being careful to keep his Eburones out of harm's way.

What he didn't expect was that Sabinus would give him a perfect opening by sending a delegation to demand indignantly of the King what he thought he was doing. Ambiorix hurried to answer in person.

"You're not going out there to talk to him, surely!" said Cotta when Sabinus began to don his armor.

"Of course I am. You ought to come along too, co-commander."

"Not I!"

Thus Sabinus went alone save for his interpreter and a guard of honor; the parley took place right outside Atuatuca's front gate, and Ambiorix was accompanied by fewer men than Sabinus had with him. No danger, no danger at all. What was Cotta on about?

"Why did you attack my camp?" Sabinus demanded angrily through his interpreter.

Ambiorix produced an exaggerated shrug and spread his hands, eyes wide with surprise. "Why, noble Sabinus, I was merely doing what every king and chieftain is doing from one end of Gallia Comata to the other," he said.

Sabinus felt the blood drain from his face. "What do you mean?" he asked, and wet his lips.

"Gallia Comata is in revolt, noble Sabinus."

"With Caesar himself sitting in Samarobriva? Rubbish!"

Another shrug, another widening of the blue eyes. "Caesar is not in Samarobriva, noble Sabinus. Didn't you know? He changed his mind and departed for Italian Gaul a month ago. As soon as he was safely gone the Carnutes murdered King Tasgetius, and the revolt began. Samarobriva is under such huge attack that it is expected to fall very soon. Marcus Crassus was massacred nearby, Titus Labienus is under siege, Quintus Cicero and the Ninth Legion are dead, and Lucius Fabius and

Lucius Roscius have withdrawn to Tolosa in the Roman Province. You are alone, noble Sabinus."

White-faced, Sabinus nodded jerkily. "I see. I thank you for your candor, King Ambiorix." He turned and almost ran back through the gate, knees shaking, to tell Cotta.

Cotta stared at Sabinus with jaw dropped. "I don't believe a word of it!"

"You had better, Cotta. Ye Gods, Marcus Crassus and Quintus Cicero are dead, so are their legions!"

"If Caesar had changed his mind about going to Italian Gaul, Sabinus, he would have let us know," Cotta maintained.

"Perhaps he did. Perhaps we never received the message."

"Believe me, Sabinus, Caesar is still in Samarobriva! You've been told lies designed to make us decide to retreat. Don't listen to Ambiorix! He's playing fox to your rabbit."

"We have to go before he comes back! *Now!*"

The only other man privy to this conversation was the Thirteenth's *primipilus* centurion, known as Gorgo because his glance turned soldiers to stone. A hoary veteran who had been in Rome's legions since Pompey's war against Sertorius in Spain, Gorgo had been given the Thirteenth by Caesar because of his talent for training and his toughness.

Cotta looked at him in appeal.

"Gorgo, what do you think?"

The head in its fantastic helmet with the great stiff sideways crest nodded several times. "Lucius Cotta is right, Quintus Sabinus," he said. "Ambiorix is lying. He wants us to panic and pull stakes. Inside this camp he can't touch us, but the moment we're on the march we're vulnerable. If we stick it out here for the winter we'll survive. If we march, we're dead men. These are real good boys, but they're green. They need a well-generaled battle with plenty of company to season them. But if they're called on to fight without some veteran legions in the line with them, they'll go down. And I don't want to see that, Quintus Sabinus, because they *are* good boys."

"I say we march! *Now!*" Sabinus shouted.

Nor could he be bent. An hour of reasoning and arguing later Sabinus was still insisting on a retreat. Nor could Cotta and Gorgo be bent. At the end of another hour they were still insisting that the Thirteenth stick it out in the winter camp.

Sabinus stormed off in search of food, leaving Cotta and Gorgo to look at each other in consternation.

"The fool!" Cotta cried, not caring that he was insulting a legate in the hearing of a centurion. "Unless you and I can talk him out of retreating, he'll get us all killed."

"Trouble is," said Gorgo thoughtfully, "he won a battle all on his unaided own, so now he thinks he knows the military manual better than

Rutilius Rufus, who wrote it. But the Venelli aren't Belgae, and Viridovix was a typical thick Gaul. Ambiorix is not typical and not thick either. He's a very dangerous man."

Cotta sighed. "Then we have to keep trying, Gorgo."

Keep trying they did. Night fell with Cotta and Gorgo still trying, while Sabinus just grew angrier and more adamant.

"Oh, give over!" Gorgo yelled in the end, patience exhausted. "For the sake of Mars, *try* to see the truth, Quintus Sabinus! If we leave this camp we're all dead men! That includes you as well as me! And you might be ready to die, but I'm not! Caesar is sitting in Samarobriva, and may all the Gods help you when he finds out what's gone on here for the last twelve hours!"

The kind of man who wouldn't stomach the attendance of King Commius at a Roman council was certainly not going to stomach this from a lowly centurion, *primipilus* veteran or not. Face purple, Sabinus went for him, one hand upraised, and slapped him with an open palm. That was too much for Cotta, who stepped between them and knocked Sabinus off his feet, then fell on him and pounded him unmercifully.

It was Gorgo who broke them up, aghast. "Please, please!" he cried. "Do you think my boys are deaf, dumb and blind? They know what's going on between us! Whatever you decide, decide it! This sort of thing isn't going to help them!"

On the verge of tears, Cotta stared down at Sabinus. "All right, Sabinus, you win. Not Caesar himself could reason with you once you've made up what passes for your mind!"

It took two days to organize the retreat, for the troops, all very young and inexperienced, couldn't be persuaded by their centurions not to overload their packs with personal treasures and souvenirs, nor to relinquish their extra gear and souvenirs in the wagons. None of it worth a sestertius, but so precious to seventeen-year-olds keen to cement their yearned-for military careers with memories.

The march when it did begin was painfully slow, not helped by the sleet driving in their faces behind a howling wind straight off the German Ocean; the ground was both soaked and icy, the wagons kept bogging to the axles and were difficult to extricate. Even so, the day passed and the rugged heights of Atuatuca disappeared behind the shifting mists. Sabinus began to crow over Cotta, who set his lips and said nothing.

But Ambiorix and the Eburones were there beyond the sleety rain, biding their time with the complacence of men who knew the terrain a great deal better than the Romans did.

Ambiorix's plan worked smoothly; he could not afford to let the Roman column, marching down the Mosa, get far enough away from Atuatuca to encounter any of Quintus Cicero's men, for Quintus Cicero and the Ninth were very much alive. The moment Sabinus led the Thirteenth into a narrow defile, Ambiorix swung his foot soldiers to block the Roman advance and unleashed his horse soldiers on the tail of the column until it turned back on itself and prevented retreat out of the steep-sided gulch, perfect for Ambiorix's purpose.

The initial reaction was blind panic as screaming hordes of Eburones swarmed into both ends of the defile, their brilliant yellow shawls abandoned so that they seemed like black shadows out of the Underworld. The unversed troops of the Thirteenth broke formation and tried to flee. Worse was Sabinus, whose fear and dismay drove all military ideas from his head.

But when the shock wore off, the Thirteenth steadied down, saved from immediate massacre by the narrow confines in which the attack took place. There was nowhere to flee, and once Cotta, Gorgo and his centurions got the milling recruits standing in proper rank and file to resist, the lads discovered to their delight that they could kill the enemy. The peculiar iron of a hopeless situation stiffened their spirits, and they resolved that they would not die alone. And while the troops at the head and the tail of the column held the Eburones at bay, the troops in the middle, helped by the noncombatants and slaves, began to throw up defensive walls.

At sunset there was still a Thirteenth, hideously smaller but far from defeated.

"Didn't I tell you they were good boys?" asked Gorgo of Cotta as they paused to catch their breath; the Eburones had drawn off to mass for another onslaught.

"I curse Sabinus!" Cotta hissed. "They *are* good boys! But they're all going to die, Gorgo, when they deserve to live and put decorations on their standards!"

"Oh, Jupiter!" came from Gorgo in a moan.

Cotta swung to look, and gasped. Carrying a stick on which he had tied his white handkerchief, Sabinus was picking his way across the dead at the mouth of the defile to where Ambiorix stood conferring with his nobles.

Ambiorix, wearing his brilliant yellow shawl because he was one of the leaders, saw Sabinus and walked a few paces forward, holding his longsword in front of him, its tip pointing at the ground. With him went two other chieftains.

"Truce, truce!" Sabinus shouted, panting.

"I accept your truce, Quintus Sabinus, but only if you give up your weapons," said Ambiorix.

"Spare those of us who are left, I beg you!" said Sabinus, throwing sword and dagger away ostentatiously.

The answer was a sudden swirling sweep of the longsword; Sabinus's head soared into the air, parting company with its Attic helmet as well as its body. One of Ambiorix's companions caught the helmet as it descended, but Ambiorix waited until the head had finished rolling before he walked to it and picked it up.

"Oh, these shorn Romans!" he cried, unable to wrap Sabinus's half-inch-long hair about his knuckles. Only by shaping his hand into a claw did he manage to lift the head high and wave it in the direction of the Thirteenth. "Attack!" he screamed. "Take their heads, take their heads!"

Cotta was killed and decapitated not long after, but Gorgo lived to see the Aquilifer, dying on his feet, summon up some last reserve of strength and fling his hallowed silver Eagle like a javelin behind the dwindling Roman line.

The Eburones drew off with the darkness, and Gorgo went the rounds of his boys to see how many were still on their feet. Pitifully few: about two hundred out of five thousand.

"All right, boys," he said to them as they huddled together in a sea of fallen comrades, "swords out. Kill every man who's still breathing, then come back to me."

"When will the Eburones return?" asked one seventeen-year-old.

"At dawn, lad, but they won't find any of us alive to burn in their wicker cages. Kill the wounded, then come back to me. If you find any of our noncombatants or slaves, offer them a choice. Go now and try to get through to the Remi, or stay with us and die with us."

While the soldiers went to obey his orders, Gorgo took the silver Eagle and looked about him, eyes used to the darkness. Ah, there! He gouged out a long, pipelike trench in some soft, bloody ground and buried the Eagle, not very deeply. After which he heaved and hauled until the spot was under a pile of bodies, then sat on a rock and waited.

At about the middle hour of the night, the surviving soldiers of the Thirteenth Legion killed themselves rather than live to be burned in wicker cages.

There were very few noncombatants or slaves left alive, for all of them had plucked swords and shields from dead legionaries and fought. But those who still lived were let through the enemy lines indifferently, with the result that Caesar got word of the fate of the Thirteenth late the following day.

"Trebonius, look after things," he said, clad in good plain steel armor, his scarlet general's cloak tied to his shoulders.

"Caesar, you can't go unprotected!" Trebonius cried. "Take the Tenth; I'll send for Marcus Crassus and the Eighth to hold Samarobriva."

"Ambiorix will be long gone," said Caesar positively. "He knows a Roman relief force will appear, and he has no intention of imperiling his victory. I've sent to Dorix of the Remi to muster his men to arms. I won't be unprotected."

Nor was he. When he reached the Sabis River some distance beyond its sources, Caesar met Dorix and ten thousand Remi cavalry. With

Caesar rode a squadron of Aeduan cavalry and one of his crop of new legates, Publius Sulpicius Rufus.

Rufus gasped in awe as they came over a rise and looked down on the massed Remi horsemen. "Jupiter, what a sight!"

Caesar grunted. "Pretty to look at, aren't they?"

Remi shawls were checkered in brilliant blue and dull crimson with a thin yellow thread interwoven, and Remi trousers were the same; Remi shirts were dull crimson, Remi horse blankets brilliant blue.

"I didn't know the Gauls rode such handsome horses."

"They don't," said Caesar. "You're looking at the Remi, who went into the business of breeding Italian and Spanish horses generations ago. That's why they greeted my advent with glee and profuse protestations of friendship. They were finding it very hard to keep their horses—the other tribes were forever raiding their herds. Fighting back turned them into superb cavalrymen themselves, but they lost many horses nonetheless, and were forced to pen their breeding stallions inside veritable fortresses. They also border the Treveri, who lust after Remi mounts. To the Remi, I was a gift from the Gods—I meant Rome had come to stay in Gaul of the Long-hairs. Thus the Remi give me excellent cavalry, and as a thank-you I send Labienus to the Treveri to terrify them."

Sulpicius Rufus shivered; he knew exactly what Caesar meant, though he knew Labienus only through the stories forever circulating in Rome. "What's wrong with Gallic horses?" he asked.

"They're not much bigger than ponies. The native stock if unmixed with other breeds is a pony. Very uncomfortable for men as tall as the Belgae."

Dorix rode up the hill to greet Caesar warmly, then swung his dish-faced, long-maned *marca* beside the General.

"Where's Ambiorix?" asked Caesar, who had preserved his calm and betrayed no sign of grief since getting the news.

"Nowhere near the battlefield. My scouts report it's quite deserted. I've brought slaves with me to burn and bury."

"Good man."

They camped that night and rode on in the morning.

Ambiorix had taken his own dead; only Roman bodies lay in the defile. Dismounting, Caesar gestured that the Remi and his own squadron of cavalry should stay back. He walked forward with Sulpicius Rufus, and as he walked the tears began to run down his seamed face.

They encountered the headless body of Sabinus first, unmistakable in its legate's armor; he had been a smallish man, Cotta much larger.

"Ambiorix has a Roman legate's head to decorate his front door," said Caesar, it seemed oblivious to his tears. "Well, he'll have no joy from it."

Almost all the bodies were headless. The Eburones, like many of the

Gallic tribes, Celtae as well as Belgae, took heads as battle trophies to adorn the door posts of their houses.

"There are traders do an excellent business selling cedar resin to the Gauls," said Caesar, still weeping silently.

"Cedar resin?" asked Sulpicius Rufus, weeping too, and finding this dispassionate conversation bizarre.

"To preserve the heads. The more heads a man has around his door, the greater his warrior status. Some are content to let them wear away to skulls, but the great nobles pickle their trophies in cedar resin. We'll recognize Sabinus when we see him."

The sight of dead bodies and battlefields was not a new experience for Sulpicius Rufus, but his youthful campaigns had all been conducted in the East, where things were, he knew now, very different. *Civilized*. This was his first visit to Gaul, and he had arrived but two days before Caesar had ordered him to come on this journey into death.

"Well, they weren't massacred like helpless women," said Caesar. "They put up a terrific fight." He stopped suddenly.

He had come to the place where the survivors had killed themselves, unmistakably; their heads remained on their shoulders and the Eburones had obviously steered a wide berth around them, perhaps frightened of that kind of courage, alien to their own kind. To die in battle was glorious. To die after it alone in the dark was horrifying.

"Gorgo!" said Caesar, and broke down completely.

He knelt beside the grizzled veteran and pulled the body into his arms, crouched there and put his cheek on the lifeless hair, keening and mourning. It had nothing to do with the deaths of his mother and daughter; this was the General grieving for his troops.

Sulpicius Rufus moved onward, shaken because he could see now how young they had all been, most of them not yet shaving. Oh, what a business! His running eyes flicked from face to face, looking for some sign of life. And found it in the face of a senior centurion, hands still clasped around the handle of his sword, buried in his belly.

"Caesar!" he shouted. "Caesar, there's one alive!"

And so they learned the story of Ambiorix, Sabinus, Cotta and Gorgo before the *pilus prior* centurion finally let go.

Caesar's tears hadn't dried; he got to his feet.

"There's no Eagle," he said, "but there should be. The Aquilifer threw it inside the defenses before he died."

"The Eburones will have taken it," said Sulpicius Rufus. "They've left nothing unturned except those who killed themselves."

"Which Gorgo will have known. We'll find it there."

Once the bodies alongside Gorgo were moved, they found the Thirteenth's silver Eagle.

"In all my long career as a soldier, Rufus, I've never seen a legion killed to the last man," said Caesar as they turned to where Dorix and the Remi waited patiently. "I *knew* Sabinus was a puffed-up fool, but because he handled himself so well against Viridovix and the Venelli, I thought him competent. It was Cotta I didn't think up to it."

"You weren't to know," said Sulpicius Rufus, at a loss for the right response.

"No, I wasn't. But not because of Sabinus. Because of Ambiorix. The Belgae have thrown up a formidable leader. He had to defeat me on his own in order to show the rest of them that he is capable of leading them. Right now he'll be sniffing at the arses of the Treveri."

"What about the Nervii?"

"They fight on foot, unusual for the Belgae. Ambiorix is a horse leader. That's why he'll be wooing the Treveri. Do you feel up to a long ride, Rufus?"

Sulpicius Rufus blinked. "I don't have your stamina in the saddle, Caesar, but I'll do whatever you require."

"Good. I must stay here to conduct the funeral rites for the Thirteenth, whose heads are missing and therefore cannot hold the coin to pay Charon. Luckily I'm Pontifex Maximus. I have the authority to draw up the necessary contracts with Jupiter Optimus Maximus and Pluto to pay Charon for all of them in one lump sum."

Completely understandable. The only Romans who were deprived of their heads under usual circumstances had also forfeited their Roman citizenship; to have no mouth in which to hold the coin to pay for the ferry ride across the river Styx meant that the dead man's shade—not a soul but a mindless remnant of life—wandered the earth instead of the Underworld. Invisible demented, akin to the living demented who roamed from place to place being fed and clothed by the compassionate, but were never invited to stay and never knew the comfort of a home.

"Take my squadron of cavalry and ride for Labienus," Caesar said, pulling his handkerchief from under the armhole of his cuirass and wiping his eyes, blowing his nose. "He's on the Mosa not far from Virodunum. Dorix will give you a couple of Remi as guides. Tell Labienus what happened here, and warn him to be very vigilant. And tell him"—Caesar drew a harsh breath—"tell him to give absolutely no quarter."

Quintus Cicero knew nothing of the fate of Sabinus, Cotta and the Thirteenth. Camped among the Nervii without benefit of a fortress like Atuatuca, Cicero's little brother and the Ninth Legion had made themselves as comfortable as possible in the midst of a flat, sleety expanse of pasture as far from the eaves of the forest as they could get, and well removed from the Mosa River.

It wasn't all bad. A stream ran through the camp, providing good fresh water where it entered and carrying the latrine sewage away as it chuckled, unfrozen, down to the distant Mosa. Of food they had plenty, and it was more varied than Quintus Cicero for one had expected after that gloomy council in Portus Itius. Wood for heating was not hard to come by, though the parties sent off to the forest to fetch it went heavily armed, stayed alert, and had a signal system in case they needed help.

The best feature about this winter cantonment was the presence of a friendly village in close proximity; the local Nervian aristocrat, one Vertico, was strongly in favor of a Roman army in Belgica, for he believed that the Belgae had more chance of fending off the Germans if they were allied to Rome. This meant that he was anxious to help in whatever ways he could, and generous to a fault in the matter of women for the Roman troops. Provided a soldier was prepared to pay, women there were. Mouth tugging itself into a smile, Quintus Cicero closed a tolerant eye to all of this, contenting himself with writing to his big brother snug in Rome and wondering on the paper if he ought to demand a share of the commission Vertico undoubtedly extracted from his obliging females, whose ranks kept swelling as word of the largesse to be found in the Ninth's camp spread far and wide.

The Ninth was composed of genuine veterans, having been enlisted in Italian Gaul during the last five months of Caesar's consulship; they had fought their way, they were fond of saying, from the Rhodanus River to Oceanus Atlanticus and from the Garumna in Aquitania to the mouth of the Mosa in Belgica. Despite which, they were all around an age of twenty-three, hard-bitten young men whom nothing frightened. Racially they were akin to the people they had been fighting for five years, for Caesar had culled them from the far side of the Padus River in Italian Gaul, where the people were the descendants of the Gauls who had fallen on Italia some centuries before. So they were on the tall side, fair or red of hair, and light-eyed. Not that this blood kinship had endeared the long-haired Gauls to them; they hated long-haired Gauls, Belgae or Celtae made no difference. Troops can live with respect for an enemy, but not with feelings of love or even pity. Hate is a mandatory emotion for good soldiering.

But Quintus Cicero's ignorance went further than oblivion about the fate of the Thirteenth; he also had absolutely no idea that Ambiorix was intriguing in the councils of the Nervii to see what damage he could do en route to his parley with the Treveri. Ambiorix's lever was simple and extremely effective: once he learned that the Nervian women were hustling themselves off to earn some money (a substance to which they normally had little access) in the Ninth's winter camp, stirring up the Nervii was easy.

"Are you really content with dipping your wicks in some Roman soldier's leavings?" he asked, blue eyes wide with astonishment. "Are your children really yours? Will they speak Nervian or Latin? Will they drink wine or beer? Will they smack their lips at the thought of butter on their bread, or hanker to soak it in olive oil? Will they listen to the lays of the Druids or prefer to see a Roman farce?"

Several days of this saw Ambiorix a happy man. He then offered to see Quintus Cicero and play the same kind of trick on him as he had on Sabinus. But Quintus Cicero was no Sabinus; he wouldn't even see Ambiorix's ambassadors, and when they became insistent he answered dourly through a messenger that he wasn't going to treat with any long-haired Gauls, no matter how highfalutin' they were, so take yourselves off (actually not quite so delicately expressed) and leave me alone.

"Real tactful," said the *primipilus* centurion, Titus Pullo, grinning hugely.

"Pah!" said Quintus Cicero, shifting his meager body on his ivory curule chair. "I'm here to do a job, not crawl up the arses of a lot of uppity savages. If they want to treat, they should go and see Caesar. It's his job to put up with them, not mine."

"The interesting thing about Quintus Cicero," said Pullo to his *pilus prior* confederate, Lucius Vorenus, "is that he can say things like that, then turn around and be as nice as a long swig of Falernian to Vertico—without ever seeing that there's any inconsistency in his behavior."

"Well, he likes Vertico," said Vorenus. "Therefore to him Vertico isn't an uppity savage. Once you're on Quintus Cicero's list of friends, doesn't matter who you are."

Which was more or less what Quintus Cicero was saying on paper to his big brother in Rome. They had corresponded for years, because all educated Romans wrote copiously to all other educated Romans. Even the rankers wrote home regularly to tell their families what life was like and what they'd been doing and what battles they'd fought and what the rest of their tent mates were like. A good number were literate upon enlistment, and those who were not discovered that some at least of winter in camp had to be spent in being tutored. Especially under generals like Caesar, who had sat and listened at Gaius Marius's knee when a child and absorbed everything Marius had to say about everything. Including the usefulness of legionaries who could read and write.

"It's the lettered version of learning to swim," Marius had mumbled through his twisted mouth. "Saves lives."

Odd, thought Quintus Cicero, that big brother Cicero grew more bearable in direct proportion to the amount of distance between them. From winter camp among the Nervii he seemed like a really ideal big brother, whereas when he was a short distance down the Via Tusculana—and likely to arrive on the doorstep unannounced—he was usually a pain in the *podex,* full of well-meaning advice Quintus just didn't want to hear while Pomponia was shrilling in the other ear and he was busy walking the tightrope of being nice to Pomponia's brother, Atticus, yet striving to be master in his own house.

Not that every letter which arrived from Cicero wasn't at least half full of advice, but among the Nervii that advice didn't need to be taken or even listened to. Quintus had perfected the art of knowing the exact syllable which would introduce a sermon, and the exact syllable which would end it, so he just skipped those many sheets and read the interesting bits. Big brother Cicero was, of course, a shocking prude who had never dared to look beyond his fearsome wife, Terentia, since he had married her over twenty-five years ago. So anywhere in his vicinity Quintus had to be similarly abstemious. Among the Nervii, however, there was no one to see what little brother Quintus got up to. And little brother Quintus got up on every possible occasion. Belgic women were on the hefty side and could flatten you with one punch, but they all fought for the attentions of the dear little commander with the lovely manners and the gratifyingly open purse. After living with Pomponia (who could also flatten you with one punch), the Belgic women were an Elysian Field of uncomplicated pleasure.

But for a day after the ambassadors from King Ambiorix had been sent away unseen and so impolitely, Quintus Cicero was conscious of a peculiar restlessness. Something was wrong; what, he didn't know. Then his left thumb started pricking and tingling. He sent for Pullo and Vorenus.

"We're in for trouble," he said, "and don't bother asking me how I know, because I don't know how I know. Let's walk around the camp and see what we can do to shore up its defenses."

Pullo looked at Vorenus; then they both looked at Quintus Cicero with considerable respect.

"Send someone to fetch Vertico—I need to see him."

That attended to, the three men and an escort of centurions set out to examine the camp with an unsparing eye.

"More towers," said Pullo. "We've got sixty, we need twice that many."

"I agree. And an extra ten feet of height on the walls."

"Do we throw up more earth or use logs?" asked Vorenus.

"Logs. The ground's full of water and freezing. Logs will be faster. We'll simply jack the breastworks up another ten feet. Get the men felling trees at once. If we come under attack we won't be able to get to the forest, so let's do it now. Just fell 'em and drag 'em in. We can pretty them up here."

Off ran one of the centurions.

"Put a lot more stakes in the bottom of the ditches," said Vorenus, "since we can't deepen 'em."

"Definitely. How are we off for charcoal?"

"We've got a bit, but not nearly enough if we want to harden sharpened points in slow fires beyond a couple of thousand," said Pullo. "The trees will give us all the branches we'll need."

"Then we'll see how much charcoal Vertico can donate." The commander pulled thoughtfully at his lower lip. "Siege spears."

"Oak won't work for them," said Vorenus. "We'll have to find birches or ash forced to grow straight up."

"More stones for the artillery," said Pullo.

"Send some men down to the Mosa."

Several more centurions ran off.

"Last," said Pullo, "what about letting Caesar know?"

Quintus Cicero had to think about that. Thanks to his big brother, who had loathed Caesar ever since he had opposed the execution of the Catilinarian conspirators, Quintus tended to mistrust Caesar too. Not that these emotions had prevented big brother Cicero from begging that Caesar take Quintus as one of his legates and Gaius Trebatius as a tribune. Nor, though Caesar was well aware how Cicero felt, did Caesar refuse. Professional courtesies between consulars were obligatory.

But what the family tradition of Caesar-detestation meant was that Quintus Cicero didn't know the General as well as most of his other legates did, nor had he yet found his feet in his dealings with the General. He had no idea how Caesar would react if one of his senior legates sent a message full of alarm when there was no better reason behind it than a pricking left thumb and a presentiment that big trouble was brewing. He had gone to Britannia with Caesar, an interesting experience, but not one which had allowed him to see what kind of latitude Caesar gave his legates. Caesar had been in personal command from beginning to end of the expedition.

A lot hinged on what answer he gave Pullo. If he made the wrong decision, he wouldn't be asked to remain in Gaul an extra year or two; he would suffer the same fate as Servius Sulpicius Galba, who had botched his campaign in the high Alps and had not been asked to stay. No use believing the senatorial dispatches; *they* had lauded Galba. Though any militarily acute individual who read them could see immediately that Galba hadn't pleased the General one little bit.

"I don't think," he said to Pullo finally, "that it would do any harm to let Caesar know. If I'm wrong, then I'll take the reprimand I'll deserve. But somehow, Pullo, I *know* I'm not wrong! Yes, I'll write to Caesar at once."

In all of this lay some good luck and some bad luck. The good luck was that the Nervii were not yet mustered to arms and therefore saw no sense in spying on the camp; they simply assumed that its denizens would be going about their normal business. This enabled Quintus Cicero to fell his trees and get them inside, and start building his walls and his extra sixty towers around the perimeter. It also enabled him to lay in a great store of good round two-pound rocks for his artillery. The bad luck was that the Nervian council had decided on war, so a watch had been put on the road south to Samarobriva, a hundred and fifty miles away.

Carried by the usual courier, Quintus Cicero's rather diffident and apologetic letter was confiscated along with every other letter the courier carried. Then the courier was killed. Some of the Druids among the Nervii read Latin, so to them went the contents of the courier's pouch for perusal. But Quintus had written in Greek, another consequence of that pricking thumb. It was only much later that he realized he must have been listening when Vertico had remarked that the Druids of the northern Belgae were schooled in Latin, not in Greek. In other parts of Gaul, the opposite might be true; usefulness determined the language.

Vertico agreed with Quintus Cicero: there was trouble coming.

"I'm so well known to be a partisan of Caesar's that I'm not welcome in the councils these days," the Nervian thane said, eyes anxious. "But several times during the last two days some of my serfs have seen warriors passing through my land, accompanied by their shield bearers and pack animals—as if going to a general muster. At this time of year they can't be going to war in someone else's territory. I think you are the target."

"Then," said Quintus Cicero briskly, "I suggest that you and your people move into camp with us. It may be a little cramped and not what you're used to, but if we can hold the camp you'll be safe. Otherwise you might find yourself the first to die. Is that acceptable?"

"Oh, yes!" cried Vertico, profoundly relieved. "You won't run short because of us—I'll bring every grain of wheat we have—all the chickens and livestock—and plenty of charcoal."

"Excellent!" said Quintus Cicero, beaming. "We'll put all of you to work, never think we won't."

Five days after the courier was killed, the Nervii attacked. Perturbed because he should have had a reply, Quintus Cicero had already sent a second letter off, but this courier too was intercepted. Instead of killing him outright, the Nervii tortured him first, and learned that Quintus Cicero and the Ninth were working frantically to strengthen the camp's fortifications.

The muster was complete; the Nervii moved immediately. Their progress was very different from a Roman march, even one at the double, for they ran at a tireless lope which ate up the miles, each warrior accompanied by his shield bearer, his body slave and a burdened pony on which were loaded his dozen spears, his mail shirt if he had one, his food, his beer, his checkered shawl of moss green and earthy orange, and a wolf pelt for warmth at night; his two servants carried their own needs upon their backs. Nor did they run in any kind of formation. The fleetest were the first to arrive, the slowest the last to arrive. But the last man of all did not come; he who arrived last to the muster was sacrificed to Esus, the god of battle, his body strung from a branch in the sacred oak grove.

It took all day for the Nervii to assemble outside the camp, while the Ninth hammered and sawed frantically; the wall and its raised breastworks were quite finished, but the extra sixty towers were still rising and the many thousands of sharpened stakes were still hardening in a hundred charcoal fires wherever there was enough vacant ground.

"Good, we'll work all night," said Quintus Cicero, pleased. "They won't attack today, they'll have a proper rest first."

A proper rest for the Nervii turned out to be about an hour; the sun had set when they stormed the walls of the camp in their thousands, filling up the ditches with leafy branches, using their gaudy, feather-bedecked spears as hand holds to haul themselves up the log walls. But the Ninth was up on top of the walls, each two men with one of the long siege spears to take the Nervii in the face as they climbed. Other men stood atop the partially finished towers, using this additional height to launch their *pila* with deadly accuracy. And all the while from within the camp the ballistae lobbed two-pound river rocks over the walls into the boiling masses of warriors.

Full night brought a cessation to the hostilities, but not to the battle frenzy of the Nervii, who leaped and shrieked and howled for a mile in every direction around the camp; the light of twenty thousand torches banished the darkness and showed up the capering figures wielding them, bare chests coppered, hair like frozen manes, eyes and teeth flashing brief sparks as they turned and reeled, bounced into the air, roared, screamed, flung up their torches, caught them like jugglers.

"Isn't this terrific, boys?" Quintus Cicero would shout as he bustled about the camp, checking on the charcoal fires, the artillerymen toiling stripped of their mail shirts, the baggage animals snorting and stamping in their stalls at so much noise. "Isn't it terrific? The Nervii are giving us all the light we need to finish our towers! Come on, boys, buckle down to it! What do you think this is, the harem of Sampsiceramus?"

Then his back began to ache, and came an agonizing pain which shot down his left leg and forced him to limp. Oh, not now! Not an attack of *that*! It sent him crawling to his bed for days on end, a moaning rag. Not now! How could he crawl off to his bed when everyone depended on him? If the commander succumbed, what would happen to morale? So Quintus Cicero clenched his teeth and limped onward, finding from somewhere the resolution to unclench his teeth, smile, joke, tell the men how terrific they were, how nice it was of the Nervii to light up the sky . . .

Every day the Nervii attacked, filled up the ditches, tried to scale the walls, and every day the Ninth repulsed them, hooked the leafy branches out of the ditches, killed Nervii.

Every night Quintus Cicero wrote another letter in Greek to Caesar, found a slave or a Gaul willing to carry it for a huge sum of money, and sent the man off through the darkness.

Every day the Nervii brought the previous night's courier to a prominent spot, brandished the letter, capered and shrieked until the courier was put to a fresh torture from the pincers or the knives or the hot irons, when they would fall silent and let the courier's screams rip through the appalled Roman camp.

"We can't give in," Quintus Cicero would say to the soldiers as he limped his rounds; "don't give those *mentulae* the pleasure or the satisfaction!"

Whereupon the men he addressed would grin, give him a wave, ask about his back, call the Nervii names big brother Cicero would have fainted to hear, and fight on.

Then came Titus Pullo, face grim. "Quintus Cicero, we have a new problem," he said harshly.

"What?" asked the commander, keeping the weariness from his voice and trying to stand straight.

"They've diverted our water. The stream's dried up."

"You know what to do, Pullo. Start digging wells. Upstream from the latrines. And start digging cesspits." He giggled. "I'd pitch in and help, but I'm afraid I'm not in a digging mood."

Pullo's face softened: was there ever such a cheerful and unquenchable commander as Quintus Cicero, bad back and all?

Twenty days after that first assault the Nervii were still attacking every morning. The supply of couriers had dried up along with the water, and Quintus Cicero had to face the fact that not one of his messages had got through the Nervian lines. Well, no other choice than to continue resistance. Fight the bastards off during the day, use the nights to repair the damage and make a supply of whatever might come in useful the following dawn—and wonder how long it would be before the dysentery and the fevers commenced. Oh, what he'd do to the Nervii if he lived to get out of this! The men of the Ninth were still unbroken, still in good spirits, still working frantically when they were not fighting frantically.

The dysentery and the fevers started, but suddenly there were worse problems to cope with.

The Nervii built a few siege towers—not a patch on Roman siege towers, naturally, but fully capable of wreaking havoc when they were close enough to serve as platforms for Nervii spears. And for a bombardment of Nervii boulders.

"Where did they get their artillery from?" cried the commander to Vorenus. "If those aren't trusty Roman ballistae, then I'm not the great Cicero's little brother!"

But since Vorenus didn't know any more than Quintus Cicero did that the artillery came from the abandoned camp of the Thirteenth Legion, the appearance of Roman ballistae was simply an additional worry—did it mean all Gaul was in revolt, that other legions had been attacked and defeated, that even if the messages had gotten through, no one was alive to answer?

The stones were bearable, but then the Nervii became more innovative. At the same moment as they launched a fresh assault on the walls, they loaded the ballistae with blazing bundles of dry sticks and shot them into the camp. Even the sick were manning the walls, so there were few to put out the fires which began all over that town of wooden houses, few to blindfold the terrified baggage animals and lead them into the open. Slaves, noncombatants and Vertico's people tried to split themselves in two and cope with this new horror while doing all the other things they had to in order to keep the Ninth fighting atop the walls. But so strong was the Ninth's morale that the soldiers never even turned their heads to see their precious possessions and food go up in flames, fanned by a bitter early winter wind. They stayed where they were and fought the Nervii to a standstill.

In the midst of the fiercest attack, Pullo and Vorenus took a bet that each was braver than the other, and demanded that the Ninth be the judges. One of the siege towers was pushed so close that it touched the camp wall; the Nervii began to use it as a bridge to leap onto the defenders. Pullo produced a torch and flung it, rising from behind the shelter of his shield; Vorenus produced another torch and rose even higher from behind his shield to fling it at the siege tower. Back and forth, back and forth, until the siege tower was blazing and the Nervii fled, their stiffened hair in flames. Pullo grabbed a bow and quiver of arrows and demonstrated that he'd served with Cretan archers by nocking and shooting in one fluid movement and never missing. Vorenus countered by stacking *pila* and throwing them with equal speed and grace—and never missing. Neither man sustained a scratch, and when the attack ebbed the Ninth shook their heads. The verdict was a draw.

"It's the turning point as well as the thirtieth day," said Quintus Cicero when the darkness came and the Nervii wandered off in undisciplined hordes.

He had summoned a little council: himself, Pullo, Vorenus and Vertico.

"You mean we'll win?" asked Pullo, astonished.

"I mean we'll lose, Titus Pullo. They're getting craftier every day, and from somewhere they've got hold of Roman gear." He groaned and beat his fist on his thigh. "Oh, ye Gods, *somehow* we have to get a message through their lines!" He turned to Vertico. "I won't ask another man to go, yet someone has to go. And right here and now we have to work out a way to make sure that whichever man we send can survive a search if he's apprehended. Vertico, you're the Nervian. How do we do it?"

"I've been thinking," said Vertico in his halting Latin. "First of all, it has to be someone who can pass for a Nervian warrior. There are Menapii and Condrusi out there too now, but I don't have access to shawls of the right pattern. Otherwise it would be better to pass the man off as one of them." He stopped, sighed. "How much food survived the fireballs?"

"Enough for seven or eight days," said Vorenus, "though the men are so sick they're not eating much. Maybe ten days."

Vertico nodded. "Then it will have to be this. Someone who can pass for a Nervian warrior because he is Nervian. I'd go myself, but I'd be recognized immediately. One of my serfs is willing to go. He's a clever fellow, thinks on his feet."

"That's well and good!" growled Pullo, face filthy, tunic of metal scales ripped from neck to sword belt. "I see the sense of it. But it's the search worries me. We put the last note up the messenger's rectum, but those bastards still found it. *Jupiter!* I mean, maybe your man will get through without being accosted, but if he is accosted, he'll be searched. They'll find a note no matter where it is, and if they don't, they'll torture him."

"Look," said Vertico, wrenching a Nervian spear out of the ground nearby.

It was not a Roman weapon, but it was workmanlike; a long wooden shaft with a large leaf-shaped iron head. As the long-haired Gauls loved color and decoration, it was not naked. At the place where the thrower held it, the shaft was covered by a woven webbing in the Nervian colors of moss green and earthy orange, and from the webbing, secured by loops, there dangled three goose feathers dyed moss green and earthy orange.

"I understand why the message has to be in writing. Caesar might not believe a message from the mouth of a Nervian warrior. But write your message in the smallest script upon the thinnest paper, Quintus Cicero. And while you write, I'll have my women unpick the webbing on a spear which looks used but not warped. Then we'll wrap the message around the spear shaft and cover it with the webbing." Vertico shrugged. "That's the best I can suggest. They search every orifice; they search every scrap of clothing, every strand of hair. But if the webbing is perfect, I don't think it will occur to them to take it off."

Vorenus and Pullo were nodding; Quintus Cicero nodded to them and limped off to his wooden house, unburned. There he sat down as he was and took the thinnest piece of paper he could find. His Greek script was tiny.

> I write in Greek because they have Latin. Urgent. Under attack from Nervii for thirty days. Water sour, latrines infested. Men sick. Holding out, don't know how. Can't much longer. Nervii have Roman gear, shooting fireballs. Food up in smoke. Get help to us or we're dead men. Quintus Tullius Cicero Legatus.

The Nervian serf belonging to Vertico was a perfect warrior type; had his station in life been higher, he would have been a warrior. But serfs were a superior kind of slave, could be put to torture, and would never be allowed to fight for the tribe. Their lot was to farm; they were lowly enough to use a plough. Yet the man stood calmly and looked unafraid. Yes, thought Quintus Cicero, he would have made a good warrior. More fool the Nervii for not allowing their lowly to fight, but lucky for me and the Ninth. He'll pass muster.

"All right," he said, "we've got a chance to get this to Caesar, but how does Caesar get his message to us? I have to be able to tell the men that help is coming or they might go under from sheer despair. It will take Caesar time to find enough legions, but I *must* be able to say that help is coming."

Vertico smiled. "Getting a message in isn't as difficult as getting one out. When my serf returns, I'll tell him to attach one yellow feather to the spear bearing Caesar's answer."

"It'll stick out like dog's balls!" cried Pullo, aghast.

"So I would hope. However, I don't think anyone will be looking too closely at spears flying into the camp. Don't worry, I'll tell him not to attach the yellow feather until just before he throws," said Vertico, grinning.

Caesar got the spear two days after the Nervian serf passed through the Nervian lines.

Because the forest to the south of Quintus Cicero's camp was too dense for a man on an urgent mission to negotiate, the serf had no choice but to travel on the road to Samarobriva. It was so heavily guarded that it was inevitable he would be stopped sooner or later, though he did well, evaded the first three watches. The fourth watch detained him. He was stripped, his orifices probed, his hair, his clothes. But the webbing on the spear was perfect; the message lay beneath it undetected. The serf had lacerated his forehead with a piece of rough bark until it looked like the result of a blow; he swayed, mumbled, rolled his eyes, endured the search ungraciously and tried to kiss the leader of the watch. Deeming him hopelessly concussed, the leader let him go south, laughing.

It was early evening when he arrived, utterly exhausted; Samarobriva was immediately plunged into a disciplined frenzy of activity. One messenger went at a gallop to Marcus Crassus, twenty-five miles away; he was ordered to bring the Eighth on the double to garrison Samarobriva in the General's absence. A second messenger galloped for Portus Itius and Gaius Fabius, who was ordered to take the Seventh and march for the lands of the Atrebates; Caesar would meet him on the Scaldis River. A third messenger galloped for the camp of Labienus on the Mosa to apprise him of developments, but Caesar didn't order his second-in-command to join the rescue mission. He left that decision to Labienus, who he privately thought might be in like case to Quintus Cicero.

At dawn the whole of Samarobriva could see Marcus Crassus's column in the distance. Caesar left with the Tenth at once.

Two legions, each a little under full strength; that was all the General could bring to the relief of Quintus Cicero. Nine thousand precious men, veterans. There could be no more of these stupid mistakes. *How many Nervii?* Fifty thousand had stayed to die on the field several years before, but it was a very populous tribe. Yes, there could be as many as fifty thousand more around the beleaguered camp of the Ninth. Good legion. Oh, not dead!

Fabius made good time to the Scaldis; he met up with Caesar as if they were engaged in a complicated drill maneuver upon the Campus Martius. Neither man had needed to wait an hour for the other. Seventy more miles to go. *But how many Nervii?* Nine thousand men, no matter how veteran, wouldn't stand a chance in the open.

Caesar had sent the Nervian serf on ahead in a gig as far as he dared, since he couldn't ride, under instructions to send the spear back into Quintus Cicero's camp with a yellow feather tied to it. But he was a serf, not a warrior. He did his best, hoping to get the spear over the breastworks into the Roman camp. Instead it buried itself in the junction between the breastworks and the log wall, and there undetected it remained for two days.

Quintus Cicero got it scant hours before a column of smoke above the trees told him that Caesar had arrived; he was on the point of despair because no one had seen a spear with a yellow feather on it, though every pair of eyes had searched until they watered, fancied yellow in everything.

> Coming. Only nine thousand men. Can't just rush in. Need to scout and find a piece of ground where nine thousand can beat many thousands. Bound to be an Aquae Sextiae here somewhere. How many of them are there? Get a message to me with details. Your Greek is good, surprisingly idiomatic. Gaius Julius Caesar Imperator.

The sight of that yellow feather sent the exhausted Ninth into paroxysms of cheers, and Quintus Cicero into a fit of weeping. Wiping his indescribably dirty face with an equally dirty hand, he sat down, aching back and crippled leg forgotten, and wrote to Caesar while Vertico got another spear and serf ready.

> Estimate sixty thousand. Whole tribe here, serious muster. Not all Nervii. Notice lots of Menapii and Condrusi, hence the numbers. We will last. Find your Aquae Sextiae. Gauls getting a bit careless,

got us burning alive in the wicker cages already. Notice more drinking, less enthusiasm. Your Greek isn't bad either. Quintus Tullius Cicero Legatus Superstes.

Caesar got the letter at midnight; the Nervii had massed to attack him, but darkness intervened, and that was one night the messenger detection squad forgot to operate. The Tenth and the Seventh were spoiling for a fight, but Caesar wouldn't oblige them until he found a field and built a camp similar to the one at which Gaius Marius and his thirty-seven thousand men had beaten a hundred and eighty thousand Teutones over fifty years before.

It took him two more days to find his Aquae Sextiae, but when he did, the Tenth and the Seventh trounced the Nervii—and accorded them no mercy. Quintus Cicero had been right: the length of the siege and its fruitless outcome had eroded both morale and temper. The Nervii were drinking heavily but not eating much, though their two allies, having come later to the war, fared better at Caesar's Aquae Sextiae.

The camp of the Ninth was a shambles. Most of its housing had crumbled to ashes; mules and oxen wandered hungrily and added their bellows to the cacophony of cheers which greeted Caesar and his two legions when they marched inside. Not one man in ten was without a wound of some kind, and all of them were sick.

The Tenth and Seventh set to with a will, undammed the stream and sent good clean water through, cheerfully demolished the log wall to build fires and heat water for baths, took the Ninth's filthy clothing and washed it, stalled the animals in some measure of comfort, and scoured the countryside for food. The baggage train came up with enough to keep men and animals content, and Caesar paraded the Ninth before the Tenth and the Seventh. He had no decorations with him, but awarded them anyway; Pullo and Vorenus, already possessed of silver torcs and *phalerae,* got gold torcs and *phalerae.*

"If I could, Quintus Cicero, I'd give you the Grass Crown for saving your legion," said Caesar.

Quintus Cicero nodded, beaming. "You can't, Caesar, I know that. Rules are rules. The Ninth saved themselves; I just helped a bit around the edges. Oh, but aren't they wonderful boys?"

"The very best."

The next day the three legions pulled out, the Tenth and the Ninth headed for the comfort and safety of Samarobriva, the Seventh for Portus Itius. Even had Caesar wanted to, it wasn't possible to keep the camp among the Nervii going. The land was eaten out where it wasn't trampled to mud, and most of the Nervii lay dead.

"I'll sort out the Nervii in the spring, Vertico," said Caesar to his partisan. "A pan-Gallic conference. You won't lose by helping me and mine, so much I promise. Take everything here and what we have left; it'll tide you over."

So Vertico and his people returned to their village, Vertico to resume the life of a Nervian thane, and the serf to go back to his plough. For it was not in the nature of those people to elevate a man above the station he was born to, even as thanks for great services; custom and tradition were too strong. Nor did the serf expect to be rewarded. He did the winter things he was supposed to, obeyed Vertico exactly as before, sat by the fire at night with his wife and children, and said nothing. Whatever he felt and thought he kept to himself.

Caesar rode upstream along the Mosa with a small escort of cavalry, leaving his legates and legions to find their own way home. It had become imperative that he see Titus Labienus, who had sent a message that the Treveri were too restless to permit of his coming to help, but had not yet summoned up the courage to attack him; his camp bordered the lands of the Remi, which meant he had help close at hand.

"Cingetorix is worried that his influence among the Treveri is waning," said Labienus. "Ambiorix is working very hard to swing the men who matter onto Indutiomarus's side. Slaughtering the Thirteenth did wonders for Ambiorix—he's now a hero."

"His slaughtering the Thirteenth gave the Celtae all sorts of delusions of power too," Caesar said. "I've just had a note from Roscius informing me that the Armorici started massing the moment they heard. Luckily they still had eight miles to go when the news of the defeat of the Nervii reached them." He grinned. "Suddenly Roscius's camp lost all its appeal. They turned round and went home. But they'll be back."

Labienus scowled. "And winter's barely here. Once spring comes, we're going to be in the shit. And we're down a legion."

They were standing in the weak sun outside Labienus's good wooden house, looking out over the serried ranks of buildings which spread in three directions before them; the commander's house was always in the center of the north side, with little behind save storage sheds and depots.

This was a cavalry camp, so it was much larger than one required to do no more than shelter and protect infantry. The rule of thumb for infantry was half a square mile per legion for a winter sojourn (a short-term camp was a fifth this size), with the men billeted ten to a house—eight soldiers and two servant noncombatants. Each century of eighty soldiers and twenty noncombatants occupied its own little lane, with the centurion's house at the open end of the lane and a stable for the century's ten mules and the six oxen or mules which pulled its single wagon closing off the other end. Houses for the legates and military tribunes were ranked along the Via Principalis on either side of the commander's quarters, together with the quaestor's quarters (which were bigger because he ran the legion's supplies, accounts, bank and burial club), surrounded by enough open space to hold issue lines; another open space on the opposite side of the commander's house served as a forum wherein the legions assembled. It was mathematically so precise that when camp was pitched every man knew exactly where he had to go, and this extended to night camps on the road or field camps when battle was imminent; even the animals knew whereabouts they had to go.

Labienus's camp was two square miles in extent, for he had two thousand Aeduan horse troopers as well as the Eleventh Legion. Each trooper had two horses and a groom as well as a beast of burden, so Labienus's camp accommodated four thousand horses and two thousand mules in snug winter stables, and their two thousand owners in commodious houses.

Labienus's camps were inevitably sloppy, for he ruled by fear rather than logic, didn't care if the stables were not mucked out once a day or if the lanes filled up with rubbish. He also permitted women to live in his winter camp. This Caesar did not object to as much as he did to the look of disorder and the stench of six thousand unclean animals plus ten thousand unclean men. Since Rome couldn't field its own cavalry, it had to rely upon non-citizen levies, and these foreigners always had their own code. They also had to be let do things their way. Which in turn meant that the Roman citizen infantry also had to be allowed women; otherwise winter camp would have been a nightmare of resentful citizens brawling with indulged non-citizens.

However, Caesar said nothing. Squalor and terror stalked one on either side of Titus Labienus, but he was brilliant. No one led cavalry better save Caesar himself, whose duties as the General did not permit him to lead cavalry. Nor was Labienus a disappointment when leading infantry. Yes, a very valuable man, and an excellent second-in-command. A pity that he couldn't tame the savage in himself, that was all. His punishments were so famous that Caesar never gave him the same legion or legions twice during long stays in camp; when the Eleventh heard that it was to winter with Labienus its men groaned, then resolved to be good boys and hoped that the following winter would see it with Fabius or Trebonius, strict commanders yet not unmerciful.

"The first thing I have to do when I return to Samarobriva is to write to Mamurra and Ventidius in Italian Gaul," Caesar said. "I'm down to seven legions, and the Fifth Alauda is grossly under-strength because I've been tapping it to plump out losses in the others. If we're going to have a hard year in the field, I need eleven legions and four thousand horse."

Labienus winced. "Four legions of raw recruits?" he asked, mouth turning down. "That's over one-third of the whole army! They'll be more a hindrance than a help."

"Just three raw," said Caesar placidly. "There's one legion of good troops sitting in Placentia right at this moment. They're not blooded, admittedly, but they're fully trained and itching for a fight. They're so bored they'll end up disaffected."

"Ah!" Labienus nodded. "The Sixth. Recruited by Pompeius Magnus in Picenum a year ago, yet still waiting to go to Spain. Ye Gods, he's slow! You're right about the boredom, Caesar. But they belong to Pompeius."

"I shall write to Pompeius and ask to borrow them."

"Will he oblige?"

"I imagine so. Pompeius isn't under any great duress in the Spains—Afranius and Petreius run both provinces for him well enough. The Lusitani are quiet, so is Cantabria. I'll offer to blood the Sixth for him. He'll like that."

"Indeed he will. There are two things you can count on with Pompeius—he never fights unless he has the numbers, and he never uses unblooded troops. What a fraud! I abominate the man, I always have!" A small pause ensued, then Labienus asked, "Are you going to enlist another Thirteenth, or skip straight to the Fourteenth?"

"I'll enlist another Thirteenth. I'm as superstitious as the next Roman, but it's essential that the men grow accustomed to thinking of thirteen as just another number." He shrugged. "Besides, if I have a Fourteenth and no Thirteenth, the Fourteenth will know it's really the Thirteenth. I'll keep the new one with me for the year. At the end of it, I guarantee that its men will be flaunting the number thirteen as a good-luck talisman."

"I believe you."

"I take it, Labienus, that you think our relations with the Treveri will break down completely," said Caesar as he began to walk down the Via Praetoria.

"Bound to. The Treveri have always wanted downright, outright war, but until now they've been too wary of me. Ambiorix has rather changed that—he's a brilliant talker, you know. With the result that Indutiomarus is gathering adherents hand over fist. I doubt Cingetorix has the thews to resist now that there are two experts working on the thanes. We can't afford to underestimate either Ambiorix or Indutiomarus, Caesar."

"Can you hold here for the winter?"

The horse's teeth gleamed. "Oh, yes. I have a little idea as to how to tempt the Treveri into a battle they can't win. It's important to push them into precipitate action. If they delay until the summer, there will be thousands upon thousands of them. Ambiorix is boating across the Rhenus regularly, trying to persuade the Germani to help; and if he succeeds, the Nemetes will decide their lands are safe from German incursions and join the Treveri muster as well."

Caesar sighed. "I had hoped Gaul of the Long-hairs would see sense. The Gods know I was clement enough during the early years! If I treated them fairly and bound them with legal agreements, I thought they'd settle down under Rome. It's not as if they don't have an example. The Gauls of the Province tried to resist for a century, yet look at them now. They're happier and better off under Rome than ever they were fighting among themselves."

"You sound like Cicero" was Labienus's comment. "They're too thick to know when they're well off. They'll fight us until they drop."

"I fear you're right. Which is why each year I get harder."

They stopped to let a long parade of horses led by grooms cross from one side of the wide thoroughfare to the other, off to the exercise yards.

"How are you going to tempt the Treveri?" Caesar asked.

"I need some help from you, and some help from the Remi."

"Ask, and you shall receive."

"I want it generally known that you're massing the Remi on their border with the Bellovaci. Tell Dorix to make it look as if he's hurrying every trooper he's got in that direction. But I need four thousand of them concealed not too far away. I'm going to smuggle them into my camp at the rate of four hundred a night—ten days to do the job. But before I begin, I'll convince Indutiomarus's spies that I'm a frightened man planning to leave because the Remi are withdrawing. Don't worry, I know who his spies are." The dark face warped itself, looked terrifying. "All women. After the Remi start coming in, I assure you that not one of them will get any messages out. They'll be too busy screaming."

"And once you have the Remi?"

"The Treveri will appear to kill me before I can leave. It will take them ten days to muster and two days to get here. I'll make it in time. Then I'll open my gates and let six thousand Aedui and Remi cut them up like pork for sausages. The Eleventh can stuff them into the skins."

Caesar left for Samarobriva satisfied.

"No one can beat you," said Rhiannon, her tone smug.

Amused, Caesar rolled onto his side and propped his head up on one hand to look at her. "That pleases you?"

"Oh, yes. You're the father of my son."

"So might Dumnorix have been."

Her teeth flashed in the gloom. "Never!"

"That's interesting."

She pulled her hair out from under her, a difficult and somewhat painful task; it lay then between them like a river of fire. "Did you have Dumnorix killed because of me?" she asked.

"No. He was intriguing to create trouble during my absence in Britannia, so I ordered him to accompany me to Britannia. He thought that meant I'd kill him over there, away from all eyes which might condemn me for it. He ran away. Whereupon I showed him that if I wanted him killed, I'd have him killed under all eyes. Labienus was pleased to oblige. He never liked Dumnorix."

"I don't like Labienus," she said, shivering.

"Not surprising. Labienus belongs to that group of Roman men who believe that the only trustworthy Gaul is a dead one," said Caesar. "That goes for Gallic women too."

"Why didn't you object when I said Orgetorix would be King of the Helvetii?" she demanded. "He is your son, yet you have no son! At the time Orgetorix was born I didn't understand how famous and influential you are in Rome. I do now." She sat up, put her hand on his shoulder. "Caesar, take him! To be king of a people as powerful as the Helvetii is a formidable fate, but to be the King of Rome is a far greater fate."

He shrugged her hand off, eyes flashing. "Rhiannon, Rome will have no king! Nor would I consent to Rome's having a king! Rome is a republic and has been for five hundred years! I will be the First Man in Rome, but that is not to be Rome's king. Kings are archaic; even you Gauls are realizing that. A people prospers better when it is administered by a group of men who change through the electoral process." He smiled wryly. "Election gives every qualified man the chance to be the best—or the worst."

"But *you* are the best! No one can beat *you*! Caesar, you were born to be king!" she cried. "Rome would thrive under your rule—you'd end in being King of the World!"

"I don't want to be King of the World," he said patiently. "Just the First Man in Rome—first among my equals. If I were king, I'd have no rivals, and where's the fun in that? Without a Cato and a Cicero to sharpen my wits, my mind would stultify." He leaned forward to kiss her breasts. "Leave things be, woman."

"Don't you want your son to be a Roman?" she asked, snuggling against him.

"It's not a matter of wanting. My son is not a Roman."

"You could make him one."

"My son is not a Roman. He's a Gaul."

She was kissing his chest, winding a rope of hair around his growing penis. "But," she mumbled, "I'm a princess. His blood is better than it could be with a Roman woman for mother."

Caesar rolled on top of her. "His blood is only half Roman—and that the half which cannot be proven. His name is Orgetorix, not Caesar. His name will remain Orgetorix, not Caesar. When the time comes, send him to your people. I rather like the idea that a son of mine will be a king. But not the King of Rome."

"What if I were a great queen, so great that even Rome saw my every virtue?"

"If you were Queen of the World, my dear, it wouldn't be good enough. You're not Roman. Nor are you Caesar's wife."

Whatever she might have said in answer to that was not said; Caesar stopped her mouth with a kiss. Because he enchanted her sexually, she left the subject to succumb to her body's pleasure, but in one corner of her mind she stored the subject for future contemplation.

And future contemplation was all through that winter, while the great Roman legates passed in and out of Caesar's stone door, paid court to her son, lay on the dining couches, talking endlessly of armies, legions, supplies, fortifications . . .

I do not understand, nor has he made me understand. My blood is far greater than the blood of any Roman woman! I am the daughter of a king! I am the mother of a king! But my son should be the King of Rome, not the King of the Helvetii. Caesar makes no sense with his cryptic answers. How can I hope to understand what he will not teach? Would a Roman woman teach me? Could a Roman woman?

So while Caesar busied himself with the preparations for his pan-Gallic conference in Samarobriva, Rhiannon sat down with an Aeduan scribe and dictated a letter in Latin to the great Roman lady Servilia. A choice of correspondent which proved that Roman gossip percolated everywhere.

> I write to you, lady Servilia, because I know that you have been an intimate friend of Caesar's for many years, and that when Caesar returns to Rome, he will resume his friendship. Or so they say here in Samarobriva.
>
> I have Caesar's son, who is now three years old. My blood is royal. I am the daughter of King Orgetorix of the Helvetii, and Caesar took me off my husband, Dumnorix of the Aedui. But when my son was born, Caesar said that he would be brought up a Gaul in Gallia Comata, and insisted that he have a Gallic name. I called him Orgetorix, but I would far rather have called him Caesar Orgetorix.
>
> In our Gallic world, it is absolutely necessary that a man have at least one son. For that reason, men of the nobility have more than one wife, lest one wife prove barren. For what is a man's career, if he has no son to succeed him? Yet Caesar has no son to succeed him, and will not hear of my son's succeeding him in Rome. I asked him why. All he would answer was that I am not Roman. I am not good enough, was what he meant. Even were I the Queen of the World, yet not Roman, I would not be good enough. I do not understand, and I am angry.
>
> Lady Servilia, can you teach me to understand?

The Aeduan secretary took his wax tablets away to transcribe Rhiannon's short letter onto paper, and made a copy which he gave to Aulus Hirtius to pass on to Caesar.

Hirtius's chance came when he informed Caesar that Labienus had brought the Treveri to battle with complete success.

"He trounced them," said Hirtius, face expressionless.

Caesar glanced at him suspiciously. "And?" he asked.

"And Indutiomarus is dead."

That news provoked a stare. "Unusual! I thought both the Belgae and the Celtae had learned to value their leaders enough to keep them out of the front lines."

"Er—they have," said Hirtius. "Labienus issued orders. No matter who or how many got away, he wanted Indutiomarus. Er—not all of him. Just his head."

"Jupiter, the man is a barbarian himself!" cried Caesar, very angry. "War has few rules, but one of them is that you don't deprive a people of its leaders through murder! Oh, one more thing I'll have to wrap up in Tyrian purple for the Senate! I wish I could split myself into as many legates as I need and do all their jobs myself! Isn't it bad enough that Rome should have displayed Roman heads on the Roman rostra? Are we now to display the heads of our barbarian enemies? He did display it, didn't he?"

"Yes, on the camp battlements."

"Did his men acclaim him imperator?"

"Yes, on the field."

"So he could have had Indutiomarus captured and kept for his triumphal parade. Indutiomarus would have died, but after he had been held in honor as Rome's guest, and understood the full extent of his glory. There's some distinction in dying during a triumph, but this was mean—shabby! How do I make it look good in my senatorial dispatches, Hirtius?"

"My advice is, don't. Tell it as it happened."

"He's my legate. My second-in-command."

"True."

"What's the matter with the man, Hirtius?"

Hirtius shrugged. "He's a barbarian who wants to be consul, in the same way Pompeius Magnus wanted to be consul. At any kind of price. Not at peace with the *mos maiorum*."

"Another Picentine!"

"Labienus is useful, Caesar."

"As you say, useful," he said, staring at the wall. "He expects that I'll choose him as my colleague when I'm consul again five years from now."

"Yes."

"Rome will want me, but it won't want Labienus."

"Yes."

Caesar began to pace. "Then I have some thinking to do."

Hirtius cleared his throat. "There is another matter."

"Oh?"

"Rhiannon."

"Rhiannon?"

"She's written to Servilia."

"Using a scribe, since she can't write herself."

"Who gave me a copy of the letter. Though I haven't let the courier take the original until you approve it."

"Where is it?"

Hirtius handed it over.

Yet another letter was reduced to ashes, this one in the brazier. "Fool of a woman!"

"Shall I have the courier take the original to Rome?"

"Oh, yes. Make sure I see the answer before Rhiannon gets it, however."

"That goes without saying."

Down came the scarlet general's cloak from its T-shaped rack. "I need a walk," said Caesar, throwing it round his shoulders and tying its cords himself. Then he looked at Hirtius, eyes detached. "Have Rhiannon watched."

"Some better news to take out into the cold, Caesar."

The smile was rueful. "I need it! What?"

"Ambiorix has had no luck yet with the Germani. Ever since you bridged the Rhenus they've been wary. Not all his pleading and cajoling has seen one German company cross into Gaul."

Winter was nearing its end and the pan-Gallic conference was looming when Caesar led four legions into the lands of the Nervii to finish that tribe as a power. His luck was with him; the whole tribe had gathered at its biggest *oppidum* to debate the question as to whether it ought to send delegates to Samarobriva. Caesar caught the Nervii armed but unprepared, and accorded them no mercy. Those who survived the battle were handed over to his men, together with enormous amounts of booty. This was one engagement from which Caesar and his legates would see no personal profit; it all went to the legionaries, including the sale of slaves. And afterward he laid waste to the Nervian lands, burning everything save the fief belonging to Vertico. The captured tribal leaders were shipped off to Rome to wait for his triumph, kept, as he had said to Aulus Hirtius, in comfort and honor. When came the day of his triumph their necks would be snapped in the Tullianum, but by then they would have learned the measure both of their glory and of Rome's.

Caesar had been holding a pan-Gallic conference every year since his coming to Gaul of the Long-hairs. The early ones had been held at Bibracte in the lands of the Aedui. This year's was the first to be held so far west, and a summons had gone out to every tribe commanding it to send delegates. The purpose was to have an opportunity to speak to the tribal leaders, be they kings, councillors or properly elected vergobrets—

an opportunity to persuade them that war with Rome could have only one outcome: defeat.

This year he hoped for better results. All those who had made war over the past five years had gone down, no matter how great their numbers and their consequent sense of invincibility. Even the loss of the Thirteenth had been turned to advantage. Surely now they would all begin to see the shape of their fate!

Yet by the time that the opening day of the conference dawned, Caesar's expectations were already dying. Three of the greatest peoples had not sent delegates: the Treveri, the Senones and the Carnutes. The Nemetes and the Triboci had never come, but their absence was understandable—they bordered the Rhenus River on the opposite shore to the Suebi, the fiercest and far the hungriest of the Germani. So dedicated were they to defending their own lands that they had almost no impact upon thought within Gaul of the Long-hairs.

The huge wooden hall hung with bear and wolf pelts was full when Caesar, his purple-bordered toga glaringly white amid so much color, mounted the dais to speak. The gathering possessed an alien splendor, each tribe in its traditional regalia: the basically scarlet checks of the Atrebates in the person of King Commius, the orange and emerald speckles of the Cardurci, the crimson and blue of the Remi, the scarlet and blue stripes of the Aedui. But no yellow and scarlet Carnutes, no indigo and yellow Senones, no dark green and light green Treveri.

"I do not intend to dwell upon the fate of the Nervii," Caesar said in the high-pitched voice he used for orating, "because all of you know what happened." He looked toward Vertico, nodded. "That one Nervian is here today is evidence of his good sense. Why fight the inevitable? Ask yourselves who is the real enemy! Is it Rome? Or is it the Germani? The presence of Rome in Gallia Comata must go to your ultimate good. The presence of Rome will ensure that you retain your Gallic customs and traditions. The presence of Rome will keep the Germani on their own bank of the Rhenus. I, Gaius Julius Caesar, have guaranteed to contend with the Germani on your behalf in every treaty I have made with you! For you cannot keep the Germani at bay without Rome's aid. If you doubt this, ask the delegates from the Sequani." He pointed to where they sat in their crimson and pink. "King Ariovistus of the Suebi persuaded them to let him settle on one-third of their lands. Wanting peace, they decided that consent was a gesture of friendliness. But give the Germani the tip of your finger and they will end in taking not only your whole arm, but your whole country! Do the Cardurci think this fate will not be theirs because they border the Aquitani in the far southwest? It will be! Mark my words, it will be! Unless all of you accept and welcome the presence of Rome, it will be!"

The Arvernian delegates occupied a whole row, for the Arverni were an extremely powerful people. The traditional enemies of the Aedui, they occupied the mountainous lands of the Cebenna around the sources of the Elaver, the Caris and the Vigemna; perhaps because of this, their shirts and trousers were palest buff, their shawls checkered in palest blue, buff and dark green. Not easy to see against snow or a rock face.

One of them, young and clean-shaven, rose to his feet.

"Tell me the difference between Rome and the Germani," he said in the Carnute dialect which Caesar was speaking, as it was the universal tongue of the Druids, therefore understood everywhere.

"No," said Caesar, smiling. "You tell me."

"I see absolutely no difference, Caesar. Foreign domination is foreign domination."

"But there are vast differences! The fact that I stand here today speaking *your* language is one of them. When I came to Gallia Comata I spoke Aeduan, Arvernian and Vocontian. Since then I have gone to the trouble of learning Druidan, Atrebatan and several other dialects. Yes, I have the ear for languages, that is true. But I am a Roman, and I understand that when men can communicate with each other directly, there is no opportunity for an interpreter to distort what is said. Yet I have not asked any of you to learn to speak Latin. Whereas the Germani would force you to speak their tongues, and eventually you would lose your own."

"Soft words, Caesar!" said the young Arvernian. "But they point out the greatest danger of Roman domination! It is subtle. The Germani are not subtle. Therefore they are easier to resist."

"This is your first pan-Gallic conference, obviously, so I do not know your name," said Caesar, unruffled. "What is it?"

"Vercingetorix!"

Caesar stepped to the very front of the dais. "First of all, Vercingetorix, you Gauls must reconcile yourselves to *some* foreign presence. The world is shrinking. It has been shrinking since the Greeks and the Punic peoples scattered themselves around the whole rim of the sea Rome now calls Our Sea. Then Rome came upon the scene. The Greeks were never united as one nation. Greece was many little nations, and, like you, they fought among each other until they exhausted the country. Rome was a city-state too, but Rome gradually brought all of Italia under her as *one* nation. Rome *is* Italia. Yet the domination of Rome within Italia does not depend upon the solitary figure of a king. All Italia votes to elect Rome's magistrates. All Italia participates in Rome. All Italia provides Rome's soldiers. For Rome *is* Italia. And Rome grows. All Italian Gaul south of the Padus River is now a part of Italia, elects Rome's magistrates. And soon all Italian Gaul north of the Padus River will be Roman too, for I have vowed it. I believe in unity. I believe that unity is strength. And I would give Gallia Comata the unity of true nationhood. That would be Rome's gift. The Germani bring no gifts worth having. Did Gallia Comata belong to the Germani, it would go backward. They have no systems of government, no systems of commerce, no systems which permit a people to lean on one single central government."

Vercingetorix laughed scornfully. "You rape, you do not govern! There is no difference between Rome and the Germani!"

Caesar answered without hesitation. "As I have said, there are many differences. I have pointed some of them out. You have not listened, Vercingetorix, because you don't want to listen. You appeal to passion, not to reason. That will bring you many adherents, but it will render you incapable of giving your adherents what they most need—sage advice, considered opinions. Consider the state of the shrinking world. Consider the place Gallia Comata will have in that shrinking world if Gallia Comata ties herself to Rome rather than to the Germani or to internal strife between her peoples. I do not want to fight you, which is not the same as unwillingness to fight. After five years of Rome in the person of Gaius Julius Caesar, you know that. Rome unifies. Rome brings her citizenship. Rome brings improvements to local life. Rome brings peace and plenty. Rome brings business opportunities, a system of commerce, new opportunities for local industries to sell their wares everywhere Rome is in the world. You Arvernians make the best pottery in Gallia Comata. As a part of Rome's world, your pots would go much further than Britannia. With Rome's legions guarding the borders of Gallia Comata, the Arverni could expand their business ventures and increase their wealth shorn of fear of invasion, pillage—and rape."

"Hollow words, Caesar! What happened to the Atuatuci? The Eburones? The Morini? The Nervii? Pillage! Slavery! *Rape!*"

Caesar sighed, spread his right hand wide, cuddled his left into the folds of his toga. "All those peoples had their chance," he said evenly. "They broke their treaties, they preferred war to submission. The submission would have cost them little. A tribute, in return for guaranteed peace. In return for no more German raids. In return for an easier, more fruitful way of life. Still worshiping their own Gods, still owning their lands, still free men, still *living*!"

"Under foreign domination," said Vercingetorix.

Caesar inclined his head. "That's the price, Vercingetorix. A light Roman hand on the bridle, or a heavy German one. That's the choice. Isolation is gone. Gallia Comata has entered Our Sea. All of you must realize that. There can be no going back. Rome is here. And Rome will stay. Because Rome too must keep the Germani beyond the Rhenus. Over fifty years ago Gallia Comata was split from end to end by three-quarters of a million Germani. All you could do was to suffer their presence. It was Rome in the person of Gaius Marius saved you then. It is Rome in the person of Gaius Marius's nephew who will save you now. Accept the continued presence of Rome, I most earnestly beseech you! If you do accept Rome, little will actually change. Ask any of the Gallic tribes in our Province—the Volcae, the Vocontii, the Helvii, the Allobroges. They are no less Gallic for being also Roman. They live at peace, they prosper mightily."

"Hah!" sneered Vercingetorix. "Fine words! They're just waiting for someone to lead them out of foreign domination!"

"They're not, you know," said Caesar conversationally. "Go and talk to them for yourself and you'll see I'm right."

"When I go to talk with them, it won't be to enquire," said Vercingetorix. "I'll offer them a spear." He laughed, shook his head incredulously. "How can you hope to win?" he asked. "There are a handful of you, that's all! Rome is a gigantic bluff! The peoples you have encountered until now have been tame, stupid, cowardly! There are more warriors in Gallia Comata than in the whole of Italia and Italian Gaul! Four million Celtae, two million Belgae! I have seen your Roman censuses—you don't have that many people! Three million, Caesar, not a person more!"

"Numbers are irrelevant," said Caesar, who appeared to be enjoying himself. "Rome possesses three things neither the Celtae nor the Belgae own—organization, technology and the ability to tap her resources with complete efficiency."

"Oh, yes, your much-vaunted technology! What of it? Did the walls you built to dam out Ocean enable you to take any of the Veneti strongholds? Did they? No! We too are a technological people! Ask your legate Quintus Tullius Cicero! We brought siege towers to bear on him, we learned to use Roman artillery! We are not tame, we are not stupid, we are not cowards! Since you came into Gallia Comata, Caesar, we have learned! And as long as you remain here, we will go on learning! Nor are all Roman generals your equal! Sooner or later you will return to Rome, and Rome will send a fool to Gallia Comata! Another like Cassius at Burdigala! Others like Mallius and Caepio at Arausio!"

"Or another like Ahenobarbus when he reduced the Arverni to nothing seventy-five years ago," said Caesar, smiling.

"The Arverni are more powerful now than they were before Ahenobarbus came!"

"Vercingetorix of the Arverni, listen to me," said Caesar strongly. "I have called for reinforcements. Four more legions. That is a total of twenty-four thousand men. I will have them in the field and ready to fight four months from the commencement of the enlistment process. They will all wear chain mail shirts, have superbly made daggers and swords on their belts, helmets on their heads, and *pila* in their hands. They will know the drills and routines so well they could do them in their sleep. They will have artillery. They will know how to build siege equipment, how to fortify. They will be able to march a minimum of thirty miles a day for days on end. They will be officered by brilliant centurions. They will come wanting to hate you and every other Gaul—and if you push them to fight, they *will* hate you.

"I will have a Fifth—a Sixth—a Seventh—an Eighth—a Ninth—a Tenth—an Eleventh—a Twelfth—a Thirteenth—a Fourteenth—and a Fifteenth Legion! All up to strength! Fifty-four thousand foot soldiers! And add to them four thousand cavalry drawn from the Aedui and the Remi!"

Vercingetorix crowed, capered. "What a fool you are, Caesar! You've just told all of us your strength in the field this year!"

"Indeed I have, though not foolishly. As a warning. I say to you, be sensible and prudent. You cannot win! Why try? Why kill the flower of your manhood in a hopeless cause? Why leave your women so destitute and your lands so vacant that I will have to settle my Roman veterans on them to marry your women and sire Roman children?"

Suddenly Caesar's iron control snapped; he grew, towered. Not realizing that he did so, Vercingetorix stepped backward.

"This year will be a year of total attrition if you try me!" Caesar roared. "Oppose me in the field and you will go down and keep on going down! *I cannot be beaten! Rome cannot be beaten!* Our resources in Italia—and the efficiency with which I can marshal them!—are so vast that I can make good any losses I sustain in the twinkling of an eye! If I so wish, I can double those fifty-four thousand men! And equip them! Be warned and take heed! I have made you privy to all of this not for today, but for the future! Roman organization, Roman technology and Roman resources alone will see you go down! And don't pin your hopes on the day when Rome sends a less competent governor to Gallia Comata! Because by the time that day comes, you won't exist! *Caesar* will have reduced you and yours to ruins!"

He swept from the dais and from the hall, leaving the Gauls and his legates stunned.

"Oh, that temper!" said Trebonius to Hirtius.

"They needed straight speaking," said Hirtius.

"Well, my turn," said Trebonius, getting to his feet. "How can I follow an act like that?"

"With diplomatic words," said Quintus Cicero, grinning.

"It doesn't matter a fig what Trebonius prattles on about," said Sextius. "They've got the fear of Caesar in them."

"The one named Vercingetorix is spoiling for a fight" from Sulpicius Rufus.

"He's young" from Hirtius. "Nor is he popular among the rest of the Arvernian delegates. They were sitting with their teeth on edge and dying to kill him, not Caesar."

While the meeting went on in the great hall, Rhiannon sat in Caesar's stone house with the Aeduan scribe.

"Read it," she said to him.

He broke the seal (which had already been broken; it had been resealed with the imprint of Quintus Cicero's ring, since Rhiannon had no idea what Servilia's seal looked like), spread the little roll, and pored over it, mumbling, for a long time.

"Read it!" Rhiannon said, shifting impatiently.

"As soon as I understand it, I will," he answered.

"Caesar doesn't do that."

He looked up, sighed. "Caesar is Caesar. No one else can read at a glance. And the more you talk, the longer I'll be."

Rhiannon subsided, picking at the gold threads woven through her long gown of brownish crimson, dying to know what Servilia said.

Finally the scribe spoke. "I can start," he said.

"Then do so!"

> "Well, I can't say I ever expected to get a letter writ in rather peculiar Latin from Caesar's Gallic mistress, but it's amusing, I must admit. So you have Caesar's son. How amazing. I have Caesar's daughter. Like your son, she does not bear Caesar's name. That is because I was married to Marcus Junius Silanus at the time. His distant relative, another Marcus Junius Silanus, is one of Caesar's legates this year. My daughter's name is therefore Junia, and as she is the third Junia, I call her Tertulla.
>
> "You say you are a princess. Barbarians do have them, I know. You produce this fact as if it could matter. It cannot. To a Roman, the only blood which matters is Roman blood. Roman blood is better. The meanest thief in some back alley is better than you, because he has Roman blood. No son whose mother was not Roman could matter to Caesar, whose blood is the highest in Rome. Never tainted with other blood than Roman. If Rome had a king, Caesar would be that king. His ancestors were kings. But Rome does not have a king, nor would Caesar allow Rome to have a king. Romans bend the knee to no one.
>
> "I have nothing to teach you, barbarian princess. It is not necessary for a Roman to have a son of his body to inherit his position and carry on the name of his family because a Roman can adopt a son. He does this very carefully. Whoever he adopts will have the necessary blood to carry on his line, and as part of the adoption the new son assumes his name. My son was adopted. His name was Marcus Junius Brutus, but when his uncle, my brother, was killed without an heir, he adopted Brutus in his will. Brutus became Quintus Servilius Caepio, of my own family. That he has preferred of late years to return to the name Marcus Junius Brutus is due to his pride in a Junian ancestor, Lucius Junius Brutus, who banished the last King of Rome and established the Roman *res publica.*

"If Caesar has no son, he will adopt a son of Julian blood and impeccably Roman ancestors. That is the Roman way. And knowing this, Caesar will proceed through his life secure in the knowledge that, should he have no son of his body, his last testament will remedy things.

"Do not bother writing back. I dislike the implication that you class yourself as one of Caesar's women. You are no more and no less than an expedient."

The scribe let the scroll curl up. "That tells us where we barbarians belong, doesn't it?" he demanded, angry.

Rhiannon snatched the letter from him and began to tear it into small pieces. "Go away!" she snarled.

Tears pouring down her face, she went then to see Orgetorix, in the custody of his nurse, one of her own servants. He was busy towing a model of the Trojan Horse around the floor; Caesar had given it to him and shown him how its side opened to disgorge the Greeks, fifty perfectly carved and painted figures each owning a name: red-haired Menelaus; red-haired Odysseus with the short legs; the beautiful Neoptolemus, son of dead Achilles; and even one, Echion, whose head fell forward, broken, when he hit the flags. Caesar had started to teach him the legend and the names, but little Orgetorix had neither the memory nor the wit to immerse himself in Homer, and Caesar gave up. If the child delighted in his gift, it was because of childish reasons: a splendid toy which moved, concealed things, could be stuffed and unstuffed, and excited admiration and envy from all who saw it.

"Mama!" he said, dropping the cord which was attached to the horse and holding out his arms.

Her tears dried; Rhiannon carried him to a chair and sat him on her lap. "You don't care," she said to him, her cheek on his brilliant curls. "You're not a Roman, you're a Gaul. But you *will* be King of the Helvetii! And you *are* Caesar's son!" Her breath hissed, her lips peeled back from her teeth. "I curse you, lady Servilia! You will never have him back again! Tonight I will go to the priestess in the tower of skulls and buy the curse of a long life spent in misery!"

News came the next day from Labienus: Ambiorix was finally having some success among the Suebic Germans, and the Treveri, far from being subdued, were boiling.

"Hirtius, I want you and Trogus to continue the conference," Caesar said as he handed the box containing the sash of his imperium to Thrayllus, packing his gear. "My four new legions have reached the Aedui, and I've sent word instructing them to march for the Senones, whom I intend to scare witless. The Tenth and Twelfth will go with me to meet them."

"What of Samarobriva?" asked Hirtius.

"Trebonius can stay to garrison it with the Eighth, but I think it's politic to shift the site of the conference to some place less tempting to our absent friends the Carnutes. Move the delegates to Lutetia among the Parisii. It's an island, therefore easily defended. Keep on trying to make the Gauls see reason—and take the Fifth Alauda with you. Also Silanus and Antistius."

"Is this war on a grand scale?"

"I hope not, quite yet. I'd rather have the time to pluck some of the raw cohorts out of the new legions and slip some of my veterans in." He grinned. "You might say, to quote the words of young Vercingetorix, that I am about to embark upon a gigantic bluff. Though I doubt the Longhairs will see it that way."

Time was galloping, but he must say goodbye to Rhiannon. Whom he found in her sitting room—ah, not alone! Vercingetorix was with her. Goddess Fortuna, you always bring me luck!

He paused in the doorway unobserved; this was his first opportunity to study Vercingetorix at close quarters. His rank was manifest in the number of massive gold torcs and bracelets he wore, in the sapphire-encrusted belt and baldric, in the size of the sapphire buried in his brooch. That he was clean-shaven intrigued Caesar, for it was very rare among the Celtae. His lime-rinsed hair was almost white and combed to imitate a lion's mane, and his face, entirely displayed, was all bones, cadaverous. Black brows and lashes—oh, he *was* different! His body too was thin; a type who lives on his nerves, thought Caesar, advancing into the room. A throwback. Very dangerous.

Rhiannon's face lit up, then fell as she took in Caesar's leather gear. "Caesar! Where are you going?"

"To meet my new legions," he said, holding out his right hand to Vercingetorix, who had risen to reveal that he was the usual Celtic six feet in height. His eyes were dark blue and regarded the hand warily.

"Oh, come!" said Caesar genially. "You won't die of poison because you touch me!"

Out came one long, frail hand; the two men performed the universal ritual of greeting, neither of them imprudent enough to turn it into a contest of strength. Firm, brief, not excessive.

Caesar raised his brows at Rhiannon. "You know each other?" he asked, not sitting.

"Vercingetorix is my first cousin," she said breathlessly. "His mother and my mother were sisters. Arverni. Didn't I tell you? I meant to, Caesar. They both married kings—mine, King Orgetorix; his, King Celtillus."

"Ah, yes," said Caesar blandly. "Celtillus. I would have said he tried to be king, rather than was one. Didn't the Arverni kill him for it, Vercingetorix?"

"They did. You speak good Arvernian, Caesar."

"My nurse was Arvernian. Cardixa. My tutor, Marcus Antonius Gnipho, was half Salluvian. And there were Aeduan tenants upstairs in my mother's insula. You might say that I grew up to the sound of Gallic."

"You tricked us neatly during those first two years, using an interpreter all the time."

"Be fair! I speak no Germanic languages, and a great deal of my first year was occupied with Ariovistus. Nor did I understand the Sequani very well. It's taken time to pick up the Belgic tongues, though Druidan was easy."

"You are not what you seem," said Vercingetorix, sitting down again.

"Is anyone?" asked Caesar, and suddenly decided to seat himself too. A few moments spent talking to Vercingetorix might be moments well spent.

"Probably not, Caesar. What do you think I am?"

"A young hothead with much courage and some intelligence. You lack subtlety. It isn't clever to embarrass your elders in an important assembly."

"Someone had to speak up! Otherwise they would all have sat there and listened like a lot of students to a famous Druid. I struck a chord in many," said Vercingetorix, looking satisfied.

Caesar shook his head slowly. "You did indeed," he said, "but that isn't wise. One of my aims is to avert bloodshed—it gives me no pleasure to spill oceans of it. You ought to think things through, Vercingetorix. The end of it all will be Roman rule, make no mistake about that. Therefore why buck against it? You're a man, not a brute horse! You have the ability to gather adherents, build a great clientele. So lead your people wisely. Don't force me to adopt measures I don't want to take."

"Lead my people into eternal captivity, that's what you're really saying, Caesar."

"No, I am not. Lead them into peace and prosperity."

Vercingetorix leaned forward, eyes glowing with the same lights as the sapphire in his brooch. "I *will* lead, Caesar! But not into captivity. Into freedom. Into the old ways, a return to the kings and the heroes. And we will spurn Your Sea! Some of what you said yesterday makes sense. We Gauls need to be one people, not many. I can achieve that. I *will* achieve that! We will outlast you, Caesar. We will throw you out, and all who try to follow you. I spoke truth too. I said that Rome will send a fool to replace you. That is the way of democracies, which offer mindless idiots a choice of candidates and then wonder why fools are elected. A people needs a king, not men who change every time someone blinks his eye. One group benefits, then another, yet never the whole people. A king is the only answer."

"A king is never the answer."

Vercingetorix laughed, a high and slightly frenzied sound. "But you are a king, Caesar! It's there in the way you move, the way you look, the way you treat others. You are an Alexander the Great accidentally given power by the electors. After you, it will fall to ashes."

"No," said Caesar, smiling gently. "I am no Alexander the Great. All I am is a part of Rome's ongoing pageant. A great part, I know that. I hope that in future ages men will say, the greatest part. Yet only a part. When Alexander the Great died, Macedon died. His country perished with him. He abjured his Greekness and relocated the navel of his empire because he thought like a king. He was the reason for his country's greatness. He did what he liked and he went where he liked. *He thought like a king, Vercingetorix!* He mistook himself for an idea. To make it bear permanent fruit, he would have needed to live forever. Whereas I am the servant of my country. Rome is far greater than any man she produces. When I am dead, Rome will continue to produce other great men. I will leave Rome stronger, richer, more powerful. What I do will be used and improved by those who follow me. Fools and wise men in equal number, and that's a better record than a line of kings can boast. For every great king, there are a dozen utter nonentities."

Vercingetorix said nothing, leaned back in his chair and closed his eyes. "I do not agree," he said finally.

Caesar got up. "Then let us hope, Vercingetorix, that we never have to decide the issue upon a battlefield. For if we do, you will go down." His voice grew warmer. "Work with me, not against me!"

"No," said Vercingetorix, eyes still closed.

Caesar left the room to find Aulus Hirtius.

"Rhiannon grows more and more interesting," Caesar said to him. "The young hothead Vercingetorix is her first cousin. In that respect, Gallic nobles are just like Roman nobles. All of them are related. Watch her for me, Hirtius."

"Does that mean she's to come to Lutetia with me?"

"Oh, yes. We must give her every opportunity to have more congress with cousin Vercingetorix."

Hirtius's small, homely face screwed up, his brown eyes pleading. "Truly, Caesar, I don't think she'd betray you, no matter who her relatives might be. She dotes on you."

"I know. But she's a woman. She chatters and she does silly things like writing to Servilia—a more stupid action is hard to think of! While I'm away, don't let her know anything I don't want her to know."

Like everyone else in on the secret, Hirtius was dying to learn what Servilia had said, but Caesar had opened her letter himself, then sealed it again with Quintus Cicero's ring before anyone had a chance to read it.

When Caesar appeared leading six legions, the Senones crumbled, capitulating without a fight. They gave hostages and begged forgiveness, then hustled delegates off to Lutetia, where the Gauls under the easygoing supervision of Aulus Hirtius squabbled and brawled, drank and feasted. They also sent frantic warnings to the Carnutes, terrified at the promptness of those four new legions, their businesslike air, their glittering armor, their latest-model artillery. It had been the Aedui who begged Caesar to be kind to the Senones; now the Remi begged him to be kind to the Carnutes.

"All right," he said to Cotus of the Aedui and Dorix of the Remi, "I'll be merciful. What else can I be, anyway? No one has lifted a sword. Though I'd be happier if I believed they meant what they say. But I don't."

"Caesar, they need time," Dorix pleaded. "They're like children who have never been gainsaid in anything, but now they have a stepfather who insists on obedience."

"They're certainly children," said Caesar, quizzing Dorix with his brows.

"Mine was a metaphor," said Dorix with dignity.

"And this is no moment for humor. I take your point. Yet however we look at them, my friends, their future welfare depends upon their honoring the treaties they've signed. That is especially true of the Senones and the Carnutes. The Treveri I consider a hopeless case; they'll have to be subdued by force. But the Celtae of central Gallia Comata are fully sophisticated enough to understand the significance of treaties and the codes they dictate. I wouldn't want to have to execute men like Acco of the Senones or Gutruatus of the Carnutes—but if they betray me, I will. Have no doubt of it, I will!"

"They won't betray you, Caesar," soothed Cotus. "As you say, they're Celtae, not Belgae."

Almost Caesar's hand went up to push at his hair in the natural gesture of weary exasperation; it stopped short of his scalp and ran itself around his face instead. Nothing could be permitted to disorder his carefully combed, scant hair. He sighed, sat back and looked at the two Gauls.

"Do you think I don't know that every retaliation I have to make is seen as Rome's heavy foot stamping on their rights? I bend over *backward* to accommodate them, and in return I'm tricked, betrayed, treated with contempt! The children metaphor is by no means inappropriate, Dorix." He drew a breath. "I'm warning both of you because both of you came forward to intercede for other tribes: if these new agreements are not honored, I'll come down hard. It's *treason* to break solemn agreements sworn by oath! And if Roman civilian citizens are murdered, I will execute the guilty men as Rome executes all non-citizen traitors and murderers—I'll flog and behead. Nor am I speaking of minions. I will execute the tribal leaders, be it treason or murder. Clear?"

He hadn't lost his temper, but the room felt very cold. Cotus and Dorix exchanged glances, shuffled. "Yes, Caesar."

"Then make sure you disseminate my sentiments. Especially to the leaders of the Senones and Carnutes." He got up. "And now," he said, smiling, "I can turn my entire mind and all my energies to war with the Treveri and Ambiorix."

Even before Caesar left headquarters he was aware that Acco, leader of the Senones, was already in violation of the treaty he had signed only days earlier. What could one do with ignoble noblemen? Men who let other men intercede for them, beg Caesar for mercy, then proceeded to break this fresh treaty as if it meant absolutely nothing? What exactly was a Gaul's concept of honor? How did Gallic honor work? Why would the Aedui guarantee Acco's good behavior when Cotus *must* have known Acco was not an honorable man? And what of Gutruatus of the Carnutes? Him too?

But first the Belgae. Caesar marched with seven legions and a baggage train to Nemetocenna in the lands of Commius's Atrebates. Here he sent the baggage train and two legions to Labienus on the Mosa. Commius and the other five accompanied him north along the Scaldis into the lands of the Menapii, who fled without fighting into their salt fens along the shores of the German Ocean. Reprisals were indirect but horrifying. Down came a swath of Menapian oaks, up went every Menapian house in flames. The freshly sown crops were raked out of the ground; the cattle, sheep and pigs slaughtered; the chickens, geese and ducks strangled. The legions ate well, the Menapii were left with nothing.

They sued for peace and gave hostages. In return Caesar left King Commius and his Atrebatan cavalry behind to garrison the place—a significant message that Commius had just been gifted with the lands of the Menapii to add to his own.

Labienus had his own problems, but by the time Caesar and his five legions arrived, he had fought the Treveri and won a great victory.

"I couldn't have done it without the two legions you sent me," he admitted cheerfully to Caesar, well aware that this gift could not detract from his own brilliance. "Ambiorix is leading the Treveri these days, and he was all set to attack when the two extra legions appeared. So he drew off and waited for his German reinforcements to come across the Rhenus."

"And did they?"

"If they did, they turned tail and went home again. I didn't want to wait for them myself, naturally."

"Naturally," said Caesar with the ghost of a smile.

"I tricked them. It never ceases to amaze me, Caesar, that they fall for the same ploy all over again. I let the Treveri spies among my cavalry think I was frightened and withdrawing"—he shook his head in wonder—"though this time I really did march. They descended on my column in their usual undisciplined hordes—my men wheeled, launched *pila,* then charged. We killed thousands of them. So many, in fact, that I doubt they'll ever give us more trouble. What Treveri are left will be too busy in the north, fending off the Germani."

"And Ambiorix?"

"Bolted across the Rhenus with some of Indutiomarus's close relatives. Cingetorix is back in Treveri power."

"Hmmmm," said Caesar thoughtfully. "Well, Labienus, while the Treveri are licking their wounds, it might be an idea to build another bridge across the Rhenus. Do you fancy a trip to Germania?"

"After months and months and months in this same stinking camp, Caesar, I'd welcome a trip to Hades!"

"It *is* on the nose, Titus, but there's so much shit on the site that it ought to grow four-hundredfold wheat for the next ten years," said Caesar. "I'll tell Dorix to grab it before the Treveri do."

Never happier than when he had a massive engineering task to tackle, Caesar bridged the Rhenus a little upstream of the place where he had bridged it two years before. The timbers were still stacked on the Gallic bank of the great river; being oak, they had seasoned rather than rotted.

If the first bridge had been a hefty structure, the second bridge was even heftier, for this time Caesar didn't intend to demolish it entirely when he left. For eight days the legions labored, driving piles into the riverbed, setting up the pylons to take the roadway, cushioning them from the swift and pounding current with huge, angled buttresses on the upstream side to divide the waters and take their force off the bridge itself.

"Is there *anything* he doesn't know how to do?" asked Quintus Cicero of Gaius Trebonius.

"If there is, I don't know of it. He can even take your wife off you if he fancies her. But he loves engineering best, I think. One of his greatest disappointments is that the Gauls have not yet offered him the chance to make the siege of Numantia look like an easy night in a brothel. Or if you want to get him started, ask him about Scipio Aemilianus's approach to the siege of Carthage—he'll tell you exactly what Aemilianus did wrong."

"It's all grist to his mill, you see," said Fabius, grinning.

"Do you think he'd take Pomponia off me if I dressed her up and thrust her under his nose?" asked Quintus Cicero wistfully.

Trebonius and Fabius howled with laughter.

Marcus Junius Silanus eyed them sourly. "If you ask me, all this is a complete waste of time. We should boat across," he said. "The bridge accomplishes nothing beyond his personal glory."

The old hands turned to stare at him contemptuously; Silanus was one of those who wouldn't be asked to stay on.

"Ye-es, we could boat across," said Trebonius slowly. "But then we'd have to boat back again. What happens if the Suebi—or the Ubii, for that matter—come charging in their millions out of the forest? Caesar never takes stupid risks, Silanus. See how he's ranged his artillery on the Gallic side? If we have to retreat in a hurry, he'll shell the bridge into splinters before a single German gets across. *One* of Caesar's secrets is speed. Another is to be prepared for every conceivable eventuality."

Labienus was snuffing the air, his eagle's beak flaring. "I can smell the *cunni*!" he said exultantly. "Oh, there's nothing like making a German wish he was burning inside a wicker cage!"

Before anyone could find an appropriate answer for this, up came Caesar, grinning delightedly. "Marshal the troops, boys!" he said. "Time to chase the Suebi into their woods."

"What do you mean, chase?" demanded Labienus.

Caesar laughed. "Unless I miss my guess, Titus, it will come to nothing else."

The legions marched in their normal eight-man-wide columns across the great bridge, the rhythmic thump of their feet amplified to a roaring drum roll as the planks vibrated and the echoes bounced off the water below. That their coming could be heard for miles was evident as the legions peeled off to either side on German soil. The Ubii chieftains were waiting in a group, but no German warriors stood behind them.

"It wasn't us!" cried their leader, whose name, inevitably, was Herman. "Caesar, we swear it! The Suebi sent men to aid the Treveri, we didn't! Not one Ubian warrior has crossed the river to help the Treveri, we swear it!"

"Calm down, Arminius," said Caesar through his interpreter, and giving the agitated spokesman the Latin version of his name. "If that's so, you have nothing to fear."

With the Ubii leaders stood another aristocrat whose black clothing proclaimed that he belonged to the Cherusci, a powerful tribe living between the Sugambri and the river Albis. Caesar's eyes kept going to him, fascinated. White skin, red-gold curls and a distinct look of Lucius Cornelius Sulla. Who had, he remembered being told, spied for Gaius Marius among the Germans. He and Quintus Sertorius. How old was this man? Hard to tell with Germans, whose air was soft and skins consequently young. But he could be sixty. Yes, very possible.

"What's your name?" he asked through the interpreter.

"Cornel," said the Cheruscian.

"Are you a twin?"

The pale eyes, so like Caesar's own, widened and filled with respect. "I was. My brother was killed in a war with the Suebi."

"And your father?"

"A great chieftain, so my mother said. He was of the Celtae."

"His name?"

"Cornel."

"And now you lead the Cherusci."

"I do."

"Do you plan war with Rome?"

"Never."

Whereupon Caesar smiled and turned away to talk to Herman. "Calm down, Arminius!" he repeated. "I accept your word. In which case, retire into your strongholds, make your supplies safe, and do nothing. I want Ambiorix, not war."

"The news was shouted down the river while your bridge was still building, Caesar. Ambiorix is gone to his own people, the Eburones. The Suebi have been shouting it constantly."

"That's considerate of them, but I think I'll look for myself," said Caesar, smiling. "However, Arminius, while I've got you here, I have a proposition for you. The Ubii are horse soldiers, they say the best in Germania, and far better than any Belgic tribe. Have I been misled?"

Herman swelled proudly. "No, you have not."

"But you find it difficult to get good horses, is that right?"

"Very, Caesar. Some we get from the Cimbric Chersonnese, where the old Cimbri bred huge beasts. And our raids into Belgica are rarely for land. We go for Italian and Spanish horses."

"Then," said Caesar in the most friendly way, "I might be in a position to help you, Arminius."

"Help *me*?"

"Yes. When next winter comes, send me four hundred of your very best horse soldiers to a place called Vienne, in the Roman Province. Don't bother mounting them well. They'll find eight hundred of the very best Remi horses waiting for them, and if they get to Vienne early enough, they'll have time to train the animals. I will also send you a gift of another thousand Remi horses, with good breeding stallions among them. I'll pay the Remi out of my own purse. Interested?"

"Yes! Yes!"

"Excellent! We'll talk about it further when I leave."

Caesar strolled then to Cornel, who had waited out of earshot with the rest of the chieftains and Caesar's superintendent of interpreters, Gnaeus Pompeius Trogus.

"One further thing, Cornel," he said. "Do you have sons?"

"Twenty-three, by eleven wives."

"And do they have sons?"

"Those who are old enough do."

"Oh, how Sulla would love that!" said Caesar, laughing. "And do you have any daughters?"

"Six whom I let live. The prettiest ones. That's why I'm here. One of them is to marry Herman's eldest son."

"You're right," Caesar said, nodding wisely. "Six are more than enough to make useful marriages. What a provident fellow you are!" He straightened, sobered. "Stay here, Cornel. On my way back to Gallia Comata I will require treaties of peace and friendship with the Ubii. And it would enormously gratify a very great Roman, long dead, if I also concluded a treaty of peace and friendship with the Cherusci."

"But we already have one, Caesar," said Cornel.

"Really? When was it made?"

"About the time I was born. I have it still."

"And I haven't done my homework. No doubt it's nailed to the wall in Jupiter Feretrius, right where Sulla put it. Unless it perished in the fire."

Sulla's German son was standing lost, but Caesar had no intention of enlightening him. Instead, he gazed about in mock bewilderment. "But I don't see the Sugambri! Where are they?"

Herman swallowed. "They'll be here when you return, Caesar."

The Suebi had retreated to the eaves of the Bacenis Forest, a limitless expanse of beech, oak and birch which eventually fused with an even mightier forest, the Hercynian, and spread untrammeled a thousand miles to far Dacia and the sources of the fabulous rivers flowing down to the Euxine Sea. It was said that a man could walk for sixty days and not reach the middle of it.

Wherever oaks and acorns were, there also were pigs; in this impenetrable fastness the boars were massive, tusked, and mindlessly savage. Wolves slunk everywhere, hunting in packs, afraid of nothing. The forests of Gaul, particularly the Arduenna, still held many boars and wolves, but the forests of Germania contained myths and fables because men had not yet forced them to retreat eastward. *Horrifying* creatures lived there! Huge elk which had to lean on trees to sleep, so heavy were their horns; aurochs the size of small elephants; and gigantic bears, dowered with claws as long as a man's fingers, teeth bigger than a lion's, bears which towered over a man when they stood upright. Deer, wild cattle and wild sheep were their food, but they were not averse to men. The Germani hunted them for their pelts, highly prized for sleeping warmth and highly valued as items of trade.

No surprise then that the troops regarded the fringes of the Bacenis Forest with trepidation, and promised innumerable rich offerings to Sol Indiges and Tellus if those Gods would only pop the thought into Caesar's head that he didn't want to go inside. For they would follow him, but do so in great dread.

"Well, as the Germani are not Druids, there seems no point in felling their trees," said Caesar to his apprehensive legates. "Nor do I intend to take my soldiers into that kind of horror. We've shown our fangs, and that's as much as we can do, I think. Back to Gallia Comata."

This time, however, the bridge didn't come down entirely. Only the two hundred feet of it closest to the German bank were demolished; Caesar left the rest still standing, erected a strongly fortified camp equipped with one tower tall enough to see into Germania for miles, and garrisoned it with the Fifth Alauda under the command of Gaius Volcatius Tullus.

It was the end of September, still high summer by the seasons; the Belgae were on their knees, but one more campaign would see a permanent cessation to Belgic resistance. From his bridge across the Rhenus, Caesar pushed westward into the lands of the Eburones, already devastated. If Ambiorix was there, he would have to be captured. The Eburones were his people, but it was impossible for a king to rule if his people no longer existed. Therefore the Eburones would disappear from the catalogue of the Druids. An objective King Commius of the Atrebates applauded; his lands were increasing rapidly, and he had the people to fill them. The title High King of the Belgae grew ever closer.

Quintus Cicero, however, was not so lucky. Because he had a happy knack with soldiers, Caesar had given him command of the Fifteenth Legion, the only one still composed entirely of raw troops who had not yet seen battle. Word of the extermination of the Eburones had flown across the river into Germania, with the result that the Sugambri decided to help Caesar in an unofficial capacity. They boated across to Belgica and contributed their mite to Belgic misery. Unfortunately the sight of a poorly formed and unruly Roman column was too much to bear; the Sugambri fell on the Fifteenth with glee, and the Fifteenth panicked so badly that Quintus Cicero and his tribunes could do nothing.

Two cohorts were needlessly killed in the confusion, but before the Sugambri could kill more, Caesar arrived with the Tenth. Shrieking with mingled joy and alarm, the Sugambri scampered off to leave Caesar and Quintus Cicero trying to restore order. Which took all day.

"I've let you down," said Quintus Cicero, tears in his eyes.

"No, not at all. They're unblooded and nervous. All that German forest. These things happen, Quintus. Had I been with them, I doubt matters would have been different. It's their vile centurions at fault, not my legate."

"If you'd been leading them, you would have seen whose fault it was and not let them fall into total disorder on the march," said Quintus Cicero, unconsoled.

Caesar threw an arm about his shoulders and shook him gently. "Perhaps," he said, "but not surely. Anyway, we shall prove the truth of it. You can have the Tenth. The Fifteenth is going to be stuck with me for many moons to come. I'll have to go across the Alps to Italian Gaul this autumn, and the Fifteenth will come with me. I'll march it into stupor and I'll drill it into puppet dolls. Including its slack centurions."

"Does this mean I'll be packing my trunks with Silanus?" Quintus Cicero asked.

"I sincerely hope not, Quintus! You're with me until you ask to go." His arm tightened, his hand squeezed. "You see, Quintus, I've come to think of you as the great Cicero's *big* brother. He might fight a superb action in the Forum, but in the field he couldn't fight his way out of a sack. To each his own. You're the Cicero I prefer any day."

Words which were to stay with Quintus Cicero during the years to come, words which were to cause much pain, greater acrimony, awful rifts within the Tullius Cicero family. For Quintus could never forget them, nor discipline himself not to love the man who said them. Blood ruled. But hearts could ache despite that. Oh, better perhaps that he had never served with Caesar! Yet had he not, the great Cicero would always have dictated his every thought, and Quintus would never have become his own man.

And so that strife-torn year wore down for Caesar. He put the legions into winter camp very early, two with Labienus in a new camp among the Treveri, two in the lands of the ever-loyal Lingones along the Sequana River, and six around Agedincum, the main *oppidum* of the Senones.

He prepared to depart for Italian Gaul, planning to escort Rhiannon and his son as far as her villa outside Arausio, and also planning to find a pedagogue for the boy. What *was* the matter with him, that he had no interest in the Greeks on the beach at Ilium for ten long years, in the rivalry between Achilles and Hector, in the madness of Ajax, in the treachery of Thersites? Had he asked these things of Rhiannon, she might have answered tartly that Orgetorix was not yet four years old; but as he said nothing of it to her, he went on interpreting the child's behavior in the light of what he had been at the same age, and didn't understand that the child of a genius might turn out to be just an ordinary little boy.

At the end of November he called another pan-Gallic assembly, this one at the Remi *oppidum* of Durocortorum. The reason for the congress was not discussion. Caesar charged Acco, the leader of the Senones, with conspiring to incite insurrection. He conducted a formal Roman trial in the prescribed manner, though in one hearing only: witnesses, cross-examination of witnesses, a jury composed of twenty-six Romans and twenty-five Gauls, advocates to speak for the prosecution and the defense. Caesar presided himself, with Cotus of the Aedui, who had interceded for the Senones, at his right hand.

All the Celtae and some of the Belgae came, though the Remi outnumbered all the other delegates (and furnished six of the twenty-five Gallic jurors). The Arverni were led by Gobannitio and Critognatus, their vergobrets, but in the party was—of course, thought Caesar with an inward sigh—Vercingetorix. Who challenged the court immediately.

"If this is to be a fair trial," he asked Caesar, "why is there one more Roman juror than Gallic juror?"

Caesar opened his eyes wide. "There is customarily an odd number of jurors to avoid a drawn decision," he said mildly. "The lots were cast; you saw them for yourself, Vercingetorix. Besides which, for the purposes of this trial all the jurors are to be regarded as Roman—all have an equal vote."

"How can it be equal when there are twenty-six Romans and only twenty-five Gauls?"

"Would you be happier if I put an extra Gaul on the jury?" asked Caesar patiently.

"Yes!" snapped Vercingetorix, uncomfortably aware that the Roman legates were laughing at him behind their eyes.

"Then I will do so. Now sit down, Vercingetorix."

Gobannitio rose to his feet.

"Yes?" asked Caesar, sure of this man.

"I must apologize for the conduct of my nephew, Caesar. It will not happen again."

"You relieve me, Gobannitio. Now may we proceed?"

The court proceeded through witnesses and advocates (with, noted Caesar, pleased, a wonderful speech in defense of Acco by Quintus Cicero—let Vercingetorix complain about *that*!) to its verdict, having taken the best part of the day.

Thirty-three jurors voted CONDEMNO, nineteen ABSOLVO. All the Roman jurors, six Remi and one Lingone had won the day. But nineteen of the Gauls, including the three Aedui on the panel, had voted for acquittal.

"The sentence is automatic," said Caesar tonelessly. "Acco will be flogged and decapitated. At once. Those who wish to witness the execution may do so. I sincerely hope this lesson is taken to heart. I will have no more broken treaties."

As the proceedings had been conducted entirely in Latin, it was only when the Roman guard formed up on either side of him that Acco truly realized what the sentence was.

"I am a free man in a free country!" he shouted, drew himself up, and walked between the soldiers out of the room.

Vercingetorix began to cheer; Gobannitio struck him hard across the face.

"Be silent, you fool!" he said. "Isn't it enough?"

Vercingetorix left the room, left the confines of the hall and strode off until he could neither see nor hear what was done to Acco.

"They say that's what Dumnorix said just before Labienus cut him down," said Gutruatus of the Carnutes.

"What?" asked Vercingetorix, trembling, face bathed in a chill sweat. "What?"

" 'I am a free man in a free country!' Dumnorix shouted before Labienus cut him down. And now his woman consorts with Caesar. This is not a free country, and we are not free men."

"You don't need to tell me that, Gutruatus. My own uncle, to strike me across the face in front of *Caesar*! Why did he do this? Are we supposed to shake in fear, get down on our knees and beg Caesar's forgiveness?"

"It's Caesar's way of telling us that we are not free men in a free country."

"Oh, by Dagda and Taranis and Esus, I swear I'll have Caesar's head on my doorpost for this!" Vercingetorix cried. "How *dare* he dress up his actions in such a travesty?"

"He dares because he's a brilliant man in command of a brilliant army," said Gutruatus through his teeth. "He's walked all over us for five long years, Vercingetorix, and we haven't got anywhere! You may as well say that he's finished the Belgae, and the only reason he hasn't finished the Celtae is that we haven't gone to war with him the way the Belgae did. Except for the poor Armorici—look at them! The Veneti sold into slavery, the Esubii reduced to nothing."

Litaviccus and Cotus of the Aedui appeared, faces grim; Lucterius of the Cardurci joined them, and Sedulius, vergobret of the Lemovices.

"That's just the point!" cried Vercingetorix, speaking to his entire audience. "Look at the Belgae—Caesar picked them off one people at a time. Never as a mass of peoples. Eburones one campaign—the Morini another—the Nervii—the Bellovaci—the Atuatuci—the Menapii—even the Treveri. *One by one!* But what would have happened to Caesar if just the Nervii, the Bellovaci, the Eburones and the Treveri had merged their forces and attacked as one army? Yes, he's brilliant! Yes, he has a brilliant army! But Dagda he is not! He would have gone down—and never managed to get up again."

"What you're saying," said Lucterius slowly, "is that we Celtae have to unite."

"That's exactly what I'm saying."

Cotus scowled. "And under whose leadership?" he demanded aggressively. "Do you expect the Aedui, for instance, to fight for an Arvernian leader in, for instance, the person of yourself, Vercingetorix?"

"If the Aedui wish to become a part of the new State of Gallia, yes, Cotus, I expect the Aedui to fight for whoever is made leader." The dark blue eyes in the skull-like face glowed beneath their strange black brows. "Perhaps the leader would be me, an Arvernian and therefore the traditional enemy of all Aedui. Perhaps the leader might be an Aeduan, in which case I would expect all the Arverni to fight under him, as I would myself. Cotus, Cotus, open your eyes! Don't you see? It's the divisions between us, the ancient feuds, will bring us to our knees! There are more of us than of them! Are they braver? No! They're better organized, that's all. They work together like some vast machine, turning like teeth through a cog—about face, wheel, form square, launch javelins, charge, march in step! Well, that we cannot change. That we have no time to learn to imitate. But we do have the numbers. If we are united, the numbers *cannot* lose!"

Lucterius drew a huge breath. "I'm with you, Vercingetorix!" he said suddenly.

"So am I," said Gutruatus. He smiled. "And I know someone else who'll be with you. Cathbad of the Druids."

Vercingetorix stared, amazed. "*Cathbad?* Then talk to him the moment you get home, Gutruatus! If Cathbad would be willing to organize all the Druids throughout all the peoples—to wheedle, cajole, persuade—half our work would be done."

But Cotus was looking steadily more frightened, Litaviccus torn, and Sedulius wary.

"It will take more than Druid talk to budge the Aedui," said Cotus, swallowing. "We take our status as Friend and Ally of the Roman People very seriously."

Vercingetorix sneered. "Hah! Then you're fools!" he cried. "It isn't so very many years ago, Cotus, that this selfsame Caesar showered that German swine Ariovistus with expensive gifts and procured *him* the title of Friend and Ally from the Roman Senate! *Knowing* that Ariovistus was raiding the Friend and Ally Aedui—stealing their cattle, their sheep, their women, their lands! Did this selfsame Caesar care about the Aedui? No! All he wanted was a peaceful province!" He clenched his fists, shook them at the sky. "I tell you, every time he mouths his sanctimonious promise to protect us from the Germani, I think of that. And if the Aedui had any sense, so would they."

Litaviccus drew a breath, nodded. "All right, I'm with you too," he said. "I can't speak for Cotus here—he's my senior, not to mention vergobret next year with Convictolavus. But I'll work for you, Vercingetorix."

"I can't promise," said Cotus, "but I won't work against you. Nor will I tell the Romans."

"More than that I don't ask for the time being, Cotus," said Vercingetorix. "Just think about it." He smiled without humor. "There are more ways of hindering Caesar than in battle. He has complete trust in the Aedui. When he snaps his fingers, he expects an Aeduan response—give me more wheat, give me more cavalry, give me more of everything! I can understand an old man like you not wanting to draw a sword, Cotus. But if you want to be a free man in a free country, you'd better think of other ways to fight Gaius Julius Caesar."

"I'm with you too," said Sedulius, the last to answer.

Vercingetorix held out his thin hand, palm up; Gutruatus put his hand on top of it, palm up; then Litaviccus; then Sedulius; then Lucterius; and, finally, Cotus.

"Free men in a free country," said Vercingetorix. "Agreed?"

"Agreed," they said.

Had Caesar delayed a day or two more, some of this might have come back to him through Rhiannon. But suddenly Gaul of the Longhairs was the last place he wanted to be. At dawn the next morning he left for Italian Gaul, the hapless Fifteenth Legion at his back, and Rhiannon on her high-stepping Italian horse. She had not seen Vercingetorix at all, nor did she understand what made Caesar so curt, so distant. Was there another woman? Always, with him! But they never mattered, and none of them had borne him a son. Who rode with his nurse in a wagon, clutching as much of his big Trojan Horse as he could. No, he cared nothing for Menelaus or Odysseus, Achilles or Ajax. But the Trojan Horse was the most wonderful beast in the world, and it belonged to him.

They had not been a day on the road before Caesar had long outdistanced them, flying like the wind in his gig harnessed to four cantering mules, dictating his senatorial dispatch to one green-faced secretary, and a letter to big brother Cicero to the other. Never becoming confused, reinforcing with Cicero the considerably modified senatorial version of Quintus Cicero and the Sugambri; all those fools in the Senate thought he tampered with the truth, but they wouldn't suspect it of the official version of Quintus Cicero and the Sugambri.

He dictated on, pausing patiently when one secretary had to lean out of the gig to vomit. Anything to get the memory of that scene in the hall at Durocortorum out of his mind, anything to forget Acco and that cry echoing Dumnorix. He hadn't wanted to single Acco out as a victim, but how else were they to learn the protocol and etiquette of civilized peoples? Talk didn't work. Example didn't work.

How else can I force the Celtae to learn the lesson I had to teach the Belgae in letters of blood? For I cannot leave with my task undone, and the years wing by. I cannot return to Rome without my *dignitas* enhanced by total victory. I am a greater hero now than Pompeius Magnus was at the height of his glory, and all of Rome is at my feet. I will do whatever I have to do, no matter the price. Ah, but the remembrance of cruelty is poor comfort in old age!

ROME

from JANUARY until
APRIL of 52 B.C.

QUINTUS CAECILIUS METELLUS PIUS SCIPIO NASICA
(METELLUS SCIPIO)

New Year's Day dawned without any magistrates entering office; Rome existed at the whim of the Senate and the ten tribunes of the plebs. Cato had been true to his word and blocked last year's elections until Pompey's nephew, Gaius Memmius, stepped down as a consular candidate. But it was not until the end of Quinctilis that Gnaeus Domitius Calvinus and Messala Rufus the augur were returned as consuls for the five months of the year remaining. Once in office, they held no elections for this year's men, their reason being the street war which broke out between Publius Clodius and Titus Annius Milo. One, Milo, wanted to be consul, and the other, Clodius, wanted to be praetor; but neither man could condone the presence of his enemy as a fellow senior magistrate. Both Clodius and Milo marshaled their gangs, and Rome erupted into constant violence. Which was not to say that everyday life in most of the city was inconvenienced; the terror was confined to the Forum Romanum and the streets nearest it. So remorseless was the urban conflict that the Senate gave up meeting in its own hallowed chamber, the Curia Hostilia, and meetings of the People and the Plebs in their tribal assemblies were not held at all.

This state of affairs seriously hampered the career of one of Clodius's greatest friends, Mark Antony. He was turned thirty and should already have gone into office as a quaestor, which carried automatic elevation to the Senate among its benefits and offered an enterprising man many opportunities to plump out his purse. If he was appointed quaestor to a province, he managed the governor's finances, usually without supervision; he could fiddle the books, sell tax exemptions, adjust contracts. It was also possible to profit from appointment as one of the three quaestors who remained inside Rome to manage the Treasury's finances; he could (for a price) alter the records to wipe out someone's debt, or make sure someone else received sums from the Treasury to which he was not entitled. Therefore Mark Antony, always in debt, was hungry to assume his quaestorship.

No one had asked for him by name among the governors, which rather annoyed him when he summoned up the energy to think about it. Caesar, the most open-handed of all governors, was his close cousin and *should* have asked for him by name. He'd asked for the sons of Marcus Crassus by name, yet the only claim they had on him was the great friendship between their father and Caesar. Then this year Caesar had asked for Servilia's son, Brutus, by name! And been turned down for his pains, a fact which Brutus's uncle Cato had trumpeted from one end of Rome to the other. While Brutus's monster of a mother, who reveled in being Caesar's mistress, tormented her half brother by feeding the gossip network with delicious little titbits about Cato's selling of his wife to silly old Hortensius!

Antony's uncle Lucius Caesar (invited to Gaul this year as one of Caesar's senior legates) had refused to ask Caesar to name him as quaestor, so Antony's mother (who was Lucius Caesar's only sister) had written instead. Caesar's reply was cool and abrupt: it would do Marcus Antonius a great deal of good to take his chances in the lots, so no, Julia Antonia, I will not request your precious oldest son.

"After all," said Antony discontentedly to Clodius, "I did very well out in Syria with Gabinius! Led his cavalry like a real expert. Gabinius never moved without me."

"The new Labienus," said Clodius, grinning.

The Clodius Club still met, despite the defection of Marcus Caelius Rufus and those two famous *fellatrices* Sempronia Tuditani and Palla. The trial and acquittal of Caelius on the charge of attempting to poison Clodius's favorite sister, Clodia, had aged that pair of repulsive sexual acrobats so strikingly that they preferred to stay at home and avoid mirrors.

While the Clodius Club flourished regardless. The members were meeting, as always, in Clodius's house on the Palatine, the new one he had bought from Scaurus for fourteen and a half million sesterces. A lovely place, spacious and exquisitely furnished. The dining room, where they all lolled at the moment on Tyrian purple couches, was adorned with startlingly three-dimensional panels of black-and-white cubes sandwiched between softly dreamy Arcadian landscapes. Since the season was early autumn, the big doors onto the peristyle colonnade were flung open, allowing the Clodius Club to gaze at a long marble pool decked with tritons and dolphins, and, atop the fountain in the pool's center, a stunning sculpture of the merman Amphitryon driving a scallop shell drawn by horses with fish's tails, superbly painted to lifelike animation.

Curio the Younger was there; Pompeius Rufus, full brother of Caesar's abysmally stupid ex-wife, Pompeia Sulla; Decimus Brutus, son of Sempronia Tuditani; and a newer member, Plancus Bursa. Plus the three women, of course. All of them belonged to Publius Clodius: his sisters, Clodia and Clodilla, and his wife, Fulvia, to whom Clodius was so devoted he never moved without her.

"Well, Caesar's asked me to come back to him in Gaul, and I'm tempted to go," said Decimus Brutus, unconsciously rubbing salt into Antony's wounds.

Antony stared at him resentfully. Not much to look at aside from a certain air of ruthless competence—slight, of average height, so white-blond that he had earned the cognomen of Albinus. Yet Caesar loved him, esteemed him so much he had been given jobs more properly in the purlieus of senior legates. Why wouldn't Caesar love his cousin Marcus Antonius? *Why?*

The pivot around whom all these people turned, Publius Clodius, was a slight man of average height too, but as dark as Decimus Brutus was fair. His face was impish, with a slightly anxious expression when it wasn't smiling, and his life had been extraordinarily eventful in a way which perhaps could not have happened to anyone other than a member of that highly unorthodox patrician clan the Claudii Pulchri. Among many other things, he had provoked the Arabs of Syria into circumcising him, Cicero into mercilessly ridiculing him in public, Caesar into permitting him to be adopted into the Plebs, Pompey into paying Milo to start up rival street gangs, and all of noble Rome into believing that he had enjoyed incestuous relations with his sisters, Clodia and Clodilla.

His greatest failing was an insatiable thirst for revenge. Once a person insulted or injured his *dignitas,* he put that person's name on his revenge list and waited for the perfect opportunity to pay the score in full. Among these persons were Cicero, whom he had succeeded in legally banishing for a time; Ptolemy the Cyprian, whom he had pushed into suicide by annexing Cyprus; Lucullus, his dead brother-in-law, whose career as one of Rome's greatest generals Clodius had sent crashing by instigating a mutiny; and Caesar's mother, Aurelia, whose celebration of the winter feast of Bona Dea, the Good Goddess of Women, he had mocked and ruined. Though this last revenge still haunted him whenever his enormous self-confidence suffered a check, for he had committed a terrible sacrilege against Bona Dea. Tried in a court of law for it, Clodius was acquitted because his wife and other women bought the jury—Fulvia because she loved him, the other women because they wanted him preserved for Bona Dea's own revenge. It would come, it would come . . . and that was what haunted Clodius.

His latest act of revenge was founded in a very old grudge. Over twenty years ago, aged eighteen, he had charged the beautiful young Vestal Virgin Fabia with unchastity, a crime punishable by death. He lost the case. Fabia's name went immediately onto his list of victims; the years passed, Clodius waited patiently while others involved, like Catilina, bit the dust. Then, aged thirty-seven and still a beautiful woman, Fabia (who, to add to her score, was the half sister of Cicero's wife, Terentia) retired. Having served her thirty years, she removed from the Domus Publica to a snug little house on the upper Quirinal, where she intended to live out the rest of her life as an honored ex–Chief Vestal. Her father had been a patrician Fabius Maximus (it was a mother she shared with Terentia), and he had dowered her richly when she had entered the Order at seven years of age. As Terentia, extremely shrewd in all money matters, had always administered Fabia's dowry with the same efficiency and acumen she brought to the management of her own large fortune (she never let Cicero get his hands on one sestertius of it), Fabia left the Order a very wealthy woman.

It was this last fact which started the seed germinating in Clodius's fertile mind. The longer he waited, the sweeter revenge became. And after a whole twenty years he suddenly saw how to crush Fabia completely. Though it was perfectly acceptable for an ex-Vestal to marry, few ever did; it was thought to be unlucky. On the other hand, few ex-Vestals were as attractive as Fabia. Or as wealthy. Clodius cast round in his mind for someone who was as penurious as he was handsome and wellborn, and came up with Publius Cornelius Dolabella. A part-time member of the Clodius Club. And of much the same kind as that other brute, Mark Antony: big, burly, bullish, bad.

When Clodius suggested that he woo Fabia, Dolabella leaped at the idea. Patrician of impeccable ancestry though he was, every father whose daughter he eyed whisked her out of sight and said a firm no to any proposal of marriage. Like another patrician Cornelius, Sulla, Dolabella had no choice other than to live on his wits. Ex-Vestals were *sui iuris*—they answered to no man; they were entirely in charge of their own lives. How fortuitous! A bride of blood as good as his own, still young enough to bear children, very rich—and no *paterfamilias* to thwart him.

But where Dolabella differed from that other brute, Antony, lay in his personality. Mark Antony was by no means unintelligent, but he utterly lacked charm; his attractions were of the flesh. Dolabella, to the contrary, possessed an easy, happy, light manner and a great talent for conversation. Antony's amours were of the "I love you, lie down!" variety, whereas Dolabella's were more "Let me drink in the sight of your dear, sweet face!"

The outcome was a marriage. Not only had the ingratiating Dolabella swept Fabia off her feet, he had also swept the female members of Cicero's household off their feet. That Cicero's daughter, Tullia (unhappily married to Furius Crassipes), should deem him divine was perhaps not surprising, but that the sour, ugly Terentia should also deem him divine rocked Rome of the gossips to its foundations. Thus Dolabella wooed Fabia with her sister's fervent blessing; poor Tullia cried.

Clodius was still enjoying his revenge, for the marriage was a disaster from its first day. A late-thirties virgin cloistered among women for thirty years required a kind of sexual initiation Dolabella was not qualified—or interested enough—to pursue. Though the rupture of Fabia's hymen could not be classified as a rape, neither was it an ecstasy. Exasperated and bored, Fabia's money safely his, Dolabella went back to women who knew how to do it and were willing at least to pretend ecstasy. Fabia sat at home and wept desolately, while Terentia kept yapping that she was a fool who didn't know how to handle a man. Tullia, on the other hand, cheered up enormously and began thinking of divorce from Furius Crassipes.

However, Clodius's genuine glee at this latest successful revenge was already beginning to pall; politics were always his first priority.

He was determined to be the First Man in Rome, but would not go about achieving this end in the usual fashion—the highest political office allied to a degree of military prowess bordering on legendary. Mainly because Clodius's talents were not martial. His method was demagoguery; he intended to rule through the Plebeian Assembly, dominated by Rome's knight-businessmen. Others had taken that path, but never the way Clodius intended to.

Where Clodius differed was in his grand strategy. He did not woo these powerful, plutocratic knight-businessmen. He intimidated them. And in order to intimidate them he employed a section of Roman society which all other men ignored as totally valueless—the *proletarii,* the Head Count who were the Roman citizen lowly. No money, no votes worth the tablets they were written on, no influence with the mighty, no other reason for existence beyond giving Rome children and enlisting as rankers in Rome's legions. Even this latter entitlement was relatively recent, for until Gaius Marius had thrown the legions open to men who had no property, Rome's armies had consisted solely of propertied men. The Head Count were not political people. Far from it. Provided their bellies were full and they were offered regular free entertainment at the games, they had no interest whatsoever in the political machinations of their betters.

Nor was it Clodius's intention to turn them into political people. He needed their numbers, that was all; it was no part of his purpose to fill them with ideas of their own worth, or draw their attention to the power their sheer numbers potentially wielded. Very simply, they were Clodius's clients. They owed him cliental loyalty as the patron who had obtained huge benefits for them: a free issue of grain once a month; complete liberty to congregate in their sodalities, colleges or clubs; and a bit of extra money once a year or so. With the assistance of Decimus Brutus and some lesser lights, Clodius had organized the thousands upon thousands of lowly men who frequented the crossroads colleges which littered Rome. On any one day when he scheduled gangs to appear in the Forum and the streets adjacent to it, he needed at most a mere one thousand men. Due to Decimus Brutus, he had a system of rosters and a set of books enabling him to distribute the load and share out the five-hundred-sestertius fee paid for a sortie among the whole of the crossroads colleges lowly; months would go by before the same man was called again to run riot in the Forum and intimidate the influential Plebs. In that way the faces of his gang members remained anonymous.

After Pompey the Great had paid Milo to set up rival gangs composed of ex-gladiators and bully-boys, the violence became complicated. Not only did it have to achieve Clodius's objective, intimidation of the Plebs, it now also had to contend with Milo and his professional thugs. Then after Caesar concluded his pact with Pompey and Marcus Crassus at Luca, Clodius was brought to heel. This had been accomplished by awarding him an all-expenses-paid embassage to Anatolia, which afforded him the chance to make a lot of money during the year he was away. Even after he returned, he was quiet. Until Calvinus and Messala Rufus were elected the consuls at the end of last Quinctilis. At this time the war between Clodius and Milo had broken out afresh.

* * *

Curio was watching Fulvia, but he had been doing that for so many years that no one noticed. Admittedly she was eminently watchable, with her ice-brown hair, her black brows and lashes, her huge dark blue eyes. Several children had only added to her charms, as did a good instinct for what clothing became her. The granddaughter of the great demagogue aristocrat Gaius Gracchus, she was so sure of her place in the highest stratum of society that she felt free to attend meetings in the Forum and barrack in the most unladylike way for Clodius, whom she adored.

"I hear," said Curio, wrenching his eyes away from his best friend's wife, "that the moment you're elected praetor you intend to distribute Rome's freedmen across the thirty-five tribes. Is that really true, Clodius?"

"Yes, it's really true," said Clodius complacently.

Curio frowned, an expression which didn't suit him. Of an old and noble plebeian family, Scribonius, at thirty-two Curio still had the face of a naughty little boy. His eyes were brown and gleamed wickedly, his skin was smothered in freckles, and his bright red hair stood up on end no matter what his barber did to smooth it down. The urchin look was strengthened when he smiled, for he was missing a front tooth. An exterior very much at odds with Curio's interior, which was tough, mature, sometimes scandalously courageous, and ruled by a first-class mind. When he and Antony, always boon companions, had been ten years younger, they had tormented Curio's ultra-conservative consular father unmercifully by pretending to be lovers, and between them had fathered more bastards than, said rumor, anyone else in history.

But now Curio frowned, so the gap in his teeth didn't show and the mischief in his eyes was quite missing. "Clodius, to distribute the freedmen across all thirty-five tribes would skew the whole of the tribal electoral system," he said slowly. "The man who owned their votes—that's you, if you do it—would be unstoppable. All he'd have to do to secure the election of the men he wanted would be to postpone the elections until there were no country voters in town. At the moment the freedmen can vote in only two urban tribes. But there are *half a million* of them living inside Rome! If they're put in equal numbers into all thirty-five tribes, they'll have the numbers to outvote the few permanent residents of Rome who belong to the thirty-one rural tribes—the senators and knights of the First Class. The true Roman Head Count are confined to the four urban tribes—*they* don't vote across all thirty-five tribes! Why, you'd be handing over control of Rome's tribal elections to a pack of non-Romans! Greeks, Gauls, Syrians, ex-pirates, the detritus of the world, all of them slaves in their own lifetimes! I don't grudge them their freedom, nor do I grudge them our citizenship. But I do bitterly grudge them control of a congress of true Roman men!" He shook his head, looked fierce. "Clodius, Clodius! They'll never let you get away with it! Nor, for that matter, will *I* let you get away with it!"

"Neither they nor you will be able to prevent me," Clodius said with insufferable smugness.

A dour and silent man who had recently entered office as a tribune of the plebs, Plancus Bursa spoke up in his passionless way. "To do that is to play with fire, Clodius," he said.

"The whole First Class will unite against you," Pompeius Rufus, another new tribune of the plebs, said in a voice of doom.

"But you intend to do it anyway," said Decimus Brutus.

"I intend to do it anyway. I'd be a fool if I didn't."

"And a fool my little brother is not," mumbled Clodia, sucking her fingers lasciviously as she ogled Antony.

Antony scratched his groin, shifted its formidable contents with the same hand, then blew Clodia a kiss; they were old bedmates. "If you do succeed, Clodius, you'll own every freedman in Rome," he said thoughtfully. "They'll vote for whomever you say. Except that owning the tribal elections won't procure you consuls in the centuriate elections."

"*Consuls?* Who needs consuls?" asked Clodius loftily. "All I need are ten tribunes of the plebs year after year after year. With ten tribunes of the plebs doing whatever I command them to, consuls aren't worth a fava bean to a Pythagorean. And praetors will simply be judges in their own courts; they won't have any legislative powers. The Senate and the First Class *think* they own Rome. The truth is that anyone can own Rome if he just finds the right way to go about it. Sulla owned Rome. And so will I, Antonius. Through freedmen distributed across the thirty-five tribes and the ten tame tribunes of the plebs they'll return—because I'll never let the elections be held while the country bumpkins are in Rome for the games. Why do you think Sulla fixed Quinctilis during the games as the time to hold elections? He wanted the rural tribes—which means the First Class—to control the Plebeian Assembly and the tribunes of the plebs. That way, everybody with clout can own one or two tribunes of the plebs. My way, I'll own all ten."

Curio was staring at Clodius as if he'd never seen him before. "I've always known that you're not quite right in the head, Clodius, but this is absolute insanity! *Don't try!*"

The women, who respected Curio's opinions greatly, began to shrink together on the couch they shared, Fulvia's beautiful brown skin paler by the moment. Then she gulped, tried to giggle, thrust out her chin pugnaciously.

"Clodius always knows what he's doing!" she cried. "He's got it all worked out."

Curio shrugged. "Be it on your own head, then, Clodius. I still think you're mad. And I'm warning you, I'll oppose you."

Back came the overindulged, atrociously spoiled youth Clodius had been; he gave Curio a look of burning scorn, sneered, slid off the couch he shared with Decimus Brutus, and flounced out of the room, Fulvia flying after him.

"They've left their shoes behind," said Pompeius Rufus, whose intellect was on a par with his sister's.

"I'd better find him," said Plancus Bursa, departing too.

"Take your shoes, Bursa!" cried Pompeius Rufus.

Which struck Curio, Antony and Decimus Brutus as exquisitely funny; they lay flat out and howled with laughter.

"You shouldn't irritate Publius," said Clodilla to Curio. "He'll sulk for days."

"I wish he'd *think*!" growled Decimus Brutus.

Clodia, not as young as she once had been but still a most alluring woman, gazed at the three men with dark eyes wide. "I know you're all fond of him," she said, "which means that you really do fear for him. But should you? He's bounced from one mad scheme to another all his life, and somehow they work to his advantage."

"Not this time," said Curio, sighing.

"He's insane," said Decimus Brutus.

But Antony had had enough. "I don't care if they brand the mad sign on Clodius's forehead," he growled. "I need to be elected quaestor! I'm scratching for every sestertius I can find, but all I do is get poorer."

"Don't tell me you've run through Fadia's money already, Marcus," said Clodilla.

"Fadia's been dead for four years!" cried Antony indignantly.

"Rubbish, Marcus," said Clodia, licking her fingers. "Rome is full of ugly daughters with plutocrat fathers scrambling up the social ladder. Find yourself another Fadia."

"At the moment it's probably going to be my first cousin, Antonia Hybrida."

They all sat up to stare, including Pompeius Rufus.

"Lots of money," said Curio, head to one side.

"That's why I'll probably marry her. Uncle Hybrida can't abide me, but he'd rather Antonia married me than a mushroom." He looked thoughtful. "They say she tortures her slaves, but I'll soon beat *that* out of her."

"Like father, like daughter," said Decimus Brutus, grinning.

"Cornelia Metella is a widow," Clodilla suggested. "Old, old family. Many thousands of talents."

"But what if she's like dear old *tata* Metellus Scipio?" asked Antony, red-brown eyes twinkling. "It's no trouble dealing with someone who tortures her slaves, but *pornographic pageants*?"

More laughter, though it was hollow. How could they protect Publius Clodius from himself if he persisted in this scheme?

* * *

Though his beloved Julia had been dead now for sixteen months and his grief had worn itself out to the point whereat he could speak her name without dissolving immediately into tears, Gnaeus Pompeius Magnus had not thought of remarriage. There was actually nothing to prevent his relocating himself in his provinces, Nearer and Further Spain, which he would be governing for another three years. Yet he had not moved from his villa on the Campus Martius, still left his provinces to the care of his legates Afranius and Petreius. He was also, of course, curator of Rome's grain supply, a job which he could use as an excuse for remaining in the vicinity of Rome; but in spite of Clodius's free grain dole and a recent drought, he had brought the grain supply so tidily into running itself that little was required of him. Like all publicly conducted enterprises, what it had needed was someone with a genius for organization and the clout to ride roughshod over those ghastly ditherers the civil servants.

The truth was that the situation in Rome fascinated him, and he couldn't bear to leave until he had sorted out his own desires, his own priorities. Namely, did he want to be appointed Dictator? Ever since Caesar had departed for Gaul, the political arena of Rome's Forum had become steadily more undisciplined. Yet what that had to do with Caesar, he didn't honestly know. Certainly it wasn't Caesar causing it. But sometimes in the midst of a white night he found himself wondering whether, were Caesar still here, it would have come to pass. And that was an enormous worry.

When he had married Caesar's daughter he hadn't thought very much about her father, except as a consummately clever politician who knew how to get his own way. There were many Caesars in the public eye, tremendously wellborn, canny, ambitious, competent. How exactly Caesar had outstripped them all escaped him. The man was some kind of magician; one moment he was standing in front of you, the next moment he was on the far side of a stone wall. You never saw how he did it, it was so fast. Nor how he managed to rise, a phoenix from its ashes, every time his formidable coterie of enemies thought they had burned him for good.

Take Luca, that funny little timber town on the Auser River just on the Italian Gaul side of the border, where three years ago he had found himself huddled with Caesar and Marcus Crassus and more or less divided the world. But why had he gone? Why did he *need* to go? Oh, at the time the reasons had seemed mountainous! But now, looking back, they seemed as small as ants' nests. What he, Pompey the Great, had gained from the conference at Luca he could have achieved unaided. And look at poor Marcus Crassus, dead, degraded, unburied. Whereas Caesar had gone from strength to strength. *How did he do that?* All through their association, which extended back to before his own campaign against the pirates, it had always seemed that Caesar was his servant. No one gave a better speech, even Cicero, and there had been times when Caesar's voice had been alone in supporting him. But he had never thought of Caesar as a man who intended to rival him. After all, Caesar had done things the proper way, everything in its time. *He* had not led legions and forced a partnership with the greatest man in Rome at a mere twenty-two years of age! *He* had not compelled the Senate to allow him to be consul before he so much as had membership in that august body! *He* had not wiped Our Sea clean of pirates in a single summer! *He* had not conquered the East and doubled Rome's tributes!

So why now did Pompey's skin prickle? Why now did he feel the cold wind of Caesar's breath on the back of his neck? How had Caesar managed to make all of Rome adore him? Once it had been Caesar who drew his attention to the fact that there were stalls in the market devoted to selling little plaster busts of Pompey the Great. Now those selfsame stalls were selling busts of Caesar. Caesar was breaking new ground for Rome; all Pompey had done was plough a fresh furrow in the same old field, the East. Of course Caesar's remarkable dispatches to the Senate had helped—why hadn't it occurred to Pompey to keep his short, riveting, a kind of chronicle of events shorn of the slightest excess verbiage? Unapologetic? Full of mentions of other men's deeds, centurions and junior legates? Caesar's swept through the Senate like a briskly invigorating wind. They earned him *thanksgivings*! There were myths about the man. The speed with which he traveled, the way he dictated to several secretaries at once, the ease with which he bridged great rivers and plucked hapless legates from the jaws of death. All so *personal*!

Well, Pompey wouldn't be going to war again just to put Caesar in his place. He'd have to do it from Rome, and before Caesar's second five years governing the Gauls and Illyricum was over. He, Pompey the Great, was the First Man in Rome. And he was going to remain the First Man in Rome for the rest of his life, Caesar or no Caesar.

They had been begging him for months to let himself be made Dictator. No one else could deal with the violence, the anarchy, the utter absence of proper procedure. Oh, it always went back to the abominable Publius Clodius! Worse than a parasite under the skin. Imagine it! Dictator of Rome. Elevated above the Law, not answerable for any measures he took as Dictator after he ceased to be Dictator.

From a practical aspect Pompey had no doubt that he could remedy what ailed Rome; it was simply a question of the proper organization, sensible measures, a light hand on government. No, execution of dictatorial powers did not dismay Pompey in the least. What dismayed him was what being Dictator might do to his reputation in the history books, his status as a popular hero. Sulla had been Dictator. And how they hated him still! Not that he'd cared. Like Caesar (that *name* again!), his birth was so august that he hadn't needed to care. A patrician Cornelius could do precisely what he pleased without diminishing his prominence in the history books of the future. Whether they portrayed him as a monster or a hero mattered not to Sulla. Only that he had mattered to Rome.

But a Pompeius from Picenum who looked far more a Gaul than a true Roman had to be very, very careful. Not for him the glory of patrician ancestry. Not for him automatic election at the top of the polls just because of the family name he bore. All that he was, Pompey had had to carve out for himself, and in the teeth of a father who had been a considerable force in Rome, yet was loathed by all of Rome. Not quite a New Man, but certainly not a Julian or a Cornelian. And on the whole, Pompey felt vindicated. His wives had all been of the very best: an Aemilia Scaura (patrician), a Mucia Scaevola (ancient plebeian), and a Julia Caesaris (top-of-the-tree patrician). Antistia he didn't count; he'd married her only because her father was the judge in a trial he hadn't wanted to take place.

But how would Rome regard him if he consented to be Dictator? The dictatorship was an ancient solution to administrative woes, designed originally to free up the consuls of the year to pursue a war, and the men who had been Dictator down the centuries had mostly been patricians. Its official duration was six months—the length of the old campaign season—though Sulla had remained Dictator for two and a half years, and had not been appointed to free up the consuls. He had forced the Senate to appoint him instead of consuls, then proceeded to have tame consuls elected.

Nor was it senatorial custom to appoint a dictator to deal with civil woes; for that, the Senate had invented the *senatus consultum de re publica defendenda* when Gaius Gracchus had tried to overthrow the State in the Forum rather than on the battlefield. Cicero had given it an easier name, the Senatus Consultum Ultimum. Infinitely preferable to a dictator because it did not, theoretically at any rate, empower one single man to do as he liked. For the trouble with a dictator was that the law indemnified him against all his actions while dictator; he could not afterward be brought to trial to answer for some action his fellow senators found odious.

Oh, why had people put the idea of becoming Dictator in his head? It had been running round there now for a year, and though before Calvinus and Messala Rufus had finally been elected consuls last Quinctilis he had firmly declined, he hadn't forgotten that the offer had been made. Now the offers were being renewed, and part of him was enormously attracted to the prospect of yet another extraordinary command. He'd piled up so many, all obtained in the teeth of bitter opposition from the senatorial ultra-conservatives. Why not another one? And it the most important one? But he was a Pompeius from Picenum who looked far more a Gaul than a true Roman.

The diehard sticklers for the *mos maiorum* were adamantly against the very idea—Cato, Bibulus, Lucius Ahenobarbus, Metellus Scipio, old

Curio, Messala Niger, all the Claudii Marcelli, all the Lentuli. Formidable. Top-heavy with clout, though none of them could lay claim to the title of the First Man in Rome, who was a Pompeius from Picenum.

Should he do it? Could he do it? Would it be a disastrous mistake, or the final accolade to crown a remarkable career?

All this irresolution occurred in his bedchamber, too grand to be termed a sleeping cubicle. Where reposed a huge, highly polished silver mirror he had taken for himself after Julia died because he had hoped to catch a glimpse of her vanishing into its swimming surface. He never had. Now, pacing up and down, he caught sight of himself, saw himself. Stopped, gazed, wept a little. For Julia he had taken care to remain the Pompey of her dreams—slim, lithe, well built. And perhaps he hadn't ever looked at himself again until this moment.

Julia's Pompey had gone. In his place stood a man in his middle fifties, overweight enough to have acquired a second chin, a sagging belly, a lower back creased by rolls of fat. His famously vivid blue eyes had disappeared into the flesh of his face, and the nose he had broken in a fall from a horse scant months ago was spread sideways. Only the hair remained as thick and lustrous as ever, but what had once been gold was now silver.

His valet coughed from the door.

"Yes?" asked Pompey, wiping his eyes.

"A visitor, Gnaeus Pompeius. Titus Munatius Plancus Bursa."

"Quickly, my toga!"

Plancus Bursa was waiting in the study.

"Good evening, good evening!" cried Pompey, bustling in. He seated himself behind his desk and folded his hands together on its surface, then looked at Bursa with the perky, enquiring gaze he had found a useful tool for thirty years.

"You're late. How did it go?" he asked.

Plancus Bursa cleared his throat loudly; he was not a natural raconteur. "Well, there was no feast following the inaugural session of the Senate, you see. In the absence of consuls, no one thought about the feast. So I went to Clodius's for dinner afterward."

"Yes, yes, but finish with the Senate first, Bursa! How did it go, man?"

"Lollius suggested that you be appointed Dictator, but just as men started agreeing with him, Bibulus launched into a speech rejecting the proposal. A good speech. He was followed by Lentulus Spinther, then Lucius Ahenobarbus. Over their dead bodies would you be made Dictator—you know the sort of thing. Cicero spoke in favor of you—another good speech. But before anyone could speak in support of Cicero, Cato began a filibuster. Messala Rufus was in the chair, and terminated the meeting."

"When's the next session?" asked Pompey, frowning.

"Tomorrow morning. Messala Rufus has convened it with the intention of choosing the first Interrex."

"Aha. And Clodius? What did you learn from him over dinner?"

"That he's going to distribute the freedmen across all thirty-five tribes the moment he's elected a praetor," said Bursa.

"Thereby controlling Rome through the tribunate of the plebs."

"Yes."

"Who was there at dinner? How did they react?"

"Curio spoke out against it very strongly. Marcus Antonius said very little. Or Decimus Brutus. Or Pompeius Rufus."

"You mean everyone except Curio was *for* the idea?"

"Oh, no. Everyone was against it. But Curio summed it up so well all the rest of us could add was that Clodius is insane."

"Does Clodius suspect that you're working for me, Bursa?"

"None of them has any inkling, Magnus. I'm trusted."

Pompey chewed his lower lip. "Hmmm . . ." He heaved a sigh. "Then we'll have to think of a way to keep Clodius from suspecting who you work for after the Senate session tomorrow. You're not going to make life any easier for Clodius at that meeting."

Bursa never looked curious, nor did he now. "What do you want me to do, Magnus?"

"When Messala Rufus has the lots brought out to draw for an *interrex,* I want you to veto the proceedings."

"Veto the appointment of an *interrex*?" Bursa asked blankly.

"That's correct, veto the appointment of an *interrex*."

"May I ask why?"

Pompey grinned. "Certainly! But I won't tell you."

"Clodius will be furious. He wants an election badly."

"Even if Milo runs for consul?"

"Yes, because he's convinced Milo won't get in, Magnus. He knows you're backing Plautius, and he knows how much money has gone out in bribes for Plautius. And Metellus Scipio, who might have backed Milo with some of his money because he's so tied to Bibulus and Cato, is running himself. He's spending his money on his own candidacy. Clodius believes Plautius will be junior consul. The senior consul is bound to be Metellus Scipio," said Bursa.

"Then I suggest that you tell Clodius after the meeting that you used your tribunician veto because you know beyond a shadow of a doubt that I'm backing Milo, not Plautius."

"Oh, clever!" Bursa exclaimed, animated for once. He thought about it, then nodded. "Clodius will accept that."

"Excellent!" beamed Pompey, rising to his feet.

Plancus Bursa got up too, but before Pompey could move round his desk, the steward knocked and entered.

"Gnaeus Pompeius, an urgent letter," he said, bowing.

Pompey took it, making sure Bursa had no chance to see its seal. After nodding absently to his tame tribune of the plebs, he went back to his desk.

Bursa cleared his throat again.

"Yes?" asked Pompey, looking up.

"A small financial embarrassment, Magnus . . ."

"After the Senate meets tomorrow."

Satisfied, Plancus Bursa departed in the wake of the steward, while Pompey broke the seal on Caesar's letter.

> I write this from Aquileia, having dealt with Illyricum. From now on I move westward through Italian Gaul. The cases have piled up in the local assizes; not surprising, since I was obliged to remain on the far side of the Alps last winter.
>
> Enough chatter. You're as busy as I am, I know.
>
> Magnus, my informants in Rome are insisting that our old friend Publius Clodius intends to distribute the freedmen across all thirty-five tribes of Roman men once he is elected praetor. This cannot be allowed to happen, as I am sure you agree. Were it to happen, Rome would be delivered into Clodius's hands for the rest of his days. Neither you nor I nor any other man from Cato to Cicero would be able to withstand Clodius short of a revolution.
>
> Were it to happen, there would indeed be a revolution. Clodius would be overpowered, executed, and the freedmen put back where they belong. However, I doubt you want this sort of solution any more than I do. Far better—and far simpler—if Clodius never becomes praetor at all.
>
> I do not presume to tell you what to do. Only rest assured that I am as much against Clodius's being elected a praetor as you and all other Roman men.
>
> I send you greetings and felicitations.

Pompey went to bed a contented man.

The following morning brought the news that Plancus Bursa had done precisely as instructed, and used the veto his office as a tribune of the plebs gave him; when Messala Rufus tried to cast the lots to see which of the patrician prefects of each decury of ten senators would become the first Interrex, Bursa vetoed. The whole House howled its outrage, Clodius and Milo loudest of all, but Bursa could not be prevailed upon to withdraw his veto.

Red with anger, Cato began to shout. "We *must* have elections! When there are no consuls to enter office on New Year's Day, this House appoints a patrician senator to serve as *interrex* for five days. And when his term as first Interrex is over, a second patrician is appointed to serve for five days. It is the duty of this second Interrex to organize the election of our magistrates. What is Rome coming to when any idiot calling himself a tribune of the plebs can stop something as necessary and constitutional as the appointment of an *interrex*? Condone the appointment of a dictator I will not, but that does not mean I condone a man's blocking the traditional machinery of the State!"

"Hear, hear!" shouted Bibulus to thunderous applause.

None of which made any difference to Plancus Bursa. He refused to withdraw his veto.

"Why?" demanded Clodius of him after the meeting ended.

Eyes shifting rapidly from side to side to make sure that no one could hear, Bursa made himself look conspiratorially furtive. "I've just discovered that Pompeius Magnus is backing Milo for consul after all," he whispered.

Which appeased Publius Clodius, but had no effect on Milo, who knew very well that Pompey was not backing him. Milo marched out to the Campus Martius to ask Clodius's question of Pompey.

"Why?" he demanded.

"Why what?" asked Pompey innocently.

"Magnus, you can't fool me! I know whose creature Bursa is—yours! He didn't dream up a veto out of his own imagination, he was acting under orders—yours! *Why?"*

"My dear Milo, I assure you that Bursa wasn't acting on any orders of mine," said Pompey rather tartly. "I suggest you ask your why of someone else with whom Bursa associates."

"You mean Clodius?" asked Milo warily.

"I *might* mean Clodius."

A big, brawny man with the face of an ex-gladiator (though he had never been anything as ignoble as a gladiator), Milo tensed his muscles and grew even larger. A display of aggression quite wasted on Pompey—which Milo knew, but did from force of habit. "Rubbish!" he snorted. "Clodius thinks I won't get in as consul, so he's all for holding the curule elections as soon as possible."

"*I* think you won't get in as consul, Milo. But you might find Clodius doesn't share my opinion. You've managed to ingratiate yourself very nicely with the faction of Bibulus and Cato. I've heard that Metellus Scipio is reconciled to having you as his junior colleague. I've also heard that he's about to announce this fact to all his many supporters, including knights as prominent as Atticus and Oppius."

"So it's *Clodius* behind Bursa?"

"It might be," said Pompey cautiously. "Bursa's certainly not acting for me, of that you can be sure. What would I have to gain by it?"

Milo sneered. "The dictatorship?" he suggested.

"I've already refused the dictatorship, Milo. I don't think Rome would like me as Dictator. You're thick with Bibulus and Cato these days, so you tell me I'm wrong."

Milo, too large a man for a room stuffed with precious relics of Pompey's various campaigns—golden wreaths, a golden grapevine with golden grapes, golden urns, delicately painted porphyry bowls—took a turn about Pompey's study. He stopped to look at Pompey, still sitting tranquilly behind his gold and ivory desk.

"They say Clodius is going to distribute the freedmen across the thirty-five tribes," he said.

"I've heard the rumor, yes."

"He'd own Rome."

"True."

"What if he didn't stand for election as a praetor?"

"Better for Rome, definitely."

"A pestilence on Rome! Would it be better for *me*?"

Pompey smiled sweetly, got up. "It couldn't help but be a great deal better for you, Milo, now could it?" he asked, walking to the door.

Milo took the hint and moved doorward too. "Could that be construed as a promise, Magnus?" he asked.

"You might be pardoned for thinking so," said Pompey, and clapped for the steward.

But no sooner had Milo gone than the steward announced yet another visitor.

"My, my, I am popular!" cried Pompey, shaking Metellus Scipio warmly by the hand and tenderly depositing him in the best chair. This time he didn't retreat behind his desk; one wouldn't treat Quintus Caecilius Metellus Pius Scipio Nasica like that! Instead, Pompey drew up the second-best chair and seated himself only after pouring wine from the flagon containing a Chian vintage so fine that Hortensius had wept in frustration when Pompey beat him to it.

Unfortunately the man with the grandest name in Rome did not have a mind to match its breathtaking sweep, though he looked what he was: a patrician Cornelius Scipio adopted into the powerful plebeian house of Caecilius Metellus. Haughty, cool, arrogant. Very plain, which was true of every Cornelius Scipio. His adopted father, Metellus Pius Pontifex Maximus, had had no sons; sadly, Metellus Scipio had no sons either. His only child was a daughter whom he had married to Crassus's son Publius three years before. Though properly a Caecilia Metella, she was always known as Cornelia Metella, and Pompey remembered her vividly because he and Julia had attended the reception following her wedding. The most disdainful-looking female he had ever seen, he had remarked to Julia, who had giggled and said Cornelia Metella always reminded her of a camel, and that she ought really to have married Brutus, who had the same sort of pedantic, intellectually pretentious mind.

The trouble was, however, that Pompey never quite knew what someone like Metellus Scipio wanted to hear—should he be jovial, distantly courteous, or crisp? Well, he had started out jovial, so it might as well be jovial.

"Not a bad drop of wine, eh?" he asked, smacking his lips.

Metellus Scipio produced a faint moue, of pleasure or pain was impossible to tell. "Very good," he said.

"What brings you all the way out here?"

"Publius Clodius," Metellus Scipio said.

Pompey nodded. "A bad business, if it's true."

"Oh, it's true enough. Young Curio heard it from Clodius's own lips, and went home to tell his father."

"Not well, old Curio, they tell me," said Pompey.

"Cancer," said Metellus Scipio briefly.

"Tch!" clucked Pompey, and waited.

Metellus Scipio waited too.

"Why come to see me?" Pompey asked in the end, tired of so little progress.

"The others didn't want me to" from Metellus Scipio.

"What others?"

"Bibulus, Cato, Ahenobarbus."

"That's because they don't know who's the First Man in Rome."

The aristocratic nose managed to turn up a trifle. "Nor do I, Pompeius."

Pompey winced. Oh, if only one of them would accord him an occasional "Magnus"! It was so wonderful to hear himself addressed as "Great" by his peers! Caesar called him Magnus. But would Cato or Bibulus or Ahenobarbus or this stiff-rumped dullard? No! It was always plain Pompeius.

"We're not getting anywhere yet, *Metellus,*" he said.

"I've had an idea."

"They're excellent things, *Metellus.*" Plebeian name again.

Metellus Scipio cast him a suspicious glance, but Pompey was sitting back in his chair, sipping soberly at his translucent rock-crystal goblet.

"I'm a very wealthy man," he said, "and so are you, Pompeius. It occurred to me that between the two of us we might be able to buy Clodius off."

Pompey nodded. "Yes, I've had the same idea," he said, and sighed lugubriously. "Unfortunately Clodius isn't short of money. His wife is one of the wealthiest women in Rome, and when her mother dies she'll come into a great deal more. He also profited hugely from his embassage to Galatia. Right at this moment he's building the most expensive villa the world has ever seen, and it's going ahead in leaps and bounds. Near my little place in the Alban Hills, that's how I know. Built on hundred-foot-high columns at its front, jutting over the edge of a hundred-foot cliff. The most stunning view across Lake Nemi and the Latin Plain all the way to the sea. He got the land for next to nothing because everyone thought the site unbuildable, then he commissioned Cyrus and now it's almost finished." Pompey shook his head emphatically. "No, Scipio, it won't work."

"Then what can we do?" asked Metellus Scipio, crushed.

"Make a lot of offerings to every God we can think of" was Pompey's advice. Then he grinned. "As a matter of fact, I sent an anonymous donation of half a million to the Vestals for Bona Dea. That's one lady doesn't like Clodius."

Metellus Scipio looked scandalized. "Pompeius, the Bona Dea is *not* in the province of men! A man can't give Bona Dea gifts!"

"A man didn't," said Pompey cheerfully. "I sent it in the name of my late mother-in-law, Aurelia."

Metellus Scipio drained his rock-crystal goblet and got up. "Perhaps you're right," he said. "I could send a donation in the name of my poor daughter."

Concern being called for, Pompey displayed it. "How is she? A terrible thing, Scipio, just terrible! To be widowed so young!"

"She's as well as can be expected," he said, walking to the door, where he waited for Pompey to open it for him. "You're recently widowed too, Pompeius," he went on as Pompey ushered him through to the front door. "Perhaps you should come and dine with us one afternoon. Just the three of us."

Pompey's face lit up. An invitation to dine with Metellus Scipio! Oh, he'd been to formal dinners there in that rather awful and too-small house, but never with the *family*! "Delighted any time, Scipio," he said, and opened the front door himself.

But Metellus Scipio didn't go home. Instead, he went to the small and drab house wherein lived Marcus Porcius Cato, who was the enemy of all ostentation. Bibulus was keeping Cato company.

"Well, I did it," Metellus Scipio said, sitting down heavily.

The other two exchanged glances.

"Did he believe you'd come to discuss Clodius?" asked Bibulus.

"Yes."

"Did he take the bait on your real purpose?"

"I think so."

Stifling a sigh, Bibulus studied Metellus Scipio for a moment, then leaned forward and patted him on the shoulder. "You're a good man, Scipio," he said.

"It's a right act," said Cato, draining his plain pottery cup at a gulp. Since he kept the plain pottery flagon close by his elbow on the desk, it was an easy matter to refill it. "Little though any one of us loves the man, we've got to nail Pompeius to us as firmly as Caesar did to himself."

"Must it be through my daughter?" asked Metellus Scipio.

"Well, he wouldn't have *my* daughter!" said Cato, neighing with laughter. "Pompeius likes patricians, make him feel terribly important. Look at Caesar."

"She'll hate it," said Metellus Scipio miserably. "Publius Crassus was of the noblest stock; she liked that. And she quite liked Publius Crassus, though she didn't know him for very long. Off to Caesar almost straight after the wedding, then off to Syria with his father." He shivered. "I don't even know how to break the news to her that I want her to marry a Pompeius from Picenum. *Strabo's* son!"

"Be honest, tell her the truth," advised Bibulus. "She's needed for the cause."

"I don't really see why, Bibulus," said Metellus Scipio.

"Then I'll go through it again for you, Scipio. We have to swing Pompeius onto our side. You do see that, don't you?"

"I suppose so."

"All right, I'll explain that too. It goes back to Luca and the conference Caesar held there with Pompeius and Marcus Crassus. Almost four years ago. April. Because Caesar's daughter held Pompeius in thrall, Caesar was able to persuade Pompeius to help legislate a second five-year command in Gaul for him. If Pompeius hadn't done that, Caesar would now be in permanent exile, stripped of everything he owns. And you'd be Pontifex Maximus, Scipio. Do remember that. He also persuaded Pompeius—and Crassus, though that was never as hard—to bring in a law which forbids the Senate to discuss Caesar's second five-year command before March of two years' time, let alone remove his command from him! Caesar bribed Pompeius and Crassus with their second consulship, but he couldn't have done that without Julia to help things along. What was to stop Pompeius's running for a second consulship anyway?"

"But Julia's dead," objected Metellus Scipio.

"Yes, but Caesar still holds Pompeius! And as long as Caesar does hold Pompeius, there's the chance that he'll manage to prolong his Gallic command beyond its present end. Until, in fact, he steps straight into a second consulship. Which he can do legally in less than four years."

"But why do you always harp on Caesar?" asked Metellus Scipio. "Isn't it Clodius who's the danger at the moment?"

Cato banged his empty cup down on the desk so suddenly that Metellus Scipio jumped. "Clodius!" he said contemptuously. "It isn't Clodius who will bring the Republic down, for all his fine plans! Someone will stop Clodius. But only we *boni* can stop the real enemy of the *boni,* Caesar."

Bibulus tried again. "Scipio," he said, "if Caesar manages to survive unprosecuted until he's consul for the second time, we will *never* bring him down! He'll force laws through the Assemblies that will make it impossible for us to arraign him in *any* court! Because now Caesar is a hero. A fabulously wealthy hero! When he was consul the first time, he had the name and little else. Ten years later, he'll be let do whatever he likes, because the whole of Rome is full of his creatures and the whole of Rome deems him the greatest Roman who ever lived. He'll get away with everything he's done—even the Gods will hear him laughing at us!"

"Yes, I do see all of that, Bibulus, but I also remember how hard we worked to stop him when he was consul the first time," said Metellus Scipio stubbornly. "We'd hatch a plot, it usually cost us a lot of money, and every time you'd say the same thing—it would be the end of Caesar. But it never was the end of Caesar!"

"That's because," said Bibulus, hanging on to his patience grimly, "we didn't have quite enough clout. Why? Because we despised Pompeius too much to make him our ally. But Caesar didn't make that mistake. I don't say he doesn't despise Pompeius to this day—who with Caesar's ancestry wouldn't?—but he *uses* Pompeius. Who has a huge amount of clout. Who even presumes to call himself the First Man in Rome, if you please! Pah! Caesar presented him with his daughter, a girl who could have married anyone, she was so highborn. A Cornelian and a Julian combined. Who was betrothed to Brutus, quite the richest and best-connected nobleman in Rome. Caesar broke that engagement. Enraged Servilia. Horrified everyone who mattered. But did he care? No! He caught Pompeius in his toils, he became unbeatable. Well, if we catch Pompeius in our toils, *we'll* become unbeatable! That's why you're going to offer him Cornelia Metella."

Cato listened, eyes fixed on Bibulus's face. The best, the most enduring of friends. A very tiny fellow, so silver of hair, brows and lashes that he seemed peculiarly bald. Silver eyes too. Sharp-faced, sharp-minded. Though he could thank Caesar for honing the razor edge on his mind.

"All right," said Metellus Scipio with a sigh, "I'll go home and talk to Cornelia Metella. I won't promise, but if she says she's willing, then I'll offer her to Pompeius."

"And that," said Bibulus when Cato returned from escorting Metellus Scipio off the premises, "is that." Cato lifted the plain pottery cup to his lips and drank again; Bibulus looked dismayed.

"Cato, must you?" he asked. "I used to think the wine never went to your head, but that isn't true anymore. You drink far too much. It will kill you."

Indeed Cato never looked well these days, though he was one of those men whose figure hadn't suffered; he was as tall, as straight, as beautifully built as ever. But his face, which used to be so bright, so innocent, had sunk to ashen planes and fine wrinkles, despite the fact that he was only forty-one years old. The nose, so large that it was famous in a city of large noses, dominated the face completely; in the old days his eyes had done that, for they were widely opened, luminously grey.

And the short-cut, slightly waving hair was no longer auburn—more a speckled beige.

He drank and he drank. Especially since he had given Marcia to Hortensius. Bibulus knew why, of course, though Cato had never discussed it. Love was not an emotion Cato could cope with, particularly a love as ardent and passionate as the love he still felt for Marcia. It tormented him, it ate at him. Every day he worried about her; every day he wondered how he could live were she to die, as his beloved brother Caepio had died. So when the addled Hortensius had asked, he saw a way out. Be strong, belong to himself again! Give her away. Get rid of her.

But it hadn't worked. He just buried himself with his pair of live-in philosophers, Athenodorus Cordylion and Statyllus, and the three of them spent each night plundering the wine flagons. Weeping over the pompous, priggish words of Cato the Censor as if Homer had written them. Falling into a stuporous sleep when other men were getting out of bed. Not a sensitive man, Bibulus had no idea of the depth of Cato's pain, but he did love Cato, chiefly for that unswerving strength in the face of all adversity, from Caesar to Marcia. Cato never gave up, never gave in.

"Porcia will be eighteen soon," said Cato abruptly.

"I know," said Bibulus, blinking.

"I haven't got a husband for her."

"Well, you had hoped for her cousin Brutus. . . ."

"He'll be home from Cilicia by the end of the month."

"Do you intend to try for him again? He doesn't need Appius Claudius, so he could divorce Claudia."

Came that neighing laugh. "Not I, Bibulus! Brutus had his chance. He married Claudia and he can stay married to Claudia."

"How about Ahenobarbus's son?"

The flagon tipped; a thin stream of red wine trickled into the plain pottery cup. The permanently haemorrhage-pinkened eyes looked at Bibulus over the rim of the cup. "How about you, old friend?" he asked.

Bibulus gasped. *"Me?"*

"Yes, you. Domitia's dead, so why not?"

"I—I—I never thought—ye Gods, Cato! *Me?"*

"Don't you want her, Bibulus? I admit Porcia doesn't have a hundred-talent dowry, but she's not poor. She's well enough born and very highly educated. And I can vouch for her loyalty." Down went some of the wine. "Pity, in fact, that she's the girl and not the boy. She's worth a thousand of him."

Eyes filling with tears, Bibulus reached out a hand across the desk. "Marcus, of course I'll have her! I'm honored."

But Cato ignored the hand. "Good," he said, and drank until the cup was empty.

On the seventeenth day of that January, Publius Clodius donned riding gear, strapped on a sword, and went to see his wife in her sitting room. Fulvia was lying listlessly on a couch, her hair undressed, delicious body still clad in a filmy saffron bed robe. But when she saw what Clodius was wearing, she sat up.

"Clodius, what is it?"

He grimaced, sat on the edge of her couch and kissed her brow. "*Meum mel,* Cyrus is dying."

"Oh, no!" Fulvia turned her face into Clodius's linen shirt, rather like the underpinnings of a military man's cuirass save that it was not padded. Then she lifted her head and stared at him in bewilderment. "But you're going out of Rome, dressed like that! Why? Isn't Cyrus here?"

"Yes, he's here," said Clodius, genuinely upset at the prospect of Cyrus's death, and not because he would then lose the services of Rome's best architect. "That's why I'm off to the building site. Cyrus has got it into his head that he made an error in his calculations, and he won't trust anyone but me to check for him. I'll be back tomorrow."

"Clodius, don't leave me behind!"

"I have to," said Clodius unhappily. "You're not well, and I'm in a tearing hurry. The doctors say Cyrus won't last longer than another two or three days, and I have to put the poor old fellow's mind at rest." He kissed her mouth hard, got up.

"Take care!" she cried.

Clodius grinned. "Always, you know that. I've got Schola, Pomponius and my freedman Gaius Clodius for company. And I have thirty armed slaves as escort."

The horses, all good ones, had been brought in from the stables outside the Servian Walls at the Vallis Camenarum, and had drawn quite a crowd of onlookers in the narrow lane into which Clodius's front door opened; so many mounts within Rome were most unusual. In these turbulent times it was customary for contentious men to go everywhere with a bodyguard of slaves or hired toughs, and Clodius was no exception. But this was a lightning trip, it had not been planned, and Clodius expected to be back before he had been missed. The thirty slaves were, besides, all young and trained in the use of the swords they wore, even if they were not equipped with cuirasses or helmets.

"Where are you off to, Soldiers' Friend?" called a man from the crowd, grinning widely.

Clodius paused. "Tigranocerta? Lucullus?" he asked.

"Nisibis, Lucullus," the man answered.

"Those were the days, eh?"

"Nearly twenty years ago, Soldiers' Friend! But none of us who were there have ever forgotten Publius Clodius."

"Who's grown old and tame, soldier."

"Where are you off to?" the man repeated.

Clodius vaulted into the saddle and winked at Schola, already mounted. "The Alban Hills," he said, "but only overnight. I'll be in Rome again tomorrow." He turned his horse and rode off down the lane in the direction of the Clivus Palatinus, his three boon companions and the thirty armed slaves falling in behind.

"The Alban Hills, but only overnight," said Titus Annius Milo thoughtfully. He pushed a small purse of silver denarii across the table to the man who had called out to Clodius from the crowd. "I'm obliged," he said, and rose to his feet.

"Fausta," he said a moment later, erupting into his wife's sitting room, "I know you don't want to come, but you are coming to Lanuvium with me at dawn tomorrow, so pack your things and be ready. That's not a request, it's an order."

To Milo, the acquisition of Fausta represented a considerable victory over Publius Clodius. She was Sulla's daughter, and her twin brother, Faustus Sulla, was an intimate of Clodius's, as was Sulla's disreputable nephew, Publius Sulla. Though Fausta had not been a member of the Clodius Club, her connections were all in that direction; she had been wife to Pompey's nephew, Gaius Memmius, until he caught her in a compromising situation with a very young, very muscular nobody. Fausta liked muscular men, but Memmius, although he was quite spectacularly handsome, was a rather thin and weary individual who was quite nauseatingly devoted to his mother, Pompey's sister. Now Publius Sulla's wife.

As he was notably muscular, even if not as young as Fausta was used to, Milo hadn't found it difficult to woo her and wed her. Clodius had screamed even louder than Faustus or Publius Sulla! Admittedly Fausta wasn't cured of her predilection for very young, very muscular nobodies; scant months ago Milo had been forced to take a whip to one Gaius Sallustius Crispus for indiscretions with her. What Milo didn't broadcast to a delighted Rome was that he had also used the whip on Fausta. Brought her to heel very nicely too.

Unfortunately Fausta hadn't taken after Sulla, a stunning-looking man in his youth. No, she took after her great-uncle, the famous Metellus Numidicus. Lumpy, dumpy, frumpy. Still, all women were the same with the lights out, so Milo enjoyed her quite as much as he did the other women with whom he dallied.

Remembering the feel of the whip, Fausta didn't argue. She cast Milo a look of anguish, then clapped her hands to summon her retinue of servants.

Milo had vanished, calling for his freedman named Marcus Fustenus, who didn't bear the name Titus Annius because he had passed into Milo's clientele after being freed from a school for gladiators. Fustenus was his own name. He was a Roman sentenced to gladiatorial combat for doing murder.

"Plans are changed a bit, Fustenus," said Milo curtly when his henchman appeared. "We're still off to Lanuvium—what a wonderful piece of luck! My reasons for heading down the Via Appia tomorrow are impeccable; I can prove that my plans to be in my hometown to nominate the new *flamen* have been in place for two months. No one will be able to say I had no right to be on the Via Appia. No one!"

Fustenus, almost as large an individual as Milo, said nothing, just nodded.

"Fausta has decided to accompany me, so you'll hire a very roomy *carpentum,*" Milo went on.

Fustenus nodded.

"Hire lots of other conveyances for the servants and the baggage. We're going to stay for some time." Milo flourished a sealed note. "Have this sent round to Quintus Fufius Calenus at once. Since I have to share a carriage with Fausta, I may as well have some decent company on the road. Calenus will do."

Fustenus nodded.

"The full bodyguard, with so many valuables in the wagons." Milo smiled sourly. "No doubt Fausta will want all her jewels, not to mention every citrus-wood table she fancies. A hundred and fifty men, Fustenus, all cuirassed, helmeted and heavily armed."

Fustenus nodded.

"And send Birria and Eudamas to me immediately."

Fustenus nodded and left the room.

It was already well into the afternoon, but Milo kept sending servants flying hither and thither until darkness fell, at which time he could lie back, satisfied, to eat heartily of a much-delayed dinner. All was in place. Quintus Fufius Calenus had indicated extreme delight at accompanying his friend Milo to Lanuvium; Marcus Fustenus had organized horses for the bodyguard of one hundred and fifty men, wagons and carts and rickety carriages for the baggage and servants, and a most comfortably commodious *carpentum* for the owners of this impressive entourage.

At dawn Calenus arrived at the house; Milo and Fausta set off with him on foot to a point just outside the Capena Gate, where the party was already assembled and the *carpentum* waited.

"Very nice!" purred Fausta, disposing herself on the well-padded seat with her back to the mules; she knew better than to usurp the seat which allowed its occupants to travel forward. On this Milo and Calenus ensconced themselves, pleased to discover that a small table had been erected between them whereon they could play at dice, or eat and drink. The fourth place, that beside Fausta, was occupied by two servants squeezed together: one female to attend Fausta, one male to wait on Milo and Calenus.

Like all carriages, the *carpentum* had no devices to absorb some of the shock of the road, but the Via Appia between Capua and Rome was very well kept, its surface smooth because a new layer of hard-tamped cement dust was laid over its stones and watered at the beginning of each summer. The inconvenience of travel was therefore more vibration than jolt or jar. Naturally the servants in the lesser vehicles were not so well off, but everyone was happy at the thought of going somewhere. About three hundred people started off down the common road which bifurcated into the Via Appia and the Via Latina half a mile beyond the Capena Gate. Fausta had brought along her maids, hairdressers, bathwomen, cosmeticians and laundresses as well as some musicians and a dozen boy dancers; Calenus had contributed his valet, librarian and a dozen other servants; and Milo had his steward, his wine steward, his valet, a dozen menservants, several cooks and three bakers. All of the more exalted slaves had their own slaves to attend them as well. The mood was merry, the pace a reasonable five miles per hour, which would get them to Lanuvium in a little over seven hours.

The Via Appia was one of Rome's oldest roads. It belonged to the Claudii Pulchri, Clodius's own family, for it had been built by his ancestor Appius Claudius the Blind, and its care and upkeep between Rome and Capua was still in the purlieus of the family. As it was the Claudian road, it was also where the patrician Claudii placed their tombs. Generations of dead Claudians lined the road on either side, though of course the tombs of other clans were also present. Not that the outlook was a serried array of tubby round monuments; sometimes a whole mile would go by between them.

Publius Clodius had been able to ascertain that the dying Cyrus had been mistaken: his calculations were perfect, there was no danger whatsoever that the daring structure the old Greek had designed would tumble to the bottom of the precipice it straddled. Oh, what a site for a villa! A view which would make Cicero choke on his own envious buckets of drool, pay the *cunnus* back for daring to erect his new house to a height which had blocked Clodius's view of the Forum Romanum. As Cicero was a compulsive collector of country villas, it wouldn't be long before he was sneaking down past Bovillae to see what Clodius was doing. And when he did see what Clodius was doing, he'd be greener than the Latin Plain stretched out before him.

Actually the checking of Cyrus's measurements had been done so quickly that Clodius might have returned to Rome that same night. But there was no moon, which made riding hazardous; best to go on to his existing villa near Lanuvium, snatch a few hours' sleep, and start back to Rome shortly after dawn. He had brought no baggage and no servants, but there was a skeleton staff at the existing villa, capable of producing a meal for himself, Schola, Pomponius and Gaius Clodius the freedman; the thirty slaves who formed his escort ate what they had brought with them in their saddlebags.

He was on the Via Appia heading in the direction of Rome by the time the sun came up, and he set a rattling pace; the truth was that Clodius so rarely traveled without Fulvia that her absence set his teeth on edge, made him snappy. He was also worried because she was unwell. Knowing him, his escort exchanged glances and made rueful faces at each other; Clodius minus Fulvia was hard to take.

At the beginning of the third hour of daylight Clodius went through Bovillae at a canter, scattering various citizens going about their business, with scant regard for their welfare or the fate of the sheep, horses, mules, pigs and chickens in their husbandage; it was market day in Bovillae. Yet a mile beyond that buzzing town all vestige of habitation was gone, though there were but thirteen miles to go to the Servian Walls of Rome. The land on either side of the road belonged to the young knight Titus Sertius Gallus, who had more than enough money to resist the many offers he had received for such lush pasturage; the fields were dotted with the beautiful horses he bred, but his luxurious villa lay so far off the road that there was no glimpse of it. The only building on the road was a small tavern.

"Big party coming," said Schola, Clodius's friend for so many years that they had long forgotten how they met.

"Huh," grunted Clodius, waving his hand in the air to signal everyone off the road itself.

The entire party took to the grass verge, which was the custom when two groups met and one contained wheeled conveyances, the other not; the group approaching definitely had many wheeled conveyances.

"It's Sampsiceramus moving his harem," said Gaius Clodius.

"No, it isn't," said Pomponius as the oncoming cavalcade grew closer. "Ye Gods, it's a small army! Look at the cuirasses!"

At which moment Clodius recognized the figure on the leading horse: Marcus Fustenus. *"Cacat!"* he exclaimed. "It's Milo!"

Schola, Pomponius and the freedman Gaius Clodius flinched, faces losing color, but Clodius kicked his horse in the ribs and increased his pace.

"Come on, let's move as quickly as we can," he said.

The *carpentum* containing Fausta, Milo and Fufius Calenus was in the exact middle of the procession; Clodius nudged his horse onto the road and scowled into the carriage, then was past. A few paces further on he turned his head to see that Milo was craning out of the window, gazing back at him fiercely.

It was a long gauntlet to run, but Clodius almost made it. The trouble developed when he drew level with the hundred-odd mounted and heavily armed men who brought up the tail of Milo's entourage. He had no difficulty getting through himself, but when his thirty slaves began to canter by, Milo's bodyguard swung sideways and put itself across the path of the slaves. Quite a few of Milo's men carried javelins, began to prick the flanks of Clodius's horses viciously; within moments several of the slaves were on the ground, while others dragged at their swords, milling about and shrieking curses. Clodius and Milo hated each other, but not as much as their men hated each other.

"Keep going!" cried Schola when Clodius pulled on his reins. "Clodius, let it happen! We're past, so keep going!"

"I can't leave my men!" Clodius came to a halt, then swung his horse around.

The two last riders in Milo's train were his most trusted bully-boys, the ex-gladiators Birria and Eudamas. And the moment Clodius was facing them, about to ride back to his men, Birria lifted the javelin he carried, aimed it casually, and threw it.

The leaflike head took Clodius high in the shoulder, with so much force behind it that Clodius shot into the air and crashed, knees first, onto the road. He lay on his back, blinking, both hands around the shaft of the spear; his three friends tumbled off their horses and came running.

With great presence of mind Schola ripped a big square piece off his cloak and folded it into a pad. He nodded to Pomponius, who pulled the spear out in the same moment as Schola pushed his makeshift dressing down onto the wound, now pouring blood.

The tavern was about two hundred paces away; while Schola held the pad in place, Pomponius and Gaius Clodius lifted Clodius to his feet, hooked their elbows beneath his armpits, and dragged him down the road at a run toward the tavern.

Milo's party had come to a halt, and Milo, sword drawn, was standing outside the carriage, staring toward the tavern. The bodyguard had made short work of Clodius's slaves, eleven of whom lay dead; some crawled about badly injured, while those who could had fled across the fields. Fustenus hurried up from the front of the cavalcade.

"They've taken him to that tavern," said Milo.

Behind him the *carpentum* was the source of bloodcurdling noises: screams, gurgles, squeals, shrieks. Milo stuck his head through the window to see Calenus and the male servant battling with Fausta and her maid, throwing themselves everywhere. Good. Calenus had his work cut out controlling Fausta; he wouldn't be emerging to see what was going on.

"Stay there," said Milo curtly to Calenus, who didn't have the freedom to look up. "Clodius. There's a fight. He started it; now I suppose we'll have to finish it." He stepped back and nodded to Fustenus, Birria and Eudamas. "Come on."

* * *

The moment the fracas on the road began, the proprietor of the little tavern sent his wife, his children and his three slaves running out the back door into the fields. So when Pomponius and Gaius Clodius the freedman hauled Clodius through the door, the proprietor was alone, eyes starting from his head in fright.

"Quick, a bed!" said Schola.

The innkeeper pointed one shaking finger toward a side room, where the three men lay Clodius on a board frame cushioned by a rough straw mattress. The pad was bright scarlet and dripping; Schola looked at it, then at the innkeeper.

"Find me some cloths!" he snapped, doing further damage to his cloak and replacing the pad.

Clodius's eyes were open; he was panting. "Winged," he said, trying to laugh. "I'll live, Schola, but there's a better chance of it if you and the others go back to Bovillae for help. I'll be all right here in the meantime."

"Clodius, I daren't!" said Schola in a whisper. "Milo has halted. They'll kill you!"

"They wouldn't dare!" gasped Clodius. "Go! Go!"

"I'll stay with you. Two are enough."

"All three of you!" ground Clodius between his teeth. "I mean it, Schola! *Go!*"

"Landlord," said Schola, "hold this hard on the wound. We'll be back as soon as we can." He gave up his place to the petrified tavern owner, and within moments came the sound of hooves.

His head was swimming; Clodius closed his eyes, tried not to think of the pain or the blood. "What's your name, man?" he asked without opening his eyes.

"Asicius."

"Well, Asicius, just make sure there's firm pressure on the pad and keep Publius Clodius company."

"Publius Clodius?" quavered Asicius.

"The one and only." Clodius sighed, lifted his lids and grinned. "What a pickle! Fancy meeting Milo."

Shadows loomed in the door.

"Yes, fancy meeting Milo," said Milo, walking in with Birria, Eudamas and Fustenus behind him.

Clodius looked at him scornfully, fearlessly. "If you kill me, Milo, you'll live in exile for the rest of your days."

"I don't think so, Clodius. You might say I'm on a promise from Pompeius." He pushed Asicius the innkeeper sprawling and leaned over to look at the wound, not bleeding as rapidly. "Well, you won't die of that," he said, and jerked his head at Fustenus. "Pick him up and take him outside."

"What about him?" asked Fustenus of the whimpering Asicius.

"Kill him."

One swift chop down the center of Asicius's head and it was done; Birria and Eudamas lifted Clodius off the bed as if he weighed nothing and dragged him out to fling him in the middle of the Via Appia.

"Take his clothes off," said Milo, sneering. "I want to see if rumor is right."

Sword sharper than a razor, Fustenus sliced Clodius's riding tunic up the center from hem to neckline; the loincloth followed.

"Will you look at that?" asked Milo, roaring with laughter. "He *is* circumcised!" He flipped Clodius's penis with the tip of his sword, drawing a single drop of precious blood. "Stand him up."

Birria and Eudamas obeyed, each with an upper arm so firmly in his grip that Clodius stood, head lolling a little, feet almost clear of the ground. But he didn't see Milo, he didn't see Birria or Eudamas or Fustenus; all of his vision was filled by a humble little shrine standing on the opposite side of the road from the tavern. A cairn of pretty stones dry-laid into the shape of a short square column, and at its navel one big single red stone into which were carved the labia and gaping slit of a woman's vulva. Bona Dea . . . a shrine to the Good Goddess here beside the Via Appia, thirteen unlucky miles from Rome. Its base littered with bunches of flowers, a saucer of milk, a few eggs.

"Bona Dea!" croaked Clodius. "Bona Dea, Bona Dea!"

Her sacred snake poked his wicked head out of the roomy slit in Bona Dea's vulva, his cold black eyes fixed upon Publius Clodius, who had profaned Bona Dea's mysteries. His tongue flickered in and out, his eyes never blinked. When Fustenus stuck his sword through Clodius's belly until it screeched off the bone of his spine and came leaping out of his back, Clodius saw nothing, felt nothing. Nor when Birria skewered him with another javelin, nor when Eudamas let his intestines tumble down upon the blood-soaked road. Until sight and life quit him in the same instant, Clodius and Bona Dea's snake stared into each other's souls.

"Give me your horse, Birria," said Milo, and mounted; the cavalcade was already some distance down the Via Appia in the direction of Bovillae. Eudamas and Birria perched precariously on one horse; the four men rode to catch it up.

Satisfied, the sacred snake withdrew his head and returned to his rest, snuggled within Bona Dea's vulva.

When Asicius's family and slaves returned from the fields they found Asicius dead, looked out the door to where the naked body of Publius Clodius lay, and fled again.

Many, many travelers passed along the Via Appia, and many passed during that eighteenth day of January. Eleven of Clodius's slaves were dead, eleven more moaned in agony and died slowly; no one stopped to succor them. When Schola, Pomponius and the freedman Gaius Clodius came back with several residents of Bovillae and a cart, they looked down on Clodius and wept.

"We're dead men too," said Schola after they had found the body of the innkeeper. "Milo will not rest until there are no witnesses left alive."

"Then we're not staying here!" said the owner of the cart, turned the vehicle and clattered off.

Moments later they were all gone. Clodius still lay in the road, his glazed eyes fixed on the shrine of Bona Dea, a lake of congealing blood and a heap of spilled guts around him.

Not until the middle of the afternoon did anyone pay the slaughter more than a horrified look before hurrying on. But then came an ambling litter, in it the very old Roman senator Sextus Teidius. Displeased when it halted amid a hubbub among his bearers, he poked his head between the curtains and looked straight at the face of Publius Clodius. Out he scrambled, his crutch propped beneath his arm; for Sextus Teidius had but one leg, having lost the other fighting in the army of Sulla against King Mithridates.

"Put the poor fellow in my litter and run with him to his house in Rome as quickly as you can," he instructed his bearers, then beckoned to his manservant. "Xenophon, help me walk back to Bovillae. They *must* know of it! Now I understand why they acted so oddly when we passed through."

And so, about an hour before nightfall, Sextus Teidius's blown bearers brought his litter through the Capena Gate and up the slope of the Clivus Palatinus to where Clodius's new house stood, looking across the Vallis Murcia and the Circus Maximus to the Tiber and the Janiculum beyond.

Fulvia came running, hair streaming behind her, too shocked to scream or weep; she parted the curtains of the litter and looked down on the ruins of Publius Clodius, his bowels thrust roughly back inside the great gash in his belly, his skin as white as Parian marble, no clothes to dignify his death, his penis on full display. "Clodius! Clodius!" she shrieked, went on shrieking.

They put him on a makeshift bier in the peristyle garden without covering his nakedness, while the Clodius Club assembled. Curio, Antony, Plancus Bursa, Pompeius Rufus, Decimus Brutus, Poplicola and Sextus Cloelius.

"Milo," growled Mark Antony.

"We don't know that," said Curio, who stood with one hand on Fulvia's hunched shoulder as she sat on a bench and stared at Clodius without moving.

"We do know that!" said a new voice.

Titus Pomponius Atticus went straight to Fulvia and sank down on the bench beside her. "My poor girl," he said tenderly. "I've sent for your mother; she'll be here soon."

"How do *you* know?" asked Plancus Bursa, looking wary.

"From my cousin Pomponius, who was with Clodius today," said Atticus. "Thirty-four of them encountered Milo and a bodyguard which outnumbered them five to one on the Via Appia." He indicated Clodius's body with one hand. "This is the result, though my cousin didn't see it. Just Birria throwing a spear. That's the shoulder wound, which wouldn't have killed him. When Clodius insisted that Pomponius, Schola and Gaius Clodius go to Bovillae for help, he was resting safely in a tavern. By the time they got back—Bovillae was behaving very strangely, wanted nothing to do with it—it was too late. Clodius was dead in the road, the innkeeper dead in his tavern. They panicked. Inexcusable, but that's what happened. I don't know where the other two are, but my cousin Pomponius got as far as Aricia, then left them to come to me. They all believe that Milo will have them killed too, of course."

"Didn't *anyone* see it?" demanded Antony, wiping his eyes. "Oh, a dozen times a month I could have murdered Clodius myself, but I *loved* him!"

"It doesn't seem that anyone saw it," said Atticus. "It happened on that deserted stretch of road alongside Sertius Gallus's horse farm." He took Fulvia's nerveless hand and began to chafe it gently. "Dear girl, it's so cold out here. Come inside and wait for Mama."

"I have to stay with Clodius," she whispered. "He's dead, Atticus! How can that be?" She began to rock. "He's dead! How can that be? How am I going to tell the children?"

Atticus's fine dark eyes met Curio's above her head. "Let your mama deal with things, Fulvia. Come inside."

Curio took her, and she went without resisting. Fulvia, who ran madly toward everything, who screamed in the Forum like a man, who fought strenuously for everything she believed in! Fulvia, whom no one had ever before seen go tamely anywhere. In the doorway her knees buckled; Atticus moved swiftly to help Curio, then together they bore her into the house.

Sextus Cloelius, who ran Clodius's street gangs these days after serving a stern apprenticeship under Decimus Brutus, was not a nobleman. Though the others knew him, he didn't attend meetings of the Clodius Club. Now, perhaps because the others were shocked into inertia, he took command.

"I suggest we carry Clodius's body just as it is down to the Forum and put it on the rostra," Cloelius said harshly. "All of Rome should see exactly what Milo did to a man who outshone him the way the sun does the moon."

"But it's dark!" said Poplicola foolishly.

"Not in the Forum. The word's spreading, the torches are lit, Clodius's people are gathering. And I say they're entitled to see what Milo did to their champion!"

"You're right," said Antony suddenly, and threw off his toga. "Come on, two of you pick up the foot of the bier. I'll carry the head."

Decimus Brutus was weeping inconsolably, so Poplicola and Pompeius Rufus abandoned their togas to obey Antony.

"What's the matter with you, Bursa?" asked Antony when the bier tipped dangerously. "Can't you see Poplicola's too small to match Rufus? Take his place, man!"

Plancus Bursa cleared his throat. "Well, actually I was going to return home. The wife's in a terrible state."

Antony frowned, then peeled his lips back from his small and perfect teeth. "What's a wife when Clodius is dead? Under the cat's foot, Bursa? Take Poplicola's place or I'll turn you into a replica of Clodius!"

Bursa did as he was told.

The word was indeed spreading; outside in the lane a small crowd had gathered, armed with spitting torches. When the massive figure of Antony appeared holding both poles projecting from the front of the bier, a murmur went up which changed to a sighing moan as the crowd saw Clodius.

"See him?" shouted Cloelius. "See what Milo did?"

A growl began, grew as the three members of the Clodius Club carried their burden to the Clivus Victoriae and paused at the top of the Vestal Steps. A natural athlete, Antony simply turned round, lifted his end of the bier high above his head, and went down the steps backward without looking or stumbling. Below in the Forum a sea of torches waited, men and women moaning and weeping as the magnificent Antony, red-brown curls alive in the flickering light, bore Clodius aloft until he reached the bottom of the steps.

Across the lower Forum to the well of the Comitia and the rostra grafted into its side; there Antony, Bursa and Pompeius Rufus set the bier's short legs upon the surface of the rostra.

Cloelius had stopped in the forefront of the crowd, and now mounted the rostra with his arm thrown about the shoulders of a very old, small man who wept desolately.

"You all know who this is, don't you?" Cloelius demanded in a great voice. "You all know Lucius Decumius! Publius Clodius's loyalest follower, his friend for years, his helper, his conduit to every man who goes, good citizen that he is, to serve in his crossroads college!" Cloelius put his hand beneath Lucius Decumius's chin, lifted the seamed face so that the light struck his rivers of tears to silver-gilt. "See how Lucius Decumius mourns?"

He turned to point a finger at the bulk of the Curia Hostilia, the Senate House, on whose steps a small group of senators had assembled:

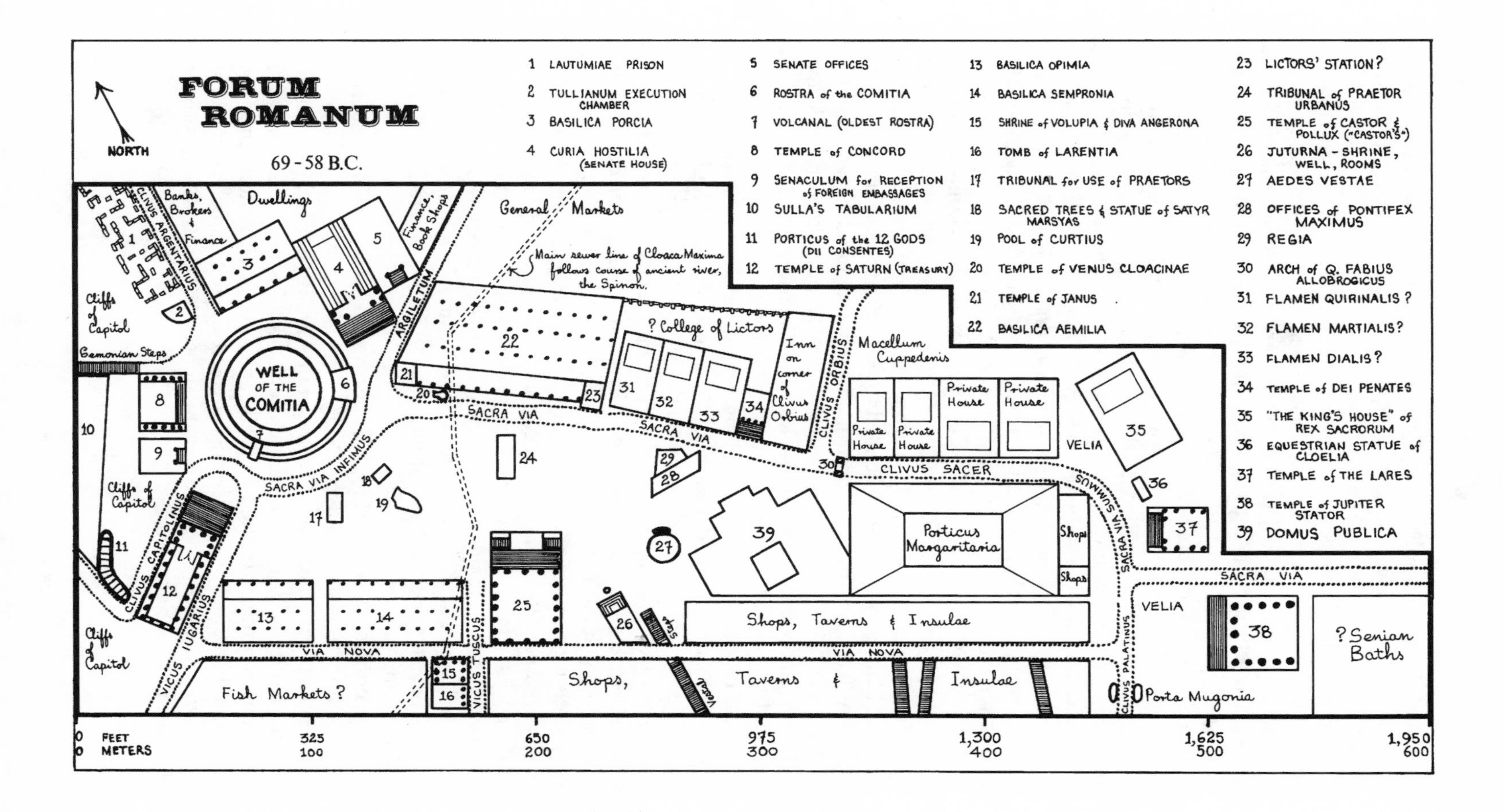
FORUM ROMANUM
69-58 B.C.
NORTH
1 LAUTUMIAE PRISON
2 TULLIANUM EXECUTION CHAMBER
3 BASILICA PORCIA
4 CURIA HOSTILIA (SENATE HOUSE)
5 SENATE OFFICES
6 ROSTRA of the COMITIA
7 VOLCANAL (OLDEST ROSTRA)
8 TEMPLE of CONCORD
9 SENACULUM for RECEPTION of FOREIGN EMBASSAGES
10 SULLA'S TABULARIUM
11 PORTICUS of the 12 GODS (DII CONSENTES)
12 TEMPLE of SATURN (TREASURY)
13 BASILICA OPIMIA
14 BASILICA SEMPRONIA
15 SHRINE of VOLUPIA & DIVA ANGERONA
16 TOMB of LARENTIA
17 TRIBUNAL for USE of PRAETORS
18 SACRED TREES & STATUE of SATYR MARSYAS
19 POOL of CURTIUS
20 TEMPLE of VENUS CLOACINAE
21 TEMPLE of JANUS
22 BASILICA AEMILIA
23 LICTORS' STATION?
24 TRIBUNAL of PRAETOR URBANUS
25 TEMPLE of CASTOR & POLLUX ("CASTOR'S")
26 JUTURNA - SHRINE, WELL, ROOMS
27 AEDES VESTAE
28 OFFICES of PONTIFEX MAXIMUS
29 REGIA
30 ARCH of Q. FABIUS ALLOBROGICUS
31 FLAMEN QUIRINALIS?
32 FLAMEN MARTIALIS?
33 FLAMEN DIALIS?
34 TEMPLE of DEI PENATES
35 "THE KING'S HOUSE" of REX SACRORUM
36 EQUESTRIAN STATUE of CLOELIA
37 TEMPLE of THE LARES
38 TEMPLE of JUPITER STATOR
39 DOMUS PUBLICA
CLIVUS ARGENTARIUS
Banks, Brokers & Finance
Dwellings
Finance, Book Shops
General Markets
Main sewer line of Cloaca Maxima follows course of ancient river, the Spinon.
ARGILETUM
Cliffs of Capitol
Gemonian Steps
WELL OF THE COMITIA
SACRA VIA
? College of Lictors
Inn on corner of Clivus Orbius
CLIVUS ORBIUS
Macellum Cuppedenis
Private House
VELIA
CLIVUS SACER
SACRA VIA INFIMUS
SACRA VIA SUMMUS
CLIVUS CAPITOLINUS
VICUS IUGARIUS
VICUS TUSCUS
Porticus Margaritaria
Shops
Shops, Taverns & Insulae
Steps
VIA NOVA
Fish Markets ?
Shops, Taverns & Insulae
Vestal
CLIVUS PALATINUS
Porta Mugonia
? Senian Baths
FEET 0 325 650 975 1,300 1,625 1,950
METERS 0 100 200 300 400 500 600

Cicero, smiling in absolute joy; Cato, Bibulus and Ahenobarbus, sober but not grief stricken; Manlius Torquatus, Lucius Caesar, the stroke-crippled Lucius Cotta, looking troubled.

"See them?" shrieked Cloelius. "See the traitors to Rome and to you? Look at the great Marcus Tullius Cicero, *smiling*! Well, we all know that *he* had nothing to lose by Milo's doing murder!" He swung aside for a moment; when he turned back, Cicero had gone. "Oh, thinks he might be next, does he? No man deserves death more than the great Cicero, who executed Roman citizens without trial and was sent into exile for it by this poor, mangled man I show you here tonight! Everything that Publius Clodius did or tried to do, the Senate opposed! Who do they think they are, the men who people that rotting body? Our betters, that's who they think they are! Better than me! Better than Lucius Decumius! Better even than Publius Clodius, who was one of them!"

The crowd was beginning to eddy, the noise of hate rising inexorably as Cloelius worked on its grief and shock, its dreadful sense of loss.

"He gave you free grain!" Cloelius screamed. "He gave you back your right to congregate in your colleges, the right *that* man"—pointing at Lucius Caesar—"stripped from you! He gave you friendship, employment, brilliant games!" He pretended to peer into the sea of faces. "There are many freedmen here to mourn, and what a friend he was to all of you! He gave you seats at the games when all other men forbade that, and he was about to give you *true* Roman citizenship, the right to belong to one of those thirty-one exclusive rural tribes!"

Cloelius paused, drew a sobbing breath, wiped the sweat from his brow. "But *they*," he cried, sweeping the sweat-smeared hand toward the Curia Hostilia steps, "didn't want that! *They* knew it meant their days of glory were over! And they conspired to murder your beloved Publius Clodius! So fearless, so determined, that nothing short of death would have stopped him! They knew it. They took it into account. And then they plotted to murder him. Not merely that ex-gladiator Milo—*all* of them were in on it! *All* of them killed Publius Clodius! Milo was just their tool! And I say there is only one way to deal with them! Show them how much we care! Show them that we will kill them all before we're done!" He looked again at the Senate steps, recoiled in mock horror. "See that? See it? They're gone! Not one of them has the backbone to face you! But will that stop us? *Will it?*"

The eddies were swirling, the torches spinning wildly. And the crowd with one voice shouted, "NO!"

Poplicola was alongside Cloelius, but Antony, Bursa, Pompeius Rufus and Decimus Brutus hung back, uneasy; two were tribunes of the plebs, one recently admitted to the Senate, and one, Antony, not yet a senator. What Cloelius was saying affected them as much as it did the group who had fled from the Senate steps, but there was no stopping Cloelius now, nor any escape.

"Then let's show them what we mean to do to them!" Cloelius screamed. "Let's put Publius Clodius in the Senate House, and dare the rest of them to remove him!"

A convulsive movement thrust the front ranks onto the top of the rostra; Clodius's bier was hoisted shoulder-high and carried on a wave of arms up the Senate steps to its ponderous bronze pair of doors, unassailably strong. In one moment they were gone, torn from their enormous hinges; the body of Publius Clodius disappeared inside. Came the sounds of things being ripped apart, splintered, smashed, reduced to fragments.

Bursa had somehow managed to get away; Antony, Decimus Brutus and Pompeius Rufus stood watching in horror as Cloelius fought his way up the Senate steps to the portico.

In the midst of which Antony's eyes found little old Lucius Decumius, still on the rostra, still mourning. He knew him, of course, from Caesar's days in the Subura, and though Antony was not a merciful man, he always had a soft spot for people he liked. No one else was interested in Lucius Decumius, so he moved to the old man's side and cuddled him.

"Where are your sons, Decumius?" he asked.

"Don't know, don't care."

"Time an old codger like you was home in bed."

"Don't want to go to bed." The tear-drenched eyes looked up into Antony's face and recognized him. "Oh, Marcus Antonius, they're *all* gone!" he cried. "She broke their hearts—she broke mine—they're all gone!"

"Who broke your heart, Decumius?"

"Little Julia. Knew her as a baby. Knew Caesar as a baby. Knew Aurelia since she was eighteen years old. Don't want to feel no more, Marcus Antonius!"

"Caesar's still with us, Decumius."

"Won't ever see him again. Caesar said to me, look after Clodius. He said, make sure while I'm away that Clodius don't come to no harm. But I couldn't do it. No one could, with Clodius."

The crowd emitted a long cry; Antony glanced toward the Curia Hostilia and stiffened. It was so old it had no windows, but high in its side where the beautiful mural adorned it were big grilles to let in air; they glowed now with a red, pulsating light and trickled smoke.

"Jupiter!" roared Antony to Decimus Brutus and Pompeius Rufus. "They've set the place on fire!"

Lucius Decumius twisted like an eel and was away; aghast, Antony watched him struggle, old man that he was, through the hordes now retreating down the Senate steps and away from the conflagration. Flames were belching out of the doorway, but Lucius Decumius never paused. His figure showed black against the fire, then disappeared inside.

Sated and exhausted, the crowd went home. Antony and Decimus

Brutus walked together to the top of the Vestal Steps and stood to watch as the fire inside the Curia Hostilia consumed Publius Clodius. Beyond it on the Argiletum stood the offices of the Senate, wherein lay the precious records of meetings, the *consulta* which were the senatorial decrees, the *fasti* which listed all the magistrates who had ever been in office. Beyond it on the Clivus Argentarius stood the Basilica Porcia, headquarters of the tribunes of the plebs and offices for brokers and bankers, again stuffed with irreplaceable records of all descriptions. Cato the Censor had built it, the first such structure to adorn the Forum, and though it was small, dingy and long eclipsed by finer edifices, it was a part of the *mos maiorum.* Opposite the Curia Hostilia on the other corner of the Argiletum stood the exquisite Basilica Aemilia, still being restored to absolute magnificence by Lucius Aemilius Paullus.

But they all went up in flames as Antony and Decimus Brutus watched.

"I loved Clodius, but he wasn't good for Rome," said Mark Antony, utterly depressed.

"And I! For a long time I truly thought that Clodius might actually make the place work better," said Decimus Brutus. "But he didn't know when to stop. His freedmen scheme killed him."

"I suppose," said Antony, turning away at last, "that things will quieten down now. I might be elected a quaestor yet."

"And I'm going to Caesar in Gaul. I'll see you there."

"Huh!" grumped Antony. "I'll probably draw the lot for Sardinia and Corsica."

"Oh no," said Decimus Brutus, grinning. "It's Gaul for both of us. Caesar's asked for you, Antonius. Told me in his letter."

Which sent Antony home feeling better.

Other things had happened during that awful night. Some in the crowd, gathered by Plancus Bursa, had gone out to the temple of Venus Libitina beyond the Servian Walls on the Campus Esquilinus, and there removed the *fasces* laid on their couches because there were no men in office to wield them. They then trudged all the way from the south side of the city to the Campus Martius, and there stood outside Pompey's villa demanding that he assume the *fasces* and the dictatorship. But the place was dark, no one answered; Pompey had gone to his villa in Etruria. Footsore, they plodded to the houses of Plautius and Metellus Scipio atop the Palatine and begged them to take the *fasces*. The doors were bolted, no one answered. Bursa had abandoned them after the fruitless mission to Pompey's villa, gone home anguished and afraid; at dawn the weary, leaderless group deposited the bundles of rods back in Venus Libitina.

No one wanted to govern Rome—that was the opinion of every man and woman who went the next day to the Forum to see the smoking ruins of so much precious history. Fulvia's undertakers were there, gloved, booted and masked, poking through the still-hot embers to find little bits of Publius Clodius. Not much, just enough to cause a rattle inside the priceless jeweled jar Fulvia had provided. Clodius must have a funeral, though it would not be at the expense of the State, and Fulvia, crushed, had yielded to her mother's command that the Forum be avoided.

Cato and Bibulus stared, appalled.

"Oh, Bibulus, Cato the Censor's basilica is gone, and I do not have the money to rebuild it!" wept Cato, looking at the crumbling, blackened walls. The column which had so inconvenienced the tribunes of the plebs stuck up through the charred beams of the collapsed roof like the stump of a rotten tooth.

"We can make a start with Porcia's dowry," said Bibulus. "I can manage without it, and so can Porcia. Besides, Brutus will be home any day. We'll get a big donation from him too."

"We've lost all the Senate records!" Cato said through his sobs. "There are not even those to tell future Romans what Cato the Censor said."

"It's a disaster, yes, Cato, but at least it means we don't have to worry about the freedmen."

Which was the chief sentiment among Rome's senators.

Lucius Domitius Ahenobarbus, who was married to Cato's sister and had given two of his own sisters to Bibulus as wives, hurried up. A short, squat man with not one hair on his head, Ahenobarbus had neither Cato's strength of principle nor Bibulus's sharpness of mind, but he was bullishly stubborn and absolutely faithful to the *boni,* the Good Men of the Senate's ultra-conservative faction.

"I've just heard the most amazing rumor!" he said breathlessly.

"What?" asked Cato apathetically.

"That Milo sneaked into Rome during the fire!"

The other two stared.

"He wouldn't have that kind of courage," said Bibulus.

"Well, my informant swears that he saw Milo watching the blaze from the Capitol, and though the doors of his house are bolted, there's definitely someone home—and I don't mean servants."

"Who put him up to it?" asked Cato.

Ahenobarbus blinked. "Did anyone have to? He and Clodius were bound to clash personally sooner or later."

"Oh, I think someone put him up to it," said Bibulus, "and I think I know who that someone was."

"Who?" asked Ahenobarbus.

"Pompeius, of course. Egged on by Caesar."

"But that's conspiracy to murder!" gasped Ahenobarbus. "We all know Pompeius is a barbarian, but he's a cautious barbarian. Caesar can't be caught, he's in Italian Gaul, but Pompeius is here. He'd never put himself voluntarily in that kind of boiling soup."

"Provided no one can prove it, why should he care?" asked Cato contemptuously. "He divorced Milo a year and more ago."

"Well, well!" said Bibulus, smiling. "It becomes steadily more important that we acquire this Picentine barbarian for our cause, doesn't it? If he's obliging enough to wag his tail and turn cartwheels at Caesar's dictate, think what he could do for us! Where's Metellus Scipio?"

"Shut in his house since they begged him to take the *fasces*."

"Then let's walk round and make him let us in," said Cato.

After forty years of enduring friendship, Cicero and Atticus had a falling-out. Whereas Cicero, who had endured paroxysms of fear because of Publius Clodius, thought Clodius's death the best news Rome could possibly get, Atticus genuinely grieved.

"I don't understand you, Titus!" Cicero cried. "You're one of the most important knights in Rome! You have business interests in almost every sort of enterprise, therefore you were one of Clodius's chief targets! Yet here you are sniveling because he's dead! Well, I am not sniveling! I am rejoicing!"

"No one should rejoice at the untimely loss of a Claudius Pulcher," said Atticus sternly. "He was brilliant and he was the brother of one of my dearest friends, Appius Claudius. He had wit and he had a good measure of erudition. I enjoyed his company very much, and I'll miss him. I also pity his poor little wife, who loved him passionately." Atticus's bony face took on a wistful look. "Passionate love is rare, Marcus. It doesn't deserve to be cut off in its prime."

"Fulvia?" squawked Cicero, outraged. "That vulgar strumpet who had the gall to barrack for Clodius in the Forum when she was so heavy with child she took up the space of two? Oh, Titus, really! She might be the daughter of Gaius Gracchus's daughter, but she's a disgrace to the name Sempronius! And the name Fulvius!"

Mouth pinched, Atticus got up abruptly. "Sometimes, Cicero, you're an insufferably puckered-up prude! You ought to watch it—there's still straw behind your Arpinate ears! You're a bigoted old woman from the outer fringes of Latium, and no Tullius had ventured to take up residence in Rome when Gaius Gracchus walked the Forum!"

He stalked out of Cicero's reception room, leaving Cicero flabbergasted.

"What's the matter with you? And where's Atticus?" barked Terentia, coming in.

"Gone to dance attendance on Fulvia, I presume."

"Well, he likes her, always did. She and the Clodias have always been very broadminded about his affection for boys."

"Terentia! Atticus is a married man with a child!"

"And what's that got to do with the price of fish?" demanded Terentia. "Truly, Cicero, you're an old woman!"

Cicero flinched, winced, said nothing.

"I want to talk to you."

He indicated the door to his study. "In there?" he suggested meekly. "Unless you don't mind being overheard?"

"It makes no difference to me."

"Then here will do, will it, my dear?"

She cast him a suspicious glance, but decided that bone was not worth a pick and said, "Tullia wants to divorce Crassipes."

"Oh, what's the matter now?" cried Cicero, exasperated.

Terentia's superbly ugly face grew uglier. "The poor girl is beside herself, that's what's the matter! Crassipes treats her like dog's mess on the sole of his boot! And where's the promise you were so convinced he showed? He's an idler and a fool!"

Hands to his face, Cicero gazed at his wife in dismay. "I am aware that he's a disappointment, Terentia, but it isn't you who has to find another dowry for Tullia, it's me! If she divorces Crassipes he'll keep the hundreds of thousands of sesterces I gave him along with her, and I'll have to find another lot on top of that! She can't stay single like the Clodias! A divorced woman is the target for every gossip in Rome."

"I didn't say she intended to stay single," said Terentia enigmatically.

Cicero missed the significance of this, concerned only about the dowry. "I know she's a delightful girl, and luckily she's attractive. But who will marry her? If she divorces Crassipes, she'll be trailing two husbands behind her at the age of twenty-five. Without producing a child."

"There's nothing wrong with her baby works," said Terentia. "Piso Frugi was so sick he didn't have the energy before he died, and Crassipes doesn't have the interest. What Tullia needs is a *real* man." She snorted. "If she finds one, it will be more than I ever did."

Why that statement should have caused a name to pop into his mind instantaneously, Cicero afterward didn't know. Just that one did. Tiberius Claudius Nero! A full patrician, a wealthy man—and a *real* man.

He brightened, forgot Atticus and Fulvia. "I know just the fellow!" he said gleefully. "Too rich to need a big dowry too! Tiberius Claudius Nero!"

Terentia's thin-lipped mouth fell open. *"Nero?"*

"Nero. Young, but bound to reach the consulship."

"Grrr!" snarled Terentia, marching out of the room.

Cicero looked after her, bewildered. What had happened to his golden tongue today? It could charm no one. For which, blame Publius Clodius.

"It's all Clodius's fault!" he said to Marcus Caelius Rufus when Caelius walked in.

"Well, we know that," Caelius said with a grin, threw an arm about Cicero's shoulders and steered him studyward. "Why are you out here? Unless you've taken to keeping the wine out here?"

"No, it's right where it always is, in the study," Cicero said, sighing in relief. He poured wine, mixed it with water, sat down. "What brings you today? Clodius?"

"In a way," said Caelius, frowning.

He was, to use Terentia's phrase, a *real* man, Caelius. Tall enough, handsome enough and virile enough to have attracted Clodia and kept her for several years. And he had been the one to do the dropping, for which Clodia had never forgiven him; the result had been a sensational trial during which Cicero, defending Caelius, had aired Clodia's scandalous behavior so effectively that the jury had been pleased to acquit Caelius of attempting to murder her. The charges had been multiple and gone much further, but Caelius got off and Publius Clodius had never forgiven him.

This year he was a tribune of the plebs in a very interesting College which was largely pro-Clodius, anti-Milo. But Caelius was pro-Milo, very definitely.

"I've seen Milo," he said to Cicero.

"Is it true he came back to town?"

"Oh, yes. He's here. Lying low until he sees which way the wind in the Forum is blowing. And rather unhappy that Pompeius chose to vanish."

"Everyone I've spoken to is siding with Clodius."

"I'm not, so much I can assure you!" snapped Caelius.

"Thank all the Gods there are for that!" Cicero swirled his drink, looked into it, pursed his lips. "What does Milo intend to do?"

"Start canvassing for the consulship. We had a long talk, and agreed that his best course is to behave as if nothing out of the way happened. Clodius encountered him on the Via Appia and attacked him. Clodius was alive when Milo and his party retreated. Well, that's the truth of it."

"Indeed it is."

"As soon as the stink of fire in the Forum dies down, I'm going to call a meeting of the Plebs," said Caelius, holding out his goblet for more wine-and-water. "Milo and I agreed that the smartest thing to do is to get in first with Milo's version of what happened."

"Excellent!"

A small silence fell, which Cicero broke by saying diffidently, "I imagine Milo has freed all the slaves who were with him."

"Oh, yes." Caelius grinned. "Can't you see all the Clodius minions demanding Milo's slaves be tortured? Yet who can believe *anything* said under torture? Therefore, no slaves."

"I hope it won't come to trial," said Cicero. "It ought not to. Self-defense precludes the need for trial."

"There'll be no trial," said Caelius confidently. "By the time there are praetors to hear the case, it will be a distant memory. One good thing about the present state of anarchy: if some tribune of the plebs who bears Milo a grudge—Sallustius Crispus, for example—tries to institute a trial in the Plebeian Assembly, I'll veto it. *And* tell Sallustius what I think of men who seize an unhappy accident as an excuse to get back at a man who flogs another man for plundering his wife's virtue!"

They both smiled.

"I wish I knew exactly where Magnus stands in all this," said Cicero fretfully. "He's grown so cagey in his old age that one can never be sure what he thinks."

"Pompeius Magnus is suffering from a terminal case of overinflated self-importance," said Caelius. "I never used to think that Julia was an influence for the good, but now she's gone I've changed my mind. She kept him busy and out of mischief."

"I'm inclined to back him for Dictator."

Caelius shrugged. "I haven't made up my mind yet. By rights Magnus ought to back Milo to the hilt, and if he does, then he's got my support." He grimaced. "The trouble is, I'm not sure he does intend to back Milo. He'll wait and see which way the wind in the Forum is blowing."

"Then make sure you give a terrific speech for Milo."

Caelius did give a terrific speech in support of Milo, who appeared dressed in the blindingly white toga of a consular candidate and stood to listen with a nice mixture of interest and humility. To strike first was a good technique, and Caelius an extremely good orator. When he invited Milo to speak as well, Milo gave a version of the clash on the Via Appia which firmly placed the blame for it on Clodius. As he had worked up his speech very carefully, he sounded splendid. The Plebs went away thoughtful, having been reminded by Milo that Clodius had resorted to violence long before any rival street gangs had come into being, and that Clodius was the enemy of both the First and the Second Classes.

Milo himself proceeded from the Forum to the Campus Martius; Pompey was definitely home again.

"I'm very sorry, Titus Annius," said Pompey's steward, "but Gnaeus Pompeius is indisposed."

A great guffaw of laughter emanated from some inner room, and Pompey's voice came clearly on its dying echoes: "Oh, Scipio, what a thing to happen!"

Milo stiffened. *Scipio?* What was Metellus Scipio doing closeted with Magnus? Milo walked back to Rome in a lather of fear.

Pompey had been so enigmatic. *Had* he made a promise? "You might be pardoned for thinking so" was what he had said. At the time it had seemed crystal clear. Do away with Clodius, and I will reward you. But was that really what he meant? Milo licked his lips, swallowed, became conscious that his heart was beating much faster than a brisk walk could provoke in such a fit man as Titus Annius Milo.

"Jupiter!" he muttered aloud. "He set me up! He's flirting with the *boni;* I'm just a handy tool. Yes, the *boni* like me. But will they go on liking me if they learn to like Magnus better?"

And to think that he had gone today prepared to tell Pompey he would step down as a candidate for consul! Well, not now. *No!*

Plancus Bursa, Pompeius Rufus and Sallustius Crispus called another meeting of the Plebeian Assembly to answer Caelius and Milo. It was equally well attended, and by the same men. The best speaker of the three was Sallust, who followed the rousing speeches of Bursa and Pompeius Rufus with an even better one.

"Absolute claptrap!" Sallust shouted. "Give me one good reason why a man accompanied by thirty slaves armed only with swords should attack a man whose bodyguard consisted of one hundred and fifty bully-boys in cuirasses, helmets and greaves! Armed with swords, daggers and spears! Rubbish! Nonsense! Publius Clodius wasn't foolish! Would Caesar himself have attacked were Caesar in a similar situation? No! Caesar does spectacular things with very few men, *Quirites,* but only if he thinks he can win! What kind of battleground is the Via Appia for a heavily out-numbered civilian? Flat as a board, no shelter, and, on the stretch where it happened, no help either! And why, if it happened the way Milo's mouthpiece Caelius—and Milo himself!—say it happened, did a defense-less, humble innkeeper die? We are supposed to believe that Clodius killed him! *Why?* It was Milo stood to gain by the despicable murder of a poor little man like the innkeeper, not Clodius! Milo, who freed his slaves, if you please, and so very generously that they've scattered far and wide—can't be traced, let alone found! But how clever to take along your hysterical wife on a mission of murder! For the only man who might have been able to give us the true story, Quintus Fufius Calenus, was so busy inside a *carpentum* dealing with a panicked woman that he can say—and I believe him, for I know the lady well!—"

Chuckles everywhere.

"—he can say he saw nothing! The only testimony we can ever hear about the circumstances in which Publius Clodius actually died is testi-mony from Milo and his henchmen, murderers all!"

Sallust paused, grinning; a neat touch, to disarm Caelius by himself referring to his affair with Fausta. He drew a long breath and launched into his peroration.

"All of Rome knows that Publius Clodius was a disruptive influence, and there are many of us who deplored his strategies and tactics. But the same can be said for Milo, whose methods are far less constitutional than Clodius's. Why murder a man who threatens your public career? There are other ways of dealing with such men! Murder is not the Roman way! Murder is inevitably an indication of even nastier things! Murder, *Quirites,* is the way a man starts to undermine the State! To take it over! A man stands in your path and refuses to get out of it, and you murder him? When you might simply pick him up—is Milo a weakling?—and lift him out of your path? This is Milo's first murder, but will it be his last? That is the real question we should all be asking ourselves! Who among us can boast a bodyguard like Milo's, far larger than the mere one hundred and fifty he had with him on the Via Appia? Cuirassed, helmeted, greaved! Swords, daggers, spears! Publius Clodius always had a bodyguard, but not like Milo's professionals! I say that Milo intends to overthrow the State! It's he who has created this climate! It's he who has started on a program of murder! Who will be next? Plautius, another consular candidate? Metellus Scipio? Pompeius Magnus, the greatest threat of all? *Quirites,* I beg you, put this mad dog down! Make sure his tally of murder remains at one!"

There were no Senate steps to stand on, but most of the Senate was standing in the well of the Comitia to hear. When Sallust was done, Gaius Claudius Marcellus Major raised his voice from the well.

"I convoke the Senate at once!" he roared. "The temple of Bellona on the Campus Martius!"

"Ah, things are happening," said Bibulus to Cato. "We're to meet in a venue Pompeius Magnus can attend."

"They'll propose that he be appointed Dictator," said Cato. "I won't hear of it, Bibulus!"

"Nor will I. But I don't think it will be that."

"What, then?"

"A Senatus Consultum Ultimum. We need martial law, and who better to enforce it than Pompeius? But *not* as Dictator."

Bibulus was right. If Pompey expected to be asked again, and this time officially, to assume the dictatorship, he gave no sign of it when the House met in Bellona an hour later. He sat in his *toga praetexta* in the front row among the consulars, and listened to the debate with just the right expression of interest.

When Messala Rufus proposed that the House pass a Senatus Consultum Ultimum authorizing Pompey to raise troops and defend the State—but not as Dictator—Pompey acceded graciously without displaying any chagrin or anger.

Messala Rufus gave him the chair gratefully; as the senior consul last year, he had perforce been conducting the meetings, but beyond organizing the appointment of an *interrex* he could do nothing. And in that he had failed.

Pompey didn't. The big jars full of water which held the little wooden balls of the lots were brought out on the spot, and the names of all the patrician leaders of the Senate's decuries were inscribed on the wooden balls. They fitted into one jar; the lid was tied down, the jar spun quickly, and out of the spout near the top a little ball popped. The name on it was Marcus Aemilius Lepidus, who was the first Interrex. But the lots proceeded until every wooden ball was ejected from the jar—not that any member of the Senate wished an endless string of *interreges,* as had happened last year. The order had to be established, that was all. Everyone confidently expected that the second Interrex, Messala Niger, would successfully hold the elections.

"I suggest," said Pompey, "that the College of Pontifices insert an extra twenty-two days in the calendar this year after the month of February. An *intercalaris* will afford the consuls something fairly close to a full term. Is that possible, Niger?" he asked of Messala Niger, second Interrex and a pontifex.

"It will be done," said Niger, beaming.

"I also suggest that I issue a decree throughout Italia and Italian Gaul that no male Roman citizen between the ages of forty and seventeen be exempted from military service."

A chorus of ayes greeted this.

Pompey dismissed the meeting, well satisfied, and returned to his villa, where he was joined shortly afterward by Plancus Bursa, who had received the nod from Pompey indicating a summons.

"A few things," said Pompey, stretching luxuriously.

"Whatever you want, Magnus."

"What I don't want, Bursa, are elections. You know Sextus Cloelius, of course."

"Well enough. He did a good job on the crowd when Clodius burned. Not a gentleman, but very useful."

"Good. Without Clodius I understand the crossroads college dissidents are leaderless, but Cloelius ran them for Clodius, and now he can run them for me."

"And?"

"I want no elections," Pompey said again. "I ask nothing else of Cloelius than that. Milo is still a strong contender for the consulship, and if he should get in, he might manage to be a bigger force in Rome than I'd care to see him become. We just can't have Claudians murdered, Bursa."

Plancus Bursa cleared his throat noisily. "Might I suggest, Magnus, that you acquire a well-armed and very strong bodyguard? And perhaps give it out that Milo has threatened you? That you fear you might become his next victim?"

"Oh, good thinking, Bursa!" cried Pompey, delighted.

"Sooner or later," Bursa said, "Milo will have to be tried."

"Definitely. But not yet. Let's wait and see what happens when the *interreges* can't manage to hold elections."

* * *

By the end of January the second Interrex was out of office and the third Interrex took over. The level of violence in Rome rose to a point whereat no shop or business within a quarter of a mile of the Forum Romanum dared open its doors, which in turn led to job dismissals, which in turn led to fresh violence, which in turn spread further throughout the city. And Pompey, empowered to care for the State in tandem with the tribunes of the plebs, spread his hands wide, opened his once-arresting blue eyes wide, said flatly that as there was no genuine revolution going on, the control of all this rested with the Interrex.

"He wants to be Dictator," said Metellus Scipio to Cato and Bibulus. "He doesn't say it, but he means to be it."

"He can't be let," said Cato tersely.

"Nor will he be let," said Bibulus calmly. "We'll work out a way to make Pompeius happy, tie him to us, and proceed to where the real enemy is. Caesar."

Who had just intruded into Pompey's nicely turning world in a manner Pompey did not appreciate. On the last day of January he received a letter from Caesar, now in Ravenna.

> I have just heard of the death of Publius Clodius. A shocking affair, Magnus. What is Rome coming to? Very wise of you to get a good bodyguard together. When assassination is so blatant, anyone is a likely victim, and you the most likely victim of all.
>
> I have several favors to ask of you, my dear Magnus, the first of which I know you won't mind granting, as my informants tell me you have already personally requested Cicero to bring his influence to bear on Caelius, make him stop stirring up trouble for you and support for Milo. If you would ask Cicero to take the journey to Ravenna—a delightful climate, so no real hardship—I would be grateful. Perhaps if my pleas are joined to yours, he will muzzle Caelius.
>
> The second favor is more complex. We have been dear friends now for eight years, six of them spent in the mutual delight of sharing our beloved Julia. Seventeen months have gone by since our girl perished, time enough to learn to live without her, even if neither of our lives will ever be the same again. Perhaps now is the time to think about renewing our relationship through marriage ties, a Roman way to show the world that we are in communion. I have already spoken to Lucius Piso, who is happy if I settle a very comfortable fortune on Calpurnia and divorce her. The poor creature is completely isolated in the female world of the Domus Publica, my mother is no longer there to keep her company, and she meets no one. She should be given the chance to find a husband with time to spend with her before she reaches an age when good husbands are not easy to find. Fabia and Dolabella are a good example.

I understand that your daughter, Pompeia, is not at all happy with Faustus Sulla, especially since his twin, Fausta, married Milo. With Publius Clodius dead, Pompeia will be forced into social contacts very much against her taste and her father's wishes. What I would propose is that Pompeia divorce Faustus Sulla and marry me. I am, as you have good reason to know, a decent and reasonable husband provided my wife keeps herself above suspicion. Dear Pompeia is all that I could ask for in a wife.

Now I come to you, a widower for seventeen months. How much I wish that I had a second daughter to offer you! Unfortunately I do not. I have one niece, Atia, but when I wrote to ask Philippus how he would feel about divorcing her, he answered that he preferred to keep her, as she is a pearl beyond price, above suspicion. Were there a second Atia, I would cast my net further, but, alas, Atia is my only niece. Atia has a daughter by the late Gaius Octavius, as you know, but again Caesar's luck is out. Octavia is barely thirteen years old, if that. However, Gaius Octavius had a child by his first wife, Ancharia, and this Octavia is now of marriageable age. A very good and solid senatorial background, and the Octavii, who hail from Velitrae in the Latin homelands, have had consuls and praetors in some of their branches. All of which you know. Both Philippus and Atia would be pleased to give this Octavia to you as a wife.

Please think deeply, Magnus. I miss my son-in-law greatly! To be your son-in-law would turn the tables nicely.

The third favor is simple. My governorship of the Gauls and Illyricum will finish some four months before the elections at which I intend to stand for my second term as a consul. As we have both been the targets of the *boni* and have no love for them from Cato to Bibulus, I do not wish to afford them the chance to prosecute me in some court rigged so hard and fast against me that I will go down. If I have to cross the *pomerium* into the city of Rome in order to declare my candidacy, I will automatically give up my imperium. Without my imperium, I can be forced to trial in a court of law. Thanks to Cicero, candidates for the consulship cannot stand for it *in absentia*. But this I need to do. Once I'm consul, I'll soon deal with any false charges the *boni* would bring against me.

But those four months must see me retain my imperium. Magnus, I hear that you will very soon be Dictator. No one could handle that office better. In fact, you will bring it back into luminous distinction after Sulla dirtied it so disgracefully. Rome need not fear proscriptions and murder under the good Pompeius Magnus! If you could see your way clear to procuring me a law enabling me to stand for the consulship *in absentia,* I would be enormously grateful.

I have just had a copy of Gaius Cassius Longinus's report to the Senate on affairs in Syria. A most remarkable document, and better writing than I thought any Cassius was capable of, apart from Cassius Ravilla. The epilogue of poor Marcus Crassus's progress to Artaxata and the court of the two kings was heartrending.

Keep well, my dear Magnus, and write to me at once. Rest assured that I remain your most loving friend, Caesar.

Pompey laid the letter down with trembling hands and then used them to cover his face. How *dare* he! Just who did Caesar think he was, to offer a man who had had three of the highest-born brides in Rome a girl who was a bigger nobody than Antistia? Oh, well, Magnus, I don't have a second daughter, and Philippus—ye Gods, *Philippus*!—won't divorce my niece for you, but my dog once piddled in your yard, so why don't you marry this nobody Octavia? After all, she shits in the same latrine as a Julian woman!

He began to grind his teeth; the fists clenched, unclenched. A moment later his horrified household heard the unmistakable sound of something they hadn't heard during Julia's time. A Pompeian temper tantrum. There would be bent metal from precious to base, smashed vessels, tufts of hair, specks of blood and shredded fabric to clear up. Oh, dear! What *had* the letter from Caesar said?

But after the spasm was over, Pompey felt much better. He sat down at his ink-splattered desk, found a pen and some untorn paper, and scribbled the draft of an answer for Caesar.

Sorry, old chap, I love you too, but afraid none of the marriage business is remotely possible. I have another bride in mind for myself, and Pompeia is perfectly happy with Faustus Sulla. Appreciate your dilemma over Calpurnia, but can't help, really, really can't help. Glad to send Cicero to Ravenna. He has to listen to you, since you're the one he owes all the money to. Won't listen to me, but then I'm a mere Pompeius from that nest of Gauls, Picenum. Happy to oblige with that little law about *in absentia*. Do it the moment I can, rest assured. Be quite a coup if I can persuade all ten tribunes of the plebs to endorse it, eh?

A runnel of blood trickled down his face from his lacerated scalp, reminding him that he had made rather a mess of his study. He clapped his hands for his steward.

"Clean up, will you?" he asked in the tone of an order, and not according Doriscus his name because he never did. "Send my secretary in. I need a good copy made of a letter."

When Brutus returned to Rome from Cilicia at the very beginning of February, he had of course first to face his wife, Claudia, and his mother, Servilia. The truth was that he infinitely preferred the company of Claudia's father to Claudia, but he and Scaptius had done so well in the moneylending business in Cilicia that he had had firmly to decline Appius Claudius's offer to keep him on as quaestor. Because that vile wretch Aulus Gabinius had passed a law which made it very difficult for Romans to lend money to non-citizen provincials, his return to Rome had become mandatory. As he was a senator now, and so superbly connected to at least half the House, he could procure senatorial decrees to exempt the firm of Matinius et Scaptius from the *lex Gabinia*. Matinius et Scaptius was a fine old company of usurers and financiers, but nowhere on its books did it record the fact that its real name ought to have been Brutus et Brutus. Senators were not permitted to engage in any business ventures unrelated to the ownership of land, a fribble which at least half the Senate had ways of getting around; most of Rome thought the worst senatorial offender in this respect was the late Marcus Licinius Crassus, but had Crassus been alive, he could have disillusioned most of Rome on that score. By far the worst offender was young Marcus Junius Brutus, who was also, thanks to a testamentary adoption, Quintus Servilius Caepio, heir to the Gold of Tolosa. Not that there was any gold; there had not been any gold for fifty and more years. It had all gone to purchase a commercial empire which was the inheritance of Servilia's only full brother. Who had died without a male heir fifteen years ago, and made Brutus his heir.

Brutus loved not so much money itself—that had been poor Crassus's abetting sin—as what money brought with it. Power. Perhaps understandable in one whose illustrious name could not fix its owner in the center of a blaze of brilliance. For Brutus was not tall, not handsome, not inspiring, not intelligent in the ways Rome admired. As to how he looked, that could not be very much improved, for the dreadful acne which had so diminished him as a youth had not gone away with maturity; the poor empustuled face could not endure a razor in a time and place when and where all men were invariably smoothly shaven. He did the best he could by clipping his dense black beard as closely as possible, but his large, heavy-lidded and very sad brown eyes looked out on his world from the midst of a facial shambles. Knowing it, hating it, he had retreated from any circumstances likely to make him the focus of ridicule, sarcasm, pity. Thus he had—or rather, his mother had—procured exemption from compulsory military service, and appeared but briefly in the Forum to learn the legalities and protocols of public life. This last was not something he was prepared to give up; a Junius Brutus could not do that. For he traced his lineage back to Lucius Junius Brutus, the founder of the Republic, and through his mother to Gaius Servilius Ahala, who had killed Maelius when he tried to restore the monarchy.

The first thirty years of his life had been spent waiting in the wings to enter upon the only stage he craved: the Senate, and the consulship. Snug within the Senate, he knew that how he looked would not militate against him. The Conscript Fathers of the Senate, his peers, respected familial clout and money far too much. Power would bring him what his face and body could not, nor his pretensions to an intellectualism no deeper than the skin on sheep's milk. But Brutus wasn't stupid, though that was what the name Brutus meant—stupid. The founder of the Republic had survived the tyrannies of Rome's last King by *seeming* to be stupid. A very big difference. No one appreciated that fact more than did Brutus.

He felt nothing for his wife, not even repugnance; Claudia was a nice little thing, very quiet and undemanding. Somehow she had managed to carve herself a tiny niche in the house her mother-in-law ran in much the same way as Lucullus had run his army—coldly, unswervingly, inhumanly. Luckily it was large enough to afford Brutus's wife her own sitting room, and there she had set herself up with her loom and her distaff, her paints and her treasured collection of dolls. Since she spun beautifully and wove at least as well as professional weavers, she was able to draw favorable comment from her mother-in-law, and even allowed to make Servilia lengths of fine and filmy fabrics for her gowns. Claudia painted flowers on bowls, birds and butterflies on plates, then sent them to the Velabrum to be glazed. They made such nice presents, a serious concern for a Claudia Pulchra, who had so many aunts, uncles, cousins, nephews and nieces that a small purse did not extend far enough.

Unfortunately she was quite as shy as Brutus, so that when he returned from Cilicia—almost a stranger, in fact, as he had married her scant weeks before leaving—she found herself in no position to deflect his attention from his mother. So far he had not visited her sleeping cubicle, which had created a pillow damp from tears each morning, and during dinner (when Brutus attended) Servilia gave her no chance to say a word—had Claudia thought of a word to say.

Therefore it was Servilia who occupied Brutus's time and Brutus's mind whenever he entered the house which was actually his, though he never thought of it as his.

She was now fifty-two years old, Servilia. Little had changed about her in many years. Her figure was voluptuous but well proportioned, hardly an inch thicker in the waist than it had been before she produced her four children, and her long, thick black hair was still long, thick and black. Two lines had etched themselves one on either side of her nose and ran down past the corners of her small, secretive mouth, but her forehead was uncreased and the skin beneath her chin enviably taut. Caesar, in fact, would have found her no different. Nor did she intend that he would when he returned to Rome.

He still dictated the terms of her life, though she did not admit that even to herself. Sometimes she ached for him with a dry, awful longing she could not assuage; and sometimes she loathed him, usually when she wrote him an infrequent letter, or heard his name spoken at a dinner party. Ever more and more, these days. Caesar was famous. Caesar was a hero. Caesar was a man, free to do as he pleased, not trammeled by the conventions of a society which Servilia found quite as repressive as Clodia and Clodilla did, but which she would not transgress as they did every day of their lives. So whereas Clodia sat demurely on the bank of the Tiber opposite the Trigarium wherein the young men swam, and sent her rowboat across with a proposition for some lovely naked fellow, Servilia sat among the arid mustiness of her account books and her specially procured verbatim records of meetings of the Senate and plotted, and schemed, and chafed, and yearned for *action*.

But why had she associated action with the return of her only son? Oh, he was impossible! No handsomer. No taller. No less enamored of her hateful half brother, Cato. If anything, Brutus was worse. At thirty, he was developing a slight fussiness of manner which reminded Servilia too painfully of that underbred upstart from Arpinum, Marcus Tullius Cicero. He didn't waddle, but he didn't stroll either, and a stroll with shoulders back was mandatory for a man to look his best in a toga. Brutus took quick little steps. He was pedantic. A trifle absent. And if her inner eye filled suddenly with a vision of Gaius Julius Caesar, so tall and golden and brazenly beautiful, oozing power, she would snarl at Brutus over dinner, and drive him away to seek solace with that frightful descendant of a slave, Cato.

Not a happy household. In which, after three or four days had gone by, Brutus spent less and less time.

It hurt to have to pay good money for a bodyguard, but one glance at the environs of the Forum, followed by a conversation with Bibulus, had decided him to pay that money. Even Uncle Cato, so fearless that he had had the same arm broken several times in the Forum over the years, now employed a bodyguard.

"Times are fine for ex-gladiators," Cato brayed. "They can pick and choose. A good man charges five hundred sesterces per *nundinae,* and then insists on plenty of time off. I exist at the beck and call of a dozen cerebrally deficient soldiers of the sawdust who eat me out of house and home and tell *me* when I can go to the Forum!"

"I don't understand," said Brutus, wrinkling his brow. "If we're under martial law and Pompeius is in charge, why hasn't the violence settled down? What's being done?"

"Nothing whatsoever, nephew."

"Why?"

"Because Pompeius wants to be made Dictator."

"That doesn't surprise me. He's been after absolute power since he executed my father out of hand in Italian Gaul. And poor Carbo, whom he wouldn't even accord privacy to relieve his bowels before he beheaded him. Pompeius is a barbarian."

Cato's ruined appearance devastated Brutus, a mere eleven years younger than Cato. Thus Cato had never seemed avuncular; more an older brother, wise and brave and so unbelievably strong in himself. Of course Brutus had not known Cato very well during his childhood and young manhood. Servilia would not permit uncle and nephew to fraternize. All that had changed from the day when Caesar had come round in the full regalia of the Pontifex Maximus and calmly announced that he was breaking the engagement between Julia and Brutus in order to marry Julia to the man who had murdered Brutus's father. Because Caesar had *needed* Pompey.

Brutus's heart had broken that day, never knit itself together again. Oh, he had loved Julia! Waited for her to grow up. Then had to see her go to a man who wasn't fit for her to wipe her shoes on. But she would see that in time; Brutus had settled back to wait, still loving her. Until she died. He hadn't seen her in months, and then she died. All he really wanted to believe was that somewhere, in some other time, he would meet her again, and she would love him as much as he loved her. So after her death he soaked himself in Plato, that most spiritual and tender of all philosophers, never having understood until she died what Plato was actually saying.

And now, gazing at Cato, Brutus understood what he was living through in a way no one else who was close to Cato could ever comprehend; for he gazed at a man whose love had gone to someone else, a man who couldn't learn to unlove. Sorrow washed over Brutus, made him bend his head. Oh, Uncle Cato, he wanted to cry out, I understand! You and I are twins in a wilderness of the soul, and we cannot find our way into the garden of peace. I wonder, Uncle Cato, if at the moments of our deaths we will think of them, you of Marcia and I of Julia. Does the pain ever go away, do the memories, does the enormity of our loss?

But he said none of this, just looked at the folds of toga in his lap until the tears went away.

He swallowed, said rather inaudibly, "What will happen?"

"One thing will not happen, Brutus. Pompeius will never be made Dictator. I will use my sword to stop my heart in the middle of the Forum before I would see it. There is no place in the Republic for a Pompeius—or a Caesar. They want to be better than all other men, they want to reduce us to pigmies in their shadow, they want to be like—like—like *Jupiter*. And we free Romans would end in worshiping them as gods. But not this free Roman! I will die first. I mean it," said Cato.

Brutus swallowed again. "I believe you, Uncle. But if we cannot cure these ills, can we at least understand how they began? Such trouble! It seems to have been there all my life, and it gets worse."

"It started with the Brothers Gracchi, particularly with Gaius Gracchus. It went then to Marius, to Cinna and Carbo, to Sulla, and now to Pompeius. But it isn't Pompeius I fear, Brutus. It never has been. I fear Caesar."

"I never knew Sulla, but people say Caesar is like him," said Brutus slowly.

"Precisely," said Cato. "Sulla. It always comes back to the man with the birthright, which is why no one feared Marius in his day, nor fears Pompeius now. To be a patrician is better. We cannot eradicate that except as my great-grandfather the Censor dealt with Scipio Africanus and Scipio Asiagenus. *Pull them down!*"

"Yet I hear from Bibulus that the *boni* are wooing Pompeius."

"Oh, yes. And I approve of it. If you want to catch the king of thieves, Brutus, bait your trap with a prince of thieves. We'll use Pompeius to bring Caesar down."

"I also hear that Porcia is to marry Bibulus."

"She is."

"May I see her?"

Cato nodded, fast losing interest; his hand strayed to the wine flagon on his desk. "She's in her room."

Brutus rose and left the study by the door opening onto the small, austere peristyle garden; its columns were severest Doric, of pool or fountain it had none, and its walls were unadorned by frescoes or hung paintings. Down one side of it were ranged the rooms belonging to Cato, Athenodorus Cordylion and Statyllus; down the other side were the rooms belonging to Porcia and her adolescent brother, Marcus Junior. Beyond them were a bathroom and latrine, with the kitchen and a servants' area at the far end.

The last time he had seen his cousin Porcia was before he left to go to Cyprus with her father, and that had been six years ago; Cato didn't encourage her to mix with those who called to see him. A thin, lanky girl, he remembered. Still, why try to remember? He was about to see her.

Her room was minute, and stunningly untidy. Scrolls, book buckets and papers literally everywhere, and in no sort of order. She was sitting at her table with her head bent over an unfurled book, mumbling her way through it.

"Porcia?"

She looked up, gasped, lumbered to her feet; a dozen pieces of paper fluttered to the terrazzo floor, the inkpot went flying, four scrolls disappeared down the gap at the back of the table. It was the den of a Stoic—dismally plain, freezingly cold, utterly unfeminine. No loom or furbelows in Porcia's quarters!

But then Porcia was dismally plain and not very feminine, though no one could accuse her of coldness. She was so *tall*! Somewhere up around Caesar's height, Brutus fancied, craning his neck. A mop of luridly red, almost kinkily waving hair, a pale yet unfreckled skin, a pair of luminous grey eyes, and a nose which bade fair to outrank her father's.

"Brutus! Dear, dear Brutus!" she cried, folding him in a hug that squeezed all the breath out of him and made it difficult for him to touch his toes to the floor. "Oh, *tata* says it is a right act to love those who are good and a part of the family, so I can love you! Brutus, how good to see you! Come in, come in!"

Dumped back on the ground again, Brutus watched his cousin flounder about sweeping a stack of scrolls and buckets off an old chair, then hunt for a duster to render its surface less likely to leave grey smears all over his toga. And gradually a smile began to tug at the corners of his doleful mouth; she was such an *elephant*! Though she wasn't fat, or even rounded. Flat chest, wide shoulders, narrow hips. Abominably dressed in what Servilia would have called a baby-cack-brown canvas tent.

And yet, he had decided by the time she had maneuvered both of them onto chairs, Porcia wasn't dismally plain at all, nor did she, despite that masculine physique, give an impression of mannishness. She crackled with life, and it endowed her with a certain bizarre attractiveness that he fancied most men, once over the initial shock, would appreciate. The hair was fantastic; so were the eyes. And her mouth was lovely, deliciously kissable.

She heaved a huge sigh, slapped her hands on her knees (far apart, but unselfconsciously so), beamed at him in simple pleasure. "Oh, Brutus! You haven't changed a bit."

His look was wry, but it didn't put her off-stride in the least; to Porcia, he was what he was, and that was not in any way a handicap. Very strangely brought up, deprived of her mother when she was six years old, unexposed since to the influence of women save for two years of Marcia (who hadn't noticed her), she had no inbuilt ideas of what beauty was, or ugliness was, or any—to her—abstract state of being. Brutus was her dearly loved first cousin, therefore he was beautiful. Ask any Greek philosopher.

"You've grown," he said, then realized how that would sound to her—oh, Brutus, *think*! She too is a freak!

But clearly she took him literally. She emitted the same neigh of laughter Cato did, and showed the same big, slightly protruding top teeth; her voice too was like his, harsh, loud and unmelodic. "Grown through the ceiling, *tata* says! I'm taller than he is by quite a bit, though he's a tall man. I must say," she whinnied, "that I'm very pleased to be so tall. I find that it gives me a great deal of authority. Odd, that people are awed by accidents of birth and nature, isn't it? Still, I have found it to be so."

The most extraordinary picture was forming in Brutus's mind, and not the sort of picture that he was prone to conjure up; but it was quite irresistible to envision tiny, frosty Bibulus trying to cover this flaming pillar of fire. Had the incongruity of the match occurred to him?

"Your father tells me you are to marry Bibulus."

"Oh, yes, isn't it wonderful?"

"You're pleased?"

The fine grey eyes narrowed, in puzzlement rather than anger. "Why would I not be?"

"Well, he's very much older than you are."

"Thirty-two years," she said.

"Isn't that rather a big gap?" he asked, laboring.

"It's irrelevant," said Porcia.

"And—and you don't mind the fact that he's a foot shorter than you are?"

"Irrelevant too," said Porcia.

"Do you love him?"

Clearly this was the most irrelevant factor of all, though she didn't say so. She said, "I love all good people, and Bibulus is good. I'm looking forward to it, I really am. Just imagine, Brutus! I'll have a much bigger room!"

Why, he thought, amazed, she's still a child! She has no idea of marriage whatsoever. "You don't mind the fact that Bibulus has three sons already?" he asked.

Another neigh of laughter. "I'm just glad he doesn't have any daughters!" she said when she could. "Don't get on with girls, they're so *silly*. The two grown-up ones—Marcus and Gnaeus—are nice, but the little one, Lucius—oh, I do like him! We have a marvelous time together. He's got the most terrific toys!"

Brutus walked home in a fever of worry for Porcia, but when he tried to talk to Servilia about her, he got short shrift.

"The girl's an imbecile!" snapped Servilia. "Still, what can you expect? She's been brought up by a drunkard and a clutch of fool Greeks! They've taught her to despise clothes, manners, good food and good conversation. She walks round in a hair shirt with her head buried in Aristotle. *I* feel sorry for Bibulus."

"Don't waste your sympathy, Mama," said Brutus, who knew these days how best to annoy his mother. "Bibulus is very well pleased with Porcia. He's been given a prize above rubies—a girl who is absolutely pure and unspoiled."

"Tchah!" spat Servilia.

The rioting in Rome continued unabated. February slipped away, a short month, then came Mercedonius, the twenty-two days intercalated by the College of Pontifices at Pompey's instigation. Each five days a new *interrex* took office and tried to organize the elections, but without success. Everyone complained; no one got anywhere by complaining. Very occasionally Pompey demonstrated that when he wanted something done, it was done, as with his Law of the Ten Tribunes of the Plebs. Passed halfway through that stormy February, it gave Caesar permission to stand for the consulship four years hence *in absentia*. Caesar was safe. He would not have to give up his imperium by crossing Rome's sacred boundary to register his candidacy in person, and thereby offer himself up for prosecution.

Milo continued to canvass for the consulship, but pressure to have him prosecuted was mounting. Two young Appius Claudiuses agitated constantly in the Forum on behalf of their dead uncle Publius, their chief grievance the fact that Milo had freed his slaves and that these slaves had disappeared into a fog of obscurity. Unfortunately Milo wasn't receiving the support from Caelius he had enjoyed just after the murder; Cicero had gone obediently to Ravenna and succeeded in muzzling Caelius on his return. Not a good omen for Milo, a worried man.

Pompey was worried too; opposition in the Senate to his being appointed Dictator was as strong as ever.

"You're one of the most prominent *boni,*" Pompey said to Metellus Scipio, "and I know you don't mind my being made Dictator. I don't want the post, mind you! That's not what I'm saying at all. Only that I can't understand why Cato and Bibulus won't have it. Or Lucius Ahenobarbus. Or any of the others. Isn't it better to have stability at any price?"

"At almost any price," said Metellus Scipio cautiously; he was a man charged with a mission, and it had taken hours for him to rehearse it with Cato and Bibulus. Not that his intentions were quite as pure as Cato and Bibulus thought. Metellus Scipio was another worried man.

"What's almost?" demanded Pompey, scowling.

"Well, there is an answer, and I've been deputed to put it to you, Magnus."

The magical thing had happened! Metellus Scipio was calling him "Magnus"! Oh, joy! Oh, sweet victory! Pompey visibly expanded, a smile growing.

"Then put it to me, Scipio." No more "Metellus."

"What if the Senate were to agree to your becoming consul without a colleague?"

"You mean sole consul? No other?"

"Yes." Frowning in an effort to remember what he had been told to say, Metellus Scipio went on. "What everyone objects to about the presence of a dictator is a dictator's invulnerability, Magnus. He can't be made to answer for anything he enacts while he is Dictator. And after Sulla, no one trusts the post. It isn't merely the *boni* who object. The knights of the eighteen senior Centuries object far more, believe me. They were the ones who felt Sulla's hand—sixteen hundred of them died in Sulla's proscriptions."

"But why should I proscribe anyone?" Pompey asked.

"I agree, I agree! Unfortunately many don't."

"Why? I'm *not* Sulla!"

"Yes, I know that. But there is a kind of man who is convinced that it isn't the person who fills the role, but the role itself at fault. Do you see what I mean?"

"Oh, yes. That anyone appointed Dictator would go mad with the power of it."

Metellus Scipio leaned back. "Exactly."

"I'm not that sort of man, Scipio."

"I know, I know! But don't accuse me, Magnus! The knights of the Eighteen won't have another Dictator any more than Bibulus and Cato will. All one has to do is say the word 'proscription' and men turn white."

"Whereas," said Pompey thoughtfully, "a sole consul in office is still constrained by the system. He can be hauled into court afterward, made to answer."

His instructions were to slip the next comment in as if it were a matter of course, and Metellus Scipio did well. He said, as if it were not important, "Not a difficulty for *you,* Magnus. You'd have nothing to answer for in a court."

"That's true," said Pompey, brightening.

"Besides which, the very concept of a consul without a colleague is a first. I mean, there have been times when a consul has served without a colleague for a few months, due to deaths in office and omens forbidding the appointment of more than one suffect consul. Quintus Marcius Rex's year, for example."

"And the year of the consulship of Julius and Caesar!" said Pompey, laughing.

Since Caesar's colleague had been Bibulus, who refused to govern with Caesar, this was not a comment which impressed Metellus Scipio; however, he swallowed and let it be. "You might say that to be consul without a colleague is the most extraordinary of all the extraordinary commands you've ever been offered."

"Do you really think so?" asked Pompey eagerly.

"Oh, yes. Undoubtedly."

"Then why not?" Pompey extended his right hand. "It's a deal, Scipio, it's a deal!"

The two men shook hands, and Metellus Scipio rose to his feet quickly, enormously relieved that he had acquitted himself to what would be the full satisfaction of Bibulus, and determined to remove himself before Pompey asked him some question not on the list he had memorized.

"You don't look very happy, Scipio," said Pompey on the way to the door.

Now how would he answer this? Was it dangerous ground? A fierce effort at thinking things through decided Metellus Scipio to be frank. "I'm not happy," he said.

"Why's that?"

"Plancus Bursa is making it generally known that he intends to prosecute me for bribery in the consular campaigning."

"*Is* he?"

"I'm afraid so."

"Dear, dear!" cried Pompey, sounding cluckily concerned. "We can't have that! Well, if I'm allowed to become consul without a colleague, Scipio, it will be a small matter to fix that up."

"Will it?"

"No trouble, I assure you! I have quite a bit of dirt on our friend Plancus Bursa. Well, he's no friend of mine really, but you know what I mean."

A huge weight lifted off Metellus Scipio. "Magnus, *I'd* be your friend forever!"

"Good," said Pompey contentedly. He opened the front door himself. "By the way, Scipio, would you care to come to dinner tomorrow afternoon?"

"I'd be delighted."

"Do you think poor little Cornelia Metella would care to accompany you?"

"I think she'd like that very much."

Pompey closed the door behind his visitor and strolled back to his study. How useful it was to have a tame tribune of the plebs who no one suspected was a tame tribune of the plebs! Plancus Bursa was worth every sestertius he was being paid. An excellent man. Excellent!

There loomed before his eyes an image of Cornelia Metella; he stifled a sigh. No Julia she. And she really did look like a camel. Not unhandsome, but insufferably proud! Couldn't *talk,* though she spoke incessantly. If it wasn't Zeno or Epicurus (she disapproved of both systems of thought), it was Plato or Thucydides. Despised mimes, farces, even Aristophanic comedy. Oh, well . . . she'd do. Not that he intended to ask for her. Metellus Scipio would have to ask him. What was good enough for a Julius Caesar was certainly good enough for a Metellus Scipio.

Caesar. Who didn't have a second daughter or a niece. Oh, that one was riding for a fall! And the consul without a colleague was just the man to do the tripping-up. Caesar had his Law of the Ten Tribunes of the Plebs, but that wasn't to say life was going to be smooth for him. Laws could be repealed. Or made redundant by other, later laws. But for the time being, let Caesar sit back and deem himself safe.

On the eighteenth day of intercalated Mercedonius, Bibulus got up in the House, meeting on the Campus Martius, and proposed that Gnaeus Pompeius Magnus be put up for election as consul, but without a colleague. The Interrex of the moment was that eminent jurist Servius Sulpicius Rufus, who listened to the House's reaction with the proper gravity becoming so famous a judge.

"It's absolutely unconstitutional!" cried Caelius from the tribunes' bench, not bothering to stand up. "There is no such man as a consul without a colleague! Why don't you just make Pompeius the Dictator and be done with it?"

"Any kind of reasonably legal government is preferable to no government at all, provided it is answerable at law for every one of its actions," said Cato. "I approve of the measure."

"I call upon the House to divide," said Servius Rufus. "All those in favor of permitting Gnaeus Pompeius Magnus to stand for election as consul without a colleague, please stand to my right. Those against the motion, please stand to my left."

Among the few men who stood to Servius Rufus's left was Brutus, attending his first meeting of the Senate. "I cannot vote for the man who murdered my father," he said loudly, chin up.

"Very well," said Servius Rufus, surveying the bulk of the Senate to his right. "I will summon the Centuries for an election."

"Why bother?" yelled Milo, who had also stood to the left. "Are we other consular candidates to be allowed to stand? For the same post, as consul without a colleague?"

Servius Rufus raised his brows. "Certainly, Titus Annius."

"Why not save time, money and a walk out to the Saepta?" Milo went on bitterly. "We all know what the result will be."

"I wouldn't accept the commission on the Senate's say-so," said Pompey with immense dignity. "Let there be an election."

"There should also be a law overriding the *lex Annalis*!" shouted Caelius. "It isn't legal for a man to run again for consul until ten years have elapsed since his last consulship. Pompeius was consul for the second time only two years ago."

"Quite right," said Servius Rufus. "Conscript Fathers, I will see another division on the motion that the House recommend as a decree to the Popular Assembly a *lex Caelia* allowing Gnaeus Pompeius Magnus to run for consul."

Which turned the tables neatly on Caelius.

By the beginning of March, Pompey the Great was consul without a colleague, and things began to happen. In Capua was sitting a legion destined for Syria; Pompey summoned it to Rome and cracked down on the street wars. Not that much effort was necessary; the moment the Centuries elected Pompey, Sextus Cloelius called off his dogs and reported to Pompey to collect a fat fee, gladly paid.

The rest of the elections were held, which meant that Mark Antony was officially appointed Caesar's quaestor—and that there were praetors in office to open the courts and start hearing the massive backlog of cases. No trials had been held since the end of the year before last, thanks to the violence which had prevailed during the five months last year's praetors had been in office. So men like Aulus Gabinius, ex-governor of Syria, who had been acquitted of treason but still had to face charges of extortion, were finally tried.

It had been Gabinius who accepted the commission to restore Ptolemy Auletes of Egypt to his throne after the irate Alexandrians had ejected him—not a senatorial commission, more the seizing of an offer and an opportunity. For a price rumored to be ten thousand silver talents. Perhaps that much had been the agreed price, but what was sure was that Gabinius had never been paid anything like it. Which didn't impress the extortion court; halfheartedly defended by Cicero, Gabinius was convicted and fined the sum of ten thousand talents. Unable to find a tenth of this fabulous sum, Gabinius went into exile.

But Cicero did better defending Gaius Rabirius Postumus, the little banker who had reorganized the finances of Egypt once its king was back on his throne. His original mission had been to collect the debts Ptolemy Auletes owed certain Roman senators for favors (Gabinius being one of them) and certain Roman moneylenders for contributing heavily to his support during his exile. Returned to Rome penniless, Rabirius Postumus accepted a loan from Caesar and bounced back. Acquitted because Cicero gave a defense as fact filled and damning as his prosecution of Gaius Verres had been years before, Rabirius Postumus was able now to devote himself to Caesar's cause.

The breach between Cicero and Atticus had not lasted long, of course; they were back together, writing to each other whenever Atticus went away on business, huddled together whenever both of them happened to be in Rome or the same town.

"There's a flurry of laws," said Atticus, frowning; he was not an ardent Pompey supporter.

"Some of which none of us like," said Cicero. "Even poor old Hortensius has started to fight back. And Bibulus and Cato, no surprise. The surprise was that they ever put up the suggestion that Magnus be elected consul without a colleague."

"Perhaps," said Atticus pensively, "they feared that Pompeius would take over the State without benefit of law. That's basically what Sulla did."

"Well, anyway," said Cicero, brightening, "Caelius and I intend that some of the prime movers in all this should suffer. The moment Plancus Bursa and Pompeius Rufus are out of office as tribunes of the plebs, we intend to prosecute them for inciting violence." He grimaced. "Since Magnus has put a new violence law on the tablets, we may as well use it."

"I can name one man who isn't pleased with our new consul without a colleague," said Atticus.

"Caesar, you mean?" No Caesar lover, Cicero beamed. "Oh, it was prettily done! I kiss Magnus's hands and feet for it!"

But Atticus, more rational about Caesar, shook his head. "It wasn't prettily done at all," he said sternly, "and it may be that one day we'll suffer for it. If Pompeius intended that Caesar not be allowed to stand for the consulship *in absentia,* why did he have the ten tribunes of the plebs pass their law saying Caesar could? Now he legislates a fresh law which forbids any man to stand *in absentia,* including Caesar."

"Huh! Caesar's creatures screamed loud enough."

Since Atticus had been one of those who screamed, he almost said something waspish, then bit his tongue. What was the use? Not all the advocates in history could persuade Cicero to see Caesar's side of things. Not after Catilina. And, like most worthy country squires, once Cicero held a grudge, he *held* it. "Fine and good," he said. "Why should they not? Everyone lobbies. But to say, 'Ooops! I forgot!' and tack a codicil onto his law which exempts Caesar, then neglect to have the codicil inscribed on bronze, is disgraceful. Sly and underhanded. I'd have liked the man better if he'd just shrugged and said, 'Too bad for Caesar; let him put up with it!' Pompeius has a swollen head and too much power. Power which he isn't using wisely. Because he's *never* used power wisely, not since he marched down the Via Flaminia with three legions—a mere youth of twenty-two!—to help Sulla ride roughshod over Rome. Pompeius hasn't changed. He's simply grown older, fatter, and craftier."

"Craft is necessary," said Cicero defensively; he had always been Pompey's man.

"Provided that the craft is aimed at men who'll fall for it. Cicero, I don't believe Caesar is the right man to choose as a target. Caesar has more craft in his little finger than Pompeius in his whole body, if for no other reason than that he employs it more rationally. But the trouble with Caesar is that he's also the most direct man I know. Craft doesn't become a habit, it's only a necessity as far as Caesar is concerned. Pompeius tangles himself in a web when he practises to deceive. Yes, he manipulates its strands well. But it's still a web. Caesar weaves a tapestry. I haven't divined exactly what the pattern is yet, but I fear him. Not for the reasons you do. But I fear him!"

"Nonsense!" cried Cicero.

Atticus closed his eyes, sighed. "It looks as if Milo will come to trial. How are you going to reconcile your allegiances then?" he asked.

"That's a way of saying that Magnus doesn't want Milo to get off," said Cicero uneasily.

"He doesn't want Milo to get off."

"I don't think he cares one way or the other."

"Cicero, grow up! Of course he cares! He put Milo up to it, you must see that!"

"I don't see it."

"Have it your own way. Will you defend Milo?"

"Not the Parthians and the Armenians combined could stop me!" Cicero declared.

The trial of Milo came on at dead of winter, which by the calendar (even after the insertion of those extra twenty-two days) was the fourth day of April. The court president was a consular, Lucius Domitius Ahenobarbus, and the prosecutors were the two young Appius Claudiuses assisted by two patrician Valerii, Nepos and Leo, and old Herennius Balbus. The defense was Olympian: Hortensius, Marcus Claudius Marcellus (a plebeian Claudian, not of Clodius's family), Marcus Calidius, Cato, Cicero and Faustus Sulla, who was Milo's brother-in-law. Gaius Lucilius Hirrus hovered on Milo's side, but as he was Pompey's close cousin he could do no more than hover. And Brutus came forward to offer himself in an advisory capacity.

Pompey had thought very carefully about how to stage this critical exercise, which was being conducted under his own violence legislation; the charge would not be murder, as no one had seen the murder. There were some innovations, among them the fact that the jury was not chosen until the final day of the case; Pompey personally drew the lots for eighty-one men, only fifty-one of whom would actually serve. By the time the final fifty-one were appointed by the lots and elimination, it would be too late to offer them bribes. The witnesses were to be heard on three consecutive days, after which, on the fourth day, their depositions were to be taken. Each witness was to be cross-examined. At the end of the fourth day, the entire court and all eighty-one potential jurors were to watch their names being inscribed on the little wooden balls, which were then to be locked up in the vaults under the temple of Saturn. And at dawn on the fifth day the fifty-one names would be drawn, with both prosecution and defense entitled to object to fifteen of the names produced.

Of slave witnesses there were very few, and none for Milo. On that first day the prosecution's chief witnesses were Atticus's cousin Pomponius and Gaius Causinius Schola: Clodius's friends who had been with him. Marcus Marcellus did all the cross-examining for the defense, and did it superbly well. When he began to work on Schola, some of Sextus Cloelius's gang members began a racket which prevented the court's hearing what was said. Pompey was not present in the court; he was on the far side of the lower Forum, hearing cases for the fiscus just outside the Treasury doors. Ahenobarbus sent a message across to Pompey, complaining that he could not conduct his court under these circumstances, and adjourned.

"Disgraceful!" said Cicero to Terentia when he went home. "I sincerely hope that Magnus does something about it."

"I'm sure he will," said Terentia absently; she had other things on her mind. "Tullia is determined, Marcus. She's going to divorce Crassipes at once."

"Oh, why does everything have to happen at once? I can't even begin to think about starting negotiations with Nero until my case is finished! And it's important that I do start negotiating—I've heard that Nero is thinking of marrying one of the Claudia Pulchra troop."

"One thing at a time," said Terentia with suspicious sweetness. "I don't think Tullia will be persuaded into another marriage hard on the heels of this one. Nor do I think that she likes Nero."

Cicero glared. "She'll do as she's told!" he snapped.

"She'll do as she wants!" snarled Terentia, sweetness gone. "She's not eighteen anymore, Cicero, she's twenty-five. You can't keep shoving her into loveless marriages tailored to suit your own social-climbing ambitions!"

"I," said Cicero, marching off to his study dinnerless, "am going to write my speech in defense of Milo!"

Rarely, in fact, did the consummate professional advocate Cicero devote the kind of time and care to a speech in someone's defense that he did to the speech he wrote for Milo. Even in early draft it ranked with his best. Necessary that it do so, as the other members of the defending team had agreed that they would donate all their time to Cicero. On him, therefore, rested the entire onus of speaking so well that the jury voted ABSOLVO. He toiled for some hours rather pleasurably, nibbling on a plate of olives, eggs and stuffed cucumbers, then retired to bed well satisfied with how the speech was shaping up.

And went off to the Forum the next morning to discover that Pompey had dealt efficiently—if extremely—with the situation. A ring of soldiers stood around the area of open space in the lower Forum where Ahenobarbus had set up his court, and beyond those soldiers were patrols of soldiers moving incessantly; of a gang member there was no sign. Wonderful! thought Cicero, delighted. The proceedings could be conducted in absolute peace and quiet. Watch Marcus Marcellus destroy Schola now!

If Marcus Marcellus did not quite destroy Schola, he certainly managed to twist his testimony into knots. For three days the witnesses gave their evidence and endured cross-examination; on the fourth day they swore their depositions, and the court watched eighty-one little wooden balls inscribed with eighty-one different names of senators or knights or *tribuni aerarii*. Including the name of Marcus Porcius Cato, working for the defense and possibly a juror as well.

Cicero's speech was perfect; he had rarely done better work. For one thing, it was not often that his co-advocates so generously yielded their time to him. The prosecution would have two hours to sum up, then the defense three hours. A whole three hours all to himself! Oh, what a man could do with that! Cicero looked forward with immense enjoyment to an oratorical triumph.

Walking home for a consular of Cicero's standing was always a parade. One's clients were there in droves; two or three of the fellows who collected Ciceronian witticisms hovered with wax tablets ready in case he uttered one; admirers clustered, talked, speculated about what he would say on the morrow. While he himself laughed, held forth, tried to think of some mot which would set the two or three collectors scribbling madly. Not a good time for the passing of a private message. Yet as Cicero started, puffing a little, up the Vestal Steps, someone brushed past him and slipped a note into his hand. How odd! Though why he didn't produce the note and read it then and there he didn't quite know. A *feeling*.

Not until he was alone in his study did he open it, peruse it, sit down with wrinkled brow. It was from Pompey, and merely instructed him to present himself at Pompey's villa on the Campus Martius that evening. Unaccompanied, please. His steward informed him that dinner was ready; he ate it in solitude, not sorry that Terentia was annoyed with him. What could Pompey want? And why so furtive?

The meal concluded, he started out for Pompey's villa by the shortest route, which took him nowhere near the Forum; he trotted down the Steps of Cacus into the Forum Boarium, and thus out to the Circus Flaminius, behind which lay Pompey's theater, hundred-pillared colonnade, senatorial meeting chamber, and villa. Which villa, he remembered with a smile, he had likened to a dinghy behind a yacht. Well, it was. Not small, just dwarfed.

Pompey was alone, greeted Cicero cheerfully, mixed him an excellent white wine with special spring water.

"All ready for tomorrow?" the Great Man asked, turned sideways on the couch so that he could see Cicero at its far end.

"Never readier, Magnus. A beautiful speech!"

"Guaranteed to get Milo off, eh?"

"It will go a long way toward doing that, yes."

"I see."

For a long moment Pompey said nothing at all, just stared ahead past Cicero's shoulder to where the golden grapes given to him by Aristobulus the Jew stood on a console table. Then he turned his eyes to Cicero and looked at him intently.

"I don't want that speech given," said Pompey.

Cicero's jaw dropped. "What?" he asked stupidly.

"I don't want that speech given."

"But—but—I have to! I've been given the whole three hours allocated to the defense's summing-up!"

Pompey got up and walked to the great closed doors which connected his study to the peristyle garden; they were of cast bronze and superbly paneled with scenes depicting the battle between the Lapiths and Centaurs. Copied from the Parthenon, of course, only those were marble bas-reliefs.

He spoke to the left-hand door. "I don't want that speech given, Marcus," he said for the third time.

"Why?"

"In case it does get Milo off," said Pompey to a Centaur.

Cicero's whole face was prickling; he felt sweat running down the back of his neck, became conscious that his hands were trembling. He licked his lips. "I would appreciate some sort of explanation, Magnus," he said with as much dignity as he could muster, and clenching his hands to still their shaking.

"I would have thought," said Pompey casually to the vein-engorged hindquarters of the Centaur, "that it was obvious. If Milo gets off, he'll be a hero to at least half of Rome. That means he'll be elected consul next year. And Milo doesn't like me anymore. He'll prosecute me the moment I lay down my imperium, which is in three years' time. As a respected and vindicated consular, he'll have clout. I don't want to have to spend the rest of my life doing what Caesar will spend the rest of his life doing—dodging prosecution on maliciously manufactured charges of everything from treason to extortion. On the other hand, if Milo is convicted, he'll go into an irreversible exile. I'll be safe. And that's why."

"But—but—Magnus, I can't!" Cicero gasped.

"You can, Cicero. What's more, you will."

Cicero's heart was behaving strangely, there was a webby mist before his eyes; he sat with them closed and drew a series of deep, strong breaths. Though he was a timid man, he was not at heart a coward. Once a sense of unfairness and injury entered into him, he could develop a surprising steeliness. And that crept into him now as he opened his eyes and stared at Pompey's podgy back, covered by a thin tunic. This was a warm room.

"Pompeius, you're asking me to give of less than my best for a client," he said. "I do understand why, truly. But I cannot consent to rigging the race as if we were driving chariots at the circus! Milo is my friend. I'll do my best for him no matter what the outcome might be."

Pompey transferred his gaze to a different Centaur; this one had a javelin wielded by a Lapith embedded in its human chest. "Do you like living, Cicero?" he asked conversationally.

The trembling increased; Cicero had to wipe his brow with a fold of toga. "Yes, I like living," he whispered.

"I imagined you did. After all, you haven't had a second consulship yet, and there's the censorship as well." The wounded Centaur was obviously interesting; Pompey bent forward to peer at the spot where the javelin entered. "It's up to you, Cicero. If you speak well enough to get Milo off tomorrow, it's all over. Your next sleep will be permanent."

Hand on one knob, Pompey tugged it, opened half the door, and went out. Cicero sat on the couch panting, lower lip held firmly in his teeth, knees vibrating. Time passed, he was not sure how much of it. But finally he put both hands on the couch and levered himself upright. His legs held. He extended a foot, began to walk. And kept on walking.

It was only at the bottom of the Palatine that he fully understood what had just transpired. What Pompey had actually told him. That Publius Clodius had died at his behest; that Milo had been his tool; that the tool's usefulness was now blunted; and that if he, Marcus Tullius Cicero, did not do as he had been told, he would be as dead as Publius Clodius. Who would do it for Pompey? Sextus Cloelius? Oh, the world was full of Pompey's tools! But what did he *want,* this Pompeius from Picenum? And where in all of this was Caesar? Yes, he was there! Clodius could not be allowed to live to be praetor. They had decided it between them.

In the darkness of his bedroom he began to weep. Terentia stirred, muttered, rolled onto her side. Cicero retreated, wrapped in a thick blanket, to the icy peristyle, and there wept as much for Pompey as for himself. The brisk, competent, oddly offhand seventeen-year-old he had met during Pompey Strabo's war against the Italians in Picenum had long, long gone. Had he known as far back as then that one day he would need the wretched youth Cicero as his tool? Was that why he had been so kind? Was that why he had saved the wretched youth Cicero's life? So that one day far in the future he could threaten to remove what he had preserved?

At dawn Rome woke to bustle and hum, though all through the night the heavy wheeled carts drawn by oxen lumbered through the narrow streets delivering goods. Goods which at dawn were put on display or put to work in some factory or foundry, when Rome rose, yawning, to begin the serious business of making money.

But on the fifth day of Milo's trial in Lucius Ahenobarbus's specially convened violence court, Rome cowered as the sun nudged upward into the sky. Pompey had literally closed the city. Within the Servian Walls no activity began; no snack bar opened its sliding doors onto the street to offer breakfast, no tavern rolled up its shutters, no bakery kindled the ovens, no stall was erected in any marketplace, no school set itself up in a quiet corner, no bank or brokerage firm tuned its abacuses, no purveyor of books or jewels opened his door, no slave or free man went to work, no crossroads college or club or brotherhood of any description met to while away the hours of a day off.

The silence was stupendous. Every street leading to the Forum Romanum was cordoned off by sour, untalkative bands of soldiers, and within the Forum itself *pila* bristled above the waving plumes of the Syrian legion's helmets. Two thousand men garrisoned the Forum itself, three thousand more the city, on that freezing ninth day of April. Walking like somnambulants, the hundred-odd men and few women who were compelled to attend the trial of Milo assembled amid the echoes, shivering with cold, staring about twitchily.

Pompey had already set up his tribunal outside the doors of the Treasury beneath the temple of Saturn, and there he sat dispensing fiscal justice while Ahenobarbus had his lictors collect the wooden balls from the vaults and brought out the lot jars. Mark Antony challenged the jurors for the prosecution, Marcus Marcellus for the defense; but when Cato's name was drawn, both sides nodded.

It took two hours to choose the fifty-one men who sat to hear the summing-up. After which the prosecution spoke for two hours. The elder of the two Appius Claudiuses and Mark Antony (who had remained in Rome to act in this trial) each spoke for half an hour, and Publius Valerius Nepos for an hour. Good speeches, but not in Cicero's league.

The jury leaned forward on its folding stools when Cicero walked forward to begin, his scroll in his hand; it was there merely for effect, he never referred to it. When Cicero gave an oration it seemed as if he were composing it as he went along, seamlessly, vividly, magically. Who could ever forget his speech against Gaius Verres, his defenses of Caelius, of Cluentius, of Roscius of Ameria? Murderers, blackguards, monsters, all grist for Cicero's undiscriminating mill. He had even made the vile Antonius Hybrida sound like every mother's ideal son.

"Lucius Ahenobarbus, members of the jury, you see me here to represent the great and good Titus Annius Milo."

Cicero paused, stared at the pleasurably expectant Milo, swallowed. "How strange it is to have an audience composed of soldiers! How much I miss the clangor of business as usual. . . ." He stopped, swallowed. "But how wise of the consul Gnaeus Pompeius to make sure that nothing unseemly happened—happens. . . ." He stopped, swallowed. "We are protected. We have nothing to fear, and least of all does my dear friend Milo have anything to fear. . . ." He stopped, waved his scroll aimlessly, swallowed. "Publius Clodius was mad; he burned and plundered. Burned. Look at the places where our beloved Curia Hostilia, Basilica Porcia . . ." He stopped, he frowned, he pushed the fingers of one hand into the sockets of his eyes. "Basilica Porcia—Basilica Porcia . . ."

By this, the silence was so profound that the chink of a *pilum* brushing against a scabbard sounded like a building crashing down; Milo was gaping at him, that loathesome cockroach Marcus Antonius was grinning, the rising sun was reflecting off the oily bald pate of Lucius Ahenobarbus the way it did off snowfields, blindingly—oh, what is the matter with my mind, why am I seeing *that*?

He tried again. "Are we to exist in perpetual misery? No! We have not since the day Publius Clodius burned! On the day Publius Clodius died, we received a priceless gift! The patriot we see here before us simply defended himself, fought for his life. His sympathies have always been with true patriots, his anger directed against the gutter techniques of demagogues. . . ." He stopped, swallowed. "Publius Clodius conspired to take the life of Milo. There can be no doubt of it, no doubt of it at all—no doubt at all—no doubt, no doubt . . . no—doubt . . ."

Face twisted with worry, Caelius crossed to where Cicero stood alone. "Cicero, you're not well. Let me get you some wine," he said anxiously.

The brown eyes staring at him were dazed; Caelius wondered if they even saw him.

"Thank you, I am well," said Cicero, and tried again. "Milo does not deny that a fight broke out on the Via Appia, though he does deny that he instigated it. He does not deny that Clodius died, though he does deny that he killed Clodius. All of which is quite immaterial. Self-defense is not a crime. Never a crime. Crime is premeditated. That was Clodius. That was premeditation. Publius Clodius. Him. Not Milo. No, not Milo. . . ."

Caelius moved back to him. "Cicero, take some wine, please!"

"No, I am well. Truly, I am well. Thank you. . . . Take the size of Milo's party. A *carpentum.* A wife. The eminent Quintus Fufius Calenus. Baggage. Servants galore. Is that the way a man plots to do murder? Clodius had no wife with him. Isn't that in itself suspicious? Clodius never moved without his wife. Clodius had no baggage. Clodius was unencumbersome—unencrumbed—unen—unencumbered. . . ."

Pompey was sitting on his tribunal hearing cases against the fiscus. Pretending the court of Ahenobarbus didn't exist. I never knew the man. Oh, Jupiter, he will kill me! *He will kill me!*

"Milo is a sane man. If it happened the way the prosecution alleges it happened, then we are looking at a madman. But Milo is not mad. It was Clodius who was mad! Everyone knew Clodius was mad! Everyone!"

He stopped, wiped the sweat out of his eyes. Fulvia swam before his gaze, sitting with her mother, Sempronia. Who was that standing with them? Oh, Curio. They were smiling, smiling, smiling. While Cicero died, died, died.

"Died. Died. Clodius died. No one denies that. We all have to die. But no one wants to die. Clodius died. Clodius brought it on himself. Milo didn't kill him. Milo is—Milo is . . ."

For a hideous half hour Cicero battled on, stumbling, stopping, faltering, tripping over simple words. Until in the end, his vision filled by Gnaeus Pompeius Magnus dispensing fiscal justice outside Saturn, he stopped for the last time. Couldn't start again.

No one on Milo's side was angry, even Milo. The shock was too enormous, Cicero's health too suspect. Perhaps he had one of those frightful headaches with flashing lights? It wasn't his heart; he didn't have that grey look. Nor his stomach. What *was* the matter with him? Was he having a stroke?

Marcus Claudius Marcellus stepped forward. "Lucius Ahenobarbus, it is clear that Marcus Tullius cannot continue. And that is a tragedy, for we all agreed to give him our time. Not one of us has prepared an address. May I humbly ask this court and its jurors to remember the kind of oration Marcus Tullius has always given? Today he is ill; we will not hear that. But we can remember. And take to your hearts, members of the jury, an unspoken oration which would have shown you, beyond a shadow of a doubt, where the guilt in this sorry business lies. The defense rests its case."

Ahenobarbus shifted in his chair. "Members of the jury, I require your votes," he said.

The jury busied itself inscribing its little tablets with a letter: *A* for ABSOLVO, *C* for CONDEMNO. Ahenobarbus's lictors collected the tablets and Ahenobarbus counted them with witnesses peering over his shoulder.

"CONDEMNO by thirty-eight votes to thirteen," Ahenobarbus announced in a level voice. "Titus Annius Milo, I will appoint a damages panel to assess your fine, but CONDEMNO carries a sentence of exile with it according to the *lex Pompeia de vi*. It is my duty to instruct you that you are interdicted against fire and water within five hundred miles of Rome. Be advised that three further charges have been laid against you. You will be tried in the court of Aulus Manlius Torquatus on charges of electoral bribery. You will be tried in the court of Marcus Favonius on charges of illegally associating with members of colleges banned under the *lex Julia Marcia*. And you will be tried in the court of Lucius Fabius on charges of violence under the *lex Plautia de vi*. Court closed."

Caelius led the almost prostrate Cicero away. Cato, who had voted ABSOLVO, crossed to Milo. It was very strange. Not even that showy termagant Fulvia was shrieking victory. People just melted away as if numbed.

"I'm sorry for it, Milo," Cato said.

"Not as sorry as I am, believe me."

"I fear you'll go down in the other courts as well."

"Of course. Though I won't be here to defend myself. I'm leaving for Massilia today."

For once Cato wasn't shouting; his voice was low. "Then you'll be all right if you've prepared for defeat. I hope you noticed that Lucius Ahenobarbus issued no order to seal your house or garnish your finances."

"I am grateful. And I'm prepared."

"I'm thunderstruck at Cicero."

Milo smiled, shook his head. "Poor Cicero!" he said. "I think he's just discovered some of Pompeius's secrets. Please, Cato, watch Pompeius! I know the *boni* are wooing him. I understand why. But in the end you'd do better to ally yourself with Caesar. At least Caesar is a Roman."

But Cato drew himself up in outrage. "Caesar? I will die first!" he shouted, then marched away.

And at the end of April a wedding took place. Gnaeus Pompeius Magnus married the widow Cornelia Metella, twenty-year-old daughter of Metellus Scipio. The charges Plancus Bursa had threatened to bring against Metellus Scipio never eventuated.

"Don't worry, Scipio," said the bridegroom genially at the wedding dinner, a small affair. "I intend to hold the elections on time in Quinctilis, and I promise that I'll have you elected as my junior consul for the rest of this year. Six months is long enough to serve without a colleague."

Metellus Scipio didn't know whether to kick him or kiss him.

Though he kept to his house for a few days, Cicero bounced back, pretended even inside his own mind that it had never happened. That Pompey was the Pompey he had always been. Yes, a headache had struck, one of those ghastly things which warped the mind, snarled the tongue. That was how he explained it to Caelius. To the world he explained that the presence of the troops had thrown him off—how could anyone concentrate in that atmosphere of silence, of military might? And if there were those who remembered that Cicero had endured worse things without being rattled, they held their tongues. Cicero was getting old.

Milo had settled down to exile in Massilia, though Fausta had gone back to her brother in Rome.

To Milo in Massilia went a couriered gift: a copy of the speech Cicero had prepared, amended to incorporate rings of soldiers and flowery references to the consul without a colleague.

"My thanks," Milo wrote to Cicero. "If you'd actually had the gumption to deliver it, my dear Cicero, I might not at this moment be enjoying the bearded mullets of Massilia."

ITALIAN GAUL, THE PROVINCE AND GAUL OF THE LONG-HAIRS

from JANUARY until
DECEMBER of 52 B.C.

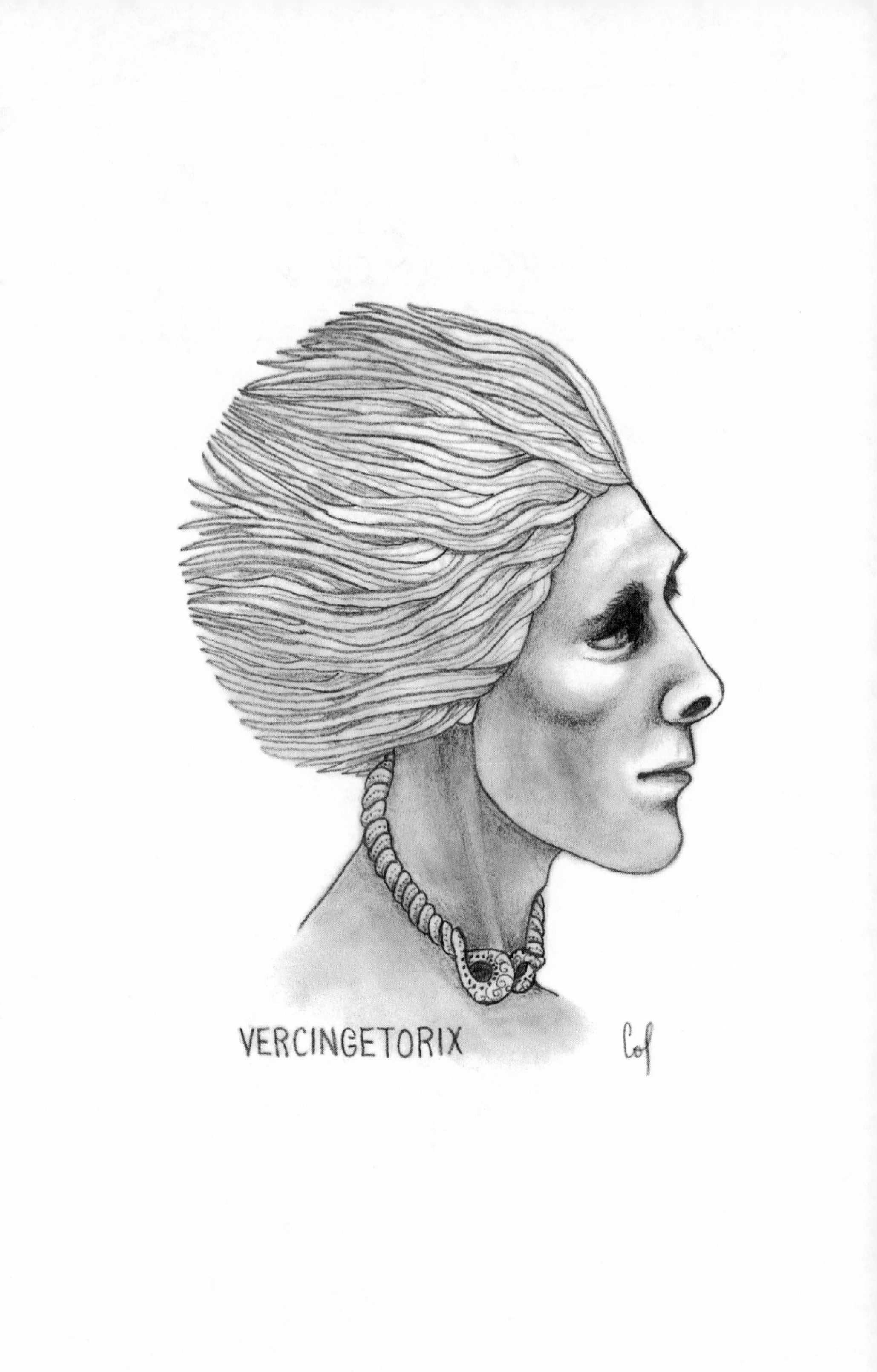
VERCINGETORIX
Col

Some years earlier, after Gnaeus Pompeius Magnus and Marcus Licinius Crassus had completed their year in office together as consuls for the second time, they looked forward to very special proconsular governorships. Caesar's legate Gaius Trebonius had been a tribune of the plebs while they were still consuls, and had carried a law which gave them enviable provinces for a full five-year term; on their mettle because Caesar was proving the effectiveness of that five-year term in Gaul, Pompey took Syria and Crassus the two Spains.

Then Julia, never fully well after her miscarriage, began to fail in health even more. Pompey couldn't take her with him to Syria; custom and tradition forbade it. So Pompey, genuinely in love with his young wife, revised his plans. He still functioned as curator of Rome's grain supply, which gave him an excellent excuse to remain in close proximity to Rome. *If* he governed a stable province. Syria was not that. Newest of Rome's territorial possessions, it bordered the Kingdom of the Parthians, a mighty empire under the rule of King Orodes, who cast wary glances at the Roman presence in Syria. Particularly if Pompey the Great was to be its governor, for Pompey the Great was a famous conqueror. Word traveled, and word had it that Rome was toying with the idea of adding the Kingdom of the Parthians to her own empire. King Orodes was a worried man. He was also a prudent and careful man.

Thanks to Julia, Pompey asked Crassus to switch provinces with him: Pompey would take both the Spains, Crassus could have Syria. A proposition Crassus agreed to eagerly. Thus it was arranged. Pompey was able to stay in the vicinity of Rome with Julia because he could send his legates Afranius and Petreius to govern Nearer and Further Spain, while Crassus set off for Syria determined to conquer the Parthians.

When news of his defeat and death at the hands of the Parthians reached Rome it created a furor, not least because the news came from the only noble survivor, Crassus's quaestor, a remarkable young man named Gaius Cassius Longinus.

Though he sent an official dispatch to the Senate, Cassius also sent a more candid account of events to Servilia, his fond friend and prospective mother-in-law. Knowing that this candid account would cause Caesar great anguish, Servilia took pleasure in transmitting it to him in Gaul. Hah! Suffer, Caesar! I do.

> I arrived in Antioch just before King Artavasdes of Armenia arrived on a State visit to the governor, Marcus Crassus. Preparations were well in hand for the coming expedition against the Parthians—or so Crassus seemed to think. A conviction I confess I didn't share once I had seen for myself what Crassus had gotten together. Seven legions, all under-strength at eight cohorts per legion instead of the proper ten, and a mass of cavalry I didn't feel would ever learn to work together well. Publius Crassus had brought a thousand Aeduan

horse troopers with him from Gaul, a gift from Caesar for his bosom friend Crassus that Caesar would have done better to withhold; they didn't get on with the Galatian horsemen, and they were very homesick.

Then there was Abgarus, King of the Skenite Arabs. I don't know why, but I mistrusted him and misliked him from the moment I met him. Crassus, however, thought him wonderful, and would hear nothing against him. It appears Abgarus is a client of Artavasdes of Armenia, and was offered to Crassus as a guide and adviser for the expedition. Along with four thousand light-armed Skenite Arab troops.

Crassus's plan was to march for Mesopotamia and strike first at Seleuceia-on-Tigris, the site of the Parthian winter court; since his campaign was to be a winter one, he expected King Orodes of the Parthians to be in residence there, and expected to capture Orodes and all his sons before they could scatter to organize resistance throughout the Parthian empire.

But King Artavasdes of Armenia and his client Abgarus of the Skenite Arabs deplored this strategy. No one, they said, could beat an army of Parthian cataphracti and Parthian horse archers on flat ground. Those mail-clad warriors on their gigantic mail-clad Median horses could not fight in the mountains effectively, said Artavasdes and Abgarus. Nor did high and rugged terrain suit the horse archers, who ran out of arrows quickly, and needed to be able to gallop across level ground to fire those fabled Parthian shots. Therefore, said Artavasdes and Abgarus, Crassus should march for the Median mountains, not for Mesopotamia. If, fighting alongside the whole Armenian army, he struck at the Parthian heartlands below the Caspian Sea and at the King's summer capital of Ecbatana, Crassus couldn't lose, said Artavasdes and Abgarus.

I thought this was a good plan—and said so—but Crassus refused to consider it. He foresaw no difficulties in beating the cataphracti and horse archers on flat ground. Frankly, I decided that Crassus didn't want an alliance with Artavasdes because he would have had to share the spoils. You know Marcus Crassus, Servilia—the world does not hold enough money to satiate his lust for it. He didn't mind Abgarus, not a paramount king and therefore not entitled to a major share of the spoils. Whereas King Artavasdes would be entitled to half of everything. Quite justifiably.

Be that as it may, Crassus said an emphatic no. The flat terrain of Mesopotamia was more suited to the maneuvers of a Roman army, he maintained; he didn't want his men mutinying as the troops of Lucullus had done when they saw Mount Ararat in the distance and realized that Lucullus expected them to climb over it. Added to which, a mountain campaign in far-off Media would have to be a

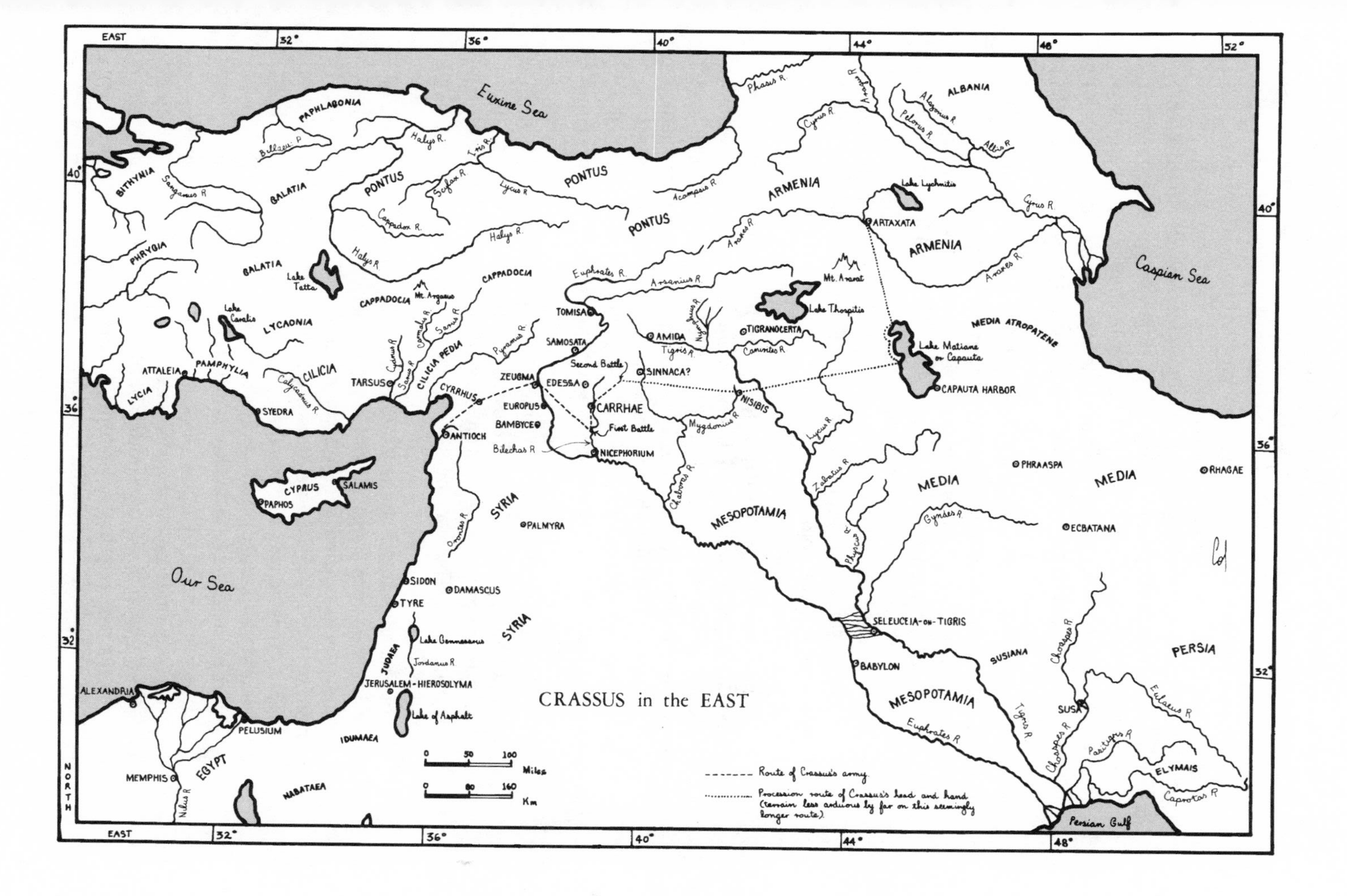
CRASSUS in the EAST
Euxine Sea
Caspian Sea
Our Sea
Persian Gulf
PAPHLAGONIA
BITHYNIA
GALATIA
PONTUS
PHRYGIA
LYCAONIA
CAPPADOCIA
CILICIA
CILICIA PEDIA
PAMPHYLIA
LYCIA
ARMENIA
ALBANIA
MEDIA ATROPATENE
MEDIA
MESOPOTAMIA
SUSIANA
PERSIA
ELYMAIS
SYRIA
JUDAEA
IDUMAEA
NABATAEA
EGYPT
CYPRUS
ATTALEIA
SYEDRA
TARSUS
CYRRHUS
ZEUGMA
EDESSA
EUROPUS
BAMBYCE
ANTIOCH
SAMOSATA
TOMISA
AMIDA
TIGRANOCERTA
SINNACA?
NISIBIS
CARRHAE
NICEPHORIUM
Second Battle
First Battle
ARTAXATA
CAPAUTA HARBOR
PHRAASPA
ECBATANA
RHAGAE
PALMYRA
SIDON
TYRE
DAMASCUS
JERUSALEM-HIEROSOLYMA
ALEXANDRIA
PELUSIUM
MEMPHIS
SALAMIS
PAPHOS
SELEUCEIA-ON-TIGRIS
BABYLON
SUSA
Lake Tatta
Lake Caralis
Lake Lychnitis
Lake Thospitis
Lake Matiane or Capauta
Lake Gennesarus
Lake of Asphalt
Mt. Argaeus
Mt. Ararat
Halys R.
Sangarius R.
Billaeus R.
Iris R.
Lycus R.
Scylax R.
Cappadox R.
Acampsis R.
Phasis R.
Cyrus R.
Alazonius R.
Pelorus R.
Albis R.
Araxes R.
Euphrates R.
Arsanius R.
Tigris R.
Centrites R.
Mygdonius R.
Chaboras R.
Bilechas R.
Pyramus R.
Cydnus R.
Sarus R.
Carmalas R.
Calycadnus R.
Orontes R.
Jordanus R.
Nilus R.
Lycus R.
Zabatus R.
Physcus R.
Gyndes R.
Choaspes R.
Eulaeus R.
Pasitigris R.
Caprotas R.
0 50 100 Miles
0 80 160 Km
Route of Crassus's army
Procession route of Crassus's head and hand (terrain less arduous by far on this seemingly longer route).
EAST
NORTH
32°
36°
40°
44°
48°
52°

summer one. His army, said Crassus, would be ready to march early in April, the beginning of winter. He thought that asking the troops to delay until Sextilis would reduce their enthusiasm. In my view, specious arguments. I saw no evidence of enthusiasm among Crassus's troops at any time for any reason.

Greatly displeased, King Artavasdes quit Antioch to go home; he had hoped, of course, to usurp the Parthian kingdom for himself through an alliance with Rome. But having been rejected, he decided to throw in his lot with the Parthians. He left Abgarus in Antioch to spy; from the time Artavasdes vanished, everything Crassus did was reported to the enemy.

Then in March an embassage arrived from King Orodes of the Parthians. The chief ambassador was a very old man named Vagises. They look so odd, Parthian nobles, with their necks throttled by coiled golden collars from chin down to shoulders; their round, brimless, pearl-encrusted hats like inverted bowls on their heads; their false beards held on by golden wires around their ears; their gold tissue finery sparkling with fabulous jewels and pearls. I think all Crassus saw was the gold, the jewels and the pearls. How much more there must be in Babylonia!

Vagises asked Crassus to abide by the treaties both Sulla and Pompeius Magnus had negotiated with the Parthians: that everything west of the Euphrates should be in the dominion of Rome, and everything east of the Euphrates in the dominion of the Parthians.

Crassus actually laughed in their faces! "My dear Vagises," he said through stifled guffaws, "tell King Orodes that I will indeed think about those treaties—*after* I've conquered Seleuceia-on-Tigris and Babylonia!"

Vagises said nothing for a moment. Then he held out his right hand, and showed its palm to Crassus. "Hair will grow here, Marcus Crassus, before you set foot in Seleuceia-on-Tigris!" he shrilled. My hackles rose. The way he said it was so eerie that it rang like a prophecy.

You perceive that Marcus Crassus was not endearing himself to any of these eastern kings, who are very touchy fellows. If any but a Roman proconsul had laughed, the joker would have parted with his head on the instant. Some of us tried to reason with him, but the trouble was that he had Publius there, his own son, who adored him and thought his father could do no wrong. Publius was Crassus's echo, and he listened to his echo, not to the voices of reason.

At the beginning of April we marched northeast from Antioch. The army was morose, and consequently slow. The Aeduan horse troopers had been unhappy enough in the fertile valley of the Orontes, but once we got into the poorer pasture around Cyrrhus, they began to behave as if someone had drugged them. Nor were the three thousand Galatians optimistic. In fact, our progress was more like a funeral procession than a march into everlasting glory. Crassus himself traveled apart from the army, in a litter because the road was too rough for a carriage. To give him his due, I doubt that he was entirely well. Publius Crassus fussed about him perpetually. It is not easy for a man of sixty-three to campaign, especially one who has not been to war for almost twenty years.

Abgarus of the Skenite Arabs was not with us. He had gone ahead a month earlier. We were to meet him on the east bank of the Euphrates at Zeugma, which we reached at the end of the month. As this proves, a very leisurely march. At the beginning of winter the Euphrates is about as low and placid as it gets. I have never seen such a river! So wide and deep and *strong*! However, we should have had no difficulty crossing it on the bridge of pontoons the engineers put together, I must say, swiftly and efficiently.

But it was not to be, like so much else on this doomed expedition. Violent storms came roaring out of nowhere. Afraid that the river would rise, Crassus refused to postpone the crossing. So the soldiers crawled on all fours while the pontoons bucked and pitched, the lightning flashed thick as hawsers in a dozen places at once, the thunder set the horses screaming and bolting, and the air became suffused with a sulfurous yellow glow, along with a sweet strange scent I associate with the sea. It was horrifying. Nor did the storms let up. One after another for days. Rain so hard that the ground dissolved into soup, while the river kept rising higher and the crossing continued nonetheless.

You never saw a more disorganized force than ours was when everyone and everything were finally on the east bank. Nothing was dry, including the wheat and other food supplies in the baggage train. The ropes and springs in the artillery were swollen and flaccid, the charcoal for the smiths was useless, the tents may as well have been made from bridal fabric, and our precious store of fortification timber was split and cracked. Imagine if you can four thousand horses (Crassus refused to allow his troopers two mounts each), two thousand mules and several thousand oxen reduced to wild-eyed terror. It took two *nundinae* to calm them down, sixteen precious days which should have seen us well along the way to Mesopotamia. The legionaries were in little better condition than the animals. The expedition, they were saying among themselves, was cursed. Just as Crassus himself was cursed. They were all going to die.

But Abgarus arrived with his four thousand light-armed infantry and horse. We held a council of war. Censorinus, Vargunteius, Megabocchus and Octavius, four of Crassus's five legates, wanted to follow the course of the Euphrates all the way. It was safer, there was grazing for the animals, and we'd pick up a bit more food as we went. I agreed with them, and was told for my pains that it was not the place of a mere quaestor to advise his seniors.

Abgarus was against hugging the Euphrates. In case you do not know, it takes a great bend westward below Zeugma, which would admittedly have added many, many miles to the march. From the confluence of the Bilechas and the Euphrates on downward into Mesopotamia its course is fairly straight and in the right direction, southeast.

Therefore, said Abgarus, we could save at least four or five days of marching if we headed due east from Zeugma across the desert until we came to the Bilechas River. A sharp turn south would then take us down the Bilechas to the Euphrates, and we'd be right where we wanted to be, at Nicephorium. With him as our guide, said Abgarus winningly, we couldn't get lost, and the march through the desert was short enough to survive comfortably.

Well, Crassus agreed with Abgarus, and Publius Crassus agreed with *tata*. We would take the short cut across the desert. Again the four legates tried to persuade Crassus not to, but he wouldn't be budged. He'd fortified Carrhae and Sinnaca, he said, and these forts were all the protection he needed—though he didn't believe he needed any protection at all. Quite so, said friend King Abgarus. There would be no Parthians this far north.

But of course there were. Abgarus had made sure of that. Seleuceia-on-Tigris knew every move we made, and King Orodes was a better strategist by far than poor, money-mad Marcus Crassus.

I imagine, dearest Rome-bound Servilia, that you do not know a great deal about the Kingdom of the Parthians, so I should tell you that it is a vast conglomeration of regions. Parthia itself is to the east of the Caspian Sea, which is why we say the King of the Parthians, and not the King of Parthia. Under the sway of King Orodes are Media, Media Atropatene, Persia, Gedrosia, Carmania, Bactria, Margiana, Sogdiana, Susiana, Elymais and Mesopotamia. More land than is contained in the Roman provinces.*

Each of these regions is ruled by a satrap who bears the title of the Surenas. Most of them are the sons, nephews, cousins, brothers or uncles of the King. The King never goes to Parthia itself; he reigns in summer from Ecbatana in the softer mountains of Media, visits Susa in the spring or the autumn, and reigns during winter from Seleuceia-on-Tigris in Mesopotamia. That he devotes his time to these most western regions of his huge kingdom is probably due to Rome. He fears us, whereas he does not fear the Indians or the Sericans, both great nations. He garrisons Bactria to keep the Massagetae at bay, as they are tribes, not a nation.

*See map on back endpapers.

It so happens that the Surenas of Mesopotamia is an extremely able satrap, and to him Orodes entrusted his campaign against Crassus. King Orodes himself journeyed north to meet with King Artavasdes of Armenia in the Armenian capital, Artaxata, taking enough troops with him to ensure that he was made very welcome in Artaxata. His son Pacorus went with him. The Pahlavi Surenas (for so he is properly called) remained in Mesopotamia to marshal a separate army to deal with us. He had ten thousand horse archers and two thousand mail-clad cataphracti. No foot at all.

An interesting man, the Pahlavi Surenas. Barely thirty years old—my own age—and a nephew of the King, he is said to be very, very beautiful in a most exquisite and effeminate way. He has no congress with women, preferring boys between thirteen and fifteen. Once they are too grown for his taste, he drafts them into his army or his bureaucracy as esteemed officers. This is acceptable Parthian conduct.

What worried him as he assembled his men was a fact well known to Crassus and the rest of us—a fact which, Abgarus assured us, would see us win comfortably. Namely that the Parthian horse archer runs out of arrows very quickly. Thus, despite his skill at shooting over his horse's rump as he flees the field, he is soon useless.

The Pahlavi Surenas devised a scheme to rectify this. He marshaled enormous camel trains and loaded the camels' panniers with spare arrows. He then got together some thousands of slaves and trained them in the art of getting fresh arrows to the archers in the midst of battle. So that when he set out north from Seleuceia-on-Tigris to intercept us with his horse archers and his cataphracti, he also took thousands of camels loaded with spare arrows, and thousands of slaves to feed the arrows to the archers in an endless chain.

How can I possibly know all this? I hear you ask. I will come to that in due time, but here I will simply say that I learned of it from a fascinating prince at the Jewish court, Antipater, whose spies and sources of information are absolutely everywhere.

There is a crossroads on the Bilechas where the caravan route from Palmyra and Nicephorium meets the caravan route to the upper Euphrates at Samosata and the one which goes through Carrhae to Edessa and Amida. It was for this junction that the army set out to march across the desert.

We had thirty-five thousand Roman foot, one thousand Aeduan horse and three thousand Galatian horse. They were terrified before they so much as started into the wilderness, and grew more terrified with each day that passed. All I had to do to ascertain this was to ride among them and listen with half an ear: Crassus was cursed, they were all going to die. Mutiny was never a risk, for mutinous troops are, to say the least, energetic. *Our* men were devoid of hope.

They simply shuffled on to meet their doom like captives going to the slave markets. The Aeduan cavalry were worst. Never in their lives had they seen a waterless waste, a dun drear landscape without shelter or beauty. They turned their eyes inward and ceased to care about anything.

Two days out, heading southeast for the Bilechas, we began to see small bands of Parthians, usually horse archers, sometimes cataphracti. Not that they bothered us. They would ride in fairly close, then spur off again. I know now that they were liaising with Abgarus and reporting back about us to the Pahlavi Surenas, who was camped outside Nicephorium, at the confluence of the Bilechas and the Euphrates.

On the fourth day before the Ides of June we reached the Bilechas, where I begged Marcus Crassus to build a strongly fortified camp and put the troops into it for long enough to enable the legates and tribunes to try to put some stiffening into them. But Crassus wouldn't hear of it. He was fretful because we'd been on the march so long already; he wanted to reach the canals where the Euphrates and the Tigris almost marry before summer clamped down, and he was beginning to wonder if he was going to succeed. So he ordered the troops to take a quick meal and march on down the Bilechas. It was still early in the afternoon.

Suddenly I became aware that King Abgarus and his four thousand men had literally disappeared. Gone! Some Galatian scouts came galloping up, shouting that the countryside was swarming with Parthians, but they had barely managed to attract anyone's attention when a storm of arrows came thrumming from every direction and the soldiers began falling like leaves, like stones—I have never seen anything as fast or as vicious as that hail of arrows.

Crassus didn't do anything. He simply let it happen.

"It'll be over in a moment," he shouted from beneath a shelter of shields; "they'll run out of arrows."

They did not run out of arrows. There were Roman soldiers fleeing all over the place, and falling. Falling. Finally Crassus had the buglers blow "form square," but it was far too late. The cataphracti moved in for the kill, huge men on huge horses dark with chain mail. I discovered that when they advance at a trot—they are too big and ponderous to move at a canter—they jingle like a million coins in a thousand purses. I wonder did Crassus find it music to his ears? The earth shakes as they pound along. The dust rises in a huge column, and they turn and tread it up around them so that they come out of it rather than ride ahead of it.

Publius Crassus gathered the Aeduan cavalry, who seemed suddenly to come to their senses. Perhaps a battle was the only familiar thing they had to cling to. The Galatians followed, and four thousand of our horsemen charged into the cataphracti like bulls with pepper up their nostrils. The cataphracti broke and fled, Publius Crassus and his horsemen behind them, into the dust fog. During this respite, Crassus managed to form his square. Then we waited for the Aeduans and the Galatians to reappear, praying to every God we knew. But it was the cataphracti who returned. They had Publius Crassus's head on a spear. Instead of attacking our square, they trotted back and forth along its sides brandishing that awful head. Publius Crassus seemed to *look* at us; we could see his eyes flash, and his face was quite unmarred.

His father was devastated—there are no words to tell that story. But it seemed to give him something I had not seen him display since the campaign began. Up and down the square he went, cheering the men on, encouraging them to hold fast, telling them that his own son had purchased the precious moments they had needed with his life, but that the grief was Crassus's alone.

"Stand!" he cried, over and over. "Stand!"

We stood, hideously thinned by the never-ending rain of arrows, until darkness fell and the Parthians drew off. They do not seem to fight at night.

Having built no camp, we had nothing to keep us there. Crassus elected to retreat at once to Carrhae, about forty miles away to the north. By dawn we began to arrive, straggling, perhaps half the infantry and a handful of horse troopers. Futile! Impossible. Carrhae owned a small fortress, but nothing capable of protecting so many men, so much disorder.

I daresay that Carrhae has stood there at the junction of the caravan routes to Edessa and Amida for two thousand years, and I daresay it hasn't changed in those two thousand years. A pathetic little collection of beehive-shaped mud brick houses in the midst of a stony, desolate wilderness—dirty sheep, dirty goats, dirty women, dirty children, dirty river—great wheels of dried dung the only source of warmth in the bitter cold, the only glory the night skies.

The prefect Coponius was in command of the garrison, a scant cohort strong. As we dribbled in, more and more, he was horrified. We had no food because the Parthians had captured our baggage train; most of the men and horses were wounded. We couldn't stay in Carrhae, so much was obvious.

Crassus held a council, and it was decided to retreat at nightfall to Sinnaca, as far away again northeast in the direction of Amida. It was much better fortified and had at least several granaries. *The wrong direction entirely!* I wanted to yell. But Coponius had brought a man of Carrhae to the council with him. Andromachus. And Andromachus swore huge oaths that the Parthians were lying in wait between Carrhae and Edessa, Carrhae and Samosata, Carrhae and anywhere along the Euphrates. Andromachus then offered to guide us to Sinnaca, and from there to Amida. Bent over with grief for Publius, Crassus accepted the offer. Oh, he *was* cursed! Whatever decision he made was the wrong one. Andromachus was the local Parthian spy.

I knew. I knew, I knew, I knew. As the day dragged on I became ever more firmly convinced that to go to Sinnaca under the guidance of Andromachus was to die. So I called my own council. Invited Crassus. He didn't come. The others did—Censorinus, Megabocchus, Octavius, Vargunteius, Coponius, Egnatius. Plus a disgustingly dirty, tattered group of local soothsayers and magi; Coponius had been in this unspeakable anus of the world for long enough to have gathered them to him as flies gather on a putrescent carcass. I told those who came that they could do whatever they liked, but that as soon as night fell I was riding southwest for Syria, not northeast for Sinnaca. If the Parthians were lying in wait, I'd take my chances. But, I said, I refused to believe they were. No more Skenite guides for me!

Coponius demurred. So did the others. It was not fit or proper for the General's legates, tribunes and prefects to abandon him. Nor for the General's quaestor to abandon him. The only one who agreed with me was the prefect Egnatius.

No, they said, they would stand by Marcus Crassus.

I lost my temper—a Cassian flaw, I admit. "Then stay to die!" I shouted. "Those who would rather live had better find a horse in a hurry, because I'm riding for Syria and trusting to none but my own star!"

The soothsayers squawked and fluttered. "No, Gaius Cassius!" wheezed the most ancient of them, hung with amulets and rodent backbones and horrible agate eyes. "Go, yes, but not yet! The Moon is still in Scorpio! Wait for it to enter Sagittarius!"

I looked at them. Couldn't help laughing. "Thank you for the advice," I said, "but this is desert. I'd far rather have the Scorpion than the Archer!"

About five hundred of us rode off at a gallop and spent the night between a walk, a trot, a canter and another gallop. By dawn we reached Europus, which the locals call Carchemish. There were no Parthians lying in wait, and the Euphrates was calm enough to boat across, horses and all. We didn't stop until we reached Antioch.

Later I learned that the Pahlavi Surenas got everyone who elected to stay with the General. At dawn on the second day before the Ides, as we rode into Europus, Crassus and the army were wandering in circles, getting not one mile closer to Sinnaca, thanks to Andromachus. The Parthians attacked again. It was a rout. A debacle. In a disastrous series of retreats and attempted stands, the Parthians cut them down. Those legates who remained with Crassus died—Censorinus, Vargunteius, Megabocchus, Octavius, Coponius.

The Pahlavi Surenas had his orders. Marcus Crassus was captured alive. He was to be saved to stand before King Orodes. How it happened no one knows, even Antipater, but shortly after Crassus was taken into custody a fight broke out. Marcus Crassus died.

Seven silver Eagles passed into the hands of the Pahlavi Surenas at Carrhae. We will never see them again. They have gone with King Orodes to Ecbatana.

Thus did I find myself the most senior Roman in Syria, and in charge of a province on the verge of panic. Everyone was convinced the Parthians were coming, and there was no army. I spent the next two months fortifying Antioch to withstand *anything,* and organized a system of watches, lookouts and beacons which would give the entire populace of the Orontes Valley time to take shelter inside the city. Then—would you believe it?—soldiers started to trickle in. Not everyone had died at Carrhae. I collected about ten thousand of them, all told. Enough to make two good legions. And according to my invaluable informant Antipater, ten thousand more who survived the first fight further down the Bilechas were rounded up by the Pahlavi Surenas and sent to the frontier of Bactria beyond the Caspian Sea, where they are to be used to keep the Massagetae from raiding. Arrows do wound, but few men die of them.

By November I felt secure enough to tour my province. Well, it is mine. The Senate has made no move to relieve me. At the age of thirty, Gaius Cassius Longinus is governor of Syria. An extraordinary responsibility, but not one which is beyond my talents.

I went to Damascus first, and then to Tyre. Because Tyrian purple is so beautiful, we tend to think that Tyre must be too. But it is a ghastly place. Stinking to the point of constant nausea with dead shellfish. There are huge hills of boiled-down murex remains all around the landward side of Tyre, taller than the buildings, which seem to kiss the sky. How the Tyrians live there on that island of festering death and fabulous incomes I do not know. However, Fortune favors the governor of Syria. I was housed in the villa of the chief *ethnarch,* Demetrius, a luxurious residence on the seaward side of the city, where the breezes blow down the length of Our Sea and the rotting shellfish are but a memory.

Here I met the man whose name I have already mentioned: Antipater. About forty-eight years old, and very powerful in the Kingdom of the Jews. Religiously he says he is a Jew, but by blood he is an Idumaean, apparently not quite the same thing as a Judaean. He offended the synod, which is the governing religious body, by marrying a Nabataean princess named Cypros. Since the Jews count citizenship in the mother's line, it means Antipater's three sons and daughter are not Jews. All of which in essence means that Antipater, a very ambitious man, cannot become King of the Jews. Nor can his sons. However, nothing will part Antipater from Cypros, who travels everywhere with him. A devoted couple. Their three sons, still adolescent, are formidable for their age. The eldest, Phasael, is impressive enough, but the second boy, Herod, is extraordinary. You might call him a perfect fusion of tortuous cunning and ferocious ruthlessness. I want to govern Syria again ten years from now just to see how Herod has turned out.

Antipater regaled me with the Parthian side of poor Marcus Crassus's fatal expedition, and then gave me more interesting news still. The Pahlavi Surenas of Mesopotamia, having done so brilliantly on the Bilechas, was summoned to the summer court at Ecbatana. Do not, if you are a subject of the King of the Parthians, fare better than your king. Orodes was delighted at the defeat of Crassus, but not at all pleased at the innovative generalship of the Pahlavi Surenas, his blood nephew. Orodes put the Pahlavi Surenas to death. In Rome, you triumph following a victory. In Ecbatana, you lose your head following a victory.

By the time I met Antipater in Tyre, I had two good legions under arms, but no campaign whereby to blood them. That changed very rapidly. The Jews were stirring now that the Parthian menace was gone. Though Aristobulus and his son Antigonus were returned to Rome by Gabinius after *their* revolt, another son of Aristobulus's named Alexander decided the time was right to throw Hyrcanus off the Jewish throne Gabinius had put him on. Thanks to Antipater's work, I add. Well, all Syria knew the governor was a mere quaestor. What an opportunity. Two other high-ranking Jews, Malichus and Peitholaus, conspired to help Alexander.

So I marched for Hierosolyma, or Jerusalem if you like that name better. Though I didn't get that far before I met the rebel Jewish army, over thirty thousand strong. The battle took place where the Jordanus River emerges from Lake Gennesarus. Yes, I was outnumbered badly, but Peitholaus, who was in command, had simply herded together an untrained mob of upcountry Galilaeans, put pots on their heads and swords in their hands, and told them to go out and beat two trained, disciplined (and, after Carrhae, chastened) Roman legions. I trounced them, and my troops have regained much of their confidence. They hailed me imperator on the field, though I doubt the Senate will award a mere quaestor a triumph. Antipater advised me to put Peitholaus to death. I followed his advice. Antipater is no Skenite traitor, though it seems many of the Jews would not agree with my evaluation. They want to rule their own little corner of the world without Rome looking over their shoulders. It is Antipater, however, who is the realist. Rome will not be going away.

Not many of the Galilaeans perished. I sent thirty thousand of them to the slave markets in Antioch, and have thus made my first personal profit from commanding an army. Tertulla is going to marry a much richer man!

Antipater is a good man. Sensible, subtle and *very* keen both to please Rome and keep the Jews from killing each other. They seem to suffer enormous internecine conflicts unless an outsider comes along to take their minds off their troubles, like Romans or (in the old days) Egyptians.

Hyrcanus still has his throne and his high priesthood. The surviving rebels, Malichus and Alexander, came to heel without a murmur.

And now I come to the last few pages in the book of Marcus Crassus's remarkable career. He died after Carrhae in that place, yes, but he had yet to make a journey. The Pahlavi Surenas cut off his head and his right hand, and sent them in the midst of an outlandish parade from Carrhae to Artaxata, the capital of Armenia far to the north amid the towering snowy mountains where the Araxes flows down to the Caspian Sea. Here King Orodes and King Artavasdes, having met, decided to be brothers rather than enemies, and to seal their pact with a marriage. Pacorus, the son of Orodes, married Laodice, the daughter of Artavasdes. Some things are the same as in Rome.

While the festivities were going on in Ataxata, the outlandish parade wended its way north. The Parthians had captured and kept alive a centurion named Gaius Paccianus because he bore a striking physical resemblance to Marcus Crassus—tall, yet so thickset that he seemed short, with that same bovine look to him. They dressed Paccianus in Crassus's *toga praetexta,* and before him they put capering clowns dressed as lictors bearing bundles of rods tied together with Roman entrails, adorned with money purses and the heads of his legates. Behind the mock Marcus Crassus pranced dancing girls and whores, musicians singing filthy songs, and some men displaying pornographic books found in the baggage of the tribune Roscius. Crassus's head and hand came next and, bringing up the rear, our seven Eagles.

Apparently King Artavasdes of Armenia is a fanatical lover of Greek drama. Orodes also speaks Greek, so several of the most famous Greek plays were staged as part of the entertainment celebrating the wedding of Pacorus and Laodice. The evening on which the parade arrived in Artaxata saw a performance of *The Bacchae* of Euripides. Well, you know that play. The part of Queen Agave was portrayed by a locally famous actor, Jason of Tralles. But Jason of Tralles is more famous for his hatred of Romans than even for his brilliant interpretation of female roles.

In the last scene, Agave comes in bearing the head of her son, King Pentheus, upon a platter, having torn his head off herself in a Bacchic frenzy.

When the time came, in walked Queen Agave. On her platter she bore the head of Marcus Crassus. Jason of Tralles put the platter down, pulled off his mask, and picked up Crassus's head, an easy thing to do because, like so many bald men, Crassus had grown the hair on the back of his head very long so he could comb it forward. Grinning triumphantly, the actor swung the head back and forth as if it were a lamp.

"Blessed is the prey I bear, new shorn from the trunk!" he cried out.

"Who slew him?" chanted the Chorus.

"Mine was that honor!" shrieked Pomaxarthres, a senior officer in the army of the Pahlavi Surenas.

They say the scene went down very well.

The head and the right hand were displayed, and as far as I know are still displayed, on the battlements of Artaxata's walls. Crassus's body was left exactly where it had fallen near Carrhae, to be picked clean by the vultures.

Oh, Marcus! That it should have come to this. Could you not see where it would all end, and how? Ateius Capito cursed you. The Jews cursed you. Your own army believed those curses, and you did nothing to disabuse them. Fifteen thousand good Roman soldiers are dead, ten thousand more sentenced to life on an alien frontier, my Aeduan cavalry are gone, most of the Galatians are gone, and Syria is being governed by an enterprising, insufferably arrogant and conceited young man whose contemptuous words about you are the words which will follow you for all time. The Parthians may have assassinated your person, but Gaius Cassius has assassinated your character. I know which fate I would prefer.

Your wonderful older son is dead. He too is vulture fodder. In the desert it is not necessary to burn and bury. Old King Mithridates tied Manius Aquillius backward on an ass, then tipped molten gold down his gullet to cure his avarice. Was that what Orodes and Artavasdes planned for you? But you cheated them of that; you died cleanly before they could do it. A poor, hapless centurion, Paccianus, probably suffered that fate in your place. And your eye sockets gaze sightlessly over a vista of endless, freezingly cold mountains toward the icy infinity of the Caucasus.

Caesar sat, remembering, for a long time. How pleased Crassus had been that the Pontifex Maximus had installed a bell he was too stingy to pay for himself. How competently and placidly he had walled Spartacus in through a time of snows. How difficult it had been to persuade him and Pompey to embrace publicly on the rostra when their first joint consulship ended. How easily he had issued the instructions which had saved Caesar from the hands of the moneylenders and permanent exile. How pleasant the many, many hours they had spent together over the years between Spartacus and Gaul. How desperately Crassus had hungered for a great military campaign and a triumph at the end of it.

The dear sight of that big, bland, impassive face at Luca.

All gone. Picked clean by the vultures. Not burned, not entombed. Caesar stiffened. Had anyone thought of it? He pulled paper toward him, dipped his reed pen in the inkwell and wrote to his friend Messala Rufus in Rome to buy the shades of those who had lost their heads a passage to the proper place.

I am, he thought, screwing up his eyes, become an authority on severed heads.

Luckily Lucius Cornelius Balbus Major was with Caesar when he received Pompey's answer to his letter proposing two marriages and requesting legislation to enable him to stand for the consulship *in absentia.*

"I am so alone," Caesar said to Balbus, but without self-pity. Then he shrugged. "Still, it happens as one grows older."

"Until," said Balbus gently, "one retires to enjoy the fruits of one's labors, and has time to lie back among friends."

The perceptive eyes began to twinkle, the generous mouth to curl up at its dented corners. "What an awful prospect! I do not intend to retire, Balbus."

"Don't you think there will ever come a time when there is nothing left to do?"

"Not for this Roman, if any Roman. When Gaul and my second consulship are over, I must avenge Marcus Crassus. I'm still reeling from that shock, let alone this." Caesar tapped Pompey's letter.

"And the death of Publius Clodius?"

The twinkle vanished, the mouth set. "The death of Publius Clodius was inevitable. His tampering with the *mos maiorum* could not be allowed to continue. Young Curio put it best in his letter to me—odd, the disparate people Clodius's activities managed to throw into the same camp. He said that Clodius was going to hand a congress of Roman men over to a parcel of non-Romans."

Balbus, a non-Roman Roman citizen, did not blink. "They say that young Curio is extremely distressed financially."

"Do they?" Caesar looked thoughtful. "Do we need him?"

"At the moment, no. But that might change."

"What do you make of Pompeius in the light of his reply?"

"What do you make of him, Caesar?"

"I'm not sure, but I do know that I made a mistake in trying to woo him with more marriages. He's grown very particular in his choice of wives, so much is sure. The daughter of an Octavius and an Ancharia isn't good enough, or so I read it between his lines. Maybe I ought to have said straight out what I imagined he would see for himself without such bluntness—that as soon as the younger Octavia was of marriageable age, I would be happy to slip the first Octavia out from under him and substitute the second girl. Though the first would have suited him very well. Not a Julian, no, but brought up by a Julian. It shows, Balbus."

"I doubt that an *air* of aristocracy operates as profoundly upon Pompeius as a pedigree," said Balbus with the ghost of a smile.

"I wonder whom he has in mind."

"That's really why I've come to Ravenna, Caesar. A little bird perched on my shoulder and chirruped that the *boni* are dangling the widow of Publius Crassus under his nose."

Caesar sat up straight. *"Cacat!"* He relaxed, shook his head. "Metellus Scipio would never do it, Balbus. Besides, I know the young woman. She's no Julia. I doubt she'd permit the likes of Pompeius to touch the hem of her robe, let alone lift it."

"One of the problems," said Balbus deliberately, "to do with your rise into Rome's firmament, despite all that the *boni* have tried to do to prevent it, is that the *boni* have grown desperate enough to contemplate using Pompeius in much the same way that you use him. And how else can they bind him except through a marriage so stellar that he wouldn't dare offend them? To dower him with Cornelia Metella is literally to admit him into their ranks. Pompeius would see Cornelia Metella as confirmation from the *boni* that he is indeed the First Man in Rome."

"So you think it's possible."

"Oh, yes. The young woman is a cool person, Caesar. If she saw herself as an absolute necessity, she'd go to the sacrifice as willingly as Iphigenia at Aulis."

"Though for far different reasons."

"Yes and no. I doubt any man will ever satisfy Cornelia Metella in the way that her own father does, and Metellus Scipio bears some resemblance to Agamemnon. Cornelia Metella is in love with her *own* aristocracy, to the extent that she would refuse to believe a Pompeius from Picenum could detract from it."

"Then," said Caesar with decision, "I won't move from this side of the Alps to the far side in a hurry this year. I'll have to monitor events in Rome too thoroughly." He clenched his teeth. "Oh, where has my luck gone? In a family famous for breeding more girls than boys, it can't produce a girl when I need one."

"It isn't your luck carries you through, Caesar," said Balbus firmly. "You'll survive."

"I take it Cicero is coming to Ravenna?"

"Very shortly."

"Good. Young Caelius has potential he ought not to waste on the likes of Milo."

"Who can't be allowed to become consul."

"He belongs to Cato and Bibulus."

But when Balbus withdrew, Caesar's thoughts did not dwell upon events in Rome. They drifted to Syria and to the loss of seven silver Eagles no doubt displayed at this moment with great ostentation in the halls of the Parthian palace at Ecbatana. They would have to be wrested from Orodes, and that meant war with Orodes. Probably also war with Artavasdes of Armenia. Ever since he'd read Gaius Cassius's letter, a part of Caesar's mind had stayed in the East, wrestling with the concept of a strategy capable of conquering a mighty empire and two mighty armies. Lucullus had shown that it could be done at Tigranocerta. Then had undone everything. Or rather, had allowed Publius Clodius to undo it. At least that was one good piece of news. Clodius was dead. *And there will never be a Clodius in any army of mine.* I will need Decimus Brutus, Gaius Trebonius, Gaius Fabius and Titus Sextius. Splendid men all. They know how my mind works, they're able to lead and to obey. But *not* Titus Labienus. I do not want him for the Parthian campaign. He can finish his time in Gaul, but after that I am finished with him.

Knitting up a structure for Gaul of the Long-hairs had proven an extremely difficult business, though Caesar knew how to do it. And one of the linchpins was to forge a good relationship with sufficient Gallic leaders to ensure two things: the first, that the Gauls themselves would feel they had a powerful say in their future; and the second, that the chosen Gallic leaders were absolutely committed to Rome. Not the Acco or Vercingetorix kind, but the Commius and Vertico kind, convinced that the best chance for the preservation of Gallic customs and traditions lay in sheltering behind the Roman shield. Oh, Commius wanted to be High King of the Belgae, yes, but that was permissible. In it were planted the seeds of Belgic fusion into one people rather than many peoples. Rome dealt well with client kings; there were a dozen within the fold.

But Titus Labienus was not a deep thinker, nor political. And he had conceived a hatred for Commius based on the fact that Commius had preferred not to use Labienus as his conduit to Caesar.

Aware of this, Caesar had always been careful to keep a distance between Labienus and King Commius of the Atrebates. Though until Hirtius had come in a hurry from Further Gaul yesterday, he hadn't realized the reason behind Labienus's request that Gaius Volusenus Quadratus, a military tribune senior enough for a prefecture, be seconded to duty with him over the winter.

"Another one who hates Commius," said Hirtius, looking worn out from his journey. "They hatched a plot."

"Volusenus hates Commius? Why?" asked Caesar, frowning.

"It happened during the second expedition to Britannia, I gather. The usual thing. They both fancied the same woman."

"Who spurned Volusenus in favor of Commius."

"Exactly. Well, why should she not? She was a Briton, and already under Commius's protection. I remember her. Pretty girl."

"Sometimes," said Caesar wearily, "I wish we just went off somewhere and *budded*. Women are a complication we men do not need to suffer."

"I suspect," said Hirtius, smiling, "that women often feel the same way."

"Which philosophical discussion is not getting us any closer to the truth about Volusenus and Labienus. What sort of plot did they hatch?"

"The report came to me from Labienus that Commius was preaching sedition."

"Is that all? Did Labienus give details?"

"Only that Commius was going about among the Menapii, the Nervii and the Eburones stirring up a new revolt."

"Among three tribes reduced to skeletons?"

"And that he was thick with Ambiorix."

"A convenient name to use. But I would have thought Commius would deem Ambiorix more a threat to his cherished high kingship than an ally willing to put him there."

"I agree. Which is why I began to smell rotting fish. A long acquaintance with Commius has convinced me that he knows very well who can assist him onto his throne—you."

"What else?"

"Had Labienus said no more, I might not have stirred out of Samarobriva," said Hirtius. "It was the last part of his typically curt letter which made me decide to seek more information about this so-called plot from Labienus himself."

"What did he say?"

"That I was not to worry. That *he* would deal with Commius."

"Ah!" Caesar sat forward and linked his hands between his knees. "So you went to see Labienus?"

"Too late, Caesar. The deed was done. Labienus summoned Commius to a parley. Instead of going himself, he deputed Volusenus to go on his behalf. With a guard of hand-picked centurions from among Labienus's cronies. Commius—who cannot have suspected any foul play—appeared with a few friends, no troops. I imagine he wasn't pleased to discover Volusenus there, though what the truth of the matter is I can have no idea. All I know is what Labienus told me with a mixture of pride in his own cleverness at thinking of the scheme, and chagrin that it went amiss."

"Are you trying to say," asked Caesar incredulously, "that Labienus intended to *assassinate* Commius?"

"Oh, yes," said Hirtius simply. "He made no secret of it. According to Labienus, you're an absolute fool for trusting Commius. Labienus *knows* he's plotting sedition."

"Without proof which would stand up to close examination?"

"He could produce none when I pressed the matter, certainly. Just kept insisting he was right and you were wrong. You know the man, Caesar. He's a force of nature!"

"What happened?"

"Volusenus had instructed one of the centurions to do the killing, while the other centurions were to concentrate on making sure none of the Atrebatans escaped. The signal for the centurion to strike was the moment in which Volusenus extended his hand to shake Commius's."

"Jupiter! What are we, adherents of Mithridates? That's the sort of ploy an eastern king would use! Ohhh . . . Go on."

"Volusenus extended his hand, Commius extended his. The centurion whipped his sword from behind his back and swung it. Either his eye was out or he misliked the task. He caught Commius across the brow, a glancing blow which didn't even break the bone or render him unconscious. Volusenus drew his sword, but Commius was gone, gushing blood. The Atrebatans formed up around their king and extricated themselves without anyone else's so much as being wounded."

"If I hadn't heard it from you, Hirtius, I would never have believed it," said Caesar slowly.

"Believe it, Caesar, believe it!"

"So Rome has lost a very valuable ally."

"I would think so." Hirtius produced a slender scroll. "I received this from Commius. It was waiting when I returned to Samarobriva. I haven't opened it because it is intended for you. Rather than write to you, I came in person."

Caesar took the scroll, broke its seal and spread it.

> I have been betrayed, and I have every reason to think that it was your doing, Caesar. You don't keep men working for you who disobey orders or act on their own initiative to this extent. I had thought you honorable, so I write this with a grief as painful as my head. You can keep your high kingship. I will throw in my lot with my own people, who are above this kind of assassination. We kill each other, yes, but not without honor. You have none. I have made a vow. That never again as long as I live will I come into the presence of a Roman voluntarily.

"The world at the moment seems to be an endless torment of severed heads," said Caesar, white about the lips, "but I tell you, Aulus Hirtius, that it would give me great pleasure to lop the head off Labienus's shoulders! A fraction of an inch at a time. But not before I had him flogged just enough."

"What do you intend to do in actuality?"

"Nothing whatsoever."

Hirtius looked shocked. *"Nothing?"*

"Nothing."

"But—but—you can at least say what happened in your next dispatch to the Senate!" cried Hirtius. "It may not be the kind of punishment you would prefer to dish out to Labienus, but it will certainly kill any hopes he might have of a public career."

The expression on Caesar's face as he turned his head and tucked his chin in was derisive, angrily amused. "I can't do that, Hirtius! Look at the trouble Cato made for me over the so-called German ambassadors! Were I to breathe a word of this to the Senate or any other persons who would leak it to Cato, *my* name would stink to the farthest reaches of the sky. Not Labienus's. Those senatorial dogs wouldn't waste an expirated breath in baying for Labienus's hide. They'd be too busy fixing their teeth in mine."

"You're right, of course," said Hirtius, sighing. "Which means that Labienus will get away with it."

"For the moment," said Caesar tranquilly. "His time will come, Hirtius. When next I see him, he'll know exactly where he stands in my estimation. And where his career is going to go if I have any say in the matter. As soon as his usefulness in Gaul is over, I'll divorce him more thoroughly than Sulla did his poor dying wife."

"And Commius? Perhaps if I worked very hard, Caesar, I could persuade him to meet with you privately. It wouldn't take long to make him see your side of it."

Caesar shook his head. "No, Hirtius. It wouldn't work. My relationship with Commius was based on complete mutual trust, and that is gone. From this time forward each of us would look askance at the other. He took a vow never again voluntarily to come into the presence of a Roman. The Gauls take such vows quite as seriously as we do. I've lost Commius."

Lingering in Ravenna was not a hardship. Caesar kept a villa there because he also kept a school for gladiators there; the climate was considered the best in all Italia and was ague-free, which made Ravenna a wonderful place for hard physical training.

Keeping gladiators was a profitable hobby, one Caesar found so absorbing he had several thousand, though most of them were billeted in a school near Capua. Ravenna was reserved for the cream of them, the ones Caesar had plans for after they finished their time in the sawdust ring.

His agents bought or acquired through the military courts none but the most promising fellows, and the five or six years these men spent exhibition-fighting were good years if Caesar was their owner. They were mainly deserters from the legions (offered a choice between disenfranchisement and life as a gladiator), though some were convicted murderers, and a few volunteered their services. These last Caesar would never accept, saying that a free Roman with a taste for battle should enlist in the legions.

They were well housed, well fed and not overworked, as indeed was true of most gladiatorial schools, which were not prisons. The men came and went as they pleased unless they were booked for a bout, before which they were expected to stay in school, remain sober and train industriously; no man who owned gladiators wanted to see his expensive investment killed or maimed in the ring.

Gladiatorial combat was an extremely popular spectator sport, though it was not a circus activity; it required a smaller venue like a town marketplace. Traditionally a rich man who had suffered a bereavement celebrated the memory of the dead relative with funeral games, and funeral games consisted of gladiatorial combat. He hired his sawdust soldiers from one of the many gladiatorial schools, usually between four and forty pairs, for whom he paid very heavily. They came to the town, they fought, they departed back to school. And at the end of six years or thirty bouts they retired, having completed their sentence. Their citizenship was secure, they had saved some money, and the really good ones had become public idols whose names were known all over Italia.

One of the reasons the sport interested Caesar lay in the fate of these men once they had served their time. To Caesar, men with the kind of skills these men had acquired were wasted once they drifted to Rome or some other city and there hired themselves out as bodyguards or bouncers. He preferred to woo them for his legions, but not as rankers. A good gladiator who hadn't suffered too many blows to the head made an excellent instructor in military training camp, and some made splendid centurions. It also amused him to send deserters from the legions back to the legions as officers.

Thus the school in Ravenna, where he kept his best men; the majority lived in the school he owned near Capua. The Capuan school of course had not seen him since he assumed his governorships, for the governor of a province could not set foot in Italia proper while ever he commanded an army.

There were other reasons too why Ravenna saw Caesar for longer than any other place in Illyricum or Italian Gaul. It was close to the Rubicon River, the boundary between Italian Gaul and Italia proper, and the roads between it and Rome, two hundred miles away, were excellent. Which meant fast travel for the couriers who rode back and forth constantly, and comfortable travel for the many people who came from Rome to see Caesar in person, since he could not go to see them.

After the death of Clodius he followed events in Rome with some anxiety, absolutely sure that Pompey was aiming at the dictatorship. For this reason had he written to Pompey with his marriage and other proposals, though afterward he wished he had not; rejection left a sour taste in the mouth. Pompey had grown so great that he didn't think it necessary to please anyone save himself, even Caesar. Who perhaps was becoming a trifle too famous these days for Pompey's comfort. Yet when Pompey's Law of the Ten Tribunes of the Plebs gave Caesar permission to stand for the consulship *in absentia,* he wondered if his misgivings about Pompey were simply the imaginings of a man forced to obtain all his news at second hand. Oh, for the chance to spend a month in Rome! But one drip of one hour was impossible. A governor with eleven legions under his command, Caesar was forbidden to cross the river Rubicon into Italia.

Would Pompey succeed in being appointed Dictator? Rome and the Senate in the persons of men like Bibulus and Cato were resisting it strenuously, but sitting in Ravenna at a distance from the convulsions which wracked Rome every day, it wasn't difficult to see whose was the hand behind the violence. Pompey's. Yearning to be Dictator. Trying to force the Senate's hand.

Then when the news came that Pompey had been made consul without a colleague, Caesar burst out laughing. As brilliant as it was unconstitutional! The *boni* had tied Pompey's hands even as they put the reins of government into them. And Pompey had been naive enough to fall for it. Yet another unconstitutional extraordinary command! While failing to see that in accepting it, he had shown all of Rome—and especially Caesar—that he did not have the sinew or the gall to keep grinding on until he was offered a perfectly constitutional command: the dictatorship.

You'll always be a country boy, Pompeius Magnus! Not quite up to every trick in town. They outfoxed you so deftly that you don't even see what they've done. You're sitting there on the Campus Martius congratulating yourself that you're the winner. But you are not. Bibulus and Cato are the winners. They exposed your bluff and you backed down. How Sulla would laugh!

The main *oppidum* of the Senones was Agedincum on the Icauna River, and here Caesar had concentrated six of his legions for the winter; he was still unsure of that very powerful tribe's loyalties, particularly in light of the fact that he had been forced to execute Acco.

Gaius Trebonius occupied the interior of Agedincum himself, and had the high command while Caesar was in Italian Gaul. Which did not mean he had been given the authority to go to war, a fact all the Gallic tribes were aware of. And were counting on.

In January Trebonius's energies were absorbed by the most exasperating task a commander knew: he had to find sufficient grain and other supplies to feed thirty-six thousand men. The harvest was coming in, so bountiful this year that, had he had fewer legions to provision, Trebonius would not have needed to go any further than the local fields. As it was, he had to buy far and wide.

The actual buying-in of grain was in the hands of a civilian Roman, the knight Gaius Fufius Cita; an old resident of Gaul, he spoke the languages and enjoyed a good relationship with the tribes of this central region. Off he trotted with his cartload of money and a heavily armed three-cohort guard to see which Gallic thanes were of a mind to sell at least a part of their harvest. In his wake trundled the high-sided wagons drawn by teams of ten oxen poled up two abreast; as each wagon filled with the precious wheat it peeled off from the column and returned to Agedincum, where it was unloaded and sent back to Fufius Cita.

Having exhausted the territory to the north of the Icauna and the Sequana, Fufius Cita and his commissioners transferred to the lands of the Mandubii, the Lingones and the Senones. At first the wagons continued to fill in a most satisfactory manner; then as the seemingly endless caravan entered the lands of the Senones, the amount of grain to be had dropped dramatically. The execution of Acco was having an effect; Fufius Cita decided that he would not prosper trying to buy from the Senones, so he moved westward into the lands of the Carnutes. Where sales picked up immediately.

Delighted, Fufius Cita and his senior commissioners settled down inside Cenabum, the Carnute capital; here was a safe haven for the cartload of money (it was, besides, not nearly as full as it had been) and no need for the three cohorts of troops who had escorted him. He sent them back to Agedincum. Cenabum was almost a second home for Fufius Cita; he would remain there among his Roman friends and conclude his purchasing in comfort.

Cenabum, in fact, was something of a Gallic metropolis. It permitted some wealthier people—mostly Romans but also a few Greeks—to live inside the walls, and had quite a township outside the walls wherein thrived a metal-working industry. Only Avaricum was larger, and if Fufius Cita sighed a little as he thought of Avaricum, he was actually well content where he was.

The pact among Vercingetorix, Lucterius, Litaviccus, Cotus, Gutruatus and Sedulius, though made in the highly emotional aftermath of Acco's execution, had not fallen by the wayside. Each man went off to his people and talked, and if some of them made no reference to unification of all the Gallic peoples under one leadership, they did harp relentlessly on the perfidy and arrogance of the Romans, the unjustifiable death of Acco, the loss of liberty. Very fertile ground to work; Gaul still hungered to throw off the Roman yoke.

Gutruatus of the Carnutes had needed little to push him into the pact with Vercingetorix; he was well aware that Caesar deemed him as guilty of treason as Acco. The next back to feel the lash and the next head to roll belonged to him. He knew it. Nor did he care, provided that before it happened he had managed to make Caesar's life a misery. So when he returned to his own lands, he did as he had promised Vercingetorix: he went straight to Carnutum, where the Druids dwelled, and sought Cathbad.

"You are right," said Cathbad when the story of Acco was finished. The Chief Druid paused, then added, "Vercingetorix is right too, Gutruatus. We must unite and drive the Romans out as one people. We cannot do it otherwise. I will summon the Druids to a council."

"And I," said Gutruatus, enthusiasm soaring, "will travel among the Carnutes to spread the warcry!"

"Warcry? What warcry?"

"The words Dumnorix and Acco both shouted before they were killed. 'A free man in a free country!' "

"Excellent!" said Cathbad. "But amend it. 'Free men in a free country!' That is the beginning of unification, Gutruatus. When a man thinks of men before he thinks in the singular."

The Carnutes met in groups, always far from Roman ears, to talk insurrection. And the smithies outside Cenabum began to make nothing but mail shirts, a change of activity which Fufius Cita did not notice any more than his fellow foreign residents did.

By mid-February the harvest was completely in. Every silo and granary across the country was full; the hams had been smoked, the pork and venison salted, the eggs and beets and apples stored down under the ground, the chickens, ducks and geese penned in, the cattle and sheep removed from the path of any marching army.

"It's time to start," said Gutruatus to his fellow thanes, "and we Carnutes will lead the way. As the leaders of Gallic thought, it behooves us to strike the first blow. And we have to do it while Caesar is on the other side of the Alps. The signs say we're going to have a hard winter, and Vercingetorix says it is imperative that we keep Caesar from returning to his legions. They won't venture out of camp without him, especially during the winter. By spring, we will have united."

"What are you going to do?" asked Cathbad.

"Tomorrow at dawn we raid Cenabum and kill every Roman and Greek it shelters."

"An unmistakable declaration of war."

"To the rest of Gaul, Cathbad, not to the Romans. I don't intend that news of Cenabum should reach Trebonius. If it did, he'd send word to Caesar immediately. Let Caesar linger on the far side of the Alps until the whole of Gaul is in arms."

"Good strategy if it works," said Cathbad. "I hope you're more successful than the Nervii were."

"We're Celtae, Cathbad, not Belgae. Besides, the Nervii kept Quintus Cicero from communicating with Caesar for a month. That's long enough. Another month will see the start of winter."

Thus did Gaius Fufius Cita and the foreign traders who lived in Cenabum discover the truth of the old Roman adage that revolt in a province always commenced with the murder of Roman civilians. Under the command of Gutruatus, a group of Carnutes swooped on their own capital, entered it, and killed every foreigner there. Fufius Cita suffered the same fate as Acco: he was publicly flogged and beheaded. Though he died under the lash. Urging on the man who wielded the whip, the Carnutes found nothing to criticize in this. Fufius Cita's head was a trophy carried in celebration to the grove of Esus and there offered up by Cathbad.

News in Gaul traveled very swiftly, though the method of its transmission inevitably meant that the further it spread from its source, the more distorted it became. The Gauls simply shouted information from one person to the next across the fields.

What had commenced as "The Romans inside Cenabum have been massacred!" became "The Carnutes are in open revolt and have killed every Roman in their lands!" by the time it had been shouted from mouth to ear for a distance of one hundred and sixty miles. It flew this far between dawn, when the raid had occurred, and dusk, when it was shouted into the main *oppidum* of the Arverni, Gergovia, and was heard by Vercingetorix.

At last! *At last!* Revolt in central Gaul instead of in the lands of the Belgae or the Celtae of the western coast! These were people he knew, people who would yield him his lieutenants when the great Army of All Gaul came together, people sophisticated enough to understand the value of a mail shirt and a helmet, to understand the way the Romans made war. If the Carnutes had rebelled, it wouldn't be long before the Senones, the Parisii, the Seussiones, the Bituriges and all the other peoples of central Gaul would boil over. And he, Vercingetorix, would be there to forge them into the Army of All Gaul!

Of course he had been working himself, but not, as was now manifest, with anything like the success Gutruatus had. The trouble was that the Arverni had not forgotten the disastrous war they had fought seventy-five years ago against the most prominent Ahenobarbus of that time. They had been defeated so completely that the slave markets of the world had received their first bulk consignment of Gallic women and children; the Arvernian men had mostly died.

"Vercingetorix, it has taken the Arverni these seventy-five years to rise again," said Gobannitio in council, striving to be patient. "Once we were the greatest of all Gallic peoples. Then in our pride we went to war against Rome. We were reduced to nothing. We yielded supremacy to the Aedui, the Carnutes, the Senones. These peoples still outrank us, but we are steadily overtaking them. So no, we will not fight Rome again."

"Uncle, Uncle, times have changed!" cried Vercingetorix. "Yes, we fell! Yes, we were crushed, humiliated, sold into slavery! But we were merely one among many peoples! And still today you talk of the Senones or the Aedui! Of Arvernian power contrasted with Aeduan power, with Carnute power! It can't be like that anymore! What is happening today is different! We are going to combine and become *one* people under *one* warcry—free men in a free country! We are not the Arverni or the Aedui or the Carnutes! We are the Gauls! We are a brotherhood! *That* is the difference! United, we will defeat Rome so decisively that Rome will never again send her armies to our country. And one day Gaul will march into Italia, one day Gaul will rule the world!"

"Dreams, Vercingetorix, silly dreams," said Gobannitio wearily. "There will never be concord among the peoples of Gaul."

The upshot of this and many other arguments in the Arvernian council chamber was that Vercingetorix found himself forbidden to enter Gergovia. Not that he moved away from the district. Instead he remained in his house on the outskirts of Gergovia and confined his energies to persuading the younger Arvernian men that he was right. And here he was far more successful. With his cousins Critognatus and Vercassivellaunus following his example, he worked feverishly to make the younger men see where their only salvation lay: in unification.

Nor did he dream. He planned. Fully aware that the hardest struggle would be to convince the leaders of the other peoples of Gaul that he, Vercingetorix, was the one who must lead the great Army of All Gaul.

So when the news of the events at Cenabum was shouted into Gergovia, Vercingetorix took it as the omen he had been waiting for. He sent out the call to arms, then walked into Gergovia, took over the council and murdered Gobannitio.

"I am your king," he said to the packed chamber of thanes, "and soon I will be King of a united Gaul! I go now to Carnutum to talk to the leaders of the other peoples, and on my way I will call every people to arms."

The tribes answered. With winter looming, men began to get out their armor, sharpen their swords, see to dispositions on the home front during a long absence. A huge wave of excitement rolled across central Gaul, and kept on rolling northward into the Belgae and westward into the Aremorici, the Celtic tribes of the Atlantic coast. Southwestward too, into Aquitania. Gaul was going to unite. Gaul united was going to drive the Romans out.

But it was in the oak grove at Carnutum that Vercingetorix had to fight his most difficult battle; here he had to summon up the power and the persuasiveness to have himself appointed leader. Too early to insist that he be called King—that would come after he had demonstrated the qualities necessary in a king.

"Cathbad is right," he said to the assembled chieftains, and careful that he kept Cathbad's name to the forefront rather than the name of Gutruatus. "We must separate Caesar from his legions until the whole of Gaul is in arms."

Many had come whom he hadn't expected, including Commius of the Atrebates. All five men with whom he had concluded his original pact were there, Lucterius chafing to be started. But it was Commius who turned the tide in Vercingetorix's favor.

"I believed in the Romans," said the King of the Atrebates, lips peeled back from his teeth. "Not because I felt a traitor to my people, but for much the same kind of reasons Vercingetorix gives us here today. Gaul needs to be one people, not many. And I thought the only way to do that was to use Rome. To let Rome, so centralized, so organized, so efficient, do what I thought no Gaul could ever do. Pull us together. Make us think of ourselves as one. But in this Arvernian, this Vercingetorix, I see a man of our own blood with the strength and the purpose we need! I am not Celtic, I am Belgic. But I am first and last a Gaul of Gaul! And I tell you, my fellow kings and princes, I will follow Vercingetorix! I will do as he asks. I will bring my Atrebatan people to his congress and tell them that a man of the Arverni is their leader, that I am merely his lieutenant!"

It was Cathbad who took the vote, Cathbad who could say to the warlords that Vercingetorix was elected leader of a united attempt to eject Rome from the homelands.

And Vercingetorix, thin, febrile, glowing, proceeded to show his fellow Gauls that he was a thinker too.

"The cost of this war will be enormous," he said, "and all our peoples must share it. The more we share, the more united we will feel. Every man is to go to the muster properly armed and outfitted. I want no brave fools stripping naked to demonstrate their valor; I want every man in mail shirt and helmet, every man carrying a full-sized shield, every man well provided with spears, arrows, whatever is his choice. And each people must work out how much food its men will eat, make sure they are not compelled to return home prematurely because they have no food left. The spoils will not be great; we cannot hope to reap enough to pay for this war. Nor are we going to ask for aid from the Germani. To do that is to open the back door for the wolves as we thrust the wild boars out the front door. Nor can we take from our own—unless our own choose to support Rome. For I warn you, any people which does not join us in this war will be deemed a traitor to united Gaul! No Remi or Lingones have come, so let the Remi and the Lingones beware!" He laughed, a breathless little sound. "With Remi horses, we will be better cavalrymen than the Germani!"

"The Bituriges aren't here either," said Sedulius of the Lemovices. "I heard a rumor that they prefer Rome."

"I had noticed their absence," said Vercingetorix. "Does anyone have more tangible evidence than rumor?"

The absence of the Bituriges was serious; in the lands of the Bituriges lay the iron mines, and iron to turn into steel had to be found in sufficient quantity to make many, many thousands of mail shirts, helmets, swords, spearheads.

"I'll go to Avaricum myself to find out why," said Cathbad.

"And what of the Aedui?" asked Litaviccus, who had come with one of the two vergobrets of that year, Cotus. "We're with you, Vercingetorix."

"The Aedui have the most important duty of all, Litaviccus. They have to pretend to be Rome's Friend and Ally."

"Ah!" Litaviccus exclaimed, smiling.

"Why," asked Vercingetorix, "should we display all our assets at once? I imagine that as long as Caesar thinks the Aedui are loyal to Rome, he will also think he has a chance to win. He will, as is his habit, royally command that the Aedui give him extra horse troopers, extra infantry, extra grain, extra meat, extra everything he needs. And the Aedui must agree to give him eagerly whatever he commands. Fall over themselves to help. Except that whatever has been promised to Caesar must never arrive."

"Always with our profuse apologies," said Cotus.

"Oh, always with those," said Vercingetorix gravely.

"The Roman Province is a very real danger we ought not to underestimate," said Lucterius of the Cardurci, frowning. "The Gauls of the Province have been well trained by the Romans—they can fight as auxiliaries in the Roman style, they have warehouses stuffed with armor and armaments, and they can field cavalry. Nor will we ever prise them away from Rome, I fear."

"It's far too early to make statements as defeatist as that! However, we should certainly make sure that the Gauls of the Province are in no condition to aid Caesar. Your job will be to make sure of it, Lucterius, since you come from a people close to the Province. Two months from now, while winter is deep, we will assemble under arms here on the plain before Carnutum. And then—*war*!"

Sedulius picked up the cry. "War! War! War!"

* * *

Trebonius in Agedincum was aware that something odd was going on, though he had no idea what. He had heard nothing from Fufius Cita in Cenabum, but nor had he heard a whisper of Fufius Cita's fate. No Roman or Greek anywhere in the vicinity had survived to tell him, nor did one Gaul come forward. The granaries in Agedincum were almost full, but there hadn't been any wagons in more than two *nundinae* when Litaviccus of the Aedui popped in to say hello on his way back to Bibracte.

It always fascinated Litaviccus that these Romans so often seemed unwarlike, unmartial; Gaius Trebonius was a perfect example. A rather small, rather grey man with a prominent thyroid cartilage in his throat always bobbing up and down as he swallowed nervously, and a pair of large, sad grey eyes. Yet he was a very good, very intelligent soldier who was greatly trusted by Caesar, and had never let Caesar down. Whatever he was told to do, he did. A Roman senator. In his time, a brilliant tribune of the plebs. Caesar's man to the death.

"Have you seen or heard anything?" asked Trebonius, looking even more mournful than he usually did.

"Not a thing," said Litaviccus blithely.

"Have you been anywhere near Cenabum?"

"Actually, no," said Litaviccus, bearing in mind that his duty was to appear Friend and Ally; no point in telling lies he might be found out in before the true loyalties of the Aedui came to light. "I've been to the wedding of my cousin in Metiosedum, so I haven't been south of the Sequana. Still, everything's quiet. Didn't hear any shouting worth listening to."

"The grain wagons have stopped coming in."

"Yes, that *is* odd." Litaviccus looked thoughtful. "However, it's common knowledge that the Senones and the Carnutes are very displeased by the execution of Acco. Perhaps they're refusing to sell any grain. Are you short?"

"No, we have enough. It's just that I expected more."

"I doubt you'll get more now," said Litaviccus cheerfully. "Winter will be here any day."

"I wish every Gaul spoke Latin!" said Trebonius, sighing.

"Oh well, the Aedui have been in league with Rome for a long time. I went to school there for two years. Heard from Caesar?"

"Yes, he's in Ravenna."

"Ravenna . . . Where's that, exactly? Refresh my memory."

"On the Adriatic not far from Ariminum, if that's any help."

"A great help," said Litaviccus, getting to his feet lazily. "I must go, or I won't go."

"A meal, at least?"

"I think not. I didn't bring my winter shawl or my warmest pair of trousers."

"You and your trousers! Didn't you learn anything in Rome?"

"When the air of Italia floats up your skirts, Trebonius, it warms whatever's up there. Whereas the air of Gaul in winter can freeze ballista boulders."

At the beginning of March well over one hundred thousand Gauls from many tribes converged on Carnutum, where Vercingetorix made his arrangements quickly.

"I don't want everyone eaten out before I begin," he said to his council as they gathered with Cathbad inside Cathbad's warm house. "Caesar is still in Ravenna, apparently more interested in what's happening in Rome than in what might be happening in Gaul. The alpine passes are blocked with snow already; he won't get here in a hurry no matter how famous he is for hurrying. And we'll be between him and his legions no matter when he comes."

Cathbad, looking tired and a little discouraged, was sitting at Vercingetorix's right hand, a pile of scrolls on the table. Whenever all eyes were upon Vercingetorix, his own eyes would go to his wife, moving quietly in the background with beer and wine. Why did he feel so cast down, so ineffectual? Like most professional priests of all lands, he had no gift of prognostication, no second sight. Those were dowered upon outcasts and strangers, doomed, as Cassandra had been, never to be believed.

I speak from painfully learned knowledge, and the sacrifices have been favorable. Perhaps what I feel at this moment is simple eclipse, he thought, striving to be fair, to be detached. Vercingetorix has some quality in common with Caesar; I sense the similarity. But one is an enormously experienced Roman man approaching fifty, and the other is a thirty-year-old Gaul who has never led an army.

"Cathbad," said Vercingetorix, interrupting the Chief Druid's internal misgivings, "I gather that the Bituriges are against us?"

"The word they used was 'fools,' " said Cathbad. "Their Druids have been trying on our behalf, but the tribe is united, and not in our direction. They're happy to sell us iron, even to steel it for us, but they won't go to war."

"Then we'll go to war against them," said Vercingetorix, not hesitating. "They have the iron, but we're not dependent on them for steeling or for smiths." He smiled, his eyes shining. "It's good, actually. If they won't join us, then we don't have to pay for their iron. We'll take it. I haven't heard that any people here today has suffered from lack of iron, but we're going to need a lot more. Tomorrow we'll march for the Bituriges."

"So soon?" gasped Gutruatus.

"The winter will get worse before it gets better, Gutruatus, and we have to use it to bring dissident Celtic peoples into the fold. By summer Gaul must be united against Rome, not divided among itself. By summer we'll be fighting Caesar, though if things go as I intend, he'll never be able to use all his legions."

"I'd like to know more before I march," said Sedulius of the Lemovices, frowning.

"That's what today is for, Sedulius!" said Vercingetorix, laughing. "I want to discuss the roll call of the peoples who are here, I want to know who else is coming, I want to send some home again to wait until the spring, I want to levy a fair war tax, I want to organize our first coinage, I want to make sure that the men who stay to march against the Bituriges are properly armed and equipped, I want to call a great muster for the spring, I want to split off a force to go to the Province with Lucterius—and these are just a few of the things we have to talk about before we sleep!"

He was visibly changing, Vercingetorix, filled with purpose and fire, impatient yet patient. If any one of the twenty men in Cathbad's house had been asked to describe what the first King of Gaul might look like, to the last one they would have painted in words a picture of some giant, bare chest massively muscled, shawl a rainbow of every tribal color, hair bristling, moustache to his shoulders, a Dagda come to earth. And yet the thin, intense man who held their attention today was no disappointment; the great thanes of Celtic Gaul were beginning to understand that what lived inside a man was more important than how he looked.

"Am I to have my own army?" asked Lucterius, astonished.

"It was you who said we must deal with the Province, and who better could I send than you, Lucterius? You'll need fifty thousand men, and you'd best choose the peoples you know—your own Cardurci, the Petrocorii, the Santoni, the Pictones, the Andes." Vercingetorix flicked the pile of scrolls with a finger, his eyes on Cathbad. "Are the Ruteni listed there, Cathbad?"

"No," said Cathbad, not needing to look. "They prefer Rome."

"Then your first task is to subjugate the Ruteni, Lucterius. Persuade them that right and might are with us, not with Rome. From the Ruteni to the Volcae is a mere step. We will talk more fully later on your strategy, but sooner or later you'll have to divide your forces and go in two directions—toward Narbo and Tolosa, and toward the Helvii and the Rhodanus. The Aquitani are dying for a chance to rebel, so it won't be long before you're turning volunteers away."

"Am I to start tomorrow?"

"Yes, tomorrow. To delay is fatal when the foe is Caesar." Vercingetorix turned to the only Aeduan present. "Litaviccus, go home. The Bituriges will be sending to the Aedui for help."

"Which will be long coming," Litaviccuus said, grinning.

"No, be more subtle than that! Bleat to Caesar's legates, ask for advice, even start an army out! I'm sure you'll find valid reasons why the army never gets there." The new King of the Gauls who had not yet asked to be called King of the Gauls shot Litaviccus a calculating look from under his black brows. "There is one factor we must thrash out now. I want no future reproaches or charges of partisan reprisals."

"The Boii," said Litaviccus instantly.

"Exactly. After Caesar sent the Helvetii back to their old lands six years ago, he allowed the Helvetian sept of the Boii to remain in Gaul—on the petition of the Aedui, who wanted them as a buffer between Aedui and Arverni. They were settled on lands we Arverni claim are ours, yet that you told Caesar were yours. But I tell you, Litaviccus," said Vercingetorix sternly, "that the Boii must go and those lands must be returned to us. Aedui and Arverni fight on the same side now; there is no need for a buffer. I want an agreement from your vergobrets that the Boii will go and those lands be returned to the Arverni. Is that agreed?"

"It is agreed," said Litaviccus. He huffed a sound of huge satisfaction. "The lands are second rate. After this war, we Aedui will be happy to acquire the lands of the Remi as adequate compensation. The Arverni can expand into the lands of the equally traitorous Lingones. Is *that* agreed?"

"It is agreed," said Vercingetorix, grinning.

He turned his attention back to Cathbad, who looked no more content. "Why hasn't King Commius come?" he demanded.

"He'll be here in the summer, not before. By then he hopes to be leading all the western Belgae left alive."

"Caesar did us a good turn in betraying him."

"It wasn't Caesar," said Cathbad scornfully. "I'd say the plot was entirely the work of Labienus."

"Do I detect a note of sympathy for Caesar?"

"Not at all, Vercingetorix. But blindness is not a virtue! If you are to defeat Caesar, you must strive to understand him. He will try a Gaul and execute him, as he did Acco, but he would deem the kind of treachery meted out to Commius a disgrace."

"The trial of Acco was rigged!" cried Vercingetorix angrily.

"Yes, of course it was," said Cathbad, persevering. "But it was *legal*! Understand that much about the Romans! They like to look legal. Of no Roman is that truer than of Caesar."

The first Gaius Trebonius in Agedincum knew of the march against the Bituriges came from Litaviccus, who galloped in from Bibracte gasping alarm.

"There's war between the tribes!" he said to Trebonius.

"Not war against us?" asked Trebonius.

"No. Between the Arverni and the Bituriges."

"And?"

"The Bituriges have sent to the Aedui for help. We have old treaties of friendship which go back to the days when we warred constantly with the Arverni, you see. The Bituriges lie beyond them, which meant an alliance between us hemmed the Arverni in on two sides."

"How do the Aedui feel now?"

"That we should send the Bituriges help."

"Then why see me?"

Litaviccus opened his innocent blue eyes wide. "You know perfectly well why, Gaius Trebonius! The Aedui have Friend and Ally status! If it were to come to your ears that the Aedui were in arms and marching west, what might you think? Convictolavus and Cotus have sent me to inform you of events, and ask for your advice."

"Then I thank them." Trebonius looked more worried than he usually did, chewed his lip. "Well, if it's internecine and has nothing to do with Rome, then honor your old treaty, Litaviccus. Send the Bituriges help."

"You seem uneasy."

"More surprised than uneasy. What's with the Arverni? I thought Gobannitio and his elders disapproved of war with anyone."

Litaviccus made his first mistake—he looked too casual; he spoke too readily, too airily. "Oh, Gobannitio is out!" he exclaimed. "Vercingetorix is ruling the Arverni."

"Ruling?"

"Yes, perhaps that's too strong a word." Litaviccus adopted a demure expression. "He's vergobret without a colleague."

Which made Trebonius laugh. And, still chuckling, Trebonius saw Litaviccus off the premises on the return section of his urgent visit. But the moment Litaviccus clattered off, he went to find Quintus Cicero, Gaius Fabius and Titus Sextius.

Quintus Cicero and Sextius were commanding legions among the six encamped around Agedincum, whereas Fabius held the two legions billeted with the Lingones, fifty miles closer to the Aedui. That Fabius was in Agedincum was unexpected; he had come, he explained, to alleviate his boredom.

"Consider it alleviated," said Trebonius, more mournful than ever. "Something is happening, and we're not being told anything like all of it."

"But they do war against each other," said Quintus Cicero.

"In *winter*?" Trebonius began to pace. "It's the news about Vercingetorix rocked me, Quintus. The sagacity of age is out and the impetuous fire of youth is in among the Arverni, and I don't understand what that means. You all remember Vercingetorix—would he be going to war against fellow Gauls, do you think?"

"He obviously is, I believe that much," said Sextius.

"It's very sudden, certainly, and you're right, Trebonius—why in winter?" asked Fabius.

"Has anyone come forward with information?"

The three other legates shook their heads.

"That in itself is odd, if you think about it," Trebonius said. "Normally there's always someone dinning in our ears, and always with moans or complaints. How many plots against Rome do we normally hear of over the course of a winter furlough?"

"Dozens," said Fabius, grinning.

"Yet this year, none. They're up to something, I swear they are. I wish we had Rhiannon here! Or that Hirtius would come back."

"I think," said Quintus Cicero, "that we should send word to Caesar." He smiled. "Surreptitiously. Not perhaps a note under the webbing on a spear, but definitely not openly."

"And not," said Trebonius with sudden decision, "through the lands of the Aedui. There was something about Litaviccus that set my teeth on edge."

"We shouldn't offend the Aedui," Sextius objected.

"Nor will we. If they don't know about any communication we might send to Caesar, they can't be offended."

"How will we send it, then?" asked Fabius.

"North," said Trebonius crisply. "Through Sequani territory to Vesontio, thence to Genava, thence to Vienne. The worst of it is that the Via Domitia pass is closed. It'll have to go the long way, around the coast."

"Seven hundred miles," said Quintus Cicero gloomily.

"Then we issue the messengers every sort of official passport, authority to commandeer the very best horses, and we expect a full hundred miles a day. Two men only, and not Gauls of any tribe. It doesn't go out of this room except to the men we pick. Two strong young legionaries who can ride as well as Caesar." Trebonius looked enquiring. "Any ideas?"

"Why not two centurions?" asked Quintus Cicero.

The others looked horrified. "Quintus, he'd *murder* us! Leave his men without centurions? Surely by now you know he'd rather lose all of us than one junior centurion!"

"Oh, yes, of course!" gasped Quintus Cicero, remembering his brush with the Sugambri.

"Leave it to me," said Fabius with decision. "Write your message, Trebonius, and I'll find boys in my legions to take it to Caesar. Less obvious. I have to be getting back anyway."

"We had better," said Sextius, "try to discover anything more we can. Tell Caesar that there'll be further information waiting for him at Nicaea on the coast road, Trebonius."

Caesar was in Placentia, so the message found him in six days. Once Lucius Caesar and Decimus Brutus arrived in Ravenna, inertia began to pall; things in Rome seemed to settle down under the consul without a colleague fairly well; Caesar saw no gain in remaining in Ravenna merely to learn what happened to Milo, bound to be sent for trial, and bound to be convicted. If anything about the business annoyed him, it was the conduct of his new quaestor, Mark Antony, who sent Caesar a brusque note to the effect that he was going to remain in Rome until Milo's trial was over, as he was one of the prosecuting advocates. Insufferable!

"Well, Gaius, you would relent and ask for him," said Antony's uncle, Lucius Caesar. "He'd not serve on any staff of mine."

"I wouldn't have relented had I not received a letter from Aulus Gabinius, who, as you well know, had Antonius in Syria. He said Antonius was a bet he'd like to take with himself. Drinks and whores too much, doesn't care enough, expends a mountain of energy on cracking a flea yet goes to sleep during a war council. Despite all that, according to Gabinius, he's worth the effort. Once he's in the field, he's a lion—but a lion capable of good thinking. So we shall see. If I find him a liability, I'll send him to Labienus. *That* ought to be interesting! A lion and a cur."

Lucius Caesar winced and said no more. His father and Caesar's father had been first cousins, the first generation in that antique family to hold the consulship in a very long time—thanks to the alliance by marriage between Caesar's Aunt Julia and the enormously wealthy upstart New Man from Arpinum, Gaius Marius. Who turned out to be the greatest military man in Rome's history. The marriage had seen money flow back into the coffers of the Julii Caesares, and money was all the family had lacked. Four years older than Caesar, Lucius Caesar luckily was not a jealous man; Gaius, of the junior branch, bade fair to becoming an even greater general than Gaius Marius. Indeed, Lucius Caesar had requested a legateship on Caesar's staff out of sheer curiosity to see his cousin in action; so proud was he of Gaius that reading the senatorial dispatches suddenly seemed very tame and secondhand. Distinguished consular, eminent juror, long a member of the College of Augurs, at fifty-two years of age Lucius Caesar decided to go back to war. Under the command of cousin Gaius.

The journey from Ravenna to Placentia wasn't too bad, for Caesar kept stopping to hold assizes in the main towns along the Via Aemilia: Bononia, Mutina, Regium Lepidum, Parma, Fidentia. But what an ordinary governor took a *nundinum* to hear, Caesar heard in one day; then it was on to the next town. Most of the cases were financial, usually civil in nature, and the need to impanel a jury was rare. Caesar listened intently, did the sums in his head, rapped the end of the ivory wand of his imperium on the table in front of him, and gave his judgement. Next case, please—move along, move along! No one ever seemed to argue with his decisions. Probably, thought Lucius Caesar in some amusement, more because Caesar's businesslike efficiency discouraged it than because of any justice involved. Justice was what the victor received; the loser never did.

At least in Placentia the pause was going to be longer, for here Caesar had put the Fifteenth Legion into training camp for the duration of his stay in Illyricum and Italian Gaul, and he wanted to see for himself how the Fifteenth was faring. His orders had been specific: drill them until they drop, then drill them until they don't drop. He had sent for fifty training centurions from Capua, grizzled veterans who slavered at the prospect of making seventeen-year-old lives a studied combination of agony and misery, and told them that they were to concentrate on the Fifteenth's centurions in their hypothetical spare time. Now the moment had come to see what over three months of training in Placentia had produced; Caesar sent word that he would review the legions on the parade ground at dawn the following morning.

"If they pass muster, Decimus, you can march them to Further Gaul along the coast road at once," he said over dinner in the midafternoon.

Decimus Brutus, munching a local delicacy of mixed vegetables lightly fried in oil, nodded tranquilly. "I hear they're really terrific troops," he said, dabbling his hands in a bowl of water.

"Who gave you that news?" asked Caesar, picking indifferently at a piece of pork roasted in sheep's milk until it was brown and crunchy and the milk was all gone.

"A purveyor of foods to the army, as a matter of fact."

"A purveyor of army supplies knows?"

"Who better? The men of the Fifteenth have worked so hard they've eaten Placentia out of everything that quacks, oinks, bleats or clucks, and the local bakers are working two shifts a day. My dear Caesar, Placentia *loves* you."

"A hit, Decimus!" said Caesar, laughing.

"I understood that Mamurra and Ventidius were to meet us here," said Lucius Caesar, a better trencherman than his cousin, and thoroughly enjoying this less-spicy-than-pepper-mad-Rome, northern kind of cuisine.

"They arrive the day after tomorrow, from Cremona."

Hirtius, too busy to eat with them, came in. "Caesar, an urgent letter from Gaius Trebonius."

Caesar sat up at once and swung his legs off the couch he shared with his cousin, one hand out for the scroll. He broke the seal, unrolled it and read it at a glance.

"Plans have changed," he said then, voice level. "How did this come, Hirtius? How long has it been on the road?"

"Six days only, Caesar, and those by the coast road too. I gather Fabius sent two legionaries who ride like the wind, loaded them with money and official pieces of paper. They did well."

"They did indeed."

A change had come over Caesar, a change Decimus Brutus and Hirtius knew of old, and Lucius Caesar not at all. The urbane consular was gone, replaced by a man as plain, as crisp and as focused as Gaius Marius.

"I'll have to leave letters for Mamurra and Ventidius, so I'm off to write them—and others. Decimus, send word to the Fifteenth to be ready to march at dawn. Hirtius, see to the supply train. No ox-wagons, everything in mule-wagons or on mules. We won't find enough to eat in Liguria, so the baggage train will have to keep up. Food for ten days, though we're not going to be ten days between here and Nicaea. Ten days to Aquae Sextiae in the Province, less if the Fifteenth is half as good as the Tenth." Caesar turned to his cousin. "Lucius, I'm marching and I'm in a hurry. You can journey on at your leisure if you prefer. Otherwise it's dawn tomorrow for you too."

"Dawn tomorrow," said Lucius Caesar, slipping into his shoes. "I don't intend to be cheated of this spectacle, Gaius."

But Gaius had vanished. Lucius raised his brows at Hirtius and Decimus Brutus. "Doesn't he ever tell you what's going on?"

"He will," said Decimus Brutus, strolling out.

"We're told when we need to know," said Hirtius, linking his arm through Lucius Caesar's and steering him gently out of the dining room. "He never wastes time. Today he'll be flying to wade through everything he has to leave behind in perfect order, because it looks to me—and to him—as if we won't be back in Italian Gaul. Tomorrow night in camp he'll tell us."

"How will his lictors cope with this march? I noticed he wore them out coming up the Via Aemilia, and that at least gave them a chance to rest every second day."

"I've often thought we should put our lictors into training camp alongside the soldiers. When Caesar's moving quickly he dispenses with his lictors, constitutional or not. They'll follow at their own pace, and he'll leave word whereabouts headquarters are going to be. That's where they'll stay."

"How will you ever find enough mules at such short notice?"

Hirtius grinned. "Most of them are Marius's mules," he said, referring to the fact that Gaius Marius had loaded thirty pounds of gear on a legionary's back, and thus turned legionaries into mules. "That's another thing you'll find out about Caesar's army, Lucius. Every mule the Fifteenth should have will be there tomorrow morning, as fit and ready for action as the men. Caesar expects to be able to start a legion moving instantly. Therefore it has to be permanently ready in every aspect."

The Fifteenth was drawn up in column at dawn the next morning when Caesar, Lucius Caesar, Aulus Hirtius and Decimus Brutus rode into camp. Whatever convulsions had wracked the Fifteenth between being informed it was marching and the actual commencement of the march didn't show; the First Cohort swung into place behind the General and his three legates with smooth precision, and the Tenth Cohort, at the tail, was moving almost as soon as the First.

The legionaries marched eight abreast in their tent octets, the rising sun glancing off mail shirts polished for a parade that hadn't happened, each man, bareheaded, girt with sword and dagger and carrying his *pilum* in his right hand. He arranged his pack on a T- or Y-shaped rod canted over his left shoulder, his shield in its hide cover the outermost item suspended from this frame, his helmet like a blister on its top. In his pack he toted five days' ration of wheat, chickpea (or some other pulse) and bacon; a flask of oil, dish and cup, all made of bronze; his shaving gear; spare tunics, neckerchiefs and linen; the dyed horsehair crest for his helmet; his circular *sagum* (with a hole in its middle for his head to poke through) made of water-resistant, oily Ligurian wool; socks and furry skins to put inside his *caligae* in cold weather; a pair of woolen breeches for cold weather; his blanket; a shallow wicker basket for carrying away soil; and anything else he could not live without, such as a lucky charm or a lock of his darling's hair. Some necessities were shared out; one man would have the flint for fire making, another the octet's salt, yet another the precious little bit of leavening for their bread, or a collection of herbs, or a lamp, or a flask of oil for it, or a small bundle of twigs for kindling. Some sort of digging implement like a *dolabra* or spade and two pickets for the marching camp palisade were strapped to the rod of the frame supporting each man's pack, making it the right size for his hand to cup comfortably.

On the octet's mule went a little mill for grinding grain, a small clay oven for baking bread, bronze cook-pots, spare *pila,* water skins and a compact, closely folded hide tent complete with guys and poles. The century's ten mules trotted behind the century, each octet's mule attended by the octet's two noncombatant servants, among whose duties on the march was the important one of keeping their octet supplied with water as they moved. Since there was no formal baggage train on this urgent march, each century's wagon, drawn by six mules, followed the century, and held tools, nails, a certain amount of private gear, water barrels, a bigger millstone, extra food, and the centurion's tent and possessions; he was the only man in the century who marched unencumbered.

Four thousand eight hundred soldiers, sixty centurions, three hundred artillerymen, a corps of one hundred engineers and artificers and sixteen hundred noncombatants made up the legion, which was fully up to strength. With it, drawn by mules, traveled the Fifteenth's thirty pieces of artillery: ten stone-hurling ballistae and twenty bolt-shooting catapultae of various sizes, together with the wagons into which were loaded spare parts and ammunition. The artillerymen escorted their beloved machines, oiling the axle sockets, fussing, caressing. They were very good

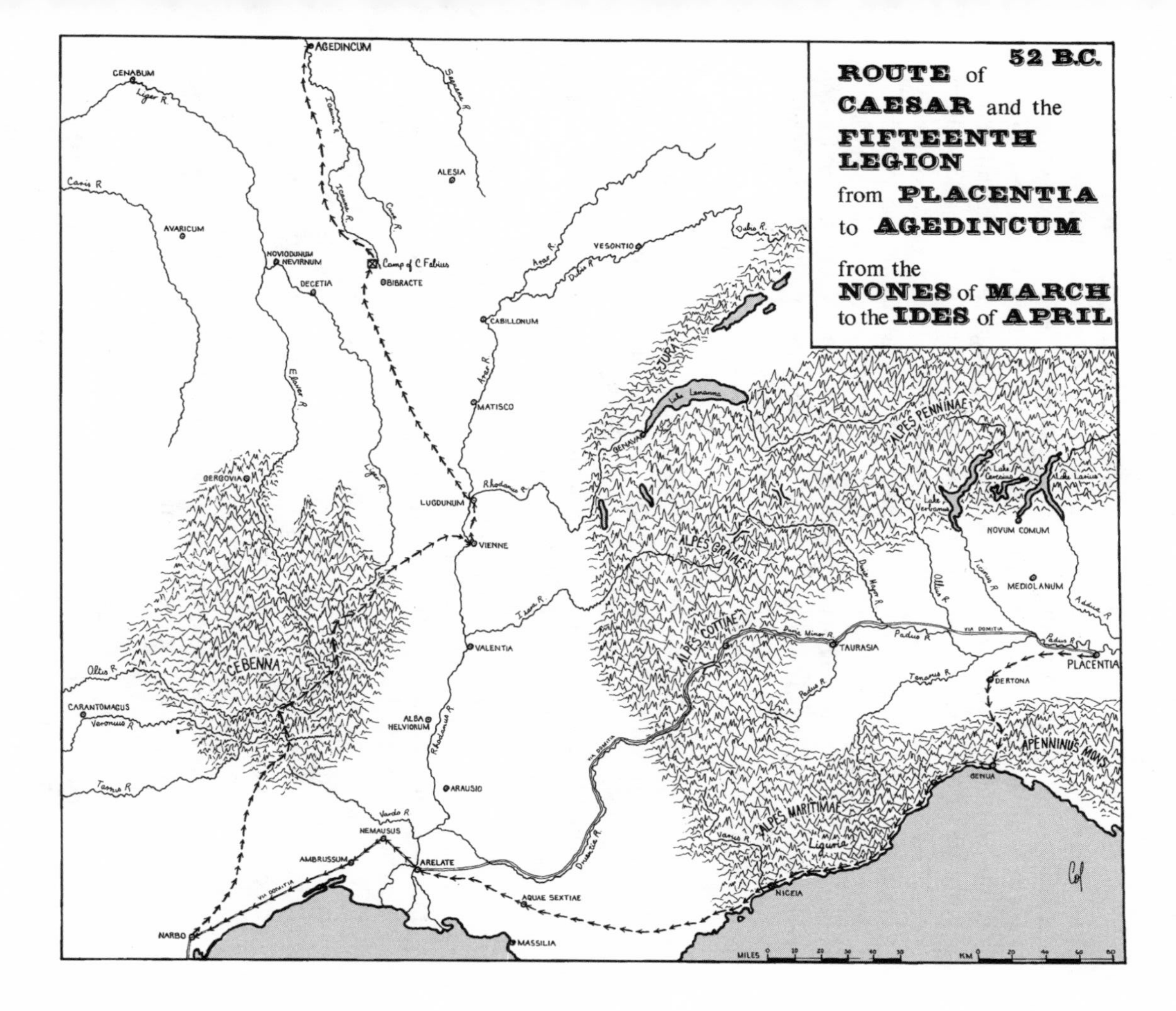
52 B.C.
ROUTE of CAESAR and the FIFTEENTH LEGION from PLACENTIA to AGEDINCUM from the NONES of MARCH to the IDES of APRIL
AGEDINCUM
CENABUM
Liger R.
Sequana R.
ALESIA
Caris R.
AVARICUM
NOVIODUNUM NEVIRNUM
DECETIA
Camp of C. Fabius
BIBRACTE
VESONTIO
Arar R.
Dubis R.
CABILLONUM
MATISCO
Elaver R.
JURA
Lake Lemannus
GENAVA
ALPES PENNINAE
Lake Verbanus
Lake Ceresius
Lake Larius
NOVUM COMUM
MEDIOLANUM
Ticinus R.
Addua R.
GERGOVIA
LUGDUNUM
Rhodanus R.
VIENNE
ALPES GRAIAE
ALPES COTTIAE
Isara R.
VALENTIA
VIA DOMITIA
Padus R.
TAURASIA
PLACENTIA
DERTONA
Tanarus R.
CEBENNA
Oltis R.
CARANTOMAGUS
ALBA HELVIORUM
ARAUSIO
Druentia R.
APENNINUS MONS
GENUA
Tarnis R.
NEMAUSUS
AMBRUSSUM
ARELATE
ALPES MARITIMAE
Liguria
Varus R.
AQUAE SEXTIAE
NICEIA
NARBO
MASSILIA
MILES 0 10 20 30 40 50
KM 0 20 40 60 80

at their job, the success of which did not depend on blind chance; they understood trajectories, and with a bolt from a catapulta they could pick off the enemy manning a ram or a siege tower with remarkable accuracy. Bolts were for human targets, stones or boulders for shelling equipment or creating terror among a mass of people.

They look good, thought Caesar with satisfaction, and dropped behind to start doing what he had to do through sixty centuries: cheer the men on and tell them where they were going and what he expected of them. A mile and a half from the first rank of the First to the last rank of the Tenth Cohort, with the artillerymen and engineers in the middle. Only after he had completed this task would Caesar dismount and walk.

"Give me forty miles a day and you can have two days at Nicaea!" he shouted, grinning widely. "Give me thirty miles a day and you can have shit duty for the rest of this war! It's two hundred miles from Placentia to Nicaea, and I have to be there in five days! That's all the food you're packing, and that's all the food you're going to get! The boys on the other side of the Alps need us, and we're going to be there before those *cunni* of Gauls know we've left! So stretch your legs, boys, and show Caesar what you're made of!"

They showed Caesar what they were made of, and it was far more than it had been when the Sugambri had surprised them not so very many months ago. The road Marcus Aemilius Scaurus had built between Dertona and Genua on the Tuscan Sea was a masterpiece of engineering which hardly rose or fell as it crossed gorges on viaducts and curled round the flanks of towering mountains, and while the road which followed the coast from Genua to Nicaea was not nearly as good, it was considerably better than it had been when Gaius Marius had led his thirty thousand men along it. Once the rhythm was established and the troops became accustomed to the routines of a long march, Caesar got his forty miles a day despite the short winter hours. Feet had long since hardened in the training camp and there were knacks to coping with the fate of Marius's mules; the Fifteenth was very conscious of its poor record to date, and very determined to expunge it.

In Nicaea the soldiers got their promised two days of rest, while Caesar and his legates wrestled with the consequences of the letter Gaius Trebonius had waiting there for him.

> We managed to get this information, Caesar, by abducting an Arvernian Druid and sending him to Labienus for interrogation. Why a Druid? you ask. Fabius, Sextius, Quintus Cicero and I talked it over and decided that a serf wouldn't know enough but that a warrior might deem it preferable to die than say anything worth hearing. Whereas the Druids are soft. If our tribunes of the plebs had half as much genuine inviolability as the most junior Druid enjoys, they'd be running Rome a great deal more ruthlessly than they do.

Labienus was elected as interrogator because—well, I don't really have to say, do I? Though I imagine the Druid was babbling what he knew long before Labienus had his irons red-hot in the fire.

Gaius Fufius Cita, his commissioners, the other Roman citizen civilians and a few Greek traders living in Cenabum were murdered at the beginning of February, though no one got through to tell us. The Carnutes shouted the news all the way to Gergovia on the same day the raid happened. Vercingetorix had been exiled from the *oppidum,* but the moment he heard about Cenabum he took over the Arvernian council and murdered Gobannitio. The next thing, he was calling himself a king. And every hothead among the Arverni was hailing him as king.

Apparently he went immediately to Carnutum and had a conference there with Gutruatus of the Carnutes and your old friend the Chief Druid, Cathbad. Our informant couldn't say who else attended, except that he thought Lucterius, vergobret of the Cardurci, was there. *And Commius!* The call to arms went out after the conference ended.

This war is no laughing matter, Caesar. The Gauls are uniting from the mouth of the Mosa to Aquitania, and right across the country from west to east. Convinced a united Gaul has the numbers to throw us out, Vercingetorix intends to unite Gaul. Under his leadership.

They mustered outside Carnutum at the beginning of March for a winter campaign. Against us? you ask. No, against any tribes which refuse to join the cause.

Lucterius and fifty thousand Cardurci, Pictones, Andes, Petrocorii and Santones started off to make war on the Ruteni and the Gabali. Once they're brought into the Gallic fold, Lucterius and his army will move on the Province, particularly at the Narbo and Tolosa end, to cut off our communications with the Spains. They're also to spread dissension among the Volcae and the Helvii.

Vercingetorix himself is leading about eighty thousand men from the Senones, Carnutes, Arverni, Suessiones, Parisii and Mandubii against the Bituriges, who refused to have anything to do with the united Gaul idea. As the Bituriges own the iron mines, it's easy to understand why Vercingetorix has to persuade them they're wrong.

As I write this, Vercingetorix and his army are on the move into the lands of the Bituriges. Our Druid informant said that Vercingetorix will move against us when spring comes. His strategy isn't bad. What he intends to do is to keep you isolated from us, on the theory that without you, we won't come out of our camps. Where he intends to besiege us.

No doubt there is one question you're burning to know the answer to: how did we come to abduct an Arvernian Druid in the first place? Why weren't we sitting back enjoying winter inertia as Vercingetorix imagined we would? Blame Litaviccus of the Aedui, Caesar. He's visited me several times since the beginning of February, each time in the most casual way—dropping in after going to a wedding, that sort of pretext. I didn't think anything of it until he arrived after the big March muster near Carnutum, when he informed me that Vercingetorix was "ruling" in Gergovia. I taxed him with the word, and he retreated too hastily, too offhandedly. He thought he was being very funny when he amended it to "vergobret without a colleague." I split my sides laughing, escorted him off the premises, and sent that first letter to you.

Caesar, I have absolutely no concrete evidence which might lead me to think that the Aedui are contemplating a part in Vercingetorix's united Gaul, but beware. My bones tell me they *are* in it. Or that the younger ones like Litaviccus are in it, even if the vergobrets are not. The Bituriges sent to the Aedui for help, the Aedui sent Litaviccus to inform me of this fact, and to ask if I'd mind their sending an army to help the Bituriges. If all that's involved is an internal squabble, I said, then go ahead, send an army.

But the fate of that army has this moment come to my attention. It set out, very strong and well armed, to march for the lands of the Bituriges. But when this force reached the east bank of the Liger, it sat down and didn't cross. After waiting several days, it marched home again. Litaviccus has just left me after coming to explain why the Bituriges were left unassisted. Cathbad, he said, had sent a warning that it was all a plot between the Bituriges and the Arverni, that the moment the Aeduan army crossed the Liger, both the Bituriges and the Arverni would fall on it.

All too pat, Caesar, though why I think this I don't know. My colleagues agree with me, especially Quintus Cicero, who seems to have a little warning voice about such things.

You will decide what to do, and it may be that we won't know what you plan until we actually see you. For I refuse to believe that a pack of Gauls, with or without the Aedui, will keep you from joining us when you're ready to join us. But be assured that we will be ready to leap into action at any moment from today until the summer. Pleading a suddenly unsanitary camp site, Fabius has picked himself and his two legions up and moved to a new camp site not far from Bibracte, on the Icauna near its sources, in case you need to know. The Aedui seemed pleased enough at this change, but who knows? I have become an Aeduan skeptic.

If you send news or troops or come yourself to Agedincum, be advised that all of us here would rather you skirted the lands of the Aedui. Genava to Vesontio, thence through the lands of the Lingones to Agedincum. That's the way we've routed our messages. I am very glad we have Quintus Cicero. His experience with the Nervii has rendered him invaluable.

Labienus sends word that he will hold himself and his two legions where he is until he hears from you. He too has moved, and is billeted outside the Remi *oppidum* of Bibrax. There doesn't seem to be any doubt that the main thrust of this insurrection will come from the Celtae of central Gaul, so we decided that we had best be situated within easy striking distance. The Belgae, Commius or no, have ceased to be a force to be reckoned with.

There was silence in the room when Caesar finished reading this communication aloud. Some of it they knew from Trebonius's first letter, but this one provided definite information.

"We deal with the Province first," said Caesar crisply. "The Fifteenth can have its two days, but after that it's going to march without a pause to Narbo. I'll have to ride on ahead—there'll be panic everywhere, and no one will want the responsibility of starting to organize resistance. It's three hundred miles from Nicaea to Narbo, but I want the Fifteenth there eight days after leaving here, Decimus. You're in command. Hirtius, you'll come with me. Make sure we have enough couriers; I'll need to correspond constantly with Mamurra and Ventidius."

"Do you want Faberius along?" asked Hirtius.

"Yes, and Trogus. Procillus can set out for Agedincum with a message for Trebonius. He'll travel straight up the Rhodanus and then go through Genava and Vesontio, as advised. He can visit Rhiannon as he passes through Arausio to tell her that she won't be leaving her home there this year."

Decimus Brutus tensed. "Then you think we'll be about this business for the entire year, Caesar?" he asked.

"If all Gaul is united, yes."

"What do you want me to do?" asked Lucius Caesar.

"You'll travel with Decimus and the Fifteenth, Lucius. I'm appointing you legate in command of the Province, so it will be your job to defend it. You'll make Narbo your headquarters. Keep in constant touch with Afranius and Petreius in the Spains, and make sure you monitor feelings among the Aquitani. The tribes around Tolosa won't give any trouble, but those further west and around Burdigala will, I think." He gave Lucius Caesar his warmest and most personal smile. "You inherit the Province because you have the experience, the consular status and the ability to function in my absence, cousin. Once I leave Narbo, I don't want to have to think about the Province for one moment. If you're in charge, my confidence won't be misplaced."

And that, thought Hirtius privately, is how he does things, cousin Lucius. He charms you into thinking you're the only possible man for the job. Whereupon you will flog yourself to death to please him, and he'll be true to his word—he won't even remember your name once he's out of your sphere.

"Decimus," said Caesar, "summon the Fifteenth's centurions to a meeting tomorrow and make sure the men have full winter gear in their packs. If there are any deficiencies, send a courier to me with a list of whatever I might have to requisition in Narbo."

"I doubt there'll be anything," said Decimus Brutus, relaxed again. "One thing I'll grant Mamurra: he's a superb *praefectus fabrum.* The bills he submits are grossly exaggerated, but he never skimps on quality or quantity."

"Which reminds me that I'll have to write to him about more artillery. I think each legion should have at least fifty pieces. I have a few ideas about increasing its use on the battlefield. We don't soften the enemy up enough before we engage."

Lucius Caesar blinked. "Artillery is a siege necessity!"

"Definitely. But why not a necessity on the battlefield too?"

By the next morning he was gone, cantering in his habitual four-mule gig, the resigned Faberius bearing him company, while Hirtius shared a second gig with Gnaeus Pompeius Trogus, Caesar's chief interpreter and his authority on everything to do with Gaul.

In every town of any size he paused briefly to see the *ethnarch* if it was Greek or the *duumviri* if it was Roman; they were apprised of the situation in Long-haired Gaul in a few succinct words, directed to start enlisting the local militia, and given authority to draw on armor and armaments from the nearest depot. By the time he departed, the local people were going busily about doing as they had been told and waiting anxiously for the arrival of Lucius Caesar.

The Via Domitia to Spain was always kept in perfect condition, so nothing slowed the two gigs down. From Arelate to Nemausus they crossed the great fens and grassy swamplands of the Rhodanus delta on the causeway Gaius Marius had constructed. From Nemausus on, Caesar's halts were more frequent and of longer duration, for this was the country of the Volcae Arecomici, who had been hearing rumors of war between the Cardurci and the Ruteni, their neighbors on the north. There was no doubt whatsoever of their loyalty to Rome, nor of their eagerness to do as Caesar commanded.

In Ambrussum a party of Helvii from the western bank of the Rhodanus were staying en route to Narbo, where they hoped to find a Roman in residence sufficiently senior to advise them. They were led by their *duumviri,* a father and son given the Roman citizenship by a Gaius Valerius; they both bore his name, but the father's Gallic name was Caburus, his son's name Donnotaurus.

"We have already received an embassage from Vercingetorix," said Donnotaurus, worried. "He expected us to leap at the chance to join his strange new federation. But when we declined, his ambassadors said that sooner or later we would beg to join."

"After that we heard that Lucterius has attacked the Ruteni and that Vercingetorix himself has moved against the Bituriges," said Caburus. "Suddenly we understood. If we do not join, then we will suffer."

"Yes, you will suffer," said Caesar. "There's no merit in trying to tell you otherwise. Will you change your minds if you are attacked?"

"No," said father and son together.

"In which case, go home and arm. Be ready. Rest assured that I'll send you help as soon as I can. However, it may be that all my available forces will be engaged in a bigger struggle elsewhere. Help might be long in coming, but it *will* come, so you must hold," said Caesar. "Many years ago I armed the citizens of Asia Province against Mithridates and asked them to fight a battle without a Roman army anywhere near. I had none. But the Asians beat the legates of old King Mithridates unaided. Just as you can beat the long-haired Gauls."

"We'll hold," said Caburus grimly.

Suddenly Caesar smiled. "Not entirely without assistance, however! You've served in Roman auxiliary legions; you know how Rome fights. All the armor and armaments you want are yours for the asking. My cousin Lucius Caesar isn't far behind me. Gauge your needs, and requisition them from him in my name. Fortify your towns and be prepared to take your villagers inside. Don't lose any more of your people than you can help."

"We've also heard," said Donnotaurus, "that Vercingetorix is dickering with the Allobroges."

"Ah!" said Caesar, frowning. "That's one people of the Province might be tempted. It's not so long since they were fighting us bitterly."

"I think you'll find," said Caburus, "that the Allobroges will listen intently, then go away and pretend to discuss the offer for many moons. The more Vercingetorix tries to hurry them, the more they'll prevaricate. You may believe us when we say they won't join Vercingetorix."

"Why not?"

"Because of you, Caesar," said Donnotaurus, surprised at the question. "After you sent the Helvetii back to their own lands, the Allobroges rested more securely. They also took uncontestable possession of the lands around Genava. They know which side is going to win."

Caesar found Narbo in a panic, and quelled it by going to work. He raised the local militia, sent commissioners into the lands of the Volcae Tectosages around Tolosa to do the same, and showed the *duumviri* who administered the city whereabouts they needed to strengthen their fortifications. Inside the forbidding stronghold of Carcasso most of the western end of the Province's armor and armaments were stored; as they came out for distribution people began to feel more confident, more settled.

Caesar had already sent to Tarraco in Nearer Spain, where Pompey's legate Lucius Afranius had his headquarters, and to Corduba in Further Spain, where Pompey's other legate, Marcus Petreius, governed. Answers from both men were waiting in Narbo; they were levying extra troops and intended to draw themselves up on the frontier, prepared to move to rescue Narbo and Tolosa if the need arose. No one understood better than these hoary *viri militares* that Rome—and Pompey—wanted no independent Gallic state on the other side of the Pyrenees.

Lucius Caesar arrived with Decimus Brutus and the Fifteenth on the day they were expected; Caesar sent his thanks to the legion and put Lucius Caesar to work at once.

"The Narbonese have steadied down remarkably since they heard I'm leaving them a consular of your standing right here to govern the Province," he said, lifting one eyebrow. "Just make sure the Volcae Tectosages, the Volcae Arecomici and the Helvii get plenty of equipment. Afranius and Petreius will be waiting on the other side of the border in case they're needed, so I'm not very worried about Narbo. It's incursions among the outlying tribes I fear." Caesar turned to Decimus Brutus. "Decimus, is the Fifteenth fully prepared for a winter campaign?"

"Yes."

"What about their feet?"

"I've had every soldier empty his kit on the ground for an inspection just to make sure. The centurions will report to me tomorrow at dawn."

"They weren't very good centurions last year. Can you trust their judgement? Ought you perhaps to inspect in person?"

"I think that would be a mistake," said Decimus Brutus evenly; he was not in the least afraid of Caesar and always spoke frankly. "I trust them because if I can't trust them, Caesar, then the Fifteenth won't do well anyway. They know what to look for."

"You're quite right. I've requisitioned all the rabbit, weasel and ferret pelts I could find, because socks won't be enough protection for the men's feet where I intend to take them. I've also got every woman in Narbo and for miles around weaving or knitting scarves for their heads and mitts for their hands."

"Ye Gods!" exclaimed Lucius Caesar. "Where are you planning to take them, to the Hyperboreans?"

"Later," said Caesar, departing.

"I know," Lucius Caesar sighed, looking ruefully at Hirtius. "I'll be told when I need to know."

"Spies," said Hirtius briefly, following Caesar out.

"Spies? *In Narbo?*"

Decimus Brutus grinned. "Probably not, but why take chances? There's always some native boiling inside with resentment."

"How long will he be here?"

"He'll be gone by the beginning of April."

"Six days from now."

"The only things which might hold him up are scarves and mitts, but I doubt that. He probably wasn't exaggerating when he said he'd put every woman to making them."

"Will he tell the soldiers where he's taking them?"

"No. He'll simply expect them to follow him. Nothing beats shouting for disseminating news, a fact of which the Gauls are well aware. To shout his intentions at an assembly of the troops would inform all of Narbo. The next thing, Lucterius would know."

Though Caesar did enlighten his legates over dinner on the last day of March—but only after the servants had been dismissed and guards posted in the corridors.

"I'm not usually so secretive," he said, reclining at his ease, "but in one respect Vercingetorix is right. Gallia Comata does have the numbers to eject us. Only, however, if Vercingetorix is given time and opportunity to get all the men he plans to marshal for his summer campaign into the field right now. At the moment he has somewhere between eighty and a hundred thousand. But when he calls a general muster in Sextilis, that number will swell to a quarter-million, perhaps many more. What I have to do is beat him by Sextilis."

Lucius Caesar drew in his breath on a hiss, but said nothing.

"He hasn't planned on any Roman activity in the field before Sextilis and high spring, which is why he hasn't got more men with him right now. All he intends to do during the winter is subdue the recalcitrant tribes. Thinking me safely on the wrong side of the Alps, and sure that when I come he can prevent my joining up with my troops. Sure that he'll have time to return to Carnutum and supervise a general muster.

"Therefore," Caesar went on, "Vercingetorix must be kept far too busy to call that general muster early. And I have to reach my legions within the next sixteen days. But if I go up the Rhodanus valley through the Province, Vercingetorix will know I'm coming before I'm halfway to Valentia. Still well down inside the Province. He'll move to block me at Vienne or Lugdunum. I'm only one man with one legion. I won't get through."

"But there's no other way you can go!" said Hirtius blankly.

"There is another way. When I leave Narbo at dawn tomorrow morning, Hirtius, I'll be marching due north. My scouts tell me that Lucterius's army is further west, besieging the Ruteni at their *oppidum* of Carantomagus. Faced with a war of this magnitude, the Gabali have decided—quite prudently, really, given their proximity to the Arverni—

to join Vercingetorix. They're very busy arming and training for the mission they've been allocated in the spring—to subdue the Helvii."

Caesar paused for maximum dramatic effect before coming to his denouement. "I intend to pass east of Lucterius and the Gabali *oppida* and enter the Cebenna massif."

Even Decimus Brutus was shocked. *"In winter?"*

"In winter. It's possible. I traversed the high Alps at a height of well over ten thousand feet when I hurried from Rome to Genava to stop the Helvetii. They said I couldn't cross through the high pass, but I did. Admittedly it was still autumn by the seasons, but at ten thousand feet winter is always there. An army couldn't have managed—the path was a goat track all the way down to Octodurum—but the Cebenna isn't as formidable as that, Decimus. The passes lie at no more than three or four thousand feet, and there are roads of a sort. The Gauls travel from one side of the massif to the other in force, so why shouldn't I?"

"I can't think of one reason why," said Decimus hollowly.

"The snow will lie deep, but we can dig our way through it."

"So you intend to enter the Cebenna at the sources of the Oltis and come down on the western bank of the Rhodanus somewhere near Alba Helviorum?" asked Lucius Caesar, who had been talking to Gauls at every opportunity and learning as much as he could ever since Caesar had given him command of the Province.

"No, I thought I'd stay in the Cebenna for somewhat longer than that," Caesar answered. "If we can manage, I'd rather come out of the massif as close as possible to Vienne. The longer we stay out of sight, the less time I afford Vercingetorix. I want him to come after me before he has a chance to call his muster. Vienne I must visit because I hope to pick up an experimental force of four hundred German horse troopers there. If Arminius of the Ubii kept his word, they should be there now getting used to handling their new horses."

"So you're giving yourself sixteen days to negotiate the Cebenna in winter and join up with your legions at Agedincum," said Lucius Caesar. "That's a distance of well over four hundred miles, a lot of it through deep snow."

"Yes. I intend to average twenty-five miles a day. We'll do many more than that between Narbo and the Oltis, and after we come down to Vienne. If we slow to fifteen miles a day across the worst of the Cebenna, we'll still be in Agedincum on time." He looked at his cousin very seriously. "I don't want Vercingetorix to know exactly where I am at any given moment, Lucius. Which means I have to move faster than he can credit. I want him utterly bewildered. Where is Caesar? Has anyone heard where Caesar is? And every time he's told, he'll discover that was four or five days earlier, so whereabouts am I now?"

"He's an amateur," said Decimus Brutus thoughtfully.

"Exactly. Large ambition, small experience. I don't say he lacks courage or even military ability. But the advantages lie with me, don't they? I have the mind, the experience—and more ambition than he'll ever know. But if I'm to beat him, I have to keep forcing him to make the wrong decisions."

"I hope you didn't neglect to pack your *sagum,*" said Lucius, grinning.

"I wouldn't part from my *sagum* for all the world! It once belonged to Gaius Marius. When Burgundus came into my service he brought it with him. It's ninety years old, it stinks to the sky no matter how many herbs I pack it in, and I hate every day I have to spend wearing it. But I tell you, they don't make a *sagum* like that anymore, even in Liguria. The rain just rolls off it, the wind can't get through it, and the scarlet is as bright as the day it came off someone's loom."

The Fifteenth left Narbo without any wagons at all. The centurions' tents were deposited upon mules; so were the extra *pila,* the tools and heavier digging equipment. Everything else, including Caesar's treasured artillery, started out the long way up the Rhodanus valley, its arrival time anybody's guess. Each legionary member of an octet carried five days' supply of food, with another eleven loaded onto a second octet mule together with the heavier gear out of his pack. The lighter by fifteen pounds, each soldier marched with a will.

And Caesar's fabled luck went with him, for the great snake coiled its way north in the midst of a thin fog which reduced visibility to a minimum and allowed it passage undetected by Lucterius or the Gabali. It entered the Cebenna in light snow and began immediately to climb; Caesar intended to cross the watershed to the east side as soon as possible, then remain within the higher crags as long as he could find reasonable ground to traverse.

The snow quickly deepened to six feet, but had stopped falling. Each century among the sixty was rotated in turn to the front of the column to take its share of digging a clear path; for safety's sake the men moved four abreast instead of eight, and the mules were led in single file over what seemed the most solid terrain. There were accidents from time to time when the path collapsed into a crevice or the mountain fell away taking a man with it, but losses were rare and rescues many. So much snow rendered tumbles easier on the bones.

Caesar remained on foot for the duration of the march and took his turn with a shovel in the digging party, mainly to cheer the men on and enlighten them as to where they were going and what they were likely to find when they got there. His presence was always a comfort; most of them had turned eighteen, but that was not the full measure of a man inside his mind or his body, and they still suffered from homesickness. Caesar wasn't a father to them, because none of them could imagine in their wildest fantasies having a father like Caesar, but he emanated a colossal confidence in himself which wasn't tarnished by a consciousness of his own importance, and with him they felt *safe*.

"You're turning into a moderately good legion," he would inform them, grinning hugely. "I doubt the Tenth could go very much faster than you are, though they've been in the field for nine years. You're only *babies*! There's hope for you yet, boys!"

His luck held. No blizzards descended to slow them down, there were no chance encounters with stray Gauls, and always a thin mist hovered to conceal them from distant sight. At first Caesar had worried about the Arverni, whose lands were on the western side of the watershed, but as time went on and no Arverni appeared, even a lost one, he began to believe that he would get to Vienne without a single warning flying to Vercingetorix.

A very thankful Fifteenth came down out of the Cebenna and moved into camp at Vienne. Three men had died, several more had sustained broken limbs, four mules had panicked and plunged over a precipice, but not one soldier had suffered frostbite and all were capable of marching onward to Agedincum.

The four hundred Ubii Germans were in residence, had been for close to four months. So delighted with their Remi horses that, said their leader in broken Latin, they would do anything Caesar asked of them.

"Decimus, take the Fifteenth to Agedincum without me," said Caesar, dressed for riding, Gaius Marius's smelly old *sagum* over his head. "I'm taking the Germans with me to the Icauna. I'll pick up Fabius and his two legions, and meet you in Agedincum."

Ninety thousand Gauls had set out from Carnutum to enter the lands of the Bituriges, Vercingetorix at their head. Progress was slow, for Vercingetorix knew that he didn't have the skill at siegecraft to attempt an investment of Avaricum, the main stronghold of the Bituriges; he had therefore sought to terrify the people by plundering and burning their farms and villages. It had the desired effect, but not until some time after the Aeduan army had returned home without crossing the Liger. The bitter truth took days to sink in, that there would be no relief and no help from the Romans sitting safe and sound behind their formidable fortifications. At the middle of April the Bituriges sent to Vercingetorix and submitted.

"We are your men to the death," said Biturgo, the King. "We will do whatever you want. When we tried to honor our treaties with the Romans, they failed to keep their end of the bargain. They did not protect us. Therefore we are your men."

Very satisfactory! Vercingetorix led his army past Avaricum and advanced on Gorgobina, the old Arvernian *oppidum* which now belonged to the Helvetian interlopers, the Boii.

Litaviccus found him before he reached Gorgobina, and paused atop a hill to marvel. So many men! How could the Romans win? One never really had much idea of the size of a Roman army because it marched in column, winding into the farthest distance at about a mile to the legion with the baggage train and the artillery in the middle. Somehow less frightening and certainly less awesome than the sight which spread itself out before Litaviccus's dazzled eyes: one hundred thousand mail-shirted, heavily armed Gallic warriors advancing on a front five miles long and a hundred men deep, with the rudimentary baggage train wandering behind. Perhaps twenty thousand of them were horsed, ten thousand bracketing either end of the front. And out in the open ahead of it rode the leaders, Vercingetorix on his own, the others in a group behind him: Drappes and Cavarinus of the Senones, Gutruatus of the Carnutes, Dad-erax of the Mandubii. And Cathbad, easy to recognize in his snow-white robe atop his snow-white horse. This was a religious war, then. The Druids were proclaiming their commitment to a united Gaul.

Vercingetorix rode a pretty fawn horse blanketed in Arvernian checks, his light trousers bound around with dark green thongs, his shawl draped across his mail shirt. Though he had insisted that his men be helmeted, he wore none himself, and his person glittered with sapphire-studded gold. Every inch a king.

Biturgo was not among the privileged just behind Vercingetorix, but he was in front of his people, and not far away. When Litaviccus approached, he drew his sword and charged.

"Traitor!" he howled. "Roman cur!"

Vercingetorix and Drappes rode between him and Litaviccus.

"Sheath your sword, Biturgo," said Vercingetorix.

"He's Aedui! Traitors! The Aedui betrayed us!"

"The Aedui did not betray you, Biturgo. The Romans did. Why do you think the Aedui went home? Not because they wanted to. It was an order from Trebonius."

Drappes persuaded Biturgo to draw off and accompanied him, still muttering, back to the ranks of his people. Litaviccus reined his horse in beside Vercingetorix. Cathbad joined them.

"News," said Litaviccus.

"Well?"

"Caesar appeared out of nowhere in Vienne with the Fifteenth Legion and left again immediately, heading north."

The fawn horse faltered; Vercingetorix turned startled eyes on Litaviccus. "In Vienne? And gone already? Why was I not told that he was coming? You said you had spies from Arausio to the gates of Matisco!"

"We did," said Litaviccus helplessly. "He didn't come that way, Vercingetorix, I swear it!"

"There is no other way."

"In Vienne they're saying that he and the Fifteenth marched through the Cebenna, that Caesar entered up the Oltis, crossed the watershed somewhere, and didn't come out until he was almost level with Vienne."

"In winter," said Cathbad slowly.

"He means to join Trebonius and his legions," said Litaviccus.

"Where is he now?"

"I have no idea, Vercingetorix, and that is the truth. The Fifteenth is marching straight for Agedincum under the command of Decimus Brutus, but Caesar isn't with him. That's why I've come. Do you want the Aedui to attack the Fifteenth? We can just manage to do it before they leave our territory."

Vercingetorix seemed subtly to have diminished a little; the first of his strategies was going to fail, and he knew it. Then he drew his shoulders back, took a deep breath. "No, Litaviccus. You must convince Caesar that you're on his side." He looked up at the surly winter sky. "Where will he go? Where is he now?"

"We should march for Agedincum," said Cathbad.

"When we're within a stone's throw of Gorgobina? Agedincum is over a hundred miles north of here, Cathbad, and I have too many men to cover that distance in less than eight or ten days. Caesar can move much faster because his army is used to working together. His men wear a drill field out long before they see an enemy face. Our advantage is in our numbers, not in our speed. No, we will go to Gorgobina as intended. We'll make Caesar come to us." He drew a deep breath. "By Dagda I swear that I will beat him! But not on a field of his choosing. We will not let him find an Aquae Sextiae."

"So you want me to tell Convictolavus and Cotus to go on pretending to help Caesar," said Litaviccus.

"Definitely. Just make sure the help never comes."

Litaviccus turned and rode off. Vercingetorix kicked his pretty fawn horse in the ribs and put distance between himself and Cathbad, who fell back to inform the others of the news Litaviccus had brought, his fair smooth face grim, for he misliked this news sorely. But Vercingetorix didn't notice; he was too busy thinking.

Where was Caesar? What did he intend? Litaviccus had lost him in *Aeduan* lands! An image of Caesar hung before his fixed gaze, but he couldn't plumb the enigma behind those cool, unsettling eyes. Such a handsome man in an almost Gallic way; only the nose and the mouth were alien. Polished. Sleek. Very fit. A man who had the blood of kings more ancient than the history of the Gauls, and who thought like a king, for all his denials. When he gave an order, he didn't expect it to be obeyed; he *knew* it would be obeyed. He would never turn away for politic reasons. He would dare all. None but another king could stop him. Oh, Esus, grant me the full strength and the instinct to defeat him! The knowledge I do not have. I am too young, too untried. But I lead a great people, and if the last six years have taught us anything, it is to *hate*.

* * *

Caesar arrived in Agedincum with Fabius and his two legions before Decimus Brutus and the Fifteenth got there.

"Thank all the Gods!" cried Trebonius, wringing his hand. "I didn't think to see you this side of spring."

"Where's Vercingetorix?"

"On his way to besiege Gorgobina."

"Good! We'll let him do that for the time being."

"While we . . . ?"

Caesar grinned. "We have two choices. If we stay inside Agedincum we can eat well and not lose a man. If we march out of Agedincum into winter, we won't eat well and we'll lose men. However, Vercingetorix has had things all his own way, so it's time to teach him that war against Rome isn't nearly as simple as war against his own peoples. I've expended a great deal of energy and thought in getting here, and by now Vercingetorix will know I'm here. That he hasn't moved in the direction of Agedincum is evidence of military talent. He wants us to venture out and meet him on a field of his choosing."

"And you intend to oblige him," said Trebonius, who knew very well that Caesar wouldn't stay inside Agedincum.

"Not immediately, no. The Fifteenth and the Fourteenth can garrison Agedincum. The rest will march with me for Vellaunodunum. We'll cut Vercingetorix's legs out from under him by going west and destroying his main bases among the Senones, Carnutes and Bituriges. Vellaunodunum first. Then Cenabum. Then into the lands of the Bituriges, to their Noviodunum. After which, Avaricum."

"All the while moving closer to Vercingetorix."

"But driving east, which separates him from reinforcements on the west. Nor can he call a general muster at Carnutum."

"How big a baggage train?" asked Quintus Cicero.

"Small," said Caesar. "I'll use the Aedui. They can keep us supplied with grain. We'll take beans, chickpea, oil and bacon with us from Agedincum." He looked at Trebonius. "Unless you think the Aedui are about to declare for Vercingetorix."

Fabius answered. "No, Caesar. I've been watching their movements closely, and there's no indication that they're giving Vercingetorix any kind of aid at all."

"Then we'll take our chances," said Caesar.

From Agedincum to Vellaunodunum was less than one day's march; it fell three days after that. The Senones, to whom it belonged, were compelled to furnish pack animals to carry all the food within it, and furnish hostages as well. Caesar moved immediately to Cenabum, which fell during the night after he had arrived. Because this was where Cita and the civilian traders had been murdered, Cenabum suffered an inevitable fate; it was plundered and burned, the booty given to the troops. After which came Noviodunum, an *oppidum* belonging to the Bituriges.

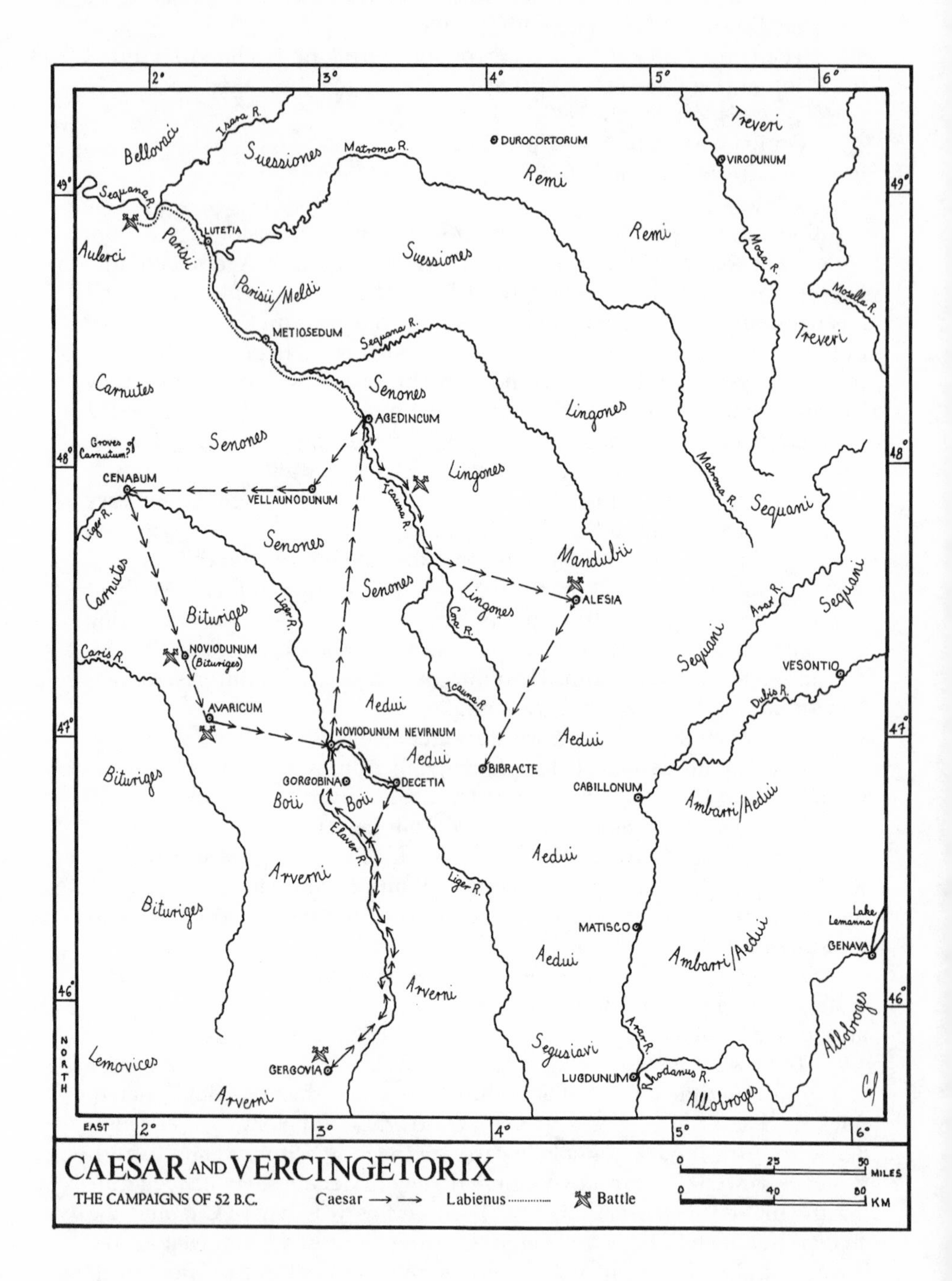

CAESAR AND VERCINGETORIX

THE CAMPAIGNS OF 52 B.C. Caesar ⟶ ⟶ Labienus .... Battle

*   *   *

"Ideal ground for cavalry," said Vercingetorix exultantly. "Gutruatus, stay here at Gorgobina with the infantry. It's too cold and capricious for a general engagement, but I can hurt Caesar with my horse; he's leading an infantry army."

Noviodunum of the Bituriges was in the process of yielding when Vercingetorix appeared, and changed its mind just as the hostages were being handed over. Some centurions and troops within the *oppidum* were trapped, but fought their way out, the Bituriges howling for their blood. In the midst of this Caesar sent the thousand Remi horse troopers he had with him out of his camp, with the four hundred Ubii in their lead. The speed of the attack took Vercingetorix by surprise; his horsemen were still coming out of their ride formation into battle lines when the Germans, shrieking a ululating cry which hadn't been heard in this part of Gaul in generations, cannoned into them broadside. The savage, almost suicidal assault caught the Gauls unprepared, and the Remi, taking heart from the Germans, followed them in. Vercingetorix broke off the engagement and retired, leaving several hundred cavalrymen dead on the field.

"He had Germans with him," said Vercingetorix. "*Germans!* But they were riding Remi horses. I thought he was busy with the town; I couldn't see how he'd get anyone into the field quickly. But he did. *Germans!*"

He had called a war council, smarting.

"We've gone down three times in eight days," growled Drappes of the Senones. "Vellaunodunum, Cenabum, and now Noviodunum."

"At the beginning of April he was in Narbo. At the end of April he's marching for Avaricum," said Daderax of the Mandubii. "Six hundred miles in a single month! How can we hope to keep up with him? Will he go on doing this? What are we to do?"

"We change our tactics," said Vercingetorix, who felt lighter after this confession of failure. "We have to learn from him, and we have to make him respect us. He walks all over us, but he won't keep on walking all over us. From now on, we make it impossible for him to campaign. We make him retreat to Agedincum and we lock him up in Agedincum."

"How?" asked Drappes, looking skeptical.

"It will require many sacrifices, Drappes. We make it quite impossible for him to eat. At this time of year and for the next six months there's nothing to be had in the fields. It's all in silos and barns. So we burn our silos and barns. We burn our own *oppida*. Anything in Caesar's path must go. And we never, never offer battle. We starve him out instead."

"If he starves, so will we," said Gutruatus.

"We'll go hungry, but we will eat something. We bring food up from those places far from Caesar's path. We send to Lucterius to give us food from the south. We send to the Armorici to bring us food from the west.

We also send to the Aedui to make sure they give the Romans nothing. *Nothing!*"

"What of Avaricum?" Biturgo asked. "It's the biggest town in Gaul and so full of food that it's threatening to sink into the marshes. Caesar's marching for it even as we speak."

"We follow him and we sit ourselves down just too far away to be compelled to give battle. As for Avaricum"—he frowned—"do we defend it or burn it?" The thin face tightened. "We burn it," said Vercingetorix with decision. "That's the right course."

Biturgo gasped. "No! No! I refuse to consent to that! You made it impossible for us Bituriges to remain aloof, and I tell you now that I will obey your orders—burn villages, burn barns, even burn our mine workings—but I will not let you burn Avaricum!"

"Caesar will take it and eat," said Vercingetorix stubbornly. "We burn it, Biturgo. We have to burn it."

"And the Bituriges will starve," said Biturgo bitterly. "He *can't* take it, Vercingetorix! No one can take Avaricum! Why else has it become the most powerful town in all our wide lands? It sits there so superbly fortified by Nature as well as by its people that it will last forever. No one can take it, I tell you! But if you burn it, Caesar will move on to some other place: Gergovia, maybe, or"—he glared at Daderax of the Mandubii—"Alesia. I ask you, Daderax—could Caesar take Alesia?"

"Never," said Daderax emphatically.

"Well, I can say the same of Avaricum." Biturgo transferred his gaze to Vercingetorix. "Please, I beg of you! Any stronghold or village or mine working that you like, but not Avaricum! Never Avaricum! Vercingetorix, I beg you! Don't make it impossible for us to follow you with our souls! Lure Caesar to Avaricum! Let him try to take it! He'll still be there trying in the summer! But he won't! He can't! No one can!"

"Cathbad?" asked Vercingetorix.

The Chief Druid thought, then nodded. "Biturgo is right. Avaricum cannot fall. Let Caesar think he can succeed, and keep him sitting before it until summer. If he's there, he can't be elsewhere. And in the spring you'll call a general muster, summon every people in the whole of Gaul. It's a good plan to keep the Romans occupied in one place. If he finds Avaricum burning, Caesar will march again and we'll lose track of him. He's like trying to eat quicksilver with a knife. Use Avaricum as an anchor."

"Very well then, we use Avaricum as an anchor. But for the rest of it, burn everything within fifty miles of him!"

Every Roman deemed Avaricum the only beautiful *oppidum* in Long-haired Gaul. Like Cenabum only much larger, it functioned as a proper town rather than a place to store foodstuffs and hold tribal meetings. It stood on a slight hill of solid ground in the midst of miles of marshy yet fertile grazing ground; the bulblike end of a spur of forested bedrock a mere three hundred and thirty feet wide outside the gates, Avaricum owed its impregnability to its very high walls and the surrounding marsh. The road into it came across this narrow bedrock causeway, but just before the gates the solid ground took a sudden downward dip which meant that the walls virtually towered right in the only spot where they might have been assailable. Elsewhere they rose out of marsh too soggy and treacherous to take the weight of siege fortifications and engines of war.

Caesar sat his seven legions down in a camp on the edge of the bedrock spur just before it narrowed into that last quarter-mile of road with the steep dip rising again to Avaricum's main gates. The city wall was made of *murus Gallicus,* a cunning interleafing of stones and wooden reinforcing beams forty feet long; the stones rendered it impervious to fire, while the gigantic wooden beams lent it the tensile strength necessary to resist battery. Even if, thought Caesar, gazing at it while the controlled frenzy of camp making went on behind him, even if I could work a ram tilted at such an angle. Or protect the men using the ram.

"This one," said Titus Sextius, "is going to be difficult."

"You'll have to build a ramp across the dip to level it out and batter the gates," said Fabius, frowning.

"No, not exactly a ramp. Too exposed. The available width is just three hundred and thirty feet. Which means the Bituriges inside have a mere three hundred and thirty feet of wall to man in order to fend us off. No, we'll have to build something more like a terrace," said Caesar, his voice betraying to his legates that he had known exactly what to do almost at first glance. "We start it right where I'm standing, which is the same height as the Avaricum battlements, and advance it fully built. It won't need to be a three-hundred-and-thirty-foot-wide platform, yet it will be three hundred and thirty feet wide. We'll flank each side of the causeway with a wall going from here to Avaricum's walls, level with its battlements. Between our two walls we'll simply ignore the dip until we can almost touch Avaricum. Then we'll build another wall between our two flank walls and connect them to each other. By advancing forward evenly we keep complete control. We'll be three quarters of the way there before we have to worry too much about the defenders' doing us serious damage."

"Logs!" exclaimed Quintus Cicero, eyes gleaming. "Thousands of logs! Axe time, Caesar."

"Yes, Quintus, axe time. You're in charge of the logging. All that experience against the Nervii will come in handy, because I want those thousands of logs in a hurry. We can't stay here more than a month. By then it has to be over." Caesar turned to Titus Sextius. "Sextius, find what stone you can. And earth. As the terrace advances, the men can tip it

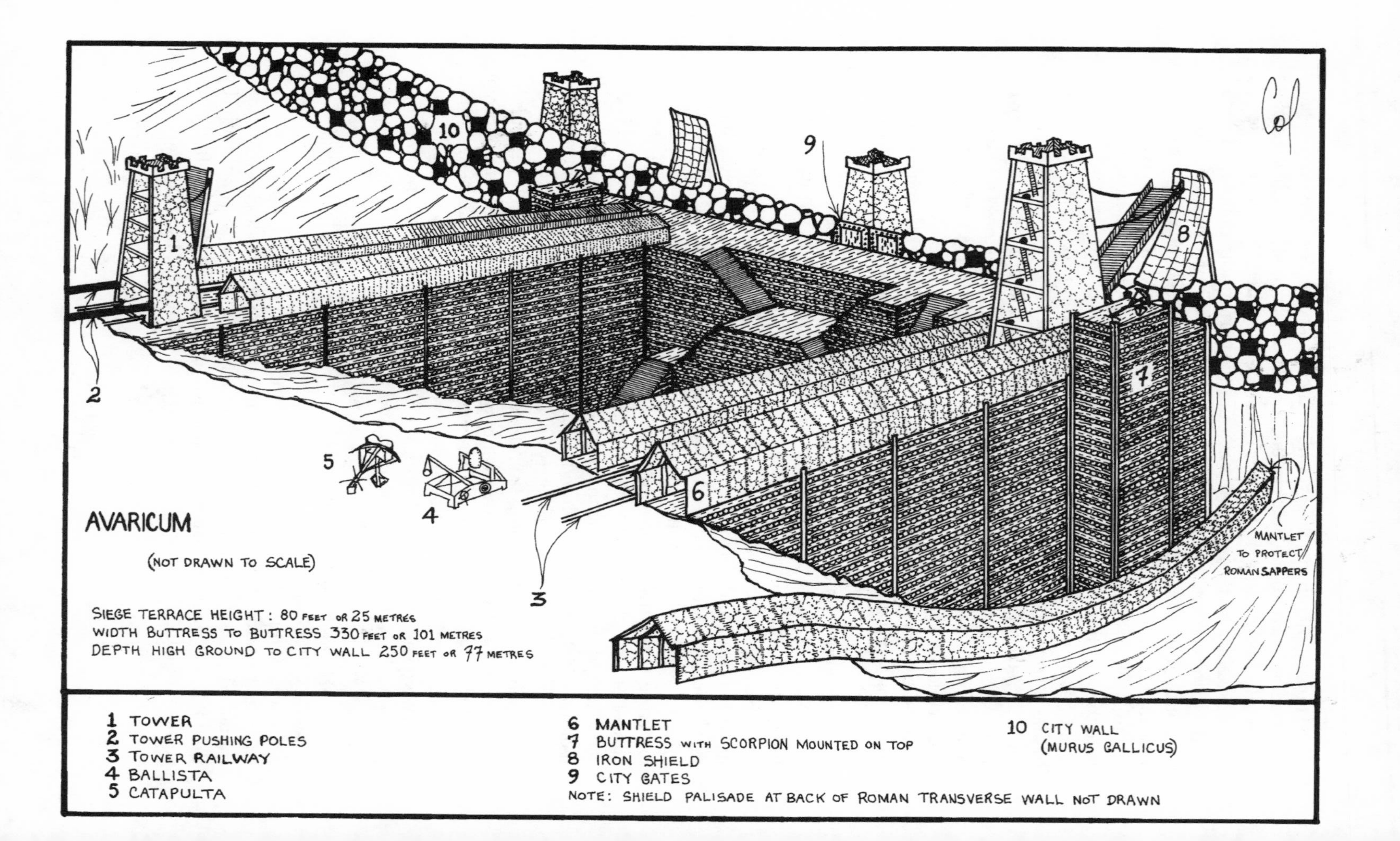
AVARICUM
(NOT DRAWN TO SCALE)
SIEGE TERRACE HEIGHT: 80 FEET OR 25 METRES
WIDTH BUTTRESS TO BUTTRESS 330 FEET OR 101 METRES
DEPTH HIGH GROUND TO CITY WALL 250 FEET OR 77 METRES
MANTLET TO PROTECT ROMAN SAPPERS
1
2
3
4
5
6
7
8
9
10
1 TOWER
2 TOWER PUSHING POLES
3 TOWER RAILWAY
4 BALLISTA
5 CATAPULTA
6 MANTLET
7 BUTTRESS WITH SCORPION MOUNTED ON TOP
8 IRON SHIELD
9 CITY GATES
10 CITY WALL (MURUS GALLICUS)
NOTE: SHIELD PALISADE AT BACK OF ROMAN TRANSVERSE WALL NOT DRAWN

over the edge into the dip for fill." It became Fabius's turn. "Fabius, you're in charge of the camp and supplies. The Aedui haven't brought up any grain yet, and I want to know why. Nor have the Boii sent any."

"We've heard nothing from the Aedui," said Fabius, looking worried. "The Boii say they don't have any food to spare, thanks to Gorgobina—and I believe them. They're not a numerous tribe and their lands don't yield a cornucopia of plenty."

"Unlike the Aedui, who have the best and most in Gaul," said Caesar grimly. "I think it's high time that I wrote a note to Cotus and Convictolavus."

His scouts informed him that Vercingetorix and his enormous army had settled down fifteen miles away in a place which prevented Caesar's leaving the area without encountering them, for the Bituriges marshes were not merely around Avaricum and the amount of solid ground was limited. Worse than this, every barn and silo within reach was in ashes. Caesar detached the Ninth and Tenth from construction work and kept them ready in camp in case the Gallic army attacked, then commenced his siege terrace.

To protect it in the early stages he put every piece of artillery he had behind a palisade on high ground, but conserved his stone ammunition for later days. The present situation was ideal for scorpions, which fired a three-foot-long bolt made very simply from a piece of wood; the business end was sharp, the other end whittled into flanges which acted like the flights on an arrow. Suitable branches lopped from the trees Quintus Cicero was logging were stockpiled, and the specialist noncombatants who did nothing save make scorpion bolts set to shaping them, checking against templates to make sure the flanges were correct.

Two parallel log walls rose on either flank of the causeway, the dip in between them only partially filled to afford the laboring troops better protection from the archers and spearmen on Avaricum's battlements. The long shelter sheds called mantlets advanced in time with the terrace. The two siege towers were built at the Roman camp end of the parallel walls, and would not be pushed down the walls until they were finished. Twenty-five thousand men toiled from sunrise to sunset every day, logging, shaping, winching, rolling, dropping the finished round beams into place, all at the rate of many hundreds of logs a day.

At the end of ten days the terrace had crept half the way to the walls of Avaricum, and at the end of ten days there was no food left save scraps of bacon and a little oil. Messengers kept coming in from the Aedui full of apologies: there had been an epidemic of winter illness, a cloudburst had bogged a train of wagons to the axles, a plague of rats had eaten all the grain in the silos closest to Avaricum, grain would have to be brought from the other side of Cabillonum, a hundred and twenty miles away . . .

Bivouacked at the terrace itself, Caesar started to make rounds. "It's up to you what I do, boys," he said to each laboring group in turn. "If you want, I'll lift the siege and we'll return to a good feed in Agedincum. This isn't a crucial business; we can beat the Gauls without taking Avaricum. Your choice."

And the answer was always the same: a pestilence on every Gaul, a bigger pestilence on Avaricum, and the biggest one of all on the Aedui!

"We've been with you for seven years, Caesar," said Marcus Petronius, centurion spokesman for the Eighth Legion. "You've been mighty good to us, and we've never brought you disgrace. To give up after all this work would be a disgrace. No, thank you, General, we'll tighten our belts and soldier on. We're here to avenge the civilians who died at Cenabum, and the taking of Avaricum is a task worth our salt!"

"We'll have to forage, Fabius," said Caesar to his second-in-command. "It'll have to be flesh, I'm afraid. They've left no granary unburned. Find sheep, cattle, anything. No one likes to eat beef, but beef is better than starvation. And where *are* our so-called allies the Aedui?"

"Still sending excuses." Fabius looked at the General very seriously. "You don't think I ought to try to get through to Agedincum with the Ninth and Tenth?" he asked.

"Not past Vercingetorix. He's hoping to see us try. Besides, if the Aedui continue to be delinquent after Avaricum falls, we'll need everything it contains." Caesar grinned. "Rather foolish of Vercingetorix, really. He's forced me to take Avaricum. I suspect it's the only place in this benighted land where I'm going to find food. Therefore Avaricum will *have* to fall."

On the fifteenth day, when the siege terrace was two-thirds of the way to the walls, Vercingetorix moved his camp closer to Avaricum and set a trap for the Tenth, foraging. He rode off with his cavalry to spring it, but the ploy came to nothing when Caesar marched with the Ninth at midnight and threatened Vercingetorix's camp. Both sides drew off without engaging, a difficult business for Caesar, whose men were spoiling for a fight.

And a difficult business for Vercingetorix, who found himself accused of treachery by none other than Gutruatus. Gutruatus was beginning to have doubts about the high command, and wondered if perhaps he would fill a king's shoes better than Vercingetorix. Who talked the war council onto his side and actually managed to gain a little ground in his struggle to be hailed as King of Gaul. For the army, on hearing that he had been forced to defend himself, cheered him mightily after the war council ended in the manner peculiar to Gallic warriors, by clashing the flats of their swords against their shield bosses. The army then gave him ten thousand volunteers to reinforce Avaricum. An easy matter to get them into the town, for the marshes held a man's weight comfortably; they were helped over the walls on the far side of Avaricum from Caesar's siege terrace.

On the twentieth day the work was nearing completion, and had approached the walls so closely that the ten thousand extra men inside the town were put to good use. A log wall joining the two parallel Roman siege tower walls was rising out of the partly leveled dip right against

Avaricum itself; Caesar intended that he would storm the battlements on as wide a front as possible. The defenders tried constantly to set the mantlets on fire, though they failed in it because Caesar had found sheets of iron inside the *oppidum* of Noviodunum, and used them to roof the mantlets at the Avaricum end of the shelter sheds. Then the defenders switched their attention to the log wall rising against Avaricum's outside, tried to demolish it with grappling hooks and windlasses, all the while pouring pitch, burning oil and blazing bundles of tinder down upon the heads of any exposed soldiers.

Avaricum's defenders put up their own breastworks and towers along the ramparts, and below the ground a different scheme progressed. Mine tunnels were dug down into the bowels of the earth until they were lower than the bottom course of the walls; they turned then and went forward until they were under Caesar's siege terrace. The Avarican miners dug upward to reach the bottom layer of Roman logs, saturated them in oil and pitch, and set fire to them.

But the logs were green and of air there was little; great billows of smoke gave the scheme away. Seeing them, the defenders decided to increase the fire's chances of taking hold by making a sortie from their walls onto the Roman walls. Skirmishes developed, the fighting grew fiercer, the Ninth and Tenth erupted out of camp to join in, the sides of the mantlets caught and burned, and so did the hide and wicker skin of the left-hand siege tower, which had been pushed most of the way toward the town. The battle raged all through the night, and was still going on when dawn broke.

Some soldiers began hacking down into the terrace with axes to make a hole to channel water in, while some of the Ninth diverted the stream supplying the camp and others manufactured a chute out of hides and sticks to carry the diverted water to the fire beneath the terrace.

A perfect opportunity for Vercingetorix, who might have won his war then and there had he brought up his army; but Gutruatus had done the Gallic cause no good turn in accusing Vercingetorix of abandoning his army to gallivant off with the cavalry. The King of the Gauls, not yet hailed as King of the Gauls, did not dare to avail himself of this wonderful chance. Until he was hailed King, he didn't have the authority to move without first calling a war council, and that was too protracted, too quarrelsome, too fruitless a business. By the time a decision might have been reached, the fighting at the walls of Avaricum was bound to be over.

At dawn Caesar brought the artillery to bear. One man on the town ramparts proved a particularly accurate marksman as he hurled lumps of fat and pitch into a fire blazing at the base of the left-hand siege tower. A bolt from a scorpion, dramatic and unexpected, plugged him through the side. When another Gaul took his place, a second bolt from the same scorpion, which had the range nicely, killed him. As fast as each new Gaul started hurling his incendiaries, the same scorpion felled him; and so it went until finally the fire was out and the Gauls had retired from the fray. It was the artillery, in fact, which won the tussle.

"I'm pleased," said Caesar to Quintus Cicero, Fabius and Titus Sextius. "We obviously do not make enough use of artillery." He shivered, drew his scarlet general's cloak closer about him. "It's going to rain and rain. Well, that will end the risk of more fires. Get everyone onto repairs."

On the twenty-fifth day the work was done. The siege terrace was eighty feet high, three hundred and thirty feet from one tower to the other, and two hundred and fifty feet from the walls of Avaricum to the Roman side of the dip. The right-hand tower was pushed forward until it was level with the left one, while icily cold, torrential rain fell remorselessly. Exactly the right time to begin the assault, for the guard atop the Avaricum battlements was sheltering from the elements, sure no attack would come in this weather. As the visible Roman troops went about their duties at an ambling pace, heads hunched into shoulders, the mantlets and siege towers filled with soldiers. The two towers winched down their gangplanks to thump onto the ramparts, while men spilled out from behind the shield palisade along the Roman wall joining the two tower walls, and put up their ladders and grapples.

The surprise was complete. The Gauls were ejected from their own wall so quickly there was hardly any fighting. They drew up then in wedge formation in the marketplace and the more open squares, determined to take Romans with them as they died.

The rain kept cascading down; the cold grew intense. No Roman troops descended from the Avaricum ramparts. Instead, they lined them and did no more than stare into the town. A reflexive panic started; the next moment the Gauls were running in all directions for the lesser gates, the walls, anywhere they thought might provide an avenue of escape. And were cut down. Of the forty thousand men, women and children inside Avaricum, some eight hundred reached Vercingetorix. The rest perished. After twenty-five days of short commons and considerable frustration, Caesar's legions were in no mood to spare anyone.

"Well, boys," Caesar shouted to his troops, assembled in the Avaricum marketplace, "now we can eat *bread*! Bean and bacon soup! Pease pottage! If I ever see a hunk of old cow again, I'll swap it for a boot! My thanks and my salutations! I wouldn't part with a single one of you!"

At first it seemed to Vercingetorix that the arrival of the eight hundred survivors of the slaughter at Avaricum was a worse crisis than Gutruatus's challenge for the leadership had been; what would the army think? So he dealt with it astutely by splitting the refugees into small groups and smuggling them to be succored well away from the army. Then the next morning he called a war council and gave it the news with complete candor.

"I should not have gone against my instincts," he said, looking directly at Biturgo. "It was futile to defend Avaricum. Which was not impregnable. Because we didn't burn it, Caesar will eat well despite the failure of the Aedui to send him supplies. Forty thousand precious people are dead, some of them the warriors of the next generation. And their mothers. And their grandparents. It wasn't lack of courage caused the fall of Avaricum. It was Roman experience. They seem to be able to look at a place we consider invulnerable and know immediately how to take it. Not because *it* possesses weaknesses. Because *they* possess strengths. We have lost four of our most important strongholds to Caesar, three of them in eight days, the fourth after twenty-five days of such incredible Roman labor that my heart stills in my breast to think of it. We have no tradition of physical work to match theirs. They march for days on end faster than our army can advance on horses. They build something like the siege apparatus at Avaricum by starting with living and innocent forests. They can pierce man after man with their bolts. They own true military excellence. *And* they have Caesar."

"We," said Cathbad softly, "have you, Vercingetorix. We also have the numbers." He turned to the silent thanes and threw off the veil of diffidence and humility which concealed his power. Suddenly he was the Chief Druid, a fount of knowledge, a great singer, the connection between Gaul and its Gods the Tuatha, the head of a huge confraternity more forceful than any other body of priests in the world.

"When a man sets himself up as the leader of a great enterprise, he also sets himself up as the man upon whose head falls the lightning, upon whose wisdom falls the blame, upon whose courage falls the judgement. In the old days it was the place of the King to stand before the Tuatha as the one who goes voluntarily to the sacrifice in the name of his people, who takes to his own breast the needs and wants and desires and hopes of every male and female creature under his shield. But you, thanes of Gaul, did not accord Vercingetorix the full extent of his power. You grudged him the title of King. You saw yourselves becoming King when he failed, as you were sure he would because in your hearts you do not believe in a united Gaul. You want supremacy for yourselves individually and for your own peoples."

No one said a word; Gutruatus moved deeper into the shadows, Biturgo closed his eyes, Drappes pulled at his moustach.

"Perhaps at this moment it does indeed seem that Vercingetorix has failed," Cathbad went on in his compelling voice, its tones honeyed. "But these are early days. He and we are still learning. What you must realize is that the Tuatha threw him up out of nothing and nowhere. Who knew him before Samarobriva?" The voice grew hard. "Chieftains of Gaul, we have but one chance to free ourselves of Rome! Of Caesar. That chance is now. The time is now. If we go down in defeat, let it not be because we could not come together in accord, because we could not bring ourselves to hail one man as King. It may be that in the future we will not need a king. But we need a king now. It was the Tuatha chose Vercingetorix, not mortal men. Not even the Druids. If you fear, love and honor the Tuatha, then bend the knee to the man *they* chose. Bend the knee to Vercingetorix, and acknowledge him openly as King of united Gaul."

One by one the great chieftains got to their feet, and one by one they went down on the left knee. Vercingetorix stood, his right hand extended, his right foot forward, the jewels and gold on his arms and neck flashing, his stiff and colorless hair like rays about his head, his clean-shaven, bony face alight.

It lasted but a moment. Yet when it was over everything had changed. He was King Vercingetorix. He was King of a united Gaul.

"It is time," he said then, "to summon all our peoples to Carnutum. They will assemble in the month the Romans call Sextilis, when the spring is almost over and the summer promises good campaign weather. I shall carefully choose envoys to go among the peoples and show them that this is our one chance to eject Rome. And who knows? Perhaps the measure of our success is in the measure of our opponent. If what we want is vast, then the Tuatha will set a vastness against us. That way, if we go down in defeat, we need not be ashamed. We will be able to say that our opponent is the greatest opponent we will ever encounter."

"But he is a man," said Cathbad strongly, "and he worships the wrong Gods. The Tuatha are the true Gods. They are greater than the Roman Gods. Ours is the right cause, the just cause. We *will* win! And we will call ourselves Gaul."

At the beginning of June, Gaius Trebonius and Titus Labienus arrived at Avaricum to find Caesar dismantling camp and preparing to move out; a great many baggage animals had been found grazing the marshes, and Avaricum's food was to go on the road with Caesar.

"Vercingetorix has adopted Fabian tactics, he won't commit himself to battle," said Caesar, "so it behooves us to force him into battle. Which I intend to do by marching for Gergovia. It's his town; he'll have to defend it. If Gergovia falls, the Arverni might think again about Vercingetorix."

"There's a difficulty," said Trebonius unhappily.

"A difficulty?"

"I've had word from Litaviccus that the Aedui are split in council and senate. Cotus has usurped Convictolavus's position as senior vergobret, and he's urging the Aedui to declare for Vercingetorix."

"Oh, I piss on the Aedui!" cried Caesar, clenching his fists. "I don't need an insurrection at my back, nor do I need to be delayed. However, it's plain that I am going to be delayed. Aaah! Trebonius, take the Fifteenth and put all the Avarican food into Noviodunum Nevirnum. What is the *matter* with the Aedui? Didn't I donate Noviodunum Nevirnum and all its lands to them when I took the place off the Senones as punishment?" Caesar turned to Aulus Hirtius. "Hirtius, summon the entire Aeduan people to a conference in Decetia immediately. I'll have to find out what's happening and settle them down before I do anything else—and do it in person. Otherwise the Aedui will drift into revolution."

Now came Labienus's turn, but now was not the right time for Caesar to raise the subject of Commius. That would have to wait. Labienus the force of nature was going to be operating on his own again, and the force of nature had to be tranquil and tractable.

"Titus Labienus, I'm going to split the army. You'll take the Seventh, the Ninth, the Twelfth and the Fourteenth. Also half the cavalry—but not the Aeduan half. Use the Remi. I want you to carry the war into the lands of the Senones, the Suessiones, the Meldi, the Parisii and the Aulerci. Keep every tribe along the Sequana River too busy even to think of reinforcing Vercingetorix. It's up to you how you proceed. Use Agedincum as your base." He beckoned to Trebonius, who walked over mournfully. Laughing, Caesar threw an arm about his shoulders. "Gaius Trebonius, don't look so sad! My word on it, there'll be plenty of work for you before the year is done. But for the moment, your orders are to hold Agedincum. Take the Fifteenth there from Noviodunum Nervirnum."

"I'll start tomorrow at dawn," said Labienus, satisfied. He shot Caesar a wary, puzzled look. "You haven't told me what you thought of the Commius incident," he said.

"That it was a pity you let Commius get away," said Caesar. "He'll prove a thorn in our paw. Let us hope, Labienus, that we find a mouse willing to withdraw it."

The business at Decetia proved to be so complex that when it was over, Caesar had no idea who was telling the truth and who was lying; the only good which came of it was the opportunity to face the assembled Aedui in person. Perhaps that was what the Aedui needed most, to see and hear Caesar himself. Cotus was ejected, Convictolavus reappointed, the young and feverish Eporedorix promoted to junior vergobret. While the Druids hovered in the background and swore to the loyalty of Convictolavus, of Eporedorix, of Valetiacus, of Viridomarus, of Cavarillus, and of that pillar of rectitude, Litaviccus.

"I want ten thousand infantry and every horseman the Aedui can muster," said Caesar. "They'll follow me to Gergovia. And they'll bring grain, is that understood?"

"I'll be leading in person," said Litaviccus, smiling. "You may rest easy, Caesar. The Aedui *will* come to Gergovia."

Thus it was the middle of June before Caesar marched for the Elaver River and Gergovia. Spring was under way, the streams so swollen from melted snows and rainy thaws that passage across them had to be by bridge, not ford.

Vercingetorix crossed from the eastern to the western bank of the Elaver immediately and demolished the bridge. Which forced Caesar to march down the eastern bank, Vercingetorix shadowing him on the other side. Demolishing all the bridges. Never good stonemasons, the Gauls preferred to build wooden bridges; the river roared and tumbled, impossible to cross. But then Caesar found what he was looking for, a wooden bridge which had been erected on stone pylons. Though the superstructure was gone, the pylons remained. That was enough. While four of his legions pretended to be six and marched southward, Caesar hid the remaining two in the forests of the eastern bank and waited until Vercingetorix moved onward. The two legions flung a new wooden bridge across the Elaver, marched over it, and were soon joined on the western bank by the other four.

Vercingetorix ran for Gergovia, but didn't enter the great Arvernian *oppidum,* which sat on a small plateau in the midst of towering crags; a spur of the Cebenna thrusting westward provided Gergovia with some of the highest peaks in the Cebenna as shelter. The hundred thousand men the King of Gaul brought with him camped among the rugged high ground behind and flanking the *oppidum,* and waited for Caesar to arrive.

The sight was truly horrifying. Every rock seemed peppered with Gauls, and one glance at Gergovia was enough to tell Caesar that it could not be stormed; the answer was a blockade, and that was going to consume valuable time. More importantly, it was going to consume valuable food. Food Caesar didn't have until the Aedui relief column arrived. But in the meantime there were things could be done, particularly seizure of a small hill with precipitous sides just below the Gergovian plateau.

"Once we own that hill, we can cut off almost all their water," said Caesar. "We can also prevent their foraging."

No sooner said than done; comfortable working in the dark, Caesar took the hill between midnight and dawn, put Gaius Fabius and two legions in a strongly fortified camp there, and extended its fortifications to join those of his main camp by means of a great double ditch.

Midnight, in fact, was to prove a crucial hour in the action before Gergovia. Two midnights later, Eporedorix of the Aedui rode into Caesar's main camp accompanied by Viridomarus, a lowborn man whom Caesar's influence had seen promoted to the Aeduan senate.

"Litaviccus has gone over to Vercingetorix," said Eporedorix, trembling. "What's worse, so has the army. They're marching for Gergovia as if to join you, but they've also sent to Vercingetorix. Once they're inside your camp, the plan is to take it from within while Vercingetorix attacks from without."

"Then I don't have time to reduce the size of my camps," said Caesar between his teeth. "Fabius, you'll have to hold the big camp and the little camp with two legions; I can't spare you a man more. I'll be back within a day, but you're going to have to last the day without me."

"I'll manage," said Fabius.

Four legions and all the cavalry moved on the double out of camp shortly after, and met the approaching Aeduan army twenty-five miles down the Elaver shortly after dawn. Caesar sent in the four hundred Germans to soften the Aedui up, then attacked. The Aedui fled, but Caesar's luck was out. Litaviccus managed to get through to Gergovia with most of the Aeduan army, and—far worse news—with all the supplies. Gergovia would eat. Caesar would not.

Two troopers arrived to tell the General that both camps were under fierce attack, but that Fabius was managing to hold them.

"All right, boys, we run the rest of the way!" Caesar shouted to those who could hear, and set off himself on foot.

Exhausted, they arrived to find Fabius still holding out.

"It was the arrows caused most of the casualties," said Fabius, wiping a trickle of blood from his ear. "It seems Vercingetorix has decided to use archers wherever he can, and they're a menace. I begin to understand how poor Marcus Crassus must have felt."

"I don't think we have much choice other than to withdraw," said Caesar grimly. "The problem is, how do we withdraw? We can't turn and run; they'd fall on us like wolves. No, we'll have to fight a battle first, frighten Vercingetorix enough to hesitate when we do withdraw."

A decision made doubly necessary when Viridomarus returned with the news that the Aedui were in open revolt.

"They ejected the tribune Marcus Aristius from Cabillonum, then attacked him, took him prisoner and stripped him of all his belongings. He gathered some Roman citizens and retreated into a small stronghold, and there he held out until some of my people changed their minds and came to beg his forgiveness. But many Roman citizens are dead, Caesar, and there will be no food."

"My luck is out," said Caesar, visiting Fabius in the small camp. He shrugged, looked toward the great citadel, and stiffened. "Ah!"

Fabius looked immediately alert; he knew that "Ah!"

"I think I've just seen a way to force a battle."

Fabius followed his gaze and frowned. A forested hill previously thick with Gauls was empty. "Oh, risky!" he said.

"We'll trick them," said Caesar.

The cavalry were too precious to waste, and there was always the chance that the bulk of it, being Aedui, would decide their skins were at too much risk. A wretched nuisance, but he did have the four hundred Germans, who knew absolutely no fear and loved to do anything dangerous. To reinforce them he took pack mules and dressed their noncombatant handlers in cavalry gear, then sent the force off under instructions to scout, learn what they could, and make a great deal of noise.

From Gergovia it was possible to see straight into both the Roman camps, but the distance rendered it difficult to see clearly; the watching

Gauls saw a great deal of activity, cavalry riding back and forth, legions marching back and forth in battle gear, everything going from the big camp into the little camp.

But the success of the enterprise, which aimed at storming the citadel itself, depended, as always, on bugle calls. Every kind of maneuver had its special short, specific tune, and the troops were exquisitely trained to obey those calls at once. Yet another difficulty concerned the Aedui, who had been deserting Litaviccus and Vercingetorix in droves, and whom Caesar had no choice other than to use combined with those Aedui loyal to him from the start. They were to form the right wing of the attack. But most of them were wearing true Gallic mail shirts instead of the customary Aeduan mail shirts, which left the right shoulder bare. Dressed for battle and therefore minus their distinctive red-and-blue-striped shawls, without that bare right shoulder they were indistinguishable from Vercingetorix's men.

At first it went well, the Eighth in the forefront of the fray. Caesar, fighting with the Tenth, had control of the bugle calls. Three of Vercingetorix's camps fell, and King Teutomarus of the Nitiobriges, asleep in his tent, was forced to escape bare-chested on a wounded horse.

"We've done enough," Caesar said to Quintus Cicero. "Bugler, sound the retreat."

The Tenth heard the call clearly, turned and retreated in good order. But the one thing no one, including Caesar, had taken into account was the complicated and precipitous terrain; the brassy voice of the bugle, propelled by a carefully chosen pair of lungs, soared up above the sound of battle so loudly that it bounced off every cliff and cranny, echoing on and on and on. The legions further from it than the Tenth didn't have any idea what the call was signaling. With the result that the Eighth didn't retreat, nor did the others. And the Gauls who had been fortifying the far side of Gergovia came running in their thousands to hurl the advance guard of the Eighth off the walls.

What was rapidly turning into a debacle increased its pace when the Aedui, on the right, were thought to be the enemy because of their mail shirts. Legates, tribunes, Caesar himself ran and shouted, hauled soldiers back, turned them round forcibly, hectored and harried. Titus Sextius, in the small camp, brought out the cohorts of the Thirteenth held in reserve, and slowly order came out of chaos. The legions reached camp and left the Gauls in command of the field.

Forty-six centurions, most of them in the Eighth, were dead, and close to seven hundred ranker soldiers. A toll which had Caesar in tears, especially when he heard that among the dead centurions were Lucius Fabius and Marcus Petronius of the Eighth; both had died making sure their men survived.

"Good, but not good enough," said Caesar to the army in assembly. "The ground was unfavorable and all of you knew it. This is Caesar's army, which means courage and daring are not the sum total of what is expected of you. Oh, it's wonderful to pay no heed to the height of citadel walls, the difficulty of camp fortifications, hideous mountain terrain. But I don't send you into battle to lose your lives! I don't sacrifice my precious soldiers, my even more precious centurions, just to say to the world that my army is composed of heroes! Dead heroes are no use. Dead heroes are burned and honored and forgotten. Valor and verve are laudable, but not everything in a soldier's life. And never in Caesar's army. Discipline and self-restraint are as prized in Caesar's army as any other virtues. My soldiers are required to think. My soldiers are required to keep a cool head no matter how fierce the passion which drives them on. For cool heads and clear thinking win more battles than bravery does. Don't make me grieve! Don't give Caesar cause to weep!"

The ranks were silent; Caesar wept.

Then he wiped his eyes with one hand, shook his head. "It wasn't your fault, boys, and I'm not angry at you. Just grieved. I like to see the same faces when I go down the files, I don't want to have to search for faces no longer there. You're my boys; I can't bear to lose any one of you. Better to lose a war than lose one's men. But we didn't lose yesterday, and we won't lose this war. Yesterday we won something. Yesterday Vercingetorix won something. We scattered his camps. He scattered us from the walls of Gergovia. It wasn't superior Gallic courage forced us back, it was shocking ground and echoes. I always had my doubts about the outcome; it's not unexpected. It won't change a thing, except that there are faces missing in my ranks. So when you think about yesterday, blame the echoes. And when you think about tomorrow, remember yesterday's lesson."

From the assembly the legions left the camp to form up in battle array on good ground, but Vercingetorix refused to come down and accept the battle offer. The faithful Germans, shrieking that ululating warcry which sent shivers down every Gallic spine, provoked a cavalry skirmish and took the honors.

"But he isn't going to commit himself to an all-out fight, even here on his home patch of Gergovia," said Caesar. "We'll parade for battle again tomorrow, though he won't come down. After that we'll get out of Gergovia. And to make sure we get out in one piece, the Aedui can bring up our rear."

Noviodunum Nevirnum lay on the north bank of the Liger, very close to its confluence with the Elaver; four days after leaving Gergovia, Caesar arrived there to find the bridges across the Liger destroyed and the Aedui in outright revolt. They had entered Noviodunum Nevirnum and burned it to deprive Caesar of food, and when the fires were slow to burn, they emptied the contents of the storehouses and granaries into the river rather than see Caesar save anything. Roman citizens living in

Aeduan lands were murdered, Roman sympathizers among the Aedui were murdered.

At which moment Eporedorix and Viridomarus found Caesar and told their tale of multiple woes.

"Litaviccus is in control, Cotus is restored to favor, and Convictolavus is doing as he's told," said Eporedorix dolefully. "Viridomarus and I have been stripped of our estates and banished. And soon Vercingetorix is going to hold a pan-Gallic conference inside Bibracte. After it, he'll call a general muster at Carnutum."

Face set, Caesar listened. "Banished or not, I expect you to return to your people," he said when the tale of woe was ended. "I want you to remind them who I am, what I am, and where I intend to go. If the Aedui attempt to stand in my way, Eporedorix, I will crush the Aedui flatter than an ox can crush a beetle. The Aedui have formal treaties with Rome and the status of Friend and Ally. But if they persist in this present lunacy, they'll lose everything. Now go home and do as I say."

"I don't understand!" cried Quintus Cicero. "The Aedui have been our allies for almost a hundred years. They were only too happy to assist Ahenobarbus when he conquered the Arverni—they're so Romanized they speak Latin! So why this change of heart?"

"Vercingetorix," said Caesar. "And let us not forget the Druids. Nor let us forget the ambitious Litaviccus."

"Let us not forget the Liger River," said Fabius. "The Aedui haven't left a bridge standing anywhere; I've had the scouts check for miles. Everyone assures me it's not fordable during spring." He smiled. "However, I've found a spot where we can ford it."

"Good man!"

The last job Caesar required of his Aeduan cavalry was to ride into the river and stand against its current, all thousand horsemen packed to form a buffer between the full force of the current and the legions, who crossed in water well above the waist without trouble.

"Except," said Mutilus, a centurion in the Thirteenth, upon the north bank, and shivering, "that there's not a *mentula* left among us, Caesar! Dropped off in the ice of that water."

"Rubbish, Mutilus!" said Caesar, grinning. "You're all *mentula*! Isn't that right, boys?" he asked the men of Mutilus's century, blue with cold.

"That's right, General!"

"Hmm!" said Caesar, and rode off.

"We're in luck," said Sextius, riding to meet him. "The Aedui may have burned Noviodunum Nevirnum, but they couldn't bear to burn their own barns and silos. The countryside is full of food. We'll eat well for the next few days."

"Good, then organize foraging parties. And if you find any Aedui, Titus, kill them."

"In front of your cavalry?" asked Sextius blankly.

"Oh, no. I'm done with the Aedui, and that goes for Aeduan cavalry too. If you come with me, you can watch me fire them."

"But you can't exist without cavalry!"

"I can exist better without cavalry aiming their lances at my soldiers' backs! But don't worry, we'll have cavalry. I've sent to Dorix of the Remi—and I've sent to Arminius of the Ubii. From now on, I don't intend to use Gallic cavalry any more than I have to. I'm going to remount and use Germans."

That night in camp he held a war council.

"With the Aedui in revolt, Vercingetorix must be absolutely convinced he'll win. In which case, Fabius, what do you think he might assume I'll do?"

"He'll assume that you're going to retreat out of Gallia Comata into the Province," said Fabius without hesitation.

"Yes, I agree." Caesar shrugged. "After all, it's the prudent alternative. We're on the run—or so he believes. We had to retreat with Gergovia untaken. The Aedui can't be trusted. How can we continue to exist in a totally hostile country? Every hand is turned against us. And we're perpetually short of food, the most important consideration of all. Without the Aedui to supply us, we *can't* continue to exist. Therefore—the Province."

"Where," said a new voice, "there's strife on all sides."

Fabius, Quintus Cicero and Sextus looked, startled, to the gaping tent flap, filled by a body so bulky that the head on its shoulders looked too small.

"Well, well," said Caesar genially. "Marcus Antonius at last! When did the trial of Milo finish? Early April? What is it now? The middle of Quinctilis? How did you come, Antonius? By way of Syria?"

Antony yanked the tent flap closed and threw off his *sagum,* quite unruffled by this ironic greeting. His perfect little white teeth gleamed in a broad smile; he ran a hand through his curly auburn hair and gazed unapologetically at his second cousin. "No, not by way of Syria," he said, and began looking about. "I know dinner's long over, but is there any chance of something to eat?"

"Why should I feed you, Antonius?"

"Because I'm full of news but little else."

"You can have bread, olives and cheese."

"Roast ox would be better, but I'll settle for bread, olives and cheese." Antony sat himself down on a vacant stool. "Ho, Fabius, Sextius! How goes it? And Quintus Cicero, no less! You do keep strange company, Caesar."

Quintus Cicero bridled, but the insult was accompanied by a winning smile, and the other two legates were grinning.

The food came, and Antony fell to eating with gusto. He took a swig from the goblet a servant had filled for him, blinked, set it down indignantly. "It's water!" he said. "I need wine!"

"I'm sure you do," said Caesar, "but you won't get it in any war camp of mine, Antonius. I run a dry operation. And if my senior legates are content with water, my humble quaestor had best be the same. Besides, once you start you can't stop. The sure sign of an unhealthy addiction to a highly poisonous substance. Campaigning with me will do you good. You'll be so sober you might actually discover that heads which don't ache are capable of serious thinking." Caesar saw Antony's mouth open to protest, and got in first. "And don't start prating about Gabinius! He couldn't control you. I can."

Antony shut his mouth, blinked his auburn eyes, looked like Aetna about to erupt, then burst out laughing. "Oh, you haven't changed since the day you kicked me so hard in the *podex* that I couldn't sit down for a week!" he said when he was able. "This man," he announced to the others, "is the scourge of our whole family. He's a terror. But when he speaks, even my monumentally silly mother stops howling and screeching."

"If you can talk so much, Antonius, I'd prefer to hear some sense," said Caesar, face straight. "What's going on in the south?"

"Well, I've been to Narbo to see Uncle Lucius—and no, I didn't take it upon myself to go, I found a summons in Arelate—who has sent you a letter about four books long." He reached into a saddlebag on the ground beside him and produced a fat scroll which he handed to Caesar. "I can summarize it for you if you like, Caesar."

"I'd be interested to hear your summary, Antonius. Proceed."

"The moment spring came, it started. Lucterius sent the Gabali and some of the southern Arverni to the eastern side of the Cebenna to make war on the Helvii. That was the worst of it," said Antony grimly. "The Helvii were overwhelmed in the open. They'd decided they had the numbers to defeat the Gabali in the field, but what they hadn't counted on was the Arvernian contingent. They went down badly. Donnotaurus was killed. But Caburus and his younger sons survived and things have gone much better since. The Helvii are now safe inside their towns and holding."

"A terrible grief for Caburus, to lose a son," said Caesar. "Have you any idea what the Allobroges are thinking?"

"Not of joining Vercingetorix, anyway! I came through their lands and found a lot of activity. Fortifications everywhere, no settlement unguarded. They're ready for any attack."

"And the Volcae Arecomici?"

"The Ruteni, the Cardurci and some of the Petrocorii have attacked all along the border of the Province between the Vardo and the Tarnis, but Uncle Lucius had armed and organized them very efficiently, so they've held out surprisingly well. Some of their more remote settlements have suffered, of course."

"And Aquitania?"

"Very little trouble so far. The Nitiobriges have declared for Vercingetorix—Teutomarus, their king, managed to hire some mercenary horse troopers among the Aquitani. But he deems himself too highborn to serve under a mere mortal like Lucterius, so he took himself off to join Vercingetorix. Aside from that, peace and quiet reign south of the Garumna." Antony paused. "All of this is from Uncle Lucius."

"Your uncle Lucius will enjoy the end of the haughty King Teutomarus's odyssey. He had to flee from Gergovia without his shirt and on a wounded horse. Otherwise he'd be walking in my triumphal parade one day," said Caesar. He inclined his head to Mark Antony, the gesture colored by a peculiar tinge of something his three legates had never seen in him before; suddenly he seemed the highest of kings, and Antony a mere worm at his feet. How extraordinary! "My thanks, Antonius."

He turned to look at Fabius, Sextius, Quintus Cicero. The usual Caesar, not a scrap different from a thousand other occasions. Imagination, thought Fabius and Sextius. He's the king of that whole family, thought Quintus Cicero. No wonder he and my brother Cicero don't get on. They're both king of the family.

"All right, the situation in the Province is stable yet perilous. No doubt Vercingetorix is quite as aware what's happening as I am at this moment. Yes, he'll expect me to retreat into the Province. So I suppose I must oblige him."

"Caesar!" gasped Fabius, eyes round. "You won't!"

"Of course I do have to go to Agedincum first. After all, I can't leave Trebonius and the baggage behind, let alone the loyal and unflagging Fifteenth. Nor can I leave without the good Titus Labienus and the four legions he has with him."

"How's he doing?" asked Antony.

"As always, very well. When he couldn't take Lutetia he moved upstream to the other big island in the Sequana, Metiosedum. It fell at once—they hadn't burned their boats. After which he returned to Lutetia. The moment he appeared the Parisii put the torch to their island fortress and scampered off to the north." Caesar frowned, shifted on his ivory curule chair. "It seems the word is being shouted from one end of Gaul to the other that I was defeated at Gergovia and that the Aedui are in revolt."

"Eh?" asked Antony, and was quelled with a glance.

"According to the letter I received late this afternoon from Labienus, he decided this wasn't the moment to become inextricably embroiled in a long campaign north of the Sequana. Amazing, how well he knows my mind! He knew I'd want my whole army." A tinge of bitterness crept into Caesar's voice. "Before he left he felt it politic to teach the Parisii—

who were led by one of the Aulerci, the old man Camulogenus—and their new allies that it doesn't pay to annoy Titus Labienus. The new allies were Commius's Atrebates and a few Bellovaci. Labienus tricked them. One always can. Most of them are dead, including Camulogenus and the Atrebates. Right at this moment Labienus is marching for Agedincum." Caesar rose to his feet. "I'm for bed. It's an early start in the morning—but not toward the Province. Toward Agedincum."

"Did Caesar really suffer a defeat at Gergovia?" Antony asked Fabius as they left the General's tent.

"*Him?* Defeated? No, of course not. It was a draw."

"Which would have been a victory," said Quintus Cicero, "if the wretched Aedui hadn't forced him to move back north of the Liger. The Gauls are a difficult enemy, Antonius."

"He didn't sound too pleased with Labienus, for all his lavish praise."

The three senior legates exchanged rueful glances. "Well, Labienus is a problem for Caesar. Not an honorable man. But brilliant in the field. Caesar hates to have to need him, we think," said Quintus Cicero.

"For more information, ask Aulus Hirtius," said Sextius.

"Where do I sleep tonight?"

"In my tent," said Fabius. "Have you much baggage? All you Syrian potentates do, of course. Dancing girls, mummers, chariots drawn by lions."

"As a matter of fact," said Antony, grinning, "I've always hankered to drive a chariot drawn by lions. But somehow I don't think Cousin Gaius would approve. So I left all the dancing girls and mummers behind in Rome."

"And the lions?"

"Still licking their chops in Africa."

"I see no reason why the Aedui should acknowledge an Arvernian as high king and commander-in-chief!" Litaviccus declared to the thanes assembled in Bibracte.

"If the Aedui wish to belong to the new and independent nation of Gaul, they must bow to the will of the majority," said Cathbad from the dais he shared with Vercingetorix.

That had started the Aeduan discontent. When the Aeduan nobles came into their own council hall, they discovered that two men only were to preside in state—and that neither man was an Aeduan. To have to argue from the floor of the chamber looking up at an *Arvernian* was intolerable! Too huge an insult to suffer!

"And on whose say-so does the majority want Vercingetorix?" Litaviccus demanded. "Has there been an election? If there has, the Aedui weren't invited! All we know is that Cathbad insisted a small group of thanes—none of whom were Aedui!—should bend the left knee to Vercingetorix as their king! *We* haven't! And nor will we!"

"Litaviccus, Litaviccus!" cried Cathbad, rising to his feet. "If we are to win—if we are to strike out as one united nation—*someone* has to be king of it until the wars to secure our autonomy are over! Then we'll have the leisure to sit down in a full council of all the peoples and determine the permanent structure our government should own. The Tuatha elected Vercingetorix to hold our peoples together in the meantime."

"Oh, I see! So it happened at Carnutum, did it?" sneered Cotus, getting up. "A Druid plot to elevate one of our traditional enemies to the high throne!"

"There was no plot, there is no plot," said Cathbad patiently. "What every Aeduan present here today must remember is that it was not an Aeduan who offered himself to the peoples of Gaul. It was not an Aeduan who inspired this convulsion of resistance which is making Caesar's life such a misery. It was not an Aeduan who went among the peoples of Gaul to drum up support. It was an Arvernian. *It was Vercingetorix!*"

"Without the Aedui, your united Gaul doesn't stand a chance," Convictolavus said, ranging himself alongside Litaviccus and Cotus. "Without the Aedui, there would have been no victory at Gergovia."

"And without the Aedui," said Litaviccus, drawing himself up proudly, "your so-called united Gaul is as hollow as a wicker man! Without the Aedui, you can't succeed! All we have to do to bring you down is apologize to Caesar and go back to work for the Romans. Give them food, give them cavalry, give them infantry, give them information. *Especially* give them information!"

Vercingetorix got up and walked to the edge of the dais on which until this day no men save Aedui had presided. Or (which the Aedui chose not to remember) Caesar.

"No one is denying the importance of the Aedui," he said in ringing tones. "No one wants to diminish the Aedui, least of all I. But *I* am the King of Gaul! There can be no getting around that, nor any possibility that the rest of the peoples of Gaul would be willing to replace me with one of you. You have great ambitions, Litaviccus. You have proven immensely valuable to our cause. I am the last man here to deny that. But it is not your face the peoples of Gaul see beneath a crown. For I will wear a crown, not a white ribbon like those who rule in the East!"

Cathbad came to stand beside him. "The answer is simple," he said. "Every people in free Gaul is represented here today except for the Remi, the Lingones and the Treveri. The Treveri send their apologies and their good wishes. They can't leave their lands because the Germans are raiding constantly for horses. As for the Remi and the Lingones, they're Rome's creatures. Their doom will come. So we will take the vote. Not to choose a king! There is only one candidate, Vercingetorix. The vote will be a simple yes or no. Is Vercingetorix the King of Gaul, or is he not?"

The vote was overwhelming. Only the Aedui voted no.

And there on the dais after the vote was taken, Cathbad took an object from under a white veil adorned with mistletoe: a jeweled golden helmet with a jeweled golden wing on either side. Vercingetorix knelt, Cathbad crowned him. When the thanes went down on their left knees, the Aedui capitulated and knelt too.

"We can wait," whispered Litaviccus to Cotus. "Let him be the sacrificial victim! If he can use us, we can use him."

Of these undercurrents Vercingetorix was well aware, but chose to ignore them. Once Gaul was rid of Rome and Caesar, he could devote his energies to defending his right to wear a crown.

"Each people will send ten hostages of highest rank to be held in Gergovia," said the King of Gaul, who had talked this over with Cathbad before the meeting. Evidence of mistrust, said Cathbad. Evidence of prudence, said Vercingetorix.

"It is not my intention to increase the size of my infantry army before the muster in Carnutum, for I am not about to pit our strength against Caesar's army in pitched battle. But I am calling for fifteen thousand extra horse warriors—to be provided at once. Such is my command as your king. With these and the cavalry I already have, I will prevent the Romans from foraging at all."

His voice swelled. "Further than that, I require a sacrifice. I command that every people anywhere in Caesar's line of march must destroy their villages, their barns, their silos. Those of us who have been in this business from the beginning have already done that. But I now command it of the Aedui, the Mandubii, the Ambarri, the Sequani and the Segusiavi. My other peoples—"

"Do you hear that? '*I* command!' '*My* other peoples!' " growled Litaviccus.

"—will feed and shelter those who must suffer in order to make the Romans suffer. It is the only way. Valor on the field is not enough. We do not fight cowards, we do not fight mythical Scandian berserkers, we not fight simpletons. Our enemy is great, brave, clever. So we must fight with every weapon in our arsenal. We must be greater, braver, cleverer. We scorch our hallowed earth, we dig our crops under, we burn anything which might aid Caesar's army or let it eat. The price is well worth it, fellow Gauls. The price is liberty, true independence, our own nation! *Free men in a free country!*"

"Free men in a free country!" howled the thanes, pounding their feet on the hollow wooden floor until it roared; then the feet fell into a rhythm and pounded the martial roll of a thousand drums while Vercingetorix, crown blazing, stared down at them.

"Litaviccus, I command you to send ten thousand Aeduan infantry and eight hundred Aeduan horsemen to the lands of the Allobroges. Make war on them until they join us," said the King.

"Do you require me to lead them in person?"

Vercingetorix smiled. "My dear Litaviccus, you're far too valuable to waste on the Allobroges," he said gently. "One of your brothers will do."

The King of Gaul raised his voice. "I have learned," he shouted, "that the Romans have commenced their march out of our lands and into the Province! The tide which began to turn with our victory at Gergovia is flooding in!"

Caesar's army was together again, though the Fifteenth Legion was no more; its men, seasoned now, were slipped into the other ten to plump them out, particularly among the more than decimated Eighth. With Labienus, Trebonius, Quintus Cicero, Fabius, Sextius, Hirtius, Decimus Brutus, Mark Antony and several other legates, it marched with everything it owned eastward from Agedincum into the lands of the ever-loyal Lingones.

"What a nice, fat bait we must look," said Caesar to Trebonius with satisfaction. "Ten legions, six thousand horse, all the baggage."

"Of which horse, two thousand are Germans," said Trebonius, grinning and turning to look at Labienus. "What do you think of our new German cavalry, Titus?"

"Worth every sestertius paid to mount them," said Labienus, grunting in content. The horse's teeth bared. "Though I imagine, Caesar, that your name isn't being uttered with love among our seriously offended military tribunes!"

Caesar laughed, raised his brows. Sixteen hundred Germans had been waiting at Agedincum, and Trebonius had striven mightily to exchange their nags for Remi steeds. Not that the Remi held back. They were charging such an inflated price for their horses that they were prepared to give up every beast they had save the breeding stock. Simply, the Remi didn't have quite enough reserves. When Caesar arrived, he solved the shortfall by compelling all his military tribunes to give up their high-stepping Italian beauties in exchange for German nags, Public Horses or no. The shriek of anguish could be heard for miles, but Caesar was unmoved.

"You can do your jobs from the backs of nags just as well as you can on Pegasus," he said. "Needs must, so *tacete, ineptes*!"

The Roman snake, fifteen miles long, scales glittering, wound its way eastward with two thousand German and four thousand Remi horsemen fussing about its sides.

"Why do they make their column so long?" asked King Teutomarus of King Vercingetorix as they sat their horses atop a hill and watched that seemingly endless procession. "Why not march on a much wider front? They could still keep to their precious columns, simply have four or five or six columns parallel to each other."

"Because," said King Vercingetorix patiently, "no army is big enough to attack along a thin column's full length. Even if I had the three or four hundred thousand men I hope to have after the muster at Carnutum, I'd be stretched thin. Though with that many men, I'd certainly try. The Roman snake is very clever. No matter whereabouts the column is attacked, the rest of it can act like wings, turn and enfold the attackers. And they are so rigorously drilled that they can form themselves into one or several squares in the time it would take us to marshal a charge. One reason I want thousands of archers. I've heard that a scant year ago the Parthians attacked a Roman column on the march, and routed it. Thanks to their archers and an all-horse army."

"Then you're going to let them go?" asked King Teutomarus.

"Not unscathed, no. I have thirty thousand horse against their six thousand. Nice odds. No infantry battle, Teutomarus. But we will have a cavalry battle. Oh, for the day when I can employ horse archers!"

Vercingetorix attacked with his cavalry in three separate groups as Caesar's army marched not far from the north bank of the Icauna River. The Gallic strategy depended upon Caesar's reluctance to allow his relatively slender horse contingent a free rein away from the infantry column; Vercingetorix was convinced Caesar would order them to hug the column, content himself with fending the Gallic assault off.

So confident were the Gauls that they had publicly sworn an oath before their king: no man who had not ridden twice through the Roman infantry column would ever know again the pleasures of his home, his wife, his children.

One of the three Gallic groups massed nine thousand strong on either Roman flank, while the third began to harry the head of the column. But the trouble was that ground for such a huge horse attack had to be fairly flat and negotiable: easy ground for the Roman foot to wheel upon, form square, draw all the baggage and artillery inside. Nor did Caesar do as Vercingetorix had expected. Instead of ordering his horse to stay close and protect the infantry, he used the infantry to protect itself and split his cavalry into three groups of two thousand. Then he sent it out under Labienus to contend with the Gauls on open ground.

The Germans on the right flank won the day; they gained the top of a ridge, dislodged the Gauls, who were terrified of German cavalry, and rode into them screaming. The Gauls broke to the south and were driven headlong to the river, where Vercingetorix himself drew up his infantry and tried to contain the panic. But nothing could stop Germans in full cry, especially superbly mounted. The Ubii warriors, hair coiled into a complicated knot on top of their bare heads, rode everyone down, in the grip of a killing frenzy. Less adventurous, the Remi felt their pride pricked, and did their best to emulate the Germans.

It was Vercingetorix who retreated, with the Germans and the Remi harassing his rear all day.

Luckily the night was a dark one; Caesar's cavalry retired, enabling the King of Gaul to put his men into a makeshift camp.

"So many Germans!" said Gutruatus, shivering.

"Mounted on Remi horses," said Vercingetorix bitterly. "Oh, we owe the Remi a reckoning!"

"And there's our main trouble," said Sedulius. "We prate of being united, but some of our peoples refuse to, and some don't have their hearts in it." He glared at Litaviccus. "Like the Aedui!"

"The Aedui proved their mettle today," said Litaviccus, his teeth clenched. "Cotus, Cavarillus and Eporedorix haven't come back. They're dead."

"No, I saw Cavarillus captured," said Drappes, "and I saw the other two in the retreat. Not everyone is here. Some took off at a tangent, I think to loop round Caesar and head west."

"What happens now?" asked Teutomarus.

"I think," said Vercingetorix slowly, "that now we wait for the general muster. Only a few days away. I had hoped to go to Carnutum in person, but this setback—I must stay with the army. Gutruatus, I entrust you with the muster at Carnutum. Take Sedulius and his Lemovices, Drappes and his Senones, Teutomarus and his Nitiobriges, and Litaviccus and his Aedui with you. I'll keep the rest of the cavalry and our eighty thousand foot with me—Mandubii, Bituriges and all my Arverni. How far is it to Alesia, Daderax?"

The chief thane of the Mandubii answered without hesitation. "About fifty miles eastward, Vercingetorix."

"Then we'll go to earth in Alesia for a few days. *Only* a few days. I don't intend another Avaricum."

"Alesia is no Avaricum," said Daderax. "It's too big, too high and too hedged in to be stormed or invested. Even if the Romans try to set up some sort of blockade similar to the one at Avaricum, they can't pen us in any more than they can attack us. When we want to leave, we'll be able to leave."

"Critognatus, how much food have we with us?" Vercingetorix asked his Arvernian cousin.

"Enough for ten days if Gutruatus and those going west let us have almost everything."

"How much food is there in Alesia, Daderax, given that there will be eighty thousand of us as well as ten thousand cavalry?"

"Enough for ten days. But we'll be able to bring more food in. The Romans can't block the whole perimeter." He chuckled. "Hardly a scrap of level ground!"

"Then tomorrow we'll split our forces as I've indicated. To Carnutum with Gutruatus, most of the cavalry and a few foot. To Alesia with me, most of the foot and ten thousand horse."

The lands which belonged to the Mandubii lay at an altitude of about eight hundred feet above sea level, with rugged hills rising another six hundred and fifty feet above that. Alesia, their principal stronghold, lay atop a flattish, diamond-shaped mount surrounded by hills of much the same height. On the two long sides, which looked north and south, these adjacent hills crowded in on it, while to the east the end of a ridge almost connected with it. In the bottom of the steep terrain on the two long sides flowed two rivers. To complete its natural excellence, Alesia was most precipitous on the west, where, in front of it, lay the only open and level ground in the area, a little three-mile-long valley where the two rivers flowed almost side by side.

Formidably walled in *murus Gallicus* style, the citadel occupied the steeper western end of the mount; the eastern end sloped gradually downward and was unwalled. Several thousand Mandubii dependents were sheltering in the town—women, children and old ones whose warrior men were off to war.

"Yes, I remember it correctly," said Caesar curtly when the army arrived on the little two-rivers plain at the western end of the mount. "Trebonius, what do the scouts report?"

"That Vercingetorix has definitely gone to earth inside, Caesar. Together with about eighty thousand foot and ten thousand horse. All the cavalry seem to be bivouacked outside the walls on the eastern end of the table. It's safe enough to ride east if you'd like to see for yourself."

"Are you implying that I wouldn't go if it wasn't safe?"

Trebonius blinked. "After all these years? I should hope not! Blame my tongue; it made hard work of what should have been a simple sentence."

Riding a very ordinary German nag, Caesar swung its mean head around ungently and kicked it several times in the ribs to get it moving.

"Ooo-er! Why is he so touchy?" whispered Decimus Brutus.

"Because he was hoping it wasn't as bad as he remembered," said Fabius.

"Why should that sour his day? He can't possibly take the place," said Antony.

Labienus shouted with laughter. "That's what you think, Antonius! Still, I'm glad we've got you. With those shoulders you'll dig magnificently."

"Dig?"

"And dig, and dig, and dig."

"Not his legates, surely!"

"It all depends how far and how much. If *he* starts digging, *we* start digging."

"Ye Gods, I'm working for a madman!"

"I wish I were half as mad," said Quintus Cicero wistfully.

In single file the legates rode behind Caesar along the river flowing past the southern side of Alesia; Antony could see how big the flattish top was, well over a mile from west to east. How it frowned. The rocky outcrops on its flanks. A man could climb to the top easily enough, yes, but not in a military assault. He'd be too short of breath when he arrived to fight, and a target for every spearman or archer atop the walls. Even the half-mile on the eastern end was difficult work for anyone trying to gain a foothold, nor was there room to maneuver.

"They've got in before us," said Caesar, pointing to the bottom of the eastern slope, where the road began to wind upward to the citadel.

The Gauls had built a six-foot wall from the banks of the north river to the south river, then fronted the wall with a ditch containing water. Two shorter walls scrambled up the north and south sides of the mount some distance behind the main one.

Manning these defenses, some of the Gallic cavalry began to call and jeer; Caesar's response was to smile, wave. But from where the legates sat on their German nags, Caesar didn't look at all genial.

Back on the little plain the legions were pitching camp with smooth efficiency.

"Marching camps only, Fabius," said Caesar. "Properly done, but not more. If we're going to finish this war here, there's no point in expending energy on something we'll replace within a very few days."

His legates, gathered round, said nothing.

"Quintus, you're the logging man. Get started at dawn. And don't throw the promising branches away: we need sharpened stakes. Cut saplings for the breastworks, battlements and tower shielding. Sextius, take the Sixth and forage. Bring in every single thing you can find. I need charcoal, so look for it. Not for hardening sharpened stakes, they'll have to go on ordinary fires. The charcoal is for working all the iron we've got. Antistius, the iron is your job. Put the smiths to building their furnaces, and tell them to search out their goad molds. Sulpicius, you're in charge of digging. Fabius, you'll build the breastworks, battlements and towers. As quartermaster, Antonius, your job is to keep my army adequately supplied. I'll strip you of your citizenship, sell you into slavery and then legally crucify you if you don't perform. Labienus, you're the defense man. Stick to cavalry if you can—I need the soldiers for construction duty. Trebonius, you're my second-in-command; you'll follow me everywhere. Decimus and Hirtius, you follow me too. I need millions of everything, and I want at least thirty days' food here, is that understood?"

No one else was asking, so Antony did. "What's the plan?"

Caesar looked at his second-in-command. "What's the plan, Trebonius?"

"We circumvallate," said Trebonius.

Antony gaped. *"Circumvallate?"*

"It is a long word, Antonius, I agree," said Caesar affably. "Cir-cum-val-late. It means we construct fortifications all the way around Alesia until, so to speak, our fortifications swallow their own tail. Vercingetorix doesn't believe I can shut him up on top of that mountain. But I can. And I will."

"It's miles!" cried Antony, still gaping. "And there's no flat land for most of the way around!"

"We fortify up hill and down dale, Antonius. If we can't go around, we go over the top. The main fortifications will embrace the entire perimeter. Two ditches, the outer one fifteen feet wide and eight feet deep, with sloping sides and a trough bottom. It will be filled with water. Right behind it, the second ditch will also be fifteen feet wide and eight feet deep, but V-shaped, no foothold in the bottom. Our wall will rise straight off the back of this ditch, twelve feet of earth excavated out of the ditches. What does that tell you about our wall, Antonius?" Caesar barked.

"That on the inside—our side—the wall will be twelve feet high, but on the outside—their side—it will be twenty feet high because it rises straight out of an eight-foot ditch," said Antony.

"Thank the Gods he's found a butt!" whispered Decimus Brutus to Quintus Cicero.

"Inevitable. Antonius is family," said Quintus Cicero, the expert on families.

"Excellent, Antonius!" said Caesar heartily. "The fighting platform inside at the top of the wall will be ten feet wide. Above it, breastworks for looking over and battlements for dodging behind when not looking over. Understand that, Antonius? Good! Every eighty feet around the perimeter, towers three storeys higher than the fighting platform. Any questions, Antonius?"

"Yes, General. You describe these as the main fortifications. What else do you have in mind?"

"Wherever the ground is flat and likely to see massed attacks, we dig a straight-sided trench twenty feet wide and fifteen feet deep, four hundred paces—that's two thousand feet, Antonius!—away from our water-filled ditch. Is that clear?"

"Yes, General. What do you intend to do with the four hundred paces—that's two thousand feet, General!—between the perpendicular trench and the water-filled ditch?"

"I thought I'd plant a garden. Trebonius, Hirtius, Decimus, let's ride. I want to measure the circumvallation."

"What's your estimate?" asked Antony, grinning.

"Between ten and twelve miles."

"He's mad," said Antony to Fabius with conviction.

"Ah, but it's such a beautiful madness!" said Fabius, smiling.

When the watchers in the citadel saw the activity begin, the surveyors moving for mile after mile all the way around the base of Alesia, the ditches and the wall starting to form, they realized what Caesar was doing. Vercingetorix's instinctive reaction was to send out all his cavalry. But the Gauls found it impossible to conquer their fear of the Germans and went down badly. The worst slaughter occurred at the eastern end of the mount, with the Gauls in full retreat. The gates in Vercingetorix's walls were too narrow to permit the panicked horsemen easy entrance; the Germans, in hot pursuit, cut down the men and made off with the mounts, for it was every German's ambition to own two superb horses.

Over the next nights the surviving Gallic troopers rode off eastward across the ridge, which told Caesar that Vercingetorix now realized his fate. He and eighty thousand foot soldiers were marooned inside Alesia.

The water-filled ditch, the V-shaped ditch, the earth wall, the breastworks, battlements and towers came into being with a speed Antony, though he had thought himself fully educated in all military matters, found unbelievable. Within thirteen days Caesar's legions had completed all of these structures over a perimeter measuring eleven miles, and dug the trench across any flat ground.

They had also finished installing Caesar's "garden" in those four hundred paces of unused land between the water-filled ditch and the trench where it existed. Deep and perpendicular though the trench was, it could be bridged, and was; raiding parties out of Alesia harassed the soldiers working on the fortifications, and did so with increasing expertise. That Caesar had always intended to do what he did was manifest, for the smiths had been casting wicked little barbed goads since camp was established. Thousands and thousands of them, until every sow and sheet of iron plundered from the Bituriges was used up.

There were three different hazards planted in those four hundred paces of Caesar's "garden." Closest to the trench the soldiers buried foot-long logs of wood into which the iron goads had been hammered. The barbed goads projected just above the ground, which was covered with rush matting and scattered leaves. Then came a series of pits three feet deep with slightly sloping sides; viciously sharpened stakes as thick as a man's thigh were planted in their bottoms, the pits filled in two-thirds of the way, the earth tamped down. Rush matting was laid over the ground, the tips of the stakes just poking through it, and leaves were sprinkled everywhere. There were eight courses of these devices, which the troops called "lilies," arranged in a most complicated series of quincunxes and diagonals. Closest to the water-filled ditch came five separate and random courses of narrow trenches five feet deep, in which sharpened, fire-

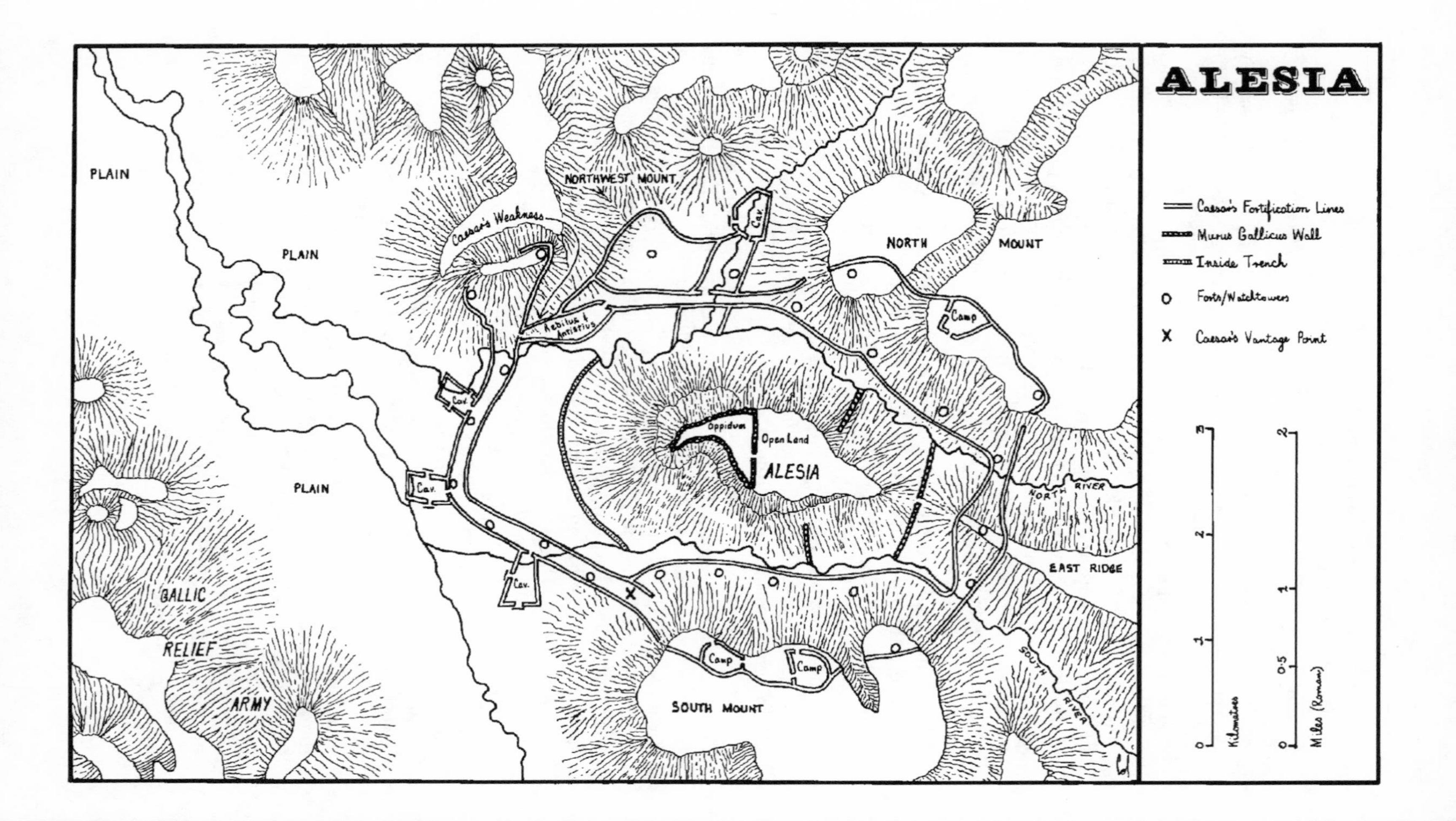
ALESIA
Caesar's Fortification Lines
Murus Gallicus Wall
Inside Trench
Forts/Watchtowers
Caesar's Vantage Point
0
1
2
3
Kilometres
0
0.5
1
2
Miles (Roman)
PLAIN
PLAIN
PLAIN
NORTHWEST MOUNT
Caesar's Weakness
Rebilus & Antistius
Cav.
Cav.
Cav.
Cav.
NORTH
MOUNT
Camp
Oppidum
Open Land
ALESIA
NORTH RIVER
EAST RIDGE
SOUTH RIVER
Camp
Camp
SOUTH MOUNT
GALLIC
RELIEF
ARMY

hardened antlered branches were fixed on a slant aiming the antlers directly into the face of a man or the breast of a horse. These the soldiers jokingly called "tombstones."

The raiding parties came no more.

"Good," said Caesar when the eleven miles were finished. "Now we do it all again on the outside. Fourteen miles by the surveyed route—we have to go up and over the tops of most of the hills, which increases the distance, of course. Do you understand that, Antonius?"

"Yes, Caesar," said Antony, eyes dancing; he enjoyed being Caesar's butt, and happily played up to the image of shambling oaf. He asked the question Caesar wanted him to ask. "Why?"

"Because, Antonius, the Gauls are mustering at Carnutum at this very moment. Before too many days have gone by, they'll arrive at Alesia to rescue Vercingetorix. Therefore we have to have fortifications to keep Vercingetorix in, and fortifications to keep the Gallic relief army out. We will exist between them."

"Ah!" cried Antony, striking his brow with the palm of his huge hand. "Like the track laid out on the Campus Martius for the race between the October Horses! We're on the track itself, with the fortifications forming the rails. Alesia is on the inside—the middle—and the Gallic relief army is on the outside."

"Very good, Antonius! An excellent metaphor!"

"How long have we got before the relief army gets here?"

"My scouts say at least another thirteen days, probably more. But the outer perimeter of fortifications must be finished within the next thirteen days. That's an order."

"It's three miles longer!"

"The troops," said Trebonius, breaking in, "are three miles better experienced, Antonius. They'll build each mile a lot faster this second time around."

They built each mile a lot faster, though the miles were more precipitous. Twenty-six days after Caesar's army arrived at Alesia, it was fenced in between two separate encirclements of fortifications, identical but mirror images of each other. At the same time a total of twenty-three forts were erected inside the lines, a very tall watchtower went up every thousand feet around the outside defenses, and both the legions and the cavalry went into separately fortified camps, the legions on high ground inside the lines, the cavalry on the outside near plenty of good water.

"It isn't a new technique," said Caesar when the inspection tour began on completion of the work. "It was used against Hannibal at Capua—Scipio Aemilianus used it twice, at Numantia and at Carthage. The idea being to keep the besieged inside and negate any possibility of aid and supplies coming from the outside. Though none of the earlier double circumvallations had to contend with relief armies of a quarter-million.

There were more inside Capua than inside Alesia, and the same at Carthage. But we definitely hold the record when it comes to relief armies."

"It's been worth the effort," said Trebonius gruffly.

"Yes. We won't be afforded the luxury of an Aquae Sextiae hereabouts. The Gauls have learned since I came here. Besides, I have no intention of losing my army." His face lit up. "Aren't they good boys?" he asked, love in his voice. "*Such* good boys!"

His legates received a stern look. "It is our responsibility to do everything in our power to keep them alive, if possible unscathed. I won't see so much work on their part go for nothing, nor so much good will. A quarter-million relief army is to err on the conservative side, so I am informed. All of this has been done to save Roman soldier lives. And to ensure victory. One way or the other, the war in Gaul will end here at Alesia." He smiled in genuine content. "However, I do not intend to lose."

The inner line of fortifications lay in the bottom of the vales around Alesia save for the eastern end, where it traversed the end of the ridge; the outer line crossed the beginning of the little plain on the west, climbed to the top of the mount south of Alesia, came down again to the southern river on the east, went over the top of the eastern ridge, down again to the northern river, then up onto the top of the mount north of Alesia. Two of the four infantry camps stood on the high ground of the southern mount, one on the high ground of the northern mount.

And here, where the northern mount descended, lay the only real weakness in the circumvallation. The mount to the northwest had proven too big to cross over. A cavalry camp on the outskirts had been connected back to the outer line of fortifications by a very strong extra line, but the fourth infantry camp lay on ground too difficult to strengthen in the same way. For this reason had the camp been put there; it was to protect a gap existing between the lines ascending the northwestern mount and the lines along the site of the infantry camp, which, to make matters worse, lay aslant a steep and rocky slope.

"If they scout well enough they'll find the weakness," said Labienus, his leather cuirass creaking as he leaned back to show his eagle's profile against the sky; alone among the senior staff, he rode his own high-stepping Italian horse. "A pity."

"Yes," Caesar agreed, "but a worse pity if we ourselves were not acutely aware it exists. The infantry camp will protect it." He looped one leg around the two front pommels—a habit of his—and turned in the saddle to point back into the southwest. "That's my vantage spot, up there on the southern hill. They'll concentrate on this western end; they'll have too many horse to attack on the north or south. Vercingetorix will come down the western end of Alesia to attack our inside fortifications at the same spot."

"Now," sighed Decimus Brutus, "we have to wait."

Perhaps because these days he had no access to wine, Mark Antony found himself so alert, so quivering with interest and energy that he drank in every word the legates said, every look on Caesar's face as well as every word he uttered. To be here at such a moment! Nothing like Alesia had ever been attempted, no matter what Caesar said about Scipio Aemilianus. Fewer than sixty thousand men defending a racetrack twelve miles in circumference, lying between eighty thousand enemy on its inside and a quarter of a million on its outside . . .

I'm *here*! I'm a part of it! Oh, Antonius, you have luck too! I am a part of it! That's why they labor for him, why they love him almost as much as he loves them. He's their passage to eternal fame because he always shares his victories with them. Without them, he's nothing. But he knows it. Gabinius didn't. Nor any of the others I've served with. He knows how they think. He speaks their language. Watching him with them is like watching him stroll through a crowd of women at a party in Rome. There's lightning in the air. But I have it too. One day they'll love me the way they love him. So all I have to do is pick up his tricks, and then when he's too old for this life, I'm going to march into his place. One day Caesar's men will be Antonius's men. Ten more years and he'll be past it. Ten more years and I'll be coming into my own. And I'll be more than Gaius Julius Caesar. Nor will he be there to eclipse me.

Vercingetorix and his thanes stood atop the western walls of Alesia where the flat top narrowed to a point jutting further west, like a wayward crystal grown out of the diamond.

"It looks as if," said Biturgo, "they've just finished riding all the way around their defenses. That's Caesar in the scarlet cloak. Who's the one on the only good horse?"

"Labienus," said Vercingetorix. "I take it that the others have donated their Italian beasts to the German beasts."

"They've been in that same spot for a long time," said Daderax.

"They're looking at the gap in their fortifications. But how when the relief army arrives can I send word to it about the weakness? It's not visible from anywhere but here," Vercingetorix said. He turned away. "Inside. It's time to talk."

There were four: Vercingetorix, his cousin Critognatus, Biturgo and Daderax.

"Food," said the King, his own increasing emaciation lending the word poignancy as well as significance. "Daderax, how much have we left?"

"The grain is gone, but we still have cattle and sheep. A few eggs if there are any chickens left unstrangled. We've been on half-rations for four days. If we halve that again, perhaps another four or five days. After that, we eat shoe leather."

Biturgo brought his fist down on the table so thunderously that the other three jumped. "Oh, Vercingetorix, stop pretending!" he cried. "The relief army should have been here four days ago, we all know that! And there's something else you're not saying, though you should say it. That you don't expect an army to come."

A silence ensued; Vercingetorix, seated at the end of the table, put his hands upon it and turned his head to stare out the huge window aperture behind him, shutters open on the mild spring day. He had been growing a beard and moustache since they had realized they were immured in Alesia, and it was easy to see now why he alone had been clean-shaven: his facial hair was scant and silver-white. Nor had he donned his crown, carefully put away.

"If it were coming," he said at last, "I believe it would be here by now." He sighed. "My hope has gone, it won't come. Therefore the food is our first consideration."

"The Aedui!" snarled Daderax. "The Aedui have betrayed us!"

"Do you mean to surrender?" asked Biturgo.

"*I* won't. But if any of you want to lead your men out and surrender to Caesar, I understand."

"We can't surrender," said Daderax. "If we do, then Gaul has nothing to remember."

"A sortie in full strength, then," said Biturgo. "We can at least go down fighting."

Critognatus was an older man than Vercingetorix and looked nothing like him; he was physically big, red-haired, blue-eyed, thin-lipped, a perfect Gaul. As if he found his chair at the table too confining, he leaped to his feet and began to pace. "I don't believe it," he said, smacking his right fist into his left palm. "The Aedui have burned their boats; they can't betray us because they daren't. Litaviccus would go in Caesar's baggage to Rome, and walk in Caesar's triumph. *He* rules the Aedui, no one else! No, I don't believe it. Litaviccus wants us to win because he wants to be King of Gaul, not some tame Roman puppet vergobret. He'll strive with everything in him to help you win, Vercingetorix—*then* he'll turn traitor! *Then* he'll make his move." He moved back to the table, looked at Vercingetorix imploringly. "Don't you see I'm right?" he asked. "The relief army *will* come! I know it will come! Why it's late, I don't know. How long it will be before it comes, I don't know. But it *will* come!"

Vercingetorix smiled, held out his hand. "Yes, Critognatus, it will come. I believe that too."

"A moment ago you said the opposite," growled Biturgo.

"A moment ago I thought the opposite. But Critognatus is right. The Aedui stand to lose too much by betraying us. No, it may be that the muster took longer because the people were slower reaching it than I had estimated. I keep thinking of how long it would have taken me to organize it, and I shouldn't. Gutruatus is a deliberate man until passion overtakes him, and there's no passion in organizing a muster."

Enthusiasm returned as Vercingetorix spoke; he looked more alive, less careworn.

"Then we halve the rations yet again," said Daderax, sighing.

"There are other things we can do to stretch the food further," said Critognatus.

"What?" asked Biturgo skeptically.

"The warriors have to survive, Biturgo. We have to be here and ready to fight when the relief army comes. Can you imagine what it would do to the relief army if they had to beat Caesar only to enter here and find us dead? What it would do to Gaul? The King dead, Biturgo dead, Daderax dead, Critognatus dead, and all the warriors, and all the Mandubii women and children? Because we didn't have enough food? Because we *starved*?"

Critognatus walked away a little and took his stand where the other three could see him from head to feet. "I say we do what we did when the Cimbri and the Teutones invaded us! I say we do as our people did then—shut themselves up in the *oppida,* and, when the food ran out, ate the useless. Those incapable of fighting. A ghastly diet, but a necessary one. That was how we Gauls survived then. And who were our enemies then? Germans! People who grew bored and restless, who drifted off to find other lands, and left us what we had before they came—our liberty, our customs and traditions, our rights. But who are our enemies now? Romans! Who won't drift off. Who will take our lands, our women, our rights, the fruits of our labors. Build their villas, put in heating furnaces, bathrooms, flower gardens! Cast us down, elevate our serfs! Take over our *oppida* and turn them into cities, with all the evils cities contain! We nobles will be slaves! And I say to you, I would far rather eat human flesh than find myself a Roman slave!"

Vercingetorix gagged, white-faced. "Awful!" he said.

"I think we must take this to the army," said Biturgo.

Daderax had slumped upon the table, head buried in his arms. "My people, my people," he mumbled. "My old ones, my women, their children. My innocents."

Vercingetorix drew a breath. "I couldn't," he said.

"*I* could," said Biturgo. "But leave it to the army to say."

"If the army is to have the say," said Critognatus, "why do we have a king?"

The chair scraped as Vercingetorix got to his feet. "Oh, no, Critognatus, this is one decision the King won't make! Kings have councils—even the greatest of the high kings had councils. And in something which brings us down to the level of the basest beasts, *all* the people must decide," he said. "Daderax, assemble everyone outside the walls on the eastern end of the mount."

"How clever!" whispered Daderax, hauling himself upright. "You know what the vote will be, Vercingetorix! But you won't have to wear the odium. They'll vote to eat my innocents. They're very hungry, and meat's meat. But I have a better idea. Let us do what all peoples do with those whom they cannot afford to feed. Let us give the innocents to the Tuatha. Let us put the innocents on the hillside, as if they were unwanted babies. Let us be like parents, unwilling to feed them, but praying that someone wanting babies will come to the place and take pity on them. It goes out of our hands and into the hands of the Tuatha. Perhaps the Romans will take pity on them, and let them through the lines. Perhaps the Romans have so much to eat that they can afford to throw scraps. Perhaps the relief army will come. Perhaps they will die on the hillside, abandoned by everyone, including the Tuatha. That I will condone. But do you seriously expect me to consent to an alternative which would force me to eat my own innocent people, or starve? I won't! *I won't!* What I will do is cast them out as a gift to the Tuatha. If I do that, we'll have several thousand fewer mouths to feed. Not warrior mouths, but the food reserves will go much, much further." His eyes, blackened by dilated pupils, glittered with tears. "And if the relief army isn't here by the time the food runs out, you can eat me first!"

The last of the livestock grazing the unwalled eastern end of Alesia was driven inside; the women, the children and the old were driven outside. Among them were Daderax's wife, his father, his aged aunt.

Until darkness fell they huddled in groups below the walls, weeping, pleading, crying out to their warrior men inside. They curled up then and slept an uneasy, hungry sleep. With the dawn they wept, begged, cried out again. No one answered. No one came. And at noon they began the slow descent to the foot of the mount, where they halted on the edge of the great trench and reached out their arms toward the Roman wall, lined with heads along the breastworks, up all the towers. But no one answered. No one beckoned. No one came riding across the exquisitely smooth, leaf-strewn ground to bridge the trench, let them in. No one threw them food. The Romans simply looked until the prospect bored them, then turned away and went about their business.

In the late afternoon the Mandubii innocents helped each other up the hill again and clustered beneath the walls to weep, to beg, to scream the names of those they knew and loved inside. But no one answered. No one came. The gates remained closed.

"Oh, Dann, mother of the world, save my people!" babbled Daderax in the darkness of his room. "Sulis, Nuadu, Bodb, Macha, save my people! Let the relief army come tomorrow! Go to Esus and intercede, I pray! Oh, Dann, mother of the world, save my people! Sulis, Nuadu, Bodb, Macha, save my people! Let the relief army come tomorrow! Go to Esus and intercede, I pray! Oh, Dann, mother of the world, save my people! Sulis, Nuadu, Bodb, Macha, save my people. . . ." Over and over again.

* * *

Daderax's prayers were answered. On the morrow the relief army arrived. It rode up from the southwest and took possession of the heights there, not so awesome a sight because the hills were forested, the men partially concealed. But by noon of the following day the three-mile plain of the two rivers was packed from end to end with horsemen, a spectacle no watcher in one of the Roman towers would ever forget. A sea of cavalry, so many thousands they could not be counted.

"So many thousands," said Caesar, standing at his vantage spot just below the summit of the southern mount on its western side, "that they'll never manage to maneuver. Why don't they ever seem to learn that more isn't necessarily better? If they fielded an eighth of the number down there, they could beat us. They'd still be sufficiently stronger numerically, and they'd have room to do what needs to be done. As it is, their numbers mean nothing."

"There's no real commander-in-chief out there," Labienus said. "Several joint commanders at least. And not fully agreed."

Caesar's beloved warhorse, Toes, was nibbling nearby, its strange toed feet almost concealed by the grass. The Roman war command was assembled, those among the legates like Trebonius who didn't already have charge of a section of the field, and thirty tribunes on their German nags ready to ride off with orders to this or that area.

"It's your day, Labienus," said Caesar. "Make it yours. I won't give you orders. Issue your own."

"I'll use the four thousand in the three camps on the plain side," said Labienus, looking fierce. "The camp on the north side I'll keep in reserve. They have to fight on the vertical axis of the plain; four thousand of mine will be more than enough. If the front ranks fall back, they'll ride their own rear down."

The four cavalry camps were extensions outward of the great perimeter rather than built on its inside wall like the infantry camps; they were heavily fortified, but the goads, the lilies and the tombstones did not mine the ground in front of them. While Caesar and his high command watched, the outside gates of the three cavalry camps impinging on the little plain flew open, and the Roman horse rode out.

"Here comes Vercingetorix," said Trebonius.

Caesar turned to where the gates at the western end of the citadel's south walls had been flung open; the Gauls were flocking out to scamper down the steep western slope, armed with trestles, ramps, planks, ropes, grapples, screens.

"At least we know they're hungry," said Quintus Cicero.

"And that they know what's in the ground waiting for them," said Trebonius. "But they don't have enough gear stored up there; it's going to take them hours to cross the goads and lilies before they have to contend with the tombstones and the real fortifications. The cavalry fight will be finished before they reach us."

Caesar whistled to Toes, which came to him immediately; he leaped up without a toss from the groom and adjusted his brilliant scarlet *paludamentum* so that it lay across the horse's rump. "Mount, everyone," he said. "Tribunes, keep your ears open. I don't want to have to repeat an order and I expect an order to reach its destination in exactly the same words you heard from me."

Though Caesar had every foot soldier at his proper post and every foot soldier knew what was expected of him, he didn't expect an attack from the enemy foot on this first day; whoever was in command clearly expected that the enormous mass of horse would win for Gaul, and soften the Roman troops up for an infantry attack on the following day. But this unknown Gallic commander was clever enough to put a few archers and spearmen among his masses of cavalry, and when the two forces met it was these men on foot who gained ground for the Gauls.

From noon until amost sunset the outcome of the battle was in doubt, though the Gauls thought they had it won. Then Caesar's four hundred original Germans, fighting together in one group, managed to mass and charge. The Gauls gave way, floundered into the huge number of unengaged horsemen behind them, and exposed the footbound archers and spearmen. Easy meat for the Germans, who killed them all. The tide turned, the German and Remi troopers all over the field pressed an attack, and the Gauls broke into retreat. They were pursued up to the Gallic camp, but Labienus, triumphant, ordered them back before foolhardy courage undid so much good work.

Vercingetorix and his army, as Trebonius had predicted, were still trying to cross the goads and the lilies when the noises from the plain outside told them where victory had gone. They packed up the gear they had got together so painfully and went back up the hill to their prison on its top. But they didn't encounter the Mandubii innocents, who were still clustered on the eastern end of the mount and too terrified to venture near the sounds of war.

The next day saw no action at all.

"They'll come across the plain in the night," said Caesar in council, "and this time they'll use foot. Trebonius, take command of the outside fortifications between the north river and the middle one of Labienus's three camps. Antonius, here's your chance. You'll command the outside fortifications from Labienus's middle camp to my spot on the slope of the southern mount. Fabius, you'll command the inside fortifications from the north to the south river in case Vercingetorix makes it across the goads, the lilies and the tombstones before we beat those attacking on the outside. They don't know what they're in for," Caesar went on with satisfaction, "but they'll have hurdles and ramps to bridge the ditches, so some of them might get through. I want torches everywhere on the ramparts, but held by soldiers, not fixed. The punishment for any man who mishandles his torch and sets fire to our works will be a flogging. I want all the scorpions and bigger catapultae on the towers, ballistae positioned on the ground where they can fire one-pounders further than our far trench. Those on ballistae can find their range while there's still daylight, but those firing bolts from the scorpions and grapeshot from the big catapultae will have to rely on torchlight. It won't be like picking off men at Avaricum, but I expect the artillery to do its best and add to Gallic confusion. Fabius, if Vercingetorix gets further than I think he will, call for reinforcements immediately. Antistius and Rebilus, keep your two legions inside your camp and watch for any sign that the Gauls have found our weakness."

The attack from the outside came at midnight, and started with a huge bellow from many thousands of throats, the signal to Vercingetorix in the citadel that an assault had begun. The faint sound of trumpets drifting down from Alesia answered the bellow; Vercingetorix was coming out and attacking too.

It was impossible for fewer than sixty thousand to man a double set of ramparts which together totaled some twenty-five miles. Caesar's strategy depended upon the Gauls' concentrating on particular areas, and sorties in the darkness were feasible only on the flat ground of the plain. Because he never underestimated his foe, Caesar didn't leave the rest of the perimeter completely undefended, but the main duty of the watchtowers was to spot enemy forces approaching and notify the high command at once. Two things governed his campaign in those last few frenzied days around Alesia: speed of troop movements and flexibility in tactics.

The Gauls on the outside had brought along a fair amount of artillery, some of it inherited from Sabinus and Cotta, most of it copied from those original pieces, and they had learned how to use it. While some of them were busy hurdling the outer trench, others shot stones onto the Roman ramparts, easy to see in the light of all those torches Caesar had ordered. They did some damage, but the one-pounders the Roman ballistae were firing constantly did more, for they had found their range, something the Gauls had not had the sophistication—or the opportunity—to do. The trench filled in or bridged, thousands upon thousands of Gauls commenced the charge to the Roman fortifications across those two thousand smooth and leafy feet of ground.

Some were ripped up by the goads, some impaled on the lilies, more ran upon the tombstones; and the closer they got, the more of them went down from scorpion bolts, the artillerymen using the better light and hardly able to miss, so great was the pack outside. In the darkness it was impossible to understand what manner of devices the Romans had planted in the ground, nor discover what if any pattern had been used. So the Gauls behind used the bodies of those who had fallen as fill, and reached the two ditches. They had brought their ramps and hurdles with them, but the light of the torches here was brilliant, and right at the junction between the earth wall and the breastworks more fire-hardened and wickedly sharp antlers had been fixed so thickly that no Gaul could find a way among them, nor manage to position his ladder over the top of them. Roman archers, slingers, spearmen and artillerymen picked them off by the hundreds.

Alert and efficient, Trebonius and Antony kept reinforcements pouring in wherever the Gauls looked likely to reach the ramparts. Many of them were wounded, but most wounds were minor, and the defenders held their own comfortably.

At dawn the Gauls outside drew off, leaving thousands of bodies strewn across the goads, the lilies, the tombstones. And Vercingetorix on the inside, still struggling to bridge the water-filled ditch, heard the noise of their retreat. The whole Roman force would transfer to his side of the lines; Vercingetorix gathered his men and equipment together and returned to the citadel up the western slope, well away from the Mandubii innocents.

From prisoners Caesar learned the dispositions of the Gallic relief army. As Labienus had guessed, a split high command: Commius the Atrebatan, Cotus, Eporedorix and Viridomarus of the Aedui, and Vercingetorix's cousin Vercassivellaunus.

"Commius I expected," said Caesar, "but where's Litaviccus? I wonder. Cotus is too old to sit well in such a youthful high command, Eporedorix and Viridomarus are insignificant. The one to watch will be Vercassivellaunus."

"Not Commius?" asked Quintus Cicero.

"He's Belgic; they had to give him a titular command. The Belgae are broken, Quintus. I don't imagine Belgic contribution to the relief army is more than a tenth of its strength. This is a Celtic revolt and it belongs to Vercingetorix, little though the Aediu might like that. Vercassivellaunus is the one to watch."

"How much longer will it go on?" asked Antony, very pleased with himself; he had, he decided, done quite as well as Trebonius.

"I think the next attack will be the hardest, and the last," said Caesar, looking at his cousin with an uncomfortable shrewdness, as if he understood very well what was going through Antony's mind. "We can't clean up the field outside on the plain, and they'll use the bodies as bridges. A great deal depends upon whether they've found our weakness. Antistius, Rebilus, I can't emphasize enough that you must be ready to defend your camp. Trebonius, Fabius, Sextius, Quintus, Decimus, be prepared to move like lightning. Labienus, you'll hover in the area, and have the German cavalry in the camp on the north side. I don't need to tell you what to do, but keep me informed every inch of the way."

* * *

Vercassivellaunus conferred with Commius, Cotus, Eporedorix and Viridomarus; Gutruatus, Sedulius and Drappes were also there, together with one Ollovico, a scout.

"The Roman defenses on the northwestern mount look excellent from here and from the plain," said Ollovico, who belonged to the Andes, but had made a great name for himself as a man who could spy out the land better than any other. "However, while the battle raged last night, I investigated at close quarters. There is a big infantry camp below the northwestern mount adjacent to the north river, and beyond it, up a narrow valley on a tributary stream, a cavalry camp. The fortifications between this cavalry camp and the main line are very heavy; there's little hope there. But the Roman encirclement is not quite complete. There is a gap on the banks of the north river beyond the infantry camp. From here or from the plain it's invisible. They've been as clever as they could given the terrain, for their fortifications go up the side of the northwestern mount, and really do look as if they go right over the top. But they do not. It's an illusion. As I've explained, there is a gap going down to the river, a tongue of unwalled land. You can't get into the Roman ring from it; that's not why finding it excited me. What it does do is enable you to attack the Roman line at the infantry camp from downhill—the fortifications are aslant the sloping flank, they don't go up and over. Nor is the ground outside the camp's double ditch and wall mined with hazards. The ground's not suitable. Much easier to get inside. Take that camp, and you will have penetrated the Roman ring."

"Ah!" said Vercassivellaunus, smiling.

"Very good," purred Cotus.

"We need Vercingetorix to tell us how best to do it," said Drappes, pulling at his moustach.

"Vercassivellaunus will cope," said Sedulius. "The Arverni are mountain people—they understand land like this."

"I need sixty thousand of our very finest warriors," said Vercassivellaunus. "I want them hand-picked from among those peoples known not to count the cost."

"Then start with Bellovaci," said Commius instantly.

"Foot, Commius, not horse. But I will take the five thousand Nervii, the five thousand Morini and the five thousand Menapii. Sedulius, I'll take you and your ten thousand Lemovices. Drappes, you and ten thousand of your Senones. Gutruatus, you and ten thousand of your Carnutes. For the sake of Biturgo I'll take five thousand from among the Bituriges, and for the sake of my cousin, the King, ten thousand of the Arverni. Is that agreeable?"

"Very much so," said Sedulius.

The others nodded gravely, though the three Aeduan co-generals, Cotus, Eporedorix and Viridomarus, looked unhappy. The command had been thrust upon them unexpectedly at Carnutum when Litaviccus, for reasons no one began to understand, suddenly climbed upon his horse and deserted the Aedui with his kinsman, Surus. One moment Litaviccus was sole leader, the next—gone! Vanished east with Surus!

Thus command of the thirty-five thousand Aeduan troops had devolved upon Cotus, old and tired, and two men who were still not sure that they wanted to be free of Rome. Besides which, their presence at this council, they suspected, was mere lip service.

"Commius, you'll command the cavalry and advance on the plain under the northwestern mount. Eporedorix and Viridomarus will take the rest of the foot to the south side of the plain and use it to make a huge demonstration. Try to force your way to the Roman ramparts—we'll keep Caesar busy there too. Cotus, you'll hold this camp. Is that clear, you three Aedui?" Vercassivellaunus asked, tone confident, voice clipped.

The three Aedui said it was clear.

"We time the attack for the hour when the sun is directly overhead. That gives the Romans no advantage, and as the sun sinks it will shine in their eyes, not in ours. I'll leave camp with the sixty thousand at midnight tonight with Ollovico as our guide. We'll climb the northwestern mount and go part of the way down the tongue before dawn, then hide ourselves in the trees until we hear a great shout. Commius, that's your responsibility."

"Understood," said Commius, whose rather homely face was grossly disfigured by a scar across his forehead, the wound Gaius Volusenus had been responsible for during that meeting primed for treachery. He burned to avenge himself; all his dreams of being High King of the Belgae were gone, his people the Atrebates so reduced by Labienus a scant month before that all he could bring with him to the muster at Carnutum was four thousand, mostly old men and underaged boys. He had hoped for his southern neighbors the Bellovaci; but of the ten thousand Gutruatus and Cathbad had demanded from the Bellovaci a mere two thousand came to Carnutum, and those only because Commius had begged them from their king, Correus, his friend and relative by marriage.

"Take two thousand if it makes you happy," said Correus, "but no more. The Bellovaci prefer to fight Caesar and Rome in their own time and in their own way. Vercingetorix is a Celt, and the Celtae don't know the first thing about attrition or annihilation. By all means go, Commius, but remember when you come back defeated that the Bellovaci will be looking for *Belgic* allies. Keep your men and my two thousand very safe. Don't die for the Celtae."

Correus was right, thought Commius, beginning to see the shape of a vast fate hovering above Alesia: the Roman Eagle. And the Celtae didn't know anything about attrition or annihilation. Ah, but the Belgae did! Correus was right. Why die for the Celtae?

* * *

By midmorning the watchers in the citadel of Alesia knew that the relief army was massing for another attack. Vercingetorix smiled in quiet satisfaction, for he had seen the flash of mail shirts and helmets among the trees on the northwestern mount above the vulnerable infantry camp. The Romans would not have from their much lower position, even including, he thought, those in the towers atop the southern mount, for the sun was behind Alesia. For a while he fretted that the watchtowers on the northern mount might have seen the telltale glitters, but the horses tethered to the feet of the towers in readiness remained tethered, drowsing with heads down. The sun was coming up over Alesia, directly opposite; yes, Alesia was definitely the only place able to see the glitters.

"This time we're going to be absolutely prepared," he said to his three colleagues. "They'll move at noon, I'd think. So we will move at noon. And we concentrate exclusively on the area around that infantry camp. If we can breach the Roman ring on our side, the Romans won't be able to hold on to both sides at once."

"Far harder for us," said Biturgo. "We're on the uphill side. Whoever is in that tongue of land is on the downhill side."

"Does that discourage you?" demanded Vercingetorix.

"No. I simply made an observation."

"There's a great deal of movement inside the Roman ring," said Daderax. "Caesar knows there's trouble coming."

"We've never thought him a fool, Daderax. But he doesn't know about our men inside the gap above his infantry camp."

At noon the relief army, horse massed to the north side of the plain and foot south of them, let out the huge bellow heralding attack and commenced to run the gauntlet of the goads, the lilies and the tombstones. A fact which registered on Vercingetorix only vaguely; his men were already halfway down the hill, converging on the inner side of the ring at the infantry camp held by Antistius and Rebilus. This time they had mantlets with them, equipped with clumsy wheels, some shelter from the scorpion bolts and grape-sized pebbles being fired from the tops of the Roman towers, and those warriors unable to squeeze beneath the mantlets locked their shields above their heads to form tortoises. The goads, the lilies and the tombstones by now had well-worn paths through them, packed with bodies or earth or hurdles; Vercingetorix reached the water-filled ditch even as the sixty thousand men belonging to Vercassivellaunus were throwing earth into the ditches on the other side, working much faster because the slope was downward.

From time to time the King of the Gauls became aware of Gallic successes elsewhere, for the infantry camp was well up the slope and enabled him to see down into the Roman ring across the end of the plain of the two rivers. Columns of smoke arose around several of the Roman towers on the outside perimeter; the Gallic foot there had reached the wall and were busy demolishing it. But he couldn't quite sustain a feeling that victory was imminent there, for out of the corner of his eye he could see the figure in the scarlet cloak, and that figure was here, there, everywhere, while cohorts held back as reserves were poured in wherever the smoke rose.

There came a huge scream of joy: Vercassivellaunus and his sixty thousand were up and over the Roman wall, there was fighting on the Roman battle platform, and the disciplined ranks of Roman foot were fending them off by using their *pila* as siege spears. At the same time the prisoners of Alesia managed to bridge the two ditches; grappling hooks were flung upward, ladders everywhere. Now it would happen! The Romans couldn't fight on two fronts at once. But from somewhere came an immense inrush of Roman reserves, and there on a dappled grey Italian horse was Labienus, coming down the hill to the north of the oblivious sixty thousand; he had brought two thousand Germans out of the cavalry camp beyond, and he was going to fall on Vercassivellaunus's rear.

Vercingetorix shrieked a warning, drowned in another noise; even as the tower to either side of him came crashing and his men scrambled onto the Roman wall, there came a deafening roar from further away. Dashing the sweat from his eyes, Vercingetorix turned to look down inside the Roman ring on the edge of the plain. And there, riding at a headlong gallop, the brilliant scarlet cloak billowing behind him, came Caesar with his high command and tribunes streaming behind him, and thousands of foot soldiers at a run. All along the Roman fighting platforms the Roman soldiers were cheering, cheering, cheering. Not at a victory—this colossal struggle wasn't over. They were cheering *him*. Caesar. So erect, so much a part of the horse he rode—the lucky horse with the toes? Was there really a horse with toes?

The beleaguered Roman troops defending the outside walls of the infantry camp heard the cheering even if they didn't see the figure of Caesar; they threw their *pila* into the enemy faces, drew their swords and attacked. So did the troops defending the inside wall against Vercingetorix. His men began to falter, were steadily pushed down from the wall; the squealing of horses and the howling of Gauls filled Vercingetorix's ears. Labienus had fallen on the Gallic rear while Caesar's soldiers went up and over the outside wall, crushing the sixty thousand warriors between them.

Many of the Arverni, Mandubii and Bituriges stayed to fight to the death, but Vercingetorix didn't want that. He managed to rally those near him, got Biturgo and Daderax doing the same—oh, where was Critognatus?—and returned up the mount to Alesia.

Once inside the citadel, Vercingetorix would speak to no one. He stood on the walls and watched for the rest of the day as the victorious Romans—how *could* they have won?—tidied up. That they were exhausted was evident, for they couldn't organize a pursuit of those who had fought along the plain, and it was almost dark when Labienus led a great host of cavalry out across the southwestern mount where the Gallic camp had been. He was going to harass the retreat, cut down as many laggards as he could.

Vercingetorix's eyes always sought Caesar, still mounted, still in that scarlet cloak, trotting about busily. What a superb craftsman! Victory his, yet the breaches in the Roman perimeter were being repaired, everything was being made ready in case of another attack. His legions had cheered him. In the midst of their great travail, beset on all sides, they had cheered him. As if they truly believed that while he bestrode his lucky horse and they could see his scarlet cloak, they couldn't lose. Did they deem him a god? Well, why should they not? Even the Tuatha loved him. If the Tuatha did not love him, Gaul would have won. A foreign darling for the Gods of the Celtae. But then, the Gods of every land most prized excellence.

In his room, lit by lamps, Vercingetorix took his golden crown from under its chaste white cover, still bearing the little sprig of mistletoe. He put it on the table and sat before it, but did not touch it as the hours dripped by and the sounds and smells came stealing through his window. A huge shout of laughter from the Roman ring. Faint mews which told him Daderax had brought his innocents into the citadel and was feeding them broth from the last of the cattle—poor Daderax! The smell of broth was nauseating. So was the stench of impaled bodies just beginning to rot among the lilies. And over everything, the brooding of the Tuatha like unspoken thunder, the lightless dawn coming, coming, coming. Gaul was finished, and so was he.

In the morning he spoke to those who still lived, with Daderax and Biturgo beside him. Of Critognatus no one had heard; he was somewhere on the field, dead or dying or captured.

"It is over," he said in the marketplace, his voice strong and even, easily understood. "There will be no united Gaul. We will have no independence. The Romans will be our masters, though I do not think an enemy as generous as Caesar will force us to pass beneath the yoke. I believe that Caesar wants to make peace with us, rather than exterminate those of us who are left. A fat and healthy Gaul is more useful to the Romans than a wilderness."

No flicker of emotion crossed his skull-like face; he went on dispassionately. "The Tuatha admire death on a battlefield, none is more honorable. But it is not a part of our Druidic tradition to put an end to our own lives. In other places, I have learned, the people of a beaten citadel like Alesia will kill themselves sooner than go into captivity. The Cilicians did it when Alexander the Great came. The Greeks of Asia have done it. And the Italians. But we do not. This life is a trial we must suffer until it comes to a natural end, no matter what shape that end might take.

"What I ask of all of you, and ask you to pass on to those who are not here, is that you turn your minds and your energies toward making a great country out of Gaul in a way the Romans will not despise. You must multiply and grow rich again. For one day—*someday*!—Gaul will rise again! The dream is not just a dream! Gaul will rise again! Gaul must endure, for Gaul is great! Through all the generations of subservience which must come, hug the idea, cherish the dream, perpetuate the reality of Gaul! I will pass, but remember me for always! One day Gaul, my Gaul, will exist! One day Gaul *will* be free!"

The listeners made no sound. Vercingetorix turned and went inside, Daderax and Biturgo following. The Gallic warriors slowly drifted away, holding the words their king had spoken within their minds to repeat to their children.

"The rest of what I have to say is for your ears only," Vercingetorix said in the empty, echoing council chamber.

"Sit," said Biturgo gently.

"No. No. It may be, Biturgo, that Caesar will take you prisoner, as the King of a great and numerous people. But I think you will go free, Daderax. I want you to go to Cathbad and tell him what I said here this morning to our men. Tell him too that I didn't embark upon this campaign for self-glory. I did it to free my country from foreign domination. Always for the general good, never for my own advancement."

"I'll tell him," said Daderax.

"And now the two of you have a decision to make. If you require my death, I will go to execution here inside Alesia, with our men witnessing it. Or I will send envoys to Caesar and offer to give myself up."

"Send envoys to Caesar," said Biturgo.

"Tell Vercingetorix," said Caesar, "that all the warriors inside Alesia must give up their weapons and their shirts of mail. This will be done tomorrow just after dawn, before I accept King Vercingetorix's surrender. They will precede him by long enough to have thrown every sword, spear, bow, arrow, axe, dagger and mace into our trench. They will divest themselves of their mail shirts and toss them in on top of the weapons. Only then may the King and his colleagues Biturgo and Daderax come down. I will be waiting there," he said, pointing to a place below the citadel just outside the Roman inner fortifications. "At dawn."

He had a little dais built, two feet higher than the ground, and on it placed the ivory curule chair of his high estate. Rome accepted this surrender, therefore the proconsul would not wear armor. He would don his purple-bordered toga, the maroon shoes with the crescent buckle of the consular, and his oak leaf chaplet, the *corona civica,* awarded for personal bravery in the field—and the only distinction Pompey the Great had never won. The plain ivory cylinder of his imperium just fitted the length of his forearm, one end tucked into his cupped palm, the other nestling in the crook of his elbow. Only Hirtius shared the dais with him.

He seated himself in the classical pose, right foot forward, left foot back, spine absolutely straight, shoulders back, chin up. His marshals stood on the ground to the right of the dais, Labienus in a gold-worked silver cuirass with the scarlet sash of his imperium ritually knotted and looped. Trebonius, Fabius, Sextius, Quintus Cicero, Sulpicius, Antistius and Rebilus were clad in their best armor, Attic helmets under their left arms. The more junior men stood on the ground to the left of the dais—Decimus Brutus, Mark Antony, Minucius Basilus, Munatius Plancus, Volcatius Tullus and Sempronius Rutilus.

Every single vantage place on the walls and up the towers was taken as the legions crowded to watch, while the cavalry stood horsed on either side of a long corridor from the trench to the dais; the goads and lilies were gone.

The remnants of Vercingetorix's eighty thousand warriors who had lived for over a month inside Alesia appeared first, as instructed. One by one they threw their weapons and mail shirts into the trench, then were herded by several squadrons of cavalry to a waiting place.

Down the hill from the citadel came Vercingetorix, Biturgo and Daderax behind him. The King of Gaul rode his fawn horse, immaculately groomed, harness glittering, feet stepping high. Every piece of gold and sapphire Vercingetorix owned was set upon his arms, neck, chest, shawl. Baldric and belt flashed. On his head he wore the golden helmet with the golden wings.

He rode sedately through the ranks of cavalry almost to the dais upon which Caesar sat. Then he dismounted, removed the baldric holding his sword, unhooked the dagger from his belt, walked forward and deposited them on the edge of the dais. He stepped back a little, folded his feet and sat cross-legged upon the ground. Off came the crown; Vercingetorix bowed his bare head in submission.

Biturgo and Daderax, already deprived of their weapons, followed their king's example.

All this happened in the midst of a huge silence; hardly a breath was drawn. Then someone in a tower let out a shriek of joy and the ovation began, went on and on.

Caesar sat without moving a muscle, his face serious and intent, his eyes upon Vercingetorix. When the cheering died down he nodded to Aulus Hirtius, also togate; Hirtius, a scroll in his hand, stepped down from the dais. A scribe hidden behind the marshals hurried forward with pen, ink and a foot-high wooden table. From which Vercingetorix deduced that had he not sat upon the ground, the Romans would have compelled him to kneel to sign this submission. As it was he simply reached out, dipped the pen in the ink, wiped its nib on the side of the well to indicate that he was properly schooled, and signed his submission where Hirtius indicated. The scribe sprinkled sand, shook it off, rolled up the single piece of paper and handed it to Hirtius, who then returned to his place on the dais.

Only then did Caesar rise to his feet. He jumped off the little dais easily and walked to Vercingetorix, right hand extended to help him up.

Vercingetorix took it and uncoiled. Daderax and Biturgo got up without assistance.

"A noble struggle with a good battle at its end," said Caesar, drawing the King of Gaul toward the place where a gap had been hewn in the Roman fortifications.

"Is my cousin Critognatus a prisoner?" asked Vercingetorix.

"No, he's dead. We found him on the field."

"Who else is dead?"

"Sedulius of the Lemovices."

"Who has been taken prisoner?"

"Your cousin Vercassivellaunus. Eporedorix and Cotus of the Aedui. Most of the relief army got away; my men were too spent to pursue them. Gutruatus, Viridomarus, Drappes, Teutomarus, others."

"What will you do to them?"

"Titus Labienus informs me that all the tribes fled in the direction of their own lands. The army broke up into tribes the moment it was over the hill. I don't intend to punish any tribe which goes home and settles down peacefully," said Caesar. "Of course Gutruatus will have to answer for Cenabum, and Drappes for the Senones. I will take Biturgo into custody."

He stopped and looked at the other two Gauls, who approached. "Daderax, you may return to your citadel and keep those among the warriors who are Mandubii. A treaty will be drawn up before I leave, and you will be required to sign it. Provided you adhere to its letter, no further reprisals will be exacted. You may take some of your men and see what you can find in the camp of the relief army to feed your people. I've taken the booty and what food I need already, but there's food left there. Those men who belong to the Arverni or the Bituriges can depart for their homelands. Biturgo, you are my prisoner."

Daderax walked forward and went down on his left knee to Vercingetorix; he embraced Biturgo, kissed him on the lips in the Gallic manner, then turned and walked back to the men gathered beyond the trench.

"What happens to Biturgo and me?" asked Vercingetorix.

"Tomorrow you'll start the journey to Italia," said Caesar. "You'll wait there until I hold my triumph."

"During which we will all die."

"No, that's not our custom. *You* will die, Vercingetorix. Biturgo won't. Vercassivellaunus won't, nor Eporedorix. Cotus may. Gutruatus will; he massacred Roman citizens, as did Cotus. Litaviccus certainly will."

"If you capture Gutruatus or Litaviccus."

"True. You'll all walk in my triumph, but only the kings and the butchers will die. The rest will be sent home."

Vercingetorix smiled, his face white, dark blue eyes huge and very sad. "I hope it won't be long before you triumph. My bones don't like dungeons."

"Dungeons?" Caesar stopped walking to look at him. "Rome has no dungeons, Vercingetorix. There's a fallen-down old jail in an abandoned quarry, the Lautumiae, where we put people for a day or two, but there's nothing to prevent their walking out unless we chain them, which is extremely rare." He frowned. "The last time we chained a man he was murdered in the night."

"Vettius the informer, while you were consul," said the captured King instantly.

"Very good! No, you will be housed in extreme comfort in a fortress town like Corfinium, Asculum Picentum, Praenestae, Norba. There are many of them. No two of you will be in the same town, nor will any of you know where the others are. You'll have the run of a good garden and will be permitted to go riding under escort."

"So you treat us like honored guests, then strangle us."

"The whole idea of the triumphal parade," said Caesar, "is to show the citizens of Rome how mighty is her army and the men who command her army. How appalling, to display some half-starved, beaten, dirty and unimpressive prisoner stumbling along in chains! That would defeat the purpose of the triumph. You'll walk clad in all your best regalia, looking every inch a king and the leader of a great people who almost defeated us. Your health and your well-being, Vercingetorix, are of paramount importance to me. The Treasury will inventory your jewels—including your crown—and take them from you, but they will be returned to you before you walk in my triumph. At the foot of the Forum Romanum you will be led aside and conducted to the only true dungeon Rome possesses, the Tullianum. Which is a tiny structure used for the ritual of execution, not to house a prisoner. I'll send to Gergovia for all your clothes and any belongings you'd like to take with you."

"Including my wife?"

"Of course, if you wish it. There will be women aplenty, but if you want your wife, you shall have her."

"I would like my wife. And my youngest child."

"Of course. A boy or a girl?"

"A boy. Celtillus."

"He will be educated in Italia, you realize that."

"Yes." Vercingetorix wet his lips. "I go tomorrow? Isn't that very soon?"

"Soon, but wiser. No one will have time to organize a rescue. Once you reach Italia, rescue is out of the question. So is escape. It isn't necessary to imprison you, Vercingetorix. Your alien appearance and your language difficulties will keep you safe."

"I might learn Latin and escape in disguise."

Caesar laughed. "You might. But don't count on it. What we will do is weld that exquisite golden torc around your neck. Not a prisoner's collar of the kind they use in the East, but it will brand you more surely than any prisoner's collar could."

Trebonius, Decimus Brutus and Mark Antony walked some paces behind; the campaign had drawn them together, despite the manifest differences in their characters. Antony and Decimus Brutus knew each other from the Clodius Club, but Trebonius was somewhat older, very much less wellborn. To Trebonius they were a breath of fresh air, for he had been in the field with Caesar for so long, it seemed, that the older legates had all the vivacity and appeal of grandfathers. Antony and Decimus Brutus were like very attractive, naughty little boys.

"What a day for Caesar," said Decimus Brutus.

"Monumental," said Trebonius dryly. "I mean that literally. He's bound to put the whole scene on a float at his triumph."

"Oh, but he's unique!" laughed Antony. "Did you ever see anyone who could be so *royal*? It's in his bones, I suppose. The Julii Caesares make the Ptolemies of Egypt look like parvenus."

"I would wish," said Decimus Brutus thoughtfully, "that a day like today could happen to me, but it won't, you know. It won't happen to any of us."

"I don't see why not," said Antony indignantly; he disliked anyone's puncturing his dreams of coming glory.

"Antonius, you're a wonder to behold, you have been for years! But you're a gladiator, not the October Horse," said Decimus Brutus. "Thank, man, *think*! There's no one like him. There never has been and there never will be."

"I wouldn't call Marius or Sulla sluggards," said Antony.

"Marius was a New Man; he didn't have the blood. Sulla had the blood, but he wasn't natural. I mean that in every way. He drank, he liked little boys, he had to learn to general troops because it wasn't in his veins. Whereas Caesar has no flaws. No weaknesses you can slip a thin dagger into and work the plates apart, so to speak. He doesn't drink wine, so his tongue never runs away with him. When he says some outrageous thing he intends to do, you know in his case it's not impossible. You called him unique, Antonius, and you were right. Don't recant because you dream of outstripping him—it's not realistic. None of us will. So why exhaust ourselves trying? Leave aside the genius, and you still have to contend with a phenomenon I for one have never plumbed—the love affair between him and his soldiers. We'll never match that in a thousand years. No, not you either, Antonius, so shut your mouth. You have a bit of it, but nowhere near all of it. He does, and today is the proof!" said Decimus Brutus fiercely.

"It won't go down well in Rome," said Trebonius. "He's just eclipsed Pompeius Magnus. I predict that our consul without a colleague will detest that."

"Eclipsed Pompeius?" asked Antony. "Today? I don't see how, Trebonius. Gaul's a big job, but Pompeius conquered the East. He has kings in his clientele."

"True. But think, Antonius, *think*! At least half of Rome believes that it was Lucullus did all the hard work in the East, that Pompeius simply strolled in when the hard work was over and took all the credit. No one can say that about Caesar in Gaul. And which story will Rome believe, that Tigranes prostrated himself before Pompeius, or that Vercingetorix hunkered down in the dust at Caesar's feet? Quintus Cicero will be writing *that* scene to his big brother this moment—Pompeius rests on more specious evidence. Who walked in Pompeius's triumphs? Certainly not a Vercingetorix!"

"You're right, Trebonius," said Decimus Brutus. "Today will ensure that Caesar becomes the First Man in Rome."

"The *boni* won't let that happen," said Antony jealously.

"I hope they have the sense to let it," said Trebonius. He looked at Decimus Brutus. "Haven't you noticed the change, Decimus? He's not more royal, but he is more autocratic. And *dignitas* is an obsession! He cares more about his personal share of public worth and standing than anyone I've ever read about in the history books. More than Scipio Africanus or even Scipio Aemilianus. I don't think there are any lengths to which Caesar wouldn't go to defend his *dignitas*. I dread the *boni*'s trying! They're such complacent couch generals—they read his dispatches and they sniff with contempt, sure he's embroidered them. Well, in some ways he does. But not in the only way which matters—his record of victories. You and I have been with the man through thick and thin, Decimus. The *boni* don't know what we know. Once Caesar's got the bit between his teeth, nothing will stop him. The will in the man is incredible. And if the *boni* try to cast him down, he'll pile Pelion on top of Ossa to stop them."

"A worry," said Decimus Brutus, frowning.

"Do you think," asked Antony plaintively, "that tonight the Old Man will let us have a jug or two of wine?"

It was Cathbad responsible for the change in Litaviccus. He had gone to the muster at Carnutum convinced that his strategy was right: assist Vercingetorix to throw the Romans out of Gaul, then start moving in on his throne. An Aeduan to bow and scrape before an Arvernian? A yokel from the mountains who spoke neither Latin nor Greek, who could pretend literacy by making his mark on a piece of paper he couldn't read? Who would have to lean on the Druids in all true matters of state? What a king for Gaul!

He took the Aedui to the muster nonetheless, and there found Cotus, Eporedorix and Viridomarus with a few more Aedui troopers. The tribes were coming in, but very, very slowly; even after the news was shouted that Vercingetorix was marooned inside Alesia, the tribes were slow. Gutruatus and Cathbad struggled manfully to speed things up, but Commius and the Belgae hadn't come, and this one, and that one. . . . Surus turned up with the Ambarri.

A great Aeduan noble (the Ambarri belonged to the Aedui), Surus was the only one Litaviccus could bear to greet when he arrived; Cotus was busy thoroughly indoctrinating Eporedorix and Viridomarus, who still shivered in their shoes at the thought of Roman vengeance should anything go wrong.

"I ask you, Surus, why would a man of Cotus's standing even worry his head about putting some iron into the backbone of an upstart like Viridomarus? *Caesar's* creature!"

They were walking between the trees of Carnutum itself, well away from the open plain where the muster was assembling.

"Cotus would do anything to irritate Convictolavus."

"Who stayed safe at home, I see!" sneered Litaviccus.

"Convictolavus pleaded that he had to guard our own lands, as he is the oldest among us," said Surus.

"Some would say too old. As can be said about Cotus."

"Just before I left Cabillonum I heard that the army we were ordered to send to subdue the Allobroges has got nowhere."

Litaviccus tensed. "My brother?"

"To the best of our knowledge, Valetiacus is unscathed. So is his army. The Allobroges chose not to fight in the open; they simply defended their borders in the Roman way." Surus stroked his luxuriant sand-colored moustach, cleared his throat. "I'm not happy, Litaviccus," he finally said.

"Oh?"

"I agree that it's time the Aedui were something more in the scheme of things than Rome's puppet, otherwise I wouldn't be here any more than you would. But how, when we're all so different from each other, can we ever hope to be united in the way our new King Vercingetorix is preaching? We're not all equal! What Celt doesn't spit on the Belgae? And how can the Celtae of Aquitania, those little dark runts, aspire to stand alongside an Aeduan? I think it's a very clever idea to unite the country, yes, but under the right circumstances. All of us Gauls, but some of us *better* Gauls. Is a Parisian boatman the equal of an Aeduan horseman?"

"No, he's not," said Litaviccus. "That's why it's going to be King Litaviccus, not King Vercingetorix."

"Oh, I see!" Surus smiled. Then the smile faded. "I have terrible misgivings about Alesia. After all Vercingetorix's homilies about not letting ourselves get shut up inside our strongholds, there's Vercingetorix shut up inside Alesia. He's the wrong man to be king right now, Litaviccus."

"Yes, I know what you're saying, Surus."

"The Aedui are committed; we can't go back. Caesar is aware we've gone over to Vercingetorix's side. It's impossible to credit that Caesar has the remotest chance to beat us when we arrive to relieve Alesia. Yet I still have terrible misgivings! What if we've ruined ourselves and our people for nothing?"

Litaviccus shivered. "We can't let it be for nothing, Surus, we *can't*! I'm a marked man. The only way out of this is for me to take the kingship from Vercingetorix after Caesar is beaten. If the roster is filled, over three hundred thousand of us will march to Alesia. We must assume that Vercingetorix will win—or rather, that Vercingetorix will be hauled out of Alesia in one piece and with his kingdom intact. That alone is a disgrace, that alone gives me a platform to challenge him. So let us think only of taking the throne off that wretched, illiterate Arvernian!"

"Yes, that's what we must think about," said Surus, but not with conviction.

They walked in silence, feet in their soft leather riding shoes making no sound on the thick carpet of moss which had grown over the ancient stone path to the grove of Dagda. Wooden statues of long-faced godheads peered between the tree trunks, squatted grotesquely with penises touching the ground.

The voice seemed suddenly to emerge from a huge oak ahead of them, so venerable and old that the path, made after its birth, divided and went around it. Cathbad's voice.

"Vercingetorix is going to prove impossible to control after we win at Alesia," Cathbad's voice was saying.

The voice of Gutruatus answered. "I've known that for quite some time, Cathbad."

Litaviccus put a hand on Surus's arm, stopped him. The two Aedui stood on the other side of the oak and listened.

"He's young and impetuous, but the germ of autocracy is there. I fear he won't defer to the Druids once he grasps the crown with both hands, and that can't be allowed to happen. The Druids are the only ones who can govern a united Gaul. Knowledge rests in their care. They make the laws, they supervise the laws, they sit in judgement. I've been thinking about it a great deal since I forced the thanes to make him King of Gaul. It's the right way to start, but the King of Gaul should be a warrior figurehead, not an autocrat who will gradually gather all the powers of government to himself. And that is what I fear will happen after Alesia, Gutruatus."

"He's not a Carnute, Cathbad."

"It will start by his elevating the Arvernian Druids to the Druidic council. The power of the Carnute Druids will wane."

"We Carnutes will be ruled by Arvernians in all ways," said Gutruatus.

"Which can't be allowed to happen."

"I agree. The King of Gaul must be a warrior figurehead. And he should be a Carnute."

"Litaviccus thinks the King of Gaul should be an Aeduan," said Cathbad dryly.

Gutruatus snorted. "Litaviccus, Litaviccus! He's a snake. Part the long grass and there he is. I'll have to part his hair with my sword."

"In time, Gutruatus, in time. First things first, and first is the defeat of Rome. Second is Vercingetorix, who will emerge from Alesia a hero. Therefore he must die a hero's death, the kind of death no Arvernian—or Aeduan!—will be able to say came at the hands of a fellow Gaul. We're between Beltine and Lugnasad at the moment. Samhain is still a long way off. So—Samhain. Perhaps we can find a special role for the new King of Gaul to play at the beginning of the Dark Months, when the harvest is all in and the people are assembled to endure the Chaos of the Souls and ask that next year's seed be blessed. Yes, here at Carnutum during Samhain . . . Maybe the new King of Gaul will disappear into a fiery mist, or be seen sailing the Liger into the west in a great swan boat. Vercingetorix must remain a hero, but become a myth."

"I'd be delighted to help," said Gutruatus.

"I'm sure you would," said Cathbad. "Thank you, Gutruatus."

"Are you going to read the signs?"

"Twice. Once for the muster, but once just for me. Today is for me, but you can come," said Cathbad, his voice dwindling.

The two Aeduans remained behind the oak for some time, eyes locked; then Litaviccus nodded and they moved forward, but not on the path. Between the oaks, inching along until the grove of Dagda opened before them, an enchanting place. The back of it was formed by a pile of boulders cushioned with lush moss, the source of a spring which gushed out from among them and fell into a deep pool endlessly rippling. Taranis like fire. Esus liked air. Dagda liked water. Earth belonged to the Great Mother, Dann. Fire and air could not commingle with earth, so Dann had married water, Dagda.

Today's offering was not for drowning, however; Cathbad was auspicating, not sacrificing. The naked victim, an enslaved German purchased specifically for this purpose, was lying face down and unbound on the altar, a simple stone slab. Beautiful in Cathbad's clear tenor voice, the prayers were sung according to the ancient ritual. They evoked no response from the victim, who was heavily drugged; his movements when they came had to leap out of the act, not out of fear or pain. Gutruatus moved a little distance away to kneel down while Cathbad picked up a very long, two-edged sword. That he found it awkward to lift was obvious, but he braced his feet apart, then with a huge effort carefully raised the sword in both hands until its blade was slightly above his head. It came down perfectly into the victim's back below the shoulder blades and severed the spine so cleanly that the blade was out and the sword on the ground a moment later.

The victim almost convulsed; Cathbad, his white robe unmarred, stood to watch every wriggle and writhe and jerk, the direction each took, the part of the body involved, clonus of head or arms or shoulders or legs, twitches in the fingers or toes, dying tics in the buttocks. It took a long time, but he stood without moving save for his lips, which formed voiceless words each time there was a short cessation in the victim's movements. When it was over he sighed, blinked, looked wearily toward Gutruatus. The Carnute lumbered to his feet as two acolytes came out of the trees and approached the altar to clear it and clean it.

"Well?" asked Gutruatus eagerly.

"I couldn't see. . . . The movements were bizarre, the pattern was alien."

"Didn't you learn anything?"

"A little. When I asked if Vercingetorix would die, there were six identical jerks of the head. I interpret that as six years. Yet when I asked if Caesar would be defeated, nothing moved at all—how am I to interpret that? I asked if Litaviccus would be king, and the answer was no. That was clear, very clear. I asked if you would be king, and the answer was no. His feet danced; you will die very soon. For the rest, I couldn't see. I couldn't see, I couldn't see. . . ."

Cathbad fell against Gutruatus, who stared at him white-faced and trembling.

The two Aeduans stole away.

Litaviccus wiped the sweat from his brow, his world in ruins. "I am not to be King of Gaul," he whispered.

Hands shaking, Surus passed them across his eyes. "Nor is Gutruatus. He's to die soon, but Cathbad didn't say you would."

"I can interpret the question about Caesar's defeat, Surus. Nothing moved at all. That means Caesar will win, that nothing in Gaul will change. Cathbad knows it, but he couldn't bear to tell Gutruatus. If he did, how would he explain the muster?"

"And the six years for Vercingetorix?"

"I don't know!" cried Litaviccus. "If Caesar wins, he can't go free. He'll walk in the triumphal parade and be throttled." A sob welled up, was swallowed. "I don't want to believe it, yet I do. Caesar will win, and I will never be King of Gaul."

They walked beside the little brook which ran out of Dagda's pool, picking their way between the wooden godheads planted on its bank. Golden shafts of light from the dying sun played with motes of pollen and drifting crystal seeds, pierced the spaces between the aged tree trunks to green the green and gild the brown.

"What will you do?" asked Surus when they emerged from the forest to find the muster swelling still, the camps of men and horses scattered as far as the eye could see.

"Get away from here," said Litaviccus, wiping his tears.

"I'll go with you."

"I don't ask that, Surus. Save what you can. Caesar will need the Aedui to bind up Gaul's wounds; we won't suffer the way the Belgae have, or the Celtic Armorici of the west."

"No, let that fate be reserved for Convictolavus! I think I'll head for the Treveri."

"As good a direction as any, if you'd like company."

The Treveri were beleaguered but unbowed.

"The abominable Labienus has killed so many of our warriors that we couldn't marshal a force to go to the relief of Alesia," said Cingetorix, still ruling.

"The Alesia rescue won't prosper," said Surus.

"I never thought it would. All this talk of a united Gaul! As if we were the same people. We're not the same people. Who does Vercingetorix think he is? Does he honestly believe that an Arvernian can call himself King of the Belgae? That we Belgae would defer to a Celt? We Treveri would vote for Ambiorix."

"Not Commius?"

"He sold himself to the Romans. A personal injury brought him over to our side, not the plight of our Belgic peoples," said Cingetorix contemptuously.

If Treves was indicative of conditions among this great and numerous group of peoples, Labienus had indeed wrought havoc. Though the *oppidum* itself was not designed to be lived in, there had once—and not too long ago—been a thriving small town around it. But few were left to populate it. What forces Cingetorix could scrape together were north of Treves, defending the precious horses from the depredations of the Ubii, just across the Rhenus.

Since Caesar had begun mounting the Germans on good horses, the Ubian appetite for them had become insatiable; Arminius of the Ubii suddenly saw a whole new vista opening up for his people, that of providing Rome with all her mounted auxiliaries. When Caesar had fired the Aedui he created a wonderful space for the Germans to move in and occupy. Arminius had not been slow to send those sixteen hundred extra men, and he intended to send more. The acquisition of true wealth was difficult for a pastoral people devoid of resources, but war on horseback was an industry Arminius understood perfectly. If he had anything to do with it, Roman generals would soon despise Gallic cavalry. Nothing but Germans would do.

Thus the grey, often stunted, dreary vastness of the Arduenna forest, suited for little save grazing and growing in the river valleys, rang to the sounds of Treveri and Ubii striving for mastery.

"I hate this place," said Litaviccus after a few days.

"Whereas I don't mind it," said Surus.

"I wish you well."

"And I you. Where will you go?"

"To Galatia."

Surus gaped. "Galatia? It's at the other end of the world!"

"Exactly. But the Galatians are Gauls, and they ride good horses. Deiotarus is bound to be looking for competent commanders."

"He's a Roman client king, Litaviccus."

"Yes. But I won't be Litaviccus. I'll be Cabachius of the Volcae Tectosages. Journeying to see my relatives in Galatia. I'll fall in love with the place and apply to stay."

"Where will you find the right shawl?"

"They gave up wearing the shawl around Tolosa a very long time ago, Surus. I'll dress like a Gaul of the Province."

First it was necessary to visit his lands and manor outside Matisco. All Gallic lands were communal, held in the name of the people, but in actual fact, of course, the great nobles of each tribe "caretook" great tracts of them. Including Litaviccus.

He rode down the Mosella and into the lands of the Sequani, who had gone to the muster at Carnutum. Because those Sequani who had not gone to Carnutum were massed closer to the Rhenus in case the Suebic Germans tried to cross, he was not challenged or opposed, nor asked any questions by some thane suspicious as to why a stray Aeduan should be riding through the lands of recent enemies with a pack horse for his only company.

Yet someone was there to shout the news. As he skirted the Sequani *oppidum* of Vesontio, Litaviccus heard it shouted across a field that Caesar had been victorious at Alesia and Vercingetorix had surrendered.

If I hadn't overheard Cathbad and Gutruatus, I'd be there in command of the Aedui. I too would be a Roman prisoner. I too would be sent to Rome to await Caesar's triumph. How then is the King of Gaul going to survive for another six years? He'll die during Caesar's triumph, no matter who else is spared. Does that mean Caesar will take a third five-year governorship of Gaul, and thus be unable to triumph for six more years? But it's over! A third period isn't necessary. He will finish us next year. Those who got away will crumble; nothing can avert total victory for Caesar. Yet I believe Cathbad saw true. Six more years. *Why?*

Because his lands lay to the east and south of Matisco, Litaviccus avoided that *oppidum* too, even though it belonged to the Aedui—and, more importantly still, even though his wife and children were living there for the duration of the war. Best not to see them. They would survive. His own survival was his first priority.

Though made of wood with a slate shingle roof, his large and comfortable house was built in the Roman manner, around a huge peristyle courtyard and owning two storeys. His serfs and slaves were overjoyed to see him, and swore an oath to breathe no word of his presence. At first he had intended to remain only long enough to empty his strong room, but summer on the sleek and sluggish Arar River was delicious, and Caesar was far away. No need for him to make one of those lightning marches in this direction. What had Caesar said? That the Arar flowed so slowly it actually flowed backward? But it was *home,* and suddenly Litaviccus was in no hurry to leave it. His people were completely loyal, nor had anyone seen him. How delightful to while away one last summer in his own land! They said Galatia was lovely—high, wide, wonderful country for horses. But it wasn't home. The Galatians spoke Greek, Pontic and a kind of Gallic not heard in any part of Gaul for two hundred years. Well, at least he had Greek, though he would have to polish it.

Then at the beginning of autumn, just as he was thinking of moving on and while his serfs and slaves were bringing in a good harvest, his brother Valetiacus arrived at the head of a hundred horse troopers who were his own adherents.

The brothers met with great affection, couldn't take their eyes off each other.

"I can't stay," said Valetiacus. "How amazing to find you here! All I came for was to make sure your people were bringing in the harvest."

"What happened against the Allobroges?" asked Litaviccus, pouring wine.

"Not very much." Valetiacus grimaced. "They fought, and I quote Caesar, 'a careful and efficient war.' "

"Caesar?"

"He's at Bibracte."

"Does he know I'm here?"

"No one knows where you are."

"What does Caesar intend to do with the Aedui?"

"Like the Arverni, we're to escape relatively lightly. We are to form the nucleus of a new, thoroughly Roman Gaul. Nor are we to lose our Friend and Ally status. Provided, that is, that we sign an enormously long treaty with Rome, and admit a great many of Caesar's creatures to our senate. Viridomarus is forgiven, but you are not. In fact, there's a price on your head, which leads me to assume that if you're captured and walk in Caesar's triumph, you'll suffer the same fate as Vercingetorix and Cotus. Biturgo and Eporedorix will walk, but then be sent home."

"What about you, Valetiacus?"

"I've been allowed to keep my lands, but I'm never to be a senior in the council, nor a vergobret," said Valetiacus bitterly.

Both the brothers were big and fine-looking men in the true Gallic way, golden-haired, blue-eyed. The muscles in Litaviccus's bare brown forearms tensed until the golden bracelets upon them bit into the flesh.

"By Dagda and Dann, I wish there was a way to be avenged!" said Litaviccus, grinding his teeth.

"Perhaps there is," said Valetiacus, smiling faintly.

"How? *How?*"

"Not far from here I encountered a party of travelers going to join Caesar in Bibracte. He intends to winter there. Three wagons, a comfortable carriage, and a lady on a prancing white horse. Very Roman looking, the group. Except for the lady, who rode astride. In the carriage with his nurse was a little boy who has a look of Caesar about him. Do you need more hints?"

Litaviccus shook his head slowly from side to side. "No," he said, and exhaled on a hiss. "Caesar's woman! Who used to belong to Dumnorix."

"What does he call her?" asked Valetiacus.

"Rhiannon."

"That's right. Vercingetorix's first cousin. Rhiannon, the wronged wife. Infamous! Dumnorix was a wronged husband."

"What did you do, Valetiacus?"

"I captured her." Valetiacus shrugged. "Why not? I'll never occupy my rightful place among our people, so what do I have to lose?"

"Everything," said Litaviccus crisply, got to his feet and put an arm about his brother's shoulders. "I can't stay, I'm a wanted man. But you *must* stay! There is my family to care for. Bide your time, be patient. Caesar will go, other governors will come. You'll resume your place in the senate and the councils. Leave Caesar's woman here with me. *She* will be my vengeance."

"And the child?"

Litaviccus clenched his hands, shook them in glee. "He's the only one who will leave here alive, because you'll leave now and take him with you. Find one of our serfs in a remote croft and give him the boy. If he talks of his mother and father, who will believe him? Let Caesar's son be raised as an Aeduan serf, doomed to be a bonded servant all his life."

They walked to the door, and there kissed. Outside in the courtyard the captives huddled, watching with round and frightened eyes. Except for Rhiannon, hands bound behind her back, feet hobbled, standing proudly. The little boy, now over five years old, stood in the shelter of his nurse's skirt, the marks of tears upon his face, his nose still running. When Valetiacus was in his saddle, Litaviccus picked the child up and handed him to his brother, who sat him across the horse's neck. He was too tired to protest, too bewildered; his head flopped back against Valetiacus and he closed his eyes wearily.

Rhiannon tried to run and fell full length. "Orgetorix! Orgetorix!" she screamed.

But Valetiacus and his hundred men were gone, Caesar's son with them.

Litaviccus brought his sword from the house and killed the Roman servants, including the nurse, while Rhiannon curled herself into a ball and cried out her son's name.

When the slaughter was over he crossed to her, put his hand in the midst of that fiery river of hair, and hauled her to her feet. "Come, my dear," he said, smiling, "I have a special treat in store for you."

He bundled her into the house and into the big room wherein the master dined and sat around his table. There he tipped her off her feet and stood for a moment looking up at the wooden beams which straddled the low ceiling. Then he nodded to himself and left the room.

When he came back he had two of his male slaves with him, terrified by the slaughter in the yard, but anxious to obey.

"Do this for me and you're both free men," said Litaviccus. He clapped his hands; a female slave came in, shrinking. "Find me a comb, woman," he said.

One of the slaves had a hook in his hand of the kind used to hang a boar for disemboweling, while the other set to work with an auger in one of the beams.

The comb was brought.

"Sit, my dear," said Litaviccus, lifting Rhiannon and pushing her into a chair. His hands pulled at her tresses until they lay down her back and pooled on the floor; he began to comb them. Slowly, carefully, yet yanking at the knots ruthlessly. Rhiannon seemed to feel no pain. She neither winced nor flinched, and all that passion and strength Caesar had so admired in her had vanished.

"Orgetorix, Orgetorix," she said from time to time.

"How beautifully clean your hair is, my dear, and how truly magnificent," said Litaviccus, still combing. "Did you plan to surprise Caesar in Bibracte, that you traveled without an escort of Roman troops? Of course you did! But he wouldn't be pleased."

Eventually he was finished. So were the two slaves. The boar hook hung from the beam, its bottom seven feet above the flags.

"Help me, woman," he said curtly to the female slave. "I want to braid her hair. Show me how."

But it took the two of them. Once Litaviccus understood the over-under-over weaving of the three separate tresses, he became quite efficient; it was the woman's job to keep the three tresses separate below Litaviccus's working fingers. Then it was done. At the base of her long white neck Rhiannon's braid was as thick as Litaviccus's arm, though it dwindled, five feet further, to a rat's tail which promptly began to unravel.

"Stand up," he said, pulling her to her feet. "Help me," to the two male slaves. Like a craftsman in a sculptor's yard he positioned Rhiannon beneath the hook, then took the braid and looped it twice about her neck. "And we still have plenty!" cried Litaviccus, stepping onto a chair. "Pick her up."

One of the slaves put his arms about Rhiannon's hips and lifted her off the ground. Litaviccus put the braid through the hook, but couldn't tie it; not only was it too thick, it was also too silky to stay taut. Down went Rhiannon again, off went one of the slaves. Finally they managed to anchor it around a second boar hook and stapled it to the beam, Rhiannon clear of the floor in the slave's embrace for the second time.

"Let go of her, but very gently!" rapped Litaviccus. "Oh, gently, gently, we don't want to break her neck, that would spoil all the fun! *Gently!*"

She didn't struggle, though it took a very long time. Her eyes, wide open, were fixed unseeingly on the top of the wall opposite, and because she didn't struggle her skin simply faded from cream to grey to blue, nor did her tongue protrude, those blind eyes begin to goggle. Sometimes her lips would move, form the word "Orgetorix!" soundlessly.

The hair stretched. First her toes and then the soles of her feet touched the floor. They dropped her like a bag of sand, not yet dead, and began the hanging all over again.

When her face was a blackish purple, Litaviccus went to write a letter; after it was finished he gave it to his steward.

"Ride with this to Bibracte," he said. "Tell Caesar's men it's from Litaviccus. Caesar will need you to guide him here. Go then and look beneath my bed for a purse of gold. Take it. Tell the rest of my people to pack their things and leave now. If they go to my brother Valetiacus, he'll take them in. No one is to touch the bodies in the yard. I want them left as they are. And she," he ended, pointing to where Rhiannon hung, "will stay like that. I want Caesar to see her for himself."

Not long after the steward set out, so did Litaviccus. He rode his best horse, wore his best clothes—but no shawl—and led three pack horses on which reposed his gold, his other jewels, his fur cloak. His goal was the Jura, where he intended to enter the lands of the Helvetii. It never occurred to him that he would not be welcomed wherever he went; he was an enemy of Rome, and every barbarian hated Rome. All he had to do was say Caesar had put a price on his head. From Gaul to Galatia, he would be feted and admired. As did happen in the Jura. Then among the sources of the Danubius he came to the lands of a people called the Verbigeni, and there was taken prisoner. The Verbigeni cared nothing for Rome or Caesar. They took Litaviccus's possessions. And his head.

"I'm glad," said Caesar to Trebonius, "that if I had to see one of the three of them dead, it is Rhiannon. I was spared it with my daughter and my mother."

Trebonius didn't know what to say, how he could express what he felt, the monumental outrage, the pain, the grief, the fierce anger, all the emotions he experienced looking at the poor, black-faced creature wound about with her own hair. Which had stretched yet again, so that she stood upon the floor, knees slightly bent. Oh, it wasn't fair! The man was so lonely, so remote, so far above all those he saw every day of his remarkable life! She had been pleasant company, she had amused him, he adored her singing. No, he hadn't loved her, but love would have been a burden. Trebonius knew that much about him by now. What was there to say? How could words ease this shock, this grossest of insults, this mad and senseless thing? Oh, it wasn't fair! It wasn't fair!

No expression had entered or left Caesar's face from the moment they rode into the courtyard and discovered the slaughter there. Then walked into the house to find Rhiannon.

"Help me," he said now to Trebonius.

They got her down, found her clothes and jewels untouched in the wagons, and dressed her for burial while some of the German troopers who had ridden with them as escort dug her grave. No Celtic Gaul liked to be burned, so she would be put into the ground with all her slain servants buried at her feet, as befitted a great lady who had been the daughter of a king.

Gotus, the commander of Caesar's original four hundred Ubii, was waiting outside.

"The little boy isn't here," he said. "We've searched for a mile in all directions—every room in the house, every other building, every well, every stall—we have missed nothing, Caesar. The little boy is gone."

"Thank you, Gotus," said Caesar, smiling.

How could he do that? wondered Trebonius. So much in command, so civil, so perfectly courteous and controlled. But what will the price of it be?

Nothing more was said until after the funeral was over; as there were no Druids to be had, Caesar officiated.

"When do you want the search for Orgetorix started?" Trebonius asked as they rode away from Litaviccus's deserted manor.

"I don't."

"What?"

"I don't want a search."

"Why?"

"The matter is ended," said Caesar. His cool, pale eyes looked straight into Trebonius's, exactly as they always did. With affection tempered by logic, with understanding tempered by detachment. He looked away. "Ah, but I will miss her singing," he said, and never referred to Rhiannon or his vanished son again.

GAUL OF THE LONG-HAIRS

from JANUARY until
DECEMBER of 51 B.C.

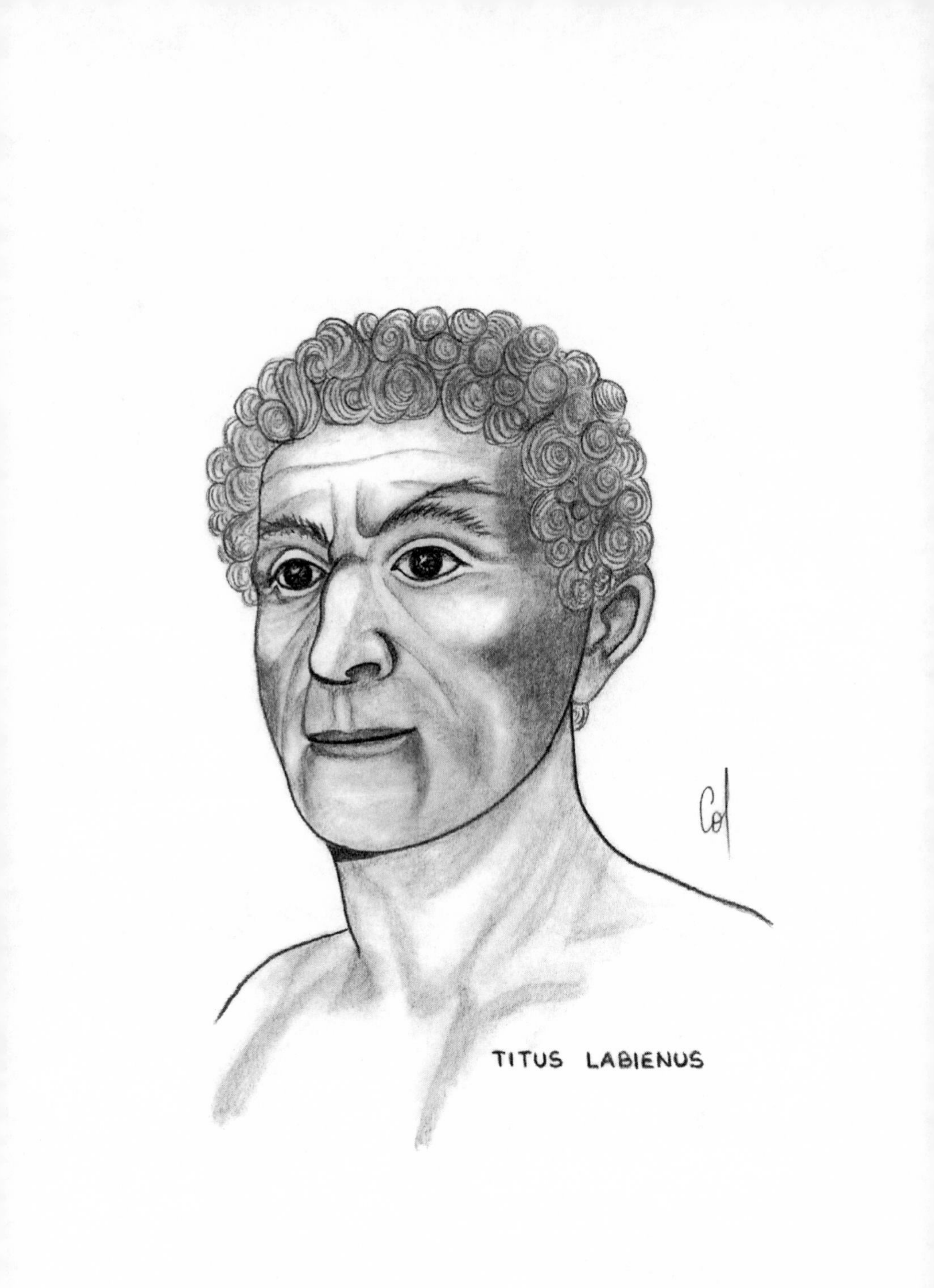

TITUS LABIENUS

When news of the defeat and capture of Vercingetorix reached Rome, the Senate decreed a thanksgiving of twenty days—which could not undo the damage Pompey and his new allies the *boni* had engineered for Caesar during that year of total war, knowing full well that Caesar did not have the time or the energy to oppose their measures personally. Though he was kept informed, the immediate urgencies of finding food for his legions, making sure his men's lives were not risked needlessly and dealing with Vercingetorix had to take first place in Caesar's priorities. And while agents like Balbus, Oppius and Rabirius Postumus the bankers strove mightily to avert disaster, they had neither Caesar's consummate grasp of politics nor his unassailable authority; precious days were wasted couriering letters and waiting for replies.

Not long after he had become consul without a colleague, Pompey had married Cornelia Metella and moved completely into the camp of the *boni*. The first evidence of his new ideological commitment came late in March, when he took a senatorial decree of the previous year and passed it into law. A harmless enough law on the surface, but Caesar saw its possibilities the moment he read Balbus's letter. From now on, a man who was in office as praetor or consul would have to wait five years before he was allowed to govern a province. A nuisance made serious because it created a pool of possible governors who could go to govern at a moment's notice: those men who, after being praetor or consul, had refused to take a province. They were now legally obliged to become governors if the Senate so directed them.

Worse than that law was one Pompey proceeded to pass which stipulated that all candidates for praetor or consul must register their candidacy personally inside the city of Rome. Every member of Caesar's extremely powerful faction protested vehemently—what about Caesar, what about the Law of the Ten Tribunes of the Plebs allowing Caesar to stand for his second consulship *in absentia*? Oops, oops! cried Pompey. Sorry about that, I clean forgot! Whereupon he tacked a codicil onto his *lex Pompeia de iure magistratuum,* exempting Caesar from its provisions. The only trouble was that he didn't have the codicil inscribed on the bronze tablet bearing his law, which gave the codicil no power in law whatsoever.

Caesar got the news that he was now barred from standing *in absentia* while he was building his siege terrace at Avaricum; after that came Gergovia, after that the revolt of the Aedui, after that the pursuit which led eventually to Alesia. As he dealt with the Aedui at Decetia he learned that the Senate had met to discuss the allocation of next year's provinces, now unavailable to the men who were currently in office as praetors or consuls. They had to wait five years. The Senate scratched its head as it asked itself where next year's governors were to come from, but the consul without a colleague laughed. Easy, Pompey said. The men who had declined to govern a province after their year in office would have to govern whether they liked it or not. Cicero was therefore ordered to govern Cilicia and Bibulus to govern Syria, a prospect which filled both of these stay-at-homes with horror.

Inside his protective ring at Alesia, Caesar got a letter from Rome informing him that Pompey had succeeded in having his new father-in-law, Metellus Scipio, elected his consular colleague for the rest of the year. And—more cheering news by far—that Cato, running for next year's consulship, had been ignominiously defeated. For all his admired incorruptibility, Cato couldn't impress the electors. Probably because the members of the First Class of centuriate voters liked to think there was some sort of chance that the consuls (for a trifling financial consideration) would do a few favors when nicely asked.

So when the New Year came in, Caesar was still in Gaul of the Longhairs. He couldn't possibly cross the Alps to monitor events in Rome from Ravenna. Two inimical consuls in Servius Sulpicius Rufus and Marcus Claudius Marcellus were just entering office, a vexatious prospect for Caesar. Though it was something of a consolation that no less than four of the new tribunes of the plebs belonged to Caesar, bought and paid for. Marcus Marcellus the junior consul was already saying that he intended to strip Caesar's imperium, provinces and army from him, though the law Gaius Trebonius had passed to give him his second five years specifically forbade the matter's so much as being discussed before March of next year, fifteen months away. Constitutionality was for lesser beings. The *boni* cared not a fig about it if their target was Caesar.

Who, through the haze of misery which greyed his life at this time, found it impossible to settle and do what he ought to do: send for people like Balbus and his dominant tribune of the plebs, Gaius Vibius Pansa, sit down with them in Bibracte and personally instruct them how to proceed. There were probably a few tactics his people could try, but only if they met with him in the flesh. Pompey was basking in *boni* approval and rejoicing in the possession of a hugely aristocratic wife, but at least he was no longer in office, and Servius Sulpicius, the new senior consul, was an approachable and deliberate member of the *boni* rather than an intemperate hothead like Marcus Marcellus.

Instead of settling to deal with Rome, Caesar went on the road to subdue the Bituriges and contented himself with dictating a letter to the Senate on the march. In view of his stunning successes in the Gauls, he said, it seemed only fair and proper that he should be treated exactly as Pompey had been treated in the matter of Pompey's governorship of the Spains. His "election" as consul without a colleague had been *in absentia* because he was governing the Spains. He was still governing the Spains, had done so throughout his term as consul. Therefore, would the Conscript Fathers of the Senate please extend Caesar's tenure of the Gauls and Illyricum until he assumed the consulship in three years' time? What was accorded to Pompey should also be accorded to Caesar. The letter did not deign to mention Pompey's law that consular candidates must register for election inside Rome; Caesar's silence on this point was a way of saying that he knew Pompey's law did not apply to him.

Three *nundinae* would elapse between the sending of this missive and any possibility of a reply; like several more *nundinae,* they were spent reducing the Bituriges to abject petitioners for mercy. His campaign was a series of forced marches of fifty miles a day; he would be in one place burning, sacking, killing and enslaving, then turn up fifty miles away even before the shouting could warn anyone. By now he knew that Gaul of the Long-hairs did not consider itself beaten. The new strategy consisted of small insurrections timed to flare up all over the country simultaneously, forcing Caesar to behave like a man obliged to stamp out ten different fires in ten different places at one and the same moment. But these insurrections presumed that there would be Roman citizens to slaughter, and there were not. Food purchasing for the legions, all scattered, was done by the legions themselves marching in force.

Caesar countered by reducing several of the most powerful tribes in turn, commencing with the Bituriges, who were angry that Biturgo had been sent to Rome to walk in Caesar's triumphal parade. He took two legions only, the Thirteenth and the new Fifteenth: the Thirteenth because it bore that unlucky number, and the Fifteenth because it consisted of raw recruits. This highest numbered legion was his "oddments box," its men seasoned and then slipped into other legions when they fell in number. The present Fifteenth was the result of Pompey's law early in the previous year stating that all Roman citizen men between seventeen and forty years of age must do military service—a law handy for Caesar, who never had trouble obtaining volunteers, but was often in trouble with the Senate for recruiting more men than he had been authorized to enlist.

On the ninth day of February he returned to Bibracte. The lands of the Bituriges were in ruins; most of the Biturigan warriors were dead and the women and children taken captive. Awaiting him in Bibracte was the Senate's answer to his request for an extended term as governor. An answer he had perhaps expected, yet in his heart had truly believed would not be so, if only because to reject his petition was the height of folly.

The answer was no: the Senate was not prepared to treat Caesar as it had treated Pompey. If he wanted to be consul in three years' time, he would have to behave like any other Roman governor: lay down his imperium, his provinces and his army, and register his candidacy in person inside Rome. What the answer didn't argue about was Caesar's calm assumption that he would be elected senior consul. Everyone knew it would happen thus. Caesar had never contested an election in which he did not come in at the top of the poll. Nor did he bribe. He didn't dare to bribe. Too many enemies were looking for an excuse to prosecute.

It was then, looking down at that coldly curt letter, that Caesar made up his mind to plan for all eventualities.

They will not let me be all that I should be. That I am *entitled* to be. Yet they will accommodate a quasi-Roman like Pompeius. Bow and scrape to him. Exalt him. Fill him with ideas of his own importance, all the while sniggering at him behind their hands. Well, that's his burden. One day he'll discover what they really think of him. When the circumstances are right their masks will drop, and Pompeius will be genuinely devastated. He's exactly like Cicero when Catilina seemed certain to be consul. The *boni* espoused the despised bumpkin from Arpinum to keep out a man who had the blood. Now they espouse Pompeius to keep me out. But I will not let that happen. I am no Catilina! They want my hide, for no better reason than that my excellence forces them to see the extent of their own inadequacies. They think they can compel me to cross the *pomerium* into Rome to declare my candidacy, and, in crossing the *pomerium,* abandon the imperium which protects me from prosecution. They'll all be there at the electoral booth ready to pounce with a dozen trumped-up suits for treason, for extortion, for bribery, for peculation—for murder, if they can find someone to swear I was seen sneaking into the Lautumiae to throttle Vettius. I'll be like Gabinius, like Milo. Condemned in so many different courts for so many different crimes that I will never be able to show my face in Italia again. I will be stripped of my citizenship, my deeds will be erased from the history books, and men like Ahenobarbus and Metellus Scipio will be popped into my provinces to take the credit, just as Pompeius took the credit for what Lucullus did.

That will not happen. I will not let it happen, no matter what I have to do to avert it. In the meantime I will continue to work to be allowed to run *in absentia,* my imperium intact until I assume the imperium of the senior consul. I do not want to be known as a man who acted unconstitutionally. Never in my life have I acted unconstitutionally. Everything has been done as the *mos maiorum* says it should be done. That is my greatest ambition: to attain my second consulship within the bounds of the law. Once I become consul, I can deal with all their trumped-up charges by using the law legally. They know that. They fear that. But they cannot bear to lose. For if they lose, they admit that I am better than they are in every conceivable way, from brilliance to blood. For I am one man, and they are many. If I defeat them within the law, they will be as chagrined as the sphinx and have no other recourse than to jump over the nearest cliff.

However, I will also plan for the worst. I will begin to do those things which will ensure that I succeed outside the law. Oh, the fools! They always underestimate me.

Jupiter Optimus Maximus, if that be the name you would like to hear; Jupiter Optimus Maximus, of whatever sex you prefer; Jupiter Optimus Maximus, who is all the Gods and forces of Rome fused into one; Jupiter Optimus Maximus, contract with me to win! Should you do this, I hereby swear that I will accord you those sacrifices which do you the greatest honor and give you the most satisfaction. . . .

The campaign to reduce the Bituriges had taken forty days. As soon as Caesar had arrived back in the camp just below the mount of Aeduan Bibracte, he assembled the Thirteenth and the Fifteenth and donated to every man in both legions one female Biturigan prisoner whom he could keep as a servant, or sell to the slavers. After which he gave every ranker a cash bonus of two hundred sesterces, and every centurion a cash bonus of two thousand sesterces. Out of his own purse.

"This is my thanks for your wonderful support," he said to his soldiers. "What Rome pays you is one thing, but it is time that I, Gaius Julius Caesar, gave you something out of my own private purse as a special thank-you. The past forty days have seen little booty, yet I've taken you out of your well-earned winter rest and asked you to march fifty miles a day for almost every one of those forty days. After a terrible winter, spring and summer in the field against Vercingetorix, you deserved to sit back and do nothing for six months at least. But did you grumble when I said you'd be marching? No! Did you complain when I asked you for Herculean efforts? No! Did you slacken pace, did you ask for more to eat, did you for one moment give me less than your best? No! No, no, no! You're the men of Caesar's legions, and Rome has never seen your like! You're my boys! As long as my life shall last, you're my beloved boys!"

They cheered him hysterically, as much for his calling them his beloved boys as for the money and the slave, who also came out of his private purse; the profits from the sale of slaves belonged exclusively to the General.

Trebonius looked sideways at Decimus Brutus. "What's he up to, Decimus? It's a wonderful gesture, but they didn't expect it and I can't work out what possessed him to make it."

"I had a letter from Curio in the same bag which brought Caesar a letter from the Senate," said Decimus Brutus, speaking too softly for Mark Antony or the tribunes to hear. "They won't let him stand *in absentia,* and the mood in the House is to strip him of his imperium as soon as possible. They want him disgraced and sent into permanent exile. So does Pompeius Magnus."

Trebonius grunted scornfully. "That last doesn't surprise me! Pompeius isn't worth one of Caesar's bootlaces."

"Nor are any of the others."

"That goes without saying." He turned and left the parade ground, Decimus walking with him. "Do you think he'd do it?"

Decimus Brutus didn't blink. "I think . . . I think they're insane to provoke him, Gaius. Because yes, if they leave him no alternative he'll march on Rome."

"And if he does?"

The invisible blond brows rose. "What do you think?"

"He'd slaughter them."

"I agree."

"So we have a choice to make, Decimus."

"*You* may have a choice to make. I don't. I'm Caesar's man through thick and thin."

"And I. Yet he's no Sulla."

"For which we ought to be thankful, Trebonius."

Perhaps because of this conversation, neither Decimus Brutus nor Gaius Trebonius was in a talkative mood over dinner; they lay together on the *lectus summus,* with Caesar alone on the *lectus medius* and Mark Antony alone on the *lectus imus,* opposite them.

"You're being mighty generous," said Antony, crunching through an apple in two bites. "I know you have a reputation for open-handedness, but"—he wrinkled his brow fiercely, eyes screwed closed—"that's a total of one hundred talents you gave away today, or near enough."

Caesar's eyes twinkled. Antony amused him intensely, and he liked that good-natured acceptance of his role as butt.

"By all that Mercury holds dear, Antonius, your mathematical skills are phenomenal! You did that sum in your head. I think it's time you took over the proper duties of quaestor and let poor Gaius Trebatius do something more suited to his inclinations, if not his talents. Don't you agree?" he asked Trebonius and Decimus Brutus.

They nodded, grinning.

"I piss on the proper duties of quaestor!" growled Antony, flexing the muscles in his thighs, a sight which would have had most of feminine Rome swooning, but was quite wasted on his present audience.

"It's necessary to know something about money, Antonius," said Caesar. "I realize you think it's liquid enough to pour like water, witness your colossal debts, but it's also a substance of great usefulness to a would-be consul and commander of armies."

"You're avoiding my point," said Antony shrewdly, tempering insolence with a winning smile. "You've just outlaid one hundred talents to the men of two of your eleven legions, and given every last one of them a slave he could sell for a thousand more sesterces. Not that many of them will this side of high spring, as you made sure they got the juiciest, youngest women." He rolled over on his couch and began flexing the muscles in his massive calves. "What I really want to know is, are you going to limit your sudden generosity to a mere two of your eleven legions?"

"That would be imprudent," said Caesar gravely. "I intend to campaign throughout the autumn and winter, taking two legions at a time. But always different legions."

"Clever!" Antony reached out to pick up his goblet, and drank deeply.

"My dear Antonius, don't oblige me to remove wine from the winter menu," said Caesar. "If you can't drink in moderation, I'll require abstinence. I suggest you water it."

"One of the many things I don't understand about you," said Antony, frowning, "is why you have this tic about one of the best gifts the Gods have ever given men. Wine's a panacea."

"It is not a panacea. Nor do I deem it a gift," Caesar said. "I'd rather call it a curse. Straight out of Pandora's box. Even taken sparingly, it blunts the sword of one's thoughts just enough to prevent splitting a hair."

Antony roared with laughter. "So that's the answer, Caesar! You're nothing but a hairsplitter!"

Eighteen days after his return to Bibracte, Caesar was off again, this time to reduce the Carnutes. Trebonius and Decimus Brutus went with him; Antony, much to his displeasure, was left to mind the shop. Quintus Cicero brought the Seventh from winter quarters in Cabillonum, but Publius Sulpicius sent the Fourteenth from Matisco, as Caesar didn't require his services.

"I came myself," said Quintus Cicero, "because my brother has just written to ask me to accompany him to Cilicia in April."

"You don't look happy at the prospect, Quintus," said Caesar gently. "I'll miss you."

"And I you. I've had the three best years of my life here with you in Gaul."

"I like to hear that, because they haven't been easy."

"No, never easy. Maybe that's why they've been so good. I—I—I appreciate your *trust* in me, Caesar. There have been times when I deserved a roaring-out, like that business with the Sugambri, but you've never roared me out. Or made me feel inadequate."

"My dear Quintus," said Caesar with his warmest smile, "why should I have roared you out? You've been a wonderful legate, and I wish you were staying until the end." The smile faded, the eyes looked suddenly into the distance. "Whatever the end may be."

Puzzled, Quintus Cicero looked at him, but the face bore no expression whatsoever. Naturally Cicero's letter had recounted events in Rome in great detail, but Quintus didn't have the truly intimate knowledge of Caesar possessed by Trebonius or Decimus Brutus. Nor had he been in

Bibracte when the General rewarded the men of the Thirteenth and Fifteenth.

Thus when Caesar set out for Cenabum, Quintus Cicero, heavy-hearted, set out for Rome and a legateship he knew perfectly well would be neither as happy nor as profitable as working with Caesar. Under big brother's thumb again! Preached at, deprecated. There were times when families were a painful nuisance. Oh, yes . . .

It was now the end of February, and winter was approaching. Cenabum was still a blackened ruin, but there were no insurgents in the area to contest Caesar's use of the *oppidum*. He pitched camp very comfortably against its walls, put some of his soldiers into any houses still standing, and had the rest thatch the roofs and sod the walls of their tents for maximum warmth.

His first order of business was to ride to Carnutum and see Cathbad, the Chief Druid.

Who looked, thought Caesar, very much older and more careworn than he had those many years ago: the bright golden hair had gone to a drabber shade of grey-and-gold, the blue eyes were exhausted.

"It was foolish to oppose me, Cathbad," the conqueror said.

Oh, he did look every inch the conqueror! Was there nothing could wipe away that incredible air of confidence, that vigorous and forthright crispness which oozed out of the man? Haloed his head, limned his body? Why did the Tuatha send Caesar to contest with us? Why him, when Rome has so many bumbling incompetents?

"I had no choice" was what Cathbad said. He lifted his chin proudly. "I assume you're here to take me captive, that I am to walk with the others in your triumphal parade."

Caesar smiled. "Cathbad, Cathbad! Do you take me for a fool? It's one thing to take warrior prisoners of war or end the activities of rebellious kings. But to victimize a country's priests is absolute insanity. You will note, I hope, that no Druid has been apprehended, nor prevented from going about his work of healing or counseling. That's my firm policy, and all my legates know it."

"Why did the Tuatha send *you*?"

"I imagine they entered into a pact with Jupiter Optimus Maximus. The world of the Gods has its laws and accommodations, just as our world does. Evidently the Tuatha felt that the forces connecting them to the Gauls were diminishing in some mysterious way. Not from lack of Gallic enthusiasm or want of religious observance. Just that nothing remains the same, Cathbad. The earth shifts, people change, times come and go. As do the Gods of all peoples. Perhaps the Tuatha are sickened by human votive sacrifices, just as other Gods became sickened. I do not believe that Gods remain static either, Cathbad."

"It's interesting that a man so welded to the political and practical attitudes of his country can also be so truly religious."

"I believe in our Gods with all my mind."

"But what about your soul?"

"We Romans don't believe in souls as you Druids do. All that outlasts the body is a mindless shade. Death is a sleep," said Caesar.

"Then you should fear it more than those who believe we live on after it."

"I think we fear it less." The pale blue eyes blazed suddenly with pain, grief, passion. "Why should any man or woman want more of this?" Caesar demanded. "It is a vale of tears, a terrible trial of strength. For every inch we gain, we fall back a mile. Life is there to be conquered, Cathbad, but the price! The price! No one will ever defeat me. I will not let them. I believe in myself, and I have set a pattern for myself."

"Then where is the vale of tears?" asked Cathbad.

"In the methods. In human obstinacy. In lack of foresight. In failing to see the best way, the graceful way. For seven long years I have tried to make your people understand that they cannot win. That for the future well-being of this land, they must submit. And what do they do? Fling themselves into my flame like moths into a lamp. Force me to kill more of them, enslave more of them, destroy more houses, villages, towns. I would far rather pursue a softer, more clement policy, but they will not let me."

"The answer is easy, Caesar. They won't give in, so you must. You have brought Gaul a consciousness of its identity, of its might and power. And having brought it, nothing can take it away. We Druids will sing of Vercingetorix for ten thousand years."

"They *must* give in, Cathbad! I cannot. That's why I've come to see you, to ask that you tell them to give in. Otherwise you leave me no choice. I'll have to do to every inch of Gaul what I've just done to the Bituriges. But that's not what I want to do. There won't be anyone left save Druids. What kind of fate is that?"

"I won't tell them to submit," said Cathbad.

"Then I'll start here at Carnutum. In no other place have I left the treasures untouched. Yet here they have been sacrosanct. Defy me, and I'll loot Carnutum. No Druid or his wife or his children will be touched. But Carnutum will lose those great piles of offerings accumulated over the centuries."

"Then go ahead. Loot Carnutum."

Caesar sighed, and meant the sigh. "The remembrance of cruelty is scant comfort in one's old age, but what I am forced to do, I will do."

Cathbad laughed joyously. "Oh, rubbish! Caesar, you must know how much all the Gods love you! Why torment yourself with thoughts you, of all men, understand have no validity? You won't live to be old, the Gods would never permit it. They'll take you in your prime. I have seen it."

His breath caught; Caesar laughed too. "For that I thank you! Carnutum is safe." He began to walk away, but said over his shoulder, still laughing, "Gaul, however, is not!"

All through the early days of a very hard and bitter winter Caesar drove the Carnutes from pillar to post. More of them died frozen in their fields than at the hands of the Seventh and the Fourteenth, for they had no shelter left, no homes, no havens. And a new attitude began to creep into Gallic behavior; where a year before the people of neighboring tribes would gladly have taken the refugees in and succored them, now they shut their doors and pretended no one cried for help. Attrition was beginning to work. Fear was conquering defiance.

At the midpoint of April, with winter at its worst, Caesar left the Seventh and Fourteenth in Cenabum with Gaius Trebonius, and set off to see what was the matter with the Remi.

"The Bellovaci," said Dorix simply. "Correus kept his men at home instead of going to the muster at Carnutum, and the two thousand he sent with Commius and his four thousand Atrebates came back from Alesia unscathed. Now Correus and Commius have allied themselves with Ambiorix, who has returned from across the great river. They've been scouring all the peatlands of Belgica for men—Nervii, Eburones, Menapii, Atuatuci, Condrusi—and further south and west too—the Aulerci, Ambiani, Morini, Veromandui, Caletes, Veliocasses. Some of these peoples did not go to Carnutum; some survived intact by running quickly. A great many men are gathering, I hear."

"Have you been attacked?" asked Caesar.

"Not as yet. But I expect it."

"Then I'd better move before you are. You've always honored your treaties with us, Dorix. Now it behooves me to act."

"I should warn you, Caesar, that the Sugambri aren't happy at developments between you and the Ubii. The Ubii are waxing fat supplying you with horse warriors, and the Sugambri resent it. All the Germani, they say, should be so favored, not just the Ubii."

"Which means the Sugambri are crossing the Rhenus to help Correus and Commius."

"So I hear. Commius and Ambiorix are very active."

This time Caesar called the Eleventh out of winter camp at Agedincum, and sent to Labienus for the Eighth and Ninth. Gaius Fabius was given the Twelfth and the Sixth and sent to garrison Suessionum on the Matroma River, dividing the lands of the Remi from those of the Suessiones. The scouts came in to report that Belgica was boiling, so the legions were shuffled round again: the Seventh was sent to Caesar, the Thirteenth was shifted to the Bituriges under Titus Sextius, and Trebonius inherited the Fifth Alauda to replace the Seventh at Cenabum.

But when Caesar and his four legions entered the lands of the Bellovaci they found them deserted; serfs, women and children were attending to affairs at home while the warriors congregated. On, the scouts reported, the only piece of elevated and dry ground in the midst of a marshy forest to the northwest.

"We'll do something a little different," said Caesar to Decimus Brutus. "Instead of marching one behind the other, we'll put the Seventh, Eighth and Ninth in columns—*agmen quadratum*—on a very broad front. That way the enemy will see our total strength immediately, and presume we're ready to wheel into full battle formation. The baggage will follow straight behind, and then we'll tuck the Eleventh into the rear of the baggage train. They'll never see it."

"We'll look as if we're frightened. And only three legions strong. Good thinking."

Sight of the enemy was a shock; there were thousands and thousands of them milling about that only piece of high, dry ground.

"More than I expected," said Caesar, and sent for Trebonius, who was to pick up Titus Sextius and the Thirteenth on his way.

There were feints and skirmishes while Caesar put his men into a very strong camp. Correus, in command, would draw up for battle, then change his mind. This despite the fact that it had been agreed he should attack while Caesar was possessed of no more than three legions.

The cavalry Caesar had sent for from the Remi and Lingones arrived ahead of Trebonius, led by Dorix's uncle Vertiscus, a doughty old warrior eager for a fight. Because the Bellovaci had not followed Vercingetorix's scorched-earth policy, there was plenty of forage and grain to be had; as the campaign looked as if it might last longer than earlier expected, Caesar was anxious to acquire whatever extra supplies he could. Though Correus's army refused to leave their high ground and attack in force, they proved a great nuisance to the foragers until the Remi came. After that it was easier. But Vertiscus was too eager for his fight. Despising the size of the Belgic group sent to harry the foraging party they were escorting, the Remi took off in pursuit and were led into an ambush. Vertiscus died, much to the delight of the Belgae; Correus decided it was time for a mass attack.

At which precise moment Trebonius marched up with the Fifth Alauda, the Fourteenth and the Thirteenth. There were now seven legions and several thousand horse troopers ringing the Belgae around, and the site which had seemed so perfect for attack or defense suddenly became a trap. Caesar built ramps across the marshes which divided the two camps, then took a ridge behind the Belgic camp and began using his artillery with devastating effect.

"Oh, Correus, you missed your chance!" cried Commius when he arrived. "What use are five hundred Sugambri now? And what do you expect me to tell Ambiorix, who's still recruiting?"

"I don't understand!" wept Correus, wringing his hands. "How did all those extra legions get here so quickly? I had no warning, and I should have had warning!"

"There is never warning," said Commius grimly. "You've held aloof until now, Correus, that's your trouble. You haven't seen the Romans at work. They move by what they call forced marches—they can cover fifty miles in a day. Then the moment they arrive they'll turn around and fight like wild dogs."

"What do we do now? How can we get out?"

That, Commius knew. He had the Belgae collect all the tinder, straw and dry brush they could find, and stockpile it. The camp was chaotic, everyone scrambling to be ready for the escape, women and hundreds of ox carts compounding the Roman-trained Commius's woes.

Correus brought all his men out in battle formation and sat them on the ground, as was their custom. The day passed; no move was made save surreptitiously to pile the wood, straw, tinder and brush in front of the lines. Then at dusk it was set on fire from end to end; the Belgae seized their chance and fled.

But the great chance had been lost. Caught while attempting an ambuscade, Correus found the steel and courage he had lacked when his position had been much better; refusing to retreat, he and the flower of his men perished. While the Belgae sued for peace, Commius crossed the Rhenus to the Sugambri and Ambiorix.

By now the winter was ending; Gaul lay quiet. Caesar went back to Bibracte, sending thanks and donatives of cash and women to all the legions, who found themselves, by legionary terms, very rich. A letter awaited him, from Gaius Scribonius Curio.

> A brilliant idea, Caesar, to issue a collected edition of your *Commentaries* on the war in Gaul and make it available to all and sundry. All and sundry are devouring it, and the *boni*—not to mention the Senate—are livid. It is not the place, roared Cato, of a proconsul conducting a war he *says* was forced upon him to puff his exalted name and exaggerated deeds throughout the city. No one takes any notice. Copies go so fast there is a waiting list. Little wonder. Your *Commentaries* are as thrilling as Homer's *Iliad,* with the advantage of being actual, of happening in our own time.
>
> You know, naturally, that Marcus Marcellus the junior consul is being thoroughly odious. Almost everyone applauded when your tribunes of the plebs vetoed his discussing your provinces in the House on the Kalends of March. You have some good men on the tribunician bench this year.
>
> It appalled me when Marcellus went a lot further in announcing that the people of the colony you set up at Novum Comum are not

Roman citizens. He maintained you have no power in law to do so—yet Pompeius Magnus has! Talk about one law for this man and another law for that man—Marcellus has perfected the art. But for the House to decree that the people living on the far side of the Padus in Italian Gaul are not citizens and never will be citizens—that's suicide. Despite the tribunician veto, Marcellus went ahead and had the decree inscribed on bronze. Then hung it publicly on the rostra.

What you probably do not know is that the result of all this is a huge shiver of fear from the Alps at the top of Italian Gaul to the toe and heel of Italia. People are very apprehensive, Caesar. In every town in Italian Gaul it's being said that they, who have given Rome so many thousands of her best soldiers, are being informed by the Senate that they are not good enough. Those living south of the Padus fear their citizenship will be stripped from them, and those living north of the Padus fear they will never, never, never be awarded the citizenship. The feeling is everywhere, Caesar. In Campania I've heard hundreds of people saying that they need Caesar back in Italia—that Caesar is the most indefatigable champion of the common people Italia has ever known—that Caesar wouldn't stand for these senatorial insults and gross injustices. It's spreading, this apprehension, but can I or anyone else get it through those blockheads in the camp of the *boni* that they're playing with fire? No.

Meantime that complacent idiot Pompeius sits like a toad in a cesspool, ignoring it all. He's *happy*. The frozen-faced harpy Cornelia Metella has her talons so deeply embedded in his insensitive hide that he nods, twitches, heaves and wallows every time she gives him a nudge. And by nudge I do not mean anything naughty. I doubt they've ever slept in the same bed. Or had one up against the atrium wall.

So why am I writing to you when I've never really been your friend? Several reasons, and I'll be honest about them all. First is that I'm sick to death of the *boni*. I used to think that any group of men with the interests of the *mos maiorum* so much at heart had to have right on their side, even when they made appalling political errors. But of late years I've seen through them, I suppose. They prate of things they know nothing about, and that is the truth. It's a mere disguise for their own negativity, for their own utter lack of gumption. If Rome began to crumble around them physically, they'd simply stand there and call it a part of the *mos maiorum* to be squashed flat by a pillar.

Second is that I abominate Cato and Bibulus. Two more hypocritical couch generals I've never encountered. They dissect your *Commentaries* in the most expert way, though neither of them could general a bun fight in a whorehouse. You could have done this better, and that more expeditiously, and whatever more diplomatically. Nor do I understand the *blindness* of their hatred for you. What did you ever do to them? As far as I can see, merely made them look as small as they really are.

Third is that you were good to Publius Clodius when you were consul. His destruction was his own doing. I daresay that Claudian streak of unorthodoxy in Clodius became a form of insanity. He had no idea when to stop. It's well over a year since he died, but I still miss him. Even though we'd fallen out a bit at the end.

Fourth is very personal, though it's all tied in with the first three reasons. I'm shockingly in debt, and I can't extricate myself. When my father died last year, I thought everything would right itself. But he left me nothing. I don't know where the money went, but it certainly wasn't there after he finished suffering. The house is all I inherited, and it's mortgaged heavily. The moneylenders are dunning me unmercifully, and the estimable house of finance which holds the house mortgage is threatening to foreclose.

Added to which, I want to marry Fulvia. Well, there you are! I hear you say. Publius Clodius's widow is one of the wealthiest women in Rome, and when her mother dies—it can't be long now—she'll be a lot richer. But I can't do that, Caesar. I can't love a woman the way I've loved her for years and years, and marry her, up to my eyebrows in debt. The thing is, I never thought she'd look at me, yet the other day she threw me a hint so broad it flattened me. I'm dying to marry Fulvia, but I can't marry Fulvia. Not until I've paid my way and can look her in the eye.

So here's my proposal. The way things are going in Rome, you're going to need the most capable and brilliant tribune of the plebs Rome has ever produced. Because they're slavering at the very thought of the Kalends of March next year, when your provinces come up for discussion in the House. Rumor has it that the *boni* will move to strip you of them immediately, and, thanks to the five-year law, they'll send Ahenobarbus to replace you. He never took a province after his consulship because he was too rich and too lazy to bother. But he'd walk upside down to Placentia for the chance to replace you.

If you pay my debts, Caesar, I give you my solemn word as a Scribonius Curio that I will be the most capable and brilliant tribune of the plebs Rome has ever produced. And always act in your interests. I'll undertake to keep the *boni* at bay until I go out of office, and that's not a hollow promise. I need at least five million.

For a long while after reading Curio's letter Caesar sat without moving. His luck was with him, and what marvelous luck. Curio as his tribune of the plebs, bought and paid for. A man of great honor, though that wasn't really a consideration. One of the most stringent rules of

Roman political behavior was the code governing those who accepted bribes. Once a man was bought, he stayed bought. For the disgrace was not in being bought, but in not staying bought. A man who accepted a bribe, then reneged on the bargain, was a social outcast from that day forward. The luck lay in being offered a tribune of the plebs of Curio's caliber. Whether he would prove quite as good as he thought was beside the point; if he was half as good as he thought, he'd still be a pearl beyond price.

Caesar turned in his chair to sit straight at his desk, picked up his pen, dipped it in the inkwell, and wrote.

> My dear Curio, I am overcome. Nothing would give me greater pleasure than to be permitted to assist you out of your financial predicament. Please believe me when I say that I do not require any services from you in return for the privilege of helping you in this matter. The decision is absolutely yours.
>
> However, if you would like the opportunity to shine as Rome's most capable and brilliant tribune of the plebs, then I would be honored to think you exerted yourself in my interests. As you say, I wear the *boni* around my neck like Medusa's snakes. Nor do I have any idea why they have fixed on me as their target for almost as many years as I have been in the Senate. The why is not important. What matters is the fact that I am indeed their target.
>
> However, if we are to succeed in blocking the *boni* when the Kalends of next March arrive, I think our little pact must remain our secret. Nor should you announce that you will stand for the tribunate of the plebs. Why don't you find some needy fellow—not in the Senate—who would be willing to announce himself as a candidate, but be prepared to step down at the very last moment? For a nice fat fee, of course. I leave that to you. Just apply to Balbus for the wherewithal. When the needy fellow steps down just as the elections are about to begin, stroll forward and offer yourself as his replacement candidate. As if the impulse came upon you. This renders you innocent of any suspicion that you might be acting in someone's interests.
>
> Even when you enter office as a tribune of the plebs, Curio, you will appear to be acting for yourself. If you want a list of useful laws, I would be happy to furnish it, though I imagine you'll have no trouble thinking of a few laws to pass without my guidance. When you introduce your veto on the Kalends of March to block discussion of my provinces, it will fall on the *boni* like a scorpion bolt.
>
> I leave it to you to devise a strategy. There's nothing worse than a man who doesn't give his colleagues sufficient rope. If you need to talk a strategy over, I am your servant. Just rest assured that I do not expect it.

Though be warned that the *boni* are not yet come to the end of their ammunition. Before you step into office, I predict that they will have thought of several more ways to make your task more difficult. And possibly more perilous. One of the marks of the truly great tribune of the plebs is martyrdom. I like you, Curio, and don't want to see the Forum knives flash in your direction. Or see you pitched off the end of the Tarpeian Rock.

Would ten million make you a completely free man? If it would, then you shall have ten million. I'll be writing to Balbus in the same bag, so you may talk to him at any time after you receive this. Despite what is seen as a tendency to gossip, he is the soul of discretion; what Balbus chooses to disseminate has been very carefully worked out beforehand.

I congratulate you on your choice of a wife. Fulvia is an interesting woman, and interesting women are rare. She believes with a true passion, and will cleave to you and your aspirations absolutely. But you know that better than I. Please give her my best regards, and tell her I look forward to seeing her when I return to Rome.

There. Ten million well spent. But when was he going to be able to return to Italian Gaul? It was June, and the prospect of being able to leave Further Gaul grew, if anything, more remote. The Belgae were probably now completely finished, but Ambiorix and Commius were still at liberty. Therefore the Belgae would have to be drubbed once more. The tribes of central Gaul were definitely finished; the Arverni and the Aedui, let off lightly, would not be listening to any Vercingetorix or Litaviccus again. As the name Litaviccus popped into his mind, Caesar shuddered; a hundred years of exposure to Rome hadn't killed the Gaul in Litaviccus. Was that equally true of every Gaul? Wisdom said that continued rule by fear and terror would benefit neither Rome nor Gaul. But how to get the Gauls to the point whereat they could see for themselves where their destiny lay? Fear and terror now, so that when it lightened they were grateful? Fear and terror now, so that they always had it to remember, even when it no longer existed? War was a passionate business to peoples other than the Roman people; those others went into war boiling with righteous anger, thirsting to kill their enemies. But that kind of emotion was difficult to sustain at the necessary fever pitch. When all was said and done, any people wanted to live at peace, pursue an ordinary and pleasant life, watch their children grow, eat plenty, be warm in winter. Only Rome had turned war into a business. That was why Rome always won in the end. Because, though Roman soldiers learned to hate their enemies healthily, they approached war with cool business heads. Thoroughly trained, absolutely pragmatic, fully confident. They understood the difference between losing a battle and losing a war. They also understood that battles were won before the first *pilum* was thrown; battles were won on the drill field and in the training camp. Discipline, restraint, thought, valor. Pride in professional excellence. No other people owned that attitude to war. And no other Roman army owned that attitude more professionally than Caesar's.

At the beginning of Quinctilis came very disturbing news from Rome. Caesar was still in Bibracte with Antony and the Twelfth, though he had already issued orders to Labienus to reduce the Treveri. He himself was about to depart for Ambiorix's lands in Belgica; the Eburones, Atrebates and Bellovaci had to be shown for once and for all that resistance was useless.

Marcus Claudius Marcellus, the junior consul, had publicly flogged a citizen of Caesar's colony at Novum Comum. Not with his own white hands, of course; the deed was done at his order. And the damage was irreparable. No Roman citizen could be flogged. He might be chastised by being beaten with the rods which made up a lictor's *fasces,* but his back was inviolate, legally protected from the touch of a knouted lash. Now Marcus Marcellus was saying to the whole of Italian Gaul and Italia that many people who deemed themselves citizens were not citizens. They could and would be flogged.

"I won't have it!" said Caesar to Antony, Decimus Brutus and Trebonius, white with anger. "The people of Novum Comum are Roman citizens! They are my clients, and I owe them my protection."

"It's going to happen more and more," said Decimus Brutus, looking grim. "All the Claudii Marcelli are cast from the same mold, and there are three of them of an age to be consul. Rumor says each of them will be consul—Marcus this year, his first cousin Gaius next year, and his brother Gaius the year after that. The *boni* are running rampant; they're dominating the elections so completely that one can't foresee two Popularis consuls getting into office until you're consul, Caesar. And even then, will you be saddled with another Bibulus? Or—ye Gods!—Bibulus himself?"

Still so angry that he couldn't laugh, Caesar thinned his lips to a straight line and glared. "I will not suffer Bibulus as my colleague, and that's that! I'll have a man *I* want, and I'll get a man *I* want, no matter what they try to do to prevent it. But that doesn't alter what's happening right now in Italian Gaul—*my* province, Decimus! How *dare* Marcus Marcellus invade my jurisdiction to flog my people?"

"You don't have a full *imperium maius,*" said Trebonius.

"Oh well, they only give that kind of imperium to Pompeius!" snapped Caesar.

"What can you do?" asked Antony.

"Quite a lot," said Caesar. "I've sent to Labienus and asked to detach the Fifteenth and Publius Vatinius. Labienus can have the Sixth instead."

Trebonius sat up. "The Fifteenth is well blooded by now," he said, "but its men have only been in the field for a year. And, as I remember, all of them come from across the Padus. Many of them come from Novum Comum."

"Exactly," said Caesar.

"And Publius Vatinius," said Decimus Brutus thoughtfully, "is your loyalest adherent."

From somewhere Caesar found a smile. "I hope no loyaler than you or Trebonius, Decimus."

"What about me?" demanded Antony indignantly.

"You're family, so pipe down," said Trebonius, grinning.

"You're going to send the Fifteenth and Publius Vatinius to garrison Italian Gaul," said Decimus Brutus.

"I am."

"I know there's nothing legal to stop you, Caesar," said Trebonius, "but won't Marcus Marcellus and the Senate take that as a declaration of war? I don't mean genuine war, I mean the kind of war which takes place between minds."

"I have a valid excuse," said Caesar, some of his usual calm returning. "Last year the Iapudes raided into Tergeste and threatened coastal Illyricum. The local militia put them down; it wasn't serious. I will send Publius Vatinius and the Fifteenth to Italian Gaul to, and I quote, 'protect the Roman citizen colonies across the Padus River from barbarian invasion.' "

"The only barbarian in sight being Marcus Marcellus," said Antony, delighted.

"I think he'll interpret the wording correctly, Antonius."

"What orders will you issue Vatinius?" asked Trebonius.

"To act in my name throughout Italian Gaul and Illyricum. To prevent Roman citizens' being flogged. To conduct the assizes. To govern Italian Gaul for me in the way I would myself were I there," said Caesar.

"And where will you put the Fifteenth?" asked Decimus Brutus. "Close to Illyricum? In Aquileia, perhaps?"

"Oh, no," said Caesar. "In Placentia."

"A stone's throw from Novum Comum."

"Quite."

"What I want to know," said Antony, "is what does Pompeius think of the flogging? After all, he established citizen colonies across the Padus in Italian Gaul too. Marcus Marcellus imperils his citizens as much as he does yours."

Caesar lifted his lip. "Pompeius said and did absolutely nothing. He's in Tarentum. Private business, I understand. But he's promised to attend a meeting of the Senate outside the *pomerium* later in the month, when he drifts through. The pretext of the meeting is to discuss army pay."

"That's a joke!" said Decimus Brutus. "The army hasn't had a pay rise in a hundred years, literally."

"True. I've been thinking about that," said Caesar.

Attrition continued; the Belgae were invaded yet again, their homes burned, their sprouting crops raked out of the ground or ploughed under, their animals killed, their women and children rendered homeless. Tribes like the Nervii, who had been able to field fifty thousand men in the early years of Caesar's campaign in Gaul, were now hard put to field one thousand. The best of the women and children had been sold into slavery; Belgica had become a land of old people, Druids, cripples and mental defectives. At the end of it Caesar could be sure that no one was left to tempt Ambiorix or Commius, and that their own tribes, such as they were, were too afraid of Rome to want anything to do with their former kings. Ambiorix, elusive as ever, was never found or captured. And Commius had gone east to help the Treveri against Labienus, quite as thorough in his campaign as Caesar was.

Gaius Fabius was sent with two legions to reinforce Rebilus and his two legions among the Pictones and the Andes, two tribes who had not suffered disastrously at Alesia, nor been in the forefront of resistance to Rome. But it seemed as if, one by one, all the peoples of Gaul determined on a dying gasp, perhaps thinking that Caesar's army, after so many years of war, must surely be exhausted and losing interest. That it was not was manifest once again: twelve thousand Andeans died in one battle at a bridge over the Liger, others in more minor engagements.

Which meant that slowly, surely, the area of Gaul still capable of fighting back was shrinking steadily southward and westward, into Aquitania. Where Lucterius was joined by Drappes of the Senones after his own people refused to shelter him.

Of all the great enemy leaders, few were left. Gutruatus of the Carnutes was turned over to Caesar by his own people, too terrified of Roman reprisals to succor him. Because he had murdered Roman citizen civilians at Cenabum, his fate was not entirely in Caesar's hands; a representative council from the army was also involved. Despite all Caesar's arguments that Gutruatus should live to walk in his triumphal parade, the army got its way. Gutruatus was flogged and beheaded.

Shortly after this, Commius encountered Gaius Volusenus Quadratus for the second time. While Caesar went south with the cavalry, Mark Antony was left in command of Belgica; he finished the Bellovaci completely, then went into camp at Nemetocenna in the lands of the Atrebates, Commius's own people. Who were so afraid of further Roman attrition that they refused to have anything to do with Commius. Having met up with a band of like-minded German Sugambri, he sought refuge in brigandage and wreaked havoc among the Nervii, in no condition to resist. When Antony received a plea for help from the ever-loyal Vertico, he sent Volusenus and a very large troop of cavalry to Vertico's assistance.

Time had not diminished Volusenus's hatred of Commius one little bit. Aware who was commanding the brigands, Volusenus set to work with enthusiastic savagery. Working systematically, he drove Commius and his Sugambri in the manner of a shepherd his sheep until finally they met. There ensued a hate-filled duel between the two men, who charged at each other with lances leveled. Commius won. Volusenus went down with Commius's lance right through the middle of his thigh; the femur was in splinters, the flesh mangled, the nerves and blood vessels severed. Most of Commius's men were killed, but Commius, on the fleetest horse, got clean away while attention was focused on the critically wounded Volusenus.

Who was conveyed to Nemetocenna. Roman army surgeons were good; the leg was amputated above the wound, and Volusenus lived.

Commius sent an envoy with a letter to see Mark Antony.

> Marcus Antonius, I now believe that Caesar had nothing to do with the treachery of that wolf's-head Volusenus. But I have taken a vow never again to come into the presence of a Roman. The Tuatha have been good to me. They delivered my enemy to me, and I wounded him so badly he will lose his leg, if not his life. Honor is satisfied.
>
> But I am very tired. My own people are so afraid of Rome that they will give me neither food nor water nor roof over my head. Brigandage is an ignoble profession for a king. I just want to be left in peace. As hostage for my good behavior I offer you my children, five boys and two girls, not all by the same mother, but all Atrebatans, and all young enough to turn into good little Romans.
>
> I gave Caesar good service before Volusenus betrayed me. For that reason, I ask that you send me somewhere to live out the rest of my days without my needing to lift a sword again. Somewhere devoid of Romans.

The letter appealed to Antony, who had a rather antique way of looking at bravery, service, the true warrior code. In his mind Commius was a Hector and Volusenus a Paris. What good would it do Rome or Caesar to kill Commius and drag him behind the victor's chariot? Nor did he think Caesar would feel differently. He sent a letter to Commius together with his envoy.

> Commius, I accept your offer of hostages, for I deem you an honest and a wronged man. Your children will be drawn to the at-

tention of Caesar himself. He will, I am sure, treat them as the children of a king.

I hereby sentence you to exile in Britannia. How you get there is your concern, though I enclose a passport you may present at Itius or Gesoriacus. Britannia is a place you know well from your days of service to Caesar. I presume you have more friends than enemies there.

So great is the length of Rome's reach that I cannot think of anywhere else to send you. Rest assured you will see no Romans. Caesar detests the place. *Vale.*

The last gasp of all happened at Uxellodunum, an *oppidum* belonging to the Cardurci.

While Gaius Fabius marched off to finish reducing the Senones, Gaius Caninius Rebilus pushed on south toward Aquitania, knowing that reinforcements would soon arrive to swell his two legions; Fabius was to return the moment he was satisfied that the Senones were utterly cowed.

Though both Drappes and Lucterius had led contingents in the army which came to relieve Alesia, they had not learned the futility of withstanding siege. Hearing of the Andean defeat and Rebilus's approach, they shut themselves up inside Uxellodunum, an extremely lofty fortress town atop a hill tucked inside a loop of the river Oltis. Unfortunately it contained no water, but it did have two sources of water nearby, one from the Oltis itself, the other a permanent spring which gushed out of rocks immediately below the highest section of wall.

Having only two legions, Rebilus when he arrived made no attempt to repeat Caesar's tactics at Alesia; besides which, the Oltis, too strong to dam or divert, made circumvallation impossible. Rebilus contented himself with sitting down in three separate camps on ground high enough to ensure that a secret evacuation of the citadel could not succeed.

What Alesia *had* taught Drappes and Lucterius was that a mountainous supply of food was essential to withstand a siege. Both men knew that Uxellodunum could not be taken by storm no matter how brilliant Caesar was, for the crag on which the stronghold stood was surrounded by other rock faces too difficult for troops to scale. Nor would a siege terrace like the one at Avaricum work; Uxellodunum's walls were so high and so perilous to approach that no feat of awesome Roman engineering could hope to surmount them. Once ensured adequate food, Uxellodunum could wait out a siege which lasted until Caesar's tenure as governor of the Gauls expired.

Therefore food had to be found, and in enormous quantities. While Rebilus was making his camps, and well before he thought of additional fortifications, Lucterius and Drappes led two thousand men out of the citadel into the surrounding countryside. The Cardurci fell to with a will, gathering grain, salt pork, bacon, beans, chickpea, root vegetables and cages of chickens, ducks, geese. Cattle, pigs and sheep were rounded up. Unfortunately the chief crop the Cardurci grew was not an edible one; they were famous for their flax, and made the best linen outside of Egypt. Which necessitated incursions into the lands of the Petrocorii and other neighboring tribes. Who were not nearly as enthusiastic about donating food to Drappes and Lucterius as the Cardurci had been. What wasn't given was taken, and when every mule and ox cart had been pressed into service, Drappes and Lucterius made for home.

While this foraging expedition was going on, those warriors left behind made life very difficult for Rebilus; night after night they attacked one or another of his three camps, so craftily that Rebilus despaired of being able to finish any fortifications designed to constrain Uxellodunum more thoroughly.

The huge food train returned and halted twelve miles short of Uxellodunum. There it camped under the command of Drappes, who was to stay with it and defend it against a Roman attack; then visitors from the citadel assured Drappes and Lucterius that the Romans were oblivious to its existence. The task of getting the food inside Uxellodunum devolved upon Lucterius, who knew the area intimately. No more carts, said Lucterius. The last miles would be on the backs of mules, and the final few hundred paces at dead of night as far as possible from any of the Roman camps.

There were many forest paths between the food train camp and the citadel; Lucterius led his contingent of mules as close as he dared and settled down to wait. Not until four hours after midnight did he move, and then with as much stealth as possible; the mules wore padded linen shoes over their hooves and were muzzled by men's hands keeping their lips together. The degree of quietness was surprising, Lucterius confident. The sentries in the watchtowers of the nearest Roman camp—nearer, indeed, than Lucterius had wished—were bound to be dozing.

But Roman sentries in watchtowers didn't doze on duty. The punishment was death by bludgeoning, and inspections of the Watch were as ruthless as unheralded.

Had there been wind or rain, Lucterius would have gotten away with it. But the night was so calm that the distant sound of the Oltis was clearly audible on this far side from it. So too were other, stranger noises clearly audible—clunks, scrapes, muffled whispers, swishes.

"Wake the General," said the chief of the Watch to one of his men, "and be a lot quieter than whatever's going on out there."

Suspecting a surprise attack, Rebilus sent out scouts and mobilized with speed and silence. Just before dawn he pounced, so noiselessly that the food porters hardly knew what happened. Panicked, they chose to flee into Uxellodunum minus the mules; why Lucterius did not remained a mystery, for though he escaped into the surrounding forest, he made no attempt to get back to Drappes and tell him what had taken place.

Rebilus learned of the location of the food train from a captured Cardurcan and sent his Germans after it. The Ubii horsemen were now accompanied by Ubii foot warriors, a lethal combination. Behind them, marching swiftly, came one of Rebilus's two legions. The contest was no contest. Drappes and his men were taken prisoner, and all the food so painstakingly gathered fell into Roman hands.

"And very glad I am of it!" said Rebilus the next day, shaking Fabius warmly by the hand. "There are two more legions to feed, yet we don't have to forage for a thing."

"Let's begin the blockade," said Fabius.

When news of Rebilus's stroke of good luck reached Caesar, he decided to push ahead with his cavalry, leaving Quintus Fufius Calenus to bring up two legions at ordinary marching pace.

"For I don't think," said Caesar, "that Rebilus and Fabius stand in any danger. If you encounter any pockets of resistance on your way, Calenus, deal with them mercilessly. It's time that Gaul put its head beneath the yoke for good and all."

He arrived at Uxellodunum to find the siege fortifications progressing nicely, though his advent came as something of a surprise; neither Rebilus nor Fabius had thought to see him there in person, but they seized him eagerly.

"We're neither of us engineers, and nor are the engineers with us worthy of the name," said Fabius.

"You want to cut off their water," said Caesar.

"I think we have to, Caesar. Otherwise we're going to have to wait until starvation drives them out, and there's every indication that they're not short of food, despite Lucterius's attempt to get more food inside."

"I agree, Fabius."

They were standing on a rocky outcrop with a full view of Uxellodunum's water supply, the path down from the citadel to the river, and the spring. Rebilus and Fabius had already begun to deal with the path to the river, by posting archers where they could pick off the water carriers without being themselves picked off by archers or spearmen on the citadel walls.

"Not enough," said Caesar. "Move up the ballistae and shell the path with two-pounders. Also scorpions."

Which left Uxellodunum with the spring, a far more difficult task for the Romans; it lay just beneath the highest part of the citadel walls, and was accessed from a gate in the base of the walls immediately adjacent to the spring. Storming it was useless. The terrain was too rugged and the location such that it couldn't be held by a cohort or two of troops, nor accommodate more.

"I think we're stuck," said Fabius, sighing.

Caesar grinned. "Nonsense! The first thing we do is build a ramp out of earth and stones from where we're standing to that spot there, fifty paces from the spring. It's all uphill, but it will give us a platform sixty feet higher than the ground we have at the moment. On the top of the ramp we build a siege tower ten storeys high. It will overlook the spring and enable the scorpions to shoot anyone trying to get water."

"During daytime," Rebilus said despondently. "They'll just visit the spring at night. Besides, our men doing the building will be shockingly exposed."

"That's what mantlets are for, Rebilus, as you well know. The important thing," Caesar said with a casual air, "is to make all this work look *good*. As if we mean it. That in turn means that the troops doing the work must believe I'm in earnest." He paused, eyes on the spring, a noble cascade gushing out under pressure. "But," he went on, "all of it is a smoke screen. I've seen many a spring of this kind before, especially in Anatolia. We mine it. It's fed by a number of underground streams, from the size of it as many as ten or twelve. The sappers will begin to tunnel at once. Each feeder stream they encounter they'll divert into the Oltis. How long the job will take I have no idea, but when every last feeder is diverted, the spring will dry up."

Fabius and Rebilus stared at him, awestruck.

"Couldn't we just mine it without the farce aboveground?"

"And have them realize what we're actually doing? There's silver and copper mining all through this part of Gaul, Rebilus. I imagine the citadel contains men skilled in mining. And I *don't* want a repeat of what happened when we besieged the Atuatuci—mines and countermines twisting around each other and running into each other like the burrowings of a squadron of demented moles. The mining here must be absolutely secret. The only ones among our men who will know of it are the sappers. That's why the ramp and the siege tower have to look like very serious trouble for the defenders. I don't like losing men—and we'll endeavor not to—but I want this business finished, and finished soon," said Caesar.

So the ramp reared up the slope, then the siege tower began to rise. The startled and terrified inhabitants of Uxellodunum retaliated with spears, arrows, stones and fire missiles. When they finally realized the ultimate height of the tower, they came out of their gate and attacked in force. The fighting was fierce, for the Roman troops genuinely believed in the efficacy of what they were doing and defended their position strenuously. Soon the tower was on fire, and the mantlets and protective fortifications on either side of the ramp under severe threat.

Because the front was so limited in extent, most of the Roman soldiers were uninvolved in the battle; they crowded as close as possible and cheered their comrades on, while the Cardurci inside the citadel lined its ramparts and cheered too. At the height of it Caesar hunted his spectator troops away, under orders to go elsewhere around the stronghold's perimeter and create a huge noise, as if a full-scale attack were being mounted on all sides.

The ruse worked. The Cardurci retired to deal with this new threat, which gave the Romans time to put the fires out.

The ten-storey siege tower began to rise again, but it was never used; beneath the ground the mines had been creeping forward inexorably, and one by one the streams feeding the spring were diverted. At about the same moment as the tower might have been manned with artillery and put into commission, the magnificent spring giving Uxellodunum water dried up for the first time ever.

It came as a bolt out of the clear sky, and something vital within the defenders died. For the message was implicit: the Tuatha had bowed down before the might of Rome, the Tuatha had deserted Gaul for love of Caesar. What was the use of fighting on, when even the Tuatha smiled on Caesar and the Romans?

Uxellodunum surrendered.

The next morning Caesar called a council consisting of all the legates, prefects, military tribunes and centurions present to participate in Gaul's last gasp. Including Aulus Hirtius, who had traveled with the two legions Quintus Fufius Calenus brought after the assault on the spring began.

"I'll be brief," he said, seated on his curule chair in full military dress, the ivory rod of his imperium lying up his right forearm. Perhaps it was the light in the citadel's meeting hall, for it poured in through a great unshuttered aperture behind the five hundred assembled men and fell directly upon Caesar's face. He was not yet fifty, but his long neck was deeply ringed with creases, though no sagging skin marred the purity of his jaw. Lines crossed his forehead, fanned out at the far edges of his eyes, carved fissures down either side of his nose, emphasized the high, sharply defined cheekbones by cleaving the skin of his face below them. On campaign he bothered not at all about his thinning hair, but today he had donned his Civic Crown of oak leaves because he wanted to set a mood of unassailable authority; when he entered a room wearing it, every person had to stand and applaud him—even Bibulus and Cato. Because of it he had entered the Senate at twenty years of age; because of it every soldier who ever served under him knew that Caesar had fought in the front line with sword and shield, though the men of his Gallic legions had seen him in the front line fighting with them on many occasions, didn't need to be reminded.

He looked desperately tired, but no man there mistook these signs for physical weariness; he was a superbly fit and enormously strong man. No, he was suffering a mental and emotional exhaustion; they all realized it. And wondered at it.

"It is the end of September. Summer is with us," he said in a clipped, terse accent which stripped the cadences in his exquisitely chosen Latin of any poetic intention, "and if this were two or three years ago, one would say that the war in Gaul was over at last. But all of us who sit here today know better. When will the people of Gallia Comata admit defeat? When will they settle down under the light hand of Roman supervision and admit that they are safe, protected, united as never before? Gaul is a bull whose eyes have been put out, but not its anger. It charges blindly time and time again, ruining itself on walls, rocks, trees. Growing steadily weaker, yet never growing calmer. Until in the end it must die, still dashing itself to pieces."

The room was utterly still; no one moved, even cleared his throat. Whatever was coming was going to matter.

"How can we calm this bull? How can we persuade it to be still, to let us apply the ointments and heal it?"

The tone of his voice changed, became more somber. "None of you, including the most junior centurion, is unaware of the terrible difficulties I face in Rome. The Senate is after my blood, my bones, my spirit . . . and my *dignitas,* my personal share of public worth and standing. Which is also your *dignitas,* because you are my people. The sinews of my beloved army. When I fall, you fall. When I am disgraced, you are disgraced. That is an omnipresent threat, but it is not why I am speaking. A by-product, no more. I mention it to reinforce what I am about to say."

He drew a breath. "I will not see my command extended. On the Kalends of March in the year after next, it will end. It may be that on the Kalends of March next year, it will end, though I will exert every ounce of myself to prevent that. I need next year to do the administrative work necessary to transform Gallia Comata into a proper Roman province. Therefore this year *must* see this futile, pointless, *wasteful* war finished for good. It gives me no pleasure to witness the battlefields after the battles are over, for there are Roman bodies lying on them too. And so many, many Gauls, Belgae and Celtae both. Dead for no good reason beyond a dream they have neither the education nor the foresight to make come true. As Vercingetorix would have found out had he been the one to win."

He got to his feet and stood with hands clasped behind his back, frowning. "I want to see the war ended this year. Not a merely temporary cessation of hostilities, but a genuine peace. A peace which will last for longer than any man in this room will live, or his children after him, or their children after them. If that doesn't happen, the Germani will conquer, and the history of Gaul will be different history. As will the history of our beloved Italia, for the Germani will not rest with the conquest of Gaul. The last time they came, Rome threw up Gaius Marius. I believe Rome has thrown up me at this time and in this place to make sure the Germani never come again. Gallia Comata is the natural frontier, not the

Alps. We must keep the Germani on the far side of the Rhenus if our world, including the world of Gaul, is to prosper."

He paced a little, came to stand in the center of his space again, and looked at them from beneath his fair brows. A long, measured, immensely serious stare.

"Most of you have served with me for a very long time. All of you have served with me long enough to know what sort of man I am. Not a naturally cruel man. It gives me no pleasure to see pain inflicted, or have to order it inflicted. But I have come to the conclusion that Gaul of the Longhairs needs a lesson so awful, so severe, so appalling that the memory of it will linger through the generations and serve to discourage future uprisings. For that reason I have called you here today. To give you my solution. Not to ask your permission. I am the commander-in-chief and the decision is mine alone to take. I have taken it. The matter is out of your hands. The Greeks believe that only the man who does the deed is guilty of the crime, if the deed be a crime. Therefore the guilt rests entirely upon my shoulders. None of you has a share in it. None of you will suffer because of it. I bear the burden. You have often heard me say that the memory of cruelty is poor comfort for old age, but there are reasons why I do not fear that fate as I did until I spoke with Cathbad of the Druids."

He returned to his curule chair, and seated himself in the formal position.

"Tomorrow I will see the men who defended Uxellodunum. I believe there are about four thousand of them. Yes, there are more, but four thousand will do. Those who scowl the most, eye us with the most hatred. I will amputate both their hands."

He said it calmly; a faint sigh echoed around the room. How good, that neither Decimus Brutus nor Gaius Trebonius was there! But Hirtius was staring at him with eyes full of tears, and Caesar found that difficult. He had to swallow, he hoped not too visibly. Then he went on.

"I will not ask any Roman to do the business. Some among the citizens of Uxellodunum can do it. Volunteers. Eighty men, each to sever the hands of fifty men. I will offer to spare the hands of any men who volunteer. It will produce enough. The artificers are working now on a special tool I have devised, a little like a sharp chisel six inches wide across the blade. It will be positioned across the back of the hand just below the the wrist bones, and struck once with a hammer. Flow of blood to the member will be occluded by a thong around the forearm. The moment the amputation is done, the wrist will be dipped in pitch. Some may bleed to death. Most won't."

He was speaking fluently now, easily, for he was out of the realm of ideas and into the practicalities.

"These four thousand handless men will then be banished to wander and beg all over this vast country. And whoever should see a man with no hands will think of the lesson learned after the siege of Uxellodunum.

When the legions disperse, as they will very shortly, each legion will take some of the handless men with it to wherever it goes into winter cantonments. Thus making sure that the handless are well scattered. For the lesson is wasted unless the evidence of it is seen everywhere.

"I will conclude by giving you some information compiled by my gallant but unsung clerical heroes. The eight years of war in Gallia Comata have cost the Gauls a million dead warriors. A million people have been sold into slavery. Four hundred thousand Gallic women and children are dead, and a quarter of a million Gallic families have been rendered homeless. That is the entire population of Italia. An awful indication of the bull's blindness and anger. It has to stop! It has to stop now. It has to stop here at Uxellodunum. When I give up my command in the Gauls, Gallia Comata will be at peace."

He nodded a dismissal; all the men filed out silently, none looking at Caesar. Save for Hirtius, who stayed.

"Don't say a word!" Caesar snapped.

"I don't intend to," said Hirtius.

After Uxellodunum surrendered, Caesar decided that he would visit all the tribes of Aquitania, the one part of Gaul of the Long-hairs least involved in the war, and therefore the one part of the country still able to field a full complement of warriors. With him he took some of the handless victims of Uxellodunum, as living testimony of Rome's determination to see an end to opposition.

His progress was peaceful; the various tribes greeted him with feverish welcomes, averted their eyes from the handless, signed whatever treaties he required, and swore mighty oaths to cleave to Rome forever. On the whole, Caesar was prepared to believe them. For an Arvernian, of all people, had turned Lucterius over to him some days after he marched for Burdigala on the first stage of his tour of Aquitania, an indication that no tribe in Gaul was prepared to shelter one of Vercingetorix's lieutenants. This meant that one of the two defenders of Uxellodunum would walk in Caesar's triumphal parade; the other, Drappes of the Senones, had refused to eat or drink, and died still resolutely opposed to the presence of Rome in Gaul of the Long-hairs.

Lucius Caesar came to see his cousin in Tolosa toward the end of October, big with news.

"The Senate met at the end of September," he told Caesar, tight-lipped. "I confess I'm disappointed in the senior consul, who I had thought was a more rational man than his junior."

"Servius Sulpicius *is* more rational than Marcus Marcellus, yes, but he's no less determined to see me fall," said Caesar. "What went on?"

"The House resolved that on the Kalends of March next year it *would* discuss your provinces. Marcus Marcellus informed it that the war in Gallia Comata was definitely over, which meant there was absolutely no reason why you should not be stripped of your imperium, your provinces and your army on that date. The new five-year law, he said, had provided a pool of potential governors able to go to replace you immediately. To delay was evidence of senatorial weakness, and quite intolerable. Then he concluded by saying that once and for all, you must be taught that you are the Senate's servant, not its master. At which statement, I gather, there were loud hear-hears from Cato."

"They'd have to be loud, since Bibulus is in Syria—or on his way there, at least. Go on, Lucius. I can tell from your face that there's worse to come."

"Much worse! The House then decreed that if any tribune of the plebs vetoed discussion on your provinces on the Kalends of next March, said veto would be deemed an act of treason. The guilty tribune of the plebs would be arrested and summarily tried."

"That's absolutely unconstitutional!" snapped Caesar. "No one can impede a tribune of the plebs in his duty! *Or* refuse to honor his veto unless there's a Senatus Consultum Ultimum in force. Does this mean that's what the Senate intends to do on the Kalends of next March? Operate under an ultimate decree?"

"Perhaps, though that wasn't said."

"Is that all?"

"No," said Lucius Caesar levelly. "The House passed another decree. That it would reserve for itself the right to decide the date on which your time-expired veterans would be discharged."

"Oh, I see! I've generated a 'first,' Lucius, haven't I? Until this moment, in the history of Rome no one has had the right to decide when time-expired soldiers are to finish their service in the legions except their commander-in-chief. I imagine, then, that on the Kalends of next March the Senate will decree that all my veterans are to be discharged forthwith."

"It seems that way, Gaius."

Caesar looked, thought Lucius, oddly unworried; he even gave a genuine smile. "Do they really think to defeat me with these kinds of measures?" he asked. "Horse piss, Lucius!" He got up from his chair and extended a hand to his cousin. "I thank you for the news, I really do. But enough of it. I feel like stretching my legs among the sacred lakes."

But Lucius Caesar wasn't prepared to leave the matter there. He followed Gaius obediently, saying, "What are you going to do to counter the *boni*?"

"Whatever I have to" was all Caesar would say.

The winter dispositions had been made. Gaius Trebonius, Publius Vatinius and Mark Antony took four legions to Nemetocenna of the Atrebates to garrison Belgica; two legions went to the Aedui at Bibracte; two were stationed among the Turoni, on the outskirts of the Carnutes to their west; and two went to the lands of the Lemovices, southwest of the Arverni. No part of Gaul was very far from an army. With Lucius Caesar, Caesar completed a tour of the Province, then went to join Trebonius, Vatinius and Mark Antony in Nemetocenna for the winter.

Halfway through December his army received a welcome and unexpected surprise; he increased the rankers' pay from four hundred and eighty sesterces a year to nine hundred—the first time in over a century that a Roman army had experienced a pay rise. In conjunction with it he gave every man a cash bonus, and informed the army that its share of the booty would be larger.

"At whose expense?" asked Gaius Trebonius of Publius Vatinius. "The Treasury's? Surely not!"

"Definitely not," said Vatinius. "He's scrupulous about the legalities, always. No, it's out of his own purse, his own share." Little crippled Vatinius frowned; he hadn't been present when Caesar got the Senate's answer to his request that he be treated as Pompey had been treated. "I know he's fabulously rich, but he spends prodigiously too. Can he afford this largesse, Trebonius?"

"Oh, I think so. He's made twenty thousand talents out of the sale of slaves alone."

"*Twenty thousand?* Jupiter! Crassus was accounted the richest man in Rome, and all he left was seven thousand talents!"

"Marcus Crassus bragged of his money, but have you ever heard Pompeius Magnus say how much *he's* worth?" asked Trebonius. "Why do you think the bankers flock around Caesar these days, anxious to oblige his every whim? Balbus has been his man forever, with Oppius not far behind. They go back to your days, Vatinius. However, men like Atticus are very recent."

"Rabirius Postumus owes him a fresh start," said Vatinius.

"Yes, but after Caesar began to flourish in Gaul. The German treasure he found among the Atuatuci was fabulous. His share of it will amount to thousands of talents." Trebonius grinned. "And if he runs a bit short, Carnutum's hoards will cease to be sacrosanct. That's in reserve. He's nobody's fool, Caesar. He knows that the next governor of Gallia Comata will seize what's at Carnutum. It's my bet that what's at Carnutum will be gone before the new governor arrives."

"My letters from Rome say he's likely to be relieved in—ye Gods, where does time go?—a little over three months. The Kalends of March are galloping toward him! What will he do then? The moment his imperium is stripped from him, he'll be arraigned in a hundred courts. And he'll go down, Trebonius."

"Oh, very likely," said Trebonius placidly.

Vatinius was nobody's fool either. "He doesn't intend to let matters go that far, does he?"

"No, Vatinius, he doesn't."

A silence fell; Vatinius studied the mournful face opposite him, chewing his lip. Their eyes met and held.

"Then I'm right," said Vatinius. "He's cemented his bond with his army absolutely."

"Absolutely."

"And if he has to, he'll march on Rome."

"Only if he has to. Caesar's not a natural outlaw; he loves to do everything *in suo anno*—no special or extraordinary commands, ten years between consulships, everything legal. If he does have to march on Rome, Vatinius, it will kill something in him. That's an alternative he knows perfectly well is available, and do you think for one moment that he fears the Senate? Any of them? Including the much-vaunted Pompeius Magnus? No! They'll go down like targets on a practice field before German lancers. He knows it. But he doesn't want it to be that way. He wants his due, but he wants it legally. Marching on Rome is the very end of his tether, and he'll battle the odds right down to the last moment rather than do it. His record is perfect. He wants it to remain so."

"He always wanted to be perfect," said Vatinius sadly, and shivered. "Jupiter, Trebonius, what will he do to them if they push him to it?"

"I hate to think."

"We'd best make offerings that the *boni* see reason."

"I've been making them for months. And I think perhaps the *boni* would see reason, save for one factor."

"Cato," said Vatinius instantly.

"Cato," Trebonius echoed.

Another silence fell; Vatinius sighed. "Well, I'm his man through thick and thin," he said.

"And I."

"Who else?"

"Decimus. Fabius. Sextius. Antonius. Rebilus. Calenus. Basilus. Plancus. Sulpicius. Lucius Caesar," said Trebonius.

"Not Labienus?"

Trebonius shook his head emphatically. "No."

"Labienus's choice?"

"Caesar's."

"Yet he says nothing derogatory about Labienus."

"Nor will he. Labienus still hopes to be consul with him, though he knows Caesar doesn't approve of his methods. But nothing is said in the senatorial dispatches, so Labienus hopes. It won't last beyond the final decision. If Caesar marches on Rome, he'll give the *boni* a gift—Titus Labienus."

"Oh, Trebonius, pray it doesn't come to civil war!"

* * *

So too did Caesar pray, even as he marshaled his wits to deal with the *boni* within the bounds of Rome's unwritten constitution, the *mos maiorum*. The consuls for next year were Lucius Aemilius Lepidus Paullus as senior, and Gaius Claudius Marcellus as junior. Gaius Marcellus was first cousin to the present junior consul, Marcus Marcellus, and also to the man predicted to be consul the year after next, another Gaius Marcellus. For this reason he was usually referred to as Gaius Marcellus Major, his cousin as Gaius Marcellus Minor. An adamant foe of Caesar's, Gaius Marcellus Major could not be hoped for. Paullus was different. Exiled for his part in the rebellion of his father, Lepidus, he had come late to the consul's curule chair, and achieved it by rebuilding the Basilica Aemilia, by far the most imposing edifice in the Forum Romanum. Then disaster had struck on the day when Publius Clodius's body had burned in the Senate House; the almost completed Basilica Aemilia burned too. And Paullus found himself without the money to start again.

A man of straw was Paullus. A fact Caesar knew. But bought him anyway. The senior consul was worth having. Paullus received sixteen hundred talents from Caesar during December, and went onto Balbus's payroll as Caesar's man. The Basilica Aemilia could be rebuilt in even greater splendor. Of more import was Curio, who had cost a mere five hundred talents; he had done exactly as Caesar suggested, pretended to stand for the tribunate of the plebs at the last moment, and—no difficulty for a Scribonius Curio—been elected at the top of the poll.

Other things could be done too. All the major towns of Italian Gaul received large sums of money to erect public buildings or reconstruct their marketplaces, as did towns and cities in the Province and in Italia itself. But all these towns had one thing in common: they had shown Caesar favor. For a while he thought about donating buildings to the Spains, Asia Province and Greece, then decided the outlay would not bring sufficient support for him if Pompey, a far greater patron in these places, chose not to permit his clients to support Caesar. None of it was done to win favor in the event of civil war; it was done to bring influential local plutocrats into his camp and prompt them to inform the *boni* that they would not be pleased were Caesar to be maltreated. Civil war was the very last alternative, and Caesar genuinely believed that it was an alternative so abominable, even to the *boni,* that it would not eventuate. The way to win was to make it impossible for the *boni* to go against the wishes of most of Rome, Italia, Italian Gaul, Illyricum and the Roman Gallic Province.

He understood most idiocies, but could not, even in his most pessimistic moods, believe that a small group of Roman senators would actually prefer to precipitate civil war rather than face the inevitable and permit Caesar what was, after all, no more than his due. Legally consul for the second time, free of prosecution, the First Man in Rome and the first name in the history books. These things he owed to his family, to his *dignitas,* to posterity. He would leave no son, but a son wasn't necessary unless the son had the ability to rise even higher. That didn't happen; everyone knew it. Great men's sons were never great. Witness Young Marius and Faustus Sulla . . .

In the meantime there was the new Roman province of Gallia Comata to think about. To craft, to settle down, to sift through for the best local men. And a few problems to solve of a more prudent nature. Including getting rid of two thousand Gauls who Caesar didn't think would bow to Rome for longer than his tenure of the new province. A thousand of them were slaves he didn't dare sell for fear of bloody reprisals, either on their new owners or in armed insurrections reminiscent of Spartacus. The second one thousand were free Gauls, mostly thanes, who had not even been cowed by the production of the handless victims of Uxellodunum.

He ended in having them marched to Massilia and loaded on board transports under heavy guard. The thousand slaves were sent to King Deiotarus of Galatia, a Gaul himself and always in need of good cavalrymen; no doubt when they arrived Deiotarus would free them and press them into service. The thousand free Gauls he sent to King Ariobarzanes of Cappadocia. Both lots of men were gifts. A little offering on the altar of Fortuna. Luck was a sign of favor among the Gods, but it never hurt to make one's luck for oneself either. A trite judgement, to attribute success to luck. No one knew better than Caesar that behind luck lay oceans of hard work and deep thinking. His troops could boast of his luck; he didn't mind that in the least. While they thought he had luck, they feared little as long as he was there to throw the mantle of his protection over them. It was luck beat poor Marcus Crassus; his days were numbered from the first moment his troops decided he was unlucky. No man was free from some sort of superstition, but men of low birth and scant education were inordinately superstitious. Caesar played on that deliberately. For if luck came from the Gods and a great man was thought to have it, he acquired a kind of reflected godhead; it did no harm for one's soldiers to deem the General just slightly below the Gods.

Just before the end of the year a letter came from Quintus Cicero, senior legate in the service of his big brother, the governor of Cilicia.

> I need not have left you so early, Caesar. That's one of the penalties of working for a man who moves as swiftly as you do. Somehow I assumed my brother Marcus would hustle himself to Cilicia. But he didn't. He left Rome early in May, and took almost two months to get as far as Athens. Why does he fawn so over Pompeius Magnus? Something to do with the days when he was seventeen and a cadet in the army of Pompeius Strabo, I know, but I think the debt Marcus fancies he owes Pompeius Magnus for his protection then is

grossly exaggerated. You will perceive from this that I had to suffer two days in Magnus's house at Tarentum en route. I cannot, try though I do, like the man.

In Athens (where we waited for Marcus's military legate, Gaius Pomptinus, to show up—I could have generaled for Marcus far more competently, you know, but he didn't trust me) we learned that Marcus Marcellus had flogged a citizen of your colony at Novum Comum—a disgrace, Caesar. My brother was equally incensed, though most of his mind was preoccupied with the Parthian threat. Hence his refusal to leave Athens until Pomptinus arrived.

Another month saw us cross the frontier into Cilicia at Laodiceia. Such a pretty place, with those dazzling crystal terraces tumbling down the cliffs! Among the warm pure pools on the top the local people have built luxurious little marble havens for such as Marcus and me, exhausted from the heat and the dust we encountered from Ephesus all the way to Laodiceia. It was delicious to spend a few days soaking in the waters—they seem to help one's bones—and frolicking like fish.

But then, journeying on, we discovered what kind of horror Lentulus Spinther and then Appius Claudius had wreaked on poor, devastated Cilicia. My brother called it "a lasting ruin and desolation," and that is no exaggeration. The province has been plundered, exploited, *raped*. Everything and everyone has been taxed out of existence. By, among others, the son of your dear friend Servilia. Yes, I am sorry to say it, but Brutus appears to have worked extremely closely with his father-in-law, Appius Claudius, in all sorts of reprehensible ways. Much though he shies away from offending important people, my brother told Atticus in a letter that he considered Appius Claudius's conduct in his province contemptible. Nor was he pleased that Appius Claudius avoided him.

We stayed in Tarsus only a very few days; Marcus was anxious to utilize the campaigning season, so was Pomptinus. The Parthians had been raiding along the Euphrates, and King Ariobarzanes of Cappadocia was in dire straits. Due largely to an army almost as skeletal as the two legions we found in Cilicia. Why were both armies so skeletal? Lack of money. One gathers that Appius Claudius garnished most of the army's wages for himself, and didn't care to increase the strength of either legion as he was paying about half the number of men his books said he was. King Ariobarzanes of Cappadocia didn't have the money to pay for a decent army, chiefly due to the fact that young Brutus, that pillar of Roman rectitude, had lent him money at an astronomical compound interest. My brother was extremely angry.

Anyway, we spent the next three months campaigning in Cappadocia, a wearying business. Oh, Pomptinus is a fool! It takes him days and days and days to reduce a pathetic fortified village you would have taken in three hours. But of course my brother doesn't know how war should be waged, so he's well satisfied.

Bibulus dallied dreadfully getting to Syria, which meant we had to wait until he got himself into order before we could start our joint campaign from both sides of the Amanus ranges. In fact, we are about to commence that business now. I gather he arrived in Antioch in Sextilis, and speeded young Gaius Cassius on his way back to Rome very coldly. Of course he had his own two young sons with him. Marcus Bibulus is in his early twenties, and Gnaeus Bibulus about nineteen. All three Bibuli were most put out to discover that Cassius had dealt with the Parthian menace very deedily, including an ambush down the Orontes which sent Pacorus and his Parthian army home in a hurry.

This martial fervor is not much to Bibulus's taste, I think. His method of dealing with the Parthians is different from Cassius's, certainly. Rather than contemplate war, he has hired a Parthian named Ornadapates, and is paying the fellow to whisper in the ear of King Orodes to the effect that Pacorus, the favorite son of Orodes, is aiming at usurping his father's throne. Clever, but not admirable, is it?

I miss Gallia Comata very much, Caesar. I miss the kind of war we fought, so brisk and practical, so devoid of machinations within the high command. Out here I seem to spend as much time placating Pomptinus as I do at anything more productive. Please write to me. I need cheering up.

Poor Quintus Cicero! It was some time before Caesar could sit to answer this rather sad missive. Typical of Cicero, to prefer a smarming nonentity like Gaius Pomptinus to his own brother. For Quintus Cicero was right. He would have proven a far more capable general than Pomptinus.

ROME

from JANUARY until DECEMBER of 50 B.C.

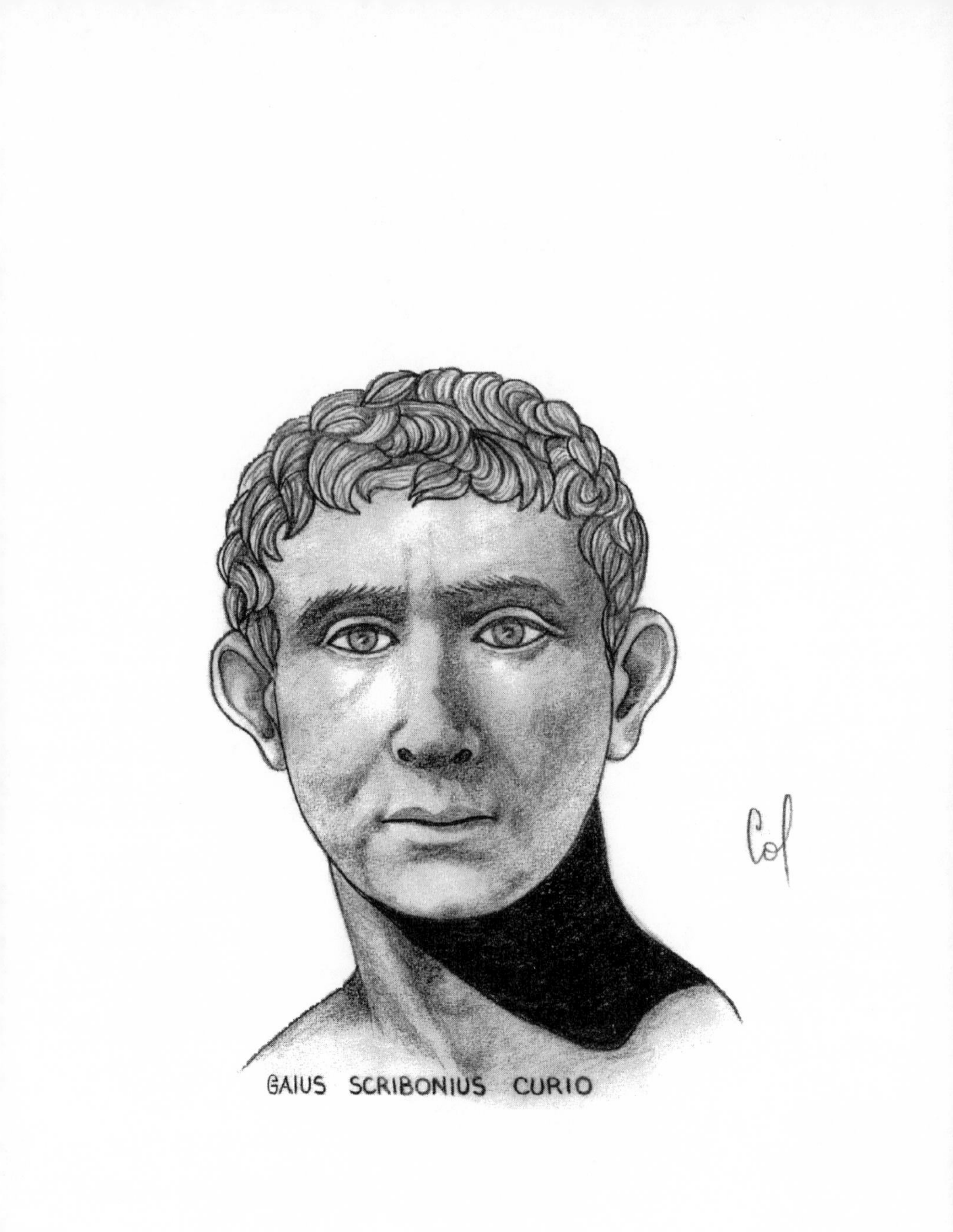
GAIUS SCRIBONIUS CURIO

When Gaius Cassius Longinus returned home after his extraordinary career as a thirty-year-old governor of a major Roman province, he found himself much admired. Very shrewdly he had declined to ask the Senate for a triumph, though his men had hailed him imperator on the field when he had trounced the Galilaean army near Lake Gennesarus.

"I think people like that as much as anything you actually did in Syria," said Brutus.

"Why draw attention to myself in a way the senatorial dotards would deplore?" asked Cassius, shrugging. "I wouldn't get a triumph anyway. Better then to pretend I don't want one. The same people who would have condemned me for my brashness now have no choice other than to praise me for my humility."

"You loved it, didn't you?"

"Syria? Yes, I did. Not while Marcus Crassus was alive, but after Carrhae it was terrific."

"What happened to all the gold and treasures Crassus took from the temples in Syria? Did he take them with him on his march to Mesopotamia?"

For a moment Cassius looked blank, then realized that Brutus, though a mere four months his junior, knew little about the logistics of provincial government beyond its monetary side. "No, they stayed in Antioch. When I left I brought them home with me." Cassius smiled sourly. "Why do you think I was so unpopular with Bibulus? He maintained they were in his charge and ought to remain until he came home. Though if I had given in, what actually arrived in Rome would have been considerably less. I could see his sticky fingers twitching at the prospect of prowling through the money chests."

Brutus looked shocked. "Cassius! Marcus Bibulus is above reproach! Cato's son-in-law to pilfer what belongs to Rome? It would never happen!"

"Rubbish," said Cassius scornfully. "What a wet fish you are, Brutus! It's what anyone would do, given half an opportunity. That I didn't was simply due to my age and my burgeoning career. After I'm consul I want Syria for my province, and I'll get it because I intend to establish myself as an expert on Syria. Had I been there as a mere quaestor, no one would remember I had been there at all. But since the quaestor turned into the governor—and made a wonderful success out of his tenure as governor—all of Rome will remember. Therefore I defended my right to bring Crassus's ill-gotten hoard back to Rome as his quaestor. Legal, and Bibulus knew it. Besides, he dithered so long in getting to Syria that I had everything crated and loaded on board a fleet of hired ships before he set foot in Antioch. How he wept to see me sail away! I wish him joy of Syria, him and those two spoiled sons of his."

Brutus said no more on the subject of Bibulus; though Gaius Cassius was the best of good fellows, he was a martial type who thought poorly of certain among the *boni* who were famous for not wanting the onus of provincial governorships, with their inevitable wars and perils. Born to the consulship though he was, Cassius would never be a political type; he lacked subtlety, tact, and the ability to win men to his way of thinking by smooth words. In fact, he looked what he was: a sturdy, close-cropped, energetic and soldierly man with scant patience for intrigue.

"I'm pleased to see you, of course," said Brutus, "but is there any reason for your coming round so soon after your return?"

Cassius's rather humorous mouth turned up at the corners; his brown and snapping eyes crinkled closed. Oh, poor Brutus! He really was a wet fish. And was there nothing would ever cure that hideously acneous skin? Or his appetite for making money in unsenatorial ways? "Actually, I'm here to see the head of the family," Cassius said.

"My mother? Why didn't you ask for her?"

Sighing, Cassius shook his head. "Brutus, *you're* the head of the family, not Servilia. I came to see you in that capacity."

"Oh! Oh, yes. I suppose I am the head of the family. It's just that Mama is so competent, and she's been a widow for so long. I suppose I'll never think of myself as superseding her."

"Until you do, Brutus, you won't."

"I'm comfortable," said Brutus. "What do you want?"

"I want to marry Junia Tertia—Tertulla. We've been betrothed for years, and I'm not getting any younger. It's time I thought of starting my family, Brutus, now that I'm in the Senate and heading for great things."

"But she's barely sixteen," said Brutus, frowning.

"I know that !" Cassius snapped. "I also know whose daughter she really is. Well, all of Rome does. And since Julian blood is somewhat higher than Junian blood, I don't object in the least to marrying Caesar's offspring. Little though I like the man for what he is, by this stage in his career he's proven that Julian blood hasn't yet achieved senility."

"*My* blood is Junian," said Brutus stiffly.

"But Brutus, not Silanus. There's a difference."

"And on our mother's side, both Tertulla and I are patrician Servilians," Brutus went on, face becoming absorbed.

"Well, that's enough of that," said Cassius hastily, knowing the signs. "May I marry Tertulla?"

"I'll have to ask my mother."

"Oh, Brutus, when will you learn? It's not Servilia's place to make that decision!"

"Which decision?" asked Servilia, walking into Brutus's study without knocking. Her large dark eyes rested not on her son (whom she found so unsatisfactory that she tried not to look at him at all), but on Cassius. Beaming, she walked to him and took his strong, tanned face between her hands. "Cassius, how lovely to see you back in Rome!" she said, and kissed him. She liked Cassius enormously, always had done since the days when he and Brutus had gone to the same school. A warrior, a *doer*. A young man with a knack for making a name for himself.

"Which decision?" she repeated, seating herself in a chair.

"I want to marry Tertulla immediately," said Cassius.

"Then let us ask her what she thinks of that idea," said Servilia smoothly, thereby removing the decision from her son. She clapped her hands to summon the steward. "Ask the lady Tertulla to come to the study," she said then. And to Cassius, "Why?"

"I'll soon be thirty-three, Servilia. Time to start my family. I realize Tertulla is underage, but we've been betrothed for a good many years, it isn't as if she doesn't know me."

"And she's nubile," said her mother with detachment.

A statement reinforced a scant moment later when Tertulla knocked and entered the room.

Cassius blinked; he hadn't seen her for close to three years, and they were three years which had wrought great changes. She had gone from thirteen to sixteen, from child to young woman. And how *beautiful* she was! She looked like Caesar's dead daughter, Julia, though she lacked Julia's frosty fairness and slight build. Her big, well-spaced eyes were a greyish yellow, her thick hair dark gold, her mouth kissable to the point of distraction. Gold skin without flaw. A pair of exquisite breasts. Oh, Tertulla!

When she saw Cassius she smiled in delight and held out her hands to him. "Gaius Cassius," she said in Julia's husky voice.

He went to her, smiling too, and took the hands. "Tertulla." Then turned to Servilia. "May I ask her?"

"Of course," said Servilia, pleased to see that they were falling in love.

Cassius's clasp on her hands tightened. "Tertulla, I've asked to marry you now. Your mother"—he gave up on Brutus; why bother so much as mentioning him?—"says the decision is yours. Will you marry me now?"

Her smile changed, became seductive; it was suddenly easy to see that she also sprang from Servilia, a most seductive lady. "I would like that very much, Gaius Cassius," she said.

"Good!" said Servilia briskly. "Cassius, take her somewhere that you can kiss her without half the house and all her relatives looking. Brutus, take care of the wedding details. It's an auspicious time of year to marry, but choose the day carefully." She frowned direfully at the happy pair. "Go on, shoo!"

They went out holding hands, which left Servilia with no other face to look at save her only son's. Pimply as ever, intolerably swarthy because he couldn't shave, with eyes as mournful as a deer hound's and lips slack from want of decision.

"I didn't know you had Cassius with you," she said.

"He'd only just arrived, Mama. I would have sent for you."

"I came to see you."

"What about?" asked Brutus, uneasy.

"Certain allegations about you. They're flying all over the city. Atticus is most distressed."

Brutus's face twisted, looked suddenly a great deal more impressive, hinted perhaps at what actually lived inside him when his mother was not there. "Cicero!" he hissed.

"Exactly. Old Loosemouth himself. Who rails at your money-lending activities in his province, in Cappadocia and in Galatia. Not to mention Cyprus."

"He can't prove a thing. The money is lent by two of my clients, Matinius and Scaptius. All I've done is exert myself to protect my clients' interests, Mama."

"My dear Brutus, you forget that I was there long before you were old enough to control your fortune! Matinius and Scaptius are your employees. My father set the firm up, along with many, many others. Well disguised, it's true. But you can't afford to give someone with Cicero's wit and acumen *any* ammunition."

"I will deal with Cicero," he said, and looked as if he could deal with Cicero.

"Better, I hope, than your esteemed father-in-law has dealt with his problems!" Servilia snapped. "He left a trail of evidence of his peculations while governor of Cilicia that a blind man could follow. With the result that he's arraigned in the Extortion Court. And you, Brutus, were his accomplice. Do you think all of Rome doesn't know about your little rackets?" She smiled humorlessly, displaying small, perfect white teeth. "Appius Claudius would threaten to billet the army on some hapless Cilician town, then you would come along and hint that a gift of one hundred talents to the governor would avoid this fate, after which the firm of Matinius and Scaptius would offer to lend the town one hundred talents. Appius Claudius popped the money in his purse, and you made even more from lending it."

"They may try Appius Claudius, but he'll be acquitted, Mama."

"I have no doubt of it, my son. But the rumors are not going to do your public career any good. Pontius Aquila says so."

The disfigured, unhappy face darkened into a snarl; the black eyes flashed dangerously. "Pontius Aquila!" he said contemptuously. "Caesar I could understand, Mama, but not an ambitious nobody like Pontius Aquila! You demean yourself."

"How dare you!" she growled, leaping to her feet.

"Yes, Mama, I am afraid of you," Brutus said steadily as she loomed over him, "but I am not a boy of twenty anymore, and in some things I have a right to speak. Things which reflect badly on our blood, our nobility. As does Pontius Aquila."

Servilia turned and walked from the room, shutting the door with ostentatious quietness. Outside in the colonnade around the peristyle garden she stood, trembling, hands clenched. How dare he! Was he absolutely bloodless? Had he ever burned, itched, howled soundlessly into the night, wrenched with hunger, loneliness, *need*? No, he hadn't. Not Brutus. Anaemic, flaccid, *impotent*. Did he think she wasn't aware of it, with his wife living in her house? A wife he never penetrated, let alone slept with. Nor did he forage in any other pastures. Whatever her son was made of—and his exact composition eluded her—it wasn't fire, thunder, volcano, earthquake. Sometimes, as today when he had spoken his mind about Pontius Aquila, he could stand up to her and voice his displeasure. But how dare he! Didn't he have any idea?

So many years since Caesar had left for Gaul, years in which she lay alone and ground her teeth, pounded her fists on the pillow. Loving him, wanting him, needing him. Limp with love, wet with want, famished with need. Those fierce confrontations, duels of will and wit, wars of strength. Oh, and the exquisite satisfaction of knowing herself bested, of measuring up to a man and being flattened by him, dominated, punished, enslaved. Knowing full well the extent of her own abilities and intellect—what more could a woman ask than a man who engendered respect? Who was more than her, yet bound to her by nothing more tangible than woman's qualities? Caesar, Caesar . . .

"You look fierce."

She gasped, turned, saw him. Lucius Pontius Aquila. Her lover. Younger than her own son at thirty, just admitted to the Senate as one of the urban quaestors. Not an old family, therefore of birth far inferior to hers. Which didn't matter the moment she laid eyes on him, as now. So handsome! Very tall, perfectly proportioned, short, curly auburn hair, truly green eyes, the face endowed with wonderful bone structure and a strong yet sensuous mouth. And the best thing about him was that he didn't remind her of Caesar.

"My thoughts were fierce," she said, leading the way to her suite of rooms.

"Love-fierce or hate-fierce?"

"Hate. Hate, hate, *hate*!"

"Then you weren't thinking of me."

"No. I was thinking of my son."

"What did he do to anger you?"

"Said that I demeaned myself, associating with you."

He locked the door, pulled the shutters closed, then turned to look at her with the smile that weakened her knees. "He's a great aristocrat, Brutus," Pontius Aquila said levelly. "I understand his disapproval."

"He doesn't know," said Servilia, unwrapping his plain white toga and placing it on a chair. "Put your foot up." She unlaced his senatorial shoe of maroon leather. "The other one." It too was removed and discarded. "Lift your arms." Off came the white tunic with the broad purple stripe over its right shoulder.

He was naked. Servilia moved back enough to see all of him, feasting her eyes, her mind, her spirit. A little dark red hair on his chest narrowed to a thin stripe which dived down to the bush of his brighter red pubic hair, out of the midst of which his dusky penis, growing already, protruded above a deliciously full and pendulous scrotum. Perfect, perfect. The thighs were slim, the calves large and well formed, the belly flat, the chest plump with muscle. Broad shoulders, long and sinewy arms.

She moved in a slow circle around him, purring over the round, firm buttocks, the narrow hips, the broad back, the way his head sat proudly atop his athlete's neck. *Beautiful!* What a man! How could she bear to touch such perfection? He belonged to Phidias and Praxiteles, to sculptural immortality.

"It's your turn," he said when the tour of his body was done.

Down came the masses of hair, black as ever save for two stark white streaks at the temples. Off came the layers of her scarlet and amber gown. Fifty-four years of age, Servilia stood naked, and felt at no disadvantage. Admittedly her skin was smoothly ivory and her full breasts were still proudly upright, but her buttocks had dropped, her waist thickened. Age, she knew, had nothing to do with it, this thing between a man and a woman. It was measured in delight, in appreciation. Never in years.

She lay down on her bed and put her hands on either side of her blackly hairy groin, pulling the lips of her vulva apart so he could see its sleek, plummy contours, the sheen of it. Hadn't Caesar said it was the most beautiful flower he had ever seen? Her confidence rested in that, in the triumph of keeping Caesar enslaved.

Oh, but the touch of this young, smooth, enormously virile man! To be covered so strongly yet so gently, to yield everything without modesty yet with intelligent restraint. She sucked at his tongue, his nipples, his penis, fought back with hungry strength, and when she reached her climax screeched her ecstasy at the top of her lungs. There, my son! I hope you heard that. I hope your wife heard that. I have just experienced a cataclysm neither of you will ever know. With a man I don't have to care about beyond this gigantic convulsion of absolute pleasure.

Afterward they sat, still naked, to drink wine and talk with the easy intimacy only physical intimacy engenders.

"I hear that Curio has just introduced a bill to set up a commission to supervise the roads of Italia, and that the head of the commission is to have a proconsular imperium," said Servilia, her feet in his lap, toes playing with that bright red hair.

"True enough, but he'll never get it past Gaius Marcellus Major," said Pontius Aquila.

"It seems an odd measure."

"So it seems to everyone."
"Does he belong to Caesar, do you think?"
"I doubt it."
"Yet the only person who might benefit from Curio's bill would be Caesar," said Servilia thoughtfully. "If he loses his provinces and his imperium on the Kalends of March, Curio's bill would provide him with another proconsulship and his imperium would continue. Not so?"
"Yes."
"Then Curio belongs to Caesar."
"I really do doubt that."
"He's suddenly free of debt."
Pontius Aquila laughed, head thrown back, and looked magnificent. "He also married Fulvia. Not before time, if the gossips are right. She's very round in the belly for a newly wedded woman."
"Poor old Sempronia! A daughter who goes from one demagogue to another."
"I haven't seen any evidence that Curio is a demagogue."
"You will," said Servilia cryptically.

For over two years the Senate had been deprived of its ancient meeting house, the Curia Hostilia, yet no one had volunteered to rebuild it. So ingrained was the Treasury's parsimoniousness that the State would not foot the bill; tradition held that some great man should undertake the task, and no great man had so far been willing. Including Pompey the Great, who seemed indifferent to the Senate's plight.
"You can always use the Curia Pompeia," he said.
"Typical of him!" snapped Gaius Marcellus Major, stumping out to the Campus Martius and Pompey's stone theater on the Kalends of March. "He wants to compel the Senate to hold all its heavily attended meetings in something he built in days when we didn't need it. Typical!"
"Yet one more extraordinary command of a sort," said Cato, striding along at a pace Gaius Marcellus Major found difficult.
"Why do we have to hurry, Cato? Paullus holds the *fasces* for March, and he'll take his time."
"Which is why Paullus is a pudding," said Cato.
The complex Pompey had built upon the green sward of the Campus Martius not far from the Circus Flaminius was most imposing; a vast stone theater which could accommodate five thousand people reared high above the sparse structures which had existed here for much longer than a mere five years. Very shrewdly Pompey had incorporated a temple to Venus Victrix at the top of the *cavea,* and thus turned what would otherwise have been an impious structure into something entirely in keeping with the *mos maiorum.* Rome's customs and traditions deplored theater as a malign moral influence on the people, so until Pompey's stone edifice

had gone up five years ago, the theater which pervaded all games and public feasts had been conducted in temporary wooden premises. What made Pompey's theater permissible was the temple to Venus Victrix.

Behind the auditorium Pompey had built a vast peristyle garden surrounded by a colonnade containing exactly one hundred pillars, each fluted and adorned with the fussy Corinthian capitals Sulla had brought back from Greece, each painted in shades of blue and lavishly gilded. The red walls along the back of the colonnade were rich with magnificently painted murals, unfortunately marred by the peculiarity of their blood-soaked subject matter. For Pompey owned a great deal more money than good taste, and nowhere did it show more than in his hundred-pillared colonnade and garden stuffed with fountains, fish, frills, frights.

At the rear of the peristyle Pompey had erected a curia, a meeting house which he had ensured was religiously inaugurated in order to house meetings of the Senate. It was very adequate in size, and in layout resembled the ruined Curia Hostilia, being a rectangular chamber containing three tiers down either side of a space ending in the dais upon which the curule magistrates sat. Each shelflike tier was broad enough to accommodate a senator's stool; upon the highest tier sat the *pedarii,* the senators who were not senior enough to speak in debate because they had never held a magistracy or won a Grass Crown or a Civic Crown for valor. The two middle tiers held senators who had attained a minor magistracy—tribune of the plebs, quaesitor or plebeian aedile—or were military heroes, and the two bottom tiers were reserved for those who had been curule aediles, praetors, consuls or censors. Which meant that those who sat on the bottom or middle tiers had more room to spread their feathers than the *pedarii* up at the top.

The old Curia Hostilia had been uninspiring within: the tiers had been blocks of unrendered tufa, the walls drably painted with a few red curliques and lines on a beige background, the curule dais more tufa stone, and the central space between the two banks of tiers tessellated in black and white marble so old it had long lost polish or majesty. In glaring contrast to this antique simplicity, Pompey's Curia was entirely done in colored marbles. The walls were purple and rose tiles laid in complicated patterns between gilded pilasters; the back tier on either side was faced in brown marble, the middle tier in yellow marble, the bottom tier in cream marble, and the curule dais in a lustrous, shimmering blue-white marble brought all the way from Numidia. The space between the two banks of tiers had been paved in patterned wheels of purple and white. Light poured in through high clerestory windows well sheltered by a wide eave on the non-colonnade side, and each aperture was covered by a gilded grille.

Though the interior of the Curia Pompeia provoked many a sniff because of its ostentation, the interior was not what really offended. *That* was the statue of himself which Pompey had erected at the back of the curule dais. Exactly his own height (therefore not an insult to the Gods), it limned him as he had been at the time of his first consulship twenty years ago: a graceful, well-knit man of thirty-six with a shock of bright gold hair, brilliantly blue eyes, and a demure, round, distinctly un-Roman face. The sculptor had been the best, so too the painter who had colored in the tones of Pompey's flesh, hair, eyes, maroon senatorial shoes fastened with the crescent buckles of the consul. Only the toga and what showed of the tunic had been done in the new way: not painted but made of highly polished marble, white for the fabric of toga and tunic, purple for the border of the toga and the *latus clavus* stripe on the tunic. As he had caused the statue to be placed on a plinth four feet tall, Pompey the Great towered over everyone and inarguably presided over any meeting of the Senate conducted there. The arrogance! The insufferable hubris!

Almost all the four hundred senators present in Rome came to the Curia Pompeia and this long-awaited meeting on the Kalends of March. To some extent Gaius Marcellus Major had been right in thinking that Pompey wanted to force the Senate to meet in his curia because the Senate had ignored his curia's existence until its own beloved chamber burned down; but Marcellus Major had neglected to take his reasoning one step further, to the fact that these days the Senate had no option other than to meet outside Rome's sacred boundary for any session likely to draw a full House. Which meant that Pompey could attend these meetings in person while comfortably retaining his imperium as governor of the Spains; as his army was in Spain and he was also curator of the grain supply, he enjoyed the luxury of living just outside Rome and traveling freely throughout Italia, two things normally forbidden to the governors of provinces.

Dawn was just paling the sky above the Esquiline Mount when the senators began to straggle into the peristyle garden, where most of them chose to linger until the convening magistrate, Lucius Aemilius Lepidus Paullus, chose to appear. They clustered in small groups of like political thinking, talking with more animation than they could usually summon up so early in the day; this promised to be a momentous meeting, and anticipation was high. Everyone likes to be present to see the idol topple, and today everyone was convinced that Caesar, idol of the People, would topple.

The leaders of the *boni* stood on the rear colonnade itself outside the Curia Pompeia doors: Cato, Ahenobarbus, Metellus Scipio, Marcus Marcellus (the junior consul of last year), Appius Claudius, Lentulus Spinther, Gaius Marcellus Major (the junior consul this year), Gaius Marcellus Minor (predicted to be consul next year), Faustus Sulla, Brutus, and two tribunes of the plebs.

"A great, great day!" barked Cato in his harsh voice.

"The beginning of the end of Caesar," said Lucius Domitius Ahenobarbus, beaming.

"He's not without support," Brutus ventured timidly. "I see Lucius Piso, Philippus, Lepidus, Vatia Isauricus, Messala Rufus and Rabirius Postumus huddled together. They look confident."

"Rabble!" said Marcus Marcellus disdainfully.

"But who knows how the backbenchers will feel when it comes to the vote?" asked Appius Claudius, under some strain thanks to the fact that his trial for extortion was still going on.

"More of them will vote for us than for Caesar," said the haughty Metellus Scipio.

At which moment the senior consul, Paullus, appeared behind his lictors and entered the Curia Pompeia. The senators streamed inside after him, each with his servant carrying his folded stool, some with scribes hovering in attendance to take private verbatim records of this historic meeting.

The prayers were said, the sacrifice made, the omens deemed to be auspicious; the House settled down on its stools, the curule magistrates on their ivory chairs atop the blue-white marble dais dominated by the statue of Pompey the Great.

Who sat on the bottom tier to the left of the dais in his purple-bordered toga and looked directly at the dais, eyes dwelling on the face of his effigy, lips faintly smiling at the delicious irony of it. What a wonderful day this one would be! The only man who seemed likely to eclipse him was going to have the feet cut out from under him. And all without one word from him, Gnaeus Pompeius Magnus. No one would be able to point the finger at him and accuse him of conspiring to unseat Caesar; it was going to happen without his needing to do more than be here. Naturally he would vote to strip Caesar of his provinces, but so would most of the House. Speak on the subject he would not, were he to be asked. The *boni* were quite capable of doing all the oratory necessary.

Paullus, holding the *fasces* during the month of March, sat with his curule chair slightly forward of Gaius Marcellus Major's, the eight praetors and two curule aediles ranked behind them.

Just below the front of the curule dais stood a very long, stout, highly polished wooden bench. On this sat the ten tribunes of the plebs, the men elected by the Plebs to safeguard their interests and keep the patricians in their place. Or so it had been at the dawn of the Republic, a time when the patricians had controlled the Senate, the consulship, the courts, the Centuriate Assembly and all aspects of public life. But that state of affairs hadn't lasted long once the Kings of Rome were dispensed with. The Plebs had risen high, held more and more of the money, and wanted a much bigger say in government. For one hundred years the duel of wits and wills between the Patriciate and the Plebs had persisted, the Patriciate fighting a losing battle. At the end of it, the Plebs had won the right to have at least one of the two consuls a plebeian, half the places in the pontifical colleges, and the right to call plebeian families noble once a member attained the rank of praetor, and had established the College of the Tribunes of the Plebs, sworn to guard plebeian interests even at the price of lives.

Over the centuries since, the role of the tribunes of the plebs had changed. Gradually their assemblage of Roman men, the Plebeian Assembly, had usurped the major share of lawmaking and moved from blocking the power of the Patriciate to protecting the interests of the knight-businessmen who formed the nucleus of the Plebeian Assembly and dictated policy to the Senate.

Then a special kind of tribune of the plebs began to emerge, culminating in the careers of two great plebeian noblemen, the brothers Tiberius and Gaius Sempronius Gracchus. Who used their office and the Plebeian Assembly to strip power from the Plebs as well as the Patriciate and give a trifle of it to those of lower status and little wealth. They had both died hideously for their pains, but their memory lived on and on. And they were followed by other great men in the job, as different in aims and ideals as Gaius Marius, Saturninus, Marcus Livius Drusus, Sulpicius, Aulus Gabinius, Titus Labienus, Publius Vatinius, Publius Clodius and Gaius Trebonius. But in Gabinius, Labienus, Vatinius and Trebonius a new phenomenon became absolutely established: they belonged to one particular man who dictated their policy; Pompey in the case of Gabinius and Labienus, Caesar in the case of Vatinius and Trebonius.

Almost five hundred years of the tribunate of the plebs was embodied in the ten men who sat on that long wooden bench on this first day of March, each clad in a plain white toga, none entitled to lictors, none constrained by the religious rituals which ringed all other Roman executives round. Eight of them had been in the Senate for two or three years before running for the tribunate of the plebs; two of them had entered the Senate upon being elected. And nine of them were nonentities, men whose names and faces would not last beyond their tenure of office.

That was not so of Gaius Scribonius Curio, who, as President of the College, occupied the middle of the tribunician bench. He looked the part of a tribune of the plebs, with that urchinish and freckled countenance, that unruly thatch of bright red hair, that vivid aura of huge energy and enthusiasm. A brilliant speaker known to be conservative in his political leanings, Curio was the son of a man who had been censor as well as consul, and young Curio had been one of Caesar's most telling opponents during the year of Caesar's consulship, even though he had not been old enough to enter the Senate at that time.

Some of his laws since entering office on the tenth day of the previous December were puzzling, seemed to hint that the bug of tribunician radical extremism had bitten him more deeply than had been expected.

First he had tried, unsuccessfully, to introduce a bill endowing a new curator of roads with a five-year proconsular imperium; many suspicious *boni* deemed this a ploy to give Caesar another, if unmilitary, command. Then as a pontifex he had tried to persuade the College of Pontifices to intercalate an extra twenty-two days into the year at the end of February. Which would have postponed the arrival of the Kalends of March and discussion of Caesar's provinces by twenty-two enormously valuable days. Again he was defeated. The road bill he had shrugged off as unimportant, but the intercalation of a Mercedonius month he clearly regarded as a very serious matter, for when the College of Pontifices kept on adamantly refusing, Curio was so irate he told them exactly what he thought of them. A reaction which provoked Cicero's great friend Caelius to write to Cilicia and inform Cicero that he thought Curio belonged to Caesar.

Luckily this shrewd guess was not arrived at by anyone else with an influential ear to whisper into, so on this day Curio sat looking as if he was interested in the scheduled proceedings, but not to any significant degree. The tribunes of the plebs had, after all, been muzzled by that unconstitutional decree forbidding them to veto discussion of Caesar's provinces in the House on pain of being automatically convicted of treason.

Paullus handed the meeting to Gaius Claudius Marcellus Major as soon as he had declared the House in session.

"Honored senior consul, censors, consulars, praetors, aediles, tribunes of the plebs, quaestors and Conscript Fathers," said Gaius Marcellus Major, on his feet, "this meeting has been convoked to deal with the proconsulship of Gaius Julius Caesar, governor of the three Gauls and Illyricum, in accordance with the law the consuls Gnaeus Pompeius Magnus and Marcus Licinius Crassus passed five years ago in the Popular Assembly. As stipulated in the *lex Pompeia Licinia,* today this House may freely discuss what to do with Gaius Caesar's tenure of office, his provinces, his army and his imperium. Under the law as it existed at the time the *lex Pompeia Licinia* was passed, the House on this day would have debated which of the senior magistrates in office this year it preferred to send to govern Gaius Caesar's provinces in March of next year, the latest date provided for under the *lex Pompeia Licinia*. However, during the sole consulship of Gnaeus Pompeius Magnus two years ago, the law was changed. It is now possible for the House to debate in a new and different way. Namely, that there is a small group of men sitting here who have been praetors or consuls, but who declined to govern a province following their tenure of office. With full legality this House may decide to utilize those reserves and appoint a new governor or governors for Illyricum and the three Gauls immediately. The consuls and praetors in office this year are disbarred from going to govern a province for five years, but we cannot possibly permit Gaius Caesar to continue to govern for five more years, can we?"

Gaius Marcellus Major paused, his dark, not unattractive face reflecting his enjoyment. No one spoke, so he pressed on.

"As all of us present here today know, Gaius Caesar has wrought wonders in his provinces. Eight years ago he started out with Illyricum, Italian Gaul and a Further Gaul which consisted of the Roman Gallic Province. Eight years ago he started out with two legions stationed in Italian Gaul and one in the Province. Eight years ago he started out to govern three provinces at peace, as they had been for a very long time. And during his first year the Senate approved of his acting to prevent the migrating tribe of the Helvetii from entering the Province. It did not authorize him to enter that region known as Gallia Comata to make war on one King Ariovistus of the Suebic Germani, titled Friend and Ally of the Roman People. It did not authorize him to recruit more legions. It did not authorize him, having subdued King Ariovistus, to march further into Gaul of the Long-hairs and pursue a war against tribes having no alliances with Rome. It did not authorize him to set up colonies of so-called Roman citizens beyond the Padus River in Italian Gaul. It did not authorize him to recruit and number his legions of non-citizen Italian Gauls as proper, fully Roman legions. It did not authorize him to make war, peace, treaties or accommodations in Gaul of the Long-hairs. It did not authorize him to maltreat ambassadors in good standing from certain Germanic tribes."

"Hear, hear!" cried Cato.

The senators murmured, shifted, looked uneasy; Curio sat on the tribunician bench, looking into the distance; Pompey sat still, gazing at his own face at the back of the curule dais; and the bald, savage-featured Lucius Ahenobarbus sat grinning unpleasantly.

"The Treasury," said Gaius Marcellus Major affably, "did not object to any of these unauthorized actions. Nor, by and large, did the members of this august body. For Gaius Caesar's activities brought great profits in their train, for Rome, for his army, and for himself. They made him a hero in the eyes of the lower classes, who adore to see Rome accumulate might, wealth, and the valorous deeds of her generals abroad. They enabled him to buy what he was unable to get from men's genuine good will—adherents in the Senate, tame tribunes of the plebs, a dominant faction in Rome's tribal assemblies, and the faces of thousands of his soldiers among the voters of the Centuries on the Campus Martius. And they enabled him to set a new style in governing: they enabled him to change Rome's hallowed *mos maiorum,* which had never permitted any Roman governor to invade non-Roman-owned territory with the object of conquering it for no better reason than to enhance his personal glory. For what did Rome stand to gain by the conquest of Gallia Comata, compared to what Rome stood to lose? The lives of her citizens, both under arms and engaged in peaceful pursuits. The hatred of peoples who know little of Rome and want no truck with Rome. Who had not—and I repeat, *had not*!—attempted to encroach upon Roman territory and Roman property in any way until Gaius Caesar provoked them. Rome in the person of Gaius Caesar and his enormous, illegally recruited army marched into the lands of peaceful peoples and laid them waste. For what real reason? To enrich himself by the sale of a million Gallic slaves, so many slaves that he could afford to look generous from time to time by donating slaves to that enormous, illegally recruited army. Rome has been enriched, yes, but Rome is already rich thanks to the absolutely legal and defensive wars fought by many who are dead and some, like our honored consular Gnaeus Pompeius Magnus, who are sitting here today. For what real reason? To make Caesar a hero to the People, to provoke that ill-educated, over-emotional rabble into burning his daughter in our revered Forum Romanum and forcing the magistrates to agree to let her be entombed on the Campus Martius among Rome's heroes. I say this without intending any insult to the honored consular Gnaeus Pompeius Magnus, whose beloved wife she was. But the fact remains that Gaius Caesar provoked that response in the People, and it was for the sake of Gaius Caesar that they did it."

Pompey sat straight now, regally inclining his head to Gaius Marcellus Major, and looked as if he was in the throes of painful grief admixed with acute embarrassment.

Curio, face impassive, sat and listened with sinking heart. The speech was very good, very reasonable, and very tailored to appeal to the members of this exclusive, superiority-conscious body. It sounded as if it was right, correct, constitutional. It was going down extremely well among the backbenchers and among those on the middle tiers whose allegiance swayed from side to side like a sapling in a vortex. For some of it *was* unanswerable. Caesar *was* high-handed. But after this speech, how to counter in the only way, which was to point out that Caesar was by no means the first or the only Roman governor and general to set out to conquer? And how to persuade these dismal mice that Caesar knew what he was doing, that all of it was really to safeguard Rome, Italia and Rome's territories from the coming of the Germans? He sighed soundlessly, hunched his head into his shoulders and thrust his feet out so that he could lean his back against the cold blue-white marble of the front of the curule dais.

"I say," Gaius Marcellus Major went on, "that it is more than high time this august body put a stop to the career of this man Gaius Julius Caesar. Whose family and connections are so elevated that he genuinely believes himself above the law, above the tenets of the *mos maiorum*. He is another Lucius Cornelius Sulla. He has the birthright, the intelligence and the ability to be whatever he wishes to be. Well, we all know what happened to Sulla. What happened to Rome under Sulla. It took over two decades to rectify the damage Sulla did. The lives he took, the indignities he inflicted upon us, the autocracy he gathered to himself and used ruthlessly.

"I do not say that Gaius Caesar has patterned himself upon Lucius Cornelius Sulla deliberately. I do not believe that is the way the men of these incredibly old patrician families think. I believe that *they* believe they are just a little under the Gods they sincerely worship, and that, if they are allowed to run amok, nothing is beyond their temerity or their ideas of entitlement."

He drew a breath and stared straight at Caesar's youngest uncle, Lucius Aurelius Cotta, who had, throughout the years of Caesar's proconsulship, maintained an imperturbable detachment.

"You all know that Gaius Caesar expects to stand for the consulship next year. You all know that this House refused to permit Gaius Caesar to stand for the consulship *in absentia*. He must cross the *pomerium* into the city to declare his candidacy, and the moment he does that, he abandons his imperium. Whereupon I and others present here today will lay charges against him for the many unauthorized actions he has taken. They are treasonous, Conscript Fathers! Recruitment of unauthorized legions—invasion of the lands of non-belligerents—bestowing our citizenship on men not entitled to it—founding colonies of such men and calling them Roman—murdering ambassadors who came in good faith—they are treasonous! Caesar will stand trial on many charges, and he will be convicted. For the courts will be special ones, and there will be more soldiers in the Forum Romanum than Gnaeus Pompeius put there for the trial of Milo. He will not escape retribution. You all know that. So think on it very carefully.

"I am going to propose a motion to strip Gaius Julius Caesar of his imperium, his provinces and his army, and I will do it *per discessionem*—by a division of the House. Further, I move that Gaius Caesar be deprived of all his proconsular authority, imperium and entitlements this very day, the Kalends of March in the year of the consulship of Lucius Aemilius Lepidus Paullus and Gaius Claudius Marcellus."

Curio didn't move, didn't sit up straight or alter the casual sprawl of his legs. He said, "I veto your motion, Gaius Marcellus."

The collective gasp which went up from almost four hundred pairs of lungs sounded like a huge wind, and was followed immediately by rustles, murmurs, scraping stools, one or two clapping hands.

Pompey goggled, Ahenobarbus emitted a long howl, and Cato sat bereft of words. Gaius Marcellus Major recovered first.

"I move," he said loudly, "that Gaius Julius Caesar be stripped of his imperium, his provinces and his army this very day, the Kalends of March in the year of the consulship of Lucius Aemilius Lepidus Paullus and Gaius Claudius Marcellus."

"I veto your motion, junior consul," said Curio.

A curious pause occurred during which no one moved, no one spoke. All eyes were riveted on Curio, whose face was invisible to those on the curule dais but visible to everyone else.

Cato leaped to his feet. "Traitor!" he roared. "Traitor, traitor, *traitor*! Arrest him!"

"Oh, rubbish!" cried Curio, got up from his bench and walked forward into the middle of the purple and white floor, where he stood with feet apart and head up. "Rubbish, Cato, and you know it! All you and your toadies passed was a senatorial decree which has no validity in law nor any, even the most transient, relevance to the constitution! No senatorial decree unsupported by martial law can deprive a properly elected tribune of the plebs of his right to interpose his veto! I veto the junior consul's motion, and I will go on vetoing it! Such is my right! And don't try to tell me that you'll march me off to a quick treason trial, then toss me off the end of the Tarpeian Rock! The Plebs would never stand for it! Who do you think you are, a patrician back in the days before the Plebs put patricians in their place? For someone who prates interminably about the arrogance and lawlessness of patricians, Cato, you behave remarkably like one yourself! Well, rubbish! Sit down and pipe down! *I veto the junior consul's motion!*"

"Oh, wonderful!" screamed a voice from beyond the open doors. "Curio, I adore you! I worship you! Wonderful, wonderful!"

And there stood Fulvia haloed by the light from the garden, the swell of her belly unmistakable beneath her orange and saffron gown, her lovely face alight.

Gaius Marcellus Major swallowed, shook all over, and lost his temper. "Lictors, remove that woman!" he shouted. "Throw her out onto the streets where she belongs!"

"Don't you lay a finger on her!" snarled Curio. "Whereabouts does it say that a Roman citizen of either sex cannot listen outside the Senate doors when they're open? Touch the granddaughter of Gaius Sempronius Gracchus and you'll be lynched by your despised, ill-educated and over-emotional rabble, Marcellus!"

The lictors hesitated; Curio grasped his chance. He strode down the length of the floor, seized his wife by the shoulders and kissed her ardently. "Go home, Fulvia, there's a good girl."

And Fulvia, smiling mistily, departed. Curio returned to the middle of the floor, grinning derisively at Marcellus Major.

"Lictors, arrest this man!" quavered Gaius Marcellus Major, so angry that beads of foam had gathered at the corners of his mouth and he trembled violently. "Arrest him! I charge him with treason and declare that he isn't fit to be at liberty! Throw him into the Lautumiae!"

"Lictors, I command you to stay where you are!" said Curio with impressive authority. "I am a tribune of the plebs who is being obstructed in the pursuit of his tribunician duties! I have exercised my veto in a legal assembly of senatorial men, as is my right, and there is no emergency decree in existence to prevent my doing so! I order you to arrest the junior consul for attempting to obstruct a tribune of the plebs who is exercising his inviolable rights! Arrest the junior consul!"

Paralyzed until now, Paullus lumbered to his feet and gestured to his chief lictor, who held the *fasces,* to drum the end of his bundle of rods on the floor. "Order! Order!" Paullus roared. "I want order! This meeting will come to order!"

"It's my meeting, not yours!" yelled Marcellus Major. "Stay out of it, Paullus, I warn you!"

"I am the consul with the *fasces,*" the normally lethargic Paullus thundered, "and that means it's my meeting, junior consul! Sit down! Everyone sit down! I will have order or I will have my lictors disband this meeting—by force, if necessary! Cato, shut your mouth! Ahenobarbus, don't even think of it! *I will have order!*" He glared at the impenitent Curio, who resembled a particularly annoying little dog, jauntily unafraid of a pack of wolves. "Gaius Scribonius Curio, I respect your right to exercise your veto, and I agree that to obstruct you is unconstitutional. But I think this House deserves to hear why you have interposed your veto. You have the floor."

Curio nodded, passed his hand over his fiery head, and looked hungry because it gave him a chance to lick his lips. Oh, for a drink of water! But to ask for one would be weakness.

"My thanks, senior consul. There is no need to dwell upon whatever legal measures certain men here may plan to take against the proconsul Gaius Julius Caesar. They are not relevant, and it was inappropriate for the junior consul to mention them in his speech. He should have confined himself to the reasons why he wishes to move that Gaius Caesar be stripped of his proconsulship and his provinces."

Curio walked to the very end of the floor and stood with his back to the doors, now closed. From this vantage point he could see every face, including the faces on the curule dais and the entirety of Pompey's statue.

"The junior consul stated that Gaius Caesar invaded peaceful non-Roman territory to enhance his own personal glory. But that is not so. King Ariovistus of the Suebic Germani had entered into a treaty with the Celtic tribe of the Sequani to settle on one-third of the Sequani lands, and it was to encourage a friendly attitude on the part of the Germani that the selfsame Gaius Caesar secured for King Ariovistus the title of Friend and Ally of the Roman People. But King Ariovistus broke his treaty by bringing many more Suebi across the river Rhenus than his treaty allowed, and dispossessing the Sequani. Who in turn threatened the Aedui, who have enjoyed the title of Friend and Ally of the Roman People for a very long time. Gaius Caesar moved to protect the Aedui, as he was obliged to do by the terms of the treaty the Aedui have with us.

"He then decided, having encountered the might of the Germani in person," Curio went on, "to seek treaties of friendship for Rome among the Celtic and Belgic peoples of Gallia Comata, and it was for that reason that he entered their lands, not to make war."

"Oh, Curio," cried Marcus Marcellus, "I never thought to see the son of your father smear himself with Gaius Caesar's shit and lick himself clean! *Gerrae!* Nonsense! A man wanting to make treaties doesn't advance at the head of an army, and that's what Caesar did!"

"Order," rumbled Paullus.

Curio shook his head as if to deplore Marcus Marcellus's stupidity. "He advanced with an army because he's a prudent man, Marcus Marcellus, not a fool like you. No Roman *pilum* was thrown in an unprovoked act of aggression, nor any tribe's land laid waste. He concluded treaties of friendship, legally binding and tangible treaties, all of which are nailed to the walls of Jupiter Feretrius—go look at them, if you doubt me! It was only when those treaties were broken by the Gallic use of force that a Roman *pilum* was thrown, a Roman sword drawn. Read Gaius Caesar's seven *Commentaries*—you can buy them at any bookshop! For it doesn't seem as if you ever listened to them when they were sent to this august body in the form of official dispatches."

"You're not worthy to call yourself a Scribonius Curio!" said Cato bitterly. "Traitor!"

"I'm worthy enough, Marcus Cato, to want to see both sides of this business aired!" snapped Curio, frowning. "I didn't veto for any other reason than that it became horribly clear to me that the junior consul and the rest of the *boni* will suffer no defense of a man who isn't here to defend himself! I do not like the idea of punishing a man without permitting a defense. And it seems to me a worthy thing for a tribune of the plebs to see that justice is done. I repeat, Gaius Caesar was not the aggressor in Gaul of the Long-hairs.

"As to those allegations that he recruited legions without the authority to do so, I would remind you that you yourselves sanctioned the recruitment of every one of those legions—and agreed to pay them!—as the seriousness of the situation in Gaul became steadily more apparent."

"After the fact!" shouted Ahenobarbus. "After the fact! And that at law does not constitute authorization!"

"I beg to disagree, Lucius Domitius. What about the many thanksgivings this House voted Caesar? And did the Treasury ever complain that the riches Gaius Caesar poured into it were riches Rome neither sanctioned, wanted, or needed? Governments *never* have enough money, because governments don't earn money—all they do is spend it."

Curio swung to look directly at Brutus, who visibly shrank. "I don't see any evidence that the *boni* find the actions of their own adherents reprehensible, yet which kind of action would the majority of this House prefer—the direct, unvarnished and very legal reprisals of Gaius Caesar in Gaul, or the furtive, cruel and very illegal reprisals Marcus Brutus made upon the elders of the city of Salamis in Cyprus when they couldn't pay the forty-eight percent compound interest Marcus Brutus's minions demanded? I have heard that Gaius Caesar tried certain Gallic chieftains and executed them. I have heard that Gaius Caesar killed many Gallic chieftains on a battlefield. I have heard that Gaius Caesar cut off the hands of four thousand Gallic men who had warred hideously against Rome at Alesia and Uxellodunum. But nowhere have I heard that Gaius Caesar lent non-citizens money, then shut them up in their own meeting hall until they starved to death! Which is what Marcus Brutus did, this eminent exemplar of everything a young Roman senator ought to be!"

"That is an infamy, Gaius Curio," said Brutus between his teeth. "The elders of Salamis did not die at my instigation."

"But you know all about them, don't you?"

"Through the malicious letters of Cicero, yes!"

Curio moved on. "As to the allegations that Caesar awarded the Roman citizenship illegally, show me where has he acted one scrap differently from our beloved but unconstitutional hero Gnaeus Pompeius Magnus? Or Gaius Marius before him? Or any one of many more provincial governors who established colonies? Who recruited men with the Latin Rights rather than the full citizenship? That is a grey area, Conscript Fathers, which cannot be said to have originated with Gaius Caesar. It has become a part of the *mos maiorum* to reward men owning the Latin Rights with full citizenship when they serve in Rome's armies legally, faithfully, and very often heroically. Nor can any of Caesar's legions be called mere auxiliary legions, filled with non-citizens! Every one of them has Roman citizens serving in it."

Gaius Marcellus Major sneered. "For someone who said this was not the time or the place to discuss the charges of treason which will be laid against Gaius Caesar the moment he lays down his imperium, Gaius Curio, you've spent a great many moments speaking as if you were leading Caesar's defense at his trial!"

"Yes, it must look that way," said Curio briskly. "However, I will now move to the crux of the matter, Gaius Marcellus. It is is contained in the letter which this body sent to Gaius Caesar early last year. Caesar had written to ask the Senate to treat him exactly as it had treated Gnaeus Pompeius Magnus, who stood for his consulship without a colleague *in absentia* because he was at the time governing both the Spains as well as looking after Rome's grain supply. Certainly, no trouble! cried the Conscript Fathers, gladly endorsing one of the most blatantly unconstitutional measures ever conceived in the fertile minds of this House and pushed with indecent haste through a poorly attended tribal assembly! But for Gaius Caesar, Pompeius Magnus's equal in all respects, this House could find nothing better to say than eat shit, Caesar!"

The doughty little terrier showed his teeth. "I will tell you what I intend to do, Conscript Fathers. Namely, I will continue to exercise my veto in the matter of Gaius Caesar's governorships of his provinces until the Senate of Rome agrees to treat Gaius Caesar exactly the way it is pleased to treat Gnaeus Pompeius Magnus. I will retract my veto on one condition: that *whatever* is done to Gaius Caesar is also done at one and the same moment to Gnaeus Pompeius! If this House strips Gaius Caesar of his imperium, his provinces and his army, then this House must in the same breath strip Gnaeus Pompeius of his imperium, his provinces and his army!"

Now they were all sitting up! Pompey was actually staring at Curio instead of admiring his own statue, and the little band of consulars who were thought to have some allegiance to Caesar bore grins from ear to ear.

"That's telling them, Curio!" cried Lucius Piso.

"Tace!" shouted Appius Claudius, who loathed Lucius Piso.

"I move," yelled Gaius Marcellus Major, "that Gaius Caesar be stripped of his imperium, his provinces and his army on this day! *Stripped!"*

"I interpose my veto to that motion, junior consul, until you add to it that Gnaeus Pompeius be stripped of his imperium, his provinces and his army on this day! *Stripped!"*

"This House decreed that it would treat the imposition of a veto on the subject of Gaius Caesar's proconsulship as treason! You are a traitor, Curio, and I'll see you die for it!"

"I veto that too, Marcellus!"

Paullus heaved himself to his feet. "Dismissed!" he roared. "The House is dismissed! Get out of here, all of you!"

Pompey sat on his stool without moving while the senators scuttled out of his curia, though he found no joy now in gazing at his own countenance on the curule dais. Nor, significantly, did Cato, Ahenobarbus, Brutus or any of the other *boni* make one overture toward him which he might have construed as a request to come and talk. Only Metellus Scipio joined him; when the egress was over, they left the dazzling chamber together.

"I'm stunned," said Pompey.

"No more than I."

"What did I ever do to Curio?"

"Nothing."

"Then why has he singled me out?"

"I don't know."

"He belongs to Caesar."

"We know that much now."

"He never did like me, though. He used to call me all kinds of nasty things when Caesar was consul, and then he kept it up after Caesar left for Gaul."

"He belonged to Publius Clodius before he sold himself to Caesar, we are all aware of that. And Clodius hated you then."

"Why did he pick on *me*?"

"Because you're Caesar's enemy, Pompeius."

The bright blue eyes tried to widen in Pompey's puffy face. "I am not Caesar's enemy!" he said indignantly.

"Rubbish. Of course you are."

"How can you say that, Scipio? You're not famous for your brilliance."

"That's true," said Metellus Scipio, unruffled. "That's why I said at first that I didn't know why he singled you out. But then I worked it out. I remembered what Cato and Bibulus always used to say, that you're jealous of Caesar's ability. That in your most secret heart, you're afraid he's better than you are."

They had not left the Curia Pompeia through its outside doors, choosing instead to exit through a small door inside; using this put them in the peristyle of the villa Pompey had tacked onto his theater complex like, as Cicero said, a dinghy behind a yacht.

The First Man in Rome bit his lips savagely and held on to his temper. Metellus Scipio always said exactly what he thought because he cared nothing for the good opinions of other men; one who was born a Cornelius Scipio and also had the blood of Aemilius Paullus in his veins did not need the good opinions of other men. Even of the First Man in Rome. For Metellus Scipio owned more than impeccable ancestries. He also owned the vast fortune which had come to him upon his adoption into the plebeian Caecilii Metelli.

Yes. Well, it was true, though Pompey couldn't voice that admission. There had been misgivings in the early years of Caesar's career in Gaul of the Long-hairs, but Vercingetorix had confirmed them, set them in concrete form. Pompey had devoured the dispatch to the Senate which detailed the exploits of that year—his own year as consul for the third time, half of it without a colleague. Eclipsed. Not a military foot wrong. How consummately skilled the man was! How incredibly quickly he moved, how decided he was in his strategies, how flexible he was in his tactics. And that army of his! How did he manage to make his men worship him as a god? For they did, they *did.* He flogged them through six feet of snow, he wore them out, he asked them to starve for him, he took them out of their winter cantonments and made them work even harder. Oh, what fools the men were who attributed it to his generosity! Avaricious troops who fought purely for money were never prepared to die for their general, but Caesar's troops were prepared to die for him a thousand times.

I have never had that gift, though I thought I did back in the days when I called up my own Picentine clients and marched off to soldier for Sulla. I believed in myself then, and I believed my Picentine legionaries loved me. Maybe Spain and Sertorius took it out of me. I had to grind through that awful campaign, I had to see my troops die because of my own military blunders. Blunders *he* has never made. Spain and Sertorius taught me that numbers do count, that it's prudent to have lots more weight than the enemy on a battlefield. I've never fought undermanned since. I never will fight undermanned again. But *he* does. He believes in himself; he is never shaken by doubt. He will breeze into a battle so outnumbered that it's ludicrous. And yet he doesn't waste men nor seek battles. He'd rather do it peacefully if he can. Then he'll turn around and lop the hands off four thousand Gauls. Calling that a way to ensure a lasting cessation of hostilities. He's probably right. How many men did he lose at Gergovia? Seven hundred? And he wept for it! In Spain I lost almost ten times that many in a single battle, but I couldn't weep. Perhaps what I fear most is his frightening sanity. Even in the midst of that shocking temper he remains capable of real thought, of turning events to his advantage. Yes, Scipio is right. In my most secret heart I am afraid that Caesar is better than I am. . . .

His wife greeted them in the atrium, offering her cool cheek for a kiss, then beaming upon that monumental fool, her father. Oh, Julia, where are you? Why did you have to go? Why couldn't this one be like you? Why did this one have to be so cold?

"I didn't think the meeting would end before sunset," said Cornelia Metella, ushering them into the dining room, "but naturally I ordered enough dinner for all of us."

She was quite handsome, no disgrace in marrying her on that account. Her lustrous, thick brown hair was rolled into sausages which partly covered each ear, her mouth was full enough to be kissable, her breasts considerably plumper than Julia's had been. And her grey eyes were widely spaced, if a trifle heavy-lidded. She had submitted to the marriage bed with commendable resignation, not a virgin because she had been married to Publius Crassus, yet not, he discovered, either experienced or ardent enough to want to learn to enjoy what men did to women. Pompey prided himself on his skills as a lover, but Cornelia Metella had defeated him. On the whole she evinced no distaste or displeasure, but six years of marriage to the deliciously responsive, easily aroused Julia had sensitized him in some peculiar way; the old Pompey would never have noticed, but the post-Julia Pompey was uncomfortably aware that a part of Cornelia Metella's mind dwelled upon the foolishness of it while he kissed her breasts or pressed himself closely against her. And on the single occasion when he had wriggled his tongue inside her labia to provoke a genuine response, he had got that response: she reared back in outraged revulsion.

"Don't *do* that!" she snarled. "It's disgusting!"

Or perhaps, thought the post-Julia Pompey, it might have led to helpless delight; Cornelia Metella wished to own herself.

Cato walked home alone, longing for Bibulus. Without him, the *boni* ranks were thin, at least when it came to ability. The three Claudii Marcelli were good enough men, and this middle one showed great promise, but they lacked the years-long, passionate hatred of Caesar that Bibulus nursed and nurtured. Nor did they know Caesar the way Bibulus did. Cato could appreciate the reason behind the five-year law about governing provinces, but neither he nor Bibulus had realized that its first victim would be Bibulus himself. So there he was, stuck in Syria and saddled with none other than that pompous, self-righteous fool Cicero right next door in Cilicia. With whom Bibulus was expected to fight his wars in tandem. How did the Senate expect a team composed of a walking horse and a pack horse to pull the chariot of Mars satisfactorily? While Bibulus dealt capably with the Parthians through his bought minion, the Parthian nobleman Ornadapates, Cicero spent fifty-seven days besieging Pindenissus in eastern Cappadocia. *Fifty-seven days!* Fifty-seven days to secure the capitulation of a nothing! And in the same year that Caesar built twenty-five miles of fortifications and took Alesia in thirty days! The contrast was so glaring it was little wonder the Senate smiled when Cicero's dispatch reached it. In forty-five days. Twelve days less to get a communication from eastern Cappadocia to Rome than consumed by the siege of Pindenissus!

Cato let himself into his house. Since he had divorced Marcia he had seen little use for many servants, and after Porcia married Bibulus and moved out, he sold off more of them. Neither he nor his two tame live-in philosophers, Athenodorus Cordylion and Statyllus, had any interest in food beyond the fact that it was necessary to eat in order to live, so the kitchen was staffed by one man who called himself a cook and one lad who assisted him. A steward was a wasteful expenditure; Cato existed without one. There was a man to do the cleaning and the marketing (Cato checked all the figures and doled out the money personally), and the bit of laundry was sent out. All of which had reduced the household expenditures to ten thousand sesterces a year. Plus the wine, which tripled it despite the fact that the wine was second pressing and quite horribly vinegary. Irrelevant. Cato and his two philosophers bibbed for the effect, not the taste. Taste was an indulgence for wealthy men, men like Quintus Hortensius, who had married Marcia.

The thought nudged, burned, prickled, wouldn't vanish on this bitterly disappointing day. Marcia. Marcia. He could still remember the look of her in that first glance, when he had gone to the house of Lucius

Marcius Philippus for dinner. Seven years ago, all save a couple of months. Elated at what he had managed to do for Rome as a result of that ghastly special command Publius Clodius had forced him to take, the annexation of Cyprus. Well, he had duly annexed Cyprus. Shrugged when informed that its Egyptian regent, Ptolemy the Cyprian, had committed suicide. Then proceeded to sell off all the treasures and works of art for good solid cash, and put the good solid cash into two thousand chests—seven thousand talents all told. Kept two sets of books, retaining one in his own custody and giving the other to his freedman Philargyrus. No one in the Senate was going to have any grounds for accusing Cato of sticky fingers! One or the other set of accounts would get to Rome intact, Cato was sure of it.

He had pressed the royal fleet into service to take the two thousand chests of money home—why spend money hiring a fleet when there was one to hand? Then he devised a way to retrieve the chests should a ship sink during the voyage, by tying one hundred feet of rope to each chest and attaching a big chunk of cork to the end of each rope; if a ship should sink, the ropes would uncoil and the corks bob to the surface, enabling the chests to be pulled up and saved. As a further safeguard, he put Philargyrus and his set of accounts on a ship far removed from his own.

The royal Cypriot ships were very pretty, but never intended to sail the open waters of Our Sea in places like Cape Taenarum at the bottom of the Peloponnese. They were undecked biremes sitting low in the water, two men to an oar, each owning a skimpy sail. This meant, of course, that there was no deck to impede the unwinding of those cork-ended ropes should a ship sink. But the weather was good, though marred by a calamitous storm as the fleet rounded the Peloponnese. Even so, only one ship sank: the ship bearing Philargyrus and the second set of account books. Searching a calm sea afterward revealed not one bobbing bit of cork, alas. Cato had severely underestimated the depth of the waters.

Still, the loss of one ship among so many wasn't bad. Cato and the rest sought shelter on Corcyra when another storm seemed likely to blow up. Unfortunately that beautiful isle could not provide roofs for a horde of unexpected visitors, who were obliged to pitch tents in the agora of the port village where they fetched up. True to the tenets of Stoicism, Cato elected a tent rather than avail himself of the richest citizen's house. As it was very cold, the Cypriot sailors built a huge bonfire to keep warm. Up came the threatened gale; brands from the bonfire blew everywhere. Cato's tent burned completely, and with it his set of accounts.

Devastated at the loss, Cato realized he would never be able to prove that he hadn't pilfered the profits of the annexation of Cyprus; perhaps because of that, he elected not to trust his money chests to the Via Appia. Instead he sailed his fleet around the Italian foot and up the west coast, made landfall at Ostia, and was able, his ships were so shallow-drafted, to sail up the Tiber right to the wharves of the Port of Rome.

Most of Rome came to greet him, so novel was the sight; among the welcoming committee was the junior consul of that year, Lucius Marcius Philippus. Gourmet, bon vivant, Epicurean. All the things Cato most despised. But after Cato had personally supervised the porterage of those two thousand chests (the ship of Philargyrus had not held a great many) to the Treasury beneath the temple of Saturn, Cato accepted Philippus's invitation to dinner.

"The Senate," said Philippus, greeting him at the door, "is consumed with admiration, my dear Cato. They have all kinds of honors for you, including the right to wear the *toga praetexta* on public occasions, and a public thanksgiving."

"No!" barked Cato loudly. "I will not accept honors for doing a duty clearly laid out in the terms of my command, so don't bother to table them, let alone vote on them. I ask only that the slave Nicias, who was Ptolemy the Cyprian's steward, be given his freedom and awarded the Roman citizenship. Without Nicias's help I could not have succeeded in my task."

Philippus, a very handsome, dark man, was moved to blink, though not to argue. He led Cato into his exquisitely appointed dining room, ensconced him in the *locus consularis* position of honor on his own couch, and introduced him to his sons, lying together on the *lectus imus.* Lucius Junior was twenty-six, as dark as his father and even handsomer; Quintus was twenty-three, less inspiring in coloring and looks.

Two chairs were set on the far side of the *lectus medius* couch where Philippus and Cato reclined, the low table which would bear the food separating chairs from couch.

"You may not know," drawled Philippus, "that I have remarried fairly recently."

"Have you?" asked Cato, ill at ease; he hated these socially obligatory dinners, for they always seemed to comprise people he had nothing in common with, from political to philosophical leanings.

"Yes. Atia, the widow of my dear friend Gaius Octavius."

"Atia . . . Who's she?"

Philippus laughed heartily; his two sons grinned. "If a woman is neither a Porcia nor a Domitia, Cato, you never know who she is! Atia is the daughter of Marcus Atius Balbus from Aricia, and the younger of Gaius Caesar's two sisters."

Feeling the skin of his jaw tighten, Cato produced a rictus of a smile. "Caesar's niece," he said.

"That's right, Caesar's niece."

Cato strove to be polite. "Whose is the other chair?"

"My only daughter's. Marcia. My youngest chick."

"Not old enough yet to be married, obviously."

"As a matter of fact, she's fully eighteen. She was engaged to young Publius Cornelius Lentulus, but he died. I haven't yet decided on another husband."

"Does Atia have children by Gaius Octavius?"

"Two, a girl and a boy. And a stepdaughter as well, Octavius's by an Ancharia," said Philippus.

At which moment the two women came in, a telling contrast in beauty. Atia was a typical Julian, golden-haired and blue-eyed, with a distinct look of Gaius Marius's wife about her and striking grace of movement; Marcia was black-haired and black-eyed, and very much resembled her older brother. Who never took his gaze away from his father's wife, had Cato noticed.

Cato didn't notice because he couldn't take his gaze away from Philippus's daughter, seated opposite him on her stiff straight chair, her hands folded demurely in her lap. Her eyes were fixed with equal intensity upon Cato.

They looked at each other and fell in love, something Cato had never believed could happen, nor Marcia believed would happen to her. Marcia recognized it for what it was; Cato did not.

She smiled at him, revealing brilliantly white teeth. "What a wonderful thing you've done, Marcus Cato," she said as the first course was brought in.

Normally Cato would have despised the fare, upon which Marcia's father had expended considerable thought: stuffed baby cuttlefish, quail's eggs, gigantic olives imported from Further Spain, smoked baby eels, oysters brought live in a tank-cart from Baiae, crabs from the same source, little shrimps in a creamy garlic sauce, the finest virgin olive oil, crunchy bread hot from the oven.

"I haven't done anything except my duty," said Cato in a voice he hadn't known he possessed, soft, almost caressing. "Rome deputed me to annex Cyprus, and I have done so."

"But with such honesty, such care," she said, eyes adoring.

He blushed deeply, dipped his head and concentrated upon eating the oysters and crabs, which were, he was forced to admit, absolutely delicious.

"Do try the shrimps," said Marcia, took his hand and guided it to the dish.

Her touch enraptured him, the more so because he couldn't do what prudence screamed at him to do—snatch the hand away. Instead he prolonged the contact by pretending the dish was elsewhere, and actually smiled at her.

How enormously attractive he was! thought Marcia. That noble nose! What beautiful grey eyes, so stern and yet so luminous. Such a mouth! And that neatly cropped head of softly waving red-gold hair . . . broad shoulders, long graceful neck, not an ounce of superfluous flesh, long and well-muscled legs. Thank all the Gods that the toga was too clumsy to dine in, that men reclined clad only in a tunic!

Cato gobbled shrimps, dying to pop one between her gorgeous lips, letting her keep on guiding his hand to the dish.

And while all this was going on, the rest of Marcia's family, startled and amused, exchanged glances and suppressed smiles. Not upon Marcia's account; about her virtue and obedience no one thought to wonder, for she was extremely sheltered and would always do as she was told. No, it was Cato fascinated them. Who would ever have dreamed *Cato* could speak softly, or relish a woman's touch? Only Philippus was old enough to remember the time not long before the war against Spartacus when Cato, a youth of twenty, had been so violently in love with Aemilia Lepida, Mamercus's daughter who had married Metellus Scipio. But that, all of Rome had long ago assumed, had killed something in Cato, who married an Attilia when he was twenty-two and proceeded to treat her with cold, harsh indifference. Then, because Caesar had seduced her, Cato had divorced her, cut her off from all contact with her daughter and son, whom he had reared in a house utterly devoid of women.

"Let me wash your hands," said Marcia as the first course was removed and the second course came in: roast baby lamb, roast baby chicken, a myriad of vegetables cooked with pine nuts or shaved garlic or crumbled cheese, roast pork in a peppery sauce, pork sausages patiently coated with layers of watered honey as they broiled gently enough not to burn.

To Philippus, constrained because he was aware that his guest ate plainly, a pedestrian meal; to Cato, an indigestibly rich one. But for Marcia's sake he ate of that and nibbled at this.

"I hear," said Cato, "that you have two stepsisters and one stepbrother."

Her face lit up. "Yes, aren't I lucky?"

"You like them, then."

"Who could not?" she asked innocently.

"Which one is your favorite?"

"Oh, that's easy," she said warmly. "Little Gaius Octavius."

"And how old is he?"

"Six, going on sixty."

And Cato actually laughed, not his habitual neigh but quite an attractive chuckle. "A delightful child, then."

She frowned, considering that. "No, not at all delightful, Marcus Cato. I'd call him fascinating. At least, that's the adjective my father uses. He's very cool and composed, and he never stops thinking. Everything is picked apart, analyzed, weighed in his balance." She paused, then added, "He's very beautiful."

"Then he takes after his great-uncle Gaius Caesar," said Cato, harshness creeping into his voice for the first time.

She noticed it. "In some ways, yes. The intellect is very formidable. But he isn't universally gifted, and he's lazy when it comes to learning. He hates Greek, and won't try at it."

"Meaning Gaius Caesar *is* universally gifted."

"Well, I think that's generally conceded," she said pacifically.

"Where are young Gaius Octavius's gifts, then?"

"In his rationality," she said. "In his lack of fear. In his self-confidence. In his willingness to take risks."

"Then he is like his great-uncle."

Marcia giggled. "No," she said. "He is more like himself."

The main course departed, and Philippus grew gastronomically animated. "Marcus Cato," he said, "I have a brand-new dessert for you to try!" He eyed the salads, raisin-filled pastries, honey-soaked cakes, huge variety of cheeses, and shook his head. "Ah!" he cried then; the brand-new dessert appeared, a pale yellow chunk of what might have passed for cheese, save that it was borne upon a platter tucked inside another big plate loaded with—*snow*?

"It's made on the Mons Fiscellus, and in another month you wouldn't have been able to taste it. Honey, eggs and the cream off milk from two-year-old ewes, churned inside a barrel inside a bigger barrel lined with salted snow, then galloped all the way to Rome packed in more snow. I call it Mons Fiscellus ambrosia."

Perhaps discussing Caesar's great-nephew had left a sour taste in Cato's mouth; he declined it, and not even Marcia could persuade him to taste it.

Soon after that the two women retired. Cato's pleasure in this visit to a den of Epicureans dimmed immediately; he began to feel nauseated, and in the end was obliged to seek the latrine to vomit discreetly. How could people live so sybaritically? Why, even the Philippus latrine was luxurious! Though, he admitted, it was very nice to be able to avail himself of a little jet of cool water to rinse out his mouth and wash his hands afterward.

On the way back down the colonnade in the direction of the dining room he passed an open door.

"Marcus Cato!"

He stopped, peered inside to see her waiting.

"Come in for a moment, please."

That was absolutely forbidden by every social rule Rome owned. But Cato went in.

"I just wanted to tell you how much I enjoyed your company," said Marcia, limpid gaze fixed not on his eyes but on his mouth.

Oh, unbearable! Intolerable! Watch my eyes, Marcia, not my mouth, or I'll have to kiss you! Don't do this to me!

The next moment, how he didn't know, she was in his arms and the kiss was real—more real than any kiss he had ever experienced, but that wasn't saying much beyond indicating the depth of his self-inflicted starvation. Cato had kissed only two women, Aemilia Lepida and Attilia, and Attilia only rarely, and never with genuine feeling. Now he found a pair of soft yet muscular lips clinging to his own with a sensuous pleasure made manifest in the way she melted against him, sighed, coiled her tongue around his, pulled his hand up to her breast.

Gasping, Cato wrenched himself away from her and fled.

He went home so confused that he couldn't remember which door on that narrow Palatine alley of a hundred doors was his, his empty stomach churning, her kiss invading his mind until he could think of nothing except the fabulous feel of her in his arms.

Athenodorus Cordylion and Statyllus were waiting for him in the atrium, agog to discover what dinner at the house of Philippus had been like, the food, the company, the conversation.

"Go away!" he shouted, and bolted for his study.

Where he walked the floor until morning dawned without one gulp of wine. He didn't want to care. He didn't want to love. Love was an entrapment, a torment, a disaster, an endless horror. All those years of loving Aemilia Lepida, and what had happened? She preferred an overbred moron like Metellus Scipio. But Aemilia Lepida and that adolescent love founded in the senses were nothing. Nothing compared to the love he had borne for his brother Caepio, who died alone and waiting for Cato to come, who died without a hand to hold or a friend to comfort him. The agony of living on without Caepio there—the ghastly spiritual amputation—the tears—the desolation which never went away, even now, eleven long years later. An all-pervasive love of any kind was a betrayal of mind, of control, of the ability to deny weakness, to live a selfless life. And it led to a grief he knew himself too old now to bear again, for he was thirty-seven, not twenty, not twenty-seven.

Yet as soon as the sun was high enough he donned a fresh, chalk-whitened toga and returned to the house of Lucius Marcius Philippus, there to request the hand of Philippus's daughter in marriage. Hoping against hope that Philippus would say no.

Philippus said yes.

"It gives me a foot in both camps," the unashamed voluptuary said cheerfully, wringing Cato's hand. "Married to Caesar's niece and guardian of his great-nephew, yet father-in-law to Cato. What a perfect state of affairs! *Perfect!*"

The marriage had been perfect too, except that the sheer joy of it gnawed at Cato perpetually. He didn't deserve it; it could not possibly be a right act to wallow in something so intensely intimate. He had received absolute proof that Philippus's daughter was a virgin on her wedding night, but where did she get that power and passion from, that *knowledge*? For Cato knew nothing of women, had no idea how much or how little girls learned from conversation, erotic murals, Priapic objects scattered around their homes, noises and glimpses through doors, sophisticated older brothers. Nor did it edify him to know that he was helpless against her wiles, that the violence of his feelings for her ruled him completely. Marcia was a bride straight from the hands of Venus, but Cato came from the iron claws of Dis.

So when, two years after the marriage, senile old Hortensius had come around begging to espouse Cato's daughter or one of Cato's nieces, he hadn't taken umbrage at Hortensius's incredible final demand: that he be permitted to marry Cato's wife. Suddenly Cato saw the only way out of his torment, the only way he could prove to himself that he did own himself. He would give Marcia to Quintus Hortensius, a disgusting old lecher who would insult her flesh in unspeakable ways, who would fart and dribble in the throes of his addiction to ecstatics and priceless vintage wines, who would compel her to fellate his limpness into some sort of rigidity, whose toothlessness, hairlessness and inelastic body would revolt her, his darling Marcia whom he couldn't bear to see hurt or made unhappy. How could he sentence her to that fate? Yet he had to, or go mad.

He did it. He actually did it. The gossip was wrong; Cato took not one sestertius from Hortensius, though of course Philippus had accepted millions.

"I am divorcing you," he said to her in his loudest, brassiest voice, "and then I'm going to marry you to Quintus Hortensius. I expect you to be a good wife to him. Your father has agreed."

She had stood absolutely erect, wide eyes full of unshed tears, then reached out and touched his cheek very gently, with so much love.

"I understand, Marcus," she said. "I do understand. I love you. I will love you beyond death."

"I don't want you to love me!" he howled, fists clenched. "I want peace, I want to be left alone, I don't want anyone loving me, I don't want to be loved beyond death! Go to Hortensius and learn to hate me!"

But all she did was smile.

And that had been almost four years ago. Four years during which the pain had never left him, never lessened by one iota. He still missed her as acutely as he had on her wedding night in Hortensius's bed, still endured the visions of what Hortensius did to her or asked her to do to him. Still could hear her saying that she understood, that she would love him beyond death. That alone said she knew him down to his very marrow, and that she loved him enough to consent to a punishment she didn't deserve, could not deserve. All so he could prove to himself that he could live without her. That he was capable of denying himself ecstasy.

Why was he thinking of her on a day when he ought to be thinking of Curio, of Caesar's despicable victory? Why did he long to have her there, to bury his face in her breasts, make love to her for half of what was going to be an unendurably sleepless night? Why was he avoiding Athenodorus Cordylion and Statyllus? He poured himself a huge goblet of unwatered wine and drank it down at one gulp; but the worst of it was that he drank so much these Marcia-less days that the wine never had enough effect in a short enough time to dull the ache.

Someone began banging on the front door. Cato hunched his head into his shoulders and tried to ignore it, willing Athenodorus Cordylion or Statyllus to answer it, or one of the three servants. But the servants were probably down in the kitchen area at the back of the peristyle, and obviously his two philosophers were sulking because he had gone straight to his study and bolted its door. The wine went down on the desk; Cato got to his feet and went to answer that insistent tattoo.

"Oh, Brutus," he said, and held the door wide. "I suppose you want to come in."

"I wouldn't otherwise be here, Uncle Cato."

"I wish you were anywhere but here, nevvy."

"It must be wonderful to have a reputation for unapologetic rudeness," said Brutus, entering the study. "I'd give a great deal to emulate it."

Cato grinned sourly. "Not with your mother, you wouldn't. She'd shell your balls out."

"She did that years ago." Brutus poured himself wine, looked vainly for water, shrugged and sipped, grimacing. "I wish you'd spend a little of your money on decent wine."

"I don't drink it to flute my appreciation and flutter my eyelashes, I drink it to get drunk."

"It's so vinegary your stomach must be like rotting cheese."

"My stomach's in better condition than yours, Brutus. *I* didn't have pimples at thirty-three. Or eighteen, for that matter."

"It's no wonder you lost at the consular elections," said Brutus, wincing.

"People don't like to hear the naked truth, but I have no intention of ceasing to tell it."

"I realize that, Uncle."

"Anyway, what brings you?"

"Today's debacle in the Curia Pompeia."

Cato sneered. "Pah! Curio will crumble."

"I don't think so."

"Why?"

"Because he produced a reason for his veto."

"There's always a reason behind a veto. Curio was bought."

Oh, thought Brutus to himself, I see why we don't function as well when Bibulus is away! Here am I trying to fill Bibulus's shoes, and failing miserably. As I do at most things except the making of money, and I don't know why I have a talent for that.

He tried again. "Uncle, to dismiss Curio as a bought man isn't clever because it isn't relevant. What is relevant is Curio's reason for the veto. Brilliant! When Caesar sent that letter asking to be treated in the same way as Pompeius, and we refused, we gave Curio his ammunition."

"How could we agree to treat Caesar identically to Pompeius? I detest Pompeius, but he's infinitely more able than Caesar. He's been a force since the days of Sulla and his career is larded with honors, special commands, highly profitable wars. He doubled our income," said Cato stubbornly.

"That was ten years ago, and in those ten years Caesar has eclipsed him in the eyes of the Plebs and the People. The Senate may run foreign policy, apportion out foreign commands and have the final word in every military decision, but the Plebs and the People *matter*. They like Caesar—no, they adore Caesar."

"I'm not responsible for their stupidity!" snapped Cato.

"Nor I, Uncle. But the fact remains that in proposing to lift his veto the moment the Senate agreed to treat Pompeius in exactly the same way as Caesar, Curio scored an immense victory. He maneuvered those of us who oppose Caesar into the wrong. He made us look petty. He made it seem that our motives are founded purely in jealousy."

"That isn't so, Brutus."

"Then what *does* drive the *boni*?"

"Ever since I entered the Senate fourteen years ago, Brutus, I've seen Caesar for what he really is," said Cato soberly. "He's Sulla! He wants to be King of Rome. And I vowed then that I would exert every fiber of my being to prevent his attaining the position and the power which would enable him to achieve his ambition. To gift Caesar with an army is suicide. But we gifted him with three legions, thanks to Publius Vatinius. And what did Caesar do? He enlisted more legions without our consent. He even managed to pay them, and keep on paying them until the Senate broke down."

"I have heard," Brutus offered, "that he took an enormous bribe from Ptolemy Auletes when he was consul and secured a decree confirming Auletes in his tenure of the throne of Egypt."

"Oh, that's a fact," said Cato bitterly. "I interviewed Ptolemy Auletes when he visited Rhodes after the Alexandrians threw him off the throne—you were convalescing in Pamphylia at the time, rather than being of use to me."

"No, Uncle, I was in Cyprus doing your preliminary culling of Ptolemy the Cyprian's treasures at the time," Brutus said. "You terminated my illness yourself, don't you remember?"

"Well, anyway," said Cato, shrugging this reproach off, "Ptolemy Auletes came to see me in Lindos. I advised him to go back to Alexandria and make peace with his people. I told him that if he went on to Rome he'd only lose more thousands of talents in useless bribes. But of course he didn't listen. He went on to Rome, squandered a fortune in bribes, and got nowhere. But one thing he did tell me—that he paid Caesar six thousand *gold* talents for those two decrees. Of which Caesar kept four thousand. Marcus Crassus got a thousand, and Pompeius got a thousand. Out of those four thousand gold talents, ably managed by that loathesome Spaniard Balbus, Caesar equipped and paid his illegally recruited legions."

"Where are you going?" asked Brutus plaintively.

"Into my reasons why I vowed never to let Caesar have command of an army. I didn't succeed because Caesar ignored the Senate and had four thousand gold talents to spend on an army. With the result that he now has eleven legions and control of all the provinces which ring Italia around—Illyricum, Italian Gaul, the Province, and the new province of Gallia Comata. He will bring down the Republic about our ears unless we stop him, Brutus!"

"I wish I could agree, Uncle, but I don't. Say the word Caesar and you over-react. Besides, Curio has found the perfect lever. He has undertaken to remove his veto on terms which will sound extremely reasonable to the Plebs, the People, and at least half the Senate. Make Pompeius step down in one and the same moment as Caesar."

"But we *can't*!" Cato yelled. "Pompeius is a Picentine oaf. He has designs on pre-eminence which I can't condone, but he doesn't have the blood to become King of Rome. Which means that Pompeius and his army are our only defense against Caesar. We can't agree to Curio's terms, nor let the Senate agree."

"I understand that, Uncle. But in stopping its happening, we're going to look very small and vindictive. And we may not, even then, succeed."

Cato's face twisted into a grin. "Oh, we'll succeed!"

"What if Caesar personally confirms that he will step down in the same moment as Pompeius?"

"I imagine he'll do just that. But it doesn't matter one little bit. Because Pompeius will never consent to step down."

Cato poured himself another goblet of wine and drained it, while Brutus sat, frowning, his own untouched.

"Don't you dare say I drink too much!" snapped Cato, seeing the frown.

"I wasn't going to," said Brutus with dignity.

"Then why the disapproving look?"

"I was thinking." Brutus paused, then looked at his uncle very directly. "Hortensius is very ill."

The indrawn breath was clearly audible. Cato stiffened. "What has that to do with me?"

"He's asking for you."

"Let him ask."

"Uncle, I think you must see him."

"He's no relation of mine."

"But," said Brutus with considerable courage, "four years ago you did him a great favor."

"I did him no favor in giving him Marcia."

"He thinks so. I've just come from his bedside."

Cato rose to his feet. "All right, then. I'll go now. You can come with me."

"I should go home," said Brutus timidly. "My mother will be wanting a report on the meeting."

The reddened, swollen grey eyes flashed. "My half sister," said Cato, "is a political amateur. Don't feed her information she will inevitably misinterpret. And probably write off to tell her lover, Caesar, all about."

Brutus emitted a peculiar noise. "Caesar has been away for a great many years, Uncle."

Cato stopped in his tracks. "Does that mean what I think it does, Brutus?"

"Yes. She's intriguing with Lucius Pontius Aquila."

"Who?"

"You heard me."

"He's young enough to be her son!"

"Oh, definitely," said Brutus dryly. "He's three years my junior. But that hasn't stopped her. The goings-on are absolutely scandalous. Or they would be if they were generally known."

"Then let us hope," said Cato, opening the front door, "that they don't become generally known. She managed to keep Caesar a deep dark secret for years."

The house of Quintus Hortensius Hortalus was one of the most beautiful residences on the Palatine, and one of the largest. It stood on what had once been the unfashionable side, looking over the Vallis Murcia and the Circus Maximus to the Aventine Mount, and it actually possessed grounds as well as a peristyle garden. In these grounds were the sumptuous marble pools housing Hortensius's darlings, his fish.

Cato had never been to his house since his marriage to Marcia; the constant invitations to dine were rejected, the invitations to pop round and taste a particularly fine vintage were rejected. What if, during one of these visits, he should set eyes on Marcia?

Now it couldn't be avoided. Hortensius had to be in his early seventies at least; due to the years of war between Sulla and Carbo followed by Sulla's dictatorship, Hortensius had come very late to his praetorship and consulship. Perhaps because of this exasperating hiatus in his political career, he had begun to abuse himself in the name of pleasure, and ended in permanently addling what had been a fine intellect.

But the vast, echoing atrium was empty save for servants when Cato and Brutus walked in. Nor was there a sign of Marcia as they were conducted to Hortensius's "reclining chamber," as he called the room too like a woman's boudoir to be a study, yet too diurnal to be a sleeping room. Striking frescoes adorned its otherwise austere walls, not erotic art. Hortensius had chosen to reproduce the wall paintings in the ruined palace of King Minos on Crete. Wasp-waisted, kilt-clad men and women with long black curls leaped on and off the backs of oddly peaceful bulls, swung from their curving horns like acrobats. No trace of green or red: blues, browns, white, black, yellows. His taste was impeccable in everything. How much Hortensius must have relished Marcia!

The room stank of age, excrement and that indefinable odor which heralds the imminence of death. There upon a great bed, lacquered in the Egyptian manner in blues and yellows reflecting the colors in the murals, lay Quintus Hortensius Hortalus, long ago the undisputed ruler of the law courts.

He had shrunk to something resembling the description in Herodotus of an Egyptian mummy, hairless, desiccated, parchmented. But the rheumy eyes recognized Cato immediately; he stuck out a liver-spotted claw and grasped Cato's hand with surprising strength.

"I'm dying," he said piteously.

"Death comes to all of us," said the master of tact.

"I am so afraid of it!"

"Why?" asked Cato blankly.

"What if some of the Greeks are right, and agony awaits me?"

"The fate of Sisyphus and Ixion, you mean?"

The toothless gums showed; Hortensius had not quite lost his sense of humor. "I'm not very good at rolling boulders uphill."

"Sisyphus and Ixion offended the Gods, Hortensius. You have merely offended men. That's not a crime worthy of Tartarus."

"Isn't it? Don't you think the Gods require that we treat men the way we treat them?"

"Men are not gods, therefore the answer to that is no."

"All of us have a black horse as well as a white horse to draw the chariot of the soul," said Brutus in a soothing voice.

Hortensius giggled. "That's the trouble, Brutus. Both my horses have been black." He twisted to look at Cato, who had moved away. "I wanted to see you to thank you," he said.

"Thank *me*? Why?"

"For Marcia. Who has given me more happiness than an old and sinful man deserves. The most dutiful and considerate of wives . . ." His eyes rolled, wandered. "I was married to Lutatia—Catulus's sister, you know. Do you know? Had my children by her. . . . She was very strong, very opinionated. Unsympathetic. My fish . . . She despised my beautiful fish. . . . I could never make her see the pleasure in watching them cruise the water so tranquilly, so very gracefully. . . . But Marcia liked to watch my fish too. I suppose she still does. Yesterday she brought me Paris, my favorite fish, in a rock-crystal tank. . . ."

But Cato had had enough. He leaned forward to kiss those awful, stringy lips, for that was a right act. "I have to go, Quintus Hortensius," he said, straightening. "Don't fear death. It is a mercy. It can be the preferable alternative to life. It is gentle, of that I am sure, though the manner of its coming may be painful. We do what is required of us, and then we are at peace. But make sure your son is here to hold your hand. No one should die alone."

"I would rather hold your hand," said Hortensius. "You are the greatest Roman of them all."

"Then," said Cato, "I will hold your hand when the time comes."

Curio's popularity in the Forum zoomed at exactly the same rate as his popularity in the Senate plummeted. He would not retract his veto, especially after he read out a letter from Caesar to the House, stating that Caesar would be happy to relinquish his imperium, his provinces and his army if Pompey the Great relinquished his imperium, provinces and army at one and the same moment. Pushed to it, Pompey had no other choice than to declare that Caesar's demand was intolerable, that he couldn't lower himself to oblige a man who was defying the Senate and People of Rome.

Which statement allowed Curio to allege that Pompey's refusal meant that it was really Pompey who had designs on the State—Caesar was willing, and didn't that mean Caesar was behaving like a faithful servant of the State? And what was all this about having designs on the State? What sort of designs?

"Caesar intends to overthrow the Republic and make himself the King of Rome!" cried Cato, tried beyond silent endurance. "He will use that army of his to march upon Rome!"

"Rubbish!" said Curio scornfully. "It's Pompeius you ought to be worried about, not Caesar. Caesar is willing to step down, but Pompeius is not. Therefore which of them intends to use his army to overthrow the State? Why, Pompeius, of course!"

And so it went through one meeting of the Senate after another; March ended, April began and ended, and still Curio maintained his veto, unintimidated by the wildest threats of trial or death. Wherever he went he was cheered deliriously, which meant that no one dared to arrest him, let alone try him for treason. He had become a hero. Pompey, on the other hand, was beginning to look more and more a villain, and the *boni* more and more a lot of jealous bigots. While Caesar was beginning to look more and more the victim of a *boni* conspiracy to set Pompey up as Rome's Dictator.

Furious at this turn in public opinion, Cato had written to Bibulus in Syria almost every day, begging for advice; he received no reply until the last day of April:

Cato, my dear father-in-law and even dearer friend, I will try to bend my mind to finding a solution for your dilemma, but events here have overwhelmed me. My eyes run tears, my thoughts return constantly to the loss of my two sons. They are dead, Cato, murdered in Alexandria.

You know, of course, that Ptolemy Auletes died in May of last year, well before I arrived in Syria. His eldest living daughter, Cleopatra, ascended the throne at seventeen years of age. Because the throne goes through the female line but cannot be held by a female alone, she is required to marry a close male relative—brother, first cousin or uncle. That keeps the royal blood untainted, though there is no doubt that Cleopatra's blood is not pure. Her mother was the daughter of King Mithridates of Pontus, whereas the mother of her younger sister and her two younger brothers was the half sister of Ptolemy Auletes.

Oh, I must strive to keep my mind on this! Perhaps I need to talk it out, and there is no one here of proper rank or *boni* persuasion to lend an ear. Whereas you are the father of my beloved wife, my friend almost forever, and the first one to whom I send this dreadful news.

When I arrived in Antioch I sent young Gaius Cassius Longinus packing—a very arrogant, cocksure young man. But would you believe he had the temerity to do what Lucius Piso did in Macedonia at the end of his governorship? He paid out his army! Maintaining that the Senate had confirmed his tenure as governor by not sending a replacement, and that this fact endowed him with all the rights, prerogatives and perquisites of a governor! Yes, Cassius paid out and discharged the men of his two legions before skipping off with every last scrap of Marcus Crassus's plunder. Including the gold from the great temple in Jerusalem and the solid gold statue of Atargatis from her temple at Bambyce.

With the Parthian threat looming (Cassius had defeated Pacorus, son of King Orodes of the Parthians, in an ambush, and the Parthians had gone home in consequence, but that did not last long), the only troops I had were the legion I brought with me from Italia. A sorry lot, as you well know. Caesar was recruiting madly, taking advantage of Pompeius's law requiring all men between seventeen and forty to serve their time in the legions, and for reasons which elude me completely those compelled to join up all preferred Caesar to Bibulus. I had to resort to pressing. So this one legion of mine was not in a mood to fight the Parthians.

I decided that for the time being my best tactic was to attempt to undermine the Parthian cause from within, so I bought a Parthian nobleman, Ornadapates, and set him to whisper in the ear of King

Orodes that his beloved son Pacorus had designs upon his throne. As a matter of fact, I have recently learned that it worked. Orodes executed Pacorus. Eastern kings are very sensitive about overthrow from within the family.

But before I knew my ploy was successful, I fretted myself into a constant state of blinding headaches because I had no decent army to protect my province. Then the Idumaean prince Antipater, who stands very high at the Jewish court of Hyrcanus, suggested that I recall the legion Aulus Gabinius left in Egypt after he reinstated Ptolemy Auletes on his throne. These, he said, were the most veteran soldiers Rome owned, for they were the last of the Fimbriani, the men who went east with Flaccus and Fimbria to deal with Mithridates on Carbo and Cinna's behalf. They were seventeen then, and during the years since they had fought for Fimbria, Sulla, Murena, Lucullus, Pompeius and Gabinius. Thirty-four years. And that, said Antipater, made them fifty-one years old. Not too old to fight, especially given their unparalleled experience in the field. They were well settled outside Alexandria, but they were not the property of Egypt. They were Romans and still under the authority of Rome.

Thus in February of this year I endowed my sons Marcus and Gnaeus with a propraetorian imperium and sent them to Alexandria to see Queen Cleopatra (her husband, her brother called Ptolemy XIII, is only nine years old) and demand that she give up the legion of Gabiniani forthwith. It would be excellent experience for them, I thought, a trifling mission in one way, yet in another way, an important diplomatic coup. Rome has had no official congress with the new ruler of Egypt; my sons would be the first.

They journeyed overland to Egypt because neither of them is comfortable upon the sea. They had six lictors each and a squadron of Galatian cavalry whom Cassius had failed to detach from duty in Syria. Antipater met them near Lake Gennesarus and personally escorted them through the Jewish kingdom, then left them to their own devices at Gaza, the border. Shortly after the beginning of March they arrived in Alexandria.

Queen Cleopatra received them very graciously. I had a letter from Marcus which didn't reach me until after I learned of his death—what a nightmarish ordeal that is, Cato! To read the words of a beloved child who is dead. He was most impressed with the girl Queen, a little wisp of a creature with a face only youth made attractive, for she has, Marcus said, a nose to rival yours. Not an endowment for a female, though noble on a male. She spoke, he said, perfect Attic Greek, and was clad in the dress of Pharaoh—a huge tall crown in two parts, white inside red; a gown of finely pleated, diaphanous white linen; and a fabulous jeweled collar ten inches wide. She even wore a false beard made of gold and blue enamel like a rounded braid. In one hand she bore a scepter like a little shepherd's crook, and in the other a fly swish of supple white linen threads with a jeweled handle. The flies in Syria and Egypt are a constant torment.

Queen Cleopatra agreed at once to free the Gabiniani from garrison duty at Alexandria. The days when it might have been necessary, she said, were long over. So my sons rode out to the Gabiniani camp, which was located beyond the eastern or Canopic Gate of the city. Where they found what was really a little town; the Gabiniani had all married local girls and gone into business as smiths, carpenters and stonemasons. Of military activity there was none.

When Marcus, who acted as spokesman, informed them that they were being recalled by the governor of Syria to duty in Syria, they refused to go! Refusal, said Marcus, was not an alternative. Sufficient ships had been hired and were waiting in the Eunostus Harbor at Alexandria; under Roman law and with the permission of the Queen of Egypt, they were to pack their belongings at once and embark. The *primipilus* centurion, a villainous oaf, stepped forward and said they were not going back to service in a Roman army. Aulus Gabinius had discharged them after thirty years under the Eagles, and left them to enjoy their retirement right where they were. They had wives, children and businesses.

Marcus grew angry. Gnaeus too. He ordered his lictors to arrest the Gabiniani spokesman, whereupon other centurions came forward and stood around the man. No, they said, they were retired, they would not leave. Gnaeus ordered his lictors to join Marcus's and arrest the lot. But when the lictors attempted to lay hands on the men, they drew their swords. There was a fight, but neither my sons nor their lictors had weapons other than the bound *fasces* containing the axes, and the Galatian cavalry had been left in Alexandria to enjoy a few days' leave.

Thus died my sons and their lictors. Queen Cleopatra acted immediately. She had General Achillas of her own army round up the Gabiniani and cast the centurions in chains. My sons were given a State funeral, and their ashes placed in the most precious little urns I have ever seen. She sent my sons' ashes and the Gabiniani leaders to me in Antioch together with a letter accepting full responsibility for the tragedy. She would wait, she said, humbly upon my decision as to what to do with Egypt. Whatever I wished would be done, even if that included the arrest of her own person. She ended by saying that the enlisted Gabiniani men were loaded onto the ships and would arrive soon in Antioch.

I sent the Gabiniani centurions back to her, explaining that she was more disinterested and would therefore judge them impartially, for I could not. And absolved her of any malicious intent. I believe that she executed the *primipilus* and *pilus prior* centurions, but that General Achillas stole the rest of them to stiffen the Egyptian army. The rankers, as she had promised, arrived in Antioch, where I have put them back under stern Roman military discipline. Queen Cleopatra had, at her own expense, hired extra ships and sent their wives, children and property too. After thinking about it, I decided that it would be wise to permit the Gabiniani to have their Egyptian families. I am not a sympathetic man, but my sons are dead, and I am no Lucullus.

As to Rome, Cato, I think that it is futile to go on encouraging Curio in the Senate. The longer the battle there goes on, the greater will his reputation be outside the Senate. Including among the senior knights of the Eighteen, whose support we desperately need. Therefore I think the *boni* will be wiser to decree a postponement of the discussion about Caesar's provinces. For long enough to let the fickle memories of the Plebs and People forget how heroic Curio has been. Postpone discussion of Caesar's provinces until the Ides of November. Curio will resume his obstructive tactics and veto yet again, but a month after that date he goes out of office. And Caesar will never get another tribune of the plebs to equal Gaius Scribonius Curio. He will be stripped of everything in December, and we can send Lucius Ahenobarbus to relieve him immediately. All that Curio will have done for him is to postpone the inevitable. I don't fear Caesar. He's a highly constitutional man, not a natural outlaw like Sulla. I know you don't agree with me there, but I have been Gaius Caesar's colleague through aedile, praetor and consul, and though he has great courage, he is not comfortable without due process.

Oh, I am feeling better. To have something to think about is some sort of anodyne for grief. And now I'm writing to you, I see you before my inner eyes, and I am comforted. But I must come home this year, Cato! I shiver in dread at the thought that the Senate might prorogue my command. Syria isn't lucky for me; nothing good will happen here. My spies say the Parthians are going to return in the summer, but if I get a replacement, I'll be gone before that. I *must* be gone!

Little though I like or esteem him, I sympathize with Cicero, who goes through the same ordeal. Two more reluctant governors than Cicero and me would be hard to find. Though he at least has enjoyed enough of a campaign to earn himself twelve million from the sale of slaves. My side of our joint campaign in the Amanus ranges yielded six goats, ten sheep and a headache so bad I went completely blind. Cicero has let Pomptinus go home, and intends to leave on the last day of Quinctilis whether he has a successor or not, provided that he has received no letter proroguing him. I may well follow his example. For though I do not fear that Caesar aims at a monarchy, I want to be there in the Senate to make sure that he is not permitted to stand for the consulship next year *in absentia*. I want to be prosecuting him for *maiestas,* make no mistake about that.

As Brutus's uncle and Servilia's—yes, I know, half!—brother, perhaps you ought to know one of the stories Cicero is busily scribbling home to Atticus, Caelius and the Gods know who else. You must know the ghastly Publius Vedius, a knight as rich as he is vulgar. Well, Cicero encountered him on the road in Cilicia somewhere at the head of a bizarre and trumpery parade which included two chariots, one containing a dog-faced baboon tricked out in woman's finery, both drawn by wild asses—an absolute disgrace for Rome. Anyway, due to a series of events with which I will not weary you, Vedius's baggage was searched. And revealed the portraits of five extremely well known young Roman noblewomen, all married to some very haughty fellows. Including the wife of Manius Lepidus, and one of Brutus's sisters. I presume that Cicero means Junia Prima, Vatia Isauricus's wife, as Junia Secunda is married to Marcus Lepidus. Unless, of course, Vedius's taste runs to cuckolding the Aemilii Lepidi. I leave it to you what to do about this story, but I warn you that it will be all over Rome very soon. Perhaps you could speak to Brutus, and he could speak to Servilia? Best she knows.

I do feel better. In fact, this is the first time that I have passed some hours without weeping. Will you break the news of my sons to those who must know? Their mother, my first Domitia. It will almost kill her. To both the Porcias, Ahenobarbus's wife and my wife. To Brutus.

Look after yourself, Cato. I cannot wait to see your dear face.

In the midst of reading Bibulus's letter Cato began to feel a peculiar, crawling dread. The basis of it he couldn't quite pin down, except that it had to do with Caesar. Caesar, Caesar, always and ever Caesar! A man whose luck was proverbial, who never put a foot wrong. What had Catulus said? Not to him, to someone else he couldn't for the life of him remember . . . that Caesar was like Ulysses; that his life strand was so strong it frayed through all those it rubbed against. Knock him down, and up he sprang again like the dragon's teeth planted in the field of death. Now Bibulus was stripped of his two eldest sons. Syria was, he said, unlucky for him. Could it be? *No!*

Cato rolled up the letter, put his misgivings from him, and sent for the hapless Brutus. Who would have to deal with the faithlessness of his sister, the wrath of his mother, and the grief of Cato's daughter, whom he would not see himself. Let Brutus do it. Brutus liked that sort of duty. He was to be seen at every single funeral; he had a deft touch with a condolence.

* * *

So it was that Brutus plodded from his own house to the house of Marcus Calpurnius Bibulus, miserably conscious of his role as the bearer of bad tidings. When informed that Junia was being a naughty girl, Servilia simply shrugged and said that she was surely old enough by now to manage her own life on whatever terms she chose. When informed of the identity of the man with whom Junia was dallying, Servilia soared higher than Ararat. A worm like Publius Vedius? Roar! Screech! Drum the heels, grind the teeth, spit worse curses than the lowliest laborer in the Port of Rome! From indifference she passed to an outrage so awful that Brutus fled, leaving Servilia to stride around the corner to Vatia Isauricus's house and confront her daughter. For the crime to Servilia was not adultery, but loss of *dignitas*. Young women with Junian fathers and patrician Servilian mothers did not gift lowborn mushrooms with access to their husbands' property.

He knocked on the door and was admitted to Bibulus's house by the steward, a man whose snobbishness exceeded that of his master. When Brutus asked to see the lady Porcia, the steward looked down his long nose and pointed silently in the direction of the peristyle. He then walked away as if to say that he wanted nothing to do with the entire situation.

Brutus had not seen Porcia since her wedding day two years ago, which was not an unusual state of affairs; on the many occasions when he had visited Bibulus, his wife was nowhere to be seen. Marriage to two Domitias, both of whom Caesar had seduced for no better reason than that he loathed Bibulus, had cured Bibulus of inviting his wife to dinner when he had male guests. Even if the male guest was his wife's first cousin, and even if his male guest was as blameless of reputation as Brutus.

As he walked toward the peristyle he could hear her loud, neighing laughter, and the much higher, lighter laughter of a child. They were galloping round the garden, Porcia handicapped by a blindfold. Her ten-year-old stepson frolicked about her, tugging her dress one moment, standing still and absolutely silent the next while she blundered within an inch of him, groping and giggling. Then he would laugh and dash away, and off she would go again in pursuit. Though, noted Brutus, the boy was considerate; he made no move toward the pool, into which Porcia might fall.

Brutus's heart twisted. Why hadn't he been dowered with a big sister like this? Someone to play with, have fun with, laugh with? Or a mother like that? He knew some men who did have mothers like that, who still romped with them when provoked. What a delight it must be for young Lucius Bibulus to have a stepmother like Porcia. Dear, galumphing elephant Porcia.

"Is anybody home?" he called from the colonnade.

Both of them stopped, turned. Porcia pulled off her blindfold and whinnied with delight. Young Lucius following, she lolloped over to

Brutus and enfolded him in a huge hug which took his feet off the terrazzo floor.

"Brutus, Brutus!" she cried, putting him down. "Lucius, this is my cousin Brutus. Do you know him?"

"Yes," said Lucius, clearly not as enthusiastic at Brutus's arrival as his stepmother was.

"*Ave,* Lucius," said Brutus, smiling to reveal that he had beautiful teeth and that the smile, were it located in a less off-putting face, possessed a winning, spontaneous charm. "I'm sorry to spoil your fun, but I must talk to Porcia in private."

Lucius, the same kind of diminutive, frosty-looking person as his father, shrugged and wandered off, kicking at the grass disconsolately.

"Isn't he lovely?" asked Porcia, conducting Brutus to her own rooms. "Isn't this lovely?" she asked then, gesturing at her sitting room proudly. "I have so much space, Brutus!"

"They say that every kind of plant and creature abhors emptiness, Porcia, and it is quite true, I see. You've managed to overcrowd it magnificently."

"Oh, I know, I know! Bibulus is always telling me to try to be tidy, but it isn't in my nature, I'm afraid."

She sat down on one chair, he on another. At least, he reflected, Bibulus kept sufficient staff to make sure his wife's shambles was dust-free and that the chairs were vacant.

Her dress sense hadn't improved, he noticed; she was wearing yet another baby-cack-brown canvas tent which emphasized the width of her shoulders and gave her a slight air of the Amazon warrior. But her mop of fiery hair was considerably longer and thus even more beautiful, and the large grey eyes were as sternly luminous as he had remembered them to be.

"What a pleasure to see you," she said, smiling.

"And to see you, Porcia."

"Why haven't you come to call before? Bibulus has been away now for almost a year."

"It isn't done to call on a man's wife in his absence."

She frowned. "That's ridiculous!"

"Well, his first two wives were unfaithful to him."

"They have nothing to do with *me,* Brutus. If it were not for Lucius, I'd have been desperately lonely."

"But you do have Lucius."

"I dismissed his pedagogue—idiotic man! I teach Lucius myself these days, and he's come ahead so well. You can't beat learning in with a rod; you have to sustain fascination with it."

"I can see he loves you."

"And I love him."

The reason for his mission gnawed at him, but Brutus found himself wanting to know a lot more about Porcia the married woman, and knew that the moment he broached the subject of death, his chance to discover her thoughts would vanish. So for the moment he pushed it away and said, "How do you like married life?"

"Very much."

"What do you like most about it?"

"The freedom." She snorted with laughter. "You've no idea how marvelous it is to live in a house without Athenodorus Cordylion and Statyllus! I know *tata* esteems them highly, but I never could. They were so jealous of him! If it looked as if I might have a few moments alone in his company, they'd rush in and spoil it. All those years, Brutus, living in the same house as Marcus Porcius Cato, knowing myself his daughter, and yet never able to be alone with him, free of his Greek leeches—I loathed them! Spiteful, petty old men. And they encouraged him to drink."

A great deal of what she said was true, but not all of it; Brutus thought Cato drank of his own volition, and that it had a great deal to do with his animosity for those he deemed unworthy of the *mos maiorum*. And Marcia. Which just went to show that Brutus too hadn't divined Cato's most fiercely guarded secret: the loneliness of life without his brother Caepio, his terror of loving other people so much that living without them was agony.

"And did you like being married to Bibulus?"

"Yes," she said tersely.

"Was it very difficult?"

Not having been raised by women, she interpreted this as a man would, and answered frankly. "The sexual act, you mean."

He blushed, but blushes didn't stand out on his dark, stubbly face; he answered with equal frankness. "Yes."

Sighing, she leaned forward with her linked hands between her widely separated knees; Bibulus clearly had not broken her of her mannish habits. "Well, Brutus, one accepts its necessity. The Gods do it too, if one believes the Greeks. Nor have I ever found any evidence in the writings of any philosopher that women are supposed to enjoy it. It is a reward for men, and if men did not seek it actively, it would not exist. I cannot say worse of it than that I suffered it, nor better of it than that it did not revolt me." She shrugged. "It is a brief business, after all, and once the pain becomes bearable, nothing truly difficult."

"But you're not supposed to feel pain after the first time, Porcia," said Brutus blankly.

"Really?" she asked indifferently. "That has not been so for me." Then she said, apparently unwounded, "Bibulus says I am juiceless."

Brutus's blush deepened, but his heart was wrung too. "Oh, Porcia! Maybe when Bibulus comes back it will be different. Do you miss him?"

"One must miss one's husband," she said.

"You didn't learn to love him."

"I love my father. I love little Lucius. I love you too, Brutus. But Bibulus I respect."

"Did you know that your father wanted me to marry you?"

Her eyes widened. "No."

"He did. But I wouldn't."

That blighted her. She said gruffly, "Why not?"

"Nothing to do with you, Porcia. Only that I gave my love to someone who didn't love me."

"Julia."

"Yes, Julia." His face twisted. "And when she died, I just wanted a wife who meant nothing to me. So I married Claudia."

"Oh, poor Brutus!"

He cleared his throat. "Aren't you curious as to what brings me here today?"

"I'm afraid I didn't think beyond the fact that you've come."

He shifted in his chair, then looked directly at her. "I'm deputed to break some painful news to you, Porcia."

Her skin paled, she licked her lips. "Bibulus is dead."

"No, Bibulus is well. But Marcus and Gnaeus were murdered in Alexandria."

The tears coursed down her face at once, but she said not one word. Brutus fished out his handkerchief and gave it to her, knowing full well that she would have put hers into service as a blotter or a mop. He let her weep for some time, then got to his feet a little awkwardly.

"I must go, Porcia. But may I come back? Would you like me to tell young Lucius?"

"No," she mumbled through the folds of linen. "I'll tell him, Brutus. But please come back."

Brutus went away saddened, though not, he realized, for the sons of Marcus Bibulus. For that poor, vital, glorious creature whose husband could say no better of her than that she was—oh, horrible word!—juiceless.

Cato was still lobbying among the minor *boni* to succeed in postponing the discussion of Caesar's provinces until the Ides of November when the word came that Quintus Hortensius was dying, and had sent for him.

The atrium was quite crowded by well-wishers, but the steward conducted Cato into the "reclining room" at once. Hortensius lay on the beautiful bed, swaddled in blankets and shivering dreadfully, the left side of his mouth drooped and drooling, his right hand picking at the bedclothes around his neck. But, as on Cato's earlier visit, Hortensius recognized him immediately. Young Quintus Hortensius, who was the same age as Brutus and well ensconced in the Senate, got up from his chair and offered it to Cato with true Hortensian courtesy.

"Won't be long," said Hortensius very thickly. "Had a stroke this morning. Can't move my left side. Can still speak but tongue gone clumsy. What a fate for me, eh? Won't be long. Another stroke soon."

Cato pulled the blankets away until he could take that feebly plucking right hand comfortably in his own; it clung pathetically.

"Left you something in my will, Cato."

"You know I don't accept inheritances, Quintus Hortensius."

"Not money, hee hee," the dying man tittered. "Know you won't take money. But will take this." Whereupon he closed his eyes and seemed to fall into a doze.

Still holding the hand, Cato had time to look about, which he did not in dread but with a steeled determination. Yes, Marcia was there, with three other women.

Hortensia he knew well; she was his brother Caepio's widow and had never remarried. Her daughter by Caepio, young Servilia, was just about of marriageable age, Cato realized with a shock—where did the years go? Was it *that* long since Caepio died? Not a nice girl, young Servilia. Did owning the name predispose them, all the Servilias? The third one was young Hortensius's wife, Lutatia, daughter of Catulus and therefore a double first cousin to her husband. Very proud. Very beautiful in an icy way.

Marcia had fixed her eyes upon a chandelier in the far corner of the room; he was free to gaze at her without fearing to meet her eyes, he knew that. The other three women he had dismissed in his misogynistic way, but he couldn't dismiss Marcia. He didn't have that kind of memory which could conjure up the exact lineaments of a beloved face, and that had been one of the saddest aspects of his ongoing sorrow since his brother Caepio had died. So he stared at Marcia in amazement. Was *that* how she looked?

He spoke, loudly and harshly; Hortensius started, opened his eyes, and kept them open, smiling gummily at Cato.

"Ladies, Quintus Hortensius is dying," he said. "Bring up chairs and sit where he can see you. Marcia and young Servilia, here by me. Hortensia and Lutatia, on the other side of the bed. A man who is dying must have the comfort of resting his eyes on all the members of his family."

Young Quintus Hortensius, now ranged around by his wife and his sister, had taken his father's paralyzed left hand in his hold; he was a rather soldierly fellow for the offspring of a most unmilitary man, but then the same could be said of Cicero's son, much younger. Sons didn't seem to take after their fathers. Cato's own son was not soldierly, not valorous, not political. How odd, that both he and Hortensius should have produced daughters eminently more suited to follow in the family footsteps. Hortensia understood the law brilliantly. Had the gift of oratory. Led a scholarly existence. And Porcia was the one who could have taken his place in Senate and public arena.

His arrangement of the family around the bed meant that he didn't have to look at Marcia, though he was intensely conscious of her body scant inches from his own.

They sat on through the hours, hardly aware that servants came in to light the lamps as darkness fell, leaving the bedside only for brief visits to the latrine. All looking at the dying man, whose eyes had fallen shut again with the going of the sun. At midnight the second stroke liberated a huge spate of blood under pressure into the vital parts of his brain and killed them so quickly, so subtly that no one realized the second stroke had taken place. Only the cooling temperature of the hand he held told Cato, who drew a deep breath and carefully untwined his numbed fingers from that clutch. He stood up.

"Quintus Hortensius is dead," he said, reached across the bed to pluck the flaccid left hand from Hortensius's son, and folded them across the chest. "Put in the coin, Quintus."

"He died so peacefully!" said Hortensia, astonished.

"Why should he not?" asked Cato, and walked from the room to seek the solitude of the cold, wintry garden.

He paced the paths for long enough to grow used to the moonless, clouded night, intent upon remaining there until the deathbed was passed into the care of the undertakers; then he would slip through the garden gate into the street without going back to the house. Not thinking of Quintus Hortensius Hortalus. Thinking of Marcia.

Who materialized before him so suddenly that he gasped. And none of it mattered. Not the years, the aged husband, the loneliness. She walked into his arms and took his face between her hands, smiling up at him.

"My exile is over," she said, and offered him her mouth.

He took it, wrung with pain, wracked with guilt, all the ardor and immensity of feeling he had passed on to his daughter liberated, uncontrollable, as fierce and wondrous as it had been in those long-forgotten days before Caepio died. His face was wet with tears, she licked them up, he pulled at her black robe and she at his, and together they fell upon the freezing ground, oblivious. Not once in the two years when she had been with him had he made love to her as he did then, holding nothing back, helpless to withstand the enormity of the emotion which invaded him. The dam had burst, he flew asunder, not all the stringent discipline of his self-inflicted and pitiless ethic could mar this stunning discovery or keep his spirit from leaping into a joy he had never known existed, there with her and within her, over and over and over again.

It was dawn when they parted, not having spoken a single word to each other; nor did they speak when he tore himself away and let himself out through the garden gate into the stirring street. While she gathered her clothing about her in some wry semblance of order and retreated unseen to her own suite of rooms in that vast house. She ached, but with triumph. Perhaps this exile had been the only way Cato could ever have come to terms with what he felt for her; smiling, she sought her bath.

Philippus came to see Cato that morning, and blinked his weary eyelids in surprise at the appearance of Rome's most famous and dedicated Stoic: vibrant with life, actually grinning!

"Don't offer me any of that ghastly piss you call wine," said Philippus, seating himself in a chair.

Cato sat to one side of his shabby desk and waited.

"I'm the executor of Quintus Hortensius's will," the visitor said, looking distinctly peevish.

"Oh yes, Quintus Hortensius said something about a bequest."

"Bequest? I'd rather call it a gift from the Gods!"

The pale red eyebrows rose; Cato's eyes twinkled. "I'm all agog, Lucius Marcius," he said.

"What's the matter with you this morning, Cato?"

"Absolutely nothing."

"Absolutely everything, I would have said. You're odd."

"Yes, but I always was."

Philippus drew a breath. "Hortensius left you the entire contents of his wine cellar," he said.

"How very nice of him. No wonder he said I'd accept."

"It doesn't mean a thing to you, does it, Cato?"

"You're quite wrong, Lucius Marcius. It means a great deal."

"Do you know what Quintus Hortensius has in his cellar?"

"Some very good vintages, I imagine."

"Oh, yes, he has that! But do you know how many amphorae?"

"No. How could I?"

"*Ten thousand* amphorae!" Philippus yelled. "Ten thousand amphorae of the finest wines in the world, and who does he go and leave it to but *you*! The worst palate in Rome!"

"I see what you mean and how you're feeling, Philippus." Cato leaned forward, put his hand on Philippus's knee, a gesture so strange from Cato that Philippus almost drew away. "I tell you what, Philippus. I'll make a bargain with you," said Cato.

"A bargain?"

"Yes, a bargain. I can't possibly accommodate ten thousand amphorae of wine in my house, and if I put it in storage down at Tusculum, the whole district would steal it. So I'll take the worst five hundred amphorae in poor old Hortensius's cellar, and give you the nine thousand five hundred best."

"You're mad, Cato! Rent a stout warehouse, or sell it! I will buy whatever I can afford of it, so I won't lose. But you can't just give away almost all of it, you just can't!"

"I didn't say I was giving it away. I said I would make a bargain with you. That means I want to trade it."

"What on earth do I have worth that much?"

"Your daughter," said Cato.

Philippus's jaw dropped. *"What?"*

"I'll trade you the wine for your daughter."

"But you divorced her!"

"And now I'm going to remarry her."

"You *are* mad! What do you want her back for?"

"That's my business," said Cato, looking extraordinarily pleased with himself. He stretched voluptuously. "I intend to remarry her as soon as Quintus Hortensius has gone into his urn."

The jaw snapped shut, the mouth worked; Philippus swallowed. "My dear fellow, you can't do that! The mourning period is a full ten months! And that is even if I did agree," he added.

The humor fled from Cato's eyes, which became their normal stern, resolute selves. He compressed his lips. "In ten months," he said, voice very harsh, "the world might have ended. Or Caesar might have marched on Rome. Or I might have been banished to a village on the Euxine Sea. Ten months are precious. Therefore I will marry Marcia immediately after the funeral of Quintus Hortensius."

"You can't! I won't consent! Rome would go insane!"

"Rome is insane."

"No, I won't consent!"

Cato sighed, turned in his chair and stared dreamily out of his study window. "Nine thousand five hundred enormous, huge, gigantic amphorae of vintage wine," he said. "How much does one amphora hold? Twenty-five flagons? Multiply nine thousand five hundred by twenty-five, and you have two hundred and thirty-seven thousand five hundred flagons of an unparalleled collection of Falernian, Chian, Fucine, Samian . . ." He sat up so suddenly that Philippus started. "Why, I do believe that Quintus Hortensius had some of that wine King Tigranes, King Mithridates and the King of the Parthians used to buy from Publius Servilius!"

The dark eyes were rolling wildly, the handsome face was a picture of confusion; Philippus clasped his hands together and extended them imploringly to Cato. "I can't! It would create a worse scandal than your divorcing her and marrying her to poor old Hortensius! Cato, *please*! Wait a few months!"

"No wine!" said Cato. "Instead, you can watch me take it down, wagonload after wagonload, to the Mons Testaceus in the Port of Rome, and personally break every amphora with a hammer."

The dark skin went absolutely white. "You wouldn't!"

"Yes, I would. After all, as you said yourself, I have the worst palate in Rome. And I can afford to drink all the ghastly piss I want. As for selling it, that would be tantamount to taking money from Quintus Hortensius. I never accept monetary bequests." Cato sat back in his chair, put his arms behind his head, and looked ironically at Philippus. "Make up your mind, man! Conduct your widowed daughter to her marriage with her ex-husband in five days' time—*and* slurp your way ecstatically through two hundred and thirty-seven thousand five hundred flagons of the world's best wine—or watch me break them into shards on the Mons Testaceus. After doing which, I will marry Marcia anyway. She's twenty-four years old, and she passed out of your hand six years ago. She's *sui iuris;* you can't stop us. All you can do is lend our second union a little respectability. For myself, I am indifferent to that kind of respectability. You know that. But I would prefer that Marcia feel comfortable enough to venture outside our door."

Frowning, Philippus studied the highly strung creature gazing at him quite indomitably. Perhaps he *was* mad. Yes, of course he was mad. Everyone had known it for years. The kind of single-minded dedication to a cause that Cato owned was unique. Look at how he kept on after Caesar. Would keep on keeping on after Caesar. Today's encounter, however, had revealed a great many more facets to Cato's madness than Philippus had suspected existed.

He sighed, shrugged. "Very well then. If you must, you must. Be it on your own heads, yours and Marcia's." His expression changed. "Hortensius never laid a finger on her, you know. At least, I suppose you must know, since you want to remarry her."

"I didn't know. I assumed the opposite."

"He was too old, too sick and too addled. He simply set her on a metaphorical pedestal as Cato's wife, and adored her."

"Yes, that makes sense. She has never ceased to be Cato's wife. Thank you for the information, Philippus. She would have told me herself, but I would have hesitated to believe her."

"Do you think so poorly of my Marcia? After husbanding her?"

"I husbanded a woman who cuckolded me with Caesar too."

Philippus got to his feet. "Quite so. But women differ as much as men." He started to walk to the door, then turned. "Do you realize, Cato, that I never knew until today that you have a sense of humor?"

Cato looked blank. "I don't have a sense of humor," he said.

Thus it was that very shortly after the funeral of Quintus Hortensius Hortalus, the seal was set upon the most delicious and exasperating scandal in the history of Rome: Marcus Porcius Cato remarried Marcia, the daughter of Lucius Marcius Philippus.

Halfway through May the Senate voted to postpone any discussion of Caesar's provinces until the Ides of November. Cato's lobbying had succeeded, though, not surprisingly, persuasion of his closest adherents proved hardest; Lucius Domitius Ahenobarbus wept, Marcus Favonius howled. Only letters from Bibulus to each of them had finally reconciled them to it.

"Oh, good!" said Curio gleefully in the House after the vote. "I can have a few months off. But don't think that I won't be interposing my veto again on the Ides of November, because I will."

"Veto away, Gaius Curio!" brayed Cato, the fabulous aura of his scandalous remarriage endowing him with considerable glamour. "You'll be out of office shortly after that, and Caesar will fall."

"Someone else will take my place," said Curio jauntily.

"But not like you" was Cato's rejoinder. "Caesar will never find another like you."

Perhaps Caesar would not, but his envisioned replacement for Curio was hurrying from Gaul to Rome. The death of Hortensius had created a gap in more than the ranks of the great advocates; he had also been an augur, which meant that his spot in the College of Augurs was up for election. And Ahenobarbus was going to try again, determined that he would put his family back into the most exclusive club in Rome, the priestly colleges. Priest or augur did not matter, though priest would have been more satisfactory for one whose grandfather had been Pontifex Maximus and brought in the law which required public election for priests and augurs.

Only candidates for consul and praetor were compelled to register in person inside the sacred boundary of Rome; for all other magistracies, including the religious ones, *in absentia* candidacy could be obtained. Thus Caesar's envisioned replacement for Curio as tribune of the plebs, hurrying from Gaul, sent ahead and registered as a candidate for the vacant augurship of Quintus Hortensius. The election was held before he reached Rome, and he won. Ahenobarbus's very vocal chagrin when he was defeated yet again seemed likely to inspire the writing of several epic poems.

"Marcus Antonius!" sniffled Ahenobarbus, his shiny hairless pate rucked into wrinkles by his writhing fingers. Rage was not possible; he had passed beyond it into despair at the last augural election, when Cicero had beaten him. "*Marcus Antonius!* I thought Cicero was as low as the electors could get, but Marcus Antonius! That oaf, that lecher, that brainless bully-boy brat! Rome is littered with his bastards! A cretin who vomits *in public*! His father committed suicide rather than come home to face his trial for treason; his uncle tortured free Greek men, women and children; his sister was so ugly they had to marry her to a cripple; his mother is undoubtedly the silliest female alive even if she is a Julia; and his two younger brothers differ from Antonius only in having even less intelligence!"

Ahenobarbus's auditor was Marcus Favonius; Cato seemed to spend every spare moment at home with Marcia these days, Metellus Scipio was off in Campania dancing attendance on Pompey, and the *boni* lesser lights were all thronging admiringly around the Marcelli.

"Do cheer up, Lucius Domitius," Favonius soothed. "Everyone knows why you lost. Caesar bought Antonius the post."

"Caesar didn't spend half the money I did on bribing," Ahenobarbus moaned, hiccuping. Then it came out. "I lost because I'm bald, Favonius! If I had one single strand of hair *somewhere* on my head it would be all right, but here I am, only forty-seven years old, and I've been as bare as a baboon's arse since I turned twenty-five! Children point and giggle and call me Egghead, women lift their lips in revulsion, and every man in Rome thinks I'm too decrepit to be worth voting for!"

"Oh, tch tch tch," clucked Favonius helplessly. He thought of something. "Caesar's bald, but he doesn't have any trouble."

"He's *not* bald!" cried Ahenobarbus. "He's still got enough hair to comb forward and cover his scalp, so he's not bald!" He ground his teeth. "He's also obliged by law to wear his Civic Crown on all public occasions, and it holds his hair in place."

At which point Ahenobarbus's wife marched in. She was that Porcia who was Cato's older full sister, and she was short, plump, sandy-haired and freckled. They had been married early and the union had proven a very happy one; the children had come along at regular intervals, two sons and four daughters, but luckily Lucius Ahenobarbus was so rich the number of sons whose careers he had to finance and daughters he had to dower was immaterial. They had, besides, adopted one son out to an Attilius Serranus.

Porcia looked, crooned, shot Favonius a glance of sympathy, and pulled Ahenobarbus's despised head against her stomach, patting his back. "My dear, stop mourning," she said. "For what reason I do not know, the electors of Rome decided years ago that they were not going to put you in a priestly college. It has nothing to do with your lack of hair. If it did, they wouldn't have voted you in as consul. Concentrate your efforts on getting our son Gnaeus elected to the priestly colleges. He's a very nice person, and the electors like him. Now stop carrying on, there's a good boy."

"But Marcus Antonius!" he groaned.

"Marcus Antonius is a public idol, a phenomenon of the same kind as a gladiator." She shrugged, rolling her hand around her husband's back like a mother with a colicky baby. "He's not like Caesar in ability, but he is like Caesar when it comes to charming the crowds. People like to vote for him, that's all."

"Porcia's right, Lucius Domitius," said Favonius.

"Of course I'm right."

"Then tell me why Antonius bothered to come to Rome? He was returned *in absentia.*"

Ahenobarbus's plaintive question was answered a few days later when Mark Antony, newly created augur, announced that he would stand for election as a tribune of the plebs.

"The *boni* are not impressed," said Curio, grinning.

For a creature who always looked magnificently well, Antony was looking, thought Curio, even more magnificently well. Life with Caesar had done him good, including Caesar's ban on wine. Rarely had Rome produced a specimen to equal him, with his height, his strongman's physique, his awesomely huge genital equipment, and his air of unquenchable optimism. People looked at him and liked him in a way they never had Caesar. Perhaps, thought Curio cynically, because he radiated masculinity without owning beauty of face. Like Sulla's, Caesar's charms were more epicene; if they were not, that ancient canard about Caesar's affair with King Nicomedes would not be so frequently trotted out, though no one could point to any suspect sexual activity since, and King Nicomedes rested on the testimony of two men who loathed Caesar, the dead Lucullus and the very much alive Bibulus. Whereas Antony, who used to give Curio lascivious kisses in public, was never for one moment apostrophized as homosexual.

"I didn't expect the *boni* to be impressed," said Antony, "but Caesar thinks I'll do very well as tribune of the plebs, even when that means I have to follow you."

"I agree with Caesar," answered Curio. "And, whether you like it or not, my dear Antonius, you are going to pay attention and learn during the next few months. I'm going to coach you to counter the *boni.*"

Fulvia, very pregnant, was lying next to Curio on a couch. Antony, who owned great loyalty to his friends, had known her for many years and esteemed her greatly. She was fierce, devoted, intelligent, supportive. Though Publius Clodius had been the love of her youth, she seemed to have transferred her affections to the very different Curio most successfully. Unlike most of the women Antony knew, Fulvia bestowed love for other than nest-making reasons. One could be sure of her love only by being brave, brilliant and a force in politics. As Clodius had been. As Curio was proving to be. Not unexpected, perhaps, in the granddaughter of Gaius Gracchus. Nor in a creature so full of fire. She was still very beautiful, though she was now into her thirties. And clearly as fruitful as ever: four children by Clodius, now one by Curio. Why was it that in a city whose aristocratic women were so prone to die in the childbed, Fulvia popped out babies without turning a hair? She destroyed so many of the theories, for her blood was immensely old and noble, her genealogy much intermarried. Scipio Africanus, Aemilius Paullus, Sempronius Gracchus, Fulvius Flaccus. Yet she was a baby manufactory.

"When's the sprog due?" asked Antony.

"Soon," said Fulvia, reaching out to ruffle Curio's hair. She smiled at Antony demurely. "We—er—anticipated our legal conjoining."

"Why didn't you get married sooner?"

"Ask Curio," she yawned.

"I wanted to be clear of debt before I married an extremely rich woman."

Antony looked shocked. "Curio, I never have understood you! Why should that worry you?"

"Because," said a new voice cheerfully, "Curio isn't like the rest of us impoverished fellows."

"Dolabella! Come in, come in!" cried Curio. "Shift over, Antonius."

Publius Cornelius Dolabella, patrician pauper, eased himself down onto the couch beside Antony and accepted the beaker of wine Curio poured and watered.

"Congratulations, Antonius," he said.

They were, thought Curio, very much the same kind of man, at least physically. Like Antony, Dolabella was tall and owned both a superb physique and unassailable masculinity, though Curio thought he probably had the better intellect, if only because he lacked Antony's intemperance. He was also much handsomer than Antony; his blood relationship to Fulvia was apparent in their features and in their coloring—pale brown hair, black brows and lashes, dark blue eyes.

Dolabella's financial position was so precarious that only a fortuitous marriage had permitted him to enter the Senate two years earlier; at Clodius's instigation, he had wooed and won the retired Chief Vestal Virgin, Fabia, who was the half sister of Cicero's wife, Terentia. The marriage hadn't lasted long, but Dolabella came out of it still legally possessed of Fabia's huge dowry—and still possessed of the affections of Cicero's wife, who blamed Fabia for the disintegration of the marriage.

"Did I hear right, Dolabella, when my ears picked up a rumor that you're paying a lot of attention to Cicero's daughter?" asked Fulvia, munching an apple.

Dolabella looked rueful. "I see the grapevine is as efficient as ever," he said.

"So you are courting Tullia?"

"Trying not to, actually. The trouble is that I'm in love with her."

"With *Tullia*?"

"I can understand that," said Antony unexpectedly. "I know we all laugh at Cicero's antics, but not his worst enemy could dismiss the wit or the mind. And I noticed Tullia years ago, when she was married to the first one—ah—Piso Frugi. Very pretty and sparkly. Seemed as if she might be fun."

"She is fun," said Dolabella gloomily.

"Only," said Curio with mock seriousness, "with Terentia for a mother, what might Tullia's children look like?"

They all roared with laughter, but Dolabella definitely did appear to be a man deeply in love.

"Just make sure you get a decent dowry out of Cicero" was Antony's last word on the subject. "He might complain that he's a poor man, but all he suffers from is shortage of cash. He owns some of the best property in Italia. And Terentia even more."

Early in June the Senate met in the Curia Pompeia to discuss the threat of the Parthians, who were expected to invade Syria in the summer. Out of which arose the vexed question of replacement governors for Cicero in Cilicia and Bibulus in Syria. Both men had adherents lobbying remorselessly to make sure that they were not prorogued for a further year, which was a nuisance, as the pool of potential governors was not large (most men took a province after their term as consul or praetor—the Ciceros and Bibuluses were rare) and the most important fish in it were all intent upon replacing Caesar, not Cicero and Bibulus. Couch generals shrank from embracing war with the Parthians, whereas Caesar's provinces seemed to be pacified for many years to come.

The two Pompeys were in attendance; the statue dominated the curule dais, and the real man dominated the bottom tier on the left-hand side. Looking very strong and rather more happily steely than of yore, Cato sat on the bottom tier of the right-hand side next to Appius Claudius Pulcher, who had emerged from his trial acquitted and promptly been elected censor. The only trouble was that the other censor was Lucius Calpurnius Piso, Caesar's father-in-law, and a man with whom Appius Claudius could not get on. At the moment they were still speaking to each other, mostly because Apppius Claudius intended to purge the Senate and, thanks to new legislation his own brother Publius Clodius had introduced while a tribune of the plebs, one censor could not take it upon himself to expel men from the Senate or alter a knight's status in the tribes or Centuries; Clodius had introduced a veto mechanism, and that meant Appius Claudius had to have Lucius Piso's consent to his measures.

But the Claudii Marcelli were still very much the center of senatorial opposition to Caesar and all other Popularis figures, so it was Gaius Marcellus Major, the junior consul, who conducted the meeting—and held the *fasces* for June.

"We know from Marcus Bibulus's letters that the military situation in Syria is critical," said Marcellus Major to the House. "He has about twenty-seven cohorts of troops all told, and that is ridiculous. Besides which, none of them are good troops, even including the Gabiniani returned from Alexandria. A most invidious situation, for a man to have to command soldiers who murdered his sons. We must send more legions to Syria."

"And where are we going to get these legions from?" asked Cato loudly. "Thanks to Caesar's remorseless recruiting—another twenty-two cohorts this year—Italia and Italian Gaul are bare."

"I am aware of that, Marcus Cato," said Marcellus Major stiffly. "Which does not alter the fact that we have to send at least two more legions to Syria."

Pompey piped up, winking at Metellus Scipio, sitting opposite him and looking smug; they were getting on splendidly together, thanks to Pompey's willingness to indulge his father-in-law's taste for pornography. "Junior consul, may I make a suggestion?"

"Please do, Gnaeus Pompeius."

Pompey got to his feet, smirking. "I understand that were any member of this House to propose that we solve our dilemma by ordering Gaius Caesar to give up some of his very many legions, our esteemed tribune of the plebs Gaius Curio would immediately veto the move. However, what I suggest is that we act entirely within the parameters which Gaius Curio has laid down."

Cato was smiling, Curio frowning.

"If we can act within those parameters, Gnaeus Pompeius, I for one would be immensely pleased," said Marcellus Major.

"It's simple," said Pompey brightly. "I suggest that I donate one of my legions to Syria, and that Gaius Caesar donate one of his legions to Syria. Therefore neither of us suffers, and both of us have been deprived of exactly the same proportion of our armies. Isn't that correct, Gaius Curio?"

"Yes," said Curio abruptly.

"Would you agree not to veto such a motion, Gaius Curio?"

"I could not veto such a motion, Gnaeus Pompeius."

"Oh, terrific!" cried Pompey, beaming. "Then I hereby serve notice on this House that I will of this day donate one of my own legions to Syria."

"Which one, Gnaeus Pompeius?" asked Metellus Scipio, hard put to keep still on his stool, so delighted was he.

"My Sixth Legion, Quintus Metellus Scipio," said Pompey.

A silence fell which Curio did not break. Well done, you Picentine hog! he said to himself. You've just pared Caesar's army of two legions, and achieved it in a way I can't veto. For the Sixth Legion had been working for Caesar for years; Caesar had borrowed it from Pompey and still possessed it. But it did not belong to him.

"An excellent idea!" said Marcellus Major, grinning. "I will see a show of hands. All those willing that Gnaeus Pompeius should donate his Sixth Legion to Syria, please show their hands."

Even Curio put his hand up.

"And all those willing that Gaius Caesar donate one of his legions to Syria, please show their hands."

Curio put up his hand again.

"Then I will write to Gaius Caesar in Further Gaul and inform him of this House's decree," said Marcellus Major, satisfied.

"And what about a new governor for Syria?" asked Cato. "I think the majority of the Conscript Fathers will agree that we ought to bring Marcus Bibulus home."

"I move," said Curio instantly, "that we send Lucius Domitius Ahenobarbus to replace Marcus Bibulus in Syria."

Ahenobarbus rose to his feet, shaking that bald head dolefully. "I would love to oblige, Gaius Curio," he said, "but unfortunately my health does not permit of my going to Syria." He pushed his chin into his chest and presented the Senate of Rome with the top of his scalp. "The sun is too strong, Conscript Fathers. I would fry my brain."

"Wear a hat, Lucius Domitius," said Curio chirpily. "What was good enough for Sulla is surely good enough for you."

"But that's the other problem, Gaius Curio," said Ahenobarbus. "I can't wear a hat. I can't even wear a military helmet. The moment I put one on, I suffer a frightful headache."

"You are a frightful headache!" snapped Lucius Piso, censor.

"And you're an Insubrian barbarian!" snarled Ahenobarbus.

"Order! Order!" shouted Marcellus Major.

Pompey stood up again. "May I suggest an alternative, Gaius Marcellus?" he asked humbly.

"Speak, Gnaeus Pompeius."

"Well, there is a pool of praetors available, but I think we all agree that Syria is too perilous to entrust to a man who has not been consul. Therefore, since I agree that we need Marcus Bibulus back in this House, may I propose that we send an ex-consul who has not yet been out of office for the full five years my *lex Pompeia* stipulates? In time the situation will settle down and problems like this will not crop up, but for the moment I do think we ought to be sensible. If the House is agreeable, we can draft a special law specifying this person for this job."

"Oh, get on with it, Pompeius!" said Curio, sighing. "Name your man, do!"

"Then I will. I nominate Quintus Caecilius Metellus Pius Scipio Nasica."

"Your father-in-law," said Curio. "Nepotism reigns."

"Nepotism is honest and just," said Cato.

"Nepotism is a curse!" yelled Mark Antony from the back tier.

"Order! I will have order!" thundered Marcellus Major. "Marcus Antonius, you are a *pedarius,* and not authorized to open your mouth!"

"*Gerrae!* Nonsense!" roared Antony. "My father is the best proof I know that nepotism is a curse!"

"Marcus Antonius, cease forthwith or I will have you thrown out of this chamber!"

"You and who else?" asked Antony scornfully. He squared up, lifted his fists in the classical boxing pose. "Come on, who's willing to try?"

"Sit down, Antonius!" said Curio wearily.

Antony sat down, grinning.

"Metellus Scipio," said Vatia Isauricus, "couldn't fight his way out of a clutch of women."

"I nominate Publius Vatinius! I nominate Gaius Trebonius! I nominate Gaius Fabius! I nominate Quintus Cicero! I nominate Lucius Caesar! I nominate Titus Labienus!" howled Mark Antony.

Gaius Marcellus Major dismissed the meeting.

"You're going to be a shocking demagogue when you're tribune of the plebs," said Curio to Antony as they walked back to the Palatine. "But don't try Gaius Marcellus too far. He's every bit as irascible as the rest of that clan."

"The bastards! They've cheated Caesar out of two legions."

"And very cleverly. I'll write to him at once."

By the beginning of Quinctilis everyone in Rome knew that Caesar, moving with his usual swiftness, had crossed the Alps into Italian Gaul, bringing Titus Labienus and three legions with him. Two were to go to Syria; Pompey's Sixth and his own Fifteenth, a legion without any experience in the field, for it was composed of raw recruits who had just emerged from a period of intensive training under Gaius Trebonius. The third legion Caesar brought with him was to remain in Italian Gaul: the Thirteenth, veteran and very proud of its unlucky number, which had not affected its performance in the field one iota. It contained Caesar's own personal clients, Latin Rights men from across the Padus River in Italian Gaul, and belonged to Caesar completely.

Whether because of Caesar's reflexive action, a ripple of fear passed up Rome's backbone; one moment there were no legions in Italian Gaul, the next moment there were three. A nucleus of potential panic began forming in Rome. All at once men started to wonder whether the Senate was being entirely responsible in acting so provocatively toward a man who was generally agreed to be the best military man since Gaius Marius—or even the best military man of all time. There was Caesar without any real barrier between himself and Italia, himself and Rome. And he was an enigma. No one really knew him. He'd been away so long! Marcus Porcius Cato was shouting to all and sundry in the Forum Romanum that

Caesar was intent on civil war, that Caesar was going to march on Rome, that Caesar would never part with any of his legions, that Caesar would bring the Republic down. Cato was noticed, Cato was listened to. Fear crept in, based upon nothing more tangible than a governor's moving himself—as he was expected to do—from one segment of his province or provinces to another. Admittedly Caesar didn't usually have a legion in constant attendance on him, even when he brought one across the Alps, and this time he was keeping the Thirteenth glued to him—but what was one legion? If it hadn't been for the other two, people would have rested easier.

Then came word that one of the many young Appius Claudiuses was escorting those two legions, the Sixth and the Fifteenth, to camp in Capua, there to await transshipment to the East. The sigh of relief was collective—why hadn't they remembered those legions no longer were Caesar's property? That he *had* to bring them with him to Italian Gaul! Oh, the Gods be praised! An attitude which burgeoned when the young Appius Claudius marched the Sixth and the Fifteenth around the outskirts of Rome, and informed the Censor, head of his clan, that the troops of both legions absolutely loathed Caesar, reviled him constantly, and had been on the point of mutiny—as indeed were the other legions in Caesar's army.

"Isn't the old boy clever?" asked Antony of Curio.

"Clever? Well, I know that, Antonius, if by the old boy you mean Caesar. Who will turn fifty in a few days—not very old."

"I mean all this claptrap about his legions being disaffected. Caesar's legions disaffected? Never happen, Curio, never! They'd lie down and let him shit on them. They'd *die* for him, every last man, including the men of Pompeius's Sixth."

"Then—?"

"He's diddling them, Curio. He's a sly old fox. You'd think even the Marcelli would realize that anyone can buy a young Appius Claudius. That's if said young Appius Claudius isn't pleased to co-operate through sheer love of making mischief. Caesar put him up to it. I happen to know that before he handed the Sixth and the Fifteenth over, Caesar held an assembly of the soldiers and told them how sorry he was to see them go. Then he gave every man a bonus of a thousand sesterces, pledged that they'd get their share of his booty, and commiserated with them about going back to standard army pay."

"The sly old fox indeed!" said Curio. Suddenly he shivered and stared at Antony anxiously. "Antonius, he wouldn't—would he?"

"Wouldn't what?" asked Antony, ogling a pretty girl.

"March on Rome."

"Oh, yes, we all think he would if he was pushed to it," said Antony casually.

"We all?"

"His legates. Trebonius, Decimus Brutus, Fabius, Sextius, Sulpicius, Hirtius, da-de-da."

Curio broke into a cold sweat, wiped his brow with a trembling hand. "Jupiter! Oh, Jupiter! Antonius, stop leering at women and come home with me right now!"

"Why?"

"So I can start coaching you in earnest, you great clod! It's up to me and then you to prevent it."

"I agree, we have to get him permission to stand for the consulship *in absentia*. Otherwise there's going to be shit from Rhegium to Aquileia."

"If Cato and the Marcelli would only shut up, there might be a chance," fretted Curio, almost running.

"They're fools," said Antony contemptuously.

When the three sets of elections were held that Quinctilis, Mark Antony was returned at the top of the poll for the tribunes of the plebs, a result which didn't dismay the *boni* one little bit. Throughout the years Curio had always shown great ability; all Mark Antony had ever shown was the outline of his mighty penis beneath a tunic drawn taut. If Caesar hoped to replace Curio with Antony, he was insane, was the *boni* verdict. These elections also threw up one of the more curious aspects of Roman political life. Gaius Cassius Longinus, still covered in glory after his exploits in Syria, was returned as a tribune of the plebs. His younger brother, Quintus Cassius Longinus, was also returned as a tribune of the plebs. But whereas Gaius Cassius was staunchly *boni,* as befitted the husband of Brutus's sister, Quintus Cassius belonged completely to Caesar. The consuls for next year were both *boni;* Gaius Claudius Marcellus Minor was the senior consul, and Lucius Cornelius Lentulus Crus the junior consul. The praetors mostly supported Caesar, save for Cato's Ape, Marcus Favonius, who came in at the bottom of the poll.

And, despite the efforts of Curio and Antony (now permitted to speak in the House, as a tribune of the plebs-elect), Metellus Scipio was deputed to replace Bibulus as governor of Syria. The ex-praetor Publius Sestius was to go to Cilicia to take over from Cicero. With him as his senior legate Publius Sestius was taking Marcus Junius Brutus.

"What are you doing leaving Rome at a time like this?" Cato demanded of Brutus, not pleased.

Brutus produced his usual hangdog look, but even Cato had come to realize that however Brutus might look, he would do what he intended to. "I must go, Uncle," he said apologetically.

"Why?"

"Because Cicero in governing Cilicia has destroyed the best part of my financial interests in that corner of the world."

"Brutus, Brutus! You've got more money than Pompeius and Caesar combined! What's a debt or two compared with the fate of Rome?"

howled Cato, exasperated. "Mark my words, Caesar is out to murder the Republic! We need every single influential man we own to counter the moves Caesar is bound to make between now and the consular elections of next year. Your duty is to remain in Rome, not gallivant around Cilicia, Cyprus, Cappadocia and wherever else you're owed money! You'd shame Marcus Crassus!"

"I'm sorry, Uncle, but I have clients affected, such as Matinius and Scaptius. A man's first duty is to his clients."

"A man's first duty is to his country."

"My country is not in any danger."

"Your country is on the brink of civil war!"

"So you keep saying," sighed Brutus, "but frankly, I don't believe you. It's your personal tic, Uncle Cato, it really is."

A repulsive thought blossomed in Cato's mind; he glared at his nephew furiously. "*Gerrae!* It's got nothing to do with your clients or unpaid debts, Brutus, has it? You're skipping off to avoid military service, just as you have all your life!"

"That's not true!" gasped Brutus, paling.

"Now it's my turn not to believe. You are never to be found anywhere there's the remotest likelihood of war."

"How can you say that, Uncle? The Parthians will probably invade before I get to the East!"

"The Parthians will invade Syria, not Cilicia. Just as they did in the summer of last year, despite all Cicero had to say in his mountainous correspondence home! Unless we lose Syria, which I very much doubt, you're as safe sitting in Tarsus as you would be in Rome. Were Rome not threatened by Caesar."

"And that too is rubbish, Uncle. You remind me of Scaptius's wife, who fussed and clucked over her children until she turned them into hypochondriacs. A spot was a cancer, a headache something frightful happening inside the cranium, a twinge in the stomach the commencement of food poisoning or summer fever. Until finally she tempted Fate with all her carrying on, and one of her children died. Not from disease, Uncle, but from negligence on her part. She was busy looking in the market stalls instead of keeping her eye on him, and he ran beneath the wheels of a wagon."

"Hah!" sneered Cato, very angry. "An interesting parable, nevvy. But are you sure that Scaptius's wife isn't really your own mother, who certainly turned you into a hypochondriac?"

The sad brown eyes flashed dangerously; Brutus turned on his heel and walked away. Only not to go home. It was the day on which he had fallen into the habit of visiting Porcia.

Who, on hearing the tale of this falling-out, huffed a huge sigh and struck her palms together.

"Oh, Brutus, *tata* really can be irascible, can't he? Please don't take umbrage! He doesn't truly mean to hurt you. It's just that he's so—so militant himself. Once he's fixed his teeth in something he can't let go. Caesar is an obsession with him."

"I can excuse your father his obsessions, Porcia, but not his wretched dogmatism!" said Brutus, still vexed. "The Gods know that I cherish no love or regard for Caesar, but all he's doing is trying to survive. I hope he doesn't. But where is he different from half a dozen others I could name? None of whom marched on Rome. Look at Lucius Piso when the Senate stripped him of his command in Macedonia."

Porcia eyed him in amazement. "Brutus, that's no kind of comparison! Oh, you're so politically dense! Why can't you see politics with the clarity you see business?"

Stiff with anger, he got to his feet. "If you're going to try to proselytize me too, Porcia, I'm going home!" he snapped.

"Oh! Oh!" Consumed with contrition, she reached out to take his hand and held it to her cheek, her wide grey eyes shining with tears. "Forgive me! Don't go home! Oh, don't go home!"

Mollified, he took back his hand and sat down. "Well, all right then. But you have to see how dense you are, Porcia. You will never hear that Cato is wrong, whereas I know he's often wrong. Like this present campaign in the Forum against Caesar. What does he think he's accomplishing? All he's managing to do is frighten people, who see his passion and can't credit that it could be mistaken. Yet everything they hear about Caesar tells them that he's behaving in an absolutely normal way. Look at the panic over his bringing three legions across the Alps. But he had to bring them! And he sent two of them straight to Capua. While your father was informing anyone who'd listen that he would die sooner than give those two legions up. He was wrong, Porcia! He was wrong! Caesar did precisely as the Senate directed."

"Yes, I agree that *tata* does tend to overstate things," she said, swallowing. "But don't quarrel with him, Brutus." A tear dropped onto her hand. "I wish you weren't going away!"

"I'm not leaving tomorrow," he said gently. "By the time I do go, Bibulus will be home."

"Yes, of course," she said colorlessly, then beamed and slapped her hands on her knees. "Look at this, Brutus. I've been delving into Fabius Pictor, and I think I've found a grave anomaly. It's in the passage where he discusses the secession of the Plebs to the Aventine."

Ah, that was better! Brutus settled down happily to an examination of the text, his eyes more on Porcia's animated face than on Fabius Pictor.

But the rumors continued to fly and proliferate. Luckily the spring that year, which fell according to the calendar's summer, was halcyon; the rain fell in the right proportion, the sun shone just warmly enough, and somehow it didn't seem at all *real* to think of Caesar sitting up there in Italian Gaul, poised like a spider to pounce on Rome. Not that the ordinary folk of Rome were much preoccupied with such things; they adored Caesar universally, were inclined to think that the Senate treated him very shabbily indeed, and rounded off their thoughts with the conclusion that it would all work out for the best because things usually did. Among the powerful knights of the eighteen senior Centuries and their less pre-eminent junior colleagues, however, the rumors acted abrasively. Money was their sole concern, and the very slightest reference to civil war caused hair to rise and hearts to accelerate.

The group of bankers who supported Caesar ardently—Balbus, Oppius and Rabirius Postumus—worked constantly in his service, talking persuasively, soothing inchoate fears, trying to make the plutocrats like Titus Pomponius Atticus see that it was not in Caesar's best interests to contemplate civil war. That Cato and the Marcelli were behaving irresponsibly and irrationally in ascribing motives to Caesar concrete evidence said he didn't have. That Cato and the Marcelli were more damaging to Rome and her commercial empire with their wild, unfounded allegations than any actions Caesar might take to protect his future career and his *dignitas*. He was a constitutional man, he always had been; *why* would he suddenly discard constitutionality? Cato and the Marcelli kept saying he would, but on what tangible evidence? There was none. Therefore, didn't it actually look as if Cato and the Marcelli were using Caesar as fuel to attain a dictatorship for Pompey? Wasn't it Pompey whose actions throughout the years smacked of unconstitutionality? Wasn't it Pompey who hankered after the dictatorship, witness his behavior after the death of Clodius? Wasn't it Pompey who had enabled the *boni* to impugn the *dignitas* and the reputation of Gaius Julius Caesar? Wasn't it Pompey behind the whole affair? Whose motives were suspect, Caesar's or Pompey's? Whose behavior in the past indicated a lust for power, Caesar's or Pompey's? Who was the real danger to the Republic, Caesar or Pompey? The answer, said Caesar's indefatigable little band of workers, always came back to Pompey.

Who, taking his ease in his villa on the coast near Campanian Neapolis, fell ill. Desperately ill, said the grapevine. A good many senators and knights of the Eighteen immediately undertook a pilgrimage to Pompey's villa, where they were received with grave composure by Cornelia Metella and given a lucid explanation of her husband's extremis, followed by a firm refusal of any access to his sickbed, no matter how august the enquirer.

"I am very sorry, Titus Pomponius," she said to Atticus, one of the first to arrive, "but the doctors forbid all visitors. My husband is fighting for his life and needs his strength for that."

"Oh," gasped Atticus, a mightily worried man, "we can't do without the good Gnaeus Pompeius, Cornelia!"

Which wasn't really what he wanted to say. That concerned the possibility of Pompey's being behind the public and senatorial campaign to impeach Caesar; Atticus, immensely wealthy and influential, needed to see Pompey and explain the effect all this political mudslinging was having on money. One of the troubles with Pompey concerned his own wealth and his ignorance of commerce. Pompey's money was managed for him, and all contained inside banks or devoted to properly senatorial investments having to do with the ownership of land. If he were Brutus, he would already have moved to squash the *boni* irascibles, for all their agitation was doing was to frighten money. And to Atticus, frightened money was a nightmare. It fled into labyrinthine shelter, buried itself in utter darkness, wouldn't come out, wouldn't do its job. *Someone* had to tell the *boni* that they were tampering with Rome's true lifeblood—money.

As it was, he went away, defeated. As did all the others who came to Neapolis.

While Pompey skulked in parts of his villa unavailable to the eyes or ears of visitors. Somehow the higher he had risen in Rome's scheme of things, the slimmer grew the ranks of his intimate friends. At the moment, for instance, his sole solace lay in his father-in-law, Metellus Scipio. With whom he had concocted the present ruse, of pretending to be mortally ill.

"I have to find out where I stand in people's opinions and affections," he said to Metellus Scipio. "Am I necessary? Am I needed? Am I loved? Am I still the First Man? This will flush them out, Scipio. I've got Cornelia making a list of everyone who comes to enquire after me, together with an account of what they say to her. It will tell me everything I need to know."

Unfortunately the caliber of Metellus Scipio's brain did not extend to nuances and subtleties, so it never occurred to him to protest to Pompey that naturally everyone who came would deliver fulsome speeches of undying affection, but that what they said might not be what they thought. Nor did it occur to him that at least half of Pompey's visitors were hoping Pompey would die.

So the two of them totted up Cornelia Metella's list with glee, played at dice and checkers and dominoes, then dispersed to pursue those activities they didn't have in common. Pompey read Caesar's *Commentaries* many times over, never with pleasure. The wretched man was more than a military genius, he was also equipped with a degree of self-confidence Pompey had never owned. Caesar didn't tear his cheeks and chest and retire to his command tent in despair after a setback. He soldiered on serenely. And why were *his* legates so brilliant? If Afranius and Petreius in the Spains were half as able as Trebonius or Fabius or Decimus Brutus, Pompey would feel more confident. Metellus Scipio, on the other hand, spent his private time composing delicious little playlets with nude actors and actresses, and directed them himself.

The mortal illness lasted for a month, after which, midway through Sextilis, Pompey popped himself into a litter and set out for his villa on the Campus Martius. Word of his grave condition had spread far and wide, and the country through which he traveled was liberally bedewed with his clients (not wanting to fall genuinely ill with a tertian or a quartan fever, he chose the inland, far healthier Via Latina route). They flocked to greet him, garlanded with flowers, and cheered him as he poked his head through the curtains of his litter to smile wanly and wave weakly. As he was not by nature a litter man, he decided to continue his journey in darkness, thinking to sleep some of the long, boring hours away. To discover, overjoyed, that people still came to greet him and cheer him, bearing torches to light his triumphant way.

"It's true!" he said delightedly to Metellus Scipio, who shared his roomy conveyance (Cornelia Metella, not wishing to have to fight off Pompey's amorous advances, had chosen to travel alone). "Scipio, they love me! They *love* me! Oh, it's true, what I've always said!"

"And what's that?" asked Metellus Scipio, yawning.

"That all I have to do to raise soldiers in Italia is to stamp my foot upon the ground."

"Uh," said Metellus Scipio, and fell asleep.

But Pompey didn't sleep. He pulled the curtains wide enough to be seen and reclined against a huge bank of pillows, smiling wanly and waving weakly for mile after mile. It was true, it was inarguably true! The people of Italia did love him. What was he afraid of Caesar for? Caesar didn't stand a chance, even if he was stupid enough to march on Rome. Not that he would. In his heart of hearts Pompey knew very well that such was not Caesar's technique. He would choose to fight in the Senate and the Forum. And, when the time came, in the courts. For it was necessary to bring him down. On that head, Pompey owned no ideological differences with the *boni;* he knew that Caesar's career in the field was far from over, and that, were he not prevented, he would end in outstripping Pompey so distantly that it would be Caesar the Great—and that the Magnus would not be self-endowed.

How did he know? Titus Labienus had begun to write to him. Humbly hoping that his patron, Gnaeus Pompeius Magnus, had long forgiven him for that deplorable slip from grace with Mucia Tertia. Explaining that Caesar had taken against him—jealousy, of course. Caesar couldn't tolerate a man who could operate alone with the dazzling success of a Titus Labienus. Thus the promised joint consulship with Caesar would not occur. For Caesar had told him as they crossed the Alps together into Italian Gaul that once the command in the Gauls was over, he would be dropping Labienus like a hot coal. But, said Labienus, marching on Rome was never an alternative in Caesar's priorities. And who would know, if Titus Labienus didn't? Not by word or look had Caesar ever indicated a wish to overthrow the State. Nor had his other legates ever referred to it, from Trebonius to Hirtius. No, what Caesar wanted to do was to have his second consulship and then embark upon a great war in the East against the Parthians. To avenge his dear dead friend Marcus Licinius Crassus.

Pompey had contemplated this missive toward the end of his self-inflicted isolation from all save Metellus Scipio, though he had not mentioned the matter to his father-in-law.

Verpa! Cunnus! Mentula! said Pompey to himself, grinning savagely. How dared Titus Labienus presume to think himself great enough these days to be forgiven? He wasn't forgiven. He would never be forgiven, the wife stealer! But, on the other hand, he might prove very useful. Afranius and Petreius were getting old and incompetent. Why not replace them with Titus Labienus? Who, like them, would never have the clout to rival Pompey the Great. Never be able to call himself Labienus the Great.

A campaign in the East against the Parthians . . . So that was where Caesar's ambitions lay! Clever, very clever. Caesar didn't want or need the headache of mastering Rome. He wanted to go into the history books as Rome's greatest-ever military man. So after the conquest of Gallia Comata—all brand-new territory—he would conquer the Parthians and add billions upon billions of *iugera* to Rome's provincial empire. How could Pompey measure up to that? All he'd done was to march over the same old Roman-owned or Roman-dominated ground, fight the traditional enemies, men like Mithridates and Tigranes. Caesar was a pioneer. He went where no Roman had gone before. And with Caesar in full command of those eleven—no, nine—fanatically devoted legions, there would be no defeat at Carrhae. Caesar would whip the Parthians. He'd walk to Serica, let alone India! He'd tread soil and see people even Alexander the Great had never dreamed existed. Bring back King Orodes to march in his triumphal parade. And Rome would worship him like a god.

Oh yes, Caesar had to go. Had to be stripped of his army and his provinces, had to be convicted so many times over in the courts that he would never be able to show his face in Italia again. Labienus, who knew him, who had fought with him for nine years, said he would never march on Rome. A judgement which was in complete agreement with Pompey's own. Therefore, he decided, buoyed up by those cheering crowds ecstatic at his recovery, he would not move to curb the *boni* in the persons of Cato and the Marcelli. Let them continue. In fact, why not help them out by spreading a few rumors to the plutocrats as well as to the Senate? Like: yes, Caesar is bringing his legions across the Alps into Italian Gaul; yes, Caesar is contemplating a march on Rome! Panic the whole city into opposing anything Caesar asked for. For when the last possible moment came, that lofty patrician aristocrat who could trace his lineage back to the goddess Venus would fold his tents and retreat with massive dignity into permanent exile.

In the meantime, thought Pompey, he would see Appius Claudius the Censor, and hint to him that it was perfectly safe to expel most of Caesar's adherents from the Senate. Appius Claudius would seize the chance eagerly—and go too far by trying to expel Curio, no doubt. Lucius Piso, the other censor, would veto that. Though probably not the smaller fry, knowing the indolent Lucius Piso.

Early in October came word from Labienus that Caesar had left Italian Gaul to journey with his usual fleetness all the way to the stronghold of Nemetocenna in the lands of the Belgic Atrebates, where Trebonius was quartered with the Fifth, Ninth, Tenth and Eleventh Legions. Trebonius had written urgently, said Labienus, to inform Caesar that the Belgae were contemplating another insurrection.

Excellent! was Pompey's verdict. While Caesar was a thousand miles from Rome, he himself would use his minions to flood Rome with all kinds of rumors—the wilder, the better. Keep the pot bubbling, boil it over! Thus the whisper reached Atticus and others that Caesar was bringing four legions—the Fifth, the Ninth, the Tenth and the Eleventh—across the Alps to Placentia on the Ides of October, where he intended to station them and intimidate the Senate into leaving his provinces alone when the matter came up for debate again on the Ides of November.

For, said Atticus in an urgent letter to Cicero, who had reached Ephesus on his journey home from Cilicia, all of Rome knew that Caesar would absolutely refuse to give up his army.

Panicking, Cicero fled across the Aegaean Sea to Athens, which he reached on the fatal Ides of October. And said in his letter to Atticus that it was preferable to be beaten on the field with Pompey than to be victorious with Caesar.

Laughing wryly, Atticus stared at Cicero's letter in amazement. What a way to put it! Was *that* what Cicero thought? Honestly? Did he genuinely think that were civil war to break out, Pompey and all loyal Romans stood no chance in the field against Caesar? An opinion, Atticus was sure, he had inherited from his brother, Quintus Cicero, who had served with Caesar through his most taxing years in Gaul of the Long-hairs. Well, if that was what Quintus Cicero thought, might it not be wise to say and do nothing to make Caesar think that Atticus was an enemy?

Thus it was that Atticus spent the next few days reforming his finances and indoctrinating his senior staff; he then left for Campania to see Pompey, back in residence in his Neapolitan villa. Rome still hummed with stories about those four veteran legions stationed in Placentia—except that everyone who knew anyone in Placentia kept getting letters which swore that there were no legions anywhere near Placentia.

But on the subject of Caesar, Pompey was very vague and would commit himself to no opinion. Sighing, Atticus abandoned the subject (silently vowing that he would proceed as common sense dictated and do nothing to irritate Caesar) and went instead to eulogizing Cicero's governance of Cilicia. In which he did not exaggerate; the couch general and stay-at-home fritterer had done very well indeed, from a fair, just and rational reorganization of Cilicia's finances to a profitable little war. Pompey agreed with all of it, his round, fleshy face bland—how would you react if I told you that Cicero thinks it preferable to be beaten on the field with you than to be victorious with Caesar? thought Atticus wickedly. Instead, he spoke aloud of Cicero's entitlement to a triumph for his victories in Cappadocia and the Amanus; Pompey said warmly that he deserved his triumph, and that he would be voting for it in the House.

That he did not attend the critical meeting of the Senate on the Ides of November was significant; Pompey did not expect to see the Senate win, and did not wish to be humiliated personally while Curio hammered away at his same old nail—whatever Caesar gave up, Pompey should give up at one and the same moment. In which Pompey was right. The Senate got nowhere; the impasse simply continued, with Mark Antony bellowing bullishly when Curio was not yapping doggedly.

The People proceeded about their daily routines without a huge interest in all this; long experience had taught them that when these internecine convulsions occurred, all the casualties and the heartaches remained the province of those at the top of the social tree. And most of them, besides, considered that Caesar would be better for Rome than the *boni*.

In the ranks of the knights, particularly those senior enough to belong to the Eighteen, sentiments were very different—and very mixed. They stood to lose the most in the event of civil war. Their businesses would crumble, debts would become impossible to collect, loans would cease to materialize, and overseas investments would become unmanageable. The worst aspect was the uncertainty: who was right, who was speaking the truth? Were there really four legions in Italian Gaul? And if there really were, why couldn't they be located? And why, if there were not four legions there, was this fact not made loudly public? Did the likes of Cato and the Marcelli care about anything other than their determination to teach Caesar a lesson? And what was the lesson all about anyway? What exactly had Caesar done that no one else had done? What would happen to Rome if Caesar was let stand for the consulship *in absentia* and extricated himself from the treason prosecutions the *boni* were so determined to levy against him? The answer to that, all men could see, save the *boni* themselves: nothing! Rome would go on in the same old way. Whereas civil war was the ultimate catastrophe. And this civil war looked as if it would be waged over a principle. Was anything more alien and less important to a businessman than a *principle*? Go to war over one? Insanity! So the knights began to exert pressure on susceptible senators to be nicer to Caesar.

Unfortunately the hardline *boni* were disinclined to listen to this plutocratic lobbying, even if the rest of the Senate was; it meant nothing to Cato or the Marcelli compared to the staggering loss of prestige and influence they would suffer in all eyes if Caesar was to win his struggle to be treated in the same manner as Pompey. And what of Pompey, still dallying in Campania? Where did he truly stand? Evidence pointed to an alliance with the *boni,* but there were still many who believed that Pompey could be prised free of them could enough words be spoken in his reluctant ear.

At the end of November the new governor of Cilicia, Publius Sestius, departed from Rome with his senior legate, Brutus. Which left a shocking vacuum in the life of his first cousin, Porcia, though not in the life of his wife, Claudia, whom he scarcely ever saw. Servilia was much thicker with her son-in-law, Gaius Cassius, than ever she had been with her son; Cassius appealed to her love of warriors, of doers, of men who would make a military mark. All of which meant that she continued discreetly to pursue her liaison with Lucius Pontius Aquila.

"I'm sure I'll see Bibulus as I go east," said Brutus to Porcia when he went to take his leave of her. "He's in Ephesus, and I gather intends to remain there until he sees what happens in Rome—Caesar, I mean."

Though she knew it was not a right act to weep, Porcia wept bitterly. "Oh, Brutus, how will I survive without you to talk to? No one else is *kind* to me! Whenever I see Aunt Servilia, she nags about how I dress and how I look, and whenever I see *tata* he's present only in the flesh—his mind is on Caesar, Caesar, Caesar. Aunt Porcia never has time, she's too involved with her children and Lucius Domitius. Whereas you've been so kind, so tender. Oh, I will miss you!"

"But Marcia is back with your father, Porcia. Surely that must make a difference. She's not an unkind person."

"I know, I know!" cried Porcia, snuffling with nauseating clarity despite making play with Brutus's handkerchief. "But she belongs to *tata* in every way, just as she did when they were married the first time. I don't exist for her. No one does for Marcia except *tata*!" She sobbed and moaned. "Brutus, I want to matter to someone's heart! And I don't! I don't!"

"There's Lucius," he said, throat constricted. Didn't he know how she felt, he who had never mattered to anyone's heart either? Freaks and uglies were despised, even by those who ought to have loved in spite of every drawback, every deficiency.

"Lucius is growing up, he's moving away from me," she said, mopping her eyes. "I understand, Brutus, and I don't disapprove. It's right and proper that his attitude changes. It's months now since he preferred my company to my father's. Politics matter more than childish games."

"Well, Bibulus will be home soon."

"Will he? Will he, Brutus? Then why do I think I'll never see Bibulus again? I have a feeling about it!"

A feeling which Brutus found himself echoing, he had no idea why. Except that Rome was suddenly an intolerable place, because something horrible was going to happen. People were thinking more of their own petty concerns than they were of Rome herself. And that went for Cato too. Bringing Caesar down was *everything*.

So he picked up her hand, kissed it, and left for Cilicia.

On the Kalends of December, Gaius Scribonius Curio summoned the Senate into session, with Gaius Marcellus Major holding the *fasces;* a disadvantage, Curio knew. As Pompey was in his villa on the Campus Martius, the meeting was held in his curia, a site Curio for one found unwelcome. I hope Caesar wins his battle, he thought as the House came to order, because at least Caesar will be willing to rebuild our own Curia Hostilia.

"I will be brief," he said to the assembled senators, "for I am just as tired of this fruitless, idiotic impasse as you are. While ever I am in office, I will continue to exercise my veto every time this body tries to move that things be done to Gaius Julius Caesar without also being done to Gnaeus Pompeius Magnus. Therefore I am going to submit a formal motion to this House, and I will insist upon a division. If Gaius Marcellus tries to block me, I will deal with him in the traditional manner of a tribune of the plebs obstructed in the exercise of his duties—I will have him thrown off the end of the Tarpeian Rock. And I mean it! I mean every word of it! If I have to summon half the Plebs—who are congregated outside in the peristyle, Conscript Fathers!—to assist me, I will! So be warned, junior consul. I will see a division of this House upon my motion."

Lips thinned, Marcellus Major sat on his ivory curule chair and said nothing; not only did Curio mean it, Curio legally could do it. The division would have to go ahead.

"My motion," said Curio, "is this: that Gaius Julius Caesar and Gnaeus Pompeius Magnus give up imperium, provinces and armies at one and the same moment. All in favor of it, please move to the right of the floor. All those opposed, please move to the left."

The result was overwhelming. Three hundred and seventy of the senators stood to the right. Twenty-two stood to the left. Among the twenty-two were Pompey himself, Metellus Scipio, the three Marcelli, the consul-elect Lentulus Crus (a surprise), Ahenobarbus, Cato, Marcus Favonius, Varro, Pontius Aquila (another surprise—Servilia's lover was not known to be her lover) and Gaius Cassius.

"We have a decree, junior consul," said Curio jubilantly. "Implement it!"

Gaius Marcellus Major rose to his feet and gestured to his lictors. "The meeting is dismissed," he said curtly, and walked out of the chamber.

A good tactic, for it all happened too quickly for Curio to summon the waiting Plebs inside. The decree was a fact, but it was not implemented.

Nor was it ever to be implemented. While Curio was speaking to an ecstatic crowd in the Forum, Gaius Marcellus Major called the Senate into session in the temple of Saturn, in close proximity to where Curio stood on the rostra, and a place from which the discomfited Pompey was debarred. For whatever happened from this day forward, Pompey would not be seen to be personally involved.

Marcellus Major held a scroll in his hand. "I have here a communication from the duumvirs of Placentia, Conscript Fathers," he announced in ringing tones, "which informs the Senate and People of Rome that Gaius Julius Caesar has just arrived in Placentia, and has four of his legions with him. He must be stopped! He is about to march on Rome, the duumvirs have heard him say it! He will not give up his army, and he intends to use that army to conquer Rome! At this very moment he is preparing those four veteran legions to invade Italia!"

The House erupted into a furor: stools overturned as men jumped to their feet, some on the back benches fled from the temple incontinently, some like Mark Antony started roaring that it was all a lie, two very aged senators fainted, and Cato began to shout that Caesar must be stopped, must be stopped, must be stopped!

Into which chaos Curio arrived, chest heaving from the effort of racing across the lower Forum and up so many steps.

"It's a lie!" he yelled. "Senators, senators, stop to think! Caesar is in Further Gaul, not in Placentia, and there are no legions in Placentia! Even the Thirteenth is not in Italian Gaul—it's in Illyricum at Tergeste!" He turned on Marcellus Major viciously. "You conscienceless, outrageous liar, Gaius Marcellus! You scum on Rome's pond, you shit in Rome's sewers! Liar, liar, *liar*!"

"House dismissed!" Marcellus Major screamed, pushed Curio aside so hard that he staggered, and left the temple of Saturn.

"Lies!" Curio went on shouting to those who remained. "The junior consul lied to save Pompeius's skin! Pompeius doesn't want to lose his provinces or his army! Pompeius, Pompeius, Pompeius! Open your eyes! Open your minds! Marcellus lied! He lied to protect Pompeius! Caesar is not in Placentia! There are not four legions in Placentia! Lies, lies, lies!"

But no one listened. Horrified and terrified, the Senate of Rome disintegrated.

"Oh, Antonius!" wept Curio when they occupied the temple of Saturn alone. "I never thought Marcellus would go so far—it never occurred to me that he'd lie! He's tainted their cause beyond redemption! Whatever happens to Rome now rests upon a lie!"

"Well, Curio, you know where to look, don't you?" snarled Antony. "It's that turd Pompeius, it's always that turd Pompeius! Marcellus is a liar, but Pompeius is a sneak. He won't say so, but he will never give up his precious position as First Man in Rome."

"Oh, where *is* Caesar?" Curio wailed. "The Gods forbid he's still in Nemetocenna!"

"If you hadn't left home so early this morning to trumpet in the Forum, Curio, you would have found his letter," Antony said. "We've both got one. And he's not in Nemetocenna. He was there just long enough to shift Trebonius and his four legions to the Mosa between the Treveri and the Remi, then he left to see Fabius. Who is now in Bibracte with the other four. Caesar is in Ravenna."

Curio gaped. "*Ravenna?* He couldn't be!"

"Huh!" grunted Antony. "He travels like the wind, and he didn't slow himself down with any legions. They're all still where they ought to be, across the Alps. But he's in Ravenna."

"What are we going to do? What can we tell him?"

"The truth," said Antony calmly. "We're just his lackeys, Curio, and never forget it. He's the one will make the decisions."

Gaius Claudius Marcellus Major had made a decision. As soon as he dismissed the Senate he walked out to Pompey's villa on the Campus Martius, accompanied by Cato, Ahenobarbus, Metellus Scipio and the two consuls-elect: his cousin Gaius Marcellus Minor and Lentulus Crus. About halfway there the servant Marcellus Major had sent running back to his house on the Palatine returned bearing Marcellus Major's own sword. Like most swords owned by noblemen, it was the usual two-foot-long, wickedly-sharp-on-both-sides Roman *gladius;* where it differed from the weapons carried by ordinary soldiers was in its scabbard, made of silver preciously wrought, and in its handle, made of ivory carved as a Roman Eagle.

Pompey met them at the door himself and admitted them into his study, where a servant poured wine-and-water for everyone save Cato, who rejected the water with loathing. Pompey waited with fretful impatience for the man to distribute these refreshments and go; in fact, he would not have offered did this deputation not look as if its members badly needed a drink.

"Well?" he demanded. "What happened?"

In answer, Marcellus Major silently extended his sheathed sword to Pompey. Startled, Pompey took it in a reflex action and stared at it as if he had never seen a sword before.

He wet his lips. "What does this mean?" he asked fearfully.

"Gnaeus Pompeius Magnus," said Marcellus Major very solemnly,

"I hereby authorize you on behalf of the Senate and People of Rome to defend the State against Gaius Julius Caesar. In the name of the Senate and People of Rome, I formally confer on you possession and use of the two legions, the Sixth and Fifteenth, sent by Caesar to Capua, and further commission you to commence recruiting more legions until you can bring your own army from the Spains. There is going to be civil war."

The brilliant blue eyes had widened; Pompey stared down at the sword again, licked his lips again. "There is going to be civil war," he said slowly. "I didn't think it would come to that. I—really—didn't. . . ." He tensed. "Where's Caesar? How many legions does he have in Italian Gaul? How far has he marched?"

"He has one legion, and he hasn't marched," said Cato.

"He hasn't marched? He—which legion?"

"The Thirteenth. It's in Tergeste," Cato answered.

"Then—then—what happened? Why are you here? Caesar won't march with one legion!"

"So we think," said Cato. "That's why we're here. To deflect him from the ultimate treason, a march on Rome. Our junior consul will inform Caesar that steps have been taken, and the whole business will come to nothing. We're getting in first."

"Oh, I see," said Pompey, handing the sword back to Marcellus Major. "Thank you, I appreciate the significance of the gesture, but I have my own sword and it is always ready to draw in defense of my country. I'll gladly take command of the two legions in Capua, but is it really necessary to start recruiting?"

"Definitely," said Marcellus Major firmly. "Caesar has to be made to see that we are in deadly earnest."

Pompey swallowed. "And the Senate?" he asked.

"The Senate," said Ahenobarbus, "will do as it's told."

"But it authorized this visit, of course."

Marcellus Major lied again. "Of course," he said.

It was the second day of December.

On the third day of December, Curio learned what had happened at Pompey's villa and went back to the House in righteous anger. Ably assisted by Antony, he accused Marcellus Major of treason and appealed to the Conscript Fathers to back him—to acknowledge that Caesar had done no wrong—to admit that there were no legions save the Thirteenth in Italian Gaul—and to see that the entire crisis had been maliciously manufactured by, at most, seven *boni* and Pompey.

But a lot stayed away, and those who came seemed so dazed and confused that they were incapable of any kind of response, let alone sensible action. Curio and Antony got nowhere. Marcellus Major continued to obstruct everything beyond Pompey's entitlement to defend the State. Which he made no attempt to legitimize.

On the sixth day of December, while Curio battled on in the Senate, Aulus Hirtius arrived in Rome, commissioned by Caesar to see what could be retrieved. But when Curio and Antony told him of the giving of the sword to Pompey, and of Pompey's accepting it, he despaired. Balbus had set up a meeting for him with Pompey on the following morning, but Hirtius didn't go. What was the use, he asked himself, if Pompey had accepted the sword? Better by far to hurry back to Ravenna and inform Caesar of events in person; all he had to go on was letters.

Pompey didn't wait overlong for Hirtius on the morning of the seventh day of December; well before noon he was on his way to inspect the Sixth and the Fifteenth in Capua.

The last day of Curio's memorable tribunate of the plebs was the ninth one of December. Exhausted, he spoke yet again in the House to no avail, then left that evening for Caesar in Ravenna. The baton had passed to Mark Antony, universally despised as a slug.

Cicero had arrived in Brundisium toward the end of November, to find himself met by Terentia; her advent did not astonish him, as she needed to make up a great deal of lost ground. For, with her active connivance, Tullia had married Dolabella. A match Cicero had opposed strongly, wanting his daughter to go to Tiberius Claudius Nero, a very haughty young patrician senator of limited intelligence and no charm.

The great advocate's displeasure was increased by his anxiety for his beloved secretary, Tiro, who had fallen ill in Patrae and had to be left behind. Then it was further exacerbated when he learned that Cato had moved a triumph for Bibulus, after which he voted against awarding a triumph to Cicero.

"How dare Cato!" fumed Cicero to his wife. "Bibulus never even left his house in Antioch, whereas I fought *battles*!"

"Yes, dear," said Terentia automatically, zeroing in on her own goals. "But will you consent to meet Dolabella? Once you do meet him you'll understand completely why I didn't oppose the union at all." Her ugly face lit up. "He's delightful, Marcus, truly delightful! Witty, intelligent—and so devoted to Tullia."

"I forbade it!" cried Cicero. "I forbade it, Terentia! You had absolutely no right to let it happen!"

"Listen, husband," hissed that redoubtable lady, thrusting her beak into Cicero's face, "Tullia is twenty-seven years old! She doesn't need your permission to marry!"

"But I'm the one who has to find the dowry, so I'm the one who should pick her husband!" roared Cicero, emboldened as the result of spending many months far away from Terentia, during which he had proven himself an admirable governor with a great deal of authority. Authority should extend to the domestic sphere.

She blinked at being defied, but she didn't back down. "Too late!"

she roared, even more loudly. "Tullia married Dolabella, and you'll find her dowry or I'll personally castrate you!"

Thus it was that Cicero journeyed up the Italian peninsula from Brundisium accompanied by a shrew of a wife who was not about to accord him the inalienable rights of the *paterfamilias*. He reconciled himself to having to meet the odious Dolabella. Which he did in Beneventum, discovering to his consternation that he was no more proof against Dolabella's charms than Terentia. To cap matters, Tullia was pregnant, a fate which had not been her lot with either of her two previous husbands.

Dolabella also informed his father-in-law about the hideous events occurring in Rome, clapped Cicero on the back and galloped off back to Rome to be, as he put it, a part of the fray.

"I'm for Caesar, you know!" he yelled from the safety of his horse. "Good man, Caesar!"

No more litters. Cicero hired a carriage in Beneventum and continued into western Campania at an accelerated pace.

He found Pompey in residence at Pompeii, where Cicero had a snug little villa himself, and sought information from one of the few men he thought might actually know what really was going on.

"I received two letters yesterday in Trebula," he said to Pompey, frowning in puzzlement. "One was from Balbus, and one from none other than Caesar himself. So sweet and friendly . . . Anything either of them could do for me, it would be an honor to witness my well-deserved triumph, did I need a trifling loan? What's the man doing that for, if he's marching on Rome? Why is he courting me? He knows very well I've never been a partisan."

"Well, actually," said Pompey uneasily, "Gaius Marcellus rather took the bit between his teeth. Did things he wasn't officially authorized to do. Though I didn't know it at the time, Cicero, I swear I didn't. You've heard he gave me a sword, and that I took it?"

"Yes, Dolabella told me."

"Trouble is, I assumed the Senate had sent him with the sword. But the Senate hadn't. So here I am betwixt Scylla and Charybdis, more or less committed to defending the State, taking over command of two legions which have fought for Caesar for years, and starting to recruit all over Campania, Samnium, Lucania and Apulia. But it isn't really legal, Cicero. The Senate didn't commission me, nor is there a Senatus Consultum Ultimum in effect. Yet I know civil war is upon us."

Cicero's heart sank. "Are you sure, Gnaeus Pompeius? Are you really sure? Have you consulted anyone other than rabid boars like Cato and the Marcelli? Have you talked to Atticus, any of the other important knights? Have you sat in the Senate?"

"How can I sit in the Senate when I'm recruiting troops?" snarled Pompey. "And I did see Atticus a few days ago. Well, quite a few days ago, actually, though it seems like yesterday."

"Magnus, are you *sure* civil war can't be averted?"

"Absolutely," said Pompey very positively. "There will be civil war, it's certain. That's why I'm glad to be out of Rome for a while. Easier to think things through. Because we can't let Italia suffer yet again, Cicero. This war against Caesar cannot be let happen on Italian soil. It must be fought abroad. Greece, I think, or Macedonia. East of Italia, anyway. The whole of the East is in my clientele; I can drum up support everywhere from Actium to Antioch. And I can bring my Spanish legions directly from Spain without landing them on Italian soil. Caesar has nine legions left, plus about twenty-two cohorts of recruits freshly levied from across the Padus. I have seven legions in the Spains, two legions in Capua, and however many cohorts I can recruit now. There are two legions in Macedonia, three in Syria, one in Cilicia and one in Asia Province. I can also demand troops from Deiotarus of Galatia and Ariobarzanes of Cappadocia. If necessary, I'll also demand an army from Egypt and bring the African legion over too. Whichever way you look at it, I ought to have upward of sixteen Roman legions, ten thousand foreign auxiliaries, and—oh, six or seven thousand horse."

Cicero sat and stared at him, heart sinking. "Magnus, you can't remove legions from Syria with the Parthians threatening!"

"My sources say there is no threat, Cicero. Orodes is having trouble at home. He shouldn't have executed the Surenas and then Pacorus. Pacorus was his own son."

"But—but oughtn't you be trying to conciliate with Caesar first? I know from Balbus's letter that he's working desperately to avert a confrontation."

"Pah!" spat Pompey, sneering. "You know nothing about it, Cicero! Balbus went to great lengths to make sure I didn't leave for Campania at dawn on the Nones, assured me that Caesar had sent Aulus Hirtius especially to see me. So I wait, and I wait, and then I discover that Hirtius turned round and went back to Caesar in Ravenna without so much as trying to keep his appointment with me! That's how much Caesar wants peace, Cicero! It's all a big front, this Balbus-instigated lobbying! I tell you straight that Caesar is bent on civil war. Nothing will deflect him. And I have made up my mind. I will not fight a civil war on Italian soil; I will fight him in Greece or Macedonia."

But, thought Cicero, scribbling a letter to Atticus in Rome, it isn't Caesar bent on civil war—or at least, not Caesar alone. Magnus is absolutely set on it, and thinks that all will be forgiven and forgotten if he makes sure Italia doesn't have to suffer the civil war on her own soil. He's found his way out.

The day was the tenth one of December when Cicero learned how Pompey felt about civil war; on the same day in Rome, Mark Antony took office as a tribune of the plebs. And proceeded to demonstrate that he was as able a speaker as his grandfather the Orator, not to mention quick-witted. He spoke tellingly of the offering of the sword and the illegality of the junior consul's actions in such a stentorian voice that even Cato understood he could not be shouted down or drowned out.

"Furthermore," he thundered, "I am authorized by Gaius Julius Caesar to say that Gaius Caesar will be happy to give up the two provinces of Gaul on the far side of the Alps together with six of his legions, if this House permits him to keep Italian Gaul, Illyricum and two legions."

"That's only eight legions, Marcus Antonius," said Marcellus Major. "What happened to the other legion and those twenty-two cohorts of recruits?"

"The ninth legion, which for the moment we will call the Fourteenth, will vanish, Gaius Marcellus. Caesar doesn't hand over an under-strength army, and at the moment all his legions are well under strength. One legion and the twenty-two cohorts of new men will be incorporated into the other eight legions."

A logical answer, but an answer to an irrelevant question. Gaius Marcellus Major and the two consuls-elect had no intention of putting Antony's proposal to a vote. The House was, besides, barely up to quorum number, so many senators were absent; some had already left Rome for Campania, others were desperately trying to squirrel away assets or collect enough cash to be comfortable in an exile long enough to cover the period of the civil war. Which now seemed to be taken for granted, though it was also becoming generally known that there were no extra legions in Italian Gaul, and that Caesar sat quietly in Ravenna while the Thirteenth Legion enjoyed a furlough on the nearest beaches.

Antony, Quintus Cassius, the consortium of bankers and all of Caesar's most important adherents inside Rome fought valiantly to keep Caesar's options open, constantly assuring everyone from the Senate to the plutocrats that Caesar would be happy to hand over six of his legions and both the further Gauls provided he could keep Italian Gaul, Illyricum and two legions. But on the day following Curio's arrival in Ravenna, Antony and Balbus both received curt letters from Caesar which said that he could no longer entirely ignore the possibility that he would need his army to protect his person and his *dignitas* from the *boni* and Pompey the Great. He had therefore, he said, sent secretly to Fabius in Bibracte to ship him two of the four legions there, and sent with equal secrecy to Trebonius on the Mosa to ship three of his four legions at once to Narbo, where they were to go under the command of Lucius Caesar and prevent Pompey's Spanish legions from marching toward Italia.

"He's ready," said Antony to Balbus, not without satisfaction.

Little Balbus was less plump these days, so great had been the strain;

he eyed Antony apprehensively with those big, brown, mournful eyes, and pursed his full lips together. "Surely we will prevail, Marcus Antonius," he said. "We *must* prevail!"

"With the Marcelli in the saddle and Cato squawking from the front benches, Balbus, we don't stand a chance. The Senate—at least that part of it which can still pluck up the courage to attend meetings—will only go on saying that Caesar is Rome's servant, not Rome's master."

"In which case, what does that make Pompeius?"

"Clearly Rome's master," said Antony. "But who runs whom, do you think? Pompeius or the *boni*?"

"Each is sure he runs the other, Marcus Antonius."

December continued to run away with frightening rapidity—attendance in the Senate dwindled even more; quite a number of houses on the Palatine and the Carinae were shut up fast, their knockers removed from their doors; and many of Rome's biggest companies, brokerages, banks and contractors were using the bitter experience accumulated during other civil wars to shore up their fortifications until they were capable of resisting whatever was to come. For it was coming. Pompey and the *boni* would not permit that it did not. Nor would Caesar bend until he touched the ground.

On the twenty-first of December, Mark Antony gave a brilliant speech in the House. It was superbly structured and rhetorically thrilling, and detailed with scrupulous chronology the entire sum of Pompey's transgressions against the *mos maiorum* from the time, aged twenty-two, when he had illegally enlisted his father's veterans and marched with three legions to assist Sulla in that civil war; it ended with the consulship without a colleague, and appended an epilogue concerning the acceptance of illegally tendered swords. The peroration was devoted to a mercilessly witty analysis of the characters of the twenty-two wolves who had succeeded in cowing the three hundred and seventy senatorial sheep.

Pompey shared his copy of the speech with Cicero; on the twenty-fifth day of December they encountered each other in Formiae, where both had villas. But it was to Cicero's villa that they repaired, therein to spend many hours talking.

"I am obdurate," said Pompey after Cicero had exhausted himself finding reasons why conciliation with Caesar was still possible. "There can be absolutely no concessions made to Caesar. The man does *not* want a peaceful settlement, I don't care what Balbus, Oppius and the rest say! I don't even care what Atticus says!"

"I wish Atticus were here," said Cicero, blinking wearily.

"Then why isn't he? Am I not good enough company?"

"He has a quartan ague, Magnus."

"Oh."

Though his throat hurt and that wretched inflammation of the eyes threatened to return, Cicero resolved to plod on. Hadn't old Scaurus once single-handedly turned around the entire Senate united against him? And Scaurus wasn't the greatest orator in the annals of Rome! That honor belonged to Marcus Tullius Cicero. The trouble was, reflected the greatest orator of all time, that ever since his illness at Neapolis, Pompey had grown overweeningly confident. No, he hadn't been there to witness it, but everyone had told him about it, first in letters, then in person. Besides, he could see for himself some of the same smugness Pompey used to own in abundance when he was seventeen years old, had still owned when he marched to help Sulla conquer. Spain and Quintus Sertorius had beaten it out of him, even though he ended in winning that tortuous war. Nor had it ever re-emerged until now. Perhaps, thought Cicero, in this cataclysmic confrontation with another military master, Caesar, he thought to relive that youth, to entrench himself for all time as the greatest man Rome produced. Only—was he? No, he surely couldn't lose (and had decided that for himself, else he wouldn't be so determined on civil war) because he was busy making sure he outnumbered Caesar at least two to one. And would forever after be hailed as the savior of his country because he refused to fight on his country's soil. That was self-evident too.

"Magnus, what's the harm in making a *tiny* concession to him? What if he were to agree to keep one legion and Illyricum?"

"No concessions," said Pompey firmly.

"But surely somewhere along the way we've all lost the plot? Didn't this start over refusing Caesar the right to stand for the consulship *in absentia*? So that he could keep his imperium and avoid being tried for treason? Wouldn't it be more sensible to let him do that? Take everything from him except Illyricum—take all his legions! Just let him keep his imperium intact and stand for the consulship *in absentia*!"

"No concessions!" snapped Pompey.

"In one way Caesar's agents are right, Magnus. You've had many concessions greater than that. Why not Caesar?"

"Because, you fool, even if Caesar were reduced to a *privatus*—no provinces, no army, no imperium, no anything!—he'd still have designs on the State! He'd still overthrow it!"

Ignoring the reference to foolishness, Cicero tried again. And again. But always the answer was the same. Caesar would never willingly give up his imperium, he would elect to keep his army and his provinces. There would be civil war.

Toward the end of the day they abandoned the major issue and concentrated instead on the draft of Mark Antony's speech.

"A distorted tissue of half truths" was Pompey's final verdict. He sniffed, flicked the paper contemptuously. "What do you think Caesar will do if he succeeds in overthrowing the State, when a tawdry, penniless minion like Antonius dares to say such things?"

With the result that a profoundly glad Cicero saw his guest off the premises, then almost resolved to get drunk. What stopped him was a horrible thought: Jupiter, he owed Caesar millions! Millions which would now have to be found and repaid. For it was the height of bad form to owe money to a political opponent.

THE RUBICON

from JANUARY 1 until
APRIL 5 of 49 B.C.

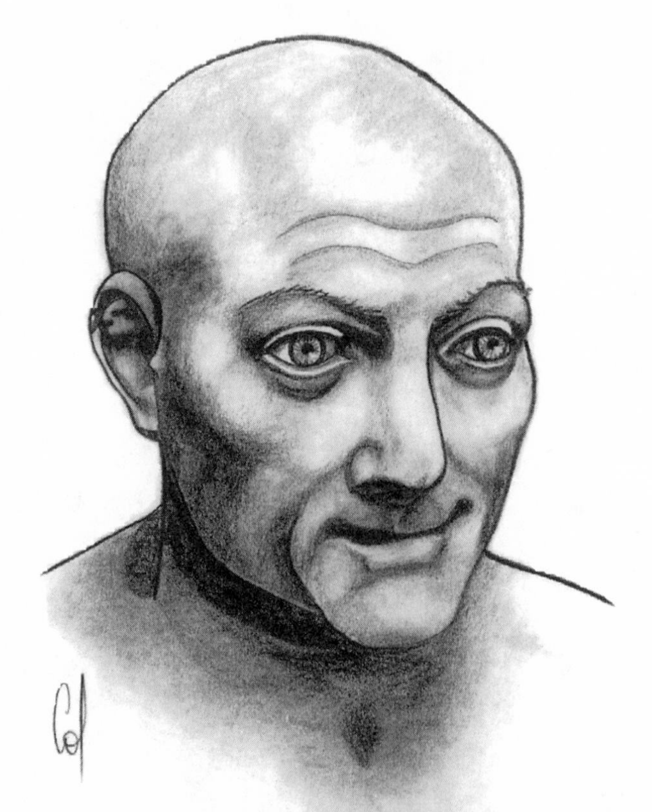

LUCIUS DOMITIUS AHENOBARBUS

ROME

At dawn on the first day of the new year, Gaius Scribonius Curio arrived at his house on the Palatine, where he was greeted ecstatically by his wife.

"Enough, woman!" he said, hugging the breath out of her, so glad was he to see her. "Where's my son?"

"You're just in time to see me give him his first meal of the day," Fulvia said, took him by the hand and led him to the nursery, where she lifted the snoozing baby Curio from his cradle and held him up proudly. "Isn't he beautiful? Oh, I always wanted to have a red-haired baby! He's your image, and won't he be *naughty*? Urchins always are."

"I haven't seen any urchin in him. He's absolutely placid."

"That's because his world is ordered and his mother transmits no anxieties to him." Fulvia nodded dismissal to the nursery maid and slipped her robe off her shoulders and arms.

For a moment she stood displaying those engorged breasts, milk beading their nipples: to Curio, the most wonderful sight he had ever seen—and all because of him. His loins ached with want of her, but he moved to a chair as she sat down in another and held the baby, still half asleep, to one breast. The reflex initiated, baby Curio began to suck with long, audible gulps, his tiny hands curled contentedly against his mother's brown skin.

"I wouldn't care," he said in a gruff voice, "if I were to die tomorrow, Fulvia, having known this. All those years of Clodius, and I never realized what a true mother you are. No wet nurses, just you. How efficient you are. How much motherhood is a part of living for you, neither a nuisance nor a universe."

She looked surprised. "Babies are lovely, Curio. They're the ultimate expression of what exists between a husband and wife. They need little in one way, lots in another. It gives me pleasure to do the natural things with them and for them. When they drink my milk, I'm exalted. It's *my* milk, Curio! I *make* it!" She grinned wickedly. "However, I'm perfectly happy to let the nursery maid change the diapers and let the laundry maid wash them."

"Proper," he said, leaning back to watch.

"He's four months old today," she said.

"Yes, and I've missed three *nundinae* of seeing him grow."

"How was Ravenna?"

He shrugged, grimaced.

"Ought I to have asked, how is Caesar?"

"I don't honestly know, Fulvia."

"Haven't you talked with him?"

"Hours every day for three *nundinae*."

"And yet you don't know."

"He keeps his counsel while he discusses every aspect of the situation lucidly and dispassionately," said Curio, frowning and leaning forward to caress the undeniably red fuzz on his son's working scalp. "If one wanted to hear a master Greek logician, the man would be a disappointment after Caesar. Everything is weighed and defined."

"So?"

"So one comes away understanding everything except the single aspect one wants most to understand."

"Which is?"

"What he intends to do."

"*Will* he march on Rome?"

"I wish I could say yes, I wish I could say no, *meum mel*. But I can't. I have no idea."

"They don't think he will, you know. The *boni* and Pompeius."

"Fulvia!" Curio exclaimed, sitting up straight. "Pompeius can't possibly be that naive, even if Cato is."

"I'm right," she said, detaching baby Curio from her nipple, sitting him up on her lap to face her and bending him gently forward until he produced a loud eructation. When she picked him up again, she transferred him to her other breast. This done, she resumed speaking as if there had been no pause. "They remind me of certain small animals—the kind which own no real aggression, but make a mock show of it because they've learned that such mock shows work. Until the elephant comes along and treads on them because he simply doesn't see them." She sighed. "The strain in Rome is enormous, husband. Everyone is petrified. Yet the *boni* keep on behaving like those mock-aggressive little animals. They posture and prate in the Forum, they send the Senate and the Eighteen into absolute paroxysms of fear. While Pompeius says all sorts of weighty and gloomy things about civil war being inevitable to mice like poor old Cicero. But he doesn't believe what he says, Curio. He *knows* that Caesar has only one legion this side of the Alps, and he has had no evidence that more are coming. He knows that were more to come, they'd be in Italian Gaul by now. The *boni* know those things too. Don't you see? The louder the fuss they make and the more upsetting it is, the greater their victory will appear when Caesar gives in. They want to cover themselves in glory."

"What if Caesar doesn't give in?"

"They'll be stepped on." She looked at Curio keenly. "You must have some sort of instinct about what will happen, Gaius. What does your instinct say?"

"That Caesar is still trying to solve his dilemma legally."

"Caesar doesn't dither."

"I am aware of that."

"Therefore it's all sorted out in his mind already."

"Yes, in that I think you're right, wife."

"Are you here for a purpose, or are you home for good?"

"I've been entrusted with a letter from Caesar to the Senate. He wants it read today at the inaugural meeting of the new consuls."

"Who's to read it out?"

"Antonius. I'm a *privatus* these days; they wouldn't listen."

"Can you stay with me for a few days at least?"

"I hope I never have to leave again, Fulvia."

Shortly thereafter Curio departed for the temple of Jupiter Optimus Maximus on the Capitol, wherein the New Year's Day meeting of the Senate was always held. When he returned several hours later, he brought Mark Antony with him.

The preparations for dinner took some moments; prayers had to be said, an offering made to the Lares and Penates, togas doffed and folded, shoes removed, feet washed and dried. During all of which Fulvia held her peace, then usurped the *lectus imus* for herself—she was one of those scandalously forward women who insisted on reclining to eat.

"Tell me everything," she said as soon as the first course was laid out and the servants had retired.

Antony ate, Curio talked.

"Our wolfing friend here read Caesar's letter out so loudly that nothing could overcome his voice," said Curio, grinning.

"What did Caesar have to say?"

"He proposed that either he should be allowed to keep his provinces and his army, or else that all other holders of imperium should step down at one and the same moment he did."

"Ah!" Fulvia exclaimed, satisfied. "He'll march."

"What makes you think that?" asked her husband.

"He made an absolutely absurd, unacceptable request."

"Well, I know that, but . . ."

"She's right," mumbled Antony, hand and mouth full of eggs. "He'll march."

"Go on, what happened next?"

"Lentulus Crus was in the chair. He refused to throw Caesar's proposal open to debate. Instead, he filibustered on the general state of the nation."

"But Marcellus Minor is the senior consul; he has the *fasces* for January! Why wasn't he in the chair?"

"Went home after the religious ceremonies," mumbled Antony. "Headache or something."

"If you're going to speak, Marcus Antonius, take your snout out of the trough!" said Fulvia sharply.

Startled, Antony swallowed and achieved a penitent smile. "Sorry," he said.

"She's a strict mother," said Curio, eyes adoring her.

"What happened next?" asked the strict mother.

"Metellus Scipio launched into a speech," said Curio, and sighed. "Ye Gods, he's boring! Luckily he was too eager to get to his peroration to waffle on interminably. He put a motion to the House. The Law of the Ten Tribunes was invalid, he said, and that meant Caesar had no right whatsoever to his provinces or his army. He would have to appear inside Rome as a *privatus* to contest the next consular elections. Scipio then moved that Caesar be ordered to dismiss his army by a date to be fixed, or else be declared a public enemy."

"Nasty," said Fulvia.

"Oh, very. But the House was all on his side. Hardly anyone voted against his motion."

"It didn't pass, surely!"

Antony gulped hastily, then said with commendable clarity, "Quintus Cassius and I vetoed it."

"Oh, well done!"

Pompey, however, didn't consider the veto well done at all. When the debate resumed in the House on the second day of January and resulted in another tribunician veto, he lost his temper. The strain was telling on him more than on anyone else in that whole anguished, terrified city; Pompey had the most to lose.

"We're getting nowhere!" he snarled to Metellus Scipio. "I want to see this business finished! It's ridiculous! Day after day, month after month—if we're not careful, the anniversary of the Kalends of March last year will roll around and we'll still have come no closer to putting Caesar in his place! I have the feeling that Caesar is running rings around me, and I don't like that feeling one little bit! It's time the comedy was ended! It's time the Senate acted once and for all! If they can't secure a law in the Popular Assembly to strip Caesar of everything, then they'll have to pass the Senatus Consultum Ultimum and leave the matter to me!"

He clapped three times, the signal for his steward.

"I want a message sent immediately to every senator in Rome," he told his steward curtly. "They are to report to me here two hours from now."

Metellus Scipio looked worried. "Pompeius, is that wise?" he ventured. "I mean, *summon* censors and consulars?"

"Yes, *summon*! I'm fed up, Scipio! I want this business with Caesar settled!"

Like most men of action, Pompey found it extremely difficult to coexist with indecision. And, like most men of action, Pompey wanted to be in absolute command. Not pushed and pulled by a parcel of incompetent, shilly-shallying senators who he knew were not his equals in anything. The situation was totally exasperating!

Why hadn't Caesar given in? And, since he hadn't given in, why was he still sitting in Ravenna with only one legion? Why wasn't he *doing* something? No, clearly he didn't intend to march on Rome—but if he didn't, what did he think he *was* going to do? Give in, Caesar! Give up, give way! But he didn't. He wouldn't. What tricks did he have up his sleeve? How could he extricate himself from this predicament if he didn't intend to give in, nor intend to march? What was going on in his mind? Did he think to prolong this senatorial impasse until the Nones of Quinctilis and the consular elections? But he would never get permission to stand *in absentia,* even if he managed to hang onto his imperium. Was it in his mind to send a few thousand of his loyalest soldiers to Rome on an innocent furlough at the time of the elections? He'd done that already, to secure the consulship for Pompeius and Crassus six years ago. But nothing got round the *in absentia,* so why? Why? Did he think to terrorize the Senate into yielding permission to stand *in absentia*? By sending thousands of his loyalest soldiers on furlough?

Up and down, up and down; Pompey paced the floor in torment until his steward came, very timidly, to inform him that there were many senators waiting in the atrium.

"I've had enough!" he shouted, striding into the room. *"I have had enough!"*

Perhaps one hundred and fifty men stood gaping at him in astonishment, from Appius Claudius Pulcher Censor to the humble urban quaestor Gaius Nerius. A pair of angry blue eyes raked the ranks and noted the omissions: Lucius Calpurnius Piso Censor, both the consuls, many of the consulars, every senator known to be a partisan of Caesar's and several who were known not to favor Caesar—but didn't favor being summoned by a man with no legal right to summon either. Still, there were sufficient to make a good beginning.

"I have had enough!" he said again, climbing onto a bench of priceless pink marble. "You cowards! You fools! You vacillating milksops! I am the First Man in Rome, and I am ashamed to call myself the First Man in Rome! Look at you! For ten months this farce has been going on over the provinces and the army of Gaius Julius Caesar, and you've gotten nowhere! Absolutely nowhere!"

He bowed to Cato, Favonius, Ahenobarbus, Metellus Scipio and two of the three Marcelli. "Honored colleagues, I do not include you in these bitter words, but I wanted you here to bear witness. The Gods know you've fought long and hard to terminate the illegal career of Gaius Caesar. But you get no real support, and this evening I intend to remedy that."

Back to the rest, some of them, like Appius Claudius Pulcher Censor, none too pleased. "I repeat! You fools! You cowards! You weak, whining, puny collection of has-beens and nowheres! I am fed up!" He drew a long, sucking breath. "I have tried. I have been patient. I have held back. I have suffered all of you. I have wiped your arses and held your heads while you puked. And don't stand there looking mortally offended, Varro! If the shoe fits, wear it! The Senate of Rome is supposed to set the tone and serve as the example to every other body politic and body public from one end of Rome's empire to the other. And the Senate of Rome is a disgrace! Every last one of you is a disgrace! Here you are, faced by one man—*one man*!—yet for ten months you've let him shit all over you! You've wavered and shivered, argued and sniveled, voted and voted and voted and voted—and gotten nowhere! Ye Gods, how Gaius Caesar must be laughing!"

By this everyone was stunned far beyond indignation; few of the men present had served in the field with Pompey in a situation which revealed his ugly side, but many of them were now grasping why Pompey got things done. Their affable, sweet-tempered, self-deprecating Gnaeus Pompeius Magnus was a martinet. Many of them had seen Caesar lose his temper, and still shivered in their boots at the memory of it. Now they saw Pompey lose his temper, and shivered in their boots. And they began to wonder: which of the two, Caesar or Pompey, would prove the harder master?

"You need me!" roared Pompey from the superior height of his bench. "You need me, and never forget it! *You need me!* I'm all that stands between you and Caesar. I'm your only refuge because I'm the only one among the lot of you who can beat Caesar on a field of battle. So you'd better start being nice to me. You'd better start bending over backward to please me. You'd better smarten up your act. You'd better resolve this mess. You'd better pass a decree and procure a law in the Assembly to strip Caesar of army, provinces and imperium! I can't do it for you because I'm only one man with one vote, and you haven't got the guts to institute martial law and put me in charge!"

He bared his teeth. "I tell you straight, Conscript Fathers, that I don't like you! If I were ever in a position to proscribe the lot of you, I would! I'd throw so many of you off the Tarpeian Rock that you'd end in falling on a senatorial mattress! I have had enough. Gaius Caesar is defying you and defying Rome. That has to stop. Deal with him! And don't expect mercy from me if I see any one of you tending to favor Caesar! The man's an outcast, an outlaw, though you don't have the guts to declare him one legally! I warn you, from this day on I will regard any man who favors Caesar as an outcast, as an outlaw!"

He waved his hand. "Go home! Think about it! And then, by Jupiter, *do something*! Rid me of this Caesar!"

They turned and left without a word.

Pompey jumped down, beaming. "Oh, that feels better!" he said to the little group of *boni* who remained.

"You certainly rammed a red-hot poker up their arses," said Cato, voice for once devoid of expression.

"Pah! They needed it, Cato. Our way one day, Caesar's way the next. I'm fed up. I want an end to the business."

"So we gathered," said Marcellus Major dryly. "It wasn't politic, Pompeius. You can't order the Senate of Rome around like raw recruits on a drill ground."

"Someone's got to!" snapped Pompey.

"I've never seen you like this," said Marcus Favonius.

"You'd better hope you never see me like this again," said Pompey grimly. "Where are the consuls? Neither of them came."

"They couldn't come, Pompeius," said Marcus Marcellus. "They are the consuls; their imperium outranks yours. To have come would have been tantamount to acknowledging you their master."

"Servius Sulpicius wasn't here either."

"I don't think," said Gaius Marcellus Major, walking toward the door, "that Servius Sulpicius answers summonses."

A moment later only Metellus Scipio was left. He gazed at his son-in-law reproachfully.

"What's wrong with you?" demanded Pompey aggressively.

"Nothing, nothing! Except perhaps that I think this wasn't wise, Magnus." He sighed dolefully. "Not wise at all."

An opinion echoed the next day, which happened to be Cicero's fifty-seventh birthday, and the day upon which he arrived outside Rome to take up residence in a villa on the Pincian Hill; granted a triumph, he could not cross the *pomerium*. Atticus came out of the city to welcome him, and was quick to apprise him of the extraordinary scene of the evening before.

"Who told you?" asked Cicero, horrified at the details.

"Your friend the senator Rabirius Postumus, not the banker Rabirius Postumus," said Atticus.

"*Old* Rabirius Postumus? Surely you mean the son."

"I mean old Rabirius Postumus. He's got a new lease on life now that Perperna is failing, wants the cachet of being the oldest."

"What did Magnus do?" asked Cicero anxiously.

"Intimidated most of the Senate still in Rome. Not many of them had seen Pompeius like that—so angry, so scathing. No elegant language, just a traditional diatribe—but delivered with real venom. He *said* he wanted an end to the senatorial dithering about Caesar. What he really wants he didn't say, but everyone was able to guess." Atticus frowned. "He threatened to proscribe, which may give you an idea of how upset he was. He followed that by threatening to throw every senator from the Tarpeian Rock—until the last fell on a mattress of the first, was how he put it. They're terrified!"

"But the Senate *has* tried—and tried hard!" protested Cicero, reliving those hours at the trial of Milo. "What does Magnus think it can do? The tribunician veto is inalienable!"

"He wants the Senate to enact a Senatus Consultum Ultimum and institute martial law with himself in command. Nothing less will satisfy him," Atticus declared strongly. "Pompeius is wearing down under the strain. He wishes it were over, and for most of his life his wishes have come true. He is an atrociously spoiled man, used to having things all his own way. For which the Senate is at least partially responsible, Cicero! Its members have given in to him for decades. They've dowered him with one special command after another and let him get away with things they won't condone in, for instance, Caesar. A man with the birthright is now demanding that the Senate treat him as it has treated Pompeius. Who do you think is really at the back of opposition to that?"

"Cato. Bibulus when he's here. The Marcelli. Ahenobarbus. Metellus Scipio. A few other diehards," said Cicero.

"Yes, but they're all political creatures, which Pompeius is not," said Atticus patiently. "Without Pompeius, they couldn't have marshaled the resistance they have. Pompeius wants no rivals, and Caesar is a formidable rival."

"Oh, if only Julia hadn't died!" said Cicero miserably.

"That's a non sequitur, Marcus. In the days when Julia was alive, Caesar was no threat. Or so Pompeius saw it. He's not a subtle creature, nor gifted with foresight. If Julia were alive today, Pompeius would be behaving no differently."

"Then I must see Magnus today," said Cicero with decision.

"With what intention?"

"To try to persuade him to come to an agreement with Caesar. Or, if he refuses, to quit Rome, retire to Spain and his army, and wait the matter out. My feeling is that, despite Cato and the rabid *boni,* the Senate will come to some sort of compromise with Caesar if they believe they haven't got Magnus to fall back on. They see Magnus as their soldier, the one capable of beating Caesar."

"And I note," said Atticus, "that you don't think he can."

"My brother doesn't think he can, and Quintus would know."

"Where is Quintus?"

"He's here, but of course he's not exiled from the city, so he's gone home to see if your sister has improved in temper."

Atticus laughed until the tears came. "Pomponia? Improve in temper? Pompeius will find harmony with Caesar before that can ever happen!"

"Why is it that neither of us Cicerones can manage to exist in domestic peace? Why are our wives such incorrigible shrews?"

Said Atticus, pragmatist supreme, "Because, my dear Marcus, both you and Quintus had to marry for money, and neither of you has the birth to find moneyed wives other men fancied."

Thus squelched, Cicero walked from the Pincian Hill across the sward of the Campus Martius (where his little contingent of Cilician soldiers was camped, awaiting his modest triumphal parade) to that dinghy behind the yacht.

But when Cicero put his proposal to Pompey, to quit Rome and retire to Spain, he was rejected with loathing.

"I'd be seen to be backing down!" Pompey said, outraged.

"Magnus, that's sheer nonsense! Pretend to agree to Caesar's demands—after all, you're not in the consul's chair, you're just another proconsul—and then settle down in Spain to wait. It's a foolish farmer who has two prize rams and keeps them in the same meadow. Once you're out of the Roman meadow, there's no contest. You'll be safe and well in Spain, an onlooker. *With your army!* Caesar will think twice about that. While you're in Italia, his troops are closer to him than yours are to you—and his troops lie between yours and Italia. Go to Spain, Magnus, *please*!"

"I've never heard such rubbish," growled Pompey. "No! No!"

While the debate in the House was raging on the sixth day of January, Cicero sent a polite note to Lucius Cornelius Balbus, asking that he come out to the Pincian Hill.

"Surely you want a peaceful solution," said Cicero when Balbus arrived. "Jupiter, you've lost weight!"

"Believe me, Marcus Cicero, I do, and yes, I have," said the little Gadetanian banker.

"I saw Magnus three days ago."

"He won't see me, alas," sighed Balbus. "Not since Aulus Hirtius left Rome without seeing him. I got the blame."

"Magnus won't co-operate," said Cicero abruptly.

"Oh, if only there were some sort of common ground!"

"Well," said Cicero, "I've been thinking. Day and night, I've been thinking. And I may have found a possibility."

"Tell me, please!"

"It will require some work on your part, Balbus, to convince Caesar. Oppius and the rest too, I imagine."

"Look at me, Marcus Cicero! Work has pared me away to nothing."

"It will necessitate an urgent letter to Caesar, best written by you, Oppius, *and* Rabirius Postumus."

"That part is easy. What should it say?"

"As soon as you leave, I'm going back to Magnus. And I will tell him that Caesar has consented to give up everything except one legion and Illyricum. Can you persuade Caesar to agree to it?"

"Yes, I'm sure we can if all of us add our weight. Caesar truly does prefer a peaceful settlement, you have my word on it. But you must see that he cannot give up everything. If he does, he will perish. They'll try him and exile him. However, Illyricum and one legion are enough. He goes from day to day, Marcus Cicero. If he keeps his imperium, he'll deal with the consular elections when the time comes. A man of more infinite resources I do not know."

"Nor I," said Cicero, rather despondently.

Back to Pompey's villa, back to another confrontation; though Cicero was not to know that Pompey had passed a series of bad nights. Once the cathartic relief of that outburst to the senators had dissipated, the First Man in Rome began to feel the recoil and remember that no one among the *boni,* including his father-in-law, had approved of what he said to the senators. Or the tone in which he said it. Autocratic arrogance. Unwise. Almost four days later Pompey was regretting his loss of control; temper had translated into elation, and then, inevitably, into depression. Yes, they needed him. But yes, he needed them. And he had alienated them. He knew it because no one had come to see him since, nor had any of the meetings of the Senate been held outside the *pomerium*. It was all going on without him, the bitter and acrimonious debates, the vetoing, the defiance of that oaf Antonius and a Cassius. A Cassius! Of a clan who ought to know better. He had whipped the horse, but not understood that he was whipping a mule. Oh, how to get out of this bind? What might the Senate do? Not put him in control, even if it did institute martial law. Why on earth had he spoken of conscriptions and the Tarpeian Rock? Too far, Magnus, too far! No matter how much it might deserve that fate, never castigate the Senate like raw recruits.

Thus Cicero found the First Man in a more malleable and doubting frame of mind, realized it, and struck hard.

"I have it on impeccable authority, Magnus, that Caesar will agree to keep Illyricum and one legion only, that he will give up everything else," said Cicero. "If you consent to this accommodation and use your influence to obtain it, you'll be a hero. You will have single-handedly averted civil war. All of Rome save Cato and a very few other men will vote you a thanksgiving, statues, every kind of honor. We both understand that the conviction and exile of Caesar are Cato's avowed goals, but they're not really your goals, are they? What you object to is being treated in like manner to Caesar—what he loses, you must lose. But this latest proposal doesn't mention you or yours."

Pompey was visibly brightening. "It's true that I don't hate Caesar the way Cato does, nor am I as rigid a man as Cato. I don't say, mind you, that I won't be voting against letting Caesar stand for the consulship *in absentia*—but that's a separate issue, and some months off. You're right, the most important thing at the moment is to avert the threat of civil war. And if Illyricum plus one legion will satisfy Caesar . . . if he doesn't require the same of me . . . well, why not? Yes, Cicero, why not? I'll agree to it. Caesar can keep Illyricum and one legion if he gives up everything else. With one legion he's powerless. Yes! I agree!"

Cicero sagged with the relief of it. "Magnus, I am not a drinking man, but I need a drop of your excellent wine."

At which moment Cato and the junior consul Lentulus Crus walked into the atrium, from which Cicero and Pompey hadn't moved, so anxious had Cicero been to make his point. Oh, the tragic misfortune of that! If they'd been ensconced in Pompey's study, the visitors would have had to be announced and Cicero would have persuaded Pompey not to see them. As it was, Pompey was unprotected.

"Join us!" said Pompey to the newcomers jovially. "We're about to drink to a peaceful accommodation with Caesar."

"You're *what*?" asked Cato, stiffening.

"Caesar has agreed to give up everything except Illyricum and one legion without asking me for anything more than my consent. No idiocies like my having to give up everything too. The threat of civil war is over; Caesar is rendered impotent," said Pompey with huge satisfaction. "We can deal with his candidacy for the consulship when the time comes. *I* have averted civil war!"

Cato emitted a sound somewhere between a screech and a howl, put his hands to his scalp and literally wrenched two clumps of hair out of his head. "You cretin!" he shrieked. "You fat, self-satisfied, over-rated, over-aged boy wonder! What do you mean, you've averted civil war? You've given in to the greatest enemy the Republic has ever had!" He ground his teeth, he raked at his cheeks with his nails, he advanced on Pompey still clutching those two hanks of hair. Pompey backed away, stupefied.

"You've taken it upon yourself to accommodate Caesar, have you? Who says you have any right to do that? You're the Senate's servant, Pompeius, not the Senate's master! And you're supposed to be teaching that lesson to Caesar, not collaborating with him on bringing down the Republic!"

Pompey in a temper was almost as awesome, but Pompey had a fatal weakness; once someone threw him off balance (as Sertorius had in Spain), he couldn't manage to regain his equilibrium nor snatch back control of the situation. Cato had wrested the offensive from him, tossed him into a state of confusion which prevented his growing angry in return, rendered him incapable of finding the right answers to explain himself. Mind whirling, he gazed at the most intimidating display of rage he had ever encountered, and he quailed. This wasn't a temper, it was a furor.

Cicero tried. "Cato, Cato, don't do this!" he shouted. "Use your ammunition in the proper way—force Caesar into court, not into civil war! *Control yourself!*"

A big and testy man, Lentulus Crus grasped Cicero by the left shoulder and spun him round, then began pushing him across the room. "Shut up! Keep out of it! Shut up! Keep out of it!" he barked, each bark punctuated by a punch to the chest which sent Cicero reeling backward.

"You are not Dictator!" Cato was screaming at Pompey. "You do not run Rome! You have no authority to enter into bargains with a traitor behind our backs! Illyricum and one legion, eh? And you think that a trifling concession, eh? It is not! It—is—not! It is a major concession! A *major* concession! And I say to you, Gnaeus Pompeius, that absolutely no concessions can be made to Caesar! He cannot be conceded the tip of a dead Roman's finger! Caesar must be taught that the Senate is his master, that he is not the Senate's master! And if you need to be taught the same lesson, Pompeius, then I am just the man to drum it into you! You want to ally yourself with Caesar, do you? Very well! Ally yourself with Caesar! Caesar the traitor! And suffer the same fate as Caesar the traitor! For I swear to you by all our Gods that I will bring you down lower than I bring Caesar down! I will have your imperium, your provinces and your army stripped from you in the same breath as Caesar's are stripped from him! All I have to do is say so in the House! And the House will vote to do it, and there will be no tribunician veto because you do not command the loyalty of a Curio or an Antonius! The only legions you have at your disposal are two legions which owe their loyalty to Caesar! Your own legions are a thousand miles away in Spain! So how can you stop me, Pompeius? I'll do it, you traitor! And I'll glory in doing it! This is no social men's club you elected to join! The *boni* are utterly committed to bringing Caesar down. And we will just as happily bring anyone down who sides with him—even you! Then perhaps it's you who will be proscribed, you who will be thrown from the Tarpeian Rock! Did you think we *boni* would condone those threats? Well, we won't! Nor will we support any man who dares to flout the authority of the Senate of Rome!"

"Stop! Stop!" gasped Pompey, extending both hands to Cato with palms out. "Stop, Cato, I beg of you! You're right! You—are—right! I admit it! Cicero talked me into it, I was—I was—I was weak! It was just a weak moment! No one's come to see me for three days! What was I to think?"

But Cato enraged was not Pompey enraged. Pompey snapped out of a temper as quickly as he fell into it, whereas it took a long time to calm Cato down, to unstopper his ears and persuade them to hear the sounds of surrender. He ranted for what seemed endless hours before he shut his mouth and stood, trembling.

"Sit down, Cato," said Pompey, fussing about him like an old woman about her lapdog. "Here, sit down, do!" He rushed to pour a goblet of wine, rushed back to hand it to Cato, wrapping both hands about its bowl and, with a shudder, removing the hair Cato still held. "There now, drink it down, please! You're right—I was wrong—I admit it freely! Blame Cicero, he caught me in a weak moment." He gazed pleadingly at Lentulus Crus. "Have some wine, do! Let's all sit down and sort out our differences, for there are none cannot be sorted out, I promise you. Please, Lucius Crus, have some wine!"

"Ohhhhh!" cried Cicero from the far side of the room.

But Pompey paid him no attention; Cicero turned and left to plod back across the Campus Martius to the Pincian Hill, trembling almost as hard as Cato had.

That was the end of it, then. That was the watershed. There could be no going back now. So close, so close! Oh, why did those two *boni* irascibles have to arrive at just the wrong moment?

"Well," he said to himself when he reached home and began to write a note to Balbus, break the news, "if there is civil war, there is only one man to blame. Cato."

At dawn the next day, the seventh one of January, the Senate met in the temple of Jupiter Stator, a site which prevented the attendance of Pompey. Though the pallid Gaius Marcellus Minor was present, he handed the meeting to his junior colleague, Lentulus Crus, as soon as the prayers and offerings were made.

"I do not intend to orate," Lentulus Crus said harshly, his florid face mottled with bluish patches, his breathing labored. "It is time and more than time, Conscript Fathers, that we dealt with our present crisis in the only sensible way. I propose that we pass the Senatus Consultum Ultimum, and that the terms of it be to grant the consuls, praetors, tribunes of the plebs, consulars and promagistrates within the vicinity of Rome full authority to protect the interests of the State against the tribunician veto."

A huge buzz of noise erupted, for the senators were genuinely astonished at the peculiar wording of this ultimate decree—and equally astonished that it did not specify Pompey by name.

"You can't do that!" roared Mark Antony, leaping off the tribunician bench. "You are proposing to instruct the tribunes of the plebs to protect the State against their own power to veto? It can't be done! Nor can a Senatus Consultum Ultimum be conjured into force to muzzle the tribunes of the plebs! The tribunes of the plebs are the servants of the State—always have been, always will be! The terms of your decree, junior consul, are completely unconstitutional! The ultimate decree is passed to protect the State from treasonous activity, and I defy you to say that any one of the ten members of my College is a traitor! But I will take the matter to the Plebs, I promise you! And have you thrown from the Tarpeian Rock for attempting to obstruct us in our sworn duty!"

"Lictors, remove this man," said Lentulus Crus.

"I veto that, Lentulus! I veto your ultimate decree!"

"Lictors, remove this man."

"They'll have to remove me too!" yelled Quintus Cassius.

"Lictors, remove both these men."

But when the dozen togate lictors attempted to lay hands on Antony and Quintus Cassius, it was an unequal fight; it took the other several dozen lictors present in the chamber to grasp hold of the furiously fighting Antony and the equally angry Quintus Cassius, who were finally ejected, bruised and bleeding, togas torn and disarrayed, into the upper Forum.

"Bastards!" growled Curio, who had quit the chamber when the lictors moved.

"Bigots," said Marcus Caelius Rufus. "Where to now?"

"Down to the well of the Comitia," said Antony, hand out to prevent Quintus Cassius from rearranging his toga. "No, Quintus! Don't tidy yourself up, whatever you do! We're going to remain exactly the way we are until we get to Caesar in Ravenna. Let him see with his own eyes what Lentulus Crus did."

Having drawn a very large crowd—no difficulty these days, when so much apprehension and bewilderment pervaded the thoughts of those who liked to frequent the Forum—Antony displayed his wounds and the wounds of Quintus Cassius.

"See us? The tribunes of the plebs have been manhandled as well as prevented from doing their duty!" he shouted. "Why? To protect the interests of a very few men who want to rule in Rome their way, which is not the accepted and acceptable way! They want to banish rule of the People and replace it with rule of the Senate! Take heed, fellow plebeians! Take heed, those patricians who do not belong to the ranks of the *boni*! The days of the People's Assemblies are numbered! When Cato and his *boni* minions take over the Senate—which they are doing at this very moment!—they will use Pompeius and military force to remove all say in government from you! They will use Pompeius and military force to strike down men like Gaius Caesar, who has always stood as protector of the People against the power of the Senate!"

He looked over the heads of the crowd to where a large group of lictors was marching down the Forum from Jupiter Stator. "This has to be a very short speech, *Quirites*! I can see the servants of the Senate coming to take me to prison, and I refuse to go to prison! I'm going to Gaius Caesar in Ravenna, together with my courageous colleague Quintus Cassius and these two champions of the People, Gaius Curio and Marcus Caelius! I'm going to show Gaius Caesar what the Senate has done! And do not forget, be you plebeian or patrician, that Gaius Caesar is the victim of a very small, very vindictive minority of senators who will not tolerate opposition! They have persecuted him, they have impugned his *dignitas*—and your *dignitas, Quirites*!—and they have made a mockery of Rome's constitution! Guard your rights, *Quirites,* and wait for Caesar to avenge you!"

With a broad grin and a genial wave of the hand, Antony left the rostra amid huge cheers, his three companions around him. By the time the lictors had managed to penetrate the crowd, they were long gone.

In the temple of Jupiter Stator things were going very much better for the *boni*. Few indeed were present to vote against the Senatus Consultum Ultimum, which passed almost unanimously. Most interesting, for those with the detachment to notice it, was the conduct and deportment of the senior consul, Gaius Marcellus Minor; he sat looking ill, said nothing, dragged himself to the right of the floor when it came time to vote, then returned wearily to his curule chair. His brother and his cousin, the ex-consuls, were far more vociferous.

By the time the lictors returned from the well of the Comitia empty-handed, the vote was taken and the decree of martial law properly recorded.

"I am adjourning the House until tomorrow," said Lentulus Crus, satisfied, "when it will meet in the Curia Pompeia on the Campus Martius. Our esteemed consular and proconsul Gnaeus Pompeius Magnus cannot be excluded from further deliberations."

"I suppose," said Servius Sulpicius Rufus, who had been the senior consul in Marcus Marcellus's year, "this means we have declared war on Gaius Caesar. Who has not moved."

"We declared war," said Marcellus Major, "when we offered Gnaeus Pompeius a sword."

"It was Caesar who declared war!" Cato hollered. "When he refused to accept the directives of this body and obey them, he outlawed himself!"

"Yet," said Servius Sulpicius gently, "you have not declared him *hostis* in your ultimate decree. He is not yet officially a public enemy. Ought you not to do that?"

"Yes, we ought!" said Lentulus Crus, whose high color and audible breathing indicated an unhappy state of affairs within his body, though it was Marcellus Minor who looked sick.

"You cannot," said Lucius Cotta, Caesar's uncle, and one of those who had voted against the ultimate decree. "So far Caesar has made no move to go to war, yet you have declared war. Until he does make that move, he is not *hostis* and cannot be declared *hostis*."

"The important thing," said Cato, "is to strike first!"

"I agree, Marcus Cato," said Lentulus Crus. "That is why we meet tomorrow on the Campus Martius, where our military expert can advise us on how to strike, and where."

But when the Senate met in Pompey's curia the next day, the eighth one of January, its military expert, Pompey, demonstrated clearly to everyone that he had not thought about striking first, nor striking anywhere. He concentrated on his military strength rather than on his military tactics.

"We must remember," he said to the House, "that all Caesar's legions are disaffected. If Caesar should ask them to march, I very much doubt they would consent. As to our own troops, there are now three legions in Italia, thanks to vigorous recruiting in the last few days. There are seven legions belonging to me in the Spains, and I have already sent word to mobilize them. The pity of it is that at this time of season, they cannot sail. Therefore it is important that they start out by road before Gaius Caesar tries to intercept them." He smiled cheerfully. "I assure you, Conscript Fathers, that there is no need to worry."

The meetings went on daily, and much was done to prepare for every eventuality. When Faustus Sulla moved that King Juba of Numidia be declared a Friend and Ally of the Roman People, Gaius Marcellus Minor emerged from his apathy to commend Faustus Sulla's motion; it passed. When, however, Faustus Sulla then suggested that he go personally to Mauretania to talk to Kings Bocchus and Bogud—a strategy Marcellus Minor again applauded—Philippus's son, a tribune of the plebs, vetoed it.

"You're like your father, a fence-sitter!" snarled Cato.

"No, Marcus Cato, I do assure you. If Caesar makes any hostile move, we will need Faustus Sulla here," said Philippus Junior firmly.

The most interesting aspect of this exchange concerned the tribunician veto itself; with a Senatus Consultum Ultimum in effect protecting the State against the tribunician veto, young Philippus's veto was accepted.

Ah, but all that was as nothing compared to the exquisite pleasure of stripping Caesar of his imperium, his provinces and his army! The Senate appointed Lucius Domitius Ahenobarbus the new governor of the further Gauls, and the ex-praetor Marcus Considius Nonianus the new governor of Italian Gaul and Illyricum. Caesar was now a *privatus;* nothing protected him. But Cato suffered too; though he had never wanted a province, he now found himself appointed governor of Sicily. Africa went to Lucius Aelius Tubero, a man whose loyalty to the *boni* was suspect but whose governorship was inevitable; the pool of available men had shrunk to nothing. This gave Pompey an excellent excuse to nominate Appius Claudius Censor to be governor of Greece as distinct from Macedonia, even though he had already had a province, and to suggest that for the moment nothing be done in Macedonia save to let it continue under the care of its quaestor, Titus Antistius. Because it was not generally known that Pompey had resolved to fight Caesar in the East rather than on Italian soil, the significance of sending Appius Claudius to Greece and preserving Macedonia for the future did not impinge on most of the senators, whose thinking had gone no further than whether Caesar would march, or wouldn't march.

"In the meantime," said Lentulus Crus, "I think we ought to make sure Italia herself is well guarded and properly defended. For which reasons I propose that we send legates endowed with proconsular imperiums to all parts of Italia. Their first duty will be to enlist soldiers—we don't have enough troops under arms to distribute everywhere."

"I'll take one of those," said Ahenobarbus instantly. "No need to go to my provinces this very moment, better to make sure Italia is prepared first. So give me charge of the Adriatic coast below Picenum. I'll travel the Via Valeria and pick up whole legions of volunteers among the Marsi and the Paeligni, who are in my clientele."

"Custody of the Via Aemilia Scaura, the Via Aurelia and the Via Clodia—which is to say, the north on the Etrurian side—I nominate should go to Lucius Scribonius Libo!" said Pompey eagerly.

That provoked a few grins. The marriage between Pompey's elder son, Gnaeus, and the daughter of Appius Claudius Censor had neither prospered nor lasted. After it ended in divorce, young Gnaeus Pompey married Scribonius Libo's daughter, a match which did not please his father but did please Gnaeus, who had insisted on it. This left Pompey with the task of finding a good job for a mediocre man. Hence Etruria, not likely to be Caesar's focus.

Quintus Minucius Thermus inherited the Via Flaminia, which was the north on the eastern side in Umbria, and was instructed to station himself in Iguvium.

Nepotism came into the picture again when Pompey suggested that his close cousin, Gaius Lucilius Hirrus, be given duty in Picenum at Labienus's hometown of Camerinum. Picenum, of course, was Pompey's own fief—and closest to Caesar in Ravenna—so other men were sent there too, Lentulus Spinther the consular to Ancona and Publius Attius Varus the ex-praetor to Pompey's hometown of Auximum.

And poor discouraged Cicero, present at these meetings because they were being held outside the *pomerium,* was ordered to go to Campania and recruit.

"There!" said Lentulus Crus at the end of it, jubilantly. "Once Caesar realizes we've done all of this, he'll think twice about marching! He won't dare!"

RAVENNA TO ANCONA

The messenger Antony and Curio had sped on ahead of their own flight from Rome reached Caesar's villa near Ravenna the day after Antony and Quintus Cassius had been ejected from the House by force. Though he arrived close to the dawning of the ninth day of January, Caesar received him at once, took the letter and sent him to a meal and a comfortable bed with a warm smile of thanks: two hundred miles in less than two days was a grueling ride.

Antony's letter was brief.

> Caesar, Quintus Cassius and I were manhandled out of the Senate when we tried to interpose our vetoes against a Senatus Consultum Ultimum. It's an odd decree. Doesn't declare you *hostis* nor specifically name Pompeius. It authorizes all the magistrates and consulars to protect the State against the tribunician veto, if you please. The sole reference to Pompeius is a mention that among those entrusted with the care of the State are "promagistrates within the vicinity of Rome." Which applies as much to Cicero, sitting awaiting his triumph, as to Pompeius, just sitting. I would imagine Pompeius is a disappointed man. But that's one thing about the *boni*—they hate awarding special commands.
>
> There are four of us coming. Curio and Caelius elected to leave the city too. We'll take the Via Flaminia.
>
> Oh, I don't know if it will be of any use to you, but I've ensured that we'll arrive in exactly the same condition as we were when the lictors finished tossing us out. Which means we'll stink a bit, so have hot baths ready.

The only trusted legate Caesar had with him was Aulus Hirtius, who came in to find Caesar sitting, the letter in his hand, staring at a mosaic wall depicting the flight of King Aeneas from burning Ilium, his aged father on his right shoulder and the Palladium tucked under his left arm.

"One of the best things about Ravenna," Caesar said without looking at Hirtius, "is the skill of the locals at mosaic. Better even than the Sicilian Greeks."

Hirtius sat down where he could see Caesar's face. It was calm and contented.

"I hear a messenger arrived in a terrific hurry," said Hirtius.

"Yes. The Senate has passed its ultimate decree."

Hirtius's breath hissed. "You're declared a public enemy!"

"No," said Caesar levelly. "The real enemy of Rome, it would appear, is the tribunician veto, and the real traitors the tribunes of the plebs. How like Sulla the *boni* are! The enemy is never without, always within. And the tribunes of the plebs must be muzzled."

"What are you going to do?"

"Move," said Caesar.

"Move?"

"South. To Ariminum. Antonius, Quintus Cassius, Curio and Caelius are traveling the Via Flaminia at this moment, though not as fast as their messenger. I imagine they'll reach Ariminum within two days, counting this one just arrived."

"Then you still have your imperium. If you move to Ariminum, Caesar, you have to cross the Rubicon into home territory."

"By the time I do, Hirtius, I imagine I will be a *privatus,* and at full liberty to go wherever I want. Sheltered by their ultimate decree, the Senate will strip me of everything at once."

"So you won't take the Thirteenth with you to Ariminum?" Hirtius asked, conscious that relief hadn't followed in the wake of Caesar's answer. He looked so relaxed, so tranquil, so much as he always did—the man in absolute control, never plagued by doubt, always in command of himself and events. Was that why his legates loved him? By definition he ought not to have been a man capable of inspiring love, yet he did. Not because he needed it. Because—because—oh, *why*? Because he was what all men wanted to be?

"Certainly I will take the Thirteenth," said Caesar. He got to his feet. "Have them ready to move within two hours. Full baggage train, everything with them including artillery."

"Are you going to tell them where they're heading?"

The fair brows rose. "Not for the time being. They're boys from across the Padus. What does the Rubicon mean to them?"

Junior legates like Gaius Asinius Pollio flew everywhere, barking orders at military tribunes and senior centurions; within those two hours the Thirteenth had struck camp and was lined up in column ready to move out. Its legionaries were fit and well rested, despite the route march Caesar had sent them on to Tergeste under the command of Pollio. They had conducted intensive military maneuvers there, then had returned to Ravenna in time for a final furlough long enough to bring them to peak fighting pitch.

The pace Caesar set was a leisurely one; the Thirteenth went into a properly fortified camp still well north of the river Rubicon, the official boundary between Italian Gaul and Italia. Nothing was said, but everyone, including the legionaries and their centurions, was aware that the Rubicon loomed. They belonged to Caesar completely, and were overjoyed that he was not going to take it lying down, that he was marching to defend his hideously insulted *dignitas,* which was also the *dignitas* of everyone who served under him, from his legates to the noncombatants.

"We're marching into history," said Pollio to his fellow junior legate, Quintus Valerius Orca; Pollio liked history.

"No one can say he didn't try to avoid this," said Orca, and laughed. "But isn't it like him, to march with only one legion? How does he know what he'll find once he's crossed into Picenum? There might be ten legions drawn up against us."

"Oh no, he's too clever for that," said Pollio. "Three or four legions, maybe, but not more. And we'll beat them hollow."

"Especially if two of them are the Sixth and the Fifteenth."

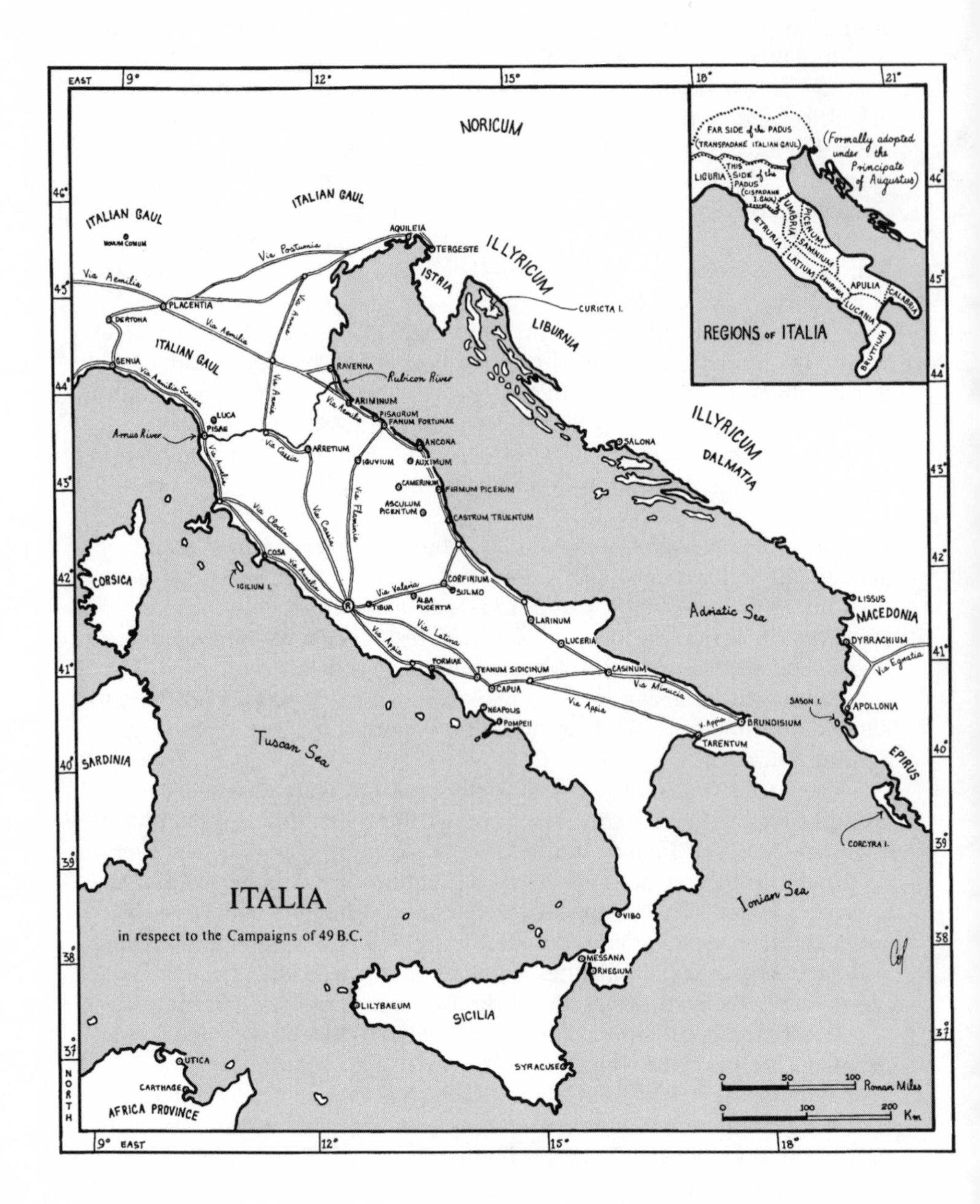

ITALIA
in respect to the Campaigns of 49 B.C.
REGIONS OF ITALIA
NORICUM
ITALIAN GAUL
ILLYRICUM
LIBURNIA
DALMATIA
MACEDONIA
EPIRUS
CORSICA
SARDINIA
SICILIA
AFRICA PROVINCE
Adriatic Sea
Tuscan Sea
Ionian Sea
Rubicon River
Arnus River
Via Aemilia
Via Postumia
Via Flaminia
Via Cassia
Via Appia
Via Latina
Via Valeria
Via Egnatia
AQUILEIA
TERGESTE
ISTRIA
PLACENTIA
DERTONA
GENUA
RAVENNA
ARIMINUM
PISAURUM
FANUM FORTUNAE
ANCONA
AUXIMUM
IGUVIUM
ARRETIUM
LUCA
PISAE
COSA
TIBUR
CORFINIUM
SULMO
LARINUM
LUCERIA
CAPUA
NEAPOLIS
POMPEII
BRUNDISIUM
TARENTUM
VIBO
MESSANA
RHEGIUM
LILYBAEUM
SYRACUSE
UTICA
CARTHAGE
SALONA
LISSUS
DYRRACHIUM
APOLLONIA
Roman Miles
Km

"True."

On the tenth day of January, fairly late in the afternoon, the Thirteenth reached the Rubicon. Its men were ordered to cross without pausing; camp was to be made on the far side.

Caesar and his little band of legates remained on the north bank, and there took a meal. At this autumnal time of year the rivers which flowed their shortish courses from the Apennines to the Adriatic Sea were at ebb; the snows had long melted, rain was unusual. Thus despite its long course, its sources almost literally a knife edge from those of the westward-flowing Arnus in the high mountains, the Rubicon's broad stream in autumn was at most knee-deep, no obstacle to any man or beast.

Little was said, though what Caesar did say was dampening in that it was so *ordinary*. He ate his usual plain and sparing fare—a little bread, a few olives, a hunk of cheese—then washed his hands in a bowl a servant tendered, and got up from his ivory curule chair, which he had not, it was noted, abandoned.

"To your horses," he said.

But the horse his groom led up for Caesar to mount was not one of his several beautiful, highly strung road animals; it was Toes. Like the two other Toes he had ridden into battle since Sulla gifted him with the original animal, this Toes—the veteran of the years in Gaul—was a sleek chestnut with long mane and tail and pretty dish face, an appropriately well-bred mount for any general who didn't (like Pompey) prefer a splashy white horse. Except that its feet were cloven into three genuine toes, each ending in a tiny hoof, behind which it had a footpad.

Mounted, the legates watched, enthralled; they had waited for a statement of war to no avail, but now they had it. When Caesar rode Toes, he was going into battle.

He nudged the animal into the lead and rode at a sedate pace across the yellowed, autumnal grass between the trees toward the sparkling stream. And there, on the vestigial bank, paused.

It is here. I can still turn back. I have not yet abandoned legality, constitutionality. But once I cross this undistinguished river I pass from servant of my country to an aggressor against her. Yet I know all this. I've known it for two years. I've gone through everything—thought, planned, schemed, striven mightily. I've made incredible concessions. I would even have settled for Illyricum and one legion. But for every step of the way, I have known and understood that they would not yield. That they were determined to spit on me, to shove my face into the dust, to make a nothing out of Gaius Julius Caesar. Who is *not* a nothing. Who will never consent to be a nothing. You wanted it, Cato. Now you can have it. You've forced me to march against my country, to turn my face against the legal way. And, Pompeius, you are about to discover what it's like to face a competent enemy. The moment Toes wets his feet, I am an outlaw. And in order to remove the slur of outlaw from my name, I will have to go to war, fight my own countrymen—and win.

What lies across the Rubicon? How many legions have they managed to get together? How much real preparation? I am basing my entire campaign on a hunch, that they have done nothing. That Pompeius doesn't know how to start a war, and that the *boni* don't know how to fight one. He's never once started a war, Pompeius, for all those special commands. He's the expert at mopping up. Whereas the *boni* have no skill at anything beyond starting a war. Once the fighting begins, how will Pompeius manage to coexist with the *boni,* who will retard him, harangue him, criticize him, attempt to constrain him? They've thought of this as a game, as a hypothesis. Never as an actuality. Still, I suppose it is a game. And *I* have the luck as well as the genius.

Suddenly he threw his head back and laughed, remembering a line from his favorite poet, Menander.

"Let the dice fly high!" he cried out in the original Greek, kicked Toes gently in the ribs, and rode across the Rubicon into Italia and rebellion.

Ariminum was in no mood to fight; when Caesar and the Thirteenth reached that prosperous town at the top of the Via Flaminia, its populace turned out armed with autumn garlands, adorned the troops and cheered Caesar deafeningly. It came, Caesar had to admit, as something of a surprise, for Ariminum lay at the top of Pompey's dominions and could well have chosen Pompey and the Senate. In which case, wondered Caesar, how much fighting might there be? He learned that Thermus was in Iguvium, Lucilius Hirrus in Camerinum, Lentulus Spinther in Ancona, and Varus in Auximum. Lentulus Spinther had succeeded in raising the most troops, about ten cohorts; the others had five cohorts each. Not very fearsome odds for the Thirteenth. Especially if the ordinary folk of Italia were on Caesar's side. Suddenly that seemed likely, a great comfort. Blood wasn't what Caesar was after; the less of it he had to spill, the better.

Antony, Quintus Cassius, Curio and Caelius reached the camp outside Ariminum early on that eleventh day of January. A sorry sight in torn and bloodied togas, faces bruised and cut, the two tribunes of the plebs were perfect for Caesar's purpose. He called the Thirteenth into assembly and presented Antony and Quintus Cassius to them in all their glory.

"This is why we're here!" said Caesar. "This is what we have marched into Italia to prevent! No body of Roman men, no matter how ancient or august, has the right to violate the sacred persons of the tribunes of the plebs, who came into being to protect the lot of the ordinary people, the vast numbers of the Plebs from the Head Count through Rome's soldiers to her business people and civil servants! For we cannot call the plebeians of the Senate anything other than would-be patricians! In treating two tribunes of the plebs the way the Senate's plebeians have treated Marcus Antonius and Quintus Cassius, they have abrogated their plebeian status and heritage!

"The person of a tribune of the plebs is inviolable, and his right to veto inalienable. *Inalienable!* All Antonius and Cassius did was to veto a scurrilous decree aimed at them and, through them, aimed at me. I have offended them, those would-be patricians of the Senate, by raising Rome's image in the eyes of the rest of the world and adding vast riches to Rome's purse. For I am not one of them. I have never been one of them. A senator, yes. A magistrate, yes. Consul, yes. But never one of that petty, small-minded, vindictive little group who call themselves the Good Men, the *boni*! Who have embarked upon a program designed to destroy the right of the People to a say in government, who have embarked upon a program to ensure that the only governing body left in Rome is the Senate. Their Senate, boys, not my Senate! My Senate is your servant. Their Senate wants to be your master. It wants to decide how much you are paid, when your service with generals like me is to be terminated, whether or not you are to receive a little parcel of land to settle on when you retire. It wants to regulate the size of your bonuses, your percentage of the booty, how many of you will walk in a triumphal parade. It even wants to decide whether or not you're entitled to the citizenship, whether or not your backs, which have bowed down serving Rome, are to be jellied by the barbed lash. It wants you, Rome's soldiers, to acknowledge it your master. It wants you cowed and sniveling like the meanest beggar in a Syrian street!"

Hirtius huffed contentedly. "He's away," he said to Curio. "It's going to be one of his best speeches."

"He can't lose," said Curio.

Caesar swept on. "This little group of men and the Senate they manipulate have impugned my *dignitas,* my right and entitlement to public honor through personal endeavor. All that I have done they want to destroy, calling what I have done treasonous! And in wanting to destroy my *dignitas,* in calling me treasonous, they are destroying your *dignitas,* calling what you have done treasonous!

"Think of them, boys! All those weary miles—those *nundinae* of empty bellies—those sword cuts, arrow punctures, spear rents—those deaths in the front line, so noble, so brave!—think of them! Think of where we've been—think of what we've done—think of the work, the sweat, the privation, the loneliness! Think of the colossal glory we've amassed for Rome! And to what avail? So that our tribunes of the plebs can be punched and kicked, so that our achievements can be sneered at, dismissed, *shit upon* by a precious little clique of would-be patricians! Poor soldiers and worse generals, every last one of them! Who ever heard of Cato the general? Ahenobarbus the conqueror?"

Caesar paused, grinned, shrugged. "But who among you even knows the name Cato? Ahenobarbus, maybe—his great-grandfather wasn't a bad soldier! So, boys, I'll give you a name you do know—Gnaeus Pompeius who awarded himself the cognomen of Magnus! Yes, Gnaeus Pompeius, who ought to be fighting for me, fighting for you! But who, in his fat and torpid old age, has elected to hold a sponge on a stick to clean the arses of his *boni* friends! Who has turned his back on the concept of the army! Who has supported this campaign against me and my boys from its very beginning! Why? Why did he do that? Because he's outfought, outgeneraled, outclassed and outraged! Because he's not 'Great' enough to admit that someone else's army is better than any army he ever commanded! Who is there to equal my boys? No one! *No one!* You're the best soldiers who ever picked up a sword and a shield in Rome's name! So here I am, and here you are, on the wrong side of a river and on our way to avenge our mangled, our despised *dignitas*!

"I would not go to war for any reason less. I would not oppose those senatorial idiots for any reason less. My *dignitas* is the center of my life; it is everything I have ever done! *I will not let it be taken from me!* Nor see your *dignitas* taken from you. Whatever I am, you are! We've marched together to cut off all three of Cerberus's heads! We've suffered through snow and ice, hail and rain! We've crossed an ocean, climbed mountains, swum mighty rivers! We've beaten the bravest peoples in the world to their knees! We've made them submit to Rome! And what can poor old has-been Gnaeus Pompeius say in answer to that? Nothing, boys, nothing! So what has he chosen to do? Try to strip it all from us, boys—the honor, the fame, the glory, the miracle! Everything we lump together and call *dignitas*!"

He stopped, held out his arms as if to embrace them. "But I am your servant, boys. I exist because of you. It's you who must make the final decision. Do we march on into Italia to avenge our tribunes of the plebs and recover our *dignitas*? Or do we about-face and return to Ravenna? Which is it to be? On or back?"

No one had moved. No one had coughed, sneezed, whispered a comment. And for a long moment after the General ceased speaking, that immense silence continued. Then the *primipilus* centurion opened his mouth.

"On!" he roared. "On, on!"

The soldiers took it up. "On! On! On! On!"

Caesar stepped down from his dais and walked into the ranks, smiling, holding out his hand to shake every hand proffered to him, until he was swallowed up in a mail-clad mass.

"What a man!" said Pollio to Orca.

But that afternoon over dinner, the four fugitives from Rome bathed and clad in leather armor, Caesar held a council of war.

"Hirtius, was my speech recorded verbatim?" he asked.

"It's being copied now, Caesar."

"I want it distributed to all my legates and read out to every one of my legions."

"Are they with us?" asked Caelius. "Your legates, I mean."

"All save Titus Labienus."

"That doesn't surprise me," said Curio.

"Why?" pressed Caelius, the least informed and therefore the most prone to ask obvious questions.

Caesar shrugged. "I didn't want Labienus."

"How did your legates know?"

"I visited Gallia Comata and my legates last October."

"So you knew about this as far back as then."

"My dear Caelius," said Caesar patiently, "the Rubicon has always been a possibility. Just one I would have preferred not to use. And, as you well know, have exerted every ounce of myself to avoid using. But it's a foolish man who doesn't thoroughly explore every possibility. Let us simply say that by last October I considered the Rubicon more a probability than a possibility."

Caelius opened his mouth again, but shut it when Curio dug him sharply in the ribs.

"Where to now?" asked Quintus Cassius.

"It's evident that the opposition isn't well organized—also that the common people prefer me to Pompeius and the *boni,*" said Caesar, popping a piece of bread soaked in oil between his lips. He chewed, swallowed, spoke again. "I'm going to split the Thirteenth. Antonius, you'll take the five junior cohorts and march at once for Arretium to hold the Via Cassia. It's more important that I keep my avenues to Italian Gaul open at this moment than try to hold the Via Flaminia. Curio, you'll stay in Ariminum with three cohorts until I send you word to march for Iguvium, from which town you'll eject Thermus. Once that's done I'll have the Via Flaminia as well as the Via Cassia. As for myself, I'm taking the two senior cohorts and continuing south into Picenum."

"That's only a thousand men, Caesar," said Pollio, frowning.

"They should be enough, but the possibility that I may need more is why Curio stays in Ariminum for the time being."

"You're right, Caesar," said Hirtius soberly. "What matters isn't the quantity of the troops, but the quality of the men leading them. Perhaps Attius Varus will offer resistance, but Thermus, Hirrus and Lentulus Spinther? They couldn't lead a tethered ewe."

"Which reminds me, I don't honestly know why," said Caesar, "that I must write to Aulus Gabinius. Time that doughty warrior was recalled from exile."

"What about recalling Milo?" asked Caelius, Milo's friend.

"No, not Milo," said Caesar curtly, and terminated the meal.

"Did you notice," said Caelius later in private to Pollio, "that Caesar spoke as if it were in his power to recall exiles? Is he really so confident?"

"He's not confident," said Pollio. "He *knows*."

"But it's on the laps of the Gods, Pollio!"

"And who," asked Pollio, smiling, "is the darling of the Gods? Pompeius? Cato? Rubbish! Never forget, Caelius, that a great man *makes* his luck. Luck is there for everyone to seize. Most of us miss our chances; we're blind to our luck. He never misses a chance because he's never blind to the opportunity of the moment. Which is why he's the darling of the Gods. They like brilliant men."

Caesar dawdled after he left Ariminum with his two cohorts, and had not gone very far when he put his men into camp on the evening of the fourteenth day of January; he wanted to be sure that he allowed the Senate every opportunity to come to agreement, nor did he relish killing fellow Romans. But not long after camp was pitched, two envoys from the Senate arrived on blown horses: young Lucius Caesar, son of Caesar's cousin at present in Narbo, and another young senator, Lucius Roscius. Both were *boni;* a grief to Lucius Caesar concerning his son, a peculiarly rigid and very un-Caesarish sprig on the Julian tree.

"We're sent to ask you your terms for a withdrawal into Italian Gaul," said young Lucius Caesar stiffly.

"I see," said his cousin, eyeing him reflectively. "Don't you think it's more important to enquire after your father first?"

Young Lucius Caesar flushed. "Since I've not heard from him, Gaius Caesar, I presume he's well."

"Yes, he is well."

"And your terms?"

Caesar opened his eyes wide. "Lucius, Lucius, patience! It's going to take me some days to work them out. In the meantime, you and Roscius will have to march with me. South."

"That's treason, cousin."

"Since I was accused of that when I kept to my own side of the border, Lucius, what difference can it make?"

"I have a letter from Gnaeus Pompeius," Roscius interrupted.

"For which I thank you," said Caesar, taking it. After a pause during which nobody moved, he inclined his head very regally. "You may go. Hirtius will look after you."

They didn't like being so dismissed by a traitor, but they went. Caesar sat down and opened Pompey's letter.

> What a sorry mess this is, Caesar. I must confess, however, that I never thought you'd do it. With one legion? You'll go down. You can't not. Italia is alive with troops.
>
> I'm writing, really, to beg you to put the interests of the Republic

ahead of your own. That's what I've done myself from the beginning of this tangle. Frankly, it's more in my interest to side with you, isn't it? Together we could rule the world. But one of us can't, because one of us isn't strong enough. *You* taught me that back before you were consul, as I remember. And reinforced it at Luca six years ago. No, seven years ago. How time flies! Seven years since I've laid eyes on you.

I hope you're not personally insulted by the fact that I've chosen to oppose you. There's nothing personal in it, I do assure you. I made my decision based on what is best for Rome and the Republic. But surely, Caesar, you of all men must realize that leading an armed insurrection is a vain hope. If you believe, as I do, that Sulla was in the right of it and simply returned to Italia to claim what was legally his, then no armed insurrection has succeeded. Look at Lepidus and Brutus. Look at Catilina. Is that what you want for yourself, an ignominious death? Think, Caesar, please.

I urge you to put aside your anger and ambitions. For the sake of our beloved Republic! If you do put aside your anger and ambitions, I'm positive an accommodation can be arrived at between you and the Senate. I'll lend such an accommodation my absolute support. I have put aside my anger and ambitions. For the sake of the Republic. Think of Rome first and always, Caesar! Don't harm the Republic! If you remain determined to harm your enemies, you must inevitably also harm the Republic. Your enemies are as much a part of the Republic as you are. Do, please, consider your alternatives. Send us back a reasonable man's answer with young Lucius Caesar and Lucius Roscius. Come to terms with us and withdraw into Italian Gaul. It's prudent. It's *patriotic*.

His smile a little twisted, Caesar screwed the short missive into a ball and tossed it among the coals on the brazier.

"What a sanctimonious fart you are, Pompeius!" he said as he watched the piece of paper flare up, dwindle. "So I have but one legion, eh? I wonder what you'd have said in that letter if you'd known I'm marching south with no more than two cohorts! A thousand men, Pompeius! If you knew, you'd come chasing after me. But you won't. The only legions with any merit you have are the Sixth and the Fifteenth, who fought for me. And you're not sure how they'd react if you ordered them to draw their swords in full sight of me, their old commander."

A thousand men were definitely enough. When Pisaurum yielded amid cheers and flowers, Caesar sent back to Ariminum and started Curio off to eject Thermus from Iguvium. Then Fanum Fortunae yielded—more cheers, more flowers. On the sixteenth day of January, with the Senate's two envoys as witnesses, Caesar accepted the surrender of the big seaport of Ancona amid cheers and flowers. He had not so far spilled one drop of Roman blood. Of Lentulus Spinther and his ten cohorts there was no sign; he had withdrawn south to Asculum Picentum. Nor did Caesar's behavior disillusion the towns which had capitulated; he exacted no reprisals of any kind and paid for whatever he requisitioned for his troops.

ROME TO CAMPANIA

On the day before Caesar received Pompey's letter, the thirteenth day of January, a man on a foundering horse had crossed the Mulvian Bridge north of Rome. The guard posted there after the Senatus Consultum Ultimum had been passed informed the man that the Senate was meeting in Pompey's curia on the Campus Martius, and gave him a fresh mount to finish the last few miles of his journey. A client of Pompey's who had taken it upon himself to keep an eye on the road between Ravenna and Ariminum, the horseman had chosen to make the ride to Rome himself because he was dying to see how the Senate took the news he was bringing. As anyone would who had a sense of history and a wish to belong to a great moment, he reflected as he spurred his horse with a loud clatter onto the terrazzo floor outside the Curia Pompeia.

He slid off the animal, walked to the closed pair of bronze doors and hammered them with his fist. A startled lictor opened one to stick his head around it; Pompey's client yanked the door wide, then strode into the chamber.

"Here, you can't enter the Senate in closed session!" cried the lictor.

"Fathers of the Senate, I have news!" the invader roared.

Every head turned; both Marcellus Minor and Lentulus Crus rose from their ivory chairs to stand gaping at him while he looked about for Pompey, whom he located in the front row on the left-hand side.

"What news, Nonius?" asked Pompey, recognizing him.

"Gaius Caesar has crossed the Rubicon and is advancing on Ariminum with one legion!"

In the act of rising, Pompey froze for a moment before he flopped limply back onto his curule chair. All feeling seemed to have gone; he was conscious only of a ghastly numbness, and could not manage to speak.

"It's civil war!" whispered Gaius Marcellus Minor.

Lentulus Crus, a more dominant man by far than Marcellus Minor, took a faltering step forward. "When, man?" he asked, face faded to grey.

"He rode his battle horse with the toes across the Rubicon shortly before sunset three days ago, honored consul."

"Jupiter!" squeaked Metellus Scipio. "He did it!"

These words acted like the opening of a sluice gate upon a dammed-up flood; the senators rushed headlong for the doors, became jammed in the aperture, fought and scrabbled to get out, fled in panic across the peristyle and away toward the city.

A moment later, only a handful of *boni* remained.

Sensation returned to Pompey, who managed to get up. "Come with me," he said curtly, going to the door which permitted entry into his villa.

Cornelia Metella took one look at their faces as the band streamed into the atrium and decided to absent herself, which left Pompey to hand his client Nonius to the steward with a request that he be well treated.

"My thanks," he said, patting the man on the shoulder.

Well pleased with his contribution to history, Nonius went off.

Pompey led the rest into his study, where everyone clustered around the console table bearing wine and poured it unwatered with shaking hands. Save Pompey, who sat in his chair behind his desk without caring what sort of insult that was to consuls and consulars.

"One legion!" he said when his guests had all found seats and were looking at him as if at the only piece of cork in a tempestuously heaving sea. "One legion!"

"The man must be insane," muttered Gaius Marcellus Minor, wiping the sweat from his face with the purple border of his toga.

But those anguished, bewildered eyes fixed on him seemed to have a more tonic effect than wine would have; Pompey threw his chest out, put his hands on his desk and cleared his throat.

"The sanity of Gaius Caesar is not the issue," he said. "He's challenged us. He's challenged the Senate and People of Rome. With one legion he's crossed the Rubicon, with one legion he's advancing on Ariminum, with one legion he intends to conquer Italia." Pompey shrugged. "He can't do it. Mars couldn't do it."

"I suspect, from all one knows about Mars, that Caesar is a better general," said Gaius Marcellus Major dryly.

Ignoring this, Pompey looked at Cato, who hadn't said one word since Nonius strode into the chamber—and had gulped down a very large quantity of unwatered wine.

"Well, Marcus Cato?" Pompey asked. "What do you suggest?"

"That," said Cato in his most unmusical tones, "those who create great crises should also be the ones to put an end to them."

"Meaning you had nothing to do with it, and I everything?"

"My opposition to Caesar is political, not military."

Pompey drew a breath. "Does this mean, then, that I am in command of resistance?" he asked Gaius Marcellus Minor, the senior consul. "Does it?" he asked the junior consul, Lentulus Crus.

"Yes, of course," said Lentulus Crus when Marcellus Minor stayed mute.

"Then," said Pompey briskly, "the first thing we have to do is send two envoys to Caesar at once and at the gallop."

"What for?" asked Cato.

"To discover on what terms he would be prepared to withdraw into Italian Gaul."

"He won't withdraw," said Cato flatly.

"One step at a time, Marcus Cato." Pompey's eyes roved over the ranks of the fifteen men who sat there and alighted upon young Lucius Caesar and his boon companion, Lucius Roscius. "Lucius Caesar, Lucius Roscius, you're elected to do the galloping. Take the Via Flaminia and commandeer fresh horses before the ones you're on fall dead under you. You don't stop, even to take a piss. Just aim backward from the saddle." He drew paper toward him and picked up a pen. "You are official envoys and you'll speak for the entire Senate, including its magistrates. But you'll also carry a letter from me to Caesar." He grinned without amusement. "A personal plea to think of the Republic first, not to injure the Republic."

"All Caesar wants is a monarchy," said Cato.

Pompey didn't reply until the letter was written and sprinkled with sand. Then he said, rolling it up and heating wax to seal it, "We don't know what Caesar wants until he tells us." He pressed his ring into the blob of wax, handed the letter to Roscius. "You keep it, Roscius, as my envoy. Lucius Caesar will do the talking for the Senate. Now go. Ask my steward for horses—they'll be better than anything you've got. We're already north of the city, so it will save time to start from here."

"But we can't ride in togas!" said Lucius Caesar.

"My man will give you riding gear, even if it doesn't fit. Now go!" barked the General.

They went.

"Spinther's in Ancona with as many men as Caesar has," said Metellus Scipio, brightening. "He'll deal with it."

"Spinther," said Pompey, showing his teeth, "was still busy dithering over sending troops to Egypt after Gabinius had already restored Ptolemy Auletes to his throne. So let's not get our hopes up by expecting great things from Spinther. I'll send word to Ahenobarbus to join up with him and Attius Varus. Then we'll see."

But every scrap of news over the next three days was dismal: Caesar had taken Ariminum, then he had taken Pisaurum, then he had taken Fanum Fortunae. With cheers and garlands, not opposition. And that was the real worry. No one had thought of the people of rural Italia and the smaller cities, the many towns. Particularly in Picenum, Pompey's own purlieu. To discover now that Caesar was advancing unopposed—*with a mere two cohorts*!—paying for what he ate and harming no one, was appalling news.

Capped in the afternoon of the seventeenth day of January by two messages: the first, that Lentulus Spinther and his ten cohorts had quit Ancona to retreat to Asculum Picentum; and the second, that Caesar had been cheered into Ancona. The Senate met at once.

"Incredible!" shouted that famous fence-sitter Philippus. "With five thousand men, Spinther wouldn't stay to meet Caesar and a thousand men! What am I doing here in Rome? Why am I not taking myself to grovel at Caesar's feet this moment? The man's got you bluffed! You're exactly what he always calls you—couch generals! And that goes for you too these days, Pompeius *Magnus*!"

"I am not responsible for deputing Spinther to defend Ancona!" Pompey roared. "That, Philippus, if you remember, was the decision of this House! And you voted for it!"

"I wish I'd voted to make Caesar the King of Rome!"

"Shut your seditious mouth!" shrieked Cato.

"And you, you pokered-up bag of meaningless political cant, can shut yours!" Philippus shouted back.

"Order!" said Gaius Marcellus Minor in a tired voice.

Which seemed to work better than a holler; Philippus and Cato sat down, glaring at each other.

"We are here to decide on a course of action," Marcellus Minor went on, "not to bicker. How much bickering do you think is going on at Caesar's headquarters? The answer to that, I imagine, is none. Caesar wouldn't tolerate it. Why should Rome's consuls?"

"Because Rome's consuls are Rome's servants, and Caesar has refused to be anyone's servant!" said Cato.

"Oh, Marcus Cato, why do you persist in being so difficult, so obstructive? I want answers, not irrelevant statements or silly questions. How do we proceed to deal with this crisis?"

"I suggest," said Metellus Scipio, "that this House confirm Gnaeus Pompeius Magnus in command of all our troops and legates."

"I agree, Quintus Scipio," said Cato. "Those who precipitate great crises should be the ones to put an end to them. I hereby nominate Gnaeus Pompeius as commander-in-chief."

"Listen," growled Pompey, acutely aware that Cato had refrained from using Magnus, "you said that to me the other day, and I resent it! *I* didn't cause this 'great crisis,' Cato! You did! You and all the rest of your *boni* confederates! I'm just the one you expect to get you out of the shit! But don't blame me for dropping us into it! You did, Cato, you did!"

"Order!" sighed Marcellus Minor. "We have a motion, but I doubt a division is necessary. I'll see hands and hear ayes."

The House voted overwhelmingly to appoint Pompey commander-in-chief of the Republic's forces and legates.

Marcus Marcellus rose to his feet. "Conscript Fathers," he said, "I hear through Marcus Cicero that recruitment in Campania is atrociously slow. How can we speed matters up? We have to lay our hands on more soldiers."

"Ha ha ha!" sneered Favonius, smarting because Pompey had chastised his beloved Cato. "Who was it always used to say that all he had to do to raise troops in Italia was stamp his foot on the ground? Who *was* that?"

"You, Favonius, have four legs, whiskers and a long, naked tail!" snarled Pompey. *"Tace!"*

"Speak as a result of the motion, Gnaeus Pompeius," said Gaius Marcellus Minor.

"Very well then, I will!" snapped Pompey. "If recruitment in Campania is proceeding at a snail's pace, one can only blame those doing the recruiting. Like Marcus Cicero, whose head is probably in some obscure manuscript when it ought to be bent over the enlistment books. There are many thousands of soldiers to be had, Conscript Fathers, and you have just made it my job—*my* job!—to produce them. I will produce them. But a lot faster if the rats who skitter around Rome's sewers get out of my way!"

"Are you calling me a rat?" yelled Favonius, leaping up.

"Oh, sit down, you dullard! I called you a rat ages ago!" said Pompey. "Attend to business, Marcus Favonius, and try to use what passes for your mind!"

"Order!" said Marcellus Minor wearily.

"That's the trouble with this wretched body!" Pompey went on wrathfully. "You all think you're entitled to your say! You all think you're entitled to run things! You all think every decision made has to be a democratic one! Well, let me tell you something! Armies can't be run on democratic principles. If they are, they founder. There's a commander-in-chief, and his word is law! *LAW!* I am now the commander-in-chief, and I won't be harassed and frustrated by a lot of incompetent idiots!"

He got to his feet and walked to the middle of the floor. "I hereby declare a state of *tumultus*! On my say-so, not your vote! We are at war! And the last vote you made was the one that gave me the high command! I am assuming it! You will do as you are told! Hear me? Hear me? *You will do as you are told!"*

"That depends," drawled Philippus, grinning.

A comment Pompey chose to ignore. "It is my command that every senator leave Rome immediately! Any senator who remains in Rome beyond tomorrow will be regarded as a partisan of Caesar's, and be treated accordingly!"

"Ye Gods," said Philippus with a huge sigh, "I hate Campania with winter coming on! Why shouldn't I remain in nice, snug Rome?"

"By all means do so, Philippus!" said Pompey. "You are, after all, husband to Caesar's niece!"

"And father-in-law to Cato," purred Philippus.

* * *

The state of absolute confusion which followed upon Pompey's order only made things worse for those in Rome below the level of senator. From the time the fleeing Conscript Fathers had broadcast the news that Caesar had crossed the Rubicon, the city had spun into a panic. The word the knights used most frequently was that frightful word which had come into existence under the dictatorship of Sulla: "proscription." The emblazoning of one's name on a list pinned to the rostra, which meant that one was declared an enemy of Rome and the dictatorship, that any person seeing one could kill one, that one's property and money was confiscate to the State. Two thousand senators and knights had died, and Sulla had filled his empty treasury on the profits.

For everyone with much to lose assumed as a matter of course that Caesar would follow in Sulla's footsteps—wasn't it exactly like that time after Sulla landed in Brundisium and marched up the peninsula? With the common folk cheering and throwing flowers? He too had paid for every leaf, sheaf, root and shoot his army ate. What was the difference between a Cornelian and a Julian, after all? They existed on a plane far above knight-businessmen, who were less to them than the dust beneath their feet.

Only Balbus, Oppius, Rabirius Postumus and Atticus tried to stem the panic, explain that Caesar was no Sulla, that all he was after was the vindication of his battered *dignitas,* that he was not about to assume the dictatorship and slaughter people indiscriminately. That he had been forced to march by the senseless, obdurate opposition of a small clique within the Senate, and that as soon as he had forced that clique to recant its policies and its decrees, he would revert to ordinary behavior.

It did little good; no one was calm enough to listen and common sense had flown away. Disaster had struck; Rome was about to be plunged into yet another civil war. Proscriptions would follow—hadn't everyone heard that Pompey too had spoken angrily of proscriptions, of thousands being thrown off the Tarpeian Rock? Oh, caught between a harpy and a siren! Whichever side won, the knights of the Eighteen were sure to suffer!

Most of the senators, packing trunks, trying to explain to wives, making new wills, had no idea exactly why they had been ordered to leave Rome. Not requested: *ordered*. If they stayed they would be regarded as Caesar's partisans, that was all they really understood. Sons over the age of sixteen were demanding to come too; daughters with a wedding date fixed shrilled and fluttered; bankers and accountants ran from one noble senatorial client to another, explaining feverishly that cash was in short supply, now was not the time to sell land, sleeping partnerships were worth nothing when business had slumped.

Little wonder, perhaps, that the most important thing of all was entirely overlooked. Not Pompey, not Cato, not any of the three Marcelli, not Lentulus Crus nor anyone else had so much as thought of emptying the Treasury.

On the eighteenth day of January, amid overladen baggage carts trundling in hundreds through the Capena Gate en route to Neapolis, Formiae, Pompeii, Herculaneum, Capua and other Campanian destinations, the two consuls and almost all the Senate fled out of Rome. Leaving the Treasury stuffed to the rafters with money and bullion, not to mention various emergency hoards of bullion in the temples of Ops, Juno Moneta, Hercules Olivarius and Mercury, and thousands of chests of money in Juno Lucina, Iuventus, Venus Libitina and Venus Erucina. The only man who had thought to draw money from the *tribuni aerarii* in charge of the Treasury had been Ahenobarbus some days earlier; he had asked for and received six million sesterces to pay the many troops he confidently expected to obtain among the Marsi and Paeligni. The public fortune of Rome remained inside Rome.

Not every senator left. Lucius Aurelius Cotta, Lucius Piso Censor and Lucius Marcius Philippus were among those who stayed. Perhaps to reinforce this decision in each other, they met for dinner on the nineteenth at Philippus's house.

"I'm a newly married man with a baby son," said Piso, his bad teeth showing. "A perilous enough situation for a man of my age without rushing off like a Sardinian bandit after a sheep!"

"Well," said Cotta, smiling gently, "I stayed because I do not believe Caesar will lose. He's my nephew, and I've never known him to act without caution, despite his reputation. It's all thought out very carefully."

"And I stayed because I'm too lazy to uproot myself. Huh!" Philippus snorted. "Fancy haring off to Campania with winter in the offing! Villas shut up, no staff to light the braziers, the fish sleepy and the diet endless plates of *cabbage*."

Which struck everyone as funny; the meal proceeded merrily. Piso had not brought his new wife, and Cotta was a widower, but Philippus's wife attended. So did her thirteen-year-old son, Gaius Octavius.

"And what do you think of it all, young Gaius Octavius?" asked Cotta, his great-great-uncle. The boy, whom he knew from many visits (Atia worried about her great-uncle, who lived alone), fascinated him. Not in the same way as Caesar had when a child, though there were similarities. The beauty, certainly. What good luck for young Gaius Octavius, however, that his ears stuck out! Caesar had had no flaw at all. The boy was very fair too, though his eyes were more widely opened and a luminous grey—not eerie eyes like Caesar's. Frowning, Cotta sought for the correct word to describe their expression, and settled upon "careful." Yes, that was it. They were careful. At first one thought them innocent and candid, until one realized that they never really told one what the mind behind them was thinking. They were permanently veiled and never passionate.

"I think, Uncle Cotta, that Caesar will win."

"In which we agree. Why do *you* think so?"

"He's better than they are." Young Gaius Octavius found a bright red apple and sank his even white teeth into it. "In the field he has no equal—Pompeius is second rate as a general. A good organizer. If you look at his campaigns, he always won because of that. There are no brilliant battles, battles wherein his strategy and tactics will inspire another Polybius. He wore his opponents down; that was his strength. Uncle Caesar has done that too, but Uncle Caesar can boast of a dozen brilliant battles."

"And one or two, like Gergovia, that were not brilliant."

"Yes, but he didn't go down in them either."

"All right," said Cotta, "that's the battlefield. What else?"

"He understands politics. He knows how to manipulate. He doesn't tangle himself in lost causes or associate with men who do. He's quite as efficient as Pompeius off the battlefield. A better speaker, a better lawyer, a better planner."

Listening to this analysis, Lucius Piso became conscious that he disliked its author. Not *proper* for a boy of that age to speak like a teacher! Who did he think he was? And so pretty. Far too pretty. Another year, and he'd be offering his arse; he had that smell about him. A very precious boy.

Pompey, the consuls and a good part of the Senate reached Teanum Sidicinum in Campania on the twenty-second day of January, and here halted to bring a little order out of the chaos of evacuating the capital. Not all the senators had tacked themselves onto Pompey's cometish tail; some had scattered to invade their shut-up villas on the coast, some preferred to be anywhere other than wherever Pompey was.

Titus Labienus was waiting; Pompey greeted him like a long-lost brother, even embraced him and kissed him on the cheek.

"Where have you come from?" Pompey asked, surrounded by his senatorial watchdogs—Cato, the three Marcelli and Lentulus Crus—and bolstered by a mournful Metellus Scipio.

"Placentia," said Labienus, leaning back in his chair.

Though all present knew Labienus by sight and remembered his activities as tribune of the plebs, it was ten years since any of them (including Pompey) had set eyes on him, for he had left Rome to take up duties in Italian Gaul while Caesar was still consul. They gazed at him now in some dismay; Labienus had changed. In his early forties, he looked exactly what he had become: a hard-bitten, ruthlessly authoritarian military man. His tight black curls were peppered with grey; his thin, liver-colored mouth bisected his lower face like a scar; the great hooked nose with its flaring nostrils gave him the look of an eagle; and his black eyes, narrow and contemptuous, gazed upon all of them, even upon Pompey, with the interest of a cruel boy in a group of insects owning potentially detachable wings.

"When did you leave Placentia?" asked Pompey.

"Two days after Caesar crossed the Rubicon."

"How many legions has he got in Placentia? Though no doubt they're already marching to join him."

The greying head reared back, the mouth opened to display huge yellow teeth; Labienus laughed heartily. "Ye Gods, you are fools!" he said. "There are no legions in Placentia! There never were. Caesar has the Thirteenth, which he sent to Tergeste and back on a training exercise which appears to have escaped your notice. Most of the time he was in Ravenna he was without troops of any kind. He's marched with the Thirteenth, and he has no other legions coming to help him. Ergo, he thinks he can do the job with the Thirteenth. From what I've seen, he is probably right."

"Then," said Pompey slowly, beginning to revise his plans to quit Italia in favor of Macedonia and Greece, "I can move to contain him in Picenum. If Lentulus Crus and Attius Varus haven't already done that. He split the Thirteenth, you see. Antonius is holding Arretium and the Via Cassia with five cohorts, and"—Pompey winced—"Curio has ejected Thermus from Iguvium with three more cohorts. All Caesar has at present are two cohorts."

"Then why are you sitting here?" demanded Labienus. "You ought to be halfway up the Adriatic coast by now!"

Pompey cast a look of burning reproach at Gaius Marcellus Major. "I was led to believe," he said with great dignity, "that Caesar possessed four legions. And though we did hear that he was marching with no more than one, we assumed the others were doing things in his rear."

"I don't think," said Labienus deliberately, "that you want to fight Caesar at all, Magnus."

"I don't think so either!" said Cato.

Oh, was he never going to be free of this carping criticism? Wasn't he the officially appointed commander-in-chief? Hadn't he informed them that democracy was over, that he'd do things his way, that they'd better pipe down? Now here was another critic, Titus Labienus, feeding lines to Cato!

Pompey drew himself up in his chair, expanded his chest until his leather cuirass creaked. "Listen, all of you," he said with commendable restraint, "it's my command, and I will do things my way, do you hear? Until my scouts inform me exactly what Caesar is doing whereabouts, I'll bide my time. If you're right, Labienus, then there's no problem. We'll advance into Picenum and finish him off. But the most important thing in my agenda is the preservation of Italia. I have sworn not to fight a civil war on her soil if it assumes anything like the dimensions of the Italian War. That ruined the country for twenty years. I won't have my name associated with that kind of odium! So until I hear what's happening in Picenum, I'll continue to bide my time. Once I know, I'll make my decision whether to attempt to contain Caesar inside Italia, or whether to remove myself, my armies and the government of Rome to the East."

"Leave Italia?" squeaked Marcus Marcellus.

"Yes, just as Carbo should have when Sulla threatened."

"Sulla beat Carbo," said Cato.

"On Italian soil. That's my whole point."

"Your whole point should be," said Labienus, "that you are indeed in Carbo's position. Handicapped by troops who'll be too old or too raw to deal with an army of veterans who've just emerged from a long and grueling foreign war. Caesar is in Sulla's shoes. He's the one with the veterans."

"I have the Sixth and the Fifteenth in Capua," said Pompey, "and I very much doubt anyone can call them either too old or too raw, Labienus!"

"The Sixth and the Fifteenth belonged to Caesar."

"But they're seriously disaffected with Caesar," said Metellus Scipio. "Appius Claudius told us!"

They're like children, thought Labienus in wonder. They've made not one single effort to establish a good intelligence force, and they're still believing whatever they're told. What has happened to Pompeius Magnus? I served with him in the East and he wasn't like this. He's either past it or intimidated. But who is doing the intimidating? Caesar or this motley crew?

"Scipio," Labienus said very slowly and distinctly, "Caesar's troops are not disaffected! I don't care how august the man is who told you, nor what evidence you've actually seen to confirm it. Just take it from one who knows—Caesar's troops are not disaffected." He turned to Pompey. "Magnus, act now! Take the Fifteenth, the Sixth and whatever other troops you can scrape together, and march to contain Caesar *now*! If you don't, other legions will arrive to reinforce him. I said there were none in Italian Gaul, but that won't last. The rest of Caesar's legates are his men to the death."

"And why aren't you, Labienus?" asked Gaius Marcellus Major.

The dark, oily skin took on a purple hue; Labienus paused, then said evenly, "I think too much of Rome, whichever Marcellus you might happen to be. Caesar is acting treasonously. *I* refuse to commit treason."

Whereabouts this turn in the conversation might have led was never known; the two envoys, Lucius Caesar Junior and Lucius Roscius, reported in.

"How long is it since you left?" asked Pompey eagerly.

"Four days," said young Lucius Caesar.

"In four days," said Labienus, drawing attention to himself, "anyone working for Caesar would have covered four hundred miles. What have you covered, less than a hundred and fifty?"

"And who," said young Lucius Caesar in freezing tones, "are you to criticize *me*?"

"I'm Titus Labienus, boy." He looked young Lucius Caesar up and down scornfully. "Your face says who *you* are, but it also says you're not in your father's league."

"Yes, yes!" snapped Pompey, temper fraying. "What was going on when you left?"

"Caesar was in Auximum. Which welcomed him with open arms. Attius Varus and his five cohorts fled before we got there, but Caesar sent his lead century after them, and caught them. There was a small engagement. Attius Varus was defeated. Most of his men surrendered and asked to join Caesar. Some scattered."

A silence fell, which Cato broke. "Caesar's lead century," he said heavily. "Eighty men. Who defeated over two thousand."

"The trouble was," said Lucius Roscius, "that Varus's troops didn't have their hearts in it. They were shivering in their boots at the very thought of Caesar. Yet once Caesar had charge of them, they cheered up and began to look like soldiers. Remarkable."

"No," said Labienus, smiling wryly. "Normal."

Pompey swallowed. "Did Caesar issue terms?"

"Yes," said young Lucius Caesar. He drew a long breath and launched into a carefully memorized speech. "I am authorized to tell you, Gnaeus Pompeius, the following: One, that you and Caesar should both disband your armies. Two, that you should withdraw at once to Spain. Three, that Italia should be completely demobilized. Four, that the reign of terror should come to an end. Five, that there should be free elections and a return to properly constitutional government by both Senate and People. Six, that you and Caesar should meet in person to discuss your differences and reach an agreement to be ratified by oath. Seven, that once this agreement is reached, Caesar should hand over his provinces to his successors. And eight, that Caesar should contest the consular elections in person inside Rome, not *in absentia*."

"What rubbish!" said Cato. "He doesn't mean a word of it! A more absurd set of conditions I've never heard!"

"That's what Cicero said when I told him," said young Lucius Caesar. "Manifestly absurd."

"And where," asked Labienus dangerously, "did you encounter Marcus Cicero?"

"At his villa near Minturnae."

"Minturnae . . . What an odd route you took from Picenum!"

"I needed to visit Rome. Roscius and I were with Caesar for much longer than we'd thought. I *stank*!"

"Now why didn't I think of that?" asked Labienus wearily. "You stank. Did Caesar stink? Or his men?"

"Not Caesar, no. But he bathes in freezing cold water!"

"That's how you keep smelling sweet on campaign, true."

Pompey attempted to regain control of proceedings. "Well, there are his terms," he said. "He's issued them officially, no matter how absurd. But I do agree. He doesn't mean them, he's just buying time." He opened his mouth and shouted. "Vibullius! Sestius!"

Two of his prefects entered the room. Lucius Vibullius Rufus belonged to the engineers, Sestius to the cavalry.

"Vibullius, go at once to Picenum and find Lentulus Spinther and Attius Varus. Urge them to come to grips with Caesar as soon as possible. He has two cohorts, therefore they can beat him—*if* they manage to explain that fact to their soldiers! Instruct them from me to do so."

Vibullius Rufus saluted and left.

"Sestius, you're ordered to proceed as an envoy to the camp of Gaius Caesar. Tell Gaius Caesar that his terms are unacceptable until he gives up the towns he is currently occupying in Picenum and returns across the Rubicon into Italian Gaul. If he does all that, I'll take it as evidence of his good faith, and then we shall see. Emphasize that there's no deal while he's on the Italian side of the Rubicon, because that means the Senate cannot return to Rome."

Publius Sestius, prefect of cavalry, saluted and left.

"Good!" said Cato, satisfied.

"What did Caesar mean, 'reign of terror'? What reign of terror?" asked Metellus Scipio.

"We think, Roscius and I," said young Lucius Caesar, "that Caesar was referring to the panic inside Rome."

"Oh, *that*!" sniffed Metellus Scipio.

Pompey cleared his throat. "Well, noble friends, we've come to the parting of the ways," he said with more satisfaction than Cato and Metellus Scipio combined. "Tomorrow Labienus and I are heading for Larinum. The Sixth and the Fifteenth are already en route. Consuls, you'll go to Capua and whip up the recruitment rate. If and when you see Marcus Cicero, tell him to stop dithering and start producing. What's he doing in Minturnae? Not enlisting men, I'll warrant! Too busy scribbling to Atticus and the Gods know who else!"

"And from Larinum," said Cato, "you'll march north toward Picenum and Caesar."

"That," said Pompey, "remains to be seen."

"I can see why the consuls are needed at Capua," said Cato, warming up, "but the rest of us will be with you, of course."

"No, you won't!" Pompey's chin trembled. "You'll all remain in Capua for the time being. Caesar has five thousand gladiators in a school there, and they'll have to be broken up. It's times like this I wish we owned a few prisons, but as we don't, I'll leave it to all you couch experts how to solve the situation. The only one I want to accompany me to Larinum is Titus Labienus."

It was true that Cicero dithered, and also true that he was not occupying himself in recruitment duties, either in Minturnae or at his next stop on that round of beautiful villas he owned from one end of the Campanian coast to the other. Misenum was next to Minturnae, therefore Misenum was his next stop. He wasn't alone; Quintus Cicero, young Quintus Cicero and his own son, Marcus, were with him; and so too were his twelve lictors, their *fasces* wreathed in laurels because Cicero was a triumphator who had not yet held his triumph. A big enough nuisance to have the male members of the family in attendance, but not half the nuisance those wretched lictors were! He couldn't move without them, and since he still held his imperium and his imperium was a foreign one, the lictors were clad in all the glory of crimson tunics broadly belted in black leather studded with brass emblems, and bore the axes in their *fasces* among the thirty rods. Imposing. But not to a man burdened with as many cares as Cicero.

He'd been visited by none other than his protégé, that most promising young advocate Gaius Trebatius Testa, who had been released from service with Caesar so thoroughly indoctrinated to Caesar's way of thinking that he would hear not one word against him. Trebatius came, podgy as ever, to beg that Cicero return at once to Rome, which desperately needed, said Trebatius, the genuine stability of a knot of consulars.

"I will not go anywhere at the behest of an outlaw!" said Cicero indignantly.

"Marcus Cicero, Caesar is no outlaw," pleaded Trebatius. "He has marched to retrieve his *dignitas,* and that is proper. All he wants is to ensure its continuance. After that—and in concert with that—he wants peace and prosperity for Rome. He feels that your presence in Rome would be a calming one."

"Well, let him feel what he likes!" snapped Cicero. "I will not be seen to betray my colleagues who are dedicated to the cause and preservation of the Republic. Caesar wants to be a king, and candidly, I believe Pompeius Magnus wouldn't refuse if he were asked to reign as King Magnus. Hah! Magnus Rex!"

Which reply left Trebatius with no alternative other than to litter himself away.

Next came a letter from Caesar himself, its brevity and off-the-point paragraph symptomatic of Caesar's exasperation.

My dear Marcus Cicero, you are one of the few people involved in this mess who may have the foresight and the courage to choose an intermediate path. Night and day I worry over the plight of Rome, left rudderless by the deplorable exodus of her government. What kind of answer is it to cry *tumultus* and then desert the ship? For that is what Gnaeus Pompeius, egged on by Cato and the Marcelli, has done. So far I have received no indication that any of them, including Pompeius, are thinking of Rome. And that despite the rhetoric.

If you would return to Rome, it would be a great help. In this, I know, I am supported by Titus Atticus. A great joy to know him recovered from that terrible bout of the ague. He doesn't take enough care of himself. I remember that Quintus Sertorius's mother, Ria—she cared for me when I almost died of the ague without a rhythm—sent me a letter after I returned to Rome advising me which herbs to hang and which herbs to throw on a brazier to avoid contracting the ague. They work, Cicero. I haven't had the ague since. But though I told him what to do, Atticus can't be bothered.

Do please consider coming home. Not for my sake. Nor will anyone apostrophize you as my partisan. Do it for Rome.

But Cicero wouldn't do it for Rome; did he do it, he would be acting to oblige Caesar. And that, he vowed, he would *never* do!

But by the time that January ended and February arrived, Cicero was very torn. Nothing he heard inspired any confidence. One moment he was assured that Pompey was marching for Picenum to finish Caesar before he got started; the next moment he was being told that Pompey was in Larinum and planning to march for Brundisium and a voyage across the Adriatic to Epirus or western Macedonia. Caesar's letter had tickled an itch, with the result that Cicero fretted about Pompey's indifference to Rome the city. Why wasn't he defending her? *Why?*

By this time the whole of the north was open to Caesar, from the Via Aurelia on the Tuscan Sea to the Adriatic coast. He held every great road or knew they contained no troops to oppose him; Hirrus had vacated Camerinum, Lentulus Spinther had fled from Asculum Picentum, and Caesar held all of Picenum. While, apparently, Pompey sat in Larinum. His prefect of engineers, Vibullius Rufus, had encountered Lentulus Spinther in disarray on the road after quitting Asculum Picentum, and stood up to the haughty consular sturdily. With the result that he took over command of Lentulus Spinther's troops and hied them, plus the dejected Lentulus Spinther, to Corfinium, where Ahenobarbus had established himself.

Of all the legates the Senate had dispatched to defend Italia back in those far-off days before Caesar crossed the Rubicon, only Ahenobarbus had fared well. In Alba Fucentia beside the Fucine Lake he had marshaled two legions of Marsi, a warlike and ardent people in his clientele. He had then proceeded with them to the fortress city of Corfinium on the river Aternus, resolved to hold Corfinium and its sister city, Sulmo, in Caesar's teeth. Thanks to Vibullius, he received Lentulus Spinther's ten cohorts— and five more cohorts Vibullius poached from Hirrus, retreating from Camerinum. Thus, or so it seemed to Cicero, Ahenobarbus looked like the only serious foe Caesar was likely to meet. For Pompey, it was clear, didn't want to meet him.

The stories about what Caesar intended to do once he owned Italia and Rome were legion and horrifying: he was going to cancel all debts; proscribe the entire knight class; hand the Senate and the Assemblies over to the rabble, the Head Count who owned nothing and could give the State nothing save children. It was perhaps something of a comfort to know that Atticus stoutly maintained Caesar would do none of these things.

"Don't dismiss Caesar as a Saturninus or a Catilina," said Atticus to Cicero in a letter. "He's a very able and clever man with a mine of common sense. Far from believing that he would do anything as foolish as cancel debts, I think him absolutely committed to protecting and ensuring the well-being of Rome's commercial sphere. Truly, Cicero, Caesar is no radical!"

Oh, how much Cicero wanted to believe that! The trouble was that he couldn't, chiefly because he listened to everyone and deemed everyone right at the time. Save those, like Atticus, who kept blowing Caesar's trumpet, no matter in how restrained and reasonable a way. For he couldn't like Caesar, couldn't trust Caesar. Not since that dreadful year when he had been consul, when Catilina had plotted to overthrow the State, and *Caesar* had accused him of executing Roman citizens without a trial. Inexcusable. Unforgivable. Out of Caesar's stand came Clodius's persecution and eighteen months in exile.

"You're an outright, downright fool!" snarled Quintus Cicero.

"I beg your pardon!" gasped Cicero.

"You heard me, big brother! You're a fool! Why won't you see that Caesar is a decent man, a highly conservative politician, and the most brilliant military man Rome has ever produced?" Quintus Cicero emitted a series of derisive raspberries. "He'll wallop the lot of them, Marcus! They do not stand a chance, no matter how much they prate about your precious Republic!"

"I will repeat," said Cicero with great dignity, "what I have already said several times. It's *infinitely* preferable to be beaten with Pompeius than victorious with Caesar!"

"Well," said Quintus, "don't expect me to feel the same way. I served with Caesar. I like him. And, by all the Gods, I admire him! So don't ask me to fight against him, because I won't."

"*I* am the head of the Tullii Cicerones!" cried big brother. "You will do what I say!"

"I'll cleave to the family in this much, Marcus—I won't enlist to fight for Caesar. But nor will I take up a sword or a command against him."

And from that stand little brother Quintus would not be budged.

Which led to more and fiercer quarrels when Cicero's wife and daughter, Terentia and Tullia, joined them at Formiae. As did Quintus's wife, Pomponia, the sister of Atticus and a worse termagant than Terentia. Terentia sided with Cicero (not always the case), but Pomponia and Tullia sided with Quintus Cicero. Added to which, Quintus Cicero's son wanted to enlist in Caesar's legions, and Cicero's son wanted to enlist in Pompey's legions.

"*Tata,*" said Tullia, big and pretty brown eyes pleading, "I do wish you'd see reason! My Dolabella says Caesar is everything a great Roman aristocrat ought to be."

"As I *know* him to be," said Quintus Cicero warmly.

"I agree, Pater," said young Quintus Cicero with equal warmth.

"My brother Atticus thinks him an excellent sort of man," said Pomponia, chin out pugnaciously.

"You're all mentally deficient!" snapped Terentia.

"Not to mention getting ready to suck up to the man you think will win!" yelled young Marcus Cicero, glaring at his cousin.

"*Tacete, tacete, tacete!*" roared the head of the Tullii Cicerones. "Shut up, the lot of you! Go away! Leave me in peace! Isn't it enough that I can't persuade anybody to enlist? Isn't it enough to be plagued by twelve lictors? Isn't it enough that the consuls in Capua have got no further than boarding out Caesar's five thousand gladiators among loyal Republican families? Where they're eating their hosts out of house and home? Isn't it enough that Cato can't make up his mind whether to stay in Capua or go to govern Sicily? Isn't it enough that Balbus writes twice a day, begging me to heal the breach between Caesar and Pompeius? Isn't it enough that I hear Pompeius is already transferring cohorts to Brundisium to ship across the Adriatic? *Tacete, tacete, tacete!*"

LARINUM TO BRUNDISIUM

It was much nicer existing without the senatorial watchdogs, Pompey had discovered. From Titus Labienus he received nothing except sound military sense delivered minus homilies, rhetoric or political analysis; Pompey began to think that he might be able to salvage something out of this hideous shipwreck. All his instincts told him that it was futile to try to halt Caesar in Italia, that his best and cleverest course was to retreat across the Adriatic and take Rome's government with him. If there was no government left in Italia, Caesar wouldn't have the opportunity to shore up his position by bluffing, bullying or bludgeoning the government into officially sanctioning his actions. He would look what he was, a treasonous conqueror who had driven the government into exile. Nor was retreating across the Adriatic a true retreat; it was the breathing space Pompey desperately needed to get his army into shape, to see his own legions shipped to him from Spain, to levy client kings in the East for additional troops and the masses of cavalry he lacked.

"Don't count on your Spanish legions," warned Labienus.

"Why ever not?"

"If you leave Italia for Macedonia or Greece, Magnus, don't expect Caesar to follow you. He'll march for Spain to destroy your base and your army there."

"Surely *I'm* his top priority!"

"No. Neutering Spain is. That's one reason why he won't bring all his legions to this side of the Alps. He knows he'll need them in the West. By now, I imagine, Trebonius will have at least three legions in Narbo. Where old Lucius Caesar has everything in perfect order as well as thousands of local troops. And they'll be waiting for Afranius and Petreius to attempt the land route to Rome." Labienus frowned, shot Pompey a look. "They haven't marched yet, have they?"

"No, they haven't. I'm still waiting to see how best to deal with Caesar himself. Whether I should go north to Picenum, or east across the Adriatic."

"You've left your run too late for Picenum, Magnus. That ceased to be an alternative a *nundinum* ago."

"Then," said Pompey with decision, "I'll send Quintus Fabius to Ahenobarbus in Corfinium today with orders that Ahenobarbus is to abandon the place and transfer himself and his troops to me."

"Good thinking. If he stays in Corfinium, he'll fall. It's Caesar will inherit his men, and we need them. Ahenobarbus has two properly formed legions and another fifteen-odd cohorts." He thought of something else. "How are the Sixth and the Fifteenth?"

"Surprisingly tractable. Largely due to you, I suspect. Since they learned you're on our side, they've been more prone to think ours is the side in the right."

"Then I've accomplished something."

Labienus got up and paced across to an unshuttered window, through which blew a cold, ominously wintry blast from the north. The camp was located on the outskirts of Larinum, which had never recovered from the treatment Gaius Verres and Publius Cethegus had doled out to it in Sulla's wake. Nor had the Apulian countryside. Verres had torn out every single tree; without windbreaks or roots to hold down the topsoil, what had been a reasonably verdant and fertile land had gone to dust and locusts.

"You're hiring seaworthy transports in Brundisium?" asked Labienus from the window, gazing out, indifferent to the cold.

"Yes, of course. Though shortly I'll have to ask the consuls for money. Some of the captains refuse to sail until they've been paid—the difference between a legitimate war and a civil one, I presume. Normally they're content to run an account."

"Then the Treasury is in Capua."

"Yes, I imagine so," Pompey answered absently. A fraction of a moment later he was sitting in his chair rigid with shock. *"Jupiter!"*

Labienus swung around immediately. "What?"

"Labienus, I can't be sure that the Treasury isn't still in Rome! Jupiter! Oh, Hercules! Minerva! Juno! Mars! I don't remember seeing any Treasury wagons on the road to Campania!" He writhed, glued his fingers to his temples, closed his eyes. "Ye Gods, I don't believe it! But the more I think about it, the more certain I am that those prize *cunni* Marcellus and Crus skipped from Rome without emptying the vaults! They're the consuls—it's their duty to deal with the money!"

Face a pasty grey, Labienus swallowed. "Do you mean we've embarked on this enterprise without a war chest?"

"It's not my fault!" wailed Pompey, hands clenched in his thick, gone-to-silver hair. "Do I have to think of *everything*? Can those *mentulae* in Capua think of *nothing*? They've hemmed me in for months, squawking and clucking, yammering in my ears until I can hardly hear my own thoughts—picking, carping, criticizing, arguing—oh, Titus, how they argue! On and on and on! It's not a right act to do this, it's a wrong act to do that; the Senate says this, the Senate says that—it's a wonder I've got as far into this campaign as Larinum!"

"Then," said Labienus, understanding that now was not the moment to castigate Pompey, "we'd better send a man at the gallop for Capua with instructions for the consuls to hustle themselves back to Rome and empty the Treasury. Otherwise it's Caesar who will pay for his war out of the public purse."

"Yes, yes!" gasped Pompey, stumbling to his feet. "I'll do it this instant—I know, I'll send Gaius Cassius! A tribune of the plebs who distinguished himself in Syria ought to be able to make them understand, eh?"

Off he reeled, leaving Labienus to stand by the window and stare at the bleak landscape with leaden heart. He's not the same man, Pompeius. He's a doll that's lost half its stuffing. Well, he's getting old. Must be pushing fifty-seven. And he's right about that clutch of political theorists—Cato, the Marcelli, Lentulus Crus, Metellus Scipio. So militarily inept they couldn't tell their arses from their swords. I've chosen the wrong side, unless I can keep closer to Magnus than the senatorial leeches. If it's left to them, Caesar will eat us. Picenum has fallen. And the Twelfth has joined the Thirteenth—Caesar possesses two veteran legions. Plus every one of our recruits he's managed to get his hands on. *They* know. I'll see Quintus Fabius myself; I must reinforce the message he's got to get through to that pigheaded *verpa* in Corfinium, Ahenobarbus—abandon the place and join us! Money. Money . . . There's bound to be some around here somewhere, even after Verres and Cethegus. They were thirty years ago. A few temple hoards, old Rabirius's house . . . And I'll see Gaius Cassius myself too. Tell him to start borrowing from the Campanian temples and towns. We need every sestertius we can find.

A wise decision on Labienus's part, one which would enable Pompey to sail. By the time Lentulus Crus answered Pompey's curt order (the senior consul, Marcellus Minor, was sick—as usual), the army had quit Larinum and was at Luceria, well south; the delighted Metellus Scipio had bundled himself off importantly with six cohorts to Brundisium under instructions to hold it, and secure in the knowledge that Caesar was a long way from Brundisium.

While Labienus watched, Pompey deciphered Lentulus Crus's letter. "I don't believe it!" he gasped, chalk-white, eyes swimming with tears of sheer rage. "Our esteemed junior consul will get up off his pampered *podex* and proceed back to Rome to empty the Treasury *if* I advance into Picenum and prevent Caesar any access to Rome! Otherwise, he says, he's staying right where he is in Capua. *Safe!* He goes on to accuse Gaius Cassius of impertinence and as punishment has sent him to Neapolis—one of *my* legates!—to gather a few ships in case the consuls and the rest of the government have to evacuate Campania in a hurry. He ends, Labienus, by informing me that he still considers it a mistake on my part to refuse to let him make a legion out of Caesar's gladiators. He's convinced they'd fight brilliantly for us and he doesn't think us military men appreciate the prowess of gladiators. Therefore he is mighty miffed that I ordered them disbanded."

Pushed beyond rage, Labienus giggled. "Oh, it's a gigantic farce! What we ought to do, Magnus, is put the whole show on the road and play every pig-shit town and village in Apulia. The yokels would deem it the funniest troupe of traveling mimers they've ever seen. Especially if we trick Lentulus Crus out as a raddled old whore with a pair of melons for tits."

But at least, thought Labienus privately, young Gaius Cassius will be raiding every temple from Antium to Surrentum. I doubt an order from the likes of Lentulus Crus to save the Senate's bacon at the expense of the army will impress that particular Cassius!

Quintus Fabius came back from Corfinium to inform Pompey that Ahenobarbus would march to join the army in Luceria four days before the Ides of February, and that he had accumulated even more troops;

refugees from the debacles in Picenum kept drifting in. One of the most cheering aspects of this was Ahenobarbus's news that he had six million sesterces with him. He had intended to pay his men, but Pompey's needs were greater, so he hadn't.

But on the eleventh day of February, two days before the Ides, Vibullius sent a dispatch telling Pompey that Ahenobarbus had now decided to remain in Corfinium. His scouts had reported that Caesar had left Picenum behind and was in Castrum Truentum. He had to be stopped! said Ahenobarbus. Therefore Ahenobarbus would stop him.

Pompey sent an urgent directive back to Corfinium instructing Ahenobarbus to leave before Caesar arrived to blockade him; his own scouts believed that a third of Caesar's veteran legions was now approaching, and the scouts knew for a fact that Antonius and Curio were back in Caesar's fold with their cohorts. With three of his old legions and a wealth of experience in blockade, Caesar would take Corfinium and Sulmo easily. Get out, get out! said Pompey's note.

Ahenobarbus ignored it and remained.

Unaware of this, on the Ides of February Pompey sent his legate Decimus Laelius to Capua with orders he insisted be obeyed. One of the two consuls was to proceed to Sicily to secure the grain harvest, just beginning to come in; Ahenobarbus and twelve cohorts of his troops would also sail for Sicily as soon as possible. The men not needed to secure Sicily were to go to Brundisium at once, cross the Adriatic to Epirus, and wait in Dyrrachium. They were to include the government. Laelius inherited the job of finding a fleet to sail for Sicily; Cassius, hinted Labienus, was very busy emptying temples and towns of their money.

News of what was happening at Corfinium filtered in very, very slowly. Though the distance between Corfinium and Luceria was only a matter of a hundred miles, dispatches took between two and four days to reach Pompey. Which meant that by the time he got the news, it was already too old to act upon. Even the awesome and frightening Labienus could not manage to improve the situation; the couriers dawdled all the way, popped in to say hello to an aged aunt, visited a tavern, lingered to dally with a woman.

"Morale," said Pompey wearily, "doesn't exist. Hardly anyone believes in this war! Those who do, refuse to take it seriously. I'm hamstrung, Labienus."

"Hang on until we get across the Adriatic" was the answer.

Though Caesar arrived at Corfinium the day after the Ides, three more days elapsed before Pompey knew; by that time Caesar had the Eighth, the Twelfth and all the Thirteenth with him. Sulmo surrendered and Corfinium had been rendered helpless by blockade. Lips tight, Pompey sent word back to Ahenobarbus that it was far too late to send help, that the situation was of Ahenobarbus's own making, and that he would have to get himself out of it.

But when Pompey's unsympathetic response reached Ahenobarbus six days after he had sent for assistance, the commander of Corfinium decided to flee secretly in the night, leaving his troops and his legates behind. Unfortunately his strange behavior gave him away; he was promptly taken into custody by Lentulus Spinther, who sent to Caesar for terms. With the result that on the twenty-first day of February, Ahenobarbus, his cronies and fifty other senators were handed over to Caesar, together with thirty-one cohorts of soldiers. And six million sesterces. For Caesar, a welcome bonus. He proceeded to require an oath of allegiance to himself from Ahenobarbus's men; he also paid them well into the future. They would be most useful, he had decided, to send to secure Sicily.

For once the messenger to Pompey hurried. Pompey reacted by striking camp in Luceria and marching for Brundisium with the fifty cohorts he possessed. Caesar was now in hot pursuit; not five hours after accepting the surrender of Corfinium, he was on the road south in the wake of Pompey. Who reached Brundisium on the twenty-fourth day of February to discover that he had sufficient transports to ship only thirty of his fifty cohorts across the sea.

The most dismaying news of all, as far as Pompey was concerned, however, was Caesar's stunning clemency at Corfinium. Instead of holding mass executions, he gave mass pardons. Ahenobarbus, Attius Varus, Lucilius Hirrus, Lentulus Spinther, Vibullius Rufus and the fifty senators were civilly commended for their valor in defending Italia, and released unharmed. All Caesar required was their word that they would cease to fight against him; did they take up arms a second time, he warned them, he might not be so merciful.

Campania was now as open to Caesar as was the north. No one was left in Capua—no troops, no consuls, no senators. Everything and everyone went to Brundisium, for Pompey had abandoned the idea of sending a force to Sicily. Everything and everyone was to sail for Dyrrachium in western Macedonia, some distance north of Epirus. The Treasury had not been emptied. But was Lentulus Crus sorry? Did he apologize for his stupidity? No, not at all! He was too indignant still over Pompey's rejection of that gladiator legion.

Brundisium was all for Caesar, which made Pompey's situation there uncomfortable. Forced to barricade and mine the port city's streets, he was also forced to expend a great deal of effort on making sure Brundisium did not betray him. But between the second and the fourth days of March he managed to send off thirty cohorts in his fleet of transports—plus one consul, many other governing magistrates, and the senators. At least they were out of his hair! The only men he retained were men he could bear to talk to.

Caesar arrived outside Brundisium before the empty transports had returned, and sent his Gallic legate Caninius Rebilus into the city to see young Gnaeus Pompey's father-in-law, Scribonius Libo. Rebilus's mission was to persuade Libo to let him see Pompey, who agreed to parley, then failed to agree to anything else.

"In the absence of the consuls, Rebilus," said Pompey, "I do not have the power to negotiate anything."

"I beg your pardon, Gnaeus Pompeius," said Rebilus firmly, "that is not true. There is a Senatus Consultum Ultimum in effect and you are the commander-in-chief under its provisions. You are at full liberty to make terms in the absence of the consuls."

"I refuse even to think of reconciliation with Caesar!" snapped Pompey. "To be reconciled with Caesar is tantamount to lying down at his feet like a cringing dog!"

"Are you sure, Magnus?" asked Libo after Rebilus had gone. "Rebilus is right, you can make terms."

"I will not make terms!" snarled Pompey, whose ordeals with the consuls and his senatorial watchdogs had passed for the moment; he was feeling much stronger, and he was growing harder. "Send for Metellus Scipio, Gaius Cassius, my son and Vibullius Rufus."

While Libo pattered off, Labienus looked at Pompey reflectively. "You're steeling rapidly, Magnus," he said.

"I am that," said Pompey between his teeth. "Was there ever a worse trick of Fortuna for the Republic than Lentulus Crus as the dominant consul in the year of the Republic's greatest crisis? Marcellus Minor may as well not have existed—he was useless."

"I think Gaius Claudius Marcellus Minor doesn't share the devotion to the *boni* cause his brother and cousin have in such abundance," said Labienus. "Otherwise, why has he been sick since he took office?"

"True. I ought not to have been surprised when he baulked and refused to sail. Still, his defection made me determined to ship the rest of them off in the first fleet. Ever since word of Caesar's clemency at Corfinium reached them, they've vacillated."

"Caesar won't proscribe," said Labienus positively. "It's not in his best interests. He'll continue to be clement."

"So I think. Though he's wrong, Labienus, he's wrong! If I win this war—*when* I win this war!—I'm going to proscribe."

"As long as you don't proscribe me, Magnus, proscribe away."

The summoned men arrived, and settled to listen.

"Scipio," said Pompey to his father-in-law, "I've decided to send you directly to your province, Syria. There you'll squeeze as much money as you can out of the place, after which you'll take the best twenty cohorts there, form them into two legions, and bring them to me in Macedonia or wherever I am."

"Yes, Magnus," said Metellus Scipio obediently.

"Gnaeus, my son, you'll come with me for the present, but later I'll ask you to raise fleets for me, I'm not sure where. I suspect my best strategy against Caesar will be naval. On land he'll always be dangerous, but if we can control the seas he'll suffer. The East knows me well, but it doesn't know Caesar at all. The East likes me, I'll get fleets." Pompey looked at Cassius, who had managed to raise a thousand talents in coin and another thousand talents in treasure from the Campanian temples and town treasuries. "Gaius Cassius, you'll come with me for the moment too."

"Yes, Gnaeus Pompeius," said Cassius, not sure if he was pleased at this news.

"Vibullius, you're going west," said the commander-in-chief. "I want you to see Afranius and Petreius in Spain. Varro is on his way already, but at this time of year you can sail. Tell Afranius and Petreius that they are not, repeat, *not* to march my legions eastward. They are to wait in Spain for Caesar, who I suspect will attempt to crush Spain before he follows me east. My Spanish army will have no trouble beating Caesar. They're hardened veterans, unlike the sorry lot I'm taking to Dyrrachium."

Good, thought Labienus, satisfied. He took my word for it that Caesar will go to Spain first. Now all I have to do is to make sure the last two legions—and this disappointing Magnus—escape from Brundisium intact.

Which they did on the seventeenth day of March, with the loss of a mere two transports.

The Senate and its executives, together with the commander-in-chief of the Republic's forces, had abandoned Italia to Caesar.

BRUNDISIUM TO ROME

Caesar's sources of information and his intelligence network were as efficient as Pompey's were inefficient, nor did his squad of couriers dally to visit aged aunts or taverns or whores. When Pompey and his last two legions sailed away, Caesar thought no more of them. First he would deal with Italia. Then he would deal with Spain. Only after that would he think again of Pompey and his Grand Army of the Republic.

With him he now had the Thirteenth Legion, the Twelfth and the very fine old Eighth, plus three over-strength legions composed of Pompeian recruits, plus three hundred horse troopers who had ridden from Noricum to serve him. That last came as a pleasant surprise. Noricum lay to the north of Illyricum and was not a Roman province, though its fairly Romanized tribes worked closely with eastern Italian Gaul; Noricum produced the best iron ore for steel and exported it down the rivers which ran into the Adriatic from Italian Gaul. Along these rivers was the series of little towns which Brutus's grandfather Caepio had established to work that magical Norican iron ore into the world's finest blade steel. For many years now Caesar had been the best customer those towns knew, therefore by association of immense value to Noricum. Not to mention that he was also greatly loved by Italian Gaul and Illyricum because he had always administered these provinces superbly and stood up for the rights of those who lived on the far side of the Padus River.

The three hundred Norican horse troopers were very welcome; as three hundred good men were enough for any campaign Caesar expected to have to wage in Italia, the Noricans meant that he didn't have to send to Further Gaul for German cavalry.

By the time he commenced to backtrack from Brundisium up the peninsula toward Campania, he knew many things. That Ahenobarbus and Lentulus Spinther were no sooner out of sight than they were planning to organize fresh resistance. That word of his clemency at Corfinium had spread faster than a fire in dry woodland, and done more to damp the panic in Rome than anything else could have. That neither Cato nor Cicero had left Italia with Pompey, and that Gaius Marcellus Minor had also elected to remain, though in hiding. That Manius Lepidus the consular and his eldest son, also pardoned at Corfinium, were planning to take their seats in the Senate in Rome if Caesar required them. That Lucius Volcatius Tullus also intended to sit in Caesar's Senate. And that the consuls had neglected to empty the Treasury.

But the one person who most preyed on Caesar's mind as he entered Campania toward the end of March was Cicero. Though he had written again to Cicero personally, and though both the Balbi and Oppius were bombarding Cicero with letters, that stubborn, shortsighted fellow would not co-operate. No, he wouldn't return to Rome! No, he wouldn't take his seat in the Senate! No, he wouldn't commend Caesar's clemency in public, no matter how much he praised it in private! No, he didn't believe Atticus any more than he believed the Balbi or Oppius!

Three days before the end of March, Caesar made it impossible for Cicero to avoid a meeting any longer; he was staying at the villa belonging to Philippus at Formiae, and Cicero's villa was just next door.

"I am commanded!" said Cicero wrathfully to Terentia. "As if I haven't got enough on my mind! Tiro so dreadfully ill, and my son coming of age—I want to be in Arpinum for that, not here in Formiae! Oh, why can't I dispense with my lictors? And look at my eyes! It takes my man half an hour each morning to sponge them open, they're so stuck together with muck!"

"Yes, you do look a sight," said Terentia, not moved to spare her husband's feelings. "However, best to get it over and done with, I say. Once the wretched man has seen you, he might leave you alone."

So off grumped Cicero clad in purple-bordered toga, preceded by his lictors and their laurel-wreathed *fasces*. Philippus's huge villa resembled nothing so much as a country fairground, with soldiers' tents everywhere, people rushing around, and such a crowd inside that the great advocate was moved to wonder whereabouts Philippus and his awkward guest laid their own heads.

But there was Caesar—ye Gods, the man never changed! How long was it? Nine years and more, though if Magnus hadn't cheated and sneaked off alone to Luca just after casually popping in to say goodbye, he might have set eyes on Caesar at Luca. However, thought Cicero, subsiding into a chair and accepting a goblet of watered Falernian, he *had* changed. The eyes had never been warm, but now they were chillingly cold. He had always radiated power, but never of this magnitude. He could always intimidate, but never with such staggering ease. I behold a mighty king! thought Cicero with a thrill of horror. He outstrips Mithridates and Tigranes combined. The man oozes an innate majesty!

"You look tired," Caesar commented. "Also half blind."

"An inflammation of the eyes. It comes and goes. But you're right, I'm tired. That's why it's bad at the moment."

"I need your counsel, Marcus Cicero."

"A most regrettable business," said Cicero, searching for some suitably banal words.

"I agree. Yet, since it has happened, we must deal with it. It's necessary that I proceed like a cat among eggs. For instance, I can't afford to offend anyone. Least of all you." Caesar leaned forward and produced his most charming smile; it reached his eyes. "Won't you help me put our beloved Republic on her feet again?"

"Since you're the one who knocked her off her feet in the first place, Caesar, no, I won't!" said Cicero tartly.

The smile left the eyes but remained glued to the lips. "I didn't do the knocking, Cicero. My opponents did. It afforded me no pleasure or sense of power to cross the Rubicon. I did so to preserve my *dignitas* after my enemies made a mockery of it."

"You're a traitor," said Cicero, course determined.

The mouth was as straight as its generous curves permitted. "Cicero, I didn't ask you to see me to argue with you. I've asked for your counsel because I value it. For the moment, let's leave the subject of the so-called government in exile and discuss the here and now—Rome and Italia, who have passed into my care. It is my vowed intention to treat both those ladies—who, in my own opinion, are one and the same—with great tenderness. You must be aware that I've been absent for many years. You must therefore be aware that I need guidance."

"I'm aware that you're a traitor!"

The teeth showed. "Stop being so obtuse!"

"Who's obtuse?" asked Cicero, splashing his wine. " 'You must be aware'—that's the language of kings, Caesar. You state the obvious as if it were not obvious. The whole population of this peninsula is 'aware' that you've been away for years!"

The eyes closed; two bright red spots burned in those ivory cheeks. Cicero knew the signs, and shivered involuntarily. Caesar was going to lose his temper. The last time he did that, Cicero found that he had made Publius Clodius into a plebeian. Oh well, the boats were burned. Let him lose his temper!

He did not. After a moment the eyes opened. "Marcus Cicero, I am on my way to Rome, where I intend to have the Senate summoned. I want you to be present in the Senate. I want you to assist me in calming the People down and getting the Senate working again."

"Huh!" snorted Cicero. "*The* Senate! *Your* Senate, you mean! You know what I'd tell the Senate if I were present, don't you?"

"As a matter of fact, no, I do not. Enlighten me."

"I'd ask the Senate to decree that you be forbidden to go to Spain, with or without an army. I'd ask the Senate to decree that you be forbidden to go to Greece or Macedonia, with or without an army. I'd ask the Senate to chain you hand and foot inside Rome until the *real* Senate was on its benches and could decree that you be sent for trial as a traitor!" Cicero smiled sweetly. "After all, Caesar, you're a stickler for the proper procedure, aren't you? We can't possibly execute you without trial!"

"You're daydreaming, Cicero," said Caesar, well in control. "It won't happen that way. The *real* Senate has absconded. Which means that the only Senate available is the one I choose to make."

"Oh!" cried Cicero, putting down his goblet with a clang. "There speaks the king! Oh, what am I doing here? My poor, sad Pompeius! Cast out of home, city, country—now there's a man, Caesar, would make ten of you!"

"Pompeius," said Caesar deliberately, "is a nothing. What I sincerely hope is that I am not forced to demonstrate his nothingness to you in a way you won't be able to ignore."

"You really do think you can beat him, don't you?"

"I *know* I can beat him, Cicero. But I hope not to have to, that's what I'm saying. Won't you put aside your absurd fantasies and look reality in the eye? The only genuine soldier pitted against me is Titus Labienus, yet he's a nothing too. The last thing I want is an outright war. Haven't I made that apparent so far? Men have not been dying, Cicero. The amount of blood I've shed thus far is minuscule. And there are men like Ahenobarbus and Lentulus Spinther—men I pardoned, Cicero!—free to thump their tubs all over Etruria in defiance of their sworn word!"

"That," said Cicero, "is it encapsulated, Caesar. Men *you* pardoned. By what right? By whose authority? You're a king and you think like a king. Your imperium was terminated, you are no more and no less than an ordinary consular senator—and that only because the *real* Senate didn't declare you *hostis*! Though the moment you crossed the Rubicon into Italia, under our constitution you became a traitor—an outlaw—*hostis*! A fig for your pardons! They're meaningless."

"I will try," said Caesar, drawing a deep breath, "just one more time, Marcus Cicero. Will you come to Rome? Will you take your seat in the Senate? Will you give me counsel?"

"I will not come to Rome. I will not sit in your Senate. I will not give you counsel," said Cicero, heart tripping.

For a moment Caesar said nothing. Then he sighed. "Very well. I see. Then I leave you with this, Cicero. Think it over very carefully. To continue to defy me isn't wise. Truly, it is not wise." He got to his feet. "If you won't give me decent and learned advice, then I'll find said advice wherever I can." The eyes were frozen as they looked Cicero up and down. "And I will go to any length that advice says I must."

He turned and vanished, leaving Cicero to find his own way out, both hands pressed against his midriff, working at the knot which threatened to asphyxiate him.

"You were right," said Caesar to Philippus, reclining at his ease in the room he had somehow managed to retain for his own use.

"He refused."

"He more than refused." A smile flashed, genuine amusement. "Poor old rabbit! I could see his heart knocking at his ribs through every fold in his toga. One must admire his courage, for it's unnatural in him, poor old rabbit. I do wish he'd see reason! I can't dislike him, you know, even at his silliest."

"Well," said Philippus comfortably, "you and I can always fall back on our ancestors for consolation. He has none, and that hurts him very much."

"I suppose that's why he can never manage to divorce himself from Pompeius. To Cicero, life for me has been a sinecure. I have the birthright. Pompeius is more to his liking in that respect. Pompeius demonstrates that ancestors are not necessary. What I wish Cicero would see is that birthright can become a handicap. Were I a Picentine Gaul like Pompeius, half those idiots who've fled across the Adriatic wouldn't have gone. I couldn't make myself King of Rome. Whereas, they think, a Julian could." He sighed, sat down on the edge of the couch opposite Philippus. "Truly, Lucius, I have absolutely no wish to be King of Rome. I simply want my entitlements. If they'd only acceded to those, none of this would ever have happened."

"Oh, I understand fully," said Philippus, yawning delicately. "I also believe you. Who in his right mind would want to king it over a litigious, cantankerous, self-willed lot of Romans?"

The boy walked unselfconsciously into the midst of their laughter and waited politely until they were done. Startled by his sudden appearance, Caesar stared, frowned.

"I know you," he said, patting the couch next to him. "Sit down, great-nephew Gaius Octavius."

"I would rather," said Gaius Octavius, "be your son, Uncle Caesar." He sat down, turned himself on his side, and produced an enchanting smile.

"You've grown a few feet, nevvy," said Caesar. "The last time I saw you, you were still unsteady on your pins. Now it rather looks as if your balls are dropping. How old are you?"

"Thirteen."

"So you'd like to be my son, eh? Isn't that somewhat of an insult to your stepfather here?"

"Is it, Lucius Marcius?"

"Thank you, I have two sons of my own. I'll gladly give you to Caesar."

"Who doesn't honestly have the time or the inclination for a son. I'm afraid, Gaius Octavius, that you'll have to continue to be my great-nephew."

"Couldn't you at least make it nephew?"

"I don't see why not."

The boy curled his feet up under him. "I saw Marcus Cicero leaving. He didn't look happy."

"With good reason," said Caesar grimly. "Do you know him?"

"Only to recognize. But I've read all his speeches."

"And what do you think of them?"

"He's a marvelous liar."

"Do you admire that?"

"Yes and no. Lies have their uses, but it's foolish to base one's whole career on them. I won't, anyway."

"So what will you base your career on, nephew?"

"Keeping my own counsel. Saying less than I'm thinking. Not making the same mistake twice. Cicero is governed by his tongue; it runs away with him. That makes him impolitic, I think."

"Don't you want to be a great military man, Gaius Octavius?"

"I would love to be a great military man, Uncle Caesar, but I don't think I have the gift of it."

"Nor do you intend to base your career on your tongue, it seems. But can you rise to the heights keeping your own counsel?"

"Yes, if I wait to see what other people do before I act myself. Extravagance," said the boy thoughtfully, "is a genuine flaw. It means one is noticed, but it also collects enemies like a fleece—no, that's incorrect grammar—*as* a fleece does burrs."

Caesar's eyes had crinkled up at their corners, but he kept his mouth straight. "Do you mean extravagance or flamboyance?"

"Extravagance."

"You're carefully tutored. Do you go to school, or learn at home?"

"At home. My pedagogue is Athenodorus Cananites of Tarsus."

"And what do you think of flamboyance?"

"Flamboyance suits flamboyant people. It suits you, Uncle Caesar, because"—his brow furrowed—"because it's a part of your nature. But there will never be another like you, and what applies to you does not apply to other men."

"Including you?"

"Oh, definitely." The wide grey eyes gazed up adoringly. "I am not you, Uncle Caesar. I never will be. But I do intend to have my own style."

"Philippus," said Caesar, laughing, "I insist that this boy be sent to me as *contubernalis* the moment he turns seventeen!"

Caesar took up residence on the Campus Martius (in Pompey's deserted villa) at the end of March, determined not to cross the *pomerium* into the city; it was no part of his plans to behave as if he admitted he had lost his imperium. Through Mark Antony and Quintus Cassius, his tribunes of the plebs, he convoked the Senate to meet in the temple of Apollo on the Kalends of April. After which he settled down to confer with Balbus and his nephew Balbus Minor, Gaius Oppius, his old friend Gaius Matius, and Atticus.

"Who is where?" he asked, of anyone.

"Manius Lepidus and his son returned to Rome after you pardoned them at Corfinium, and I gather are debating whether to take their seats in the Senate tomorrow," said Atticus.

"Lentulus Spinther?"

"Sulking at his villa near Puteoli. He may end in going to Pompeius across the water, but I doubt he'll raise fresh resistance against you in Italia," said Gaius Matius. "It seems two tastes of Ahenobarbus were enough for Lentulus Spinther—first Corfinium, then Etruria. He's ended in preferring to go to earth."

"And Ahenobarbus?"

Balbus Minor answered. "He chose the Via Valeria back to Rome after Corfinium, skulked at Tibur for a few days, then went to Etruria. He's been recruiting there with considerable success. The man is inordinately wealthy, of course, and withdrew his funds from Rome before—before you crossed the Rubicon."

"In fact," said Caesar levelly, "one would have to say that the intemperate Ahenobarbus acted more prudently and logically than any of the others. Save for his decision to remain in Corfinium."

"True," said Balbus Minor.

"And what does he intend to do with his Etrurian recruits?"

"He's gathered two small fleets, one in Cosa harbor and one on the island of Igilium. From which," said Balbus Minor, "it seems he intends to quit Italia. Probably to go to Spain. I've been traveling extensively in Etruria, and that's the rumor."

"How is Rome?" Caesar asked Atticus.

"Much calmer after the news of your clemency at Corfinium, Caesar. Also once everyone began to realize that you're not slaughtering soldiers in the field. As civil wars go, it's being said, this is a remarkably bloodless one."

"Let us keep offering to the Gods that it remains bloodless."

"The trouble is," said Gaius Matius, remembering days when two little boys played together in the courtyard of Aurelia's insula, "that your enemies don't have the same objectivity. I doubt any of them—except Pompeius himself, perhaps—cares how much blood is shed, provided you're brought down."

"Oppius, tell me all about Cato."

"He's gone to Sicily, Caesar."

"Well, he was appointed its governor."

"He was, but he's not well liked by the majority of those senators who stayed in Rome after you crossed the Rubicon. So they got around Cato's governorship by deciding to appoint a man specifically to secure the grain supply. They chose, of all people, Lucius Postumius. But Postumius declined the commission. Asked why, he expressed unease at supplanting Cato, still the titular governor. They begged him to go. Finally he said he would—provided Cato came with him. Naturally Cato didn't want the job. He doesn't like being out of Italia, as we all know. However, Postumius stood firm, so in the end Cato agreed to go too. After which his Ape, Favonius, offered to accompany him."

Caesar listened to this with a smile. "Lucius Postumius, eh? Ye Gods, they have an inspired ability to pick the wrong men! A more precious, pedantic and fiddling man I don't know."

"You're absolutely right," said Atticus. "The moment he had the commission, he refused to leave for Sicily! Wouldn't budge until young Lucius Caesar and Lucius Roscius came back with your terms. After that he refused to sail until Publius Sestius returned with your answer to Pompeius's terms."

"Dear, dear. So when did this wonderful little clutch of hens finally depart?"

"Midway through February."

"With any troops, since there's no legion in Sicily?"

"Absolutely none. The understanding was that Pompeius would ship twelve cohorts of Ahenobarbus's troops to them, but you know what happened to that. Every man Pompeius possesses has gone to Dyrrachium."

"They haven't thought very much about the welfare of Rome, have they?"

Gaius Matius shrugged. "They didn't need to, Caesar. They know you won't see Rome or Italia starve."

"Well, at least taking Sicily shouldn't present any great difficulties," said Caesar, acknowledging the truth of Matius's statement. He raised his brows to the older Balbus. "I find it hard to credit, but is it really true that no one emptied the Treasury?" he asked.

"Absolutely true, Caesar. It's stuffed with bullion."

"I hope it's stuffed with coin too."

"You'll garnish the Treasury?" asked Gaius Matius.

"I have to, oldest friend. Wars cost money, staggering amounts of it, and civil wars don't bring booty in their train."

"But surely," said Balbus Minor, frowning, "you don't mean to drag thousands of wagons of gold, silver and coins with you wherever you go?"

"Ah, you're thinking that I don't dare to leave it in Rome," said Caesar, very relaxed. "However, that's exactly what I'll do. Why should I not? Pompeius has to climb over the top of me before he can enter Rome—he abandoned her. All I'll remove is what I need for the moment. About a thousand talents in coin, if there's that much there. I'll have to fund a war in Sicily and Africa as well as my own campaign in the West. But one thing you can count on, Minor—I won't relinquish control of the Treasury once it's mine. And by mine, I mean establishing myself and those senators still in Rome as the legitimate government."

"Do you think you can do that?" asked Atticus.

"I sincerely hope so," said Caesar.

But when the Senate met on the first day of April in the temple of Apollo, it was so thinly attended that it didn't constitute a quorum. A terrific blow to Caesar. Of the consulars, only Lucius Volcatius Tullus and Servius Sulpicius Rufus came, and Servius was unsympathetic. Nor had every *boni* tribune of the plebs departed, a contingency which Caesar hadn't counted on. There beside Mark Antony and Quintus Cassius on the tribunician bench was Lucius Caecilius Metellus, very *boni* indeed. A worse blow to Caesar, who had made his reason for crossing the Rubicon the injuries done to his tribunes of the plebs. Which meant that now he couldn't react with force or intimidation if any of his motions were to be vetoed by Lucius Metellus.

Despite the fact that there were not enough senators present to pass any decrees, Caesar spoke at length on the perfidies of the *boni* and his own perfectly justified march into Italia. The lack of bloodshed was dwelled upon. The clemency at Corfinium was dwelled upon.

"What must be done immediately," he said in conclusion, "is for this House to send a deputation to Gnaeus Pompeius in Epirus. The deputation will be formally charged with the duty of negotiating a peace. I do not want to fight a civil war, be that civil war in Italia or elsewhere."

The ninety-odd men shuffled, looked desperately unhappy.

"Very well, then, Caesar," said Servius Sulpicius. "If you think a deputation will help, we will send it."

"May I have the names of ten men, please?"

But no one would volunteer.

Tight-lipped, Caesar looked at the urban praetor, Marcus Aemilius Lepidus; he was the most senior man left among the elected government. The youngest son of a man who had rebelled against the State and died for it—some said of pneumonia, others of a broken heart—Lepidus was determined to reinstate his patrician family among the most powerful people in Rome. A handsome man who bore a sword scar across his nose, Lepidus had realized some time ago that the *boni* would never trust him (or his elder brother, Lucius Aemilius Lepidus Paullus); Caesar's advent had come as a salvation.

Thus he got to his feet eager to do as he had been asked before the meeting commenced. "Conscript Fathers, the proconsul Gaius Caesar has requested that he be granted free access to the funds of the Treasury. I hereby move that permission to advance Gaius Caesar whatever he needs from the Treasury be granted. Not without profit for the Treasury. Gaius Caesar has offered to take what he needs on loan at ten percent simple interest."

"I veto that motion, Marcus Lepidus," said Lucius Metellus.

"Lucius Metellus, it's a good deal for Rome!" cried Lepidus.

"Rubbish!" said Lucius Metellus scornfully. "First of all, you can't pass a motion in a House which does not constitute a quorum. And, more importantly by far, what Caesar is actually asking is to be formally invested with the legitimate cause in this present difference of opinion between himself and the true government of Rome. I veto his being granted loans from the Treasury, and I will go on vetoing! If Caesar can't find money, he'll have to desist in his aggression. Therefore I veto."

An able enough man, Lepidus countered. "There is a Senatus Consultum Ultimum in effect forbidding the tribunician veto, Lucius Metellus."

"Ah," said Lucius Metellus, smiling brilliantly, "but that was the old government! Caesar marched to protect the rights and persons of the tribunes of the plebs, and this is his Senate, his government. One must presume that its cornerstone is the right of a tribune of the plebs to interpose his veto."

"Thank you," said Caesar, "for refreshing my memory, Lucius Metellus."

Dismissing the Senate, Caesar called the People into a formal assembly in the Circus Flaminius. This meeting was far better attended—and by those who had no love for the *boni*. The crowd listened receptively to the same speech Caesar had delivered to the Senate, prepared to believe in Caesar's clemency and anxious to help in whatever way possible. Especially after Caesar told the People that he would continue Clodius's free grain dole and give three hundred sesterces to every Roman man.

"But," said Caesar, "I do not want to look like a dictator! I am in the midst of pleading with the Senate to govern, and I will continue until I have persuaded it to govern. For which reason, I do not ask you at this moment to pass any laws."

Which proved to be a mistake; the impasse in the Senate went on. Servius Sulpicius harped constantly on peace at any price, no one would volunteer to be a part of the deputation to Pompey, and Lucius Metellus kept interposing his veto every time Caesar asked for money.

At dawn on the fourth day of April, Caesar crossed the *pomerium* into the city, attended by his twelve lictors (in their crimson tunics and bearing the axes in their *fasces*—something only a dictator was permitted to do within the sacred boundary). With him went his two tribunes of the plebs, Antony and Quintus Cassius, and the urban praetor, Lepidus. Antony and Quintus Cassius were clad in full armor and wore their swords.

He went straight to the basement of the temple of Saturn, wherein lay the Treasury.

"Go ahead," he said curtly to Lepidus.

Lepidus applied a fist. "Open the doors to the *praetor urbanus*!" he shouted.

The right-hand leaf opened; a head poked out. "Yes?" it enquired, a look of terror on its face.

"Admit us, *tribunus aerarius*."

It seemed out of nowhere, Lucius Metellus appeared and put himself squarely across the doorway. He was alone. "Gaius Caesar, you have abandoned whatever imperium you say you own. You are inside the *pomerium*."

A small crowd was gathering, its ranks swelling quickly.

"Gaius Caesar, you have no authority to invade these premises and no authority to remove one single sestertius from them!" cried Lucius Metellus in his loudest voice. "I have vetoed your access to Rome's public purse, and here and now I veto you again! Go back to the Campus Martius, or go to the official residence of the Pontifex Maximus, or go wherever else you wish. I will not obstruct you. But I will not let you enter Rome's Treasury!"

"Stand aside, Metellus," said Mark Antony.

"I will not."

"Stand aside, Metellus," Antony repeated.

But Metellus spoke to Caesar, not to Antony. "Your presence here is a direct infingement of every law on Rome's tablets! You are not dictator! You are not proconsul! At best you are a *privatus* senator, at worst you are a public enemy. If you defy me and enter these portals, every man watching will know which of the two you really are—an enemy of the People of Rome!"

Caesar listened impassively; Mark Antony stepped forward, sword scabbard pushed into drawing position.

"Stand aside, Metellus!" roared Antony. "I am a legally elected tribune of the plebs, and I order you to stand aside!"

"You're Caesar's creature, Antonius! Don't loom over me like my executioner! I will not stand aside!"

"Well," said Antony, putting his hands on Metellus's arms below the shoulders, "look at it this way, Metellus. I'm going to lift you aside. Intrude again, and I *will* execute you."

"*Quirites,* bear witness! Armed force has been used against me! I have been obstructed in my duty! My life has been threatened! Remember it well against the day when all these men are tried for the highest treason!"

Antony lifted him aside. His purpose accomplished, Lucius Metellus walked away into the crowd proclaiming his violated status and begging all men present to bear witness.

"You first, Antonius," said Caesar.

For Antony, never an urban quaestor, this was a new experience. He ducked his head to enter, though it wasn't necessary, and almost collided with the terrified *tribunus aerarius* in charge of the Treasury that fateful morning.

Quintus Cassius, Lepidus and Caesar followed; the lictors remained outside.

Openings covered by grilles permitted a wan light to soak into darkened tufa block walls on either side of a narrow passage ending in a very ordinary door, the entrance to the warren in which the Treasury officials worked amid lamps, cobwebs and paper mites. But to Antony and Quintus Cassius that door was nothing; off the interior wall of the corridor there opened dark chambers, each one sealed with a massive gate of iron bars. Inside in the gloom were dull glitters, gold in this chamber, silver in that, all the way to the office door.

"It's the same on the other side," said Caesar, leading the way. "One vault after another. The law tablets get whisked in and out of one room at the very back." He entered the outer office and proceeded through its cluttered space to the stuffy cubicle wherein the senior man worked. "Your name?" he asked.

The *tribunus aerarius* swallowed. "Marcus Cuspius," he said.

"How much is here?"

"Thirty million sesterces in minted coin. Thirty thousand talents of silver in talent sows. Fifteen thousand talents of gold in talent sows. All stamped with the Treasury seal."

"Excellent!" purred Caesar. "More than a thousand talents in coin. Sit down, Cuspius, and make out a paper. The urban praetor and these two tribunes of the plebs will bear witness. Record on your paper that Gaius Julius Caesar, proconsul, has this day borrowed thirty million sesterces in coin to fund his legitimate war in the name of Rome. The terms are for two years, the interest ten percent simple." Caesar perched himself on the edge of the desk as Marcus Cuspius wrote; when the document was complete he leaned over and put his name to it, then nodded to the witnesses.

Quintus Cassius wore a peculiar expression.

"What's the matter, Cassius?" Caesar asked, handing his pen to Lepidus.

"Oh! Oh, nothing, Caesar. Just that I never realized gold and silver have a smell."

"Do you like the smell?"

"Very much."

"Interesting. Personally I find it suffocating."

The document signed and witnessed, Caesar handed it back to Cuspius with a smile. "Keep it safe, Marcus Cuspius." He lifted himself off the desk. "Now listen to me, and mark me well. The contents of this building are in my care from this day forward. Not one sestertius will leave it unless I say so. And to make sure my orders are obeyed, there will be a permanent guard of my soldiers at the Treasury entrance. They will allow no one access save those who work here and my designated agents, who are Lucius Cornelius Balbus and Gaius Oppius. Gaius Rabirius Postumus—the banker, not the senator—is also authorized as my agent when he returns from his travels. Is that understood?"

"Yes, noble Caesar." The *tribunus aerarius* wet his lips. "Er—what about the urban quaestors?"

"No urban quaestors, Cuspius. Just my named agents."

"So that's how you do it," said Antony as the group walked back to Pompey's villa on the Campus Martius.

"No, Antonius, that's not how you do it. It's how I've been forced to do it. Lucius Metellus has put me in the wrong."

"Worm! I should have killed him."

"And martyred him? Certainly not! If I read him correctly—and I think I do—he'll spoil his victory by prating of it to all and sundry night and day. It isn't wise to prate." Suddenly Caesar thought of young Gaius Octavius's words on the subject of keeping one's counsel, and smiled. He might go far, that boy. "Men will grow tired of listening to him, just as men grew tired of Marcus Cicero and his struggle to prove Catilina a traitor."

"It's a pity all the same," said Antony. He grimaced. "Why is it, Caesar, that there's always a man like Lucius Metellus?"

"If there were not, Antonius, this world might work better. Though if this world worked better, there'd be no place in it for men like me," said Caesar.

At Pompey's villa he gathered his legates and Lepidus in the huge room Pompey had called his study.

"We have money," he said, sitting in Pompey's chair behind Pompey's desk. "That means I move tomorrow, the Nones of April."

"For Spain," said Antony with pleasure. "I'm looking forward to that, Caesar."

"Don't bother, Antonius. You're not coming. I need you here in Italia."

Brow darkening, Antony scowled ferociously. "That's not fair! I want to go to war!"

"Nothing is fair, Antonius, nor do I run things to keep you happy. I said I needed you in Italia, so in Italia you'll stay. As my—er—unofficial Master of the Horse. You'll take command of everything outside the first milestone from Rome. Particularly those troops I intend to leave behind to garrison Italia. You will recruit—and not like a Cicero. I want results, Antonius. You'll be required to make all the executive decisions and all the dispositions necessary to keep this entire country peaceful. No one of senatorial status may leave Italia for a foreign destination without first obtaining permission from you. Which means I want a garrison in every port capable of harboring ships for hire. You will also be required to deal with the Italian end of the grain supply. No one can be let go hungry. Listen to the bankers. Listen to Atticus. And listen to the voice of good sense." The eyes grew very cold. "You may junket and carouse, Antonius—provided the work is done to my satisfaction. If it is not, I'll strip you of your citizenship and send you into permanent exile."

Antony swallowed, nodded.

Now came Lepidus's turn.

"Lepidus, as urban praetor you'll govern the city of Rome. It won't be as difficult for you as it has been for me these last few days, because you won't have Lucius Metellus to veto you. I have given instructions to some of my troops to escort Lucius Metellus to Brundisium, where they will put him on a boat and send him, with my compliments, to Gnaeus Pompeius. You will make use of the guard outside the Treasury should you need it. Though the normal rule allows the urban praetor to be absent from the city for up to ten days at a time, you will never be absent. I expect full granaries, a continuation of the free grain dole, and peace on Rome's streets. You will persuade the Senate to authorize the minting of one hundred million sesterces in coin, then hand the Senate's directive to Gaius Oppius. My own building programs will continue—at my own expense, of course. When I return I expect to see Rome prosperous, well cared for and content. Is that clear?"

"Yes, Caesar," said Lepidus.

"Marcus Crassus," said Caesar in a softer voice. This was one legate he prized, the last living link with his friend Crassus, and a loyal subordinate in Gaul. "Marcus Crassus, to you I hand my province of Italian Gaul. Care for it well. You will also begin a census of all those inhabitants of Italian Gaul who do not as yet hold the full citizenship. As soon as I have the time, I will be legislating the full citizenship for everyone. Therefore a census will shorten the procedure."

"Yes, Caesar," said Marcus Crassus.

"Gaius Antonius," said Caesar, voice neutral. Marcus he thought a good man provided his duties were spelled out and dire punishment promised if he failed, but this middle of the three Antonian brothers he couldn't care for at all. Almost as large as Marcus, but not nearly as bright. An untutored oaf. Family, however, was family. Therefore Gaius Antonius would have to be given a job with some responsibility. A pity. Whatever he was given would not be done well.

"Gaius Antonius, you will take two legions of locally recruited troops and hold Illyricum for me. When I say hold, I mean just that. You will not conduct assizes or function as governor—Marcus Crassus in Italian Gaul will look after that side of Illyricum. Base yourself at Salona, but keep your communications with Tergeste open at all times. Do not tempt Pompeius; he's fairly close to you. Understood?"

"Yes, Caesar."

"Orca," said Caesar to Quintus Valerius Orca, "you will go to Sardinia with one legion of local recruits and hold it for me. Personally I wouldn't care if the whole island sank to the bottom of Our Sea, but the grain it produces is valuable. Safeguard it."

"Yes, Caesar."

"Dolabella, I'm giving you the Adriatic Sea. You'll raise a fleet and defend it against any navy Pompeius may have. Sooner or later I'll be using the crossing from Brundisium to Macedonia, and I expect to be able to use it."

"Yes, Caesar."

Now came one of the more surprising Caesareans, the son of Quintus Hortensius. He had gone to Caesar in Gaul as a legate after his father's death, and proved a good worker in the short time his duties lasted. Liking him and learning that he possessed good diplomatic skills, Caesar had found him very useful in settling the tribes down. Present with Caesar in Italian Gaul, he had been a part of the group who had crossed the Rubicon in their commander's wake. Yes, a surprise. But a very pleasant one.

"Quintus Hortensius, I'm giving you the Tuscan Sea. You'll raise a fleet and keep the sea lanes open between Sicily and all the western ports from Rhegium to Ostia."

"Yes, Caesar."

There remained the most important of the independent commands;

every pair of eyes turned to the cheerful, freckled face of Gaius Scribonius Curio.

"Curio, good friend, huge help, faithful ally, brave man . . . you'll take all the cohorts Ahenobarbus had in Corfinium, and recruit sufficient extra men to form four legions. Levy in Samnium and Picenum, not in Campania. You will proceed to Sicily and eject Postumius, Cato and Favonius from it. Holding Sicily is absolutely essential, as you well know. Once Sicily is secured and properly garrisoned, you'll go on to Africa and secure it too. That will mean the grain supply is completely ours. I'm sending Rebilus with you as second-in-command, and Pollio for good measure."

"Yes, Caesar."

"All commands will carry propraetorian imperium."

Mischief nudged the elated Curio's tongue, made him ask, "If I'm propraetor, I have six lictors. May I wreath their *fasces* in laurels?"

The mask slipped for the first time. "Why not? Since you assisted me to conquer Italia, Curio, of course you may," said Caesar with venomous bitterness. "What a thing to have to say! I *conquered* Italia. But there was no one to defend her." He nodded brusquely. "That is all. Good day."

Curio tore home to the Palatine whooping, whirled Fulvia off her feet and kissed her. Not confined to the Campus Martius as Caesar was, he had been home now for five days.

"Fulvia, Fulvia, I'm to have my own command!" he cried.

"Tell me!"

"I'm to lead four legions—four legions, imagine it!—to Sicily and then to Africa! My own war! I'm *propraetore,* Fulvia, and I'm to wreath my *fasces* in laurels! I'm in command! I have six lictors! My second-in-command is a hoary Gallic veteran, Caninius Rebilus! I'm his superior! I've got Pollio too! Isn't it wonderful?"

And she, so loyal, so wholehearted a supporter, beamed, kissed him all over his dear freckled face, hugged him and exulted for him. "My husband the propraetor," she said, and had to kiss his face again many times. "Curio, I'm so pleased!" Her expression changed. "Does that mean you have to leave at once? When will your imperium be conferred?"

"I don't know that it ever will be," said Curio, undismayed. "Caesar gave all of us propraetorian status, but, strictly speaking, he's not authorized to. So I daresay we'll have to wait for our *leges curiatae.*"

Fulvia stiffened. "He means to be dictator."

"Oh, yes." Curio sobered, frowned. "It was the most amazing meeting I've ever attended, *meum mel*. He sat there and he dished out the jobs without, it seemed, drawing breath. Crisp, succinct, absolutely specific. Over and done with in mere moments. The man's a phenomenon! Fully aware that he has no authority whatsoever to depute anyone to do anything, yet—for how long has he been thinking of it? He's a complete autocrat. I suppose ten years in Gaul as master of everyone and everything would have to change a man, but—ye Gods, Fulvia, he was born a dictator! If I don't understand any aspect of him, it's how he ever managed to hide what he is for so long. Oh, I remember how he used to irritate me when he was consul—I thought him royal then! But I actually believed that Pompeius pulled *his* strings. I know now that no one has ever pulled Caesar's strings."

"He certainly pulled my Clodius's strings, little though my Clodius would care to hear me say that."

"He won't be gainsaid, Fulvia. And somehow he'll manage to do it without spilling oceans of Roman blood. What I heard today was the dictator sprung fully armed from the brow of Zeus."

"Another Sulla."

Curio shook his head emphatically. "Oh, no. Never Sulla. He doesn't have Sulla's weaknesses."

"Can you continue to serve someone who will rule Rome as an autocrat?"

"I think so. For one reason. He's so eminently capable. What I would have to do, however, is make sure that Caesar didn't change our way of looking at things. Rome needs to be ruled by Caesar. But he's unique. Therefore no one can be permitted to rule after him."

"A mercy then that he has no son," said Fulvia.

"Nor any member of his family to claim his place."

Down in the damp and shady cleft which was the Forum Romanum stood the residence of the Pontifex Maximus, a huge and chilly structure without architectural distinction or physical beauty. With winter just arriving, the courtyards were too cold to permit their being used, but the mistress of the house had a very nice sitting room well warmed by two braziers, and here she ensconced herself cozily. The suite had belonged to the mother of the Pontifex Maximus, Aurelia, and in her days its walls had been impossible to see for pigeonholes, book buckets and accounts. All of that impedimenta had gone; the walls once more shone dully crimson and purple, the gilded pilasters and moldings glittered, the high ceiling was a honeycomb of plum and gold. It had taken considerable persuasion to coax Calpurnia down from her suite on the top floor; Eutychus the steward, now into his seventies, had managed it by hinting that all the servants were too decrepit these days to climb the stairs. So Calpurnia had moved down, and that had been almost five years ago—long enough by far not to feel the presence of Aurelia these days as anything more than an additional warmth.

Calpurnia sat with three kittens in her lap, two tabby and one black-and-white, her hands lying lightly on their fat bodies. They were asleep.

"I love the abandonment of their sleep," she said to her visitors in a grave voice, smiling down. "The world might end, and they would dream on. So lovely. We of the *gens humana* have lost the gift of perfect sleep."

"Have you seen Caesar?" asked Marcia.

The large brown eyes lifted, looked sad. "No. I think he is too busy."

"Haven't you tried to contact him?" asked Porcia.

"No."

"Don't you think you ought?"

"He's aware I'm here, Porcia." It wasn't said with a snap or a snarl; it was a simple statement of fact.

A peculiar trio, some intruder might have thought, coming upon Caesar's wife entertaining Cato's wife and Cato's daughter. But she and Marcia had been friends ever since Marcia had gone to be wife to Quintus Hortensius, into an exile of the spirit and the flesh. Not unlike, Marcia had thought then, the exile poor Calpurnia dwelled in. They had found each other's company very pleasant, for each was a gentle soul without much liking for intellectual pursuits and no liking at all for the traditional women's occupations—spinning, weaving, sewing, embroidering; painting plates, bowls, vases and screens; shopping; gossiping. Nor was either woman a mother.

It had started with a courtesy call after the death of Julia, and another after Aurelia's death not much more than a month later. Here, thought Marcia, was an equally lonely person: someone who would not pity her, someone who would not find fault with her for acceding so tamely to her husband's actions. Not all Roman women were so compliant, no matter what their social status. Though, they found as the friendship prospered, they both envied the lot of women in the lower classes—they could be professionally qualified as physicians or midwives or apothecaries, or work in trades like carpentering or sculpting or painting. Only the upper-class women were constrained by their status into ladylike homebound activities.

Not a cat fancier, Marcia had found Calpurnia's chief hobby a little unbearable at first, though she discovered after some exposure to them that cats were interesting creatures. Not that she ever yielded to Calpurnia's pleas that she take a kitten for herself. She also shrewdly concluded that if Caesar had given his wife a lapdog, Calpurnia would now be surrounded by puppies.

Porcia's advent was quite recent. When Porcia had realized after Marcia's return to Cato's household that she was friendly with Caesar's wife, Porcia had had a great deal to say. None of it impressed Marcia, nor, when Porcia complained to Cato, was he moved to censure his wife.

"The world of women is not the world of men, Porcia," he shouted in his normal way. "Calpurnia is a most respectable and admirable woman. Her father married her to Caesar, just as I married you to Bibulus."

But after Brutus had left for Cilicia a change had come over Porcia—the stern Stoic who had no truck with the world of women lost her fire, secretly wept. Dismayed, Marcia saw what Porcia herself was trying desperately to hide, would not speak about: she had fallen in love with someone who had refused her when offered her, someone who had now gone away. Someone who was not her husband. With her young stepson moving out of her ken, Porcia needed a warmer kind of stimulus than philosophy and history. She was moldering. Sometimes Marcia worried that she was dying the subtlest death of all—she mattered to no one.

Thus, badgered into consenting and under solemn oath not to embark upon political talk or speak scathingly of her father's and her husband's most hated enemy, Porcia too began to visit. Miraculously, she enjoyed these outings. As both were good people at heart, Porcia found herself quite unable to despise Calpurnia. Goodness recognized goodness. Besides which, Porcia liked cats. Not that she had ever seen one at close quarters before; cats slunk through the night, yowled for mates, ate rodents or lived around kitchens begging for scraps. But from the moment Calpurnia held out her enormously fat and complacent orange Felix and Porcia found herself holding this soft, cuddly, thrumming creature, she liked cats. Friendship with Calpurnia aside, it kept her coming back to the Domus Publica, for she knew better than to think that father or husband would approve of enjoying the company of an animal, dog or cat or fish.

Loneliness, Porcia began to see, was not her own exclusive province. Nor was unrequited love. And in these two things she grieved for Calpurnia as much as for herself. No one to fill her life, no one to look at her with love. Except her cats.

"I still think you should write," Porcia persisted.

"Perhaps," said Calpurnia, rolling one kitten over. "And yet, Porcia, that would be an intrusion. He is so busy. I don't understand any of it, and I never will. I just make offerings to keep him safe."

"So do we all for our men," said Marcia.

Old Eutychus staggered in with steaming hot sweet wine and a plate loaded with goodies; no one save he was allowed to wait on this last living one of the beloved Domus Publica ladies.

The kittens were returned to the padded box with their mother, which opened its green eyes wide and looked at Calpurnia reproachfully.

"That was unkind," said Porcia, sniffing the mulled wine and wondering why Bibulus's staff never thought of it on these cold, misty days. "Poor mama cat was enjoying a little peace."

The last word fell, echoed, lay between them.

Calpurnia broke off a piece of the best-looking honey-cake and took it across to the shrine of the Lares and Penates.

"Dear Gods of the Household," she prayed, "grant us peace."

"Grant us peace," prayed Marcia.

"Grant us peace," prayed Porcia.

THE WEST, ITALIA AND ROME, THE EAST

from APRIL 6 of 49 B.C. until
SEPTEMBER 29 of 48 B.C.

POMPEY
GNAEUS POMPEIUS MAGNUS

Because the winter in the Alps was a snowy one, Caesar marched his legions to the Province along the coast road, and moved with his customary speed. Having left Rome on the fifth day of April, he arrived outside Massilia on the nineteenth day. The distance covered on that tortuously winding road was closer to six than to five hundred miles.

But he marched in a mood of profound gladness; the years away from home had been too many, and the difficulties when he finally returned home too exasperating. On the one hand he could see how desperately a strong and autocratic hand was needed. The city itself was more sloppily governed than ever—not enough notice or respect was given to the commercial sector—not enough had been done to safeguard, let alone improve, everything from the grain supply to the grain dole. Were it not for his own many building projects, Rome's workmen would have gone wanting. Temples were shabby, the cobbles of city streets were lifting, no one was regulating the chaotic traffic, and he suspected that the State granaries along the cliffs below the Aventine were rat infested and crumbling. The public moneys were being hoarded, not spent. On the other hand he didn't honestly welcome the job of putting it all to rights. Thankless, mined with obstacles, an intrusion into duties more properly those of other magistrates—and Rome the city was a minute problem compared to Rome the institution, Rome the country, Rome the empire.

He was not, Caesar reflected as the miles strode by, a city-bound man by temperament. Life on the road at the head of a fine strong army was infinitely preferable. How wonderful, that he had been able to assure himself in all truth that he couldn't afford to waste time in Rome, that Pompey's army in the Spains had to be contained and rendered ineffectual very quickly! There was no life like it, marching at the head of a fine army.

The only true city between Rome and the Spains was located on a superb harbor about forty miles to the east of the Rhodanus delta and its marshes: Massilia. Founded by the Greeks who had roamed Our Sea establishing colonies centuries before, Massilia had maintained its independence and its Greekness ever since. It had treaties of alliance with Rome, but governed its own affairs—had its own navy and army (purely for defense, said the treaty) and sufficient of the hinterland to supply itself with produce from market gardens and orchards, though it bought in grain from the Roman Province, which surrounded its borders. The Massiliotes guarded their independence fiercely, despite the fact that they could not afford to offend Rome, that upstart interloper in the previously Greek and Phoenician world.

Hastening out of the city to Caesar's camp (carefully sited on unused ground), the Council of Fifteen which governed Massilia sought an audience with the man who had conquered Gallia Comata and made himself the master of Italia.

Caesar received them with great ceremony, clad in the full regalia of the proconsul, and wearing his *corona civica* upon his head. Aware too that in all his time in Further Gaul, he had never been to Massilia nor intruded upon Massiliote affairs. The Council of Fifteen was very cold and very arrogant.

"You are not here legally," said Philodemus, leader of the Council, "and Massilia's treaties are with the true government of Rome, as personified in Gnaeus Pompeius Magnus and those individuals who were forced to flee at your advent."

"In fleeing, Philodemus, those individuals abrogated their rights," said Caesar evenly. "I am the true government of Rome."

"No, you are not."

"Does this mean, Philodemus, that you will give aid to Rome's enemies in the persons of Gnaeus Pompeius and his allies?"

"Massilia prefers to give aid to neither side, Caesar. Though," said Philodemus, smiling complacently, "we have sent a delegation to Gnaeus Pompeius in Epirus confirming our allegiance to the government in exile."

"That was impudent as well as imprudent."

"If it was, I don't see what you can do about it," Philodemus said jauntily. "Massilia is too strongly defended for you to reduce."

"Don't tempt me!" said Caesar, smiling.

"Go about your business, Caesar, and leave Massilia alone."

"Before I can do that, I need better assurances that Massilia will remain neutral."

"We will help neither side."

"Despite your delegation to Gnaeus Pompeius."

"That is ideological, not practical. Practically speaking, we will maintain absolute neutrality."

"You had better, Philodemus. If I see any evidence to the contrary, you'll find yourself under siege."

"You can't afford to besiege a city of one million people," said Philodemus smugly. "We are not Uxellodunum or Alesia."

"The more mouths there are to feed, Philodemus, the more certain it is that any place will fall. You've heard, I'm sure, the story of the Roman general besieging a town in Spain. It sent him a gift of food, with the message that it had sufficient in store to eat for ten years. The general sent a message back thanking its people for their candor, and informing them that he would take it in the eleventh year. The town surrendered. They knew he meant every word. Therefore I warn you: do not aid my enemies."

Two days later Lucius Domitius Ahenobarbus arrived with a fleet and two legions of Etrurian volunteers. The moment he hove to off the harbor, the Massiliotes removed the great chain which barred the entrance and permitted him to sail in.

"Fortify everything," said the Council of Fifteen.

Sighing, Caesar resigned himself to besieging Massilia, a delay which was by no means as disastrous as Massilia clearly thought it was; winter would make the Pyrenees difficult to cross for Pompey's troops as much as for his own, and contrary winds would prevent their leaving Spain by sea.

The best part about it all was that Gaius Trebonius and Decimus Brutus arrived at the head of the Ninth, Tenth and Eleventh Legions.

"I left the Fifth on the Icauna behind massive fortifications," said Trebonius, gazing at Caesar with an almost bemused fondness. "The Aedui and the Arverni have fallen nicely into line, and have good Roman-style troops available if the Fifth needs strengthening. I can tell you that the news of your victory in Italia was all any of the Gallic tribes needed to fall into docile torpor. Even the Bellovaci, who still mutter. They've tasted your mettle, and Italia proves it. I predict that Gallia Comata will lie very low this year."

"Good, because I can't afford to garrison it with more men than the Fifth," said Caesar. He turned to his other loyalest legate. "Decimus, I'm going to need a good fleet if we're to beat Massilia into submission. You're the naval man. According to my cousin Lucius, Narbo has developed an excellent shipbuilding industry and is dying to sell us a few stout decked triremes. Go there now and see what's available. And pay them well." He laughed soundlessly. "Would you believe that Pompeius and the consuls forgot to empty the Treasury before they scuttled off?"

Trebonius and Decimus Brutus gaped.

"Ye Gods!" said Decimus Brutus, to whom the question had been directed. "I couldn't even contemplate fighting alongside anyone but you anyway, Caesar, but that news makes me *religiously* glad I know you! The fools!"

"Yes, but what it really tells us is how confused and ill prepared they are to wage any sort of war. They strutted, postured, waved their fists in my face, insulted me, thwarted me—yet all the time, I realize now, they didn't believe for one moment that I would march. They have no strategy, no real idea what to do. And no money to do it with. I've left instructions with Antonius not to impede the sale of any of Pompeius's properties, nor to prevent the money's going out of Italia."

"Should you do that?" asked Trebonius, looking as worried as ever. "Surely cutting Pompeius off from any source of funding is one way to win bloodlessly."

"No, it would be a postponement," said Caesar. "What Pompeius and the others sell to finance their war can't go back to them. Our Picentine friend is one of the two or three wealthiest men in the whole country. Ahenobarbus would be in the top six or seven. I want them bankrupted. Penniless great men have clout—but no power."

"I think," said Decimus Brutus, "that you're really saying you don't intend to kill them when it's over. Or even exile them."

"Exactly, Decimus. I won't be apostrophized as a monster like Sulla. No one on either side is a traitor. We simply see Rome's future course in different ways. I want those I pardon to resume their positions in Rome and give me a few challenges. Sulla was wrong. No man functions at his best without opposition. I truly cannot bear the thought of being surrounded by sycophants! I'll be the First Man in Rome the proper way—by constantly striving."

"Do you consider us sycophants?" asked Decimus Brutus.

That provoked a laugh. "No! Sycophants don't lead legions capably, my friend. Sycophants lie on couches and trumpet fulsome praise. *My* legates aren't afraid to tell me when I'm wrong."

"Was it very hard, Caesar?" asked Trebonius.

"To do what I warned you I would? To cross the Rubicon?"

"Yes. We wondered and worried."

"Hard, yet not hard. I have no wish to go down in the history books as one of a series of men who marched on their homeland. Simply, I had no option. Either I marched, or I retired into a permanent exile. And had I done the latter, Gaul would have been in a ferment of rebellion within three years, and Rome would have lost control of all her provinces. It's high time the Claudii, the Cornelii and their ilk were prevented at law from raping their provinces. Also the *publicani*. Also men like Brutus, who hides his commercial doings behind a wall of senatorial respectability. I'm necessary to institute some badly needed reforms, after which I intend to march for the Kingdom of the Parthians. There are seven Roman Eagles in Ecbatana. And a great, misunderstood Roman to avenge. Besides which," said Caesar, "we have to pay for this war. I don't know how long it will last. Reason says a few months only, but instinct says much longer. I'm fighting fellow Romans—stubborn, persistent, pigheaded. They won't go down any easier than the Gauls, though I hope with less bloodshed."

"You've been mighty continent in that respect so far," said Gaius Trebonius.

"And I intend to remain so—without going down myself."

"You've got the contents of the Treasury," said Decimus Brutus. "Why worry about paying for the war?"

"The Treasury belongs to the People of Rome, not the Senate of Rome. This is a war between factions in the Senate, having little to do with the People save those who are called upon to fight. I have borrowed, not taken. I will continue to do that. I can't let my troops plunder, there will be no booty. Which means I'll have to recompense them from my own funds. Extremely considerable funds. However, I'll still have to pay the Treasury back. How? You can bet Pompeius is busy squeezing the East dry to fund his side of things, so I'll find nothing there. Spain is penniless aside from its metals, and the profits from those will be going to Pompeius. Not to Rome. Whereas the Kingdom of the Parthians is immensely wealthy. One place we've never managed to tap. I will tap it, I promise you."

"I'll go with you," said Trebonius quickly.

"And I," said Decimus Brutus.

"But in the meantime," said Caesar, very pleased, "we have to deal with Massilia and Spain."

"And Pompeius," said Trebonius.

"First things first," said Caesar. "I want Pompeius ejected from the West completely. To do that is to take money from him."

Very well fortified and defended—particularly now that Ahenobarbus had arrived to swell its naval and military resources—Massilia held out easily against Caesar's land blockade because it still dominated the seas. Its granaries were full, perishable foods were brought in by water, and so confident of Caesar's inability to win were the other Greek colonies along the Province coast that they hastened to supply Massilia.

"I wonder why it is that none of them think I can beat a tired old man like Pompeius?" asked Caesar of Trebonius at the end of May.

"The Greeks have never been good judges of generals," said Trebonius. "They don't know you. Pompeius is an enduring legend because of his campaign against the pirates, I think. This entire coast sampled his activities and talents at that time."

"My conquest of Gallia Comata wasn't very far away."

"Yes, Caesar, but they're Greeks! Greeks never have warred with barbarians; they've always preferred to enclose themselves in coastal cities and avoid the barbarian inland. That's as true of their colonies in the Euxine as it is in Our Sea."

"Well, they are about to learn that they've backed the wrong side," said Caesar, nettled. "I'm leaving for Narbo in the morning. Decimus ought to be on his way back with a fleet. He's in charge on the sea, but you're in overall command. Push them hard and don't give too much quarter, Trebonius. I want Massilia humbled."

"How many legions?"

"I'll leave you the Twelfth and the Thirteenth. Mamurra tells me there's a new Sixth freshly recruited in Italian Gaul—I've instructed him to send it to you. Train it, and if possible blood it. Far better to blood it on Greeks than Romans. Though actually that's one of my great advantages in this war."

"What?" asked Trebonius, bewildered.

"My men are from Italian Gaul, and a great many of them from across the Padus. Pompeius's soldiers are properly Italian save for the Fifteenth. I realize Italians look down on Italian Gauls, but Italian Gauls absolutely loathe Italians. No brotherly love."

"Come to think of it, a good point."

Lucius Caesar had gone native, regarded Narbo as his home; when Cousin Gaius arrived at the head of four legions—the Ninth, the beloved Tenth, the Eighth and the Eleventh—he found the Province's governor so well ensconced that he had three mistresses, a brace of superb cooks and the love of all of Narbo.

"Have my cavalry arrived?" Caesar asked, eating with relish for once. "Oh, I had forgotten how deliciously light and tasty—how *digestible*—the dug-mullets of Narbo are!"

"That," said Lucius Caesar smugly, "is because I've taken to doing them the Gallic way—fried in butter rather than in oil. Oil's too strong. The butter comes from the lands of the Veneti."

"You've degenerated into a Sybarite."

"But kept my figure."

"A family trait, I suspect. The cavalry?"

"All three thousand you called up by name are here, Gaius. I decided to pasture them south of Narbo around the mouth of the Ruscino. On your way, so to speak."

"I gather Fabius is sitting at Illerda."

"With the Seventh and the Fourteenth, yes. I sent several thousand Narbonese militia with him to force passage across the Pyrenees, but when you reach him I'd appreciate your returning them. They're good and loyal, but not citizens."

"And are Afranius and Petreius still facing him?"

"Across the Sicoris River. With five legions. The other two are still in Further Spain with Varro." Lucius Caesar grinned. "Varro isn't quite as confident as everyone else that you'll lose, so he hasn't done much to bestir himself. They've been spending a cozy winter in Corduba."

"A long march from Illerda."

"Precisely. I think all you have to worry about are the five legions with Afranius and Petreius. Do try the oysters."

"No, I prefer the dug-mullets. How clever of your cook to bone them so thoroughly."

"An easy fish to bone, as a matter of fact. They're so flat." Lucius Caesar looked up. "What you may not know," he said, "is that Pompeius sent from Epirus and borrowed heavily from the men of his Spanish legions. They gave him everything they had and agreed to waive pay until you're defeated."

"Ah! Pompeius is feeling the pinch."

"He deserves to, forgetting to empty the Treasury."

Caesar's shoulders shook with silent laughter. "He'll never manage to live that down, Lucius."

"I hear my son has elected Pompeius."

"I'm afraid so."

"He never was very bright."

"Speaking of brightness, I met a remarkable member of the family in Formiae," said Caesar, transferring his attention to the cheeses. "All of thirteen years old."

"Who's that?"

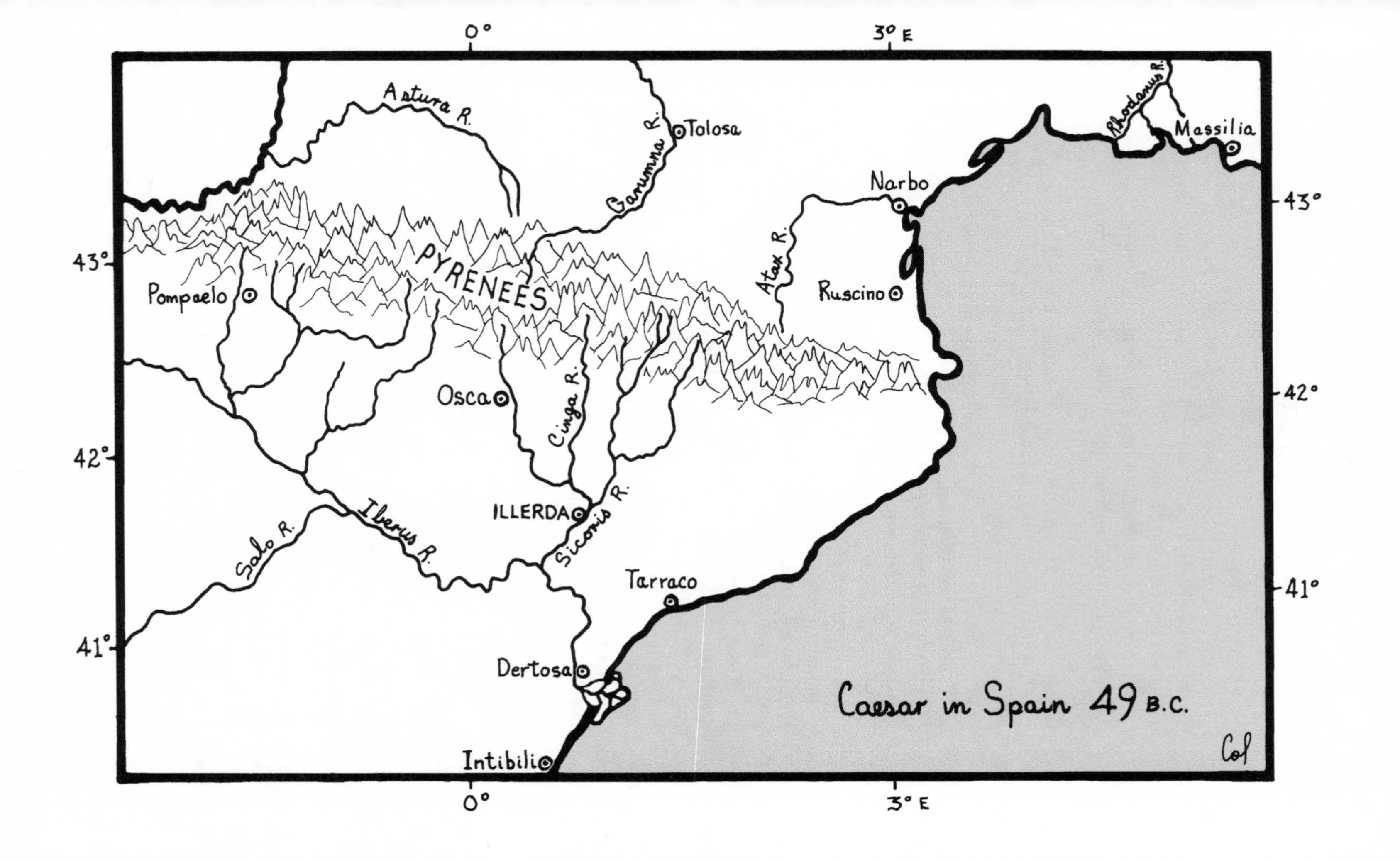
Caesar in Spain 49 B.C.
0°
3° E
43°
42°
41°
Astura R.
Garumna R.
Tolosa
Rhodanus R.
Massilia
Narbo
Atax R.
Ruscino
PYRENEES
Pompaelo
Osca
Cinga R.
ILLERDA
Sicoris R.
Iberus R.
Salo R.
Tarraco
Dertosa
Intibili
Col

"Atia's son by Gaius Octavius."

"Another Gaius Julius Caesar in the making?"

"He says not. No military talent, he informed me. A very cold fish, but a very bright one."

"He's not tempted to espouse Philippus's life style?"

"I saw no evidence of it. What I did see was huge ambition and considerable shrewdness."

"That branch of the Octavii have never had a consul."

"They will in my great-nephew," said Caesar positively.

Caesar arrived to reinforce Gaius Fabius toward the end of June, bringing the strength of his forces up to six legions; the Narbonese militia were thanked and sent home.

"Lucius Caesar told you that Pompeius has borrowed this army's savings?" asked Gaius Fabius.

"He did. Which means they have to win, doesn't it?"

"So they think. Afranius and Petreius were bitten too."

"Then we'd better reduce them to penury."

But it seemed that Caesar's fabled luck was out. The winter dissipated early in continuous downpours which extended into the high Pyrenees and brought a spate down the Sicoris which knocked out every bridge across it. A problem for Caesar, who had to bring his supplies over those bridges. A narrow but fast-flowing stream even when not in flood, the Sicoris continued to defy the new arrivals; when finally its level dropped, the presence of Afranius and Petreius on its far side prevented rebuilding of the bridges. The rain persisted, camp was a misery, food was low.

"All right, boys," said Caesar at assembly, "we're going to have to do it the hard way."

The hard way was to slog with two legions twenty miles upstream, mired to the ankles in mud, and there throw up a bridge without the knowledge of the Pompeians. Once this was done, food flowed in again—even if camp was no drier.

"And that," said Caesar to Fabius, "is what Caesar's luck really consists of—hard work. Now we sit through the rains and wait for fine weather."

Of course the couriers galloped between Rome and Caesar's camp, between Massilia and Caesar's camp; Caesar never liked to be more than two *nundinae* behind events. Among the many letters from Rome came one from Mark Antony, carried very swiftly.

> The word in Rome is that you're stuck, Caesar. All the Sicoris bridges out, and no food. When certain senators heard, they staged a joyful celebration outside Afranius's house on the Aventine. Lepidus and I thought it might be amusing to watch, so we went along—no, I didn't need to cross the *pomerium*! They had singers, dancers,

tumblers, a couple of rather horrible freaks, and plenty of shrimps and oysters from Baiae. Between ourselves, Lepidus and I thought it a bit premature. By now, we think, you will have solved your supply problems and be dealing with the Pompeians.

One further effect of this news that you were in serious trouble concerns the Senate; the celebration concluded, all the waverers—about forty, all told—departed for Pompeius in eastern Macedonia. I believe that when they get there, these anxious-to-be-on-the-right-side senators will not suffer any deprivations in the field. Pompeius has taken up residence in the governor's palace at Thessalonica, and they're all living mighty high.

Neither Lepidus nor I prevented this mass exodus, in which I hope we did right. Our assumption was that you're better off without these creatures in Italia—let Pompeius have the joy of them. By the way, I let Cicero leave too. His noises of opposition didn't diminish, and he didn't care much for my style of governing. I've got this terrific chariot drawn by four lions, and made a show of driving it whenever I was in Cicero's neighborhood. Truth to tell, Caesar, it's a pain in the *podex*. I had male lions with black manes—huge and very imposing animals. But they refused to work. Lazy! Every two paces they'd flop down and go to sleep. I had to substitute females. Even so, lions do not make good chariot pullers. Which makes me skeptical about Dionysos and his car drawn by leopards.

Cicero left from Caieta about the Nones of June, but not with brother Quintus. As you well know, Quintus's son is minded to side with you. Been listening to *tata,* I suspect. Both brother Quintus and nephew Quintus elected to stay in Italia, though for how long remains a mystery. Cicero is playing on family feelings. Full of moans right up to his departure. His eyes were in a shocking mess when I saw him at the beginning of May. I know you wanted him to stay here, but he's better gone. He's too incompetent to make any difference to Pompeius's chances of success (which I rate very low), and he'll never come round to your way of thinking. A voice like his is better removed to someplace it can't be heard. His boy, Marcus, went too.

Tullia, by the way, gave birth to a seven-months child in May—a boy. But it died on the same day in June that old Perperna died. Fancy that! The senior senator and senior consular. Still, if I live to be ninety-eight, I'll be happy.

A letter which both pleased and displeased Caesar. Was there anything could make a sensible man out of Antonius? Lions! He and Lepidus were right about the senatorial exodus—better without such men, they'd only make it difficult for Lepidus to pass much needed legislation. Cicero was another matter. He should not have been let leave the country.

The news from Massilia was cheering. Decimus Brutus and his inexplicable gift for doing well on water had paid dividends. The blockade of Massilia's harbor he instituted had begun to hurt the city so badly that Ahenobarbus led the Massiliote fleet out to do battle. With the result that Ahenobarbus went down, sustaining very heavy losses. Decimus Brutus's blockade was still firmly in place, and Massilia was eating less well. Also, it would seem, developing a dislike of Ahenobarbus.

"That," said Fabius, "is not surprising."

"Massilia picked the wrong side," said Caesar. He compressed his lips. "I don't know why these places deem me incapable of winning when I can't lose."

"Pompeius has a much longer record of success, Caesar. But they'll learn."

"As Afranius and Petreius are about to learn."

By the middle of Quinctilis, Afranius and Petreius were worried men. Though there had been no major engagement between the two armies, Caesar's three thousand Gallic cavalry were hitting the Pompeians hard along their supply lines. Very short of horse troopers themselves, Pompey's two old retainers decided to pull out and move south of the great river Iberus, into country Caesar didn't know. Country which was absolutely loyal to Pompey, which would not supply Caesar with food. To compound the Pompeian woes, some of the bigger Spanish towns north of the Iberus were starting to think Caesar's chances were better. Led by Sertorius's old capital, Osca, they declared for Caesar, who was related to Gaius Marius, who was related to Sertorius.

South of the Iberus that kind of defection wouldn't occur; definitely time to withdraw. Marcus Petreius went ahead with the corps of engineers and some laborers to build a bridge of boats across the river, while Afranius kept up appearances opposite Caesar. Unfortunately for the Pompeians, Caesar's network of informers was excellent. He knew exactly what was going on. In the same moment as Afranius was surreptitiously pulling out, Caesar was surreptitiously leading his army upstream.

The ground had dried out, the terrain was reasonable; Caesar marched with all his customary speed, and caught up with Afranius's rear guard by midafternoon. And kept on marching, right into Afranius's ranks. The rougher country ahead of Afranius's column contained a defile for which the Pompeian army had been heading, but, still five miles short of it, Caesar's remorseless harrying forced Afranius to halt and build a strongly fortified camp. Minus the moral support of Petreius, he spent a long and miserable night, dying to sneak away, yet unable to do so because he knew Caesar liked to attack at night. His main worry was the spirit among his troops; in civil war disaffection was always possible, and there had been muttering. What he overlooked was his own mood.

It had been many years since Afranius had campaigned as strenuously—if he ever had. At dawn Caesar struck camp much faster and reached the defile first; Afranius had no choice other than to pitch camp at the mouth of the ravine. Petreius, returning from the Iberus, found him lackluster and depressed, unable to think what must be done; he hadn't even ensured his water supply. Angry, Petreius set about building a fortified line to the river.

But while Petreius, the engineers and some of the men busied themselves with this, most of the Pompeian soldiers were idle. Caesar's camp was so close to theirs that his sentries were within speaking distance; Pompeians began to talk with Caesareans, who urged them to surrender.

"You can't beat Caesar" was the constantly repreated refrain. "Give in now, while you're still alive. Caesar doesn't want to fight fellow Romans, but most of us are dying for a good battle—and pressing Caesar to give us one! Best surrender while you can."

A Pompeian deputation of senior centurions and military tribunes went to Caesar. Among them was Afranius's son, who begged Caesar to pardon his father. In fact, discipline had relaxed so much that while the Pompeian deputation parleyed with Caesar, some of Caesar's soldiers strolled into the Pompeian camp. When Afranius and Petreius discovered them, they were appalled to learn that their senior officers—together with Afranius's own son!—were conferring with the enemy. Afranius wanted to send the Caesarean soldiers home; Petreius refused to hear of it and had his Spanish bodyguard kill them on the spot. Retaliation was typical of this new, clement Caesar. He sent the Pompeians back to their camp with courteous words and an offer of service in his own legions. The contrast between his behavior and Petreius's did not go unnoticed; while Afranius and Petreius were deciding to head for Illerda rather than cross the Iberus, disaffection in the Pompeian ranks was spreading rapidly.

The retreat toward Illerda was a frantic scramble, with Caesar's cavalry harassing the rear guard all day. That night when the Pompeians went into camp, Caesar threw up some quick fortifications and deprived them of water.

Afranius and Petreius sued for peace.

"Fine by me," said Caesar, "provided that negotiations are conducted in a full assembly of both armies."

Caesar's terms were reasonable and acceptable. The Pompeian troops—and Afranius and Petreius—were pardoned. Any men who fancied joining Caesar's ranks were admitted if they swore an oath of allegiance to Caesar, but none were coerced; men enlisted against their will would form the first nucleus of disaffection. Pompeians who lived in Spain might return to their homes after giving up their arms; Roman Pompeians would be marched back to the river Varus, which was the boundary between the Province and Liguria, and there discharged.

The war in Spain was over, and again had been virtually a bloodless one. Quintus Cassius and two legions marched for the southern Spanish province, wherein Marcus Terentius Varro had done little to prepare for war save decide to shut himself up in Gades. But before he could do so, the entire populace and both legions of Further Spain went over to Caesar without a fight. Varro met Quintus Cassius at Corduba and surrendered.

In only one aspect did Caesar make a mistake, and that was to place Quintus Cassius in the governorship of Further Spain. Those aurally and argently sensitized nostrils flared like a hound's as they sniffed the gold and silver which the further province still produced in abundance; Quintus Cassius waved a cheerful goodbye to Caesar and settled down to plunder his new charge ruthlessly.

By mid-September, Caesar was back in Massilia. Just in time to receive that city's surrender. The chastened and disillusioned Council of Fifteen was forced to admit that Ahenobarbus had sailed away, leaving them without the strength to resist Decimus Brutus's blockade. Leaving them to starve. Caesar permitted Massilia to retain its independent status, but without any troops or warships to defend itself—and with its hinterland pared back almost to nothing. Just to make sure, Caesar left two legions of ex-Pompeian troops behind to garrison it. Pleasant duty in a pleasant land; the ex-Pompeians would stay loyal. The Fourteenth Legion was sent back to Gaul of the Long-hairs under the command of Decimus Brutus, who would govern that new province in Caesar's absence. Trebonius, Fabius, Sulpicius and the others were to march with him for Rome and Italia, where most of them would remain to serve as praetors.

Rome had settled down fairly well. When Curio sent the news that he had secured Sicily at the end of June, everyone breathed a sigh of relief. With Orca holding Sardinia and Curio holding Sicily, enough grain would flow in good harvest years. Africa was insurance against famine should Curio manage to take it.

At the moment it was firmly in the hands of the Pompeians; the capable legate Quintus Attius Varus had gone from Corfinium to Sicily and from there to Africa Province, where he wrested control from Aelius Tubero, ejected him, and formed an alliance with King Juba of Numidia. Africa's single legion was now augmented by troops levied from among Roman veterans settled in Africa, their sons, and Juba's large army of infantry. Juba had, besides, his famous Numidian cavalry, men who rode bareback, wore no armor and fought as lancers rather than at cut-and-thrust close quarters.

Matters were much easier for Lepidus after the second exodus of senators from Rome. He had his instructions from Caesar and now began to implement them. The first thing he did was to reduce the number of senators necessary to form a quorum; the decree was easily obtained from a Senate now consisting of Caesar's men and a few neutrals, and the

Popular Assembly saw no reason why it shouldn't pass the law. Henceforth sixty senators would constitute a quorum.

Lepidus did nothing further save keep in constant touch with Mark Antony, who was proving a popular governor of Italia. Between the litterloads of mistresses, the entourages of dwarves, dancers, acrobats and musicians, and that famous lion-drawn chariot, the rural people and the townsfolk of Italia thought him marvelous. Always jolly, always affable, always approachable, always ready to quaff a bucket or two of unwatered wine, he yet managed to get his duties done—and did not make the mistake of appearing in ridiculous guise when he visited his troops or port garrisons. Life was a bower of the exquisite roses which rambled all over Campania (his favorite destination), a heady mixture of frolic and authority. Antony was enjoying himself hugely.

News from Africa continued to be good. Curio had established himself in Utica without difficulty, and had dealt skillfully with Attius Varius and Juba in a number of skirmishes.

Then in Sextilis events in Illyricum and Africa soured. Mark Antony's middle brother, Gaius, had set himself down with fifteen cohorts of troops on the island of Curicta at the head of the Adriatic; there he was surprised by the Pompeian admirals Marcus Octavius and Lucius Libo, who attacked. Despite the valor of some of his men, Gaius Antonius knew himself in desperate trouble; he sent for help to Caesar's admiral in the Adriatic, Dolabella. Leading forty slow and under-armed ships, Dolabella responded. A sea battle developed and Dolabella was forced out of the water; his fleet was lost—and so was Gaius Antonius. Together with his troops, Gaius Antonius was captured. Falsely emboldened by his success, Marcus Octavius went on to attack the Dalmatian coast at Salona, which shut its gates and defied him. In the end he was forced to break off operations and return to Epirus, bearing as his captives Gaius Antonius and those fifteen cohorts. Dolabella got away.

Not happy news for Mark Antony, who cursed his brother's stupidity heartily, then settled down to work out how he could engineer Gaius Antonius's escape. The brunt of his disapproval, however, fell on Dolabella's head—what had Dolabella been about, to lose not only a battle but all of his ships? Nor was he prepared to listen when more detached people explained to him that the Pompeian ships were infinitely superior to the tubs poor Dolabella had under his command.

Fulvia had adjusted to life without Curio. Not happily, but adequately. Her three children by Publius Clodius were some years older than baby Curio: Publius Junior was now sixteen and would become a man at the festival of Juventas in December; Clodia was fourteen and had a head filled with dreams of husbands; and little Clodilla was eight, delightfully obsessed with baby Curio, who was now approaching a year in age and was walking and talking.

She still kept up with Clodius's own two sisters, Clodia the widow of Metellus Celer, and Clodilla the divorced widow of Lucius Lucullus. Those two ladies had declined to marry again, preferring the freedom they enjoyed because they were wealthy and not in any man's custody. But to some extent Fulvia's interests became ever more divergent from Clodius's sisters'; she liked her children and she liked being married. Nor was she tempted to have affairs.

Her best friend was not a woman.

"At least," she grinned, "not in the anatomical sense."

"I don't know why I put up with you, Fulvia," said Titus Pomponius Atticus, grinning back. "I'm a happily married man, and I have a delightful little daughter."

"You needed an heir to all that money, Atticus."

"Perhaps so." He sighed. "Bother these warring generals! I can't travel to Epirus with the freedom I used to have, nor do I dare show my nose in Athens, which is full of Pompeians of high birth strutting about obnoxiously."

"But you maintain good relations with both sides."

"True. However, lovely lady, it's more prudent for a rich man to rub noses with Caesar's adherents rather than Pompeius's. Pompeius is ravenous for money—he asks anyone he thinks has any for a loan. And, candidly, I think Caesar's going to win. Therefore to be inveigled into lending Pompeius or his adherents money is tantamount to throwing it into the sea. Thus—no Athens."

"And no delicious boys."

"I can live without them."

"I know. I'm just sorry you have to."

"So are they," said Atticus dryly. "I'm a generous lover."

"Speaking of lovers," she said, "I miss Curio dreadfully."

"Odd, that."

"Odd, what?"

"Men and women usually fall in love with the same kind of person every time. But you didn't. Publius Clodius and Curio are very different, in nature as well as looks."

"Well, Atticus, that makes marriage an adventure. I missed being married very much after Clodius died, and Curio was always there. I never used to notice him as a man. But the more I looked, the more the differences between him and Clodius became interesting. The freckles, the homeliness. That awful mop of disobedient hair. The missing tooth. The thought of having a red-haired baby."

"The way babies turn out has nothing to do with their sire," said Atticus thoughtfully. "I've come to the conclusion that their mothers force them *in utero* into whatever sort of baby they want."

"Rubbish!" said Fulvia, chuckling.

"No, it really isn't. If babies emerge a disappointment, that's because their mothers don't care enough to force. When my Pilia was pregnant with Attica, she was determined to produce a girl with tiny little ears. She didn't care about anything save the sex and those ears, though big ears run on both sides of the family. Yet Attica has tiny little ears. And she's a girl."

These were the things the best friends spoke about; for Fulvia, a masculine view of feminine concerns, and for Atticus, a rarely accorded chance to be himself. They had no secrets from each other, nor any wish to impress each other.

But the pleasure and inconsequence of that particular visit from Atticus was interrupted by Mark Antony, whose appearance inside the sacred boundary was so disturbing in itself that Fulvia paled at sight of him, began to shake.

He looked very grim yet was curiously aimless—couldn't sit, couldn't speak, looked anywhere except at Fulvia.

Her hand went out to Atticus. "Antonius, *tell me*!"

"It's Curio!" he blurted. "Oh, Fulvia, Curio is dead!"

Her head seemed stuffed with wool, her lips parted, the dark blue eyes stared glassily. She got to her feet and went to her knees in the same movement, a reflex from somewhere outside; inside herself she couldn't assimilate it, couldn't believe it.

Antony and Atticus lifted her, put her into a high-backed chair, chafed her nerveless hands.

Her heart—where was it going? Tripping, stumbling, booming, dying. No pain yet. That would come later. There were no words, no breath to scream, no power to run. Just the same as Clodius.

Antony and Atticus looked at one another above her head.

"What happened?" asked Atticus, trembling.

"Juba and Varus led Curio into a trap. He'd been doing well, but only because they didn't want him to do otherwise. Curio's not a military man. They cut his army to pieces—hardly any of his men survived. Curio died on the field. Fighting."

"He's one man we couldn't afford to lose."

Antony turned to Fulvia, stroked the hair from her brow and took her chin in one huge hand. "Fulvia, did you hear me?"

"I don't want to hear," she said fretfully.

"Yes, I know that. But you must."

"Marcus, I *loved* him!"

Oh, why was he here? Save that he had to come, imperium or no. The news had reached him and Lepidus by the same messenger; Lepidus had gone galloping out to Pompey's villa on the Campus Martius, where Antony, following Caesar's example, had taken up residence when in the vicinity of Rome. Curio's best friend since adolescence, Antony took his death very hard, wept for those old days and for what Curio might have become in Caesar's government. The fool, with his laurel-wreathed *fasces*! Going off so blithely.

To Lepidus, a rival had been removed from his path. Ambition hadn't blinded him, it simply drove him. And Curio dead was a bonus. Unfortunately he didn't have the wit to hide his satisfaction from Antony, who, being Antony, dashed his tears away as soon as Lepidus arrived and swore that he would have his revenge on Attius Varus and King Juba; Lepidus interpreted this swift change in mood as lack of love for Curio on Antony's part, and spoke his mind.

"A good thing if you ask me," he said with satisfaction.

"How do you arrive at that conclusion?" asked Antony quietly.

Lepidus shrugged, made a moue. "Curio was bought, therefore he wasn't to be trusted."

"Your brother Paullus was bought too. Does that go for him?"

"The circumstances were very different," said Lepidus stiffly.

"You're right, they were. Curio gave value for Caesar's money. Paullus swallowed it up without gratitude or return service."

"I didn't come here to quarrel, Antonius."

"Just as well. You're not up to my weight, Lepidus."

"I'll convene the Senate and give it the news."

"Outside the *pomerium,* please. And I'll give it the news."

"As you wish. I suppose that means I inherit the job of telling the ghastly Fulvia." Lepidus produced a smile. "Still, I don't mind. It will be an experience to break that kind of news to someone. Especially someone I dislike. It won't cause me any grief at all to do so."

Antony got to his feet. "*I'll* tell Fulvia," he said.

"You can't!" gasped Lepidus. "You can't enter the city!"

"I can do whatever I like!" roared Antony, unleashing the lion. "Leave it to an icicle like you to tell her? I'd sooner be dead! That's a great woman!"

"I must forbid it, Antonius. Your imperium!"

Antony grinned. "What imperium, Lepidus? Caesar gave it to me without any authority to do so beyond his own confidence that one day he'll be able to make it real. Until he does—until I receive my *lex curiata*—I'll come and go as I please!"

He'd always liked her, always thought her the final touch in Clodius's world. Sitting at the base of old Gaius Marius's statue after that terrific riot in the Forum—lying on a couch, adding her mite to Clodius's machinations—shrewdly tempering Clodius's craziness by playing on it—not so much transferring her affections to Curio as willing herself to live and love again—and the only woman in Rome who didn't have an unfaithful bone in her delectable body. The gall of Lepidus, to apostrophize her as "ghastly"! And he married to one of Servilia's brood!

"Marcus, I *loved* him!" she repeated.

"Yes, I know. He was a lucky man."

The tears began to fall; Fulvia rocked. Torn with pity, Atticus drew up his chair closer and cradled her head against his chest. His eyes met

Antony's; Antony relinquished her hand and her care to Atticus, and went away.

Twice widowed in three years. For all her proud heritage and her strength, the granddaughter of Gaius Gracchus couldn't bear to look at a life suddenly emptied of purpose. Was this how Gaius Gracchus had felt in the grove of Lucina beneath the Janiculum eighty-two years ago? His programs toppled, his adherents dead, his enemies baying for his blood. Well, they hadn't got that. He killed himself. They had had to be satisfied with lopping off his head and refusing his body burial.

"Help me die, Atticus!" she mourned.

"And leave your children orphans? Is that all you think of Clodius? Of Curio? And what of little Curio?"

"I want to *die*!" she moaned. "Just let me die!"

"I can't, Fulvia. Death is the end of all things. You have children to live for."

The Senate's comprising none but Caesar's adherents (or the careful neutrals like Philippus, Lucius Piso and Cotta) meant that it was no longer capable of opposing Caesar's wishes. Confident and persuasive, Lepidus went to work to fulfill Caesar's orders.

"I do not like alluding to a time best forgotten," he said to that thin and apprehensive body, "beyond drawing your attention to the fact that Rome in the aftermath of the battle at the Colline Gate was utterly exhausted and completely incapable of governing. Lucius Cornelius Sulla was appointed Dictator for one reason: he represented Rome's only chance to recover. Things needed to be done which could not be done in an atmosphere of debate, of many different opinions on how they ought to be done. From time to time in the history of the Republic, it has been necessary to hand the welfare of this city and her empire into the care of one man alone. The Dictator. The strong man with Rome's best interests at heart. The pity of it is that our most recent experience of the Dictator was Sulla. Who did not step down at the end of the obligatory six months, nor respect the lives and property of his country's most influential citizens. He proscribed."

The House listened gloomily, wondering how Lepidus thought he could ever persuade a tribal Assembly to ratify the decree he was clearly going to ask the Senate to hand down. Well, they were Caesar's men; they had no choice in it. But the tribal Assemblies were dominated by the knights, the very people whom Sulla had chosen for his proscription victims.

"Caesar," said Lepidus in tones of absolute conviction, "is no Sulla. His only aim is to establish good government and heal the wounds of this disgraceful exodus, the disappearance of Gnaeus Pompeius and his tame senators. Business is languishing, economic affairs are a shambles, both debtors and creditors are suffering. Consider the career of Gaius Caesar, and you will realize that this is no bigoted fool, no partisan preferrer. What has to be done, he will do. In the only way possible—by being appointed Dictator. It is not without precedent that I, a mere praetor, ask for this decree. As you well know. But we need elections, we need stability, we need that strong hand. Not my hand, Conscript Fathers! I do not so presume. We need to appoint Gaius Julius Caesar the Dictator of Rome."

He got his decree without difficulty, and took it to the Popular Assembly, which was the whole People gathered in its tribes, patricians as well as plebeians. He ought perhaps to have gone to the whole People in its Centuries, but the Centuriate Assembly was far too weighted in favor of the knights. Those who would oppose the appointment of a dictator most bitterly.

The move was very carefully timed; it was early September, and Rome was filled with country visitors in town for the games, the *ludi Romani.* Both the curule aediles, responsible for staging the games, had fled to Pompey. Nothing daunted, Lepidus as temporary ruler of the city appointed two senators to take their place for the purpose of the games, and funded them from Caesar's private moneys. Harping on the fact that the absent curule aediles had abrogated their duty to honor Jupiter Optimus Maximus, and that Caesar had stepped into the breach.

When there were sufficient country people in Rome, a tribal Assembly could not be manipulated by the First Class of voters; rural voters, despite their reasonable prosperity, tended to want the men whose names they knew—and the thirty-one rural tribes constituted a massive majority. Pompey had done himself no good in their eyes by speaking openly of proscriptions Italia-wide, whereas Caesar had behaved with clemency and great affection for country people. They liked Caesar. They believed in Caesar. And they voted in the Popular Assembly to appoint Caesar the Dictator of Rome.

"Don't be alarmed," said Atticus to his fellow plutocrats. "Caesar is a conservative man, not a radical. He won't cancel debts and he won't proscribe. Wait and see."

At the end of October, Caesar arrived in Placentia with his army, secure in the knowledge that he was now Dictator. The governor of Italian Gaul, Marcus Crassus Junior, met him there.

"All's well, save for Gaius Antonius's fiasco in Illyricum," said Crassus, and sighed. "I wish I could say that was a freak mischance, but I can't. Why on earth he chose to base himself on an island, I don't know. And the local people were so supportive! They adore you, therefore any legate of yours has to be worthwhile. Would you believe that a group of them built a raft and tried to help fend Octavius's fleet off? They hadn't anything beyond spears and stones—no ballistae, no catapultae. All day they took what Octavius threw at them. When night came, they committed suicide rather than fall into enemy hands."

Caesar and his legates listened grimly.

"I wish," said Caesar savagely, "that we Romans didn't hold the family in such reverence! I *knew* Gaius Antonius would manage to stuff up whatever command I gave him! The pity of it is that wherever I sent him, things would have gone the same way. Well, I can bear losing him. Curio is a tragedy."

"We've lost Africa, certainly," said Trebonius.

"And will have to do without Africa until Pompeius is beaten."

"His navy is going to be a nuisance, I predict," said Fabius.

"Yes," said Caesar, tight-lipped. "It's time Rome admitted that the best ships are all built at the eastern end of Our Sea. Where Pompeius is obtaining his fleets, while we're at the mercy of Italians and Spaniards. I took every ship Ahenobarbus left behind at Massilia, but the Massiliotes don't build much better than the shipyards in Narbo, Genua and Pisae. Or Novum Carthago."

"The Liburnians of Illyricum build a beautiful little galley," said Crassus. "Very fast."

"I know. Unfortunately they've done it in the past to equip pirates; it's not a well-organized industry." Caesar shrugged. "Well, we shall see. At least we're aware of our deficiencies." He looked at Marcus Crassus enquiringly. "What of preparations to give all Italian Gauls the full citizenship?"

"Just about done, Caesar. I appreciate your sending me Lucius Rubrius. He conducted a brilliant census."

"Will I be able to legislate it when I'm next in Rome?"

"Give us another month, and yes."

"That's excellent, Crassus. I've put *my* Lucius Roscius onto the Roman end, which means I ought to be able to have the whole matter finished by the end of the year. They've waited since the Italian War for their citizenships, and it's twenty years since I first gave them my word that I'd enfranchise them. Yes, high time."

There were eight legions encamped around Placentia—the new Sixth, the Seventh, Eighth, Ninth, Tenth, Eleventh, Twelfth and Thirteenth. The bulk of Caesar's Gallic army. The men of the Seventh, Eighth, Ninth and Tenth had been under the Eagles now for ten years, and were at the peak of their fighting ability; in age they were between twenty-seven and twenty-eight, and had been enlisted in Italian Gaul. The Eleventh and Twelfth were a little younger, and the Thirteenth, whose men were only twenty-one years old, was a mere baby by comparison. The Sixth, recruited earlier in this year and still unblooded, was a legion of shavelings looking very forward to some real fighting. As Caesar had remarked to

Gaius Trebonius, his was an army composed of Italian Gauls, many of whom were from the far side of the Padus. Well, shortly these men could no longer be dismissed as non-citizens by certain senatorial fools.

Recruitment was flourishing as Italian Gaul across the Padus realized that its forty-year battle to attain the full citizenship was over, and Caesar was its hero. He wanted twelve legions to take east to fight Pompey; Mamurra, Ventidius and their staff had labored to achieve Caesar's figure, and informed him when he reached Placentia that there would indeed be a Fifteenth, Sixteenth, Seventeenth and Eighteenth by the time he was ready to ship them to Brundisium.

Serene in the knowledge that his veteran troops belonged to him completely, Caesar went about the business of a governor. He paid a special visit to his colony at Novum Comum, where Marcus Marcellus had ordered a citizen flogged two years before, and personally paid the man compensation at a public meeting in the town marketplace. From there he visited the people of Marius's old colony at Eporedia, dropped in to see how things were at the big and thriving town of Cremona, and toyed with the idea of going further east along the foothills of the Alps to give out the news of impending citizenship. This was a great coup, for it meant that the large population still disenfranchised in Italian Gaul would, when citizens, come into his clientship.

A courier came from Gaius Trebonius in Placentia, demanding that Caesar return there immediately.

"Trouble," said Trebonius curtly when Caesar arrived.

"What kind of trouble?"

"The Ninth is disaffected."

For the first time in their long association, Trebonius saw the General bereft of words, stunned.

"It can't be," he said slowly. "Not my boys!"

"I'm afraid it is."

"Why?"

"I'd rather they told you. There's a deputation coming here this afternoon."

It consisted of the Ninth's senior centurions, and was led by the chief centurion of the Seventh Cohort, one Quintus Carfulenus. A Picentine, not an Italian Gaul. Perhaps, thought Caesar, face flinty, Carfulenus was in the clientele of Pompey. If so, he gave no sign of it.

The General received the men, ten in all, clad in full armor and seated in his curule chair; on his head he wore a chaplet of oak leaves to remind them—but how could the Ninth forget?—that he too was no mean soldier in the front line.

"What is this?" he asked.

"We're fed up," said Carfulenus.

Caesar looked not at Carfulenus but at his *primipilus* centurion, Sextus Cloatius, and his *pilus prior* centurion, Lucius Aponius. Two good men, yet very ill at ease; Carfulenus, a hard-bitten man of forty, was ten years their senior in age. Not satisfactory, thought Caesar, seeing an unsuspected problem for the first time. He would have to order his legates to examine the pecking order in their legions' centurions. Quintus Carfulenus, a senior man yet eleven grades junior to Cloatius and Aponius, was the dominant influence in this legion, under the command of Sulpicius Rufus.

Behind Caesar's set face and cold eyes a turmoil seethed; of grief, awful anger, incredulity. He had never believed this could happen to *him*—never believed for one moment that any of his beloved boys would cease to love him, plot to bring him down. Not a humbling experience, to find that his confidence had been misplaced; rather a disillusionment of huge proportions, in the wake of which roared an iron determination to reverse the process, to make the Ninth his again, to strike Carfulenus and any who genuinely felt as he did down to the dust. Literally, dust. Dead.

"What are you fed up with, Carfulenus?" he asked.

"This war. Or better say, this non-war. No fighting worth a lead denarius. I mean, that's what soldiering is all about. The fighting. The plunder. But so far all we've done is march until we drop, freeze in wet tents, and go hungry."

"You've done that for years in Gallia Comata."

"Why, that's exactly the point, General. We've done it for years in Gallia Comata. And that war's over. Been over for near two years. But where's the triumph, eh? When are we going to march in your triumph? When are we going to be discharged to a nice little plot of good land with our share of the spoils in our own purses and our legion savings accounts cashed in?"

"Do you doubt my word that you'll march in my triumph?"

Carfulenus drew a breath; he was truculent and on his guard, but not quite sure of himself. "Yes, General, we do."

"And what leads you to that conclusion?"

"We think you're deliberately stalling, General. We think you're trying to wriggle out of paying us our due. That you're going to take us to the other end of the world and leave us there. This civil war is a farce. We don't believe it's real."

Caesar stretched his legs out and looked at his feet, no expression on his face. Then the unsettling eyes came up and stared into the eyes of Carfulenus, who moved uncomfortably; they shifted to Cloatius, who looked agonized, then to Aponius, clearly wishing he was somewhere else, and slowly, horribly, at each of the other seven men.

"What are you going to do if I tell you that you're marching for Brundisium within a few days?"

"Simple," said Carfulenus, gaining assurance. "We won't go to Brundisium. The Ninth won't march a step. We want to be paid out and discharged here in Placentia, and we'd like our land around Verona. Though I want my piece in Picenum."

"Thank you for your time, Carfulenus, Cloatius, Aponius, Munatius, Considius, Apicius, Scaptius, Vettius, Minicius, Pusio," said Caesar, demonstrating that he knew the name of every member of the delegation. He didn't rise; he nodded. "You may go."

Trebonius and Sulpicius, who had witnessed this extraordinary interview, stood without a word to say, sensing the gathering of some terrible storm but unable to divine the form it was going to take. Odd, that such control, such lack of emotion, could give off emanations of impending doom. Caesar was angry, yes. But he was also shattered. And that never happened to Caesar. How would he cope with it? What might he do?

"Trebonius, summon the Ninth to an assembly on the parade ground at dawn tomorrow. Have the First Cohort of every other legion present as well. I want my whole army to participate in this affair, even if only as onlookers," said Caesar. He looked at Sulpicius. "Rufus, there's something very wrong with a legion whose two most senior centurions are dominated by a man of lower rank. Take the military tribunes who are liked by the rankers and start investigating who in the Ninth among the centurions has the gumption and the natural authority to fulfill the proper roles of *primipilus* and *pilus prior*. Cloatius and Aponius are nothings."

It became Trebonius's turn again. "Gaius, the legates in command of my other legions will have to undertake the same sort of investigation. Look for troublemakers. Look for centurions who are dominating more senior men. I want the army swept from top to tail."

At dawn the five thousand–odd men of the Ninth Legion were joined on the parade ground by the six hundred men of the First Cohort of seven other legions, a total of four thousand two hundred extra men. To speak to ten thousand men was feasible, particularly for Caesar, who had worked out his technique while campaigning in Further Spain as propraetor thirteen years ago. Specially chosen clerks with stentorian voices were positioned at intervals through the assembled soldiers. Those close enough to hear Caesar repeated what he said three words behind him; the next wave repeated what they heard, and so on through the crowd. Few speakers could do it, for the shouted repeats formed a colossal echo and made it extremely difficult to keep going against what had already been said. By making his mind tune the echoes out, Caesar could do it.

The Ninth was apprehensive yet determined. When Caesar mounted the dais in full armor he scanned the faces, which didn't blur with distance; his eyes, thank the Gods, were still keen both near and far. A thought popped into his head having nothing to do with legionary discontent: what were Pompeius's eyes like these days? Sulla's eyes had gone, and made him mighty touchy. Things happened to eyes in middle age—look at Cicero.

Though he had often wept at assemblies, today there were no tears. The General stood with feet apart and hands by his sides, his *corona civica* on his head, the scarlet cloak of his high estate attached to the shoulders of his beautifully worked silver cuirass. No helmet. His legates stood to either side of him on the dais, his military tribunes in two groups on either side below the dais.

"I am here to rectify a disgrace," he cried in the high, carrying voice he had found went further than his naturally deep tones. "One of my legions is mutinous. You see it here in its entirety, representatives of my other legions. The Ninth."

No one murmured in surprise; word got round, even when men were quartered in different camps.

"The Ninth! Veterans of the whole war in Gallia Comata, a legion whose standards groan with the weight of awards for valor, whose Eagle has been wreathed with laurel a dozen times, whose men I have always called my boys. But the Ninth has mutinied. Its men are no longer my boys. They are rabble, stirred and turned against me by demagogues in the guise of centurions. *Centurions!* What would those two magnificent centurions Titus Pullo and Lucius Vorenus call these shabby men who have replaced them at the head of the Ninth?" Caesar's right hand went out, pointed close by. "See them, men of the Ninth? Titus Pullo and Lucius Vorenus! Gone to the honorable duty of training other centurions here in Placentia, but present today to weep at their old legion's dishonor. See their tears? They weep for you! But I cannot. I am too filled with contempt, too consumed by anger. The Ninth has broken my perfect record; I can no longer say no legion of mine has ever mutinied."

He didn't move. The hands remained by his sides.

"Representatives of my other legions, I have called you together to witness what I will do to the men of the Ninth. They have informed me that they will not move from Placentia, that they wish to be discharged here and now, paid out and paid up, including their share of the spoils of a nine-year war. Well, they can have their discharge—but it will not be an honorable one! Their share of the spoils of that nine-year war will be divided up among my faithful legions. They will have no land, and I will strip every last one of them of his citizenship! I am the Dictator of Rome. My imperium outranks the imperium of the consuls, of the governors. But I am no Sulla. I will not abuse the power inherent in the dictatorship. What I do here today is not an abuse of that power. It is the just and rational decision of a commander-in-chief whose soldiers have mutinied.

"I tolerate much. I don't care if my legionaries stink of perfume and ram each other up the arse, provided they fight like wildcats and remain utterly loyal to me! But the men of the Ninth are disloyal. The men of the Ninth have accused me of deliberately cheating them of their entitlements. Accused *me*! Gaius Julius Caesar! Their commander-in-chief for ten long years! My word isn't good enough for the Ninth! The Ninth has mutinied!"

His voice swelled; he roared, something he never did in a soldier assembly. "I WILL NOT TOLERATE MUTINY! Do you hear me? I WILL NOT TOLERATE MUTINY! Mutiny is the worst crime soldiers can commit! Mutiny is high treason! And I will treat the mutiny of the Ninth as high treason! I will strip its men of their rights, their entitlements, and their citizenships! And I will decimate!"

He waited then until the last of the echoing voices died away. No one made a sound, save for Pullo and Vorenus, weeping. Every eye was riveted on Caesar.

"How could you?" he cried then to the Ninth. "Oh, you have no idea how profoundly I have thanked all of our Gods that Quintus Cicero is not here today! But this isn't his legion—these men can't be the same men who held off fifty thousand Nervii for over thirty days, who all bore wounds, who all sickened, who all watched their food and baggage go up in flames—AND WHO SOLDIERED ON! No, these aren't the same men! These men are puling, avaricious, mean, *unworthy*! I won't call men like these my boys! I don't want them!"

Both hands went out. "How could you? How could you believe the men who whispered among you? What have I ever done to deserve this? When you were hungry, did I eat better? When you were cold, did I sleep warm? When you were afraid, did I deride you? When you needed me, wasn't I there? When I gave you my word, did I ever go back on it? What have I done? *What have I done?*" The hands shook, clenched. "Who are these men among you, that you believe them before you believe me? What laurels are on their brows that I have not worn? Are they the champions of Mars? Are they greater men than I? Have they served you better than I? Have they enriched you more than I? No, you haven't had your share of the triumphal spoils yet—nor has any other among my legions! But you've had much from me despite that—cash bonuses I found out of my own purse! I doubled your pay! Is your pay in arrears? No, it is not! Haven't I compensated you for the lack of booty a civil war forbids? What have I done?"

The hands fell. "The answer is, Ninth, that I have done nothing to merit a mutiny, even were mutiny an accepted prerogative. But mutiny is not an accepted prerogative. Mutiny is high treason, were I the stingiest, cruelest commander-in-chief in the entire history of Rome! You have spat on me. I do not dignify you by spitting back. I simply call you unworthy to be my boys!"

A voice rang out: Sextus Cloatius, tears streaming down his face. "Caesar, Caesar, don't!" he wailed, walking out of the front rank and up to the dais. "I can bear the discharge. I can bear the loss of money. I can bear being decimated if the lot falls on me. But I can't bear not to be one of your boys!"

Out they came, all of the ten men who had formed the Ninth's deputation, weeping, begging forgiveness, offering to die if only Caesar would call them his boys, accord them the old respect. The grief spread; the rankers sobbed and moaned. Genuine, heartfelt.

They're such children! thought Caesar, listening. Swayed by fair words out of foul mouths. Gulled like Apulians in congress with charlatans. Children. Brave, hard, sometimes cruel. But not men in the true sense of that word. Children.

He let them have their tears.

"Very well," he said then, "I won't discharge you. I won't deem you all guilty of high treason. But there are terms. I want the one hundred and twenty ringleaders in this mutiny. They will all be discharged, they will all forfeit their citizenship. And I will decimate them, which means twelve of them will die in the traditional way. Produce them now."

Eighty of them constituted Carfulenus's entire century, the first of the Seventh Cohort; the other forty included Carfulenus's centurion friends. And Cloatius and Aponius.

The lots to choose the twelve men who would die had been rigged; Sulpicius Rufus had made his own enquiries as to the true ringleaders. One of whom, the centurion Marcus Pusio, was not among the one hundred and twenty men the Ninth indicated.

"Is there any innocent man here?" asked Caesar.

"Yes!" cried a voice from the depths of the Ninth. "His centurion, Marcus Pusio, nominated him. But Pusio is guilty!"

"Step out, soldier," said Caesar.

The innocent man stepped out.

"Pusio, take his place."

Carfulenus, Pusio, Apicius and Scaptius drew death lots; the other eight doomed men were all rankers, but heavily implicated. The sentences were carried out immediately. In each decury of the nominated men, the nine whom the lots let live were given cudgels and ordered to beat the owner of the death lot until he was unrecognizable pulp.

"Good," said Caesar when it was over. But it wasn't good. He could never again say that his troops were innocent of mutiny. "Rufus, have you a revised list of centurion seniority for me?"

"Yes, Caesar."

"Then restructure your legion accordingly. I've lost over twenty of the Ninth's centurions today."

"I'm glad we didn't have to lose the whole Ninth," said Gaius Fabius, sighing. "What an awful business!"

"One really bad man," said Trebonius, sad face sadder. "If it hadn't been for Carfulenus, I doubt it would have happened."

"Perhaps so," said Caesar, voice hard, "but it did happen. I will never forgive the Ninth."

"Caesar, they're not all bad!" said Fabius, perturbed.

"No, they're simply children. Yet why do people expect that children must be forgiven? They're not animals, they're members of the *gens humana*. Therefore they ought to be able to think for themselves. I will never forgive the Ninth. As they will discover when this civil war is over and I do discharge them. They won't get land in Italia or Italian Gaul. They can go to a colony near Narbo." He nodded dismissal.

Fabius and Trebonius walked to their own quarters together, very quiet at first.

Finally, from Fabius: "Trebonius, is it my imagination, or is Caesar changing?"

"Hardening, you mean?"

"I'm not sure that's the right word. Perhaps . . . yes, more conscious of his specialness. Does that make sense?"

"Definitely."

"Why?"

"Oh, the march of events," said Trebonius. "They'd have broken a lesser man. What's held him together is that he's never doubted himself. But the mutiny of the Ninth has fractured something in him. He never dreamed of it. He didn't think it could ever, ever happen to him. In many ways, I think a worse Rubicon for Caesar than that piddling river."

"He still believes in himself."

"He'll still believe in himself while he's dying," said Gaius Trebonius. "It's just that today tarnished his idea of himself. Caesar wants perfection. Nothing must diminish him."

"He asks with increasing frequency why no one will believe he can win this war," said Fabius, frowning.

"Because he's getting angrier at the foolishness of other people. Imagine, Fabius, what it must be like to *know* that there is no one in your league! Caesar knows. He can do anything! He's proven it too many times to enumerate. All he really wants is to be acknowledged for what he is. Yet it doesn't happen. He gets opposition, not recognition. This is a war to prove to other people what you and I—and Caesar—already know. He's turned fifty, and he's still battling for what he considers his due. Little wonder, I think, that he's growing thin-skinned."

At the beginning of November the eight legions gathered at Placentia marched for Brundisium, with almost two months to complete that five-hundred-and-fifty-mile journey; once they reached the Adriatic coast they were to proceed down its length, rather than cross the Apennines to skirt the vicinity of Rome. The pace was set at twenty miles a day, which meant that every second or third day was one of rest. To Caesar's legions, a glorious holiday, especially at this autumnal time of year.

From Ariminum, which welcomed him just as enthusiastically at the end of this year as it had at its beginning, Caesar turned to take the Via Flaminia to Rome. Up and over the lovely mountains of the homeland, their little fortified towns sitting atop this crag and that, the grass richly yellowed for nutritious grazing, the great forests of fir, larch, pitch-pine and pine stretching to the heights of the peaks, enough building timber for centuries to come. The careful husbanding which saw virtue in pure beauty, the natural affinity all Italians seemed to have for visual harmony. For Caesar, a kind of healing, that journey, taken at something less than his usual headlong pace; he stopped in every town of any size to enquire how things were, what was needed, where Rome's omissions lay. Speaking to the duumvirs of the smallest *municipia* as if they mattered to him quite as much as the Senate of Rome. Truth was, he reflected, they mattered more. Like all great cities, Rome was to some extent an artificial growth; as with all such excrescences, it sucked vitality unto itself, and often at the expense of the less numerous and less powerful places doomed to feed it. The cuckoo in the Italian nest. Owning the numbers, Rome owned the clout. Owning the numbers, its politicians favored it. Owning the numbers, it overshadowed all else.

Which it did, he had to admit, approaching it from the north; that other visit at the beginning of April had been a dim and nightmarish business, so much so that he hadn't noticed the city herself. Not as he did now, looking at the seven hills asprawl with orange-tiled roofs, glitters of gold from gilded temple eaves, tall cypresses, umbelliferous pines, arched aqueducts, the deep blue and strongly flowing width of Father Tiber with the grassy plains of Martius and Vaticanus on either bank.

They came out to meet him in thousands upon thousands, faces beaming, hands throwing flowers like a heady carpet for Toes to walk upon—would he have entered riding any but Toes? They cheered him, they blew him kisses, they held up their babies and small children for him to smile at, they shouted love and encouragement. And he, clad in his finest silver armor, his Civic Crown of oak leaves upon his head, rode at a slow walk behind the twenty-four crimson-clad lictors who belonged to the Dictator and carried the axes in their bundles of rods. Smiling, waving, vindicated at last. Weep, Pompeius! Weep, Cato! Weep, Bibulus! Never once for any of you, this ecstasy. What matters the Senate, what matters the Eighteen? These people are Rome, and these people still love me. They outnumber you as the stars do a cluster of lanterns. And they belong to *me*.

He rode into the city through the Fontinalis Gate alongside the Arx of the Capitol and down the Hill of the Bankers to the fire-blackened ruins of the Basilica Porcia, the Curia Hostilia and the Senate offices; good then to find that Paullus had used that huge bribe to better effect than he had his consulship by finishing the Basilica Aemilia. And his own Basilica Julia on the opposite side of the lower Forum, where the Basilicae Opimia and Sempronia had been, was growing from nothing. It would cast the Basilica Aemilia in the shade. So would the Curia Julia, the new home of the Senate, once he had seen the architects and commenced. Yes, he would put that temple pediment on the Domus Publica, make it more appealing from the Sacra Via, and clothe its facade all the way around with marble.

But his first visit was to the Regia, tiny temple of the Pontifex Maximus; there he entered alone, saw to his satisfaction that the hallowed place was clean and free from vermin, its altar unstained, its twin laurel trees thriving. A brief prayer to Ops, then it was out and across to his home, the Domus Publica. Not a formal occasion; he went in through his own entrance and closed its door upon the sighing, satiated crowd.

As Dictator he could wear armor within the *pomerium,* have his lictors bear the axes; when he disappeared within the Domus Publica they nodded genially to the people and walked to their own College behind the inn on the corner of the Clivus Orbius.

But the formalities were not over for Caesar, who had not set foot inside the Domus Publica on that hasty visit in April; he had now as Pontifex Maximus to greet his charges, the Vestal Virgins. Who waited for him in the great temple common to both sides of that divided house. Oh, where had the time gone? The Chief Vestal had been little more than a child when he had departed for Gaul—how Mater had railed at her liking for food! Quinctilia, now twenty-two and Chief Vestal. No thinner, but, he saw now with relief, a jolly young woman whose good sense and practical disposition shone out of her round, homely face. Beside her, Junia, not much younger, quite pretty. And there was his blackbird, Cornelia Merula, a tall and fine young lady of eighteen. Behind them, three little girls, all new since his time here. The three adult Vestals were clad in full regalia, white robes, white veils perched upon the mandatory seven sausages of wool, their *bulla* medallions upon their breasts. For the children, white robes but no veils; they wore wreaths of flowers instead.

"Welcome, Caesar," said Quinctilia, smiling.

"How good it is to be home!" he said, longing to embrace her, knowing he could not. "Junia and Cornelia, grown up too!"

They smiled, nodded.

"And who are the little ones?"

"Licinia Terentia, daughter of Marcus Varro Lucullus."

Yes, she had that look—long face, grey eyes, brown hair.

"Claudia, daughter of the Censor's eldest son."

Dark and pretty, very Claudian.

"Caecilia Metella, of the Caprarian Metelli."

A stormy one, fierce and proud.

"Fabia, Arruntia and Popillia, all gone!" he marveled. "I have been away too long."

"We have kept Vesta's hearth burning," said Quinctilia.

"And Rome is safe because of you."

Smiling, he dismissed them and turned then to enter his own half of the great house. An ordeal without Aurelia.

It was indeed a reunion full of tears, but these were tears that had to be shed. They had all come to see him who belonged to the days in the Subura—Eutychus, Cardixa and Burgundus. How *old* they were! Seventies? Eighties? Did it matter? They were so glad to see him! Oh, all those sons of Cardixa and Burgundus! Some of *them* were grizzled! But no one was allowed to remove the scarlet cloak, the cuirass and the skirt of *pteryges* save Burgundus; Caesar had to fight to remove the sash of his imperium himself.

Then finally he was free to find his wife, who had not come to him. That was her nature, to wait. Patient as Penelope weaving her shroud. He found her in Aurelia's old sitting room, though it bore no sign of his mother anymore. Barefoot, he moved as quietly as one of her cats; she didn't see him. Sitting in a chair with fat orange Felix in her lap. Had he ever realized she was lovely? It didn't seem so, from this distance. Dark hair, long and graceful neck, fine cheekbones, beautiful breasts.

"Calpurnia," he said.

She turned at once, dark eyes wide. *"Domine,"* she said.

"Caesar, not *domine*." He bent to kiss her, the perfectly correct salutation for a wife of scant months not seen for many years: affectionate, appreciative, promising more. He sat down in a chair close to her, where he could see her face. Smiling, he pushed a strand of hair off her brow; the dozing cat, sensing a foreign presence, opened one yellow eye and rolled onto its back, all four feet in the air.

"He likes you," she said, surprise in her voice.

"So he should. I rescued him from a watery grave."

"You never told me that."

"Didn't I? Some fellow was about to toss him into Father Tiber."

"Then he and I are grateful, Caesar."

Later that night, his head comfortably cushioned between her breasts, Caesar sighed and stretched. "I am very glad, wife," he said, "that Pompeius refused to let me marry that battle-axe of a daughter of his. I'm fifty-one, a little old for tantrums and power tactics in my home as well as my public life. You suit me well."

If perhaps in the very depths of her that wounded Calpurnia, yet she was able to see both the sense of it and the lack of malice in it. Marriage was a business, no less so in her own case than it would have been in the case of the strapping, pugnacious Pompeia Magna. Circumstances had conspired to keep her Caesar's wife, stave off the advent of Pompeia Magna. Which had delighted her at the time. Those *nundinae* between her father's informing her that Caesar wished to divorce her in order to marry Pompey's daughter and the news that Pompey had turned Caesar's offer down had been fraught with anxiety, with terrible misgivings. All Lucius Calpurnius Piso, her father, had seen was the huge endowment Caesar was willing to give Calpurnia in order to be free of her; all Calpurnia had seen was another marriage which her father would, of course, arrange. Even had love not formed a part of Calpurnia's attachment to Caesar, she would have hated it—the moving, the loss of her cats, the adjusting to a completely different kind of life. The cloistered style of the Domus Publica suited her, for it had its freedoms too. And when Caesar did visit, it was a visitation from some god who knew so perfectly how to please, how to make love comfortable. Her husband was the First Man in Rome.

Publius Servilius Vatia Isauricus was a quiet man. Loyalty ran in the family; his father, a great plebeian aristocrat, had cleaved to Sulla and remained one of Sulla's greatest supporters until that difficult, contrary man died. But because the father too had been a quiet man, he adjusted to life in a post-Sullan Rome with grace and some style, did not lose the massive clout which an old name and a huge fortune brought with it. Probably seeing something of Sulla in Caesar, the father before his death had liked him; the son simply carried on the family tradition. He had been a praetor in the year Appius Claudius Censor and Ahenobarbus were consuls, and had soothed *boni* fears by prosecuting one of Caesar's legates. Not an aberration but a deliberate ploy; Gaius Messius was not important to Caesar.

In the years since he was always to be found on Caesar's side of any senatorial division, nor could he be intimidated. No surprise then that when Pompey and the bulk of the Senate fled, Vatia Isauricus remained in Rome. Caesar, it was clear, mattered more to him than the alliances his marriage to Servilia's eldest daughter, Junia, might have predicated. Though when Cicero blabbed all over Rome that Junia's portrait was one of those in the baggage of a lowbred scoundrel, Vatia Isauricus did not divorce her. A loyal man remains loyal in all respects.

The day after Caesar arrived in Rome, Mark Antony sent word that he was waiting on the Campus Martius in Pompey's villa, and Marcus Aemilius Lepidus, who had secured the dictatorship for Caesar, waited in the Domus Publica for an interview. But it was Vatia Isauricus whom Caesar saw first.

"I can't stay long, alas," said Caesar.

"That I expected. You'll have to get your army to the other side of the Adriatic before the equinoctial gales."

"And lead it myself. What do you think of Quintus Fufius Calenus?"

"You had him as a legate. Don't you know?"

"In that respect, a good man. But this campaign against Pompeius necessitates that I restructure my high command—I won't have Trebonius, Fabius, Decimus Brutus or Marcus Crassus, yet I do have more legions than ever. What I need from you is an assessment of Calenus's ability to handle high command rather than a legion."

"Aside from his role in the regrettable affair of Milo and Clodius, I think him ideal for your purpose. Besides, in all fairness to poor Calenus, he accepted a ride in Milo's carriage without any knowledge of what Milo was planning. If anything, Milo's selecting him is a very good reference. Calenus is probably unimpeachable."

"Ah!" Caesar settled back in his chair and gazed at Vatia Isauricus intently. "Do you want the job of running Rome in my absence?" he asked.

Vatia Isauricus blinked. "You want *me* to act as your Master of the Horse?"

"No, no! I don't intend to remain Dictator, Vatia."

"You don't? Then why did Lepidus organize it?"

"To give me dictatorial clout for long enough to start things moving again. Really, just until I can have myself and one other man of my choice elected consul for the coming year. I'd like you as my consular colleague."

That was very evidently good news; Vatia Isauricus beamed. "Caesar, a great honor!" He frowned, not in anxiety but in thought. "Will you do as Sulla did and nominate two candidates only for the consular elections?" he asked.

"Oh, no! I don't mind how many men want to run against us."

"Well, you'll get no opposition from the Senate, but the men of the Eighteen are terrified of what you might do to the economy. The election results might not be what you want."

Which statement provoked a laugh. "I assure you, Vatia, that the knights of the Eighteen will scramble to vote for us. Before I hold elections, I intend to bring a *lex data* before the Popular Assembly to regulate the economy. It will quieten all those fears that I intend a general cancellation of debts, not to mention other, equally irresponsible acts. What Rome needs is proper legislation to restore faith in business circles and enable people on both sides of the debt fence to cope. My *lex data* will do that in the most sensible and moderate way. But the man I leave behind to govern Rome has to be a sensible and moderate man. That's why I want you as my colleague. With you, I know Rome will be safe."

"I won't destroy your faith in me, Caesar."

Next came Lepidus, a very different sort of man.

"In two years, Lepidus, I expect you'll be consul," said Caesar pleasantly, eyes never leaving that handsome and vaguely disquieting face; a man of great hauteur, riddled with weaknesses.

Lepidus's face changed, twisted in disappointment. "Not any sooner than two years, Caesar?" he asked.

"Under the *lex Annalis,* it can't possibly be sooner. I do not intend that Rome's *mos maiorum* be disturbed any more than is necessary. Though I follow in Sulla's footsteps, I am no Sulla."

"So you keep saying," said Lepidus bitterly.

"You have a very old patrician name and high ambitions to enhance it," said Caesar coolly. "You've chosen the winning side, and you'll prosper, that I promise you. But patience, my dear Lepidus, *is* a virtue. Practise it."

"I can practise it as well as the next man, Caesar. It's my purse is impatient."

"A revealing statement which doesn't augur well for Rome under your authority. However, I'll make a bargain with you."

"What?" asked Lepidus warily.

"Keep me informed of everything, and I'll have Balbus pop a little something in your hungry purse regularly."

"How much?"

"That depends on the accuracy of the information, Lepidus. Be warned! I don't want the facts warped to suit your own ends. I want exact transcriptions of the truth. Yours won't be my only sources of information, and I am no fool."

Mollified yet disappointed, Lepidus departed.

Which left Mark Antony.

"Am I to be your Master of the Horse?" was Antony's first question, asked eagerly.

"I won't be Dictator long enough to need one, Antonius."

"Oh, what a pity! I'd make a terrific Master of the Horse."

"I'm sure you would, if your conduct in Italia these past months is anything to go by. Though I must protest strongly against lions, litters, mistresses and mummers. Luckily next year you won't have any chance to behave like the New Dionysus."

The heavy, pouting face lowered. "Why?"

"Because, Antonius, you're going with me. Italia will be stable without you because Italia will have a *praetor peregrinus,* Marcus Caelius. I need you as a member of my high command."

The red-brown eyes lit up. "Now that's more like it!"

And that, Caesar reflected, was one man he had managed to please. A pity the Lepiduses of this world were choosier.

Caesar's *lex data* found immediate favor with the knights of the eighteen senior Centuries—and with many, many thousands more of lower status in Rome's commercial sphere. Its scope was wider than merely the city; it provided for Italia as well. Property, loans and debts were regulated through a series of provisos which favored neither creditors nor debtors. Those creditors who classified their debts as hopeless were directed to take land as settlement, but the value of the land was to be assessed by impartial arbitrators supervised by the urban praetor. If the interest payments on loans were up to date, the debtors received a deduction from the capital sum owed of two years' interest at twelve percent. No one was allowed to have more than sixty thousand sesterces in cash. The ceiling on all new loans was to be ten percent simple interest. And, most enormous relief of all, Caesar's *lex data* contained a clause which severely punished any slave who sought to inform on his master. As Sulla had encouraged slave informers and paid them well with money and freedom, this clause told Rome's businessmen that Caesar was no Sulla. There would be no proscriptions.

Overnight the world of commerce began to right itself, for debtors used Caesar's law as much as creditors, and both kinds of man vowed the law was an excellent one. Sensible and moderate. Atticus, who had been saying ever since the Rubicon that Caesar was no radical, preened himself, said "I told you so!" to everyone, and blandly accepted congratulations on his perspicacity.

Little wonder then that when the elections were held for all ranks of magistrates—the curule men in the Centuries, the quaestors and tribunes of the soldiers in the People's tribes, and the tribunes of the plebs and plebeian aediles in the tribal Plebs—Caesar's candidates, discreetly indicated, were all returned. The consular elections saw several candidates other than merely Caesar and Vatia Isauricus, but Caesar was returned as senior consul and Vatia as his junior. The Eighteen's way of saying thank you, thank you, thank you!

Vacancies in the priestly colleges were filled and a belated Latin Festival held on the Alban Mount. Things *happened*. But then, men were remembering, didn't things always happen when Caesar was in government? And this time he had no Bibulus to retard his progress.

Because he would not assume the consulship until the first day of the New Year, Caesar retained his dictatorship until then. Under its auspices he legislated the full citizenship for every man of Italian Gaul; the old, bitterly resented wrong was gone.

He restored the right to stand for public office to the sons and grandsons of Sulla's proscribed, then brought home those exiles whom he chose to repatriate as improperly banished. With the result that Aulus Gabinius was once more a Roman citizen in good standing, whereas Titus Annius Milo and Gaius Verres, among others, were not.

By way of thanks to the People, he gave an extra free grain dole to every Roman citizen man, paying for it out of a special treasure stored in the temple of Ops. The Treasury was still very full, but he would have to borrow another large sum from it to fund his campaign in Macedonia against Pompey.

On the tenth day of this sojourn in Rome, he finally had the leisure to summon a full meeting of the Senate, which he had convened on two earlier days in such a hurry that he left the senators quite winded; many of them had forgotten what Caesar in a hurry was like.

"I leave tomorrow," he said from the curule dais in Pompey's curia, a deliberate choice of venue; it amused him to stand below that hubristic statue of the man who was no longer the First Man in Rome. There were those who had pressed him to remove it; he had firmly declined, saying that Pompeius Magnus should witness the doings of Caesar Dictator.

"You will note that I have instituted no laws to remove their citizen status from that group of men who wait for me across the Adriatic. I do not regard them as traitors because they have chosen to oppose my occupation of the consuls' chair, nor because they sought to destroy my *dignitas*. What I have to do is show them that they are wrong, misguided, blind to Rome's welfare. Without, I sincerely hope, much if any bloodshed. There is no merit in shedding the blood of fellow citizens, as my conduct so far in this difference of opinion has conclusively shown. What I find hardest to forgive in them is that they abandoned their country to chaos, that they left it in no condition to continue. That it is now in good condition is due to me. Therefore the reckoning must be paid. Not to me, but to Rome.

"I have given Enemy of the People status to only one man, King Juba of Numidia, for the foul murder of Gaius Scribonius Curio. And I have given Friend and Ally status to Kings Bocchus and Bogud of Mauretania.

"How long I will be away I do not know, but I go secure in the knowledge that Rome and Italia, and their provinces in the West, will prosper under proper and sensible government. I also go with the intention of returning to Rome and Italia their provinces in the East. Our Sea must be united."

Even the fence-sitters were there that day: Caesar's uncle Lucius Aurelius Cotta, his father-in-law Lucius Calpurnius Piso, and his nephew-in-law Lucius Marcius Philippus. Looking very stern and above such things as internecine strife. Excusable in Cotta, still rather crippled by two strokes, and excusable perhaps in Philippus, constitutionally incapable of taking sides in anything. But Lucius Piso, so tall, so dark and so ferocious looking that Cicero had once had a fine old time describing him as a barbarian, was irritating. A complete self-server whose daughter was far too nice to deserve him as a father.

Lucius Piso cleared his throat.

"You wish to speak?" asked Caesar.

"I do."

"Then speak."

Piso rose to his feet. "Before committing us to a war, Gaius Caesar, might it not be politic to approach Gnaeus Pompeius and ask for peace negotiations?"

Vatia Isauricus answered, and tartly. "Oh, Lucius Piso!" he said, making a rude noise with his lips. "Don't you think it's a little late for that? Pompeius has been living high in the palace at Thessalonica for months, with plenty of time to sue for peace. He doesn't want peace. Even if he did, Cato and Bibulus wouldn't permit it. Sit down and shut up!"

"I loved it!" chuckled Philippus over dinner that afternoon. " 'Sit down and shut up!' So *delicately* put!"

"Well," said Caesar, grinning, "I suppose he thought it was time he said *something*. Whereas you, you reprobate, sail on as serenely as Ptolemy Philopator's barge."

"I like the metaphor. I'd also love to see that barge."

"The biggest ship ever built."

"Sixty men to an oar, they say."

"Rubbish!" said Caesar, snorting. "With that many men on an oar, it would act like a ballista."

Young Gaius Octavius, grey eyes wide, sat listening raptly.

"And what do you say, young Octavius?" asked Caesar.

"That a country which can build a ship that big and cover it in gold must be very, very rich."

"Of that there is no doubt," said Caesar, assessing the boy coolly. Fourteen now. There had been some changes associated with puberty, though the beauty had not diminished. He was beginning to have an Alexandrine look to him, and wore his luxuriantly waving golden hair long enough to cover the tips of those jutting ears. More worrying to Caesar, sensitive on that subject, was a certain—not precisely effeminacy, more a lack of the adolescent version of masculinity. To his surprise, he found that he cared about the future of this lad, didn't want to see him set off in a direction which would make his public career painfully difficult. No time now to speak privately with young Gaius Octavius, but somewhere in his crowded schedule he would have to make that time a fact.

His last call in Rome was upon Servilia, whom he found alone in her sitting room.

"I like those two white ribbons in your hair," he said, easing himself into a chair after kissing her lips like a friend.

"I had hoped to see you somewhat sooner," she said.

"Time, Servilia, is my enemy. But clearly not yours. You don't look a day older."

"I'm well serviced."

"So I hear. Lucius Pontius Aquila."

She stiffened. "How do you know that?"

"My informants constitute a positive ocean."

"They must, to have prised that little item out of hiding!"

"You must miss him now he's gone to help Pompeius."

"There are always replacements."

"I daresay. I hear that Brutus has also gone to help the good Pompeius."

Her small, secretive mouth turned down at its corners. "Hah! I don't understand it in him. Pompeius murdered his father."

"That was a long time ago. Perhaps his uncle Cato means more to him than an old deed."

"Your fault! If you hadn't broken off his engagement to Julia, he'd be in your camp."

"As are two of your three sons-in-law, Lepidus and Vatia Isauricus. But with Gaius Cassius and Brutus on the other side, you can't very well lose, can you?"

She shrugged, disliking this cold conversation. He was not going to resume their affair; his every look and movement showed it. And, setting eyes on him again for the first time in almost ten years, she found herself impaled again on his power. Yes, power. That had always been the great attraction. After Caesar, all other men were *insulsus*. Even Pontius Aquila, a scratch for an itch, no more. Immeasurably older, yet not one day older, that was Caesar. Graven with lines speaking of action, life in hard climes, obstacles conquered. The body as fit and workmanlike as ever. As no doubt was that part of him she couldn't see, would never see again.

"Whatever happened to that silly woman who wrote to me from Gaul?" she asked harshly.

His face closed. "She died."

"And her son?"

"He disappeared."

"You don't have much of that luck with women, do you?"

"Since I have so much of it in other, more important areas, Servilia, I don't find that surprising. Goddess Fortuna is a very jealous mistress. I propitiate her."

"One day she'll desert you."

"Oh, no. Never."

"You have enemies. They might kill you."

"I will die," said Caesar, getting to his feet, "when I am quite ready."

While Caesar conquered in the West, Pompey the Great contended with Epirus, a wet, rugged and mountainous land which was a small enclave of territory between western Macedonia to the north and western Greece to the south. Not, as Pompey soon discovered, an easy place to assemble and train an army. He had headquartered himself on fairly flat land near the prosperous port city of Dyrrachium, convinced now that he would not see Caesar for some time to come. Caesar would attempt to neutralize the Spanish army first. It would be a titanic struggle between one veteran force and another—but fought on Pompeian ground in Pompeian country. Nor would Caesar have all nine legions at his disposal; he would have to garrison Italia, Illyricum, Gallia Comata—and find enough troops to equip someone to wrest the grain provinces from the true government. Even with whatever soldiers he had managed to persuade to change sides after Corfinium, he'd be lucky to be able to match the five legions of Afranius and Petreius.

This mood of optimism about the outcome in the West was to last for some months yet, and was bolstered by the enthusiastic response Pompey received from all over the East; no one from King Deiotarus of Galatia and King Ariobarzanes of Cappadocia to the Greek *socii* of Asia could imagine the great Pompeius losing a war. Who was this Caesar? How could he equate some miserable victories over miserable foes like Gauls with the

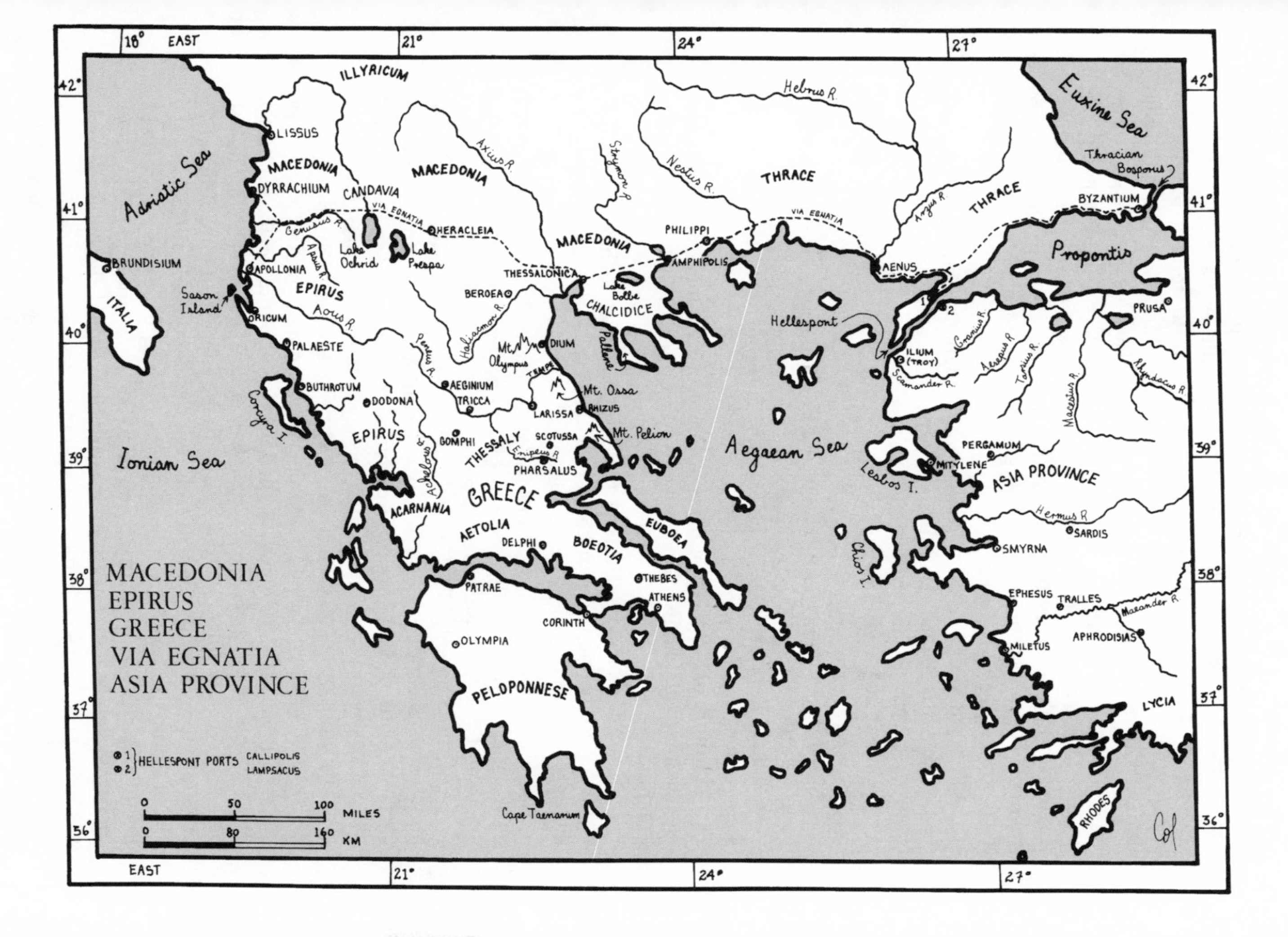
MACEDONIA
EPIRUS
GREECE
VIA EGNATIA
ASIA PROVINCE
1 CALLIPOLIS
2 LAMPSACUS
HELLESPONT PORTS
0 50 100 MILES
0 80 160 KM
EAST
Adriatic Sea
Ionian Sea
Aegaean Sea
Euxine Sea
Propontis
Thracian Bosporus
Hellespont
ILLYRICUM
MACEDONIA
THRACE
EPIRUS
THESSALY
GREECE
ACARNANIA
AETOLIA
BOEOTIA
EUBOEA
CHALCIDICE
PELOPONNESE
ASIA PROVINCE
LYCIA
ITALIA
CANDAVIA
VIA EGNATIA
LISSUS
DYRRACHIUM
APOLLONIA
ORICUM
PALAESTE
BUTHROTUM
DODONA
BRUNDISIUM
Sason Island
Corcyra I.
HERACLEIA
THESSALONICA
BEROEA
AEGINIUM
TRICCA
GOMPHI
DIUM
LARISSA
RHIZUS
SCOTUSSA
PHARSALUS
PHILIPPI
AMPHIPOLIS
AENUS
BYZANTIUM
PRUSA
ILIUM (TROY)
PERGAMUM
MITYLENE
SMYRNA
SARDIS
EPHESUS
TRALLES
MILETUS
APHRODISIAS
DELPHI
THEBES
ATHENS
CORINTH
PATRAE
OLYMPIA
Cape Taenarum
RHODES
Lesbos I.
Chios I.
Lake Ochrid
Lake Prespa
Lake Bolbe
Pallene
Mt. Olympus
Tempe
Mt. Ossa
Mt. Pelion
Genusus R.
Apsus R.
Aous R.
Axius R.
Haliacmon R.
Peneus R.
Achelous R.
Enipeus R.
Strymon R.
Nestus R.
Hebrus R.
Argus R.
Granicus R.
Aesepus R.
Tarsius R.
Scamander R.
Macestus R.
Rhyndacus R.
Hermus R.
Maeander R.
18°
21°
24°
27°
36°
37°
38°
39°
40°
41°
42°

glorious career of Pompeius Magnus, conqueror of Mithridates and Tigranes? Kingbreaker, kingmaker, sovereign in all but name himself. The promises of armies came in, together with a little—a very little—money.

It had been a Herculean act of self-control to be civil to Lentulus Crus, who had left the Treasury for Caesar to plunder. Where would he be without the two thousand talents Gaius Cassius had managed to squeeze out of Campania, Apulia and Calabria? But it was going nowhere. Dyrrachium was making hay in more ways than in its fields, autumnally replete; every bale of the stuff cost ten times its value, not to mention every *medimnus* of wheat, every side of bacon, every pea and bean, every pig and chicken.

Off went Gaius Cassius to see what might be found in the great temple sanctuaries all over Epirus, especially at holy Dodona, while Pompey called his "government" into session.

"Do any of you doubt that we'll win this war?" he demanded very aggressively.

Murmurs of protest, mutters of not liking the tone of voice. Finally, from Lentulus Crus: "Of course not!"

"Good! Because, Conscript Fathers, you are going to have to put some money on our war chariot."

Murmurs of surprise, mutters of inappropriate metaphors for a senatorial meeting. Finally, from Marcus Marcellus: "What do you mean, Pompeius?"

"I mean, Conscript Fathers, that you're going to have to send to Rome for all the money your bankers will advance you, and when it isn't enough, start selling land and businesses."

Murmurs of horror, mutters of what intolerable presumption. Finally, from his son's father-in-law, Lucius Scribonius Libo: "I can't sell my land! I'd lose my senatorial census!"

"At the moment, Libo," said Pompey through his teeth, "your senatorial census is not worth a fart in a flagon! Make up your minds to it: every last one of you is going to have to stick his fingers down his financial throat and spew up enough money to keep this enterprise going!"

Murmurs of outrage, mutters of such language, such language. Finally, from Lentulus Crus: "Rubbish! What's mine is mine!"

Pompey lost his temper, launched into his variation on the traditional diatribe of insults. "You," he roared, "are entirely responsible for the fact that we have no money, Crus! You ingrate, you leech, you ulcer on the brow of Jupiter Optimus Maximus! You pissed yourself in fear and shot out of Rome like a bolt from a catapulta, leaving the Treasury stuffed to the gills! And when I instructed you to go back to Rome and rectify that—that *gross* dereliction of your consular duty, you had the temerity to answer that you'd do so when I advanced into Picenum to meet Caesar and rendered him unable to touch your fat, pampered *capon* of a carcass! You, to tell *me* that I'm talking rubbish? You, to refuse to share in the funding of this war? I shit on your prick, Lentulus! I piss in your ugly face, Lentulus! I fart up your snobby nostrils, Lentulus! And if you're not very careful, Lentulus, I'll slit you up the middle from guts to gizzard!"

Of murmurs there were none, of mutters there were none. Frozen to stone, ears ringing at a saltiness few if any of them had ever heard from a commanding officer in the days of their military service, so sheltered and indulged had they been, the senators stood, jaws dropped, bowels gone liquid with fear.

"There's not one of you here apart from Labienus could fight a room full of feathers! Nor one of you has the remotest idea what waging war entails! Therefore," said Pompey, taking a long, deep breath, "it's time you found out. The major item you need to wage a war is money. Do any of you remember what Crassus used to say, that a man ought not to dare call himself rich if he couldn't afford to fund and maintain a legion? When he died he was worth seven thousand talents, and that was probably half what he was worth before he buried some where we'll never find it! *Money!* We need money! I've already started liquidating my assets in Lucania and Picenum, and I expect every man here to do the same! Call it an investment against the rosy future," he said chattily, a great deal happier now that he had them where any decent commander ought to have them—under his heel. "When Caesar is beaten and Rome belongs to us, we'll reap what we put in now a thousandfold. So open up the purse strings, all of you, and empty the contents into our communal war chest. Is that understood?"

Murmurs of assent, mutters of if only they'd known, if only they'd thought a little harder. Finally, from Lentulus Spinther: "Gnaeus Pompeius is right, Conscript Fathers. When Rome belongs to us, we'll reap what we put in now a thousandfold."

"I'm glad we sorted that out," said Pompey pleasantly. "Now comes the division of labor. Metellus Scipio is already on his way to Syria, where he will gather what money he can, and what troops he can. Gaius Cassius, once he returns from seeing what he can get from the Epirote and Greek temple treasures, will follow Scipio to Syria and there gather a fleet. Gnaeus, my son, you'll go to Egypt and commandeer a fleet, transports and grain from the Queen. Aulus Plautius in Bithynia will need a little prodding—it's your job to apply the goad, Piso Frugi. Lentulus Crus, you'll go to Asia Province and proceed to raise money, troops and a fleet. You can have Laelius and Valerius Triarius to help with the ships. Marcus Octavius, levy ships from Greece. Libo, levy ships from Liburnia—they're nice little galleys. I want fast ships, decked ships big enough to take artillery, but no monstrosities—triremes for main preference, biremes not bad, quadriremes and quinqueremes if they're trim and maneuverable."

"Who'll be commanding what?" asked Lentulus Spinther.

"That remains to be seen. First, round up the flocks. Then worry about the shepherds." Pompey nodded. "You can go."

Titus Labienus lingered. "That was very good," he said.

"Pah!" said Pompey contemptuously. "A more incompetent, addled lot I've never seen! How did Lentulus Spinther ever think he could lead an army to Egypt while he was governor of Cilicia?"

"There is no Trebonius, Fabius or Decimus Brutus, to be sure." Labienus cleared his throat. "We have to move from Dyrrachium before winter makes Candavia impassable, Magnus. Relocate ourselves somewhere on the plains near Thessalonica."

"I agree. It's the end of March. I'll wait out April to make sure Caesar does head west. Then it's off to a sunnier climate than rain, rain, rain in Epirus." Pompey looked gloomy. "Besides, if I wait here a bit longer, some better men might turn up."

Labienus lifted his lip. "I suppose you mean Cicero, Cato and Favonius?"

Pompey closed his eyes, shuddered. "Oh, Labienus, pray all the Gods, not! Let Cicero stay in Italia, and Cato and Favonius in Sicily. Or Africa. Or the land of the Hyperboreans. Or *anywhere*!"

This prayer was not answered. At the middle of April, Cato and Favonius, with Lucius Postumius in tow, arrived in Dyrrachium to tell of their ejection from Sicily by Curio.

"Why didn't you go on to Africa?" asked Pompey.

"It seemed better to join you," said Cato.

"I am ecstatic," said the commander-in-chief, secure in the knowledge that irony would pass straight over the top of Cato's head.

Two days later, however, a more useful man did turn up: Marcus Calpurnius Bibulus, who had dallied in Ephesus on his way home from governing Syria until events shaped themselves enough for him to perceive a proper course. Not that he was any more deferential or understanding than Cato, simply that his resolution to oppose Caesar was allied to a strong desire to be genuinely helpful rather than needlessly critical.

"I'm so glad to see you!" said Pompey fervently, wringing his hand. "There's no one here apart from Labienus and me with any idea of how to go about this war."

"Yes, that's obvious," said Bibulus coolly. "Including my esteemed father-in-law, Cato. Put a sword in his hand and he does well. But a leader he is not." He listened while Pompey summarized his preparations, nodding approval. "An excellent idea, to get rid of Lentulus Crus. But what's your strategy?"

"To train my army to think like an army. Spend the winter and spring, possibly also the early summer, near Thessalonica. It's closer to Asia Minor, a shorter march for troops sourced there. Nor will Caesar deal with me until he's tried to deal with my Spanish army. After he loses in Spain he'll regroup and come after me—he has to, or else submit, and he won't do that until he's not got a man left. It's mandatory that I control the seas. *All* the seas. Ahenobarbus has set himself up to take over Massilia, which has told me that it respects its ties with our government. That will slow Caesar down and oblige him to split his forces even more. I want him to experience the old, familiar Roman headache—a shortage of grain in Italia. We must dominate the seas between Africa, Sicily, Sardinia and the Italian coast. I also have to deny Caesar passage across the Adriatic at whatever time he decides to come east."

"Ah, yes," purred Bibulus, "pen him in and starve Rome out. Excellent, excellent!"

"I have you in mind as admiral-in-chief of all my fleets."

That came as a surprise. Immensely gratified, Bibulus put out his right hand and clasped Pompey's with unusual warmth. "My dear Pompeius, an honor you will not find misplaced. I give you my word that I'll do the job properly. Ships are strange, but I'll learn. And learn well."

"Yes, I think you will, Bibulus," said Pompey, beginning to believe that this decision was the right one.

Cato was not so sure. "To love my son-in-law is a right act," he said in his usual hectoring tones to Pompey. "However, he knows absolutely nothing about boats."

"Ships," said Pompey.

"Things that float on water and are rowed. His nature is Fabian, not Marian. Impede, stall, delay, stalk, but never engage. You need a more aggressive admiral-in-chief."

"Like you?" asked Pompey with deceptive mildness.

Cato reared back in horror. "No! No! I was thinking of Favonius and Postumius, actually."

"Good men, I do agree. However, they're not consulars, and the admiral-in-chief must be a consular."

"Yes, that is in keeping with the *mos maiorum*."

"Would you prefer that I appoint Lentulus Spinther, one of the Marcelli, or perhaps recall Ahenobarbus?"

"No! No!" Cato sighed. "Very well, it must be Bibulus. I'll spend a lot of time talking to him about developing considerably more aggression. And I must talk to Lentulus Spinther and both the Marcelli. And Labienus. Ye Gods, that man is dirty and untidy!"

"I have a better idea," said Pompey, holding his breath.

"What?"

"Hie yourself off—I'll have the Senate give you propraetor's imperium—to southern Asia Province and raise a fleet for me. I imagine Lentulus Crus, Laelius and Triarius will have enough to do in the north. Go to Rhodes, Lycia, Pamphylia."

"But—I won't be at the center of things, Pompeius. I'm needed at the center of things! Everyone is so *disorderly*! You need me here with you to smarten everyone up," said Cato, dismayed.

"Yes, but the trouble is that you're so famous in places like Rhodes,

Cato. Who, other than the wise, incorruptible and much respected Cato, can persuade the Rhodians to back us?" Pompey patted Cato's hand. "I tell you what. Leave Favonius behind with me. Give him instructions. Depute him to do what you'd do."

"That might work," said Cato, brightening.

"Of course it will!" said Pompey heartily. "Off you go, man! The sooner, the better."

"It's terrific to be rid of Cato, but you've still got that fart Favonius around your neck," said Labienus, displeased.

"The Ape is not the equal of the Master. I'll sool him onto those who need a boot up the arse. And those," said Pompey with a huge smile, "whom I personally detest."

When the news came that Caesar was sitting before Massilia and that Ahenobarbus was confident he would get no further, Pompey decided to pull stakes and march east. Winter was upon him, but his scouts were confident that the highest passes through Candavia were still negotiable.

At which point Marcus Junius Brutus arrived from Cilicia.

Quite why the sight of that mild, mournful, singularly unwarlike face caused Pompey to throw both arms around Brutus and weep into his overlong black curls, Pompey never afterward knew. Except that from the very beginning this inevitable civil war had been a series of disastrous bungles, conflicting voices, unjust criticisms, disobedience, doubt. Then in walked Brutus, a completely unmartial and gentle soul—Brutus wouldn't rasp, wouldn't carp, wouldn't try to usurp authority.

"Do we have Cilicia?" he asked after he had composed himself, poured watered wine, ensconced Brutus in the best chair.

"I'm afraid not," said Brutus sadly. "Publius Sestius says he won't actively support Caesar—but he won't do anything to offend Caesar either. You'll get no help from Tarsus."

"Oh, Jupiter!" cried Pompey, clenching his fists. "I need Cilicia's legion!"

"You'll have that much, Pompeius. When word came that you'd left Italia, I had the legion in Cappadocia—King Ariobarzanes was very delinquent in his loan repayments. So I didn't send it back to Tarsus. I sent it on through Galatia and Bithynia to the Hellespont. It will be with you in winter quarters."

"Brutus, you're the best!" The level of wine in Pompey's goblet went down considerably; he smacked his lips and leaned back contentedly. "Which leads me," he said casually, "to another, more important subject. You're the richest man in Rome, and I haven't enough money to fight this war. I'm selling up my own interests in Italia, so are the others. Oh, I don't expect you to go so far as to sell your house in the city, or *all* your country estates. But I need a loan of four thousand talents. Once we've won the war, we'll have Rome and Italia to carve up between us. You won't lose."

The eyes so earnestly and kindly fixed on Pompey's widened, filled with tears. "Pompeius, I daren't!" he gasped.

"You daren't?"

"Truly, I daren't! My mother! She'd kill me!"

Mouth open, Pompey stared back, stunned. "Brutus, you're a man of thirty-four! Your fortune belongs to you, not to Servilia!"

"*You* tell her that," said Brutus, shivering.

"But—but—Brutus, it's easy! *Just do it!*"

"I can't, Pompeius. She'd kill me."

And from that stand Brutus would not be budged. He blundered out of Pompey's comfortable house in tears, colliding with Labienus.

"What's wrong with him?"

Pompey was gasping. "I don't believe it! I can't believe it! Labienus, that spineless little worm just refused to lend us one sestertius! He's the richest man in Italia! But no, he daren't open his purse! His mother would kill him!"

The sound of Labienus's laughter filled the room. "Oh, well done, Brutus!" he said when he was able, wiping his eyes. "Magnus, you have just been defeated by an expert. What a perfect excuse! There's nothing in the world will ever part Brutus from his money."

By the beginning of June, Pompey had put his army into camp near the town of Beroea, some forty miles from Thessalonica, the capital of Macedonia, and moved into the governor's palace in that great and heavily fortified city—together with his entourage of consulars and senators.

Things were going better. Apart from the five legions he had brought with him from Brundisium, he now had one legion of Roman veterans settled in Crete and Macedonia, the Cilician legion (very under-strength), and two legions the chastened Lentulus Crus had managed to raise in Asia Province. Forces were beginning to dribble in from King Deiotarus of Galatia, some infantry and several thousand cavalry; the debt-crippled King Ariobarzanes of Cappadocia (who owed Pompey even more than he owed Brutus) sent a legion of foot and a thousand horse; the petty kingdoms of Commagene, Sophene, Osrhoene and Gordyene contributed light-armed troops; Aulus Plautius the governor of Bithynia-Pontus had found several thousand volunteers; and various other tetrarchies and confederations were also sending soldiers. Even money was beginning to appear in sufficient quantity to ensure that Pompey could feed what promised to be an army containing thirty-eight thousand Roman foot, fifteen thousand other foot soldiers, three thousand archers, a thousand slingers, and seven thousand horse troopers. Metellus Scipio had written to say that he had two full-strength legions of surprisingly excellent troops ready to move, though he would have to march them overland due to a shortage of transport vessels.

Then in Quinctilis came a delightful surprise. Bibulus's admirals Marcus Octavius and Scribonius Libo had captured fifteen cohorts of troops on the island of Curicta—together with Gaius Antonius, their commander. Since the troops were all prepared to swear allegiance to Pompey, his army was even bigger. That sea battle in which Octavius and Libo destroyed Dolabella's forty ships was the first of many victories for Pompey's navy, swelling rapidly. And very ably commanded, as it turned out, by the inexperienced Bibulus, who learned ruthlessly and developed a talent for his job.

Bibulus divided his navy into five large flotillas, only one of which was still theoretical by the time that September came. One flotilla, commanded by Laelius and Valerius Triarius, consisted of the one hundred very good ships levied from Asia Province; Gaius Cassius came back from Syria with seventy ships to inherit command of them; Marcus Octavius and Libo controlled fifty ships from Greece and Liburnia; and Gaius Marcellus Major and Gaius Coponius took charge of the twenty superb triremes Rhodes had donated to the distressingly persistent Cato, who refused to leave without them. *Anything* to get rid of Cato! cried the Rhodians.

The fifth flotilla was to consist of whatever ships young Gnaeus Pompey managed to extract from Egypt.

Full of himself because his father had given him this hugely important job, Gnaeus Pompey set out by sea for Alexandria, determined that he would excel. Twenty-nine this year, had Caesar not intruded he would have entered the Senate as quaestor next year. A fact which didn't worry him. Gnaeus Pompey never for one moment doubted that his father had the ability and the strength to squash that presumptuous Julian beetle to pulp.

Unfortunately he had not been quite old enough to serve in the East during Pompey's campaigns there; his cadetship had been spent in Spain during a disappointingly peaceful time. He had, of course, done the obligatory tour of Greece and Asia Province after he finished his military service, but he had never managed to reach either Syria or Egypt. He disliked Metellus Scipio only one degree less than he disliked his stepmother, Cornelia Metella, thus his decision to sail to Egypt along the African coast rather than go overland through Syria. An insufferable pair of snobs was Gnaeus Pompey's verdict about Metellus Scipio and his daughter. Luckily his little brother Sextus, born thirteen years later, got on very well with his stepmother, though, like all Pompey the Great's three children, he had mourned the passing of Julia bitterly. She had made everyone in the family so happy. Whereas Cornelia Metella, Gnaeus Pompey suspected, didn't even manage to make his status-conscious father happy.

Why he was thinking these things as he leaned on his ship's poop rail watching the dreary desert of Catabathmos slide by, he didn't know, save that time dragged and thoughts winged their own airy passage. He missed his young wife, Scribonia, dreamed of her by day as well as night.

Oh, that ghastly marriage to Claudilla! Yet one more evidence of his father's insecurity, his determination to obtain none but the highest wives and husbands for all his family. A drab, sat-upon girl too young for marriage, so utterly devoid of the kind of stimulus Gnaeus Pompey had needed. And what ructions when he had set eyes on Libo's daughter, announced that he was divorcing Claudilla and marrying this exquisite little Latin partridge with the glossy feathers and plump contours his mind and body craved! Pompey had thrown one of his best tantrums. In vain. His oldest son stuck to his resolve with true Pompeian tenacity, and had his way. With the result that Appius Claudius Censor had to be given the sinecure of governing Greece for the government in exile. Where, if rumor was right, he had gone even more peculiar, spent his time probing the geometry of pylons and muttering about fields of force, invisible fingers of power, and similar claptrap.

Alexandria burst on Gnaeus Pompey like Aphrodite upon the world. More numerous even than Antioch or Rome, its three million people inhabited what was arguably Alexander the Great's most perfect gift to posterity. His empire had perished within a single generation, but Alexandria went on forever. Though so flat that its biggest hill, the dreamy garden of the Panaeum, was a man-made mound two hundred feet high, it seemed to Gnaeus Pompey's dazzled eyes more something constructed by the Gods than by clumsy, mortal men. Part blinding white, part a rainbow of colors, liberally dewed with trees carefully chosen for slenderness or roundness, Alexandria upon the farthest shore of Our Sea was magnificent.

And the Pharos, the great lighthouse of Pharos Island! Far taller than any other building Gnaeus Pompey had ever seen, a three-tiered hexagon faced with shimmering white marble, the Pharos was a wonder of the world. The sea around it was the color of an aquamarine, sandy-bottomed and crystal clear, for the great sewers which underlay Alexandria emptied into the waters west of the city, ensuring that their contents were carried away. What air! Balmy, caressing. See the Heptastadion, the causeway connecting Pharos Island with the mainland, marching for almost a mile in white majesty! Two arches pierced its center, each arch spacious enough to permit the passage of a big ship between the Eunostus and the Great Harbors.

There directly before him reared the great palace complex, joined at its far end to a crag climbing out of the sea that used to be a fortress and now cupped a shell-like amphitheater within its hollow. This, Gnaeus Pompey realized, was a *real* palace. The only one in the world. So vast that it paled the heights of Pergamum into insignificance. At first glance its many hundreds of pillars looked severely Doric, save that they owned a more ponderous girth, were far taller and were vividly painted with tiers of pictures, each one the height of a column drum; yet proper pediments sat atop them, with proper metopes, everything a truly Greek building of importance should have. Except that the Greeks built on the ground. Like the Romans, the Alexandrians had elevated their palace complex upon a stone plateau thirty steps high. Oh, and the palms! Some graceful fans, some horny and stumpy, some with fronds like feathers.

In an ecstatic daze, Gnaeus Pompey saw his ship tied up at the royal wharf, supervised the disposition of his other ships, donned the purple-bordered toga his propraetor's imperium entitled him to wear, and set off behind six crimson-clad lictors bearing the axes in their *fasces* to seek palace accommodation and an audience with the seventh Queen Cleopatra of Egypt.

Having ascended the throne at seventeen years of age, she was now nearing twenty.

The two years of her reign had been fraught with triumphs and perils: first the glory of skimming down Nilus in her huge gilded barge with its purple sail embroidered in gold, the native Egyptians abasing themselves before her as she stood with her nine-year-old brother/husband by her side (but one step down); in Hermonthis the bringing home of the Buchis Bull, found because the curls in his flawless long black coat grew the wrong way round, her vessel afloat in a sea of flower-decked barges, herself clad in the solemn regalia of Pharaoh but wearing only the tall white crown of Upper Egypt; the journey past ruined Thebes to the First Cataract and the island of Elephantine, to be at the first, most important Nilometer on the very day when the rising waters would predict the final height of the Inundation.

Every year at the beginning of summer, Nilus mysteriously rose, broke its banks and spread a coat of thick, black mud replete with nutrition over the fields of that strange kingdom, seven hundred miles long but only four or five miles wide except for the anabranch valley of Ta-she and Lake Moeris, and the Delta. There were three kinds of Inundation: the Cubits of Surfeit, the Cubits of Plenty and the Cubits of Death. Measured in the Nilometers, a series of graduated wells dug to one side of the mighty river. It took a month for the Inundation to travel from the First Cataract to the Delta, which was why the reading of the Nilometer at Elephantine was so important: it gave warning to the rest of the kingdom what kind of Inundation it would experience that summer. By autumn Nilus was receding back within its banks, the soil deeply watered and enriched.

That first year of her reign had seen the reading low in the Cubits of Plenty, a good omen for a new monarch. Any level above thirty-three Roman feet was in the Cubits of Surfeit, which meant disastrous flooding. Any level between seventeen and thirty-two feet was in the Cubits of Plenty, which meant a good Inundation; the ideal Inundation level was twenty-seven feet. Below seventeen feet lay the Cubits of Death, when Nilus didn't rise high enough to break its banks and famine was the inevitable result.

That first year saw the real Egypt—Egypt of the river, not the Delta—seem to revive under the rule of its new Queen, who was also Pharaoh—the God on Earth who her father, King Ptolemy Auletes, had never been. The immensely powerful faction of the priests, who were native Egyptians, controlled much of the destiny of Egypt's Ptolemaic rulers, descendants of one of Alexander the Great's marshals, the first Ptolemy. Only by fulfilling the true religious criteria and earning the blessing of the priests could the King and Queen be crowned Pharaoh. For the titles of King and Queen were Macedonian, whereas the title of Pharaoh belonged to the awesome agelessness of Egypt itself. The ankh of Pharaoh was the key to more than religious sanction; it was also the key to the vast treasure vaults beneath the ground of Memphis, as they were in the custody of the priests and bore no relation to Alexandria, wherein the King and Queen lived their Macedonian-oriented lives.

But the seventh Cleopatra belonged to the priests. She had spent three years of her childhood in their custody at Memphis, spoke both formal and demotic Egyptian, and came to the throne as Pharaoh. She was the first Ptolemy of the dynasty to speak Egyptian. Being Pharaoh meant that she had complete, godlike authority from one end of Egypt to the other; it also meant that she had access, should she ever need it, to the treasure vaults. Whereas in un-Egyptian Alexandria being Pharaoh could not enhance her standing. Nor did the economy of Egypt and Alexandria depend upon the contents of the treasure vaults; the public income of the monarch was six thousand talents per year, the private income as much again. Egypt contained nothing in private ownership; it all went to the monarch and the priests.

Thus the triumphs of Cleopatra's first two years were more related to Egypt than to Alexandria, isolated to the west of the Canopic Nilus, the westernmost arm of the Delta. They also related to a mystical enclave of people who occupied the eastern Delta, the Land of Onias, separate and complete in itself and owning no allegiance to the religious beliefs of either Macedonia or Egypt. The Land of Onias was the home of the Jews who had fled from Hellenized Judaea after refusing to acknowledge a schismatic high priest, and it kept its fervent Jewishness still. It also supplied Egypt with the bulk of its army and controlled Pelusium, the other important seaport Egypt possessed upon the shores of Our Sea. And Cleopatra, who spoke both Hebrew and Aramaic fluently, was the darling of the Land of Onias.

The first peril she had handled well, the murder of the two sons of Bibulus. But her present peril was much graver. When the time came for the second Inundation of her reign, it fell in the Cubits of Death. The Nilus didn't break its banks, the muddy water did not flow across the fields, and the crops failed to poke their bright green blades above the parched ground. For the sun blazed down upon the Kingdom of

Egypt every day of every year; life-giving water was the gift of Nilus, not the skies, and Pharaoh was the deified personification of the river.

When Gnaeus Pompey sailed into the Royal Harbor of Alexandria, that city was stirring ominously. It took two or three famines in a row to deprive the native Egyptians along the river of all food sources, but that was not so in Alexandria, which produced little save bureaucrats, businessmen and bonded servants. Alexandria was the quintessential middleman, unproductive of itself yet making most of the money. It manufactured fancies like astonishing glass made up of thin, multicolored strands; it turned out the world's finest scholars; it controlled the world's paper. Without being able to feed itself. That, it expected Egypt of the Nilus to do.

The people were of several kinds: the pure Macedonian stock composing the aristocracy and jealously guarding all the highest positions in the bureaucracy; the merchants, manufacturers and other commercial persons who were a hybrid mixture of Macedonian and Egyptian; a very considerable Jewish ghetto at the eastern end of the city in Delta District, mostly artisans, craftsmen, skilled laborers and scholars; the Greek rather than Macedonian scribes and clerks who filled the lower echelons of the bureaucracy, worked as masons and sculptors, teachers and tutors—and plied the oars of both naval and merchant vessels; and even a few Roman knights. The language was Greek, the citizenship not Egyptian but Alexandrian. Only the three hundred thousand Macedonian noblemen owned the full Alexandrian citizenship, a source of complaint and bitter resentment among the other groups in the population. Save for the Romans, who sniffed at such an inferior kind of suffrage. To be Roman was to be better than anyone, including an Alexandrian.

Food was still to be had in plenty; the Queen was buying in grain and other stuffs from Cyprus, Syria and Judaea. What caused that ominous stirring was the rise in prices. Unfortunately the Alexandrians of all walks except the peaceful and inwardly turned Jews were aggressive, extremely independent and absolutely uncowed by monarchs. Time and time again they had risen and ejected this Ptolemy from the throne, replaced him or her by a different Ptolemy, then done it all over again the moment prosperity trembled or the cost of living soared.

All of which Queen Cleopatra knew as she readied herself to receive Gnaeus Pompey in audience.

Complicated by the fact that her brother/husband was now almost twelve years old, and could no longer be dismissed as a mere child. Not yet pubertal beyond those first physical tremors which preceded the massive changes still to come, the thirteenth Ptolemy was nonetheless becoming increasingly difficult to control. Mostly due to the malign influence of the two men who dominated his life, his tutor, Theodotus, and the Lord High Chamberlain, Potheinus.

They were already waiting in the audience chamber when the Queen strode in, and she did stride; to do so, she had discovered, spoke of confidence and authority, neither of which her meager bodily endowments reinforced. The little King was seated on his throne, a smaller edifice one step lower than the great ebony and gilt chair which was her own seat. Until he had proven his manhood by quickening his sister/wife, he would not be elevated any higher. Clad in the purple tunic and cape of the Macedonian kings, he was an attractive boy in a very Macedonian way, blond, blue-eyed, more Thracian than Greek. His mother had been his father's half sister, her mother a princess of Arabian Nabataea. But the Semite didn't show at all in the thirteenth Ptolemy, whereas in Cleopatra, his half sister, it did. Her mother had been the daughter of the awesome King Mithridates of Pontus, a big, tall woman with the dark yellow hair and dark yellow eyes peculiar to the Mithridatidae. Therefore the thirteenth Ptolemy had more Semitic blood than his half sister; yet she looked the Semite.

A Tyrian purple cushion encrusted with gold and pearls enabled the Queen of Alexandria and Egypt to sit on that too-big chair and place her feet on something solid; without it, her toes could not touch the dais of purple marble.

"Is Gnaeus Pompey on his way?" she asked.

Potheinus answered. "Yes, lady."

She could never make up her mind which of the two she disliked more, Potheinus or Theodotus. The Lord High Chamberlain was the more imposing, and bore witness to the fact that eunuchs were not necessarily short, plump and effeminate. His testicles had been enucleated in his fourteenth year, a little late perhaps, and at the direction of his father, a Macedonian aristocrat with huge ambitions for his very bright son. Lord High Chamberlain was the greatest position at court and could be held only by a eunuch, a peculiar result of the crisscrossed Egyptian and Macedonian cultures; it was inflicted upon one of pure Macedonian blood because the ancient Egyptian traditions dictated it. A subtle, cruel and very dangerous man, Potheinus. Mouse-colored curls, narrow grey eyes, handsome features. He was, of course, plotting to spill her from the throne and replace her with her half sister Arsinoë, the full sister of the thirteenth Ptolemy.

Theodotus was the effeminate one, despite his intact testicles. Willowy, pale, deceptively weary. Neither a good scholar nor a true teacher, he had been a great intimate of her father, Auletes, and owed his position to that happy chance. Whatever he taught the thirteenth Ptolemy had nothing to do with history, geography, rhetoric or mathematics. He liked boys, and one of the most galling facts of Cleopatra's life was the knowledge that Theodotus would have sexually initiated her brother well before her brother was deemed old enough to consummate their marriage. I will have to take, she thought, Theodotus's leavings. If I live that long. Theodotus too wants to replace me with Arsinoë. He and Potheinus know that they cannot manipulate me. What fools they are! Don't they understand that Arsinoë is as unmanageable as I am? Yes, the war to own Egypt has begun. Will they kill me, or will I kill them? But one thing I have vowed. The day Potheinus and Theodotus die, my brother will die too. Little viper!

The audience chamber was not the throne room. In that vast conglomeration of buildings there were rooms, even palaces within the palace, for every kind of function and functionary. The throne room would have stunned a Crassus; the audience chamber was enough to stun Gnaeus Pompey. The architecture of the complex, inside as well as outside, was Greek, but Egypt had a say too, as much of the adornment fell to the lot of the priest-artists of Memphis. Thus the audience chamber walls were partially covered in gold leaf, partially in murals of a sort foreign to this Roman ambassador. Very flat and stilted, two-dimensional people, animals, palms and lotuses. There were no statues and no items of furniture other than the two thrones on the dais.

To either side of the dais stood a gigantic man so bizarre Gnaeus Pompey had only heard of such people, apart from a woman in a side show at the circus during his childhood days; though she had been very beautiful, she did not compare to these two men. They were clad in gold sandals and short leopard-skin kilts belted with jeweled gold, and had gold collars flashing with jewels about their throats. Each one gently plied a massive fan on a long gold rod, its base more jeweled gold, its breeze-making part the most wonderful feathers dyed many colors, huge and fluffy. All of which was as nothing compared to the beauty of their skins, which were *black*. Not brown, black. Like a black grape, thought Gnaeus Pompey, glossy yet powdered with plummy must. Tyrian purple skins! He had seen faces like theirs before on little statues; when a good Greek or Italian sculptor was lucky enough to see one, he seized upon the amazing person immediately. Hortensius had owned a statue of a boy, Lucullus the bronze bust of a man. But again, mere shadows alongside the reality of these living faces. High cheekbones, aquiline noses, very full but exquisitely delineated lips, black eyes of a peculiar liquidity. Topped by close-cropped hair so tightly curled that it had the look of the foetal goat pelt from Bactria that the Parthian kings prized so much they alone were allowed to wear it.

"Gnaeus Pompeius Magnus!" gushed Potheinus, rushing forward in his purple tunic and *chlamys* cloak with the chain of his high estate draped athwart his shoulders. "Welcome, welcome!"

"I am *not* Magnus!" snapped Gnaeus Pompey, very annoyed. "I am plain Gnaeus Pompeius! Who are you, the crown prince?"

The female on the bigger, higher throne spoke in a strong, melodic voice. "That is Potheinus, our Lord High Chamberlain," she said. "We are Cleopatra, Queen of Alexandria and Egypt. In the names of Alexandria and Egypt we bid you welcome. As for you, Potheinus, if you wish to stay, step back and don't speak until you're spoken to."

Oho! thought Gnaeus Pompey. She doesn't like him. And he doesn't like taking orders from her one little bit.

"I am honored, great Queen," Gnaeus Pompey said, three lictors to either side of him. "And this, I presume, is King Ptolemy?"

"Yes," said the Queen curtly.

She weighed about as much as a wet dishcloth was Gnaeus Pompey's verdict, was probably not five Roman feet tall when she stood up, had thin little arms and a scrawny little neck. Lovely skin, darkly olive yet transparent enough to display the blueness of the veins beneath it. Her hair was a light brown and done in a peculiar fashion, parted in a series of inch-wide bands back from brow to a bun on the nape of her neck; all he could think of was the similarly banded rind of a summer melon. She wore the white ribbon of her sovereign's diadem not across her forehead but behind the hairline, and was simply clad in the Greek style, though her robe was the finest Tyrian purple. No precious thing on her person save for her sandals, which looked as if they were never designed to be walked in, so flimsy was their gold.

The light, which poured in through unshuttered apertures high in the walls, was good enough for him to see that her face was depressingly ugly, only the single charm of youth to soften it. Wide eyes that he fancied were green-gold, or perhaps hazel. A good mouth for kissing save that it was held grimly. And a nose to rival Cato's for size, a mighty beak hooked like a Jew's. Hard to see any Macedonian in this young woman. A purely eastern type.

"It is a great honor to receive you in audience, Gnaeus Pompeius," she went on in that powerfully mellifluous voice, her Greek perfect and Attic. "We are sorry we cannot speak to you in Latin, but we have never had the opportunity to learn it. What may we do for you?"

"I imagine that even at this remotest end of Our Sea, great Queen, you are aware that Rome is engaged in a civil war. My father—who *is* called Magnus—has been obliged to flee from Italia in the company of Rome's legitimate government. At the moment he is in Thessalonica preparing to meet the traitor Gaius Julius Caesar."

"We are aware, Gnaeus Pompeius. You have our sympathy."

"That's a start," said Gnaeus Pompey with all the cheerful lack of politesse his father had made famous, "but not enough. I am here to ask for material aid, not expressions of condolence."

"Quite so. Alexandria is a long journey to obtain expressions of condolence. We *had* gathered that you have come to seek our—er—material aid. What kind of aid?"

"I want a fleet consisting of at least ten superior warships, sixty good transport vessels, sailors and oarsmen in sufficient numbers to power them, and every one of the sixty transports filled to the brim with wheat and other foodstuffs," Gnaeus Pompey chanted.

The little King moved on his minor throne, turned his head—which also wore the white ribbon of the diadem—to look at the Lord High Chamberlain and the slender, effeminate man beside him. His elder sister, who was also his wife—how decadently convoluted these eastern monarchies were!—promptly reacted exactly as a Roman elder sister might have. She was holding a gold and ivory scepter, and used it to rap him across the knuckles so hard that he let out a yelp of pain. His pretty, pouting face returned to the front and stayed there, his bright blue eyes winking away tears.

"We are delighted to be asked to give you material aid, Gnaeus Pompeius. You may have all the ships you require. There are ten excellent quinqueremes in the boat sheds attached to the Cibotus Harbor, all designed to carry plenty of artillery, all endowed with the best oaken rams, and all highly maneuverable. Their crews are rigorously trained. We will also commandeer sixty large, stout cargo vessels from among those belonging to us. We own all the ships of Egypt, commercial as well as naval, though we do not own all the merchant ships of Alexandria."

The Queen paused, looked very stern—and very ugly. "However, Gnaeus Pompeius, we cannot donate you any wheat or other foodstuffs. Egypt is in the midst of famine. The Inundation was down in the Cubits of Death; no crops germinated. We do not have sufficient to feed our own people, particularly those of Alexandria."

Gnaeus Pompey, who looked very like his father save that his equally thick crop of hair was a darker gold, sucked his teeth and shook his head. "That won't do!" he barked. "I want grain and I want food! Nor will I take no for an answer!"

"We have no grain, Gnaeus Pompeius. We have no food. We are not in a position to accommodate you, as we have explained."

"Actually," said Gnaeus Pompey casually, "you don't have any choice in the matter. Sorry if your own people starve, but that's not my affair. Quintus Caecilius Metellus Pius Scipio Nasica the governor is still in Syria, and has more than enough good Roman troops to march south and crush Egypt like a beetle. You're old enough to remember the arrival of Aulus Gabinius and what happened then. All I have to do is send to Syria and you're invaded. And don't think of doing to me what you did to the sons of Bibulus! I am Magnus's son. Kill me or any of mine and you'll all die very painfully. In many ways annexation would be best for my father and the government in exile. Egypt would become a province of Rome and everything Egypt possesses would go to Rome. In the person of my father. Think it over, Queen Cleopatra. I'll return tomorrow."

The lictors wheeled and marched out, faces impassive, Gnaeus Pompey strolling behind them.

"The arrogance!" gasped Theodotus, flapping his hands. "Oh, I don't *believe* the arrogance!"

"Hold your tongue, tutor!" the Queen snapped.

"May I go?" the little King asked, his tears overflowing.

"Yes, go, you little toad! And take Theodotus with you!"

Out they went, the man's arm possessively about the boy's heaving shoulders.

"You'll have to do as Gnaeus Pompeius has ordered you to do," purred Potheinus.

"I am well aware of that, you self-satisfied worm!"

"And pray, mighty Pharaoh, Isis on Earth, Daughter of Ra, that Nilus rises into the Cubits of Plenty this summer."

"I intend to pray. No doubt you and Theodotus—and your minion Achillas, commander-in-chief of my army!—intend to pray just as hard to Serapis that Nilus remains in the Cubits of Death! Two failed Inundations in a row would dry up the Ta-she and Lake Moeris. No one in Egypt would eat. My income would shrink to a point whereat, Potheinus, I could find little money for buying in. If there is grain to buy in. There is drought from Macedonia and Greece to Syria and Egypt. Food prices will keep on rising until the Nilus rises. While you and your two cronies urge a third kind of rise—the Alexandrians against me."

"As Pharaoh, O Queen," said Potheinus smoothly, "you have the key to the treasure vaults of Memphis."

The Queen looked scornful. "Certainly, Lord High Chamberlain! You know perfectly well that the priests will not allow me to spend the Egyptian treasures to save Alexandria from starvation. Why should they? No native Egyptian is permitted to live in Alexandria, let alone have its citizenship. Something I do not intend to rectify for one good reason. I don't want my best and loyalest subjects to catch the Alexandrian disease."

"Then the future does not bode well for you, O Queen."

"You deem me a weak woman, Potheinus. That is a very grave mistake. You'd do better to think of me as Egypt."

Cleopatra had hundreds upon hundreds of servants; only two of them were dear to her, Charmian and Iras. The daughters of Macedonian aristocrats, they had been given to Cleopatra when all three were small children, to be the royal companions of the second daughter of King Ptolemy Auletes and Queen Cleopatra Tryphaena, a daughter of King Mithridates of Pontus by his queen. The same age as Cleopatra, they had been with her through all the stormy years since—through Ptolemy Auletes's divorce of Cleopatra Tryphaena and the arrival of a stepmother—through the banishment of Auletes—through three years of exile in Memphis while the oldest daughter, Berenice, reigned with her mother, Cleopatra Tryphaena—through the awful time after Cleopatra Tryphaena's death when Berenice searched frantically for a husband acceptable to the Alexandrians—through the return of Ptolemy Auletes and his resumption of the throne—through the day when Auletes had murdered Berenice, his own daughter—through the first two years of Cleopatra's reign. So long!

They were her only confidantes, so it was to them that she poured out the story of her audience with Gnaeus Pompey.

"Potheinus is becoming insufferably confident," she said.

"Which means," said Charmian, dark and very pretty, "that he will move to dethrone you as soon as he can."

"Oh, yes. I need to journey to Memphis and sacrifice in the true way to the true Gods," Cleopatra said fretfully, "but I daren't. To leave Alexandria would be a fatal mistake."

"Would it help to write for advice to Antipater at the court of King Hyrcanus?"

"No use whatsoever. He's all for the Romans."

"What was Gnaeus Pompeius like?" asked Iras, who always thought of personalities, never of politics. She was fair and very pretty.

"In the same mold as the great Alexander. Macedonian."

"Did you *like* him?" Iras persisted, blue eyes fondly misty.

Cleopatra looked exasperated. "As a matter of fact, Iras, I disliked the man intensely! Why do you ask such silly questions? I am Pharaoh. My hymen belongs to my equal in blood and deity. If you fancy Gnaeus Pompeius, go and sleep with him. You're a young woman; you should by rights be married. But I am Pharaoh, God on Earth. When I mate, I do so for Egypt, not for my own pleasure." Her face twisted. "Believe me, for no lesser reason than Egypt will I summon the fortitude to give my untouched body to the little viper!"

It was with a sense of enormous relief that Pompey the Great set out at the beginning of December to march westward along the Via Egnatia all the way to Dyrrachium. Sharing the palace in Thessalonica with more than half of Rome's Senate had proven a nightmare. For they had all returned, of course, from Cato to his beloved older son, who had sailed in from Alexandria with a superb fleet of ten quinqueremes and sixty transports, the latter loaded to creaking point. Their cargo was supposed to be wheat, barley, beans and chickpea, but turned out to consist mostly of dates. Sweet and tasty for an Epicurean snack, unpalatable fare for soldiers.

"That stringy she-wolf monster!" Gnaeus Pompey had snarled after he discovered that only ten of the transports held wheat; the other fifty contained dates in jars he had *seen* filled with wheat. "She tricked me!"

His father, worn down by a combination of Cato and Cicero, chose to see the funny side, laughed himself to tears he couldn't shed any other way. "Never mind," he soothed his irate son, "after we've beaten Caesar we'll hie ourselves off to Egypt and pay for this war out of Cleopatra's treasury."

"It will give me great pleasure personally to torture her!"

"Tch, tch!" clucked Pompey. "Not loverlike language, Gnaeus! There's a rumor going round that you had her."

"The only way I'd have her is roasted and stuffed with dates!"

Which reply set Pompey laughing again.

Cato had returned just before Gnaeus Pompey, very pleased with the success of his mission to Rhodes, and full of the story of his encounter with his half sister, Servililla, divorced wife of the dead Lucullus, and her son, Marcus Licinius Lucullus.

"I don't understand her any more than I do Servilia," he said frowning. "When I encountered Servililla in Athens—she seemed to think she'd be proscribed if she stayed in Italia—she swore never again to leave me. Sailed the Aegaean with me, came to Rhodes. Started bickering with Athenodorus Cordylion and Statyllus. But when it came time to leave Rhodes, she said she was staying there."

"Women," said Pompey, "are queer fish, Cato. Now go away!"

"Not until you agree to tighten up on discipline among the Galatian and Cappadocian cavalry. They're behaving disgracefully."

"They are here to help us win against Caesar, Cato, and we do not have to pay for their upkeep. As far as I'm concerned, they are welcome to violate the female population of all Macedonia, *and* beat up the male population. Now go away!"

Next to arrive was Cicero, accompanied by his son. Exhausted, miserable, full of complaints about everyone from his brother and nephew, the Quintuses, to Atticus, who refused to speak out against Caesar and was busy smoothing Caesar's path in Rome.

"I was surrounded by traitors!" he fulminated to Pompey, his poor oozing eyes red and crusted. "It took months to manage my escape, and then I had to leave without Tiro."

"Yes, yes," said Pompey wearily. "There's a marvelous wisewoman lives outside the Larissa gate, Cicero. Go and see her about those eyes. *Now!* Please!"

In October came Lucius Afranius and Marcus Petreius from Spain, the harbingers of their own doom. With them they brought a few cohorts of troops, which was no consolation to Pompey, shattered by the news that his Spanish army was no more—and that Caesar had won another almost bloodless victory. To make matters worse, the advent of Afranius and Petreius provoked a frenzied fury in men like Lentulus Crus, returned from Asia Province.

"They're traitors!" Lentulus Crus yelled in Pompey's ear. "I demand that our Senate try them and condemn them!"

"Oh, shut up, Crus!" said Titus Labienus. "At least Afranius and Petreius know their way around a battlefield, which is more than anyone can say of you."

"Magnus, who is this lowborn worm?" gasped Lentulus Crus, outraged. "Why do we have to tolerate him? Why do I, a patrician Cornelius, have to be insulted by men who aren't fit to polish my boots? Tell him to take himself off!"

"Take yourself off, Lentulus!" said Pompey, close to tears.

Those tears finally overflowed at night upon his pillow after Lucius Domitius Ahenobarbus sailed in with the news that Massilia had capitulated to Caesar, and that Caesar was in complete control of every land to the west of Italia.

"However," said Ahenobarbus, "I have a good little flotilla, and I intend to make use of it."

Bibulus journeyed late in December to find Pompey as his huge army plodded across the high passes of Candavia.

"Ought you to be here?" asked Pompey nervously.

"Calm down, Magnus! Caesar won't be landing in Epirus or Macedonia in the near future," said Bibulus comfortably. "For one thing, there aren't anything like enough transports in Brundisium for Caesar to get his troops across the Adriatic. For another, I have your son's fleet in the Adriatic as well as my own two under Octavius and Libo, and Ahenobarbus patrolling the Ionian Sea."

"You know, of course, that Caesar has been appointed Dictator and that the whole of Italia is for him? And that he hasn't any intention of proscribing?"

"I do. But cheer up, Magnus, it isn't all bad. I've sent Gaius Cassius and those seventy trim Syrian ships to the Tuscan Sea with orders to patrol it between Messana and Vibo and block all shipments of grain from Sicily. His presence will also prevent Caesar's sending any of his troops to Epirus from the west coast."

"Oh, that is good news!" cried Pompey.

"I think so." Bibulus smiled the restrained smile of real satisfaction. "If we can pen him up in Brundisium, can you imagine how Italia will feel if the countryside has to feed *twelve* legions through the winter? After Gaius Cassius gets through with the grain supply, Caesar will have enough trouble feeding the civilian populace. And we hold Africa, don't forget."

"That's true." Pompey lapsed back into gloom. "However, Bibulus, I'd be a far happier man if I'd received those two Syrian legions from Metellus Scipio before I left Thessalonica. I'm going to need them when and if Caesar manages to get across. Eight of his legions are completely veteran."

"What prevented the Syrian legions reaching you?"

"According to Scipio's latest letter, he's having terrible trouble forcing the Amanus. The Skenite Arabs have taken up residence in the passes and they're obliging him to fight every inch of the way. Well, you know the Amanus, you campaigned there."

Bibulus frowned. "Then he still has to march the entire length of Anatolia before he reaches the Hellespont. I doubt you'll see Scipio before spring."

"So let us hope, Bibulus, that we don't see Caesar either."

A vain hope. Pompey was still in Candavia negotiating the heights north of Lake Ochris when Lucius Vibullius Rufus located him fairly early in January.

"What are *you* doing here?" asked Pompey, astonished. "We thought you in Nearer Spain!"

"I'm the first evidence of what happens to a man who, having been pardoned by Caesar—after Corfinium—goes off and opposes him again. He took me prisoner after Illerda, and he's kept me with him ever since."

Pompey could feel himself go pale. "You mean—?"

"Yes, I mean Caesar loaded four legions into every transport he could find and sailed from Brundisium the day before the Nones." Vibullius smiled mirthlessly. "He never even saw a single warship and landed safely on the coast at Palaestae."

"Palaestae?"

"Between Oricum and Corcyra. The first thing he did was to send me to see Bibulus on Corcyra—to inform him that he'd missed his chance. And to ask for your whereabouts. You see in me Caesar the Dictator's ambassador."

"Ye Gods, he has hide! *Four legions?* That's all?"

"That's all."

"What's his message?"

"That enough Roman blood has been spilled. That now's the time to discuss the terms of a settlement. Both sides, he says, are evenly matched but uncommitted."

"Evenly matched," said Pompey slowly. "Four legions!"

"They're his words, Magnus."

"And his terms?"

"That you and he apply to the Senate and People of Rome to set the terms. After you and he have dismissed your armies. That he requires within three days of my return to him."

"The Senate and People of Rome. *His* Senate. *His* People," said Pompey between his teeth. "He's been elected senior consul, he's no longer Dictator. Everyone in Rome and Italia deems him a wonder. Certainly no Sulla!"

"Yes, he rules through fair words, not foul means. Oh, he is clever! And all those fools in Rome and Italia fall for it."

"Well, Vibullius, he's the hero of the hour. Ten years ago, I was the hero of the hour. There are fashions in public heroes too. Ten years ago, the Picentine prodigy. Today, the patrician prince." Pompey's manner changed. "Tell me, whom did he leave in charge at Brundisium?"

"Marcus Antonius and Quintus Fufius Calenus."

"So he has no cavalry with him in Epirus."

"Very little. Two or three squadrons of Gauls."

"He'll be making for Dyrrachium."

"Undoubtedly."

"Then I'd better summon my legates and start this army moving at the double. I have to beat him to Dyrrachium or he'll inherit my camp and access to Dyrrachium itself."

Vibullius stood up, taking this as a dismissal. "What about an answer to Caesar?"

"Let him whistle!" said Pompey. "Stay here and be useful."

Pompey beat Caesar to Dyrrachium, but only just.

The west coast of the landmass which comprised Greece, Epirus and Macedonia was only vaguely demarcated; the southern boundary of Epirus was generally taken as the north shore of the Gulf of Corinth, but that was also Grecian Acarnania, and the northern border of Epirus was largely anywhere an individual fancied. To a Roman general, the Via Egnatia, which ran from the Hellespont for close to seven hundred miles through Thrace and Macedonia to the Adriatic, was definitely in Macedonia. Some fifteen miles from the west coast it branched north and south; the northern branch terminated at Dyrrachium and the southern branch at Apollonia. Therefore most Roman generals classified Dyrrachium and Apollonia as part of Macedonia, not as part of Epirus.

To Pompey, arriving in haste and disorder at Dyrrachium, it came as a colossal shock to discover that all of Epirus proper had declared for Caesar, and so had Apollonia, the southern terminus of the Via Egnatia. Everything south of the river Apsus, in fact, now belonged to Caesar. Who had ejected Torquatus from Oricum and Staberius from Apollonia without bloodshed and in the simplest way: the local people cheered for Caesar and made life for a garrison too difficult. From where he had landed at Palaestae, the distance along a poorly surveyed and built local road to Dyrrachium was a little over a hundred miles, yet he almost beat Pompey, marching the Roman Via Egnatia, to Dyrrachium.

To make matters more distressing for Pompey, Dyrrachium too decided to support Caesar. His local recruits and the townsfolk refused to co-operate with the Roman government in exile at all, and began a program of subversive action. With seven thousand horses and nearly eight thousand mules to feed, Pompey could not afford to sit himself down in hostile country.

"Let me deal with them," said Titus Labienus, a look in his fierce dark eyes that Caesar—or Trebonius, or Fabius, or Decimus Brutus, for that matter—would have recognized instantly for what it was: the lust for savagery.

Unaware of the extent of the barbarian streak in Labienus, Pompey asked an innocent question. "How can you deal with them in a way others cannot?"

The big yellow teeth showed in a snarl. "I'll give them a taste of what the Treveri came to dread."

"All right, then," said Pompey, shrugging, "do so."

Several hundreds of shockingly maimed Epirote bodies later, Dyrrachium and the surrounding countryside decided it was definitely more prudent to cleave to Pompey, who, having heard the tales flying through his enormous camp, elected to say and do nothing.

When Caesar retired to the south bank of the Apsus, Pompey and his army followed to set up camp on the north bank immediately opposite; at this ford across the big river, the south branch of the Via Egnatia crossed on its way to Apollonia.

No more than a stream of water between himself and Caesar . . . Six legions of Roman troops, seven thousand horse soldiers, ten thousand foreign auxiliaries, two thousand archers and a thousand slingers—against four veteran Gallic legions, the Seventh, the Ninth, the Tenth and the Twelfth. Pompey's was an enormous numerical advantage! Surely, surely, surely more than enough! How could a huge force like his go down in a battle against four legions of Roman foot? It couldn't. It simply couldn't. He'd *have* to win!

Yet Pompey sat on the north bank of the Apsus, so close to Caesar's camp fortifications that he might have pitched a stone and hit some veteran of the Tenth on the helmet. And didn't move.

In his mind he was back in the Spains facing Quintus Sertorius, who could march out of nowhere eluding every scout, inflict a terrible defeat on a relatively huge army, then disappear again into nowhere. Pompey was back under the walls of Lauro, he was back gazing up at Osca, he was back dragging his tail between his legs as he retreated across the Iberus, he was back seeing Metellus Pius win the laurels.

And Lucius Afranius and Marcus Petreius, who ought to have brought pressure to bear on Pompey, were back in Nearer Spain facing Sertorius too, remembering also how laughably easily Caesar had outmaneuvered them in Nearer Spain a mere six months earlier. Nor was Labienus there to deride Caesar in his customary way, stiffen Pompey's failing resolve; Labienus had been left behind to garrison Dyrrachium and keep its people loyal. Together with those nagging couch generals, Cato, Cicero, Lentulus Crus, Lentulus Spinther and Marcus Favonius. No one actually in camp with Pompey had either the vision or the steel to cope with Pompey in a doubting mood.

"No," he said to Afranius and Petreius after several *nundinae* of inaction, "I'll wait for Scipio and the Syrian legions before I give battle. In the meantime, I'll sit here and contain him."

"Good strategy," said Afranius, relieved. "He's suffering, Magnus, suffering badly. Bibulus has almost strangled his seaborne supply lines; he has to rely on what comes overland from Greece and southern Epirus."

"Good. Winter ought to starve him out. It's coming early, and coming fast."

But not early enough and not fast enough. Caesar had Publius Vatinius with him. The proximity of the two camps meant that some degree of communication went on across the little river between the sentries; this swelled to include legionaries with time on their hands, and was to Caesar's advantage. His men, so lauded and admired for their valor and unquenchable determination during the Gallic War, became the target of many questions from the curious Pompeians. Observing this largely unconscious reverence, Caesar sent Publius Vatinius to the middle of the nearest fortification tower and had him speak to the Pompeians. Why go on shedding Roman blood? Why dream of defeating the absolutely unbeatable Caesar? Why didn't Pompey offer battle if he wasn't terrified of losing? *Why were they there at all?*

When he heard what was going on, Pompey's reaction was to send to Dyrrachium for his chief problem-solver, Labienus, with a special request to Cicero that he come along as well in case counter-oration was necessary. With the result that every couch general decided to come (they were so *bored*!), including Lentulus Crus, who at the time was listening to a great deal of subtle persuasion in the form of offers of money from Balbus Minor, sent by Caesar to win him over. Praying that no one in Pompey's camp recognized him, Balbus Minor perforce came too.

Labienus arrived on the very day that negotiations were scheduled to commence between Caesar and a Pompeian delegation led by one of the Terentii Varrones. The conference never happened, broken up when Labienus appeared, shouted Vatinius down, and then launched a volley of spears across the river. Cowed by Labienus, the Pompeians scuttled away, never to parley again.

"Don't be a fool, Labienus!" Vatinius called. "Negotiate! Save lives, man, save lives!"

"There'll be no dickering with traitors while I'm here!" yelled Labienus. "But send me Caesar's head and I'll reconsider!"

"You haven't changed, Labienus!"

"Nor will I ever!"

While this was going on, Cicero was comfortably and cozily partaking of wine and a chat in Pompey's command house, delightfully undisturbed for once.

"You seem very perky and chirpy," said Pompey gloomily.

"With excellent reason," said Cicero, too full of his joyous news—

and too bursting with the compulsion of a wordsmith to communicate—to curb his tongue. "I've just come into a very nice inheritance."

"Have you now?" asked Pompey, his eyes narrowing.

"Oh, truly, Magnus, it couldn't have come at a better moment!" caroled Cicero, oblivious to impending disaster. "The second installment of Tullia's dowry is due—two hundred thousand, if you please!—and I still owe Dolabella sixty thousand of the first installment. He's sending me a letter a day about it." Cicero gave his charming giggle. "I daresay he has *iugera* of time to write, since he's an admiral with no ships."

"How much did you get?"

"A round million."

"Just the sum I need!" said Pompey. "As your commander-in-chief and friend, Cicero, lend it to me. I'm at my wit's end to pay the army's bills—I mean, I've borrowed from every Roman soldier I own, and that's an unthinkable predicament for a commander! My troops are my creditors. Now I hear that Scipio's stuck in Pergamum until the winter's over. I was hoping to pull myself out of the boiling oil with the Syrian money, but . . ." Pompey shrugged. "As it is, your million will be a big help."

Mouth dry, throat closed up like a sphincter, Cicero sat for long moments unable to speak, while the puffy, brilliantly blue eyes of his nemesis stared into his very marrow.

"I did send you to that wisewoman in Thessalonica, didn't I? She did cure your eyes, didn't she?"

Swallowing painfully, Cicero nodded. "Yes, Magnus, of course. You shall have the million." He shifted in his chair, drank a little watered wine to stroke that sphincter open. "Er—I don't suppose you'd let me keep enough to pay Dolabella?"

"Dolabella," said Pompey, rearing up in righteous indignation, "works for Caesar! Which makes your own loyalty suspect, Cicero."

"You shall have the million," Cicero repeated, lip trembling. "Oh, dear, what can I tell Terentia?"

"Nothing she doesn't already know," said Pompey, grinning.

"And my poor little Tullia?"

"Tell her to tell Dolabella to ask Caesar for the money."

Well based on the island of Corcyra, Bibulus was faring much better against Caesar than the timorous Pompey. It had hurt badly to learn that Caesar had successfully run his blockade—wasn't that typical of Caesar, to send a captive Pompeian legate to inform him of it? Ha ha ha, beat you, Bibulus! Nothing could have spurred Bibulus on more energetically than that derisive gesture. He had always worked hard, but from the time of Vibullius's visit he flogged himself and his legates remorselessly.

Every ship he could lay his hands on was sent out to patrol the Adriatic; Caesar would rot before he saw the rest of his army! First blood was empty blood, but tasty blood for all that. Out on the water himself, he intercepted thirty of the transports Caesar had used to cross, captured them and burned them. There! Thirty less ships for Antonius and Calenus to use.

One of Bibulus's two objectives was to make it impossible for Antony and Fufius Calenus in Brundisium to obtain enough ships to ferry eight legions and a thousand German horse to Epirus. To ensure this, he sent Marcus Octavius to patrol the Adriatic north of Brundisium on the Italian side, Scribonius Libo to maintain a station immediately off Brundisium, and Gnaeus Pompey to cover the Greek approaches. Whether Antony and Calenus tried to get ships from the northern Adriatic ports, or from Greece, or from the ports of the Italian foot on its western side, they would not succeed!

His second objective was to deprive Caesar of all seaborne supplies, including those sent from Greece through the Gulf of Corinth or around the bottom of the Peloponnese.

He had heard a fantastic tale that Caesar, alarmed at his enforced isolation, had tried to return to Brundisium in a tiny open boat, and in the teeth of a terrible storm off Sason Island. In disguise to avoid alarming his men—so the story went—Caesar revealed his identity to the captain when a decision was made to turn back, appealing to the man to continue because he carried Caesar and Caesar's luck. A second attempt was made, but in the end the pinnace was forced to return to Epirus and deposit Caesar unharmed among his men. True? Bibulus had no idea. Just like the man's conceit, to make that appeal to the captain! But why would he bother? What did he think he could do in Brundisium that his legates—two good men, Bibulus admitted—could not?

Nevertheless, legends like this one caused Bibulus to push himself even harder. When the equinoctial gales rendered a breakout from Brundisium impossible, he ought by rights to have taken a rest. He did not. No one save the admiral-in-chief was available to patrol the Epirote coast between Corcyra and Sason Island. So the admiral-in-chief patrolled it, out in all weathers, never warm, never dry, never comfortable enough to sleep except in snatches.

In March he caught cold, but refused to return to Corcyra until the decision was taken out of his hands. Head on fire, hands and feet frozen, chest laboring, he collapsed at his post on his flagship. His deputy, Lucretius Vespillo, ordered the fleet to return to base, and there Bibulus was put to bed.

When his condition failed to improve, Lucretius Vespillo took another executive decision: to send to Dyrrachium for Cato. Who arrived in a pinnace much like the one in the legend about Caesar, tormented by the fear that once again he would be too late to hold the hand of a beloved man before he died.

Cato's ears told him that Bibulus still lived before he entered the room; the whole snug little stone house on a sheltered Corcyran cove reverberated with the sound of Bibulus's breathing.

So tiny! Why had he forgotten that? Huddled in a bed far too big for him, his silver hair and silver brows invisible against skin gone to silver scales from exposure to the elements. Only the silver-grey eyes, enormous in that sunken face, looked alive. They met Cato's across the room and filled with tears. A hand came out.

Down on the edge of the bed, that hand enfolded between his own two strong ones; Cato leaned forward and kissed Bibulus's brow. Almost he leaped back, so hot was the skin, fancying that as the slow tears trickled from the outer corner of each eye toward the temples, he would hear a hiss, see steam rise. Burning up! On fire. The chest was working like a bellows in loud dry rasps, and oh, the pain! There in the weeping eyes, shining through their liquid film with a simple, profound love. Love for Cato. Who was going to be alone again.

"Doesn't matter now you're here," he said.

"I'm here for as long as you want me, Bibulus."

"Tried too hard. Can't let Caesar win."

"We will never let Caesar win, even if by our dying."

"Destroy the Republic. Has to be stopped."

"We both know that."

"Rest of them don't care enough. Except Ahenobarbus."

"The old trio."

"Pompeius is a pricked bladder."

"And Labienus a monster. I know. Don't think about it."

"Look after Porcia. And little Lucius. Only son I have now."

"I will take care of them. But Caesar first."

"Oh, yes. Caesar first. Has a hundred lives."

"Do you remember, Bibulus, when you were consul and shut yourself up in your house to watch the skies? How he *hated* that! We ruined his consulship. We forced him to be unconstitutional. We laid the foundation for the treason charges he'll have to answer when all this is over. . . ."

That innately loud, unmusical, hectoring voice continued to talk for hours so softly, so tenderly, so kindly and even happily, gentling Bibulus into the cradle of his final sleep with the same cadences as a lullaby. It fell sweetly upon the listening ears, provoked the same rapt and permanent smile a child will maintain while listening to the most wonderful story in the world. And so, still smiling, still watching Cato's face, Bibulus slipped away.

The last thing he said was "We will stop Caesar."

This time was not like Caepio. This time there was no huge outpouring of grief, no frantic scrabble to deny the presence of death. When the last rattle faded away to nothing, Cato got up from the bed, folded the hands across Bibulus's breast and passed his open hand across the fixed eyes, brushing their lids down and closed. He had known, of course, from the moment he got the message in Dyrrachium, so the gold denarius was there in Cato's belt. He slipped it inside the open mouth, strained still by the effort of that last breath, then pushed the chin up and set the lips back into a faint smile.

"*Vale,* Marcus Calpurnius Bibulus," he said. "I do not know if we can destroy Caesar, but he will never destroy us."

Lucius Scribonius Libo was waiting outside the room with Vespillo, Torquatus and some others.

"Bibulus is dead," Cato announced at a shout.

Libo sighed. "That makes our task harder." He made a courteous gesture to Cato. "Some wine?"

"Thank you, a lot of it. And unwatered."

He drank deeply but refused food. "Can we find a place to build a pyre in this storm?"

"It's being attended to."

"They tell me, Libo, that he tried to trick Caesar by asking Caesar to a parley in Oricum. And that Caesar came."

"Yes, it's true. Though Bibulus wouldn't see Caesar personally. He made me tell Caesar that he didn't dare be in the same room with him for fear of losing his temper. What we hoped was to get the wretched man to relax his vigilance along the coast—he makes it difficult for us to victual our ships by land."

"But the ploy didn't work," said Cato, refilling his cup.

Libo grimaced, spread his hands. "Sometimes, Cato, I think that Caesar isn't a mortal man. He laughed at me and walked out."

"Caesar is a mortal man," said Cato. "One day he will die."

Libo lifted his cup, splashed a little of the wine in it onto the floor. "A libation to the Gods, Cato. That I live to see the day it happens."

But Cato smiled and shook his head. "No, I'll not make that libation. My bones tell me I'll be dead first."

The distance across the Adriatic Sea from Apollonia to Brundisium was eighty miles. At sunrise on the second day of April, Caesar in Apollonia entrusted a letter to the commander of a kind of boat he had grown very attached to during his expeditions to Britannia—the pinnace. The seas were falling, the wind out of the south no more than a breeze, and the horizon from the top of a hill showed no sign of a ship, let alone a Pompeian fleet.

At sunset in Brundisium, Mark Antony took possession of the letter, which had had a swift, uneventful voyage. Caesar had written it himself, so it was easier to read than most communications; the writing was scribe-perfect though distinctive, and the first letter of each new word was indicated by a dot above it.

> Antonius, the equinoctial gales have blown themselves out. Winter is here. Our weather patterns indicate that the usual lull is about to occur. We may hope to enjoy as many as two calm *nundinae* before the next barrage of storms begins.
>
> I would deeply appreciate it if you got yourself up off your overdeveloped arse and brought me the rest of my army. Now. Whatever troops you can't squeeze into however many transports you have, you will leave behind. Veterans and cavalry first, new legions lowest priority.
>
> Do it, Antonius. I am fed up with waiting.

"The old boy's touchy," said Antony to Quintus Fufius Calenus. "Sound the bugles! We go in eight days."

"We have enough transports for the veterans and the cavalry. And the Fourteenth has arrived from Gaul. He'll have nine legions."

"He's fought better men with fewer," said Antony. "What we need is a decent fleet outside Brundisium to fend Libo off."

The most difficult part of it was loading over a thousand horses and four thousand mules: seven days and torchlit nights of brilliantly organized toil. Because Brundisium was a big harbor containing gulflike branches sheltered from the elements, it was possible to load each ship from a wharf, then push it off to anchor and wait. One by one the animal transports filled and were sent to wait with grooms, stablehands, harness hands and German horse troopers jammed into the spaces between hooves attached to equine bodies. The legions' wagons and artillery had been loaded long since; getting the infantry on board was quick and easy by comparison.

The fleet put out into the roads well before dawn on the tenth day of April and turned into a stiff southwesterly, which meant sails could be hoisted as well as oars manned.

"We'll be blown there too fast for Libo!" laughed Antony.

"Let's hope we stay together," said Calenus dourly.

But Caesar's luck extended its reach to protect them—or so thought the men of the Sixth, Eighth, Eleventh, Thirteenth and Fourteenth as the ships scudded up the Adriatic on a following sea with the wind swelling the sails. Of Libo's fleet there was no sign, nor did storm clouds darken the paling vault.

Off Sason Island another Pompeian fleet picked them up and started in pursuit, assisted by the same wind propelling Antony's fleet steadily further away from any desirable destination.

"Ye Gods, we're likely to be blown to Tergeste!" Antony cried as the promontory beyond Dyrrachium flew by. But even as he spoke—as if the Gods had required him to—the wind began to drop.

"Turn inshore while we can," he said curtly to the captain, standing on the poop; the man nodded to the two helmsmen on the huge rudder oars, who leaned against their tillers as if pushing boulders.

"That's Coponius's fleet," said Calenus. "He'll catch us."

"Not before we beach, if beach we have to."

Thirty-five miles north of Dyrrachium was Lissus, and here Antony turned his ships bow-on to present smaller targets for the rams of Coponius's war galleys, a scant mile from his stragglers and already rowing at close to ramming speed.

Suddenly the wind turned, blew a minor gale from the north. Cheering hysterically, everyone aboard Antony's ships watched as the thwarted Pompeians dwindled and disappeared below the horizon.

All Lissus was on hand to welcome Caesar's army, sympathies in line with those of every other settlement along that coast, and set to work with a will to help get the thousands of animals ashore in a place not nearly as well endowed with wharfage as Brundisium.

A very happy man, Antony paused only long enough to let his charges regain their land legs with a sleep and a meal, then, with tribunes and centurions and cavalry prefects harrying the men into marching order, he set off south to meet Caesar.

"Or Pompeius," said Calenus.

Eyes rolling, Antony slapped one mighty thigh in exasperation. "Calenus, you ought to know better! Do you honestly believe that a slug like Pompeius will reach us first?"

Keeping watch on top of the highest hill in the area around his camp on the Apsus, Caesar saw his fleet in the distance and breathed a sigh of relief. But then, helpless to do anything about it, he had to witness the wind carrying it away to the north.

"Strike camp, we march."

"Pompeius is readying to march too," said Vatinius. "He'll get there first."

"Pompeius is a routine commander, Vatinius. He'll want to choose his battle site, so he won't venture north of Dyrrachium because he doesn't know the lie of the land well enough. I think he'll go to earth on the Genusus near Asparagium, a long way south of Dyrrachium—but on the Via Egnatia. Pompeius hates marching on bad roads. And he has to prevent my joining up with Antonius. So why not lie in wait at a point he knows—or thinks he knows—the rest of my army will have to use?"

"So what will you do?" asked Vatinius, eyes dancing.

"Skirt him, of course. I'll ford the Genusus ten miles inland on that country road we scouted," said Caesar.

"Ah!" Vatinius exclaimed. "Pompeius thinks Antonius will reach Asparagium before you do!"

"It's true that Antonius marches my way—I trained him well in Gaul to move fast. But he's no fool, our Antonius. Or put it this way—he has more than his share of low cunning."

An accurate assessment. Marching on a minor road some miles to the west of Dyrrachium, Antony had indeed moved swiftly. Though not blindly. His scouts were scrupulous. Near sunset on the eleventh day of June they informed him that some local people had revealed that Pompey was lying in wait just north of the Genusus. Antony promptly stopped, pitched camp, and expected Caesar.

On the twelfth day of June the two parts of Caesar's army combined, a joyous reunion for the veterans.

Antony himself was hopping up and down in glee. "I have a big surprise for you!" he told Caesar the moment they met.

"Not unpalatable, I hope."

Like one of the magicians he so loved to include in his wild parades through Campania, Antony conjured his hands at a wall of his legates. It parted to reveal a tall, handsome man in his middle forties, sandy-haired and grey-eyed.

"Gnaeus Domitius Calvinus!" cried Caesar. "I *am* surprised!" He walked forward, wrung Calvinus's hand. "What are you doing in such disreputable company? I felt sure you'd be with Pompeius."

"Not I," said Calvinus emphatically. "I admit that I've been a loyal member of the *boni* for years—until, in fact, March of last year." His eyes grew flinty. "But, Caesar, I cannot adhere to a group of miserable cowards who abandoned their country. When Pompeius and his court left Italia, they broke my heart. I'm your man to the death. You've treated Rome and Italia like a sensible man. Sensible laws, sensible government."

"You might have remained there with my good wishes."

"Not I! I'm a handy man with an army, and I want to be there when Pompeius and the rest submit. For they will. They will!"

Over a simple dinner of bread, oil and cheese, Caesar made his dispositions. Present were Vatinius, Calvinus, Antony, Calenus, Lucius Cassius (a first cousin of Gaius and Quintus), Lucius Munatius Plancus, and Gaius Calvisius Sabinus.

"I have nine good legions at full strength and a thousand German cavalry," said the General, munching a radish. "Too many to feed while we're here in Epirus, and enduring winter. Pompeius won't engage in this kind of country, nor will he engage in this weather. He'll move east to Macedonia or Thessaly in spring. If there is to be a battle at all, it will be there. It behooves me to win Greece to my side—I'm going to need supplies as well as support. Therefore I'll split my army. Lucius Cassius and Sabinus, you'll take the Seventh and deal with western Greece—

Amphilochia, Acarnania and Aetolia. Behave very nicely. Calenus, you'll take the five senior cohorts of the Fourteenth and half my cavalry and persuade Boeotia that Caesar's side is the right one. Which will give me central Greece too. Avoid Athens, it's not worth the effort. Concentrate on Thebes, Calenus."

"It leaves you very under Pompeius's strength, Caesar," said Plancus, frowning.

"I think I could probably bluff Pompeius with two legions," said Caesar, unperturbed. "He won't engage until he has Metellus Scipio and the two Syrian legions."

"But that's ridiculous!" said Calenus. "If he hit you with everything he has, you'd go down."

"I'm well aware of it. But he won't, Calenus."

"I hope you're right!"

"Calvinus, I have a special job for you," said Caesar.

"Anything I can do, I will."

"Good. Take the Eleventh and the Twelfth and see if you can find Metellus Scipio and those two Syrian legions before they join Pompeius."

"You want me in Thessaly and Macedonia."

"Exactly. Take a squadron of my Gallic cavalry with you. They can act as scouts."

"Which leaves you with another squadron of Gallic horse and five hundred Germans," said Calvinus. "Pompeius has thousands."

"Eating him out of house and home, yes." Caesar turned his head to Antony. "What did you do with the three legions you left in Brundisium, Antonius?"

"Sent 'em to Italian Gaul," mumbled Antony through a huge mouthful of oily bread. "Wondered if you mightn't want some of 'em for Illyricum, so I told the Fifteenth and Sixteenth to march for Aquileia. Other one's going to Placentia."

"My dear Antonius, you are a pearl beyond price! That is exactly right. Vatinius, I'm giving you command of Illyricum. You'll go overland from here, it's quicker." The pale eyes looked on Antony kindly. "Don't worry about your brother, Antonius. I hear he's being treated well."

"Good," said Antony gruffly. "A bit of a fool, I know, but he's my brother."

"A pity," said Calvinus, "that you allowed so many of those wonderful legates from Gallic days to remain in Rome this year."

"They've earned it," said Caesar placidly. "They'd rather be here, but they have careers to get on with. None of them can be consuls until they've been praetors." He sighed. "Though I do miss Aulus Hirtius. No one runs the office like Hirtius."

After the meal ended only Vatinius and Calvinus remained to keep Caesar company; Caesar wanted news from Rome and Italia.

"What on earth got into Caelius?" he asked Calvinus.

"Debt," said Calvinus abruptly. "He'd staked everything on your bringing in a general cancellation of debts, and when you didn't, he was done for. Such a promising fellow in some ways—Cicero absolutely doted on him. And he did well when he was aedile—fought the water companies to a standstill and brought in some much-needed reforms."

"I detest the aedileship," said Caesar. "The men who hold it—including me in my day!—spend money they can't afford to throw wonderful games. And never get out of debt."

"You did," said Vatinius, smiling.

"That's because I'm Caesar. Go on, Calvinus. With the sea not mine to sail upon freely, I've heard little. Tell me."

"Well, as foreign praetor, I suppose Caelius thought he had the authority to do pretty much as he liked. He tried to put his own cancellation of debts through the Popular Assembly."

"And Trebonius tried to stop him, I know that."

"Unsuccessfully. The meeting was shockingly violent. Not one man in need of a general cancellation of debts wasn't there—and wasn't determined to see it pass."

"So Trebonius went to Vatia Isauricus, I imagine," said Caesar.

"You know these men, so your guess is better educated than mine. Vatia passed the Senatus Consultum Ultimum at once. When two tribunes of the plebs tried to veto it, he expelled them under its terms. He did very well, Caesar. I approved."

"So Caelius fled Rome and went to Campania to try to drum up support and troops around Capua. That's the last I've heard."

"We heard," said Calvinus slyly, "that you were so worried you even tried to return to Brundisium in an open boat."

"*Edepol,* these stories do get round!" said Caesar, grinning.

"Your nephew Quintus Pedius was the praetor delegated to march the Fourteenth Legion to Brundisium, and he happened to be in Campania at the moment when Caelius met none other than Milo sneaking back from exile in Massilia."

"Aaah!" said Caesar, drawing the word out slowly. "So Milo thought he'd mount a revolution of his own, did he? I presume that the Senate under Vatia and Trebonius wasn't foolish enough to give him permission to come home."

"No, he landed illegally at Surrentum. He and Caelius fell on each other's shoulders and agreed to combine forces. Caelius had managed to scrape up about three cohorts of debt-ridden Pompeian veterans—all addicted to wine and grand ideas. Milo volunteered to help scrape up a few more."

Calvinus sighed, shifted. "Vatia and Trebonius sent word to Quintus Pedius to deal with the situation in Campania under the Senatus Consultum Ultimum."

"In other words, they authorized my nephew to make war."

"Yes. Pedius swung his legion around and met them not far from Nola. There was a battle of a kind. Milo died in it. Caelius managed to get away, but Quintus Pedius pursued him and killed him. That was the end of it."

"Good man, my nephew. Very reliable."

It was Vatinius's turn to sigh. "Well, Caesar, I imagine that will be the last of any troubles in Italia this year."

"I sincerely hope so. But, Calvinus, at least you know now why I left so many of my loyalest legates behind in Rome. They're men of action, not dithery old women."

Pompey decided to settle more permanently on the Genusus River at Asparagium, secure in the fact that he was still north of Caesar's main camp and that Dyrrachium was safe. Whereupon, shades of the Apsus River, Caesar appeared on the south bank of the Genusus and paraded every day for battle. Most embarrassing for Pompey, who was aware that Caesar had halved his cavalry and split off at least three legions to forage in Greece; he didn't know that Calvinus was heading to Thessalia to intercept Metellus Scipio, though he had heard in letters that Calvinus was now openly for Caesar.

"I can't fight!" he was reported to Caesar as saying. "It's too wet, sleety, cold and miserable to expect a good performance from my troops. I'll fight when Scipio joins me."

"Then," said Caesar to Antony, "let's make him warm his troops up a little."

He broke camp with his usual startling rapidity and disappeared. At first Pompey thought he had retreated south due to lack of food; then his scouts informed him that Caesar had crossed the Genusus a few miles inland and headed up a mountain pass toward Dyrrachium. Horrified, Pompey realized that he was about to be cut off from his base and huge accumulation of supplies. Still, he was marching the Via Egnatia, while Caesar was stuck getting his army over what the scouts described as a track. Yes, he'd beat Caesar easily!

Caesar was in the lead along that track, surrounded by the hoary young veterans of the Tenth.

"Oh, this is more like it, Caesar!" said one of these hoary young veterans as the Tenth struggled around boulders and over rocks. "A *decent* march for once!"

"Thirty-five miles of it, lad, so I've been told," Caesar said, grinning broadly, "and it's got to be done by sunset. When Pompeius strolls up the Via Egnatia, I want the bastard to be pointing his snub nose at our arses. He thinks he's got some Roman soldiers. *I* know he hasn't. The real Roman soldiers belong to me."

"That's because," said Cassius Scaeva, one of the Tenth's centurions, "real Roman soldiers belong to real Roman generals, and there's no Roman general realer than Caesar."

"That remains to be seen, Scaeva, but thanks for the kind words. From now on, boys, save your breath. You're going to need it before sunset."

By the end of the day Caesar's army occupied some heights about two miles from Dyrrachium just east of the Via Egnatia; orders were to dig in for the duration, which meant a big camp bristling with fortifications.

"Why not the higher heights over there, the ones the locals call Petra?" asked Antony, pointing south.

"Oh, I think we'll leave that for Pompeius to occupy."

"But it's better ground, surely!"

"Too close to the sea, Antonius. We'd spend most of our time fending off Pompeius's fleets. No, he's welcome to Petra."

Coming up the Via Egnatia the next morning to find Caesar between himself and Dyrrachium, Pompey seized the heights of Petra and established himself there impregnably.

"Caesar would have done better to keep me out of here," said Pompey to Labienus. "It's far better ground, and I'm not cut off from Dyrrachium because I'm on the sea." He turned to one of his more satisfactory legates, his son-in-law, Faustus Sulla. "Faustus, get messages to my fleet commanders that all my supplies are to be landed here in future. And have them start ferrying what's in Dyrrachium." He lifted his lip. "We can't have Lentulus Crus complaining that there's no quail or *garum* sauce for his chefs to conjure their marvels."

"It's an impasse," said Labienus, scowling. "All Caesar is intent on doing is demonstrating that he can run rings around us."

A curiously prophetic statement. Within the next days the Pompeian high command in Petra noticed that Caesar was fortifying a line of hills about a mile and a half inland from the Via Egnatia, starting at his own camp's walls and moving inexorably south. Then entrenchments and earthworks were flung up between the forts, linking them together.

Labienus spat in disgust. "The *cunnus*! He's going to circumvallate. He's going to wall us in against the sea and make it impossible for us to get enough grazing for our mules and horses."

Caesar had called his army to an assembly.

"Here we are, a thousand and more miles from our old battleground in Gallia Comata, boys!" he shouted, looking cheerful and—well, didn't he always?—confident. "This last year must have seemed strange to you. More marching than digging! Not too many days going hungry! Not too many nights freezing! A romp in the hay from time to time! Plenty of money going into the legion banks! A nice, brisk sea voyage to clear the nostrils!

"Dear, dear," he went on mildly, "you'll be getting soft at this rate! But we can't have that, can we, boys?"

"NO!" roared the soldiers, thoroughly enjoying themselves.

"That's what I thought. Time, I said to myself, that those *cunni* in my legions went back to what they do best! What do you do best, boys?"

"DIG!" roared the soldiers, beginning to laugh.

"Go to the top of Caesar's class! Dig it is! It looks like Pompeius might nerve himself to fight one of these years, and we can't have you going into battle without having first shifted a few million basketloads of earth, can we?"

"NO!" roared the soldiers, hysterical with mirth.

"That's what I thought too. So we're going to do what we do best, boys! We're going to dig, and dig, and dig! Then we'll dig some more. I've a fancy to make Alesia look like a holiday. I've a fancy to shut Pompeius up against the sea. Are you with me, boys? Will you dig alongside Caesar?"

"YES!" they roared, flapping their kerchiefs in the air.

"Circumvallation," said Antony thoughtfully afterward.

"Antonius! You remembered the word!"

"How could anyone forget Alesia? But why, Caesar?"

"To make Pompeius respect me a little more," said Caesar, his manner making it impossible to tell whether he was joking. "He's got over seven thousand horses and nine thousand mules to feed. Not terribly difficult around here, where there's winter rain rather than winter snow. The grass doesn't wither, it keeps on growing. Unless, that is, he can't send his animals out to pasture. If I wall him in, he's in trouble. A circumvallation also renders his cavalry ineffectual. No room to maneuver."

"You've convinced me."

"Oh, but there's more," said Caesar. "I want to humiliate Pompeius in the eyes of his client kings and allies. I want men like Deiotarus and Ariobarzanes to chew their nails down wondering and worrying whether Pompeius will *ever* get up the courage to fight. He's outnumbered me two to one since I landed. Yet he will not fight. If it goes on long enough, Antonius, some of his foreign kings and allies might decide to withdraw their support, bring their levies home. After all, they're paying, and the men who pay are entitled to see results."

"I'm convinced, I'm convinced!" cried Antony, palms up in surrender.

"It's also necessary to demonstrate to Pompeius what five and a half legions like mine can do," said Caesar as if no one had interrupted. "He's well aware that these are my Gallic veterans, and that they've marched two thousand miles over the course of the last year. Now I'm going to ask them to work their arses off doing however many miles of digging are necessary. Probably, knowing I'm strapped, short of food. Pompeius will have his fleets patrolling endlessly, and I don't see any deterioration in their efficiency since Bibulus died."

"Odd, that."

"Bibulus never did know when enough was enough, Antonius." Caesar sighed. "Though, candidly, I'll miss him. He's the first of my old enemies to go. The Senate won't be the same."

"It'll improve considerably!"

"In terms of ease, yes. But not when it comes to the kind of opposition every man should have to contend with. If there's one thing I fear, Antonius, it's that this wretched war will end in my having no opponents left. Which won't be good for me."

"Sometimes," said Antony, pursing his lips and touching the tip of his nose with them, "I don't understand you, Caesar. Surely you don't hanker for the kind of anguish Bibulus gave you! These days you can do what has to be done. Your solutions are the right ones. Men like Bibulus and Cato made it impossible for you to improve the way Rome works. You're better off without the sort of opposition that watches the skies rather than governs—that has a dual standard—one set of rules for their own conduct, a different set for your conduct. Sorry, I think losing Bibulus is almost as good as losing Cato would be. One down, one to go!"

"Then you have more faith in my integrity than I do at times. Autocracy is insidious. Perhaps there's no man ever born, even me, with the strength to resist it unless opposed," said Caesar soberly. He shrugged. "Still, none of this will bring Bibulus back."

"Pompeius's son might end in being more dangerous with those terrific Egyptian quinqueremes. He's knocked out your naval station at Oricum and burned thirty of my transports in Lissus."

"Pah!" said Caesar contemptuously. "They're nothings. When I return my army to Brundisium, Antonius, it will be in Pompeius's transports. And what's Oricum? I'll live without those warships. What Pompeius doesn't yet understand is that he will never be free of me. Wherever he goes, I'll be there to make his life a misery."

During the relentless rains of May a bizarre race began, both sides digging frantically. Caesar raced to get ahead of Pompey and squeeze his available territory in; Pompey raced to get ahead of Caesar and expand his available territory. Caesar's task was made harder by a constant bombardment of arrows, sling stones and ballista boulders, but Pompey's task was made harder from within: his men detested digging, were reluctant to dig, and did so only out of fear of Labienus, who understood Caesar and the capacity of Caesar's men for hard work under grueling conditions. With more than twice Caesar's manpower, Pompey did manage to keep that precious lead, but never by enough to strike well eastward.

Occasional skirmishes occurred, not usually to Pompey's advantage; his terror of exposing his men to Caesar in sufficient numbers to permit a spontaneous outbreak of hostilities hampered him badly. Nor at first did Pompey fully understand the handicap of being westward in a land where the many little rivers all flowed westward. Caesar occupied their sources, therefore Caesar came to control Pompey's water supply.

One of Pompey's greatest comforts was the knowledge that Caesar lacked a patent supply line. Everything had to come up from western Greece overland; the roads were earthen and mud-bound, the terrain rugged, the easier coastal routes cut off because of those Pompeian fleets.

But then Labienus brought him several slimy grey bricks of a fibrous, gluey substance.

"What are these?" asked Pompey, completely at a loss.

"These are Caesar's staple rations, Pompeius. These are what Caesar and his men are subsisting on. The roots of a local plant, crushed, mixed with milk and baked. They call it 'bread.' "

Eyes wide, Pompey took one of the bricks and worked at a recalcitrant corner until he managed to tear a small piece off. He put it in his mouth, choked, spat it out.

"They don't eat this, Labienus! They *couldn't* eat this!"

"They can and they do."

"Take it away, take it away!" squealed Pompey, shuddering. "Take it away and burn it! And don't you dare breathe a word about it to any of the men—or my legates! If they knew what Caesar's soldiers are willing to eat in order to fence me in—oh, they'd give up in despair!"

"Don't worry, I'll burn the stuff and say nothing. And if you're wondering how I got them, Caesar sent them to me with his compliments. No matter what the odds, he's always cocky."

By the end of May the grazing situation within Pompey's territory was becoming critical; he summoned transports and shipped several thousand of his animals to good pasture north of Dyrrachium. The little city lay on the tip of a small peninsula which almost kissed the mainland half a mile east of the port; a bridge carried the Via Egnatia across the narrow gap. The inhabitants of Dyrrachium saw the arrival of these animals with dismay. Precious grazing land, needed for themselves, was no longer theirs. Only fear of Labienus stilled their tongues and prevented retaliation.

Through the month of June the race continued unabated, while Pompey's horses and mules still penned within his lines grew ever thinner, weaker, more prone to succumb to the diseases a wet and muddy land made inevitable. By the end of June they were dying in such numbers that Pompey, still digging frantically, had not the manpower to dispose of the carcasses properly. The stench of rotting flesh permeated everywhere.

Lentulus Crus was the first to complain. "Pompeius, you cannot expect us to live in this—this *disgusting* miasma!"

"I can't keep anything down for the smell," said Lentulus Spinther, handkerchief to his nose.

Pompey smiled seraphically. "Then I suggest that you pack your trunks and go back to Rome," he said.

Unfortunately for Pompey, the two Lentuli preferred to go on complaining.

For Pompey, a minor matter; Caesar was busy damming all the little rivers and cutting off his water supply.

When Pompey's lines attained a length of fifteen miles—and Caesar's seventeen miles—he was fenced in, could go no further. Pompey's predicament was desperate.

With Labienus's assistance, he persuaded a group of the inhabitants of Dyrrachium to go to Caesar and offer to let him take the city. The weather was not much improved by the arrival of spring; Caesar's men were flagging on that diet of "bread." Yes, Caesar thought, it's worth a try to get at Pompeius's supplies.

On the eighth day of Quinctilis he attacked Dyrrachium. While he was so engaged, Pompey struck, launching a three-pronged assault against the forts in the center of Caesar's line. The two forts which took the brunt of the attack were manned by four cohorts belonging to the Tenth Legion, under the command of Lucius Minucius Basilus and Gaius Volcatius Tullus; so well engineered were the defenses that they held off five of Pompey's legions until Publius Sulla managed to relieve them from Caesar's main camp. Publius Sulla then proceeded to prevent the five Pompeian legions from returning behind their own lines. Stranded in the No Man's Land between the two sets of circumvallations, they huddled and took what was thrown at them for five days. By the time Pompey managed to retrieve them, they had lost two thousand men.

A minor victory for Caesar, smarting at being tricked. He paraded the four cohorts of the Tenth before his army and loaded their standards with yet more decorations. When shown the shield of the centurion Cassius Scaeva, bristling like a sea urchin with one hundred and twenty arrows, Caesar gave Scaeva two hundred thousand sesterces and promoted him to *primipilus*.

Dyrrachium did not fare so well. Caesar sent sufficient troops to build a wall around it—then drove Pompey's grazing horses and mules within the narrow corridor between the city and the fields its people could no longer reach. Having no other alternative, Dyrrachium was forced to commence eating Pompey's supplies. The city also sent the mules and horses back to Pompey.

On the thirteenth day of Quinctilis, Caesar turned fifty-two. Two days after that, Pompey finally admitted to himself that he had to break out or perish from a combination of no water and rotting carcasses. But how to do it, *how*? Cudgel his brain as he might, Pompey couldn't devise a scheme to break out that did not also entail giving battle.

Chance offered him the answer in the persons of two officers from Caesar's squadron of Aeduan cavalry, whom Caesar used mainly to gallop from one end of his circumvallation to the other with notes, messages, dispatches. The two officers had been embezzling their squadron's funds. Though not Roman, the Aedui followed Roman methods of military accounting, and had a savings fund, a burial fund and a pay fund. The difference lay in the fact that they managed these financial affairs themselves through two officers elected for the purpose; Roman legions had proper clerical staffs to do the same sort of thing, and audited as regularly as ruthlessly. Thus the two managers of the squadron's finances had been peculating since their departure from Gaul. Chance found them out. And chance brought them fleeing for refuge to Pompey.

They told him exactly how Caesar's forces were disposed—then told him exactly where Caesar's great weakness was situated.

Pompey attacked at dawn on the seventeenth day of Quinctilis. Caesar's great weakness was situated at the far southern end of his lines, where they turned west and ran to the sea. Here he was still in the process of finishing a second wall outside his main wall; this outer wall was undefended, and from the seaward side neither wall could be held securely.

The Ninth garrisoned the area for Caesar; all six of Pompey's Roman legions began a frontal assault while Pompey's slingers, archers and some light Cappadocian infantry sneaked around behind the undefended wall, entered and surprised the Ninth from the rear. A small force Lentulus Marcellinus brought up from the nearest fort couldn't help; the Ninth was routed.

Things changed when Caesar and Antony arrived with enough reinforcements, but Pompey had used his time well. He pulled five of the six legions into a new camp on the far side of Caesar's walls and sent the sixth to occupy a disused little camp nearby. Caesar retaliated by sending thirty-three cohorts to dislodge the single legion, but was unable to follow through because of an entangling fortification in his path. Sensing victory, Pompey sent all the cavalry he was able to mount against Caesar himself. Who withdrew with such incredible speed that Pompey ended in grasping at air rather than at opportunity. He sat back, pleased, to recover his wind instead of ordering his cavalry to pursue the vanished Caesar.

"What a fool the man is!" growled Caesar to Antony when he had his whole army safely within the ramparts of his main camp. "If he'd kept his cavalry on our tails, he'd have won this war here and now. But he didn't, Antonius. Caesar's luck consists in fighting a fool."

"Do we hold?" asked Antony.

"Oh, no. Dyrrachium has outworn its usefulness. We strike camp and steal away in the night."

Pompey's blindness was complete. Returning jubilant to Petra, he failed to see from his superior height that Caesar was readying his army to march.

In the morning the silent line of fortifications and the lack of smoke from Caesar's camp told the tale: Caesar was gone.

Pompey bestirred himself sufficiently to order some cavalry south to the Genusus to prevent Caesar's crossing, but they failed to reach the river first. Overconfident at yesterday's success, they forded it only to run into an arm of Caesar's forces no one had really encountered before—his German horse troopers. Who, assisted by a few cohorts of infantry, drove the Pompeian cavalry off with heavy losses.

Not far up the Via Egnatia they met up with Pompey, who had decided to follow. That night the two armies camped on opposite banks of the Genusus.

At noon the next day Caesar moved out southward. Pompey did not. Oblivious to the urgency of Pompey's need to keep up with Caesar, some of Pompey's soldiers had defied orders and returned to Petra to collect various items out of their gear. Always anxious to have the numbers, Pompey elected to wait for them. He never did catch up. Like a wraith from the Underworld, Caesar simply disappeared off the face of the earth, somewhere to the south of Apollonia.

By the twenty-second day of Quinctilis, Pompey and his army had returned to Petra, there to celebrate a great victory, send the news of it hurrying across the Adriatic to Italia and Rome. No more Caesar! A beaten man, Caesar was in headlong retreat. And if anyone wondered whether a Caesar in headlong retreat with all save a thousand of his men intact was truly a beaten man, he kept his wondering to himself.

The troops celebrated too, but no one had a happier day than Titus Labienus, who paraded the several hundred members of the Ninth captured during the battle. In front of Pompey, Cato, Cicero, the Lentuli Spinther and Crus, Faustus Sulla, Marcus Favonius and many others, Labienus demonstrated the absoluteness of his ferocity. The men of the Ninth were first derided, insulted, slapped about; after which Labienus settled down to business with the red-hot irons, the tiny knives, the pincers, the barbed lash. Only after every man was blinded, deprived of his tongue and genitals and flogged to jelly did Labienus finally behead them.

Pompey watched helplessly, so appalled and sickened that he seemed not to comprehend that it was within his power to order Labienus to desist. He did nothing, he said nothing, neither then nor afterward as he wandered about Petra in a daze.

"That man," said Cato, hunting him down, "is a monster! Why did you let him do such things, Pompeius? What's the matter with you? Here we've just defeated Caesar, yet you stand there demonstrating the fact that you can't control your own legates!"

"Aaargh!" cried Pompey, eyes full of tears. "What do you want of me, Cato? What do you expect of me, Cato? I'm not a genuine commander-in-chief, I'm a puppet everyone thinks himself entitled to jerk this way and that! *Control Labienus?* I didn't see you stepping forward to try! How do you control an earthquake, Cato? How do you control a volcano, Cato? How do you control a man who terrified the life out of *Germans*?"

"I cannot continue," said Cato, sticking to his principles, "to support the efforts of an army commanded by the likes of Titus Labienus! If you won't banish him from our ranks, Pompeius, then I refuse to serve with you!"

"Good! That's one fewer nuisance I'll have to suffer! Go away!" He thought of something, yelled after Cato's retreating back: "You cretin, Cato! Don't you understand? None of you can fight! None of you can general troops! But Labienus can!"

He returned to his house to find Lentulus Crus waiting for him. Oh, *abominable* man!

"What a shambles," said Lentulus Crus, sniffing disdainfully. "My dear Pompeius, must you keep animals like Labienus around? Can you do nothing right? What are you doing, claiming a great victory over Caesar when you've done nothing to eliminate the man? He has escaped! Why are you still here?"

"I wish *I* could escape," said Pompey through his teeth. "Unless you have something constructive to offer, Crus, I suggest you go back to your hypocaust-heated house and pack up all your gold plate and ruby quizzing glasses! We're marching."

And on the twenty-fourth day of Quinctilis, Pompey did just that. In Dyrrachium he left behind fifteen cohorts of wounded men under the command of Cato.

"If you don't mind, Magnus, I'll stay here too," said Cicero apprehensively. "I'm afraid I'm not much use in a war, but I can perhaps be of some use in Dyrrachium. Oh, I do wish my brother Quintus would join you! He's a handy man in a war."

"Yes, stay," said Pompey tiredly. "You won't be in any danger, Cicero. Caesar is going to Greece."

"How do you know that? What if he settles at Oricum and elects to prevent your returning to Italia?"

"Not he! He's a leech, Cicero. A burr."

"Afranius is very keen for you to abandon this eastern campaign, steal a march on Caesar and return to Italia now."

"I know, I know! And then hasten west to recover the Spains. A lovely dream, Cicero, nothing more. It's suicide for our cause to leave

Caesar unopposed in Greece or Macedonia. I'd lose all my eastern levies and all my support from the client kings." Pompey patted Cicero on the shoulder. "Don't worry about me, please. I know what to do. Prudence dictates that I keep on waging Fabian war against Caesar, never engage him, but the others won't have it. I see that now very clearly. Even marching at the pace he does, Caesar has a long way to go. He'll be days behind me. I'll have the time I need to replace my horses and mules—I've bought them from the Dacians and Dardani; they'll be waiting in Heracleia. Not up to much, I imagine, but better than none." Pompey smiled. "Scipio ought to be in Larissa with the Syrian legions by now."

Cicero did not make any comment. He had had a letter from Dolabella urging him to return to Italia, and most of him wanted desperately to go. At least by remaining in Dyrrachium he was no more than the width of the Adriatic from his beloved homeland.

"I envy you, Cicero" was Pompey's parting shot. "The sun might come out here occasionally from now on, and the air's soft. All you'll have to suffer is Cato. Who informs me that he's going to send Favonius with me to keep me 'pure.' His word, not mine. That leaves me with curs like Labienus, voluptuaries like Lentulus Crus, critics like Lentulus Spinther, and a wife and son to worry about. With just a morsel of Caesar's luck, I might survive."

Cicero stopped, looked back. "A wife and son?"

"Yes. Cornelia Metella has decided that Rome is too far away from *tata* and me. With Sextus egging her on. He's mad keen to be my *contubernalis*. They're joining me in Thessalonica."

"Thessalonica? Do you plan to go that far?"

"No. I've already sent word there and told her to take Sextus to Mitylene. They'll be safe enough on Lesbos." Pompey's hands went out, a curiously pathetic gesture. "Do try to understand, Cicero! I *can't* go west! If I do, I abandon my own father-in-law and two good legions to Caesar's famous clemency. He will control the East and my wife and son will pass into his custody. The outcome *must* take place somewhere in Thessaly."

Thus it was Cicero who stood watching as Pompey turned to walk away. A mist descended in front of Cicero's eyes, he winked away tears. Poor Magnus! How old he suddenly seemed.

In Heracleia, on the Via Egnatia as it began to come down to the gentler lands around Alexander the Great's home of Pella, those who had been absent on other duties joined Pompey's army again: men like Brutus, who had tried to be useful by trotting off obediently to places as far afield as Thessalonica; and Lucius Domitius Ahenobarbus, who left his fleet and hastened to catch up.

In Heracleia, Pompey took delivery of several thousand good horses and mules, sufficient to replace those he had lost. Their Dacian herdsmen had brought along none other than the King of Dacia, Burebistas, who had heard of the defeat of Gaius Caesar at Dyrrachium. Nothing would do than that King Burebistas should come himself to make a treaty of accord with this mammoth force in world events, the conqueror of the mighty Gaius Caesar, the kings Mithridates and Tigranes, and some quaint relic out of the far West named Quintus Sertorius. King Burebistas also wanted to boast to his subjects back home that he had shared a cup of wine with the fabled Pompey the Great. Who was truly Great.

Events like the arrival of King Burebistas tended to cheer Pompey up; so too did the news that the elusive Metellus Scipio and his Syrian legions were encamped at Beroea and ready to march south to Larissa the moment Pompey gave the word.

What Pompey didn't know was that Gnaeus Domitius Calvinus, leading Caesar's Eleventh and Twelfth Legions, was approaching Heracleia in quest of Caesar. He had encountered Metellus Scipio and the Syrian legions on the Haliacmon River and done everything in his power to tempt Scipio into battle. When Scipio and the countryside proved uncooperative, Calvinus decided to head for the Via Egnatia, sure that Caesar would come that way, and that he would be ahead of Pompey. News of Pompey's great victory at Dyrrachium had flown all over Greece and Macedonia, so Calvinus presumed that Caesar would be retreating before the wrathful and triumphant victor. Bitterly disappointing news, but not news capable of persuading Calvinus to change sides, even if his legions had let him. *They* refused to believe it, and clamored to join Caesar as soon as possible. All Caesar needed, they said, was the full complement of his Gallic veterans. Once he had that, he'd wallop Pompey and the entire world.

With Calvinus was Caesar's other squadron of Aeduan cavalry, sixty men on horseback; Calvinus used them as scouts. Riding in the lead with two of the Aeduans for company and aware that Heracleia was no more than four hours away, Calvinus kept looking for signs of Caesar's imminence. Confirmed, he thought, when he saw two Aeduan cavalrymen canter over a hill in his path. His two Aeduan companions whooped at sight of the red-and-blue-striped shawls, kicked their horses in the ribs and galloped to meet the newcomers.

An ecstatic reunion took place while Calvinus let his horse's head drop to graze the springtime greening. Quick chat went back and forth in Aeduan, continued for some moments. Then his own two Aeduans returned as the other two trotted off in the direction of Heracleia.

"How far to Caesar?" he asked Caragdus, who spoke Latin.

"Caesar's not anywhere in Macedonia," said Caragdus, scowling. "Can you imagine it, General? Those two bastards skipped off to Pompey with their squadron's money! Thought it such a great joke that they couldn't wait to tell us. Veredorix and I decided to keep our mouths shut and find out what we could. Just as well."

"The Gods are passing strange," said Calvinus slowly. "What did they know?"

"There was a battle in Dyrrachium, and Pompeius did win it—but it wasn't a great victory, General. The idiots let Caesar get away with his army intact. Well, he lost about a thousand men—those captured alive were tortured and executed by Labienus." The Aeduan shivered. "Caesar went south. Those two think he's on the way to Gomphi, wherever that might be."

"Southern Thessaly," said Calvinus automatically.

"Oh. Anyway, the army in Heracleia belongs to Pompeius. He's meeting with King Burebistas of the Dacians. But we'd better scuttle off in a hurry, General. Those two bastards betrayed all Caesar's dispositions to the enemy. Veredorix and I thought of killing them, but then we decided to leave well enough alone."

"What did you tell them about our presence here?"

"That we were scouting ahead of a foraging party. Just a couple of cohorts strong," said Caragdus.

"Good man!" Calvinus jerked his horse's head up. "Come on, boys, we're going to scuttle off south in search of Caesar."

Caesar had not gone the long way across the range of sere mountains which spined Greece and Macedonia on the west. Below Apollonia lay the river Aous, one of the major streams which came down from the backbone itself. A very poor road followed it into the Tymphe Mountains, traversed a pass and descended to Thessaly at the headwaters of the river Peneus. Rather than march an extra one hundred and fifty miles, Caesar and his army turned off the better roads of Epirus and proceeded at their usual thirty to thirty-five miles a day along a road which meant they needed to build only a rudimentary camp each night; they saw no one save shepherds and sheep, emerged into Thessaly well to the north of Gomphi at the town of Aeginium.

Thessaly had declared for Pompey. Like the other regions of Greece, it was organized into a league of towns, which had a council called the Thessalian League. On hearing of Pompey's great victory at Dyrrachium, the leader of the League, Androsthenes of Gomphi, sent out word to every town to support Pompey.

Dazed at the speed with which a fit and businesslike army proceeded to reduce it, Aeginium sent frantic messages to all the other towns of the Thessalian League that a far-from-defeated-looking Caesar was in the neighborhood. Tricca was the next place to fall; Caesar moved on to Gomphi, from which city Androsthenes sent an urgent message to Pompey that Caesar had arrived long before he was expected. Gomphi fell.

Though the month was early Sextilis, the season was still spring;

there were no ripe crops anywhere and the rains had been poor east of the ranges. A minor famine threatened. For this reason Caesar ensured the submission of western Thessaly; it gave him a source of supplies. He was also waiting for the rest of his legions to join him. Word had gone out recalling the Seventh, Fourteenth, Eleventh and Twelfth.

With Lucius Cassius, Sabinus, Calenus and Domitius Calvinus back in the fold, Caesar advanced due east en route to the better roads which led to the city of Larissa and the pass into Macedonia at Tempe. The best way was along the river Enipeus to Scotussa, where Caesar planned to turn north toward Larissa.

Less than ten miles short of Scotussa, Caesar dug himself a stout camp north of the Enipeus outside the village of Pharsalus; he had heard that Pompey was coming, and the lay of the land at Pharsalus was battleworthy. Typical of Caesar, he didn't choose the best ground for himself. It always paid to seem at a bit of a disadvantage; routine generals—and he classified Pompey as a routine general—tended to go by what the manuals said, accept them as doctrine. Pompey would like Pharsalus. A line of hills to the north sloping to a little plain about two miles wide, then the swampy course of the Enipeus River. Yes, Pharsalus would do.

Pompey received the message from Androsthenes in Gomphi as he skirted his old training camp at Beroea. He turned immediately and headed for the pass into Thessaly at Tempe. There was no other easy way to go; the massif of Mount Olympus and its sprawling, rugged foothills prevented a straighter march. Outside the city of Larissa he was finally reunited with Metellus Scipio, and breathed a sigh of relief for many reasons, not the least important of which was those two extra and veteran legions.

Relations within the tents of the high command had deteriorated even further since leaving Heracleia. Everyone had decided it was time to put Pompey in his place, and in Larissa the long-simmering resentments and grudges all surfaced together.

It started when one of Pompey's senior military tribunes, an Acutius Rufus, chose to summon the high command to a hearing in a military court he had taken it upon himself to convene. And there in front of Pompey and his legates he formally charged Lucius Afranius with treason for deserting his troops after Illerda; the chief prosecutor was Marcus Favonius, adhering religiously to Cato's instructions to keep Pompey "pure."

Pompey's temper snapped. "Acutius, dismiss this illegal court!" he roared, fists clenched, face mottling. "Go on, get out before I arraign you on treason charges! As for you, Favonius, I would have thought that your experience in public life would have taught you to avoid unconstitutional prosecutions! Get out! Get out! *Get out!*"

The court dissolved, but Favonius wasn't done. He began to lie in wait for Pompey, to hector him at every opportunity with Afranius's falseness, and Afranius, almost deprived of breath at the impudence of it, hammered away in Pompey's other ear with demands that he dismiss Favonius from his service. Petreius sided with Afranius, naturally, and hammered away too.

Active command of the army had devolved upon Labienus, whose lightest punishment for the most minor infringement was a flogging; the troops muttered and shivered, looked sideways with darkling glances, plotted how to expose Labienus to the spears during the battle everyone knew was coming.

Over dinner, Ahenobarbus struck.

"And how's our dear Agamemnon, King of Kings?" he enquired as he strolled in on Favonius's arm.

Jaw dropped, Pompey stared. "What did you call me?"

"Agamemnon, King of Kings," said Ahenobarbus, sneering.

"Meaning?" asked Pompey dangerously.

"Why, that you're in the same position as Agamemnon, King of Kings. Titular head of the army of a thousand ships, titular head of a group of kings, any one of whom has as much right to call himself King of Kings as you do. But it's over a millennium since the Greeks invaded Priam's homeland. You'd think something would have changed, wouldn't you? But it hasn't. In modern Rome we still suffer Agamemnon, King of Kings."

"Cast yourself in the role of Achilles, have you, Ahenobarbus? Going to sulk beside your ships while the world goes to pieces and the best men die?" asked Pompey, lips white.

"Well, I'm not sure," said Ahenobarbus, comfortably disposed on his couch between Favonius and Lentulus Spinther. He selected a hothouse grape from bunches ferried across from Chalcidean Pallene, where this profitable little industry had grown up inside linen-draped frames. "Actually," he went on, spitting out seeds and reaching for the whole bunch, "I was thinking more of the role of Agamemnon, King of Kings."

"Hear, hear," barked Favonius, searching in vain for some simpler fare—and profoundly glad that Cato wasn't present to see how Pompey's high command were living in this Romanized land of luxurious plenty. Hothouse grapes! Chian wine twenty years in the amphora! Sea urchins galloped from Rhizus and sauced with an exotic version of *garum*! Baby quail filched from new mothers to slide down the gullet of Lentulus Crus!

"Want the command tent, do you, Ahenobarbus?"

"I'm not sure I'd say no."

"Why," asked Pompey, tearing savagely at some cheesed bread, "would you want the aggravation?"

"The aggravation," said Ahenobarbus, bald pate sporting a pretty wreath of spring flowers, "lies in the fact that Agamemnon, King of Kings, never wants to give battle."

"A wise course," said Pompey, hanging onto his temper grimly. "My strategy is to wear Caesar down by Fabian means. Engaging the man is an unnecessary risk. We lie between him and good supply lines. Greece is in drought. As summer comes in, he'll be hungry. By autumn he will have looted Greece of everything edible. And in winter he'll capitulate. My son Gnaeus is so snugly based in Corcyra that he'll get nothing across the Adriatic, Gaius Cassius has won a big victory against Pomponius off Messana—"

"*I* heard," Lentulus Spinther interrupted, "that after this much-lauded victory, Gaius Cassius went on to do battle with Caesar's old legate Sulpicius. And that a legion of Caesar's watching from the shore became so fed up with the way Sulpicius was handling the battle that they rowed out, boarded Cassius's ships, and trounced him. He had to slip over the side of his flagship to get away."

"Well, yes, that is true," Pompey admitted.

"Fabian means," said Lentulus Crus between mouthfuls of succulent squid sauced with their own sepia ink, "are ridiculous, Pompeius. Caesar can't win; we all know that. You're always griping about our lack of money, so why are you so determined on these Fabian tactics?"

"Strategy, not tactics," said Pompey.

"Whatever—who cares?" asked Lentulus Crus loftily. "I say that the moment we find Caesar, we give battle. Get it over and done with. Then head home for Italia and a few proscriptions."

Brutus lay listening to all this in growing horror. His own participation in the siege of Dyrrachium had been minuscule; at any chance he volunteered to ride for Thessalonica or Athens or anywhere far from that frenzied, revolting cesspool. Only at Heracleia had he realized what kind of dissension was going on between Pompey and his legates. At Heracleia he heard of the doings of Labienus. At Heracleia he began to realize that Pompey's own legates would end in ruining him.

Oh, why had he ever left Tarsus, Publius Sestius and that careful state of neutrality? How could he collect the interest on debts from people like Deiotarus and Ariobarzanes while they were funding Pompey's war? How would he manage if these intransigent boars did manage to thrust Pompey into the battle he so clearly didn't want? He was right, he was right! Fabian tactics—strategy—would win in the end. And wasn't it worth it, to spare Roman lives, ensure a minimum of bloodshed? *What would he do if someone thrust a sword into his hand and told him to fight?*

"Caesar's done for," said Metellus Scipio, who didn't agree with his son-in-law in this matter. He sighed happily, smiled. "I will be the Pontifex Maximus at last."

Ahenobarbus sat bolt upright. "You'll what?"

"Be the Pontifex Maximus at last."

"Over my dead body!" yelled Ahenobarbus. "That's one public honor belongs to me and my family!"

"Gerrae!" said Lentulus Spinther, grinning. "You can't even get yourself elected a priest, Ahenobarbus, let alone get yourself elected Pontifex Maximus. You're a born loser."

"I will do what my grandfather did, Spinther! I'll be voted in as pontifex and Pontifex Maximus at the same election!"

"No! It's going to be a race between me and Scipio."

"Neither of you stands a chance!" gasped Metellus Scipio, outraged. *"I'm* the next Pontifex Maximus!"

The clang of a knife thrown against precious gold plate set everyone jumping; Pompey slid off his couch and walked from the room without looking back.

On the fifth day of Sextilis, Pompey and his army arrived at Pharsalus to find Caesar occupying the ground on this north side of the river, but to the east.

"Excellent!" said Pompey to Faustus Sulla, who, dear boy, was just about the only one among the legates he could bear to talk to. Never criticized, just did what *tata*-in-law said. Well, there was Brutus. Another good fellow. But he skulked so! Kept himself out of sight, never wanted to attend the councils or even the dinners. "If we put ourselves here on this nice slope up to the hills, Faustus, we're well above Caesar's lie and between him and Larissa, Tempe and access to Macedonia."

"Is it going to be a battle?" asked Faustus Sulla.

"I wish not. But I fear so."

"Why are they so determined on it?"

"Oh," said Pompey, sighing, "because they're none of them soldiers save Labienus. They don't understand."

"Labienus is set on fighting too."

"Labienus wants to pit himself against Caesar. He's dying for the chance. He believes he's the better general."

"And is he?"

Pompey shrugged. "In all honesty, Faustus, I have absolutely no idea. Though Labienus should. He was Caesar's right-hand man for years in Gallia Comata. Therefore I'm inclined to say yes."

"Is it for tomorrow?"

Seeming to shrink, Pompey shook his head. "No, not yet."

The morrow brought Caesar out to deploy. Pompey did not follow suit. After a wait of some hours, Caesar sent his troops back into his camp and put them in the shade. Only spring, yes, but the sun was hot and the air, perhaps because of the swampiness of the river, was suffocatingly humid.

That afternoon Pompey called his legates together. "I have decided," he announced, on his feet and inviting no one to sit. "We will give battle here at Pharsalus."

"Oh, good!" said Labienus. "I'll start the preparations."

"No, no, not tomorrow!" cried Pompey, looking horrified.

Nor the next day. Thinking to stretch his men's legs, he led them out for a walk—or so his legates assumed, since he put them in places where only a fool would have attacked after a long uphill run. Since Caesar was not a fool, he didn't attack.

But on the eighth day of Sextilis, with the sun sliding down behind his camp, Pompey called his legates together again, this time in his command tent and around a large map his cartographers had drawn up for him upon calfskin.

"Tomorrow," said Pompey tersely, and stepped back. "Labienus, explain the plan."

"It's to be a cavalry battle," Labienus began, moving up to the map and beckoning everyone to cluster around. "By that I mean that we'll use our enormous superiority in cavalry as the lever to defeat Caesar, who has only a thousand Germans. Note, by the way, that our skirmish with them revealed that Caesar has armed some of his foot in the same way the Ubii foot fight among the Ubii horse. They're dangerous, but far too few. We'll deploy here, with our long axis positioned between the river and the hills. At nine Roman legions we'll outnumber Caesar, who must keep one of his nine in reserve. That's where we're lucky. We have fifteen thousand foreign auxiliary infantry as our reserve. The ground favors us; we're slightly uphill. For that reason, we'll draw up further away from Caesar's front line than usual. Nor will we charge. Puff his men out before they reach our front line. We're going to pack our infantry tightly because I'm massing six thousand cavalry on the left wing—here, against the hills. A thousand cavalry on our right, against the river—the ground's too swampy for good horse work. A thousand archers and slingers will be interposed between the first legion of foot on the left and my six thousand horse."

Labienus paused, glared at each of the men around him with fierce intensity. "The infantry will be drawn up in three separate blocks each comprising ten ranks. All three blocks will charge at the same moment. We have more weight than Caesar, who I'm very reliably informed has only four thousand men per legion due to his losses over the months in Epirus. Our legions are at full strength. We'll let him charge us with breathless men and roll his front line back. But the real beauty of the plan is in the cavalry. There's no way Caesar can resist six thousand horse charging his right. While the archer-slinger unit bombards the legion on his far right, my cavalry will drive forward like a landslide, repulse Caesar's scant cavalry, then swing behind his lines and take him in the rear." He stepped back, grinning broadly. "Pompeius, it's all yours."

"Well, I haven't much more to add," said Pompey, sweating in the humid air. "Labienus will command the six thousand horse on my left. As to the infantry, I'll put the First and Third Legions on my left wing. Ahenobarbus, you'll command. Then five legions in the center, including the two Syrian. Scipio, you'll command the center. Spinther, you'll command my right, closest to the river. You'll have the eighteen cohorts not in legions. Brutus, you'll second-in-command Spinther. Faustus, you'll second-in-command Scipio. Afranius and Petreius, you'll second-in-command Ahenobarbus. Favonius and Lentulus Crus, you're in charge of the foreign levies drawn up in reserve. Young Marcus Cicero, you can have the cavalry reserve. Torquatus, take the reserve archers and slingers. Labienus, depute someone to command the thousand horse on the river. The rest of you can sort yourselves out among the legions. Understood?"

Everyone nodded, weighed down by the solemnity of the moment.

Afterward Pompey went off with Faustus Sulla. "There," he said, "they have what they wanted. I couldn't hold out any longer."

"Are you well, Magnus?"

"As well as I'll ever be, Faustus." Pompey patted his son-in-law in much the same affectionate way as he had patted Cicero on leaving Dyrrachium. "Don't worry about me, Faustus, truly. I'm an old man. Fifty-eight in less than two months. There's a time . . . It's hollow, all this ripping and clawing for power. Always a dozen men drooling at the prospect of tearing the First Man down." He laughed wearily. "Fancy finding the energy to quarrel over which one of them will take Caesar's place as Pontifex Maximus! As if it matters, Faustus. It doesn't. They'll all go too."

"Magnus, don't talk like this!"

"Why not? Tomorrow decides everything. I didn't want it, but I'm not sorry. A decision of any kind is preferable to a continuation of life in my high command." He dropped an arm about Faustus's shoulders. "Come, it's time to call the army to assembly. I have to tell them that tomorrow is the day."

By the time the army had been summoned and the obligatory pre-battle oration given, darkness had fallen. An augur, Pompey then took the auspices himself. Because no cattle were available, the victim was to be a pure white sheep; a round dozen animals had been herded into a pen, washed, combed, readied for the augur's expert eye to choose the most suitable offering. But when Pompey indicated a placid-looking *bidentalis* ewe and the *cultarius* and *popa* opened the gate, all twelve animals bolted for freedom. Only after a chase was the victim, dirtied and distressed, caught and sacrificed. Not a good omen. The army stirred and muttered; Pompey took the trouble to descend from the augural platform after the sacrifice and go among them, speaking reassuringly. The liver had been perfect, all was well, nothing to worry about.

Then the worst happened. The men were facing east toward Caesar's camp, still milling and murmuring, when a mighty fireball streaked across the indigo sky like a falling comet of white flames. Down, down, down, leaving a trail of sparks in its wake, not to fall on Caesar's camp—which might have been a good omen—but to disappear into the darkness far beyond. The unrest began all over again; this time Pompey couldn't dispel it.

He went to bed in fatalistic mood, convinced that whatever the morrow might bring, it would be to his ultimate good. Why was a fireball a bad omen? What might Nigidius Figulus have made of it, that walking encyclopaedia of ancient Etruscan augural phenomena? Might the Etruscans not have thought it a good omen? Romans went only as far as livers, with the occasional foray into entrails and birds, whereas the Etruscans had catalogued everything.

The thunder woke him up several hours before dawn, sitting straight up in bed and wondering if he had leaped as high as the leather ceiling. Because his sleep had been interrupted at the right moment, he could remember his dream as vividly as if it were still going on. The temple of Venus Victrix at the top of his stone theater, where the statue of Venus had Julia's face and slender body. He had been in it and decorating it with trophies of battle, while crowds and crowds in the auditorium applauded in huge delight. Oh, such a good omen! Except that the trophies of battle were trophies from his own side: his best silver armor, unmistakable with its cuirass depicting the victory of the Gods over the Titans; Lentulus Crus's enormous ruby quizzing glass; Faustus Sulla's lock of hair from his father Sulla's bright red-gold tresses; Scipio's helmet, which had belonged to his ancestor Scipio Africanus and still bore the same moth-eaten, faded egret's feathers in its crest; and, most horrifying trophy of all, the glossy-pated head of Ahenobarbus on a German spear. Flower wreathed.

Shivering from cold, sweating from heat, Pompey lay down again and closed his eyes upon the flaring white lightning, listened as the thunder rolled away across the hills behind him. When the drumming rain came down in torrents, he drifted back into an uneasy sleep, his mind still going over the details of that awful dream.

Dawn brought a thick fog and windless, enervating air. In Caesar's camp all was stirring; the mules were being loaded up, the wagon teams harnessed, everyone getting into marching mode.

"He *won't* fight!" Caesar had barked when he came to wake Mark Antony a good hour before first light. "The river's running a banker after this storm, the ground's soggy, the troops are wet, da de da de da . . . Same old Pompeius, same old list of excuses. We're moving for Scotussa, Antonius, before Pompeius can get up off his arse to stop our slipping by him. Ye Gods, what a slug he is! Will *nothing* tempt him to fight?"

From which exasperated diatribe the sleepy Antony deduced that the old boy was touchy again.

In that grey, lustrous pall it was impossible to see as far as the lower ground between his own camp and Pompey's; the pulling of stakes continued unabated.

Until an Aeduan scout came galloping up to where Caesar stood watching the beautiful order of nine legions and a thousand horse troopers preparing to move out silently, efficiently.

"General, General!" the man gasped, sliding off his horse. "General, Gnaeus Pompeius is outside his camp and lined up for—for *battle*! It really looks as if he means to fight!"

"Cacat!"

That exclamation having escaped his lips, no more followed. Caesar started barking orders in a fluent stream.

"Calenus, have the noncombatants get every last animal to the back of the camp! At the double! Sabinus, start the men tearing the front ramparts to pieces and filling in the ditch—I want every man out quicker than the *capite censi* can fill the bleachers at the circus! Antonius, get the cavalry saddled up for war, not a ride. You—you—you—you—form up the legions as we discussed. We'll fight exactly as planned."

When the fog lifted, Caesar's army waited on the plain as if no march had ever been on the agenda for that morning.

Pompey had drawn his lines up facing east—which meant he had the rising sun facing him—on a front a mile and a half long between the line of hills and the river, a huge host of cavalry on his left wing, a much smaller contingent on his right.

Caesar, though he had the smaller army, strung his infantry front out a little longer, so that the Tenth, on his right, faced Pompey's archer-slinger detachment and part of Labienus's horse. From right to left he put the Tenth, Seventh, Thirteenth, Eleventh, Twelfth, Sixth, Eighth and Ninth. The Fourteenth, which he had thinned down from ten to eight cohorts when re-forming his legions at Aeginium, he positioned concealed behind his thousand German horse on the right wing. They were curiously armed; instead of their customary *pila* the men each carried a long, barbed siege spear. His left, against the river, would have to fend for itself without cavalry to stiffen it. Publius Sulla, a knacky soldier, had command of Caesar's right; his center went to Calvinus; his left was in the charge of Mark Antony. He had nothing in reserve.

Positioned on a rise behind those eight cohorts of the Fourteenth armed with siege spears, Caesar sat Toes in his usual fashion, side on, one leg hooked round the two front pommels. Risky for any other horseman, not so for Caesar, who could twist in the tiniest fraction of time fully into the saddle and be off at a gallop. He liked his troops to see, should they cast a glance behind, that the General was absolutely relaxed, totally confident.

Oh, Pompeius, you fool! You fool! You've let Labienus general this battle. You've staked your all on three silly, flimsy things—that your horse has the weight to outflank my right and come round behind me to roll me up—that your infantry has the weight to knock my boys back—and that you'll tire my boys out by making them run all the way to you. Caesar's eyes went to where Pompey sat on his big white Public Horse behind his archer-slingers, neatly opposite Caesar. I am sorry for you, Pompeius. You can't win this one, and it's the big one.

Every detail had been worked out three days before, gone over each day since. When Labienus's cavalry charged, Pompey's infantry did not, though Caesar's infantry did. But they paused halfway to get their breath back, then punched into Pompey's line like a great hammer. The thousand Germans on Caesar's right fell back before Labienus's charge without truly engaging; rather than waste time pursuing them, Labienus wheeled right the moment he got to the back third of the Tenth. And ran straight into a wall of siege spears the eight cohorts of the Fourteenth—who had practised the technique for three days—jabbed into the faces of Galatians and Cappadocians. Exactly, thought Labienus, mind whirling, like an old Greek phalanx. His cavalry broke, which was the signal for the Germans to fall upon his flank like wolves, and the signal for the Tenth to wheel sideways and slaughter the archer-slinger contingent before wading fearlessly into Labienus's disarrayed cavalry, horses screaming and going down, riders screaming and going down, panic everywhere.

Elsewhere the pattern was the same; Pharsalus was more a rout than a battle. It lasted a scant hour. Pompey's foreign auxiliaries held in reserve fled the moment they saw the horse begin to falter. Most of the legions stayed to fight, including the Syrian, the First and the Third, but the eighteen cohorts against the river on Pompey's right scattered everywhere, leaving Antony complete victor along the Enipeus.

Pompey left the field at an orderly trot the moment he realized he was done for. Rot Labienus and his scornful dismissal of Caesar's soldiers as raw recruits from across the Padus! Those were veteran legions out there and they fought as one unit, so competently and with such businesslike, rational flair! I was right, my legates were wrong. Just what is Labienus up to? No one will ever defeat Caesar on a battlefield. The man is on top of everything. Better strategy, better tactics. I'm done for. Is that what Labienus has been aiming for all along, high command?

He rode back to his camp, entered his general's tent and sat with his head between his hands for a long time. Not weeping; the time for tears was past.

And so Marcus Favonius, Lentulus Spinther and Lentulus Crus found him, sitting with his head between his hands.

"Pompeius, you must get up," said Favonius, going across to put a hand on his silver-sheathed back.

Pompey said no word, made no movement.

"Pompeius, you must get up!" cried Lentulus Spinther. "It's finished, we're broken."

"Caesar will be inside our camp, you must escape!" gasped Lentulus Crus, trembling.

His hands fell; Pompey lifted his head. "Escape where?" he asked apathetically.

"I don't know! Anywhere, anywhere at all! Please, Pompeius, come with us now!" begged Lentulus Crus.

Pompey's eyes cleared enough to see that all three men were clad in the dress of Greek merchants—tunic, *chlamys* cape, broad-brimmed hat, ankle boots. "Like that? In disguise?" he asked.

"It's better," said Favonius, who bore another and similar outfit. "Come, Pompeius, stand up, do! I'll help you out of your armor and into these."

So Pompey stood and allowed himself to be transformed from a Roman commander-in-chief to a Greek businessman. When it was attended to, he looked about the confines of his tent dazedly, then seemed to come to himself. He chuckled, followed his shepherds out.

They left the camp through the gate nearest to the Larissa road on horseback and cantered off before Caesar reached the camp. Larissa was only thirty miles away, a short enough journey not to need a change of horse, but all four horses were blown before they rode in through the Scotussa gate.

Even so, the news of Caesar's victory at Pharsalus had preceded them; Larissa, emphatically attached to Pompey's cause, was thronged with confused townsfolk who wandered this way and that, audibly wondering what would be their fate when Caesar came.

"He'll not harm you," said Pompey, dismounting in the agora and removing his hat. "Go about your normal business. Caesar is a merciful man; he'll not harm you."

Of course he was recognized, but not, thanks be to all the Gods, reviled for losing. What was it I once said to Sulla? asked Pompey of himself, surrounded by weeping partisans offering help. What was it I said to Sulla on that road outside Beneventum? When he was so drunk? More people worship the rising than the setting sun. . . . Yes, that was it. Caesar's sun is rising. Mine has set.

A half-strength squadron of thirty Galatian horse troopers rallied around, offering to escort Pompey and his companions wherever they would like to go—provided, that is, that it was eastward along the road back to Galatia and a little peace. They were all Gauls, a part of those thousand men Caesar had sent to Deiotarus as a gift, a way of making sure the men didn't die, but couldn't live to rebel either. Mostly Treveri who had learned a little broken Greek since being relocated so far from home.

Freshly mounted, Pompey, Favonius and the two Lentuli rode out of Larissa's Thessalonica Gate, hidden between the troopers. When they reached the Peneus River inside the Tempe Pass, they encountered a seagoing barge whose captain, ferrying a load of homegrown vegetables to the market in Dium, offered to take the four fugitives as far as Dium. With thanks to the Gallic horsemen, Pompey and his three friends boarded the barge.

"More sensible," said Lentulus Spinther, recovering faster than the other three. "Caesar will be looking for us on the road to Thessalonica, but not on a barge full of vegetables."

In Dium, a few miles up the coast from the mouth of the Peneus River, the four had another stroke of luck. There tied up at a wharf, having just emptied its cargo of millet and chickpea from Italian Gaul, was a neat little Roman merchantman with a genuinely Roman captain named Marcus Peticius.

"No need to tell me who you are," said Peticius, shaking Pompey warmly by the hand. "Where would you like to go?"

For once Lentulus Crus had done the right thing; before he left the camp, he filched every silver denarius and sestertius he could find, perhaps as atonement for forgetting to empty Rome's money and bullion out of the Treasury. "Name your price, Marcus Peticius," he said magnificently. "Pompeius, where to?"

"Amphipolis," said Pompey, plucking a name out of his memory.

"Good choice!" said Peticius cheerfully. "I'll pick up a nice load of mountain ash there—hard to get in Aquileia."

For Caesar, victor and owner of the field of Pharsalus, a very mixed day, that ninth one of Sextilis. His own losses had been minimal; the Pompeian losses at six thousand dead might have been far worse.

"They would have it thus," he said sadly to Antony, Publius Sulla, Calvinus and Calenus when the tidying-up began. "They held my deeds as nothing and would have condemned me had I not appealed to my soldiers for help."

"Good boys," said Antony affectionately.

"Always good boys." Caesar's lips set. "Except the Ninth."

The bulk of Pompey's army had vanished; Caesar did not exert himself to pursue it. Even so, it was nearing sunset when he finally found the time to enter and inspect Pompey's camp.

"Ye Gods!" he breathed. "Weren't they sure of winning!"

Every tent had been decorated, including those of the ranker soldiers. Evidence that a great feast had been ordered lay all over the place: piles of vegetables, fish which must have been sent fresh that morning from the coast and placidly put in shade to the sound of battle, hundreds upon hundreds of newly slaughtered lamb carcasses, mounds of bread, pots of stew, jars of softened chickpea and ground sesame seed in oil and garlic, cakes sticky with honey, olives by the tub, many cheeses, strings of sausages.

"Pollio," said Caesar to his very junior legate, Gaius Asinius Pollio, "there's no point in transferring all this food from their camp to ours. Start moving our men over here to enjoy a victory feast donated to them by the enemy." He grunted. "It will have to take place tonight. By tomorrow, a lot of this stuff will have perished. I don't want sick soldiers."

However, it was the tents of Pompey's legates really opened every pair of eyes. By ironic coincidence, Caesar reached Lentulus Crus's quarters last. "Shades of that palace on the sea at Gytheum!" he said (a reference no one understood), shaking his head. "No wonder he couldn't be bothered emptying the Treasury! A man might be pardoned for presuming he'd looted the Treasury for himself."

Gold plate was strewn everywhere, the couches were Tyrian purple, the pillows pearl embroidered, the tables in the corners were priceless citrus-wood; in Lentulus Crus's sleeping chamber the inspection party found a huge bathtub of rare red marble with lion's paw feet. The kitchen, an open area behind the tent's back, yielded barrels packed with snow in which reposed the most delicate fish—shrimps, sea urchins, oysters, dug-mullets. More snow-packed barrels contained various kinds of little birds, lambs' livers and kidneys, herbified sausages. The bread was rising, the sauces all lined up in pots ready to heat.

"Hmmm," said Caesar, "this is where we feast tonight! And for once, Antonius, you'll be able to eat and drink to your heart's content. Though," he ended with a chuckle, "it's back to the same old stuff tomorrow night. I will not live like Sampsiceramus when I'm on campaign. I daresay Crus got the snow from Mount Olympus."

Accompanied only by Calvinus, he sat down in Pompey's command tent to investigate the chests of papers and documents found there.

"One has to trot out that old saw and proclaim to the world that one has burned the enemy's papers—Pompeius did that once, in Osca after Sertorius died—but it's a foolish man who doesn't have a good look first."

"Will you burn them?" Calvinus asked, smiling.

"Oh, definitely! In great public state, as Pompeius did. But I read at a glance, Calvinus. We'll establish a system. I'll con everything first, and anything I think might be worth reading at leisure I'll hand to you."

Among many dozens of fascinating pieces of paper was the last will and testament of King Ptolemy Auletes, late of Egypt.

"Well, well!" said Caesar thoughtfully. "I think this is one document I won't sacrifice to the fire. It might come in quite handy in the future."

Everyone rose rather late the following morning, Caesar included; he had stayed up until nearly dawn reading those chests and chests of papers. Very informative indeed.

While the legions completed the burning of bodies and other inevitable duties consequent upon victory, Caesar and his legates rode out along the road to Larissa. Where they encountered the bulk of Pompey's Roman troops. Twenty-three thousand men cried for pardon, which Caesar was pleased to grant. He then offered places in his own legions for any men who wanted to volunteer.

"Why, Caesar?" asked Publius Sulla, astonished. "We've won the war here at Pharsalus!"

The pale, unsettling eyes rested on Sulla's nephew with cool irony. "Rubbish, Publius!" he said. "The war's not over. Pompeius is still at large. So too are Labienus, Cato, all Pompeius's fleet commanders—and fleets!—and at least a dozen other dangerous men. This war won't be over until they've all submitted to me."

"Submitted to *you*?" Publius Sulla frowned, then relaxed. "Oh! You mean submitted to Rome."

"I," said Caesar, "am Rome, Publius. Pharsalus has proved it."

For Brutus, Pharsalus was a nightmare. Wondering whether Pompey had understood his torment, he had been enormously grateful for the fact that Pompey had deputed him to Lentulus Spinther on the right flank at the river. But Antony and the Eighth and Ninth had faced them, and though the Ninth in particular had been replenished with the more inexperienced men of the Fourteenth, no one could say afterward that they hadn't punished the enemy. Given a horse and told to look after the outermost cohorts, Brutus sat the animal in serviceable steel armor and eyed the ivory eagle hilt of his sword like a small animal fascinated by a snake.

He never did draw it. Suddenly chaos broke loose, the world was filled with his own men screaming "Hercules Invictus!" and the men of the Ninth screaming some unintelligible warcry; he discovered, appalled, that hand-to-hand combat in a legion's front line was not a precious pairing-off of one man against another, but a massive push, push, push of mail-clad bodies while other mail-clad bodies pushed, pushed, pushed in the opposite direction. Swords stabbed and flickered, shields were used like rams and levers—how did they ever remember who was who, friend or enemy? Did they really have time to look at the color of a helmet crest? Transfixed, Brutus simply sat his horse and watched.

The news of the collapse of Pompey's left and his cavalry traveled down the line in some way he didn't understand, except that men ceased to cry "Hercules Invictus!" and started crying quarter instead. Caesar's Ninth wore blue horsehair plumes. When the yellow plumes of his own cohorts seemed suddenly to vanish before a sea of blue ones, Brutus kicked his restive mount in the ribs and bolted for the river.

All day and into the night he hid in the swampy overflow of the Enipeus, never for a moment letting go of his horse's reins. Finally, when the cheers, shouts and laughter of Caesar's feasting and victorious troops began to die away with the embers of their fires, he pulled himself upon the horse's back and rode off toward Larissa.

There, given civilian Greek clothing by a sympathetic man of Larissa who also offered him shelter, Brutus sat down at once and wrote to Caesar.

> Caesar, this is Marcus Junius Brutus, once your friend. Please, I beg you, pardon me for my presumption in deciding to ally myself with Gnaeus Pompeius Magnus and the Senate in exile. For many months I have regretted my action in leaving Tarsus and Publius

Sestius and my legateship there. I deserted my post like a silly boy in quest of adventure. But this kind of adventure has not proven to my taste. I am, I discover, unmartial to the point of ridiculousness and quite without the will to wage war.

I have heard it broadcast through the town that you are offering pardon to all Pompeians of all ranks provided they have not been pardoned before. I also heard that you are willing to pardon any man a second time if one of your own men intercedes for him. That is not necessary in my case. I cry for pardon as a first offender. Will you extend it to me, if not for my own unworthy sake, for the sake of my mother and your dear dead daughter, Julia?

It was in answer to this letter that Caesar rode down the road to Larissa with his legates.

"Find me Marcus Junius Brutus," he said to the town ethnarch, who presented himself at once to plead for his people. "Bring him to me and Larissa will suffer no consequences."

The Brutus who came, still in Greek dress, was abject, thin, hangdog, unable to lift his face to the man on the horse.

"Brutus, Brutus, what is this?" he heard the familiar deep voice say, then felt two hands on his shoulders. Someone took him into strong, steely arms; Brutus felt the touch of a pair of lips. He finally looked up. Caesar. Who else had eyes like that? Who else combined enough power and beauty to devastate his mother?

"My dear Brutus, I am so delighted to see you!" said Caesar, one arm around his shoulders, walking away from his legates, still mounted and watching sardonically.

"Am I pardoned?" whispered Brutus, who thought the weight and heat of that arm was about equal to his mother's, and terribly reminiscent of her. Lead to burden him down, kill him.

"I wouldn't presume to think you needed to be pardoned, my boy!" said Caesar. "Where's your stuff? Have you a horse? You're coming with me this moment, I need you desperately. As usual, I have no one with the kind of mind capable of dealing with facts, figures, minutiae. And I can promise you," that warm and friendly voice went on, "that in years to come you will do better by far under my aegis than ever you could have under Pompeius's."

"What do you intend to do about the fugitives, Caesar?" asked Antony that afternoon, back at Pharsalus.

"Follow Pompeius's tracks, first and foremost. Is there any word? Has he been seen since he left Larissa?"

"There are stories of a ship in Dium," said Calenus, "and of Amphipolis."

Caesar blinked. "Amphipolis? Then he's heading east, not west or south. What of Labienus, Faustus Sulla, Metellus Scipio, Afranius, Petreius?"

"The only one we can be sure of, Caesar—aside from dear little Marcus Brutus—is Ahenobarbus."

"That is true, Antonius. The only one of the great men to die on the field of Pharsalus. And the second one of my enemies to go. Though I confess I won't miss him the way I will Bibulus. Are his ashes taken care of?"

"On their way to his wife already," said Pollio, who found himself entrusted with all kinds of tasks.

"Good."

"We march tomorrow?" asked Calvinus.

"That we do."

"There might be a large number of refugees heading in the direction of Brundisium," said Publius Sulla.

"For which reason I've already sent to Publius Vatinius in Salona. Quintus Cornificius can maintain Illyricum for the moment. Vatinius can go to command Brundisium and turn the refugees away." Caesar grinned at Antony. "And you may rest easy, Antonius. I've heard that Gnaeus Pompeius the son has released your brother from detention on Corcyra. Safe and well."

"I'll offer to Jupiter for that!"

In the morning, Pharsalus returned to a sleepy, swampy river valley amid the Thessalian hills; Caesar's army dispersed. With him on the road to Asia Province, Caesar took two legions only, both made up of volunteers from Pompey's defeated legions. His own veterans were to return to a well-deserved furlough in Italian Campania under the command of Antony. With Caesar went Brutus and Gnaeus Domitius Calvinus, whom Caesar found himself liking more and more. A good man in a hard situation, that was Calvinus.

The march to Amphipolis was done in Caesar's usual swift manner; if Pompey's old legionaries found the pace a little more hectic than they were used to, they didn't complain. The truth was that Caesar ran a *good* army; a man always knew where he stood.

Eighty miles east of Thessalonica on the Via Egnatia and located where the widened river Strymon flowed out of Lake Cercinitis on its short course to the sea, Amphipolis was a shipbuilding and timber town. The trees grew far inland and were sent down the Strymon as logs to be dismembered and reconstructed in Amphipolis.

Here Marcus Favonius waited alone for the pursuit he knew would come.

"I cry pardon, Caesar," he said when they met, another one whom defeat at Pharsalus had changed out of all recognition. His strident manner and his aping of Cato were gone.

"I grant it with great good will, Favonius. Brutus is with me, and very anxious to see you."

"Ah, you pardoned him too."

"Of course. It's no part of my policy to punish decent men for mistaken ideals. What I hope is to see us all together in Rome one day, working together for Rome's well-being. What do you want to do? I'll give you a letter for Vatinius in Brundisium saying whatever you wish."

"I wish," said Favonius, tears on his lashes, "that none of this had ever happened."

"So do I," said Caesar sincerely.

"Yes, I can understand that." He drew a breath. "For myself, I want only to retire to my estates in Lucania and live a quiet life. No war, no politics, no strife, no dissent. Peace, Caesar. That's all I want. Peace."

"Do you know where the others have gone?"

"Mitylene was their next port of call, but I doubt they have any intention of staying there. The Lentuli say they'll remain with Pompeius, at least for the time being. Just before he left, Pompeius had messages from some of the others. Labienus, Afranius, Petreius, Metellus Scipio, Faustus Sulla and some others have headed for Africa. I know nothing else."

"And Cato? Cicero?"

"Who knows? But I think Cato will head for Africa once he finds out so many others are going there. After all, there is a pro-Pompeian government in Africa Province. I doubt it will submit to you without a fight, Caesar."

"I doubt that too. Thank you, Marcus Favonius."

That evening there was a quiet dinner alone with Brutus, but at dawn Caesar was on his way toward the Hellespont, Calvinus by his side and Brutus, to whom Caesar was most tender, ensconced in a comfortable gig with a servant to minister to him.

Favonius rode out to watch, he hoped for the last time, the silvery column of Roman legions stride off down a Roman-made road, straight where it could be straight, easily graded, unexhausting. But in the end all Favonius saw was Caesar, riding a mettlesome brown stallion with the ease and grace of a much younger man. He would, Favonius knew, be scarcely out of sight of the Amphipolan walls before he was down and marching on his feet. Horses were for battles, parades and spectacles. How could a man so sure of his own majesty be so down to earth? A most curious mixture, Gaius Julius Caesar. The sparse gold hair fluttered like ribbons in the keen wind off the Aegaean Sea, the spine was absolutely straight, the legs hanging down unsupported as powerful and sinewy as ever. One of the handsomest men in Rome, yet never pretty like Memmius or effete like Silius. Descended from Venus and Romulus. Well, who knew? Maybe the Gods did love their own best. Oh, Cato, don't go on resisting him! No one can. He will be King of Rome—but only if he wants to be.

Mitylene was panic stricken too. Panic was spreading all over the East at the result of this clash between two Roman titans, so unexpected, so horrifying. For no one knew this Caesar save at second or third or fourth hand; all his governorships had been in the West, and those far-off days when he had been in the East were obscure. Mitylene knew that when Lucullus besieged it in Sulla's name, this Gaius Caesar had fought in the front lines and won a *corona civica* for valor. Hardly anyone knew of the battle he had generaled against the forces of Mithridates outside Tralles in Asia Province, though Tralles knew that it had erected a statue of him in a little temple to Victory near the site of the battle, and flocked now to tidy the temple up, make sure the statue was in good repair. To find, awestruck, that a palm seed had germinated between the flags at the base of Caesar's statue, the sign of a great victory. And the sign of a great man. Tralles talked.

Rome had dominated the world of Our Sea for so long now that any convulsion within the ranks of the Roman powerful sent cracks racing through every land around it like the cracks which spread after an earthquake. What was going to happen? What would the new structure of the world be like? Was Caesar a reasonable man of Sulla's kind, would he institute measures to relieve the squeezing of governors and tax farmers? Or would he be another Pompeius Magnus, encourage the depredations of governors and tax farmers? In Asia Province, utterly exhausted by Metellus Scipio, Lentulus Crus and one of Pompey's minor legates, Titus Ampius Balbus, every island, city and district scrambled to tear down its statues of Pompey the Great and erect statues to Gaius Caesar; traffic was very heavy to the temple of Victory outside Tralles, where an authentic likeness of the new First Man in Rome existed. In Ephesus some of the coastal cities of Asia Province clubbed together to commission a copy of Caesar's Tralles statue from the famous studios at Aphrodisias. It stood in the center of the agora and said on its plinth: GAIUS JULIUS CAESAR, SON OF GAIUS, PONTIFEX MAXIMUS, IMPERATOR, CONSUL FOR THE SECOND TIME, DESCENDED FROM ARES AND APHRODITE, GOD MADE MANIFEST AND COMMON SAVIOR OF MANKIND. Heady stuff, particularly because it chose to put Caesar's descent from Mars and his son, Romulus, ahead of his descent from Venus and her son, Aeneas. Asia Province was very busy doing its homework.

It was into this atmosphere of mingled panic and sycophantic adulation that Pompey stepped when he disembarked with the two Lentuli in Mitylene harbor on the big island of Lesbos. All of Lesbos had declared for him long since, but to receive him, a beaten man, was difficult and delicate. His arrival indicated that he was not yet forced from the arena, that perhaps in time to come there would be another Pharsalus. Only—

could he *win*? The word was that Caesar had never lost a battle (the "great victory" in Dyrrachium was now being called hollow), that no one could defeat him.

Pompey handled the situation well, maintaining his Greek dress and informing the ethnarchs in council that Caesar was most famous for his clemency.

"Be nice to him" was his advice. "He rules the world."

Cornelia Metella and young Sextus were waiting for him. A curious reunion, dominated by Sextus, who threw his arms about his adored father and wept bitterly.

"Don't cry," said Pompey, stroking the brown, rather straight hair; Sextus was the only one of his three children to inherit Mucia Tertia's darker coloring.

"I should have been there as your cadet!"

"And you would have been, had events marched slower. But you did a better job, Sextus. You looked after Cornelia for me."

"Women's work!"

"No, men's work. The family is the nucleus of all Roman thought, Sextus, and the wife of Pompeius Magnus is a very important person. So too his sons."

"I won't leave you again!"

"I hope not. We must offer to the Lares and Penates and Vesta that one day we are *all* reunited." Pompey eased Sextus out of his arms, gave him his handkerchief to blow his nose and dry his eyes. "Now you can do me a good turn. Start a letter to your brother, Gnaeus. I'll be with you soon to finish it."

Only after Sextus, sniffling and clutching the handkerchief, had gone off to do his father's bidding did Pompey have the opportunity to look at Cornelia Metella properly.

She hadn't changed. Still supercilious looking, haughty, a trifle remote. But the grey eyes were red-rimmed, swollen, and gazed at him with genuine grief. He walked forward to kiss her hand.

"A sad day," he said.

"Tata?"

"Gone in the direction of Africa, I think. In time we'll find out. He wasn't hurt at Pharsalus." How hard to say that word! "Cornelia," he said, playing with her fingers, "you have my full permission to divorce me. If you do, your property will remain yours. At least I was clever enough to put the villa in the Alban Hills in your name. I didn't lose that when I had to sell so much to fund this war. Nor the villa on the Campus Martius. Nor the house on the Carinae. Those are mine, you and my sons may lose them to Caesar."

"I thought he wasn't going to proscribe."

"He won't proscribe. But the property of the leaders in this war will be confiscate, Cornelia. That's custom and tradition. He won't stand in the way of it. Therefore I think it's safer and more sensible for you to divorce me."

She shook her head, gave one of her rare and rather awkward smiles. "No, Magnus. I am your wife. I will remain your wife."

"Then go home, at least." He released her hand, waved his own about aimlessly. "I don't know what will become of me! I don't know what's the best thing to do. I don't know where to go from here, but I can't stay here either. Life with me won't be very comfortable, Cornelia. I'm a marked man. Caesar knows he has to apprehend me. While I'm at liberty I represent a nucleus for the gathering of another war."

"Like Sextus, I won't leave you again. But surely the place to go is Africa. We should sail for Utica at once, Magnus."

"Should we?" The vivid blue eyes were emerging once more from his puffy face, shrinking, like his body, from the anguish, the pain, the blow to his pride he still found impossible to govern. "Cornelia, it has been terrible. I don't mean Caesar or the war, I mean my associates in this venture. Oh, not your father! He's been a tower of strength. But he wasn't there for most of it. The bickering, the carping, the constant fault-finding."

"They found fault with *you*?"

"Perpetually. It wore me down. Perhaps I could have coped better with Caesar if I'd had control of my own command tent. But I didn't. Labienus generaled, Cornelia, not me. That man! How did Caesar ever put up with him? He's a barbarian. I do believe that he can only achieve physical satisfaction from putting men's eyes out—oh, worse acts I can't speak of to you! And though Ahenobarbus died very gallantly on the field, he tormented me at every opportunity. He called me Agamemnon, King of Kings."

The shocks and dislocations of the past two months had done much for Cornelia Metella; the spoiled amateur scholar had gained a measure of compassion, some much-needed sensitivity to the feelings of others. So she didn't make the mistake of interpreting Pompey's words as evidence of self-pity. He was like a noble old rock, worn away by the constant dripping of corrosive water.

"Dear Magnus, I think the trouble was that they deemed war as another kind of Senate. They didn't begin to understand that politics has nothing to do with military matters. They passed the Senatus Consultum Ultimum to make sure Caesar wouldn't be able to order them about. How then could they let you order them about?"

He smiled wryly. "That is very true. It should also tell you why I shrink from going to Africa. Your *tata* will go, yes. But so will Labienus and Cato. What would be different in Africa? I wouldn't own my command tent there either."

"Then we should seek shelter with the King of the Parthians, Magnus," she said decisively. "You sent your cousin Hirrus to see Orodes.

He hasn't come back, though he's safe. Ecbatana is one place won't see either Caesar or Labienus."

"But what would it be like to look up at seven captured Roman Eagles? I'd be living with the shade of Crassus."

"Where else is there?"

"Egypt."

"It's not far enough away."

"No, but it's a place to jump off from. Can you imagine how much the people of the Indus or Serica might pay to gain a Roman general? I could win that world for my employer. The Egyptians know how to get to Taprobane. In Taprobane there will be someone who knows how to get to Serica or the Indus."

She smiled broadly, a nice sight. "Magnus, that's brilliant! Yes, let's you and I and Sextus go to Serica!"

He didn't stay long in Mitylene, but when he heard that the great philosopher Cratippus was there, he went to seek an audience.

"I am honored, Pompeius," said the old man in the pure white robe with the pure white beard flowing down its front.

"No, the honor is mine." Pompey made no attempt to sit down, stood looking into the rheumy eyes and wondering why they showed no sign of wisdom. Didn't philosophers always look wise?

"Let us walk," said Cratippus, putting his arm through Pompey's. "The garden is so beautiful. Done in the Roman style, of course. We Greeks have not the gift of gardening. I have always thought that the Roman appreciation of Nature's beauty is an indication of the innate worth of the Roman people. We Greeks deflected our love of beauty into man-made things, whereas you Romans have the genius to insert your man-made things into Nature as if they belonged there. Bridges, aqueducts . . . So perfect! We never understood the beauty of the arch. Nature," Cratippus rambled on, "is never linear, Gnaeus Pompeius. Nature is round, like the globe."

"I have never grasped the roundness of the globe."

"Didn't Eratosthenes prove it when he measured the shadow on the same plane in Upper and Lower Egypt? Flatness has an edge. And if there is an edge, why don't the waters of Oceanus flow off it like a cataract? No, Gnaeus Pompeius, the world is a globe, closed on itself like a fist. The tips of its fingers kiss the back of its palm. And that, you know, is a kind of infinity."

"I wondered," said Pompey, searching for words, "if you could tell me anything about the Gods."

"I can tell you much, but what did you want to know?"

"Well, something about their form. What godhead is."

"I think you Romans are closer to that answer than we Greeks. We set up our Gods as facsimiles of men and women, with all the failings, desires, appetites and evils thereof. Whereas the Roman Gods—the true Roman Gods—have no faces, no sex, no form. You say *numina.* Inside the air, a part of the air. A kind of infinity."

"But how do they exist, Cratippus?"

The watery eyes, Pompey saw, were very dark but had a pale ring around the outside of each iris. *Arcus senilis,* the sign of coming death. He was not long for this world. This globe.

"They exist as themselves."

"No, what are they *like*?"

"Themselves. We can have no comprehension of what that might be because we do not know them. We Greeks gave them human personae because we could grasp at nothing else. But in order to make them Gods, we gave them superhuman powers. I believe," said Cratippus gently, "that all the Gods are actually a part of one great God. Again, you Romans come closer to that truth. You know that all your Gods are a part of your great God, Jupiter Optimus Maximus."

"And does this great God live in the air?"

"I think *it* lives everywhere. Above, below, inside, outside, around, about. I think we are a part of *it*."

Pompey wet his lips, came at last to what preyed on his mind. "Do we live on after we die?"

"Ah! The eternal question. A kind of infinity."

"By definition, the Gods or a great God are immortal. We die. But do we continue to live?"

"Immortality is not the same as infinity. There are many different kinds of immortality. The long life of God—but is it infinitely long? I do not think so. I think God is born and reborn in immeasurably long cycles. Whereas infinity is unchanging. It had no beginning, it will have no end. As for us—I do not know. Beyond any doubt, Gnaeus Pompius, *you* will be immortal. Your name and your deeds will live on for millennia after you are vanished. That is a sweet thought. And is it not to own godhead?"

Pompey went away no more enlightened. Well, wasn't that what they always said? Try to pin a Greek down and you ended with nothing. A kind of infinity.

He set sail from Mitylene with Cornelia Metella, Sextus and the two Lentuli and island-hopped down the eastern Aegaean Sea, staying nowhere longer than an overnight sleep, encountering no one he knew until he rounded the corner of Lycia and docked in the big Pamphylian city of Attaleia. There he found no less than sixty members of the Senate in exile. None terribly distinguished, all terribly bewildered. Attaleia announced its undying loyalty and gave Pompey twelve neat and seaworthy triremes together with a letter from his son Gnaeus, still on the island of Corcyra. How *did* word get around so quickly?

Father, I have sent this same letter to many places. Please, I beg of you, don't give up! I have heard of your frightful ordeals in the command tent from Cicero, who was here but has now gone. That Labienus! Cicero told me.

He arrived with Cato and a thousand recovered wounded troops. Then Cato announced that he would take the soldiers on to Africa, but that it was inappropriate for a mere praetor to command when a consular—he meant Cicero—was available for command. His aim was to put himself and the men under Cicero's authority, but you know that old bag of wind better than I do, so you can imagine what his answer was. He wanted nothing to do with further resistance, troops or Cato. When Cato realized that Cicero was secretly bent on going back to Italia, he lost his temper and went for Cicero with feet and fists. I had to drag him off. The moment he could, Cicero fled to Patrae, taking his brother Quintus and nephew Quintus with him. They had been staying with me. I imagine the three of them are now squabbling in Patrae.

Cato took my transports—I have no need of them—and set sail for Africa. Unfortunately I had no one I could give him as a pilot, so I told him to point the bows of his ships south and let the winds and currents take him. One consolation is that Africa shuts Our Sea in on the south, so he can't help but fetch up *somewhere* in Africa.

What this tells me is that the war against Caesar is far from over. Resistance will crystallize in Africa Province as the refugees all head there. We are still alive and kicking, and we still own the seas. Please, I beg you, my beloved father, gather what ships you can and come either to me or to Africa.

Pompey's answer was brief.

My dearest son, forget me. I can do nothing to help the Republican cause. My day is over. Nor, candidly, can I face the thought of the command tent with Cato and Labienus breathing down my neck. My race is run. What you do is your choice. But beware Cato and Labienus. The one is a rigid ideologue, the other a savage.

Cornelia, Sextus and I are going far, far away. I will not say where in case this letter is intercepted. The two Lentuli, who have accompanied me until now, will leave me before I reveal my destination. I hope to elude them here in Attaleia.

Look after yourself, my son. I love you.

Early in September came the time for departure; Pompey's ship slipped out of harbor without the knowledge of the two Lentuli or the sixty refugee senators. He had taken three of the triremes but left the other nine to be sent to Gnaeus in Corcyra.

They called in to Cilician Syedra briefly, then crossed the water to Paphos in Cyprus. The prefect of Cyprus, now under Roman rule from Cilicia, was one of the sons of Appius Claudius Pulcher Censor and very keen to do what he could to help Pompey.

"I am so sorry your father died so suddenly," said Pompey.

"And I," said Gaius Claudius Pulcher, who didn't look sorry. "Though he'd quite gone off his head, you know."

"I had heard something of it. At least he was spared things like Pharsalus." How *hard* it was to say that word "Pharsalus"!

"Yes. He and I have always been yours, but I can't say the same for the whole patrician Claudian clan."

"All the Famous Families are split, Gaius Claudius."

"You can't stay here, unfortunately. Antioch and Syria have declared for Caesar, and Sestius in the governor's palace at Tarsus has always inclined toward Caesar. He'll declare openly any day."

"How is the wind for Egypt?"

Gaius Claudius stiffened. "I wouldn't go there, Magnus."

"Why not?"

"There's civil war."

The third Inundation of Cleopatra's reign was the lowest on record in a land where records of the Inundation had been kept for two thousand years. Not merely down in the Cubits of Death: eight feet, a new bottom for the Cubits of Death.

The moment Cleopatra heard, she understood that there would be no harvest this coming year, even in the lands of Ta-she and Lake Moeris. She did what she could to stave off disaster. In February she issued a joint edict with the little King directing that every scrap of grain produced or stored in Middle Egypt was to be sent to Alexandria. Middle and Upper Egypt were to feed themselves by irrigating the narrow valley of the Nilus from the First Cataract to Thebes. As every grain of wheat and barley grown in Egypt was the property of the Double Crown, she was fully entitled to issue this edict—and to exact the punishment for any transgression by grain merchant or bureaucrat: death and confiscation of all property. Informants were offered cash rewards; slave informants were offered their freedom as well.

The response was immediate and frantic. In March the Queen thought it politic to issue a second edict. This one assured those possessed of Letters Regnant exempting them from taxation or military service that their exemptions would be honored—on the sole condition that they were engaged in agriculture. The whole kingdom outside Alexandria had to be driven to grow in the most painful way, by irrigation minus Inundation.

The letters of protest flooded in. So too did requests for seed grain

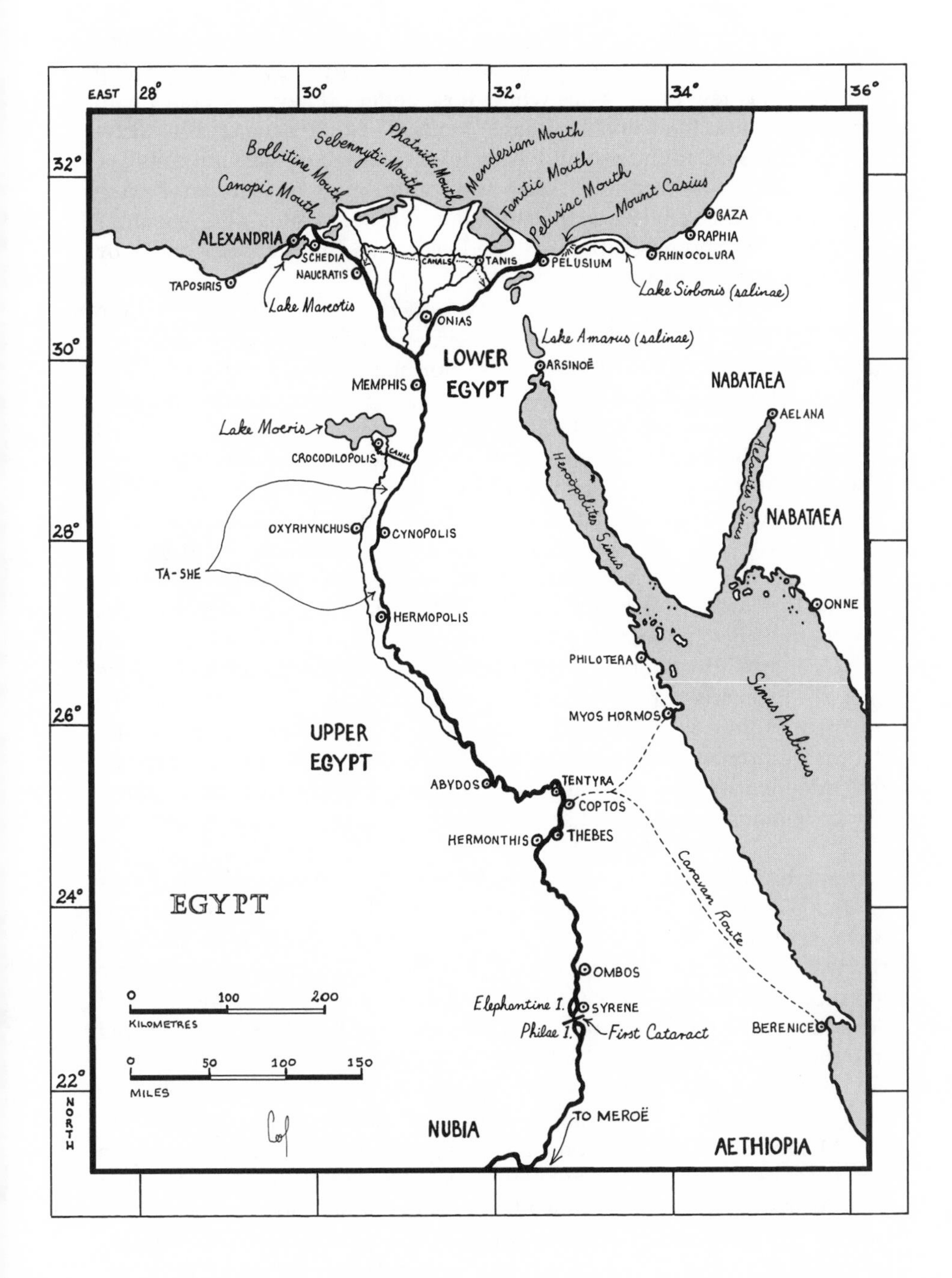
EAST
28°
30°
32°
34°
36°
32°
30°
28°
26°
24°
22°
NORTH
Canopic Mouth
Bolbitine Mouth
Sebennytic Mouth
Phatnitic Mouth
Mendesian Mouth
Tanitic Mouth
Pelusiac Mouth
Mount Casius
GAZA
RAPHIA
RHINOCOLURA
ALEXANDRIA
SCHEDIA
NAUCRATIS
CANALS
TANIS
PELUSIUM
TAPOSIRIS
Lake Sirbonis (salinae)
Lake Mareotis
ONIAS
Lake Amarus (salinae)
LOWER EGYPT
ARSINOË
MEMPHIS
NABATAEA
AELANA
Lake Moeris
CROCODILOPOLIS
CANAL
Heroöpolites Sinus
Aelanites Sinus
NABATAEA
OXYRHYNCHUS
CYNOPOLIS
TA-SHE
HERMOPOLIS
ONNE
PHILOTERA
Sinus Arabicus
MYOS HORMOS
UPPER EGYPT
ABYDOS
TENTYRA
COPTOS
HERMONTHIS
THEBES
Caravan Route
EGYPT
OMBOS
0
100
200
KILOMETRES
Elephantine I.
SYRENE
Philae I.
First Cataract
BERENICE
0
50
100
150
MILES
NUBIA
TO MEROË
AETHIOPIA

and remissions in taxes, neither of which the Double Crown was in a position to grant.

Worse than this, Alexandria was in ferment. Food prices were spiraling, the poorer people scraping money together to buy food by selling their precious few possessions while those better off began to hoard both their money and their non-perishable foods. The little King and his sister Arsinoë smirked; Potheinus and Theodotus, assisted by General Achillas, went far and wide through Alexandria commiserating with the simmering citizens and suggesting that the shortage was a ploy of Cleopatra's to reduce the more seditious-minded elements among the people by starving them out of the city.

In June the trio struck. Alexandria boiled over; a mob set out from the Agora to the Royal Enclosure. Potheinus and Theodotus unbarred the gates, and the mob, led by Achillas, stormed inside. To discover that Cleopatra had gone. Nothing daunted, Arsinoë was presented to the mob as the new Queen and the little King spoke fair promises of improved conditions. The mob went home; Potheinus, Theodotus and Achillas were content. But they faced severe difficulties. There was no extra food to be had. However, power seized had to be defended and retained; Potheinus sent a fleet to raid the granaries of Judaea and Phoenicia, secure in the knowledge that the war between Pompey the Great and Gaius Caesar was occupying so much attention elsewhere that a few Egyptian raids would go, if not unnoticed, certainly unpunished.

One difficulty loomed very large. Cleopatra had vanished. While ever she was free, she would be working indefatigably to ensure the downfall of little King Ptolemy's palace cabal. Only where had she gone? All the dethroned Ptolemies took ship and sailed away! Yet nowhere on that huge waterfront could any of the cabal's spies discover the slightest evidence that Cleopatra had sailed away.

She had not sailed away. Accompanied by Charmian, Iras and a gigantic, black-skinned eunuch named Apollodorus, Cleopatra left the Royal Enclosure clad in the clothes of a well-to-do Alexandrian lady and riding on a donkey. Passing through the Canopic Gate scant hours before the mob stormed the palace, they boarded a small barge at the town of Schedia, where the canal from Lake Mareotis behind Alexandria flowed into the Canopic arm of the Nilus Delta. The distance to Memphis, which lay on the Nilus itself just before it fanned into the Delta, was not more than eight hundred Greek *stadia*—a hundred Roman miles.

Memphis had again become the most powerful nucleus of worship in Egypt. Centered around the cult of the creator-god Ptah, under the first and middle pharaohs it had contained the treasure vaults and the most august priests. From the time of Pharaoh Senusret it sank from favor, superseded by Amon in Thebes. Religious power shifted from Memphis to Thebes. So did custody of the treasures. But with the fluctuating fortunes of Egypt after the last of the truly Egyptian pharaohs had died out, Amon too declined. Then came the Ptolemies and Alexandria. Memphis began to rise again, perhaps because it was much closer to Alexandria than was Thebes; the first Ptolemy, a brilliant man, had conceived the idea of bonding Alexandria to Egypt by having the high priest of Ptah, one Manetho, carve out a hybrid religion, part Greek, part Egyptian, under the godhead of Zeus-Osirapis-Osiris-Apis and an Artemis-Isis.

The fall of Thebes occurred when it rebelled against Ptolemaic rule during the time of the ninth Ptolemy, called Soter II in the inscriptions and Lathyrus (which meant Chickpea) by his subjects. Chickpea massed his Jewish army and his shallow-drafted war galleys and rowed down Nilus to teach Thebes a lesson. He sacked it and razed it to the ground. Amon suffered terribly.

However, the three-thousand-year-old priestly hierarchy of Egypt knew all there was to know about looting. Every pharaoh who had been laid to rest surrounded by incredible wealth was a target for tomb robbers, who went to any lengths to plunder the dead. While Egypt was strong these bandits were kept at bay; after Egypt became the prey of foreign incursions, most of the royal tombs were denuded. Only those secretly located remained unpillaged. As did the treasure vaults.

By the time Ptolemy Chickpea tore Thebes apart (looking for the treasure vaults), those vaults were back in Memphis. He was desperate for money; Chickpea's mother, the third Cleopatra, was Pharaoh, but made sure he was not. She loathed him, preferring his younger brother, Alexander, whom she finally succeeded in putting on the throne in his place. A fatal act for Egypt. After Alexander murdered her, the two brothers warred for the throne. When both were dead, Sulla the Dictator sent Alexander's son to rule Egypt. He was the last legitimate male of the line, but not capable of siring children. His will bequeathed Egypt to Rome, and Egypt had lived in fear ever since.

Cleopatra came ashore on the west bank and rode on her ass to the west pylon of an enclosure half a square mile in extent. It embraced the temple of Ptah, the house in which the Apis Bulls were embalmed, a conglomeration of buildings devoted to the priests and their varied duties, and numerous smaller temples established in honor of long-dead pharaohs. Beneath it were honeycombs of chambers, rooms, tunnels which proliferated as far as the pyramid fields several miles away. That part of the labyrinth entered from the embalming house of the Apis Bulls held the mummy of every Apis Bull which had ever lived, as well as mummified cats and ibises. That part of the labyrinth entered from a secret room within the temple of Ptah itself contained the treasure vaults.

The Ue'b came to meet her, accompanied by his reciter priest the *cherheb,* his treasurer, his officials and the *mete-en-sa,* who were the ordinary priests. Not five Roman feet tall and weighing no more than a talent and a half, Cleopatra stood there while two hundred shaven-headed men prostrated themselves, their brows pressed against the polished red granite flags.

"Goddess on Earth, Daughter of Ra, Incarnation of Isis, Queen of Queens," said the High Priest of Ptah, getting to his feet in an expertly managed, gradually lessening series of additional obeisances while his priests remained prostrated.

"Sem of Ptah, Neb-notru, *wer-kherep-hemw,* Seker-cha'bau, Ptahmose, Cha'em-uese," said Pharaoh, smiling at him lovingly. "My dearest Cha'em, how good it is to see you!"

The only item of apparel which distinguished Cha'em from his underlings was a necklace-collar. For the rest, he shaved his head and wore nothing save a thick white linen skirt which began just below his nipples and flared gently to mid-calf. The necklace-collar, the badge of office of the High Priest of Ptah since the first Pharaoh, was a wide gold plate extending from his throat to the tips of his shoulders and down to his nipples like a pectoral. Its outer border was studded with lapis lazuli, carnelian, beryl and onyx in a much thicker, twisted gold band which was fashioned into a jackal on the left side and two human feet and a lion's paw on the right side. Two zigzagging courses of heavy gold connected the lapis nipple studs with his throat. Over it he wore three carefully distributed necklaces of gold rope which ended in carnelian-studded discs; over these he wore six more necklaces of gold rope which ended in even-sided jeweled crosses, three lower, three higher.

"You're disguised," he said in Old Egyptian.

"The Alexandrians have deposed me."

"Ah!"

Cha'em led the way to his palace, a small blockish building of limestone painted with hieroglyphs and the cartouche of every High Priest of Ptah who had ever served the creator-god who made Ra, who was also Amon. Statues of the Memphis Triad of Ptah flanked the door: Ptah himself, a skullcapped straight human figure wrapped in mummy bandages to his neck; Sekhmet, his wife, lioness-headed; and the lotus god Nefertem, crowned with the sacred blue lotus and white ostrich plumes.

Inside was cool and white, yet vivid with paintings and ornaments, furnished with chairs and tables of ivory, ebony, gold. A woman came into the room at the sound of voices; she was very Egyptian, very beautiful in that expressionless way the caste of Egyptian priests had perfected over the millennia. She wore a black wig cut to bare the tips of her shoulders, a tubelike under-dress of opaque white linen and a flare-sleeved, open over-dress of that fabulous linen only Egypt could make—a transparent, finely pleated.

She too prostrated herself.

"Tach'a," said Cleopatra, embracing her. "My mother."

"I was for three years, that's true," said the wife of Cha'em. "Are you hungry?"

"Have you enough?"

"We manage, Daughter of Ra, even in these hard times. My garden has a good canal to Nilus; my servants grow for us."

"Can you feed my people? There are only three, but poor Apollodorus eats a lot."

"We will manage. Sit, sit!"

Over a simple meal of flattish bread, some small fish fried whole and a platter of dates, all washed down with barley beer, Cleopatra told her story.

"What do you intend to do?" asked Cha'em, dark eyes hooded.

"Command you to give me enough money to buy myself an army in Judaea and Nabataea. Phoenicia too. Potheinus was talking of raiding their granaries, so I imagine I won't find it hard to enlist good troops. When Metellus Scipio quit Syria last year he left no one of ability behind—Syria has been left to its own devices. Provided I avoid the coast, I should have no difficulties."

Tach'a cleared her throat. "Husband, you have something else to discuss with Pharaoh," she said in the tone all wives develop.

"Patience, woman, patience! Let us finish with this first. How can we deal with Alexandria?" Cha'em asked. "I understand why it was built in the first place and I admit it is good to have a port onto the Middle Sea less vulnerable and mud-plagued than old Pelusium. But Alexandria is a parasite! It takes everything from Egypt and gives Egypt nothing in return."

"I know. And didn't you train me for that when I lived here? If my throne were secure I'd be remedying that. But I have to make my throne secure. You know that Egypt cannot secede from Macedonian Alexandria, Cha'em. The damage is done. Were I as Pharaoh to leave it and govern real Egypt from Memphis, Alexandria would simply import massive armies and move to crush us. Egypt is Nilus. There is nowhere to flee beyond the river. It would be so easy, didn't Chickpea demonstrate that? The winds blow the war galleys from the Delta all the way south to the First Cataract, and the Nilus current speeds them back. True Egypt would become a slave to Macedonians, hybrids and Romans. For it's Roman armies would come."

"Which leads me, Goddess on Earth, to a most delicate topic."

The yellow-green eyes narrowed; Cleopatra frowned. "The Cubits of Death," she said.

"Twice in a row. This last one only eight feet—unheard of! The people of Nilus are murmuring."

"About the famine? Naturally."

"No, about Pharaoh."

"Explain."

Tach'a did not remove herself. A priestess-musician of the temple and the wife of the Ue'b, she was privileged.

"Daughter of Ra, it is being said that Nilus will remain in the Cubits of Death until female Pharaoh is quickened and brings forth a male child. It is the duty of female Pharaoh to be fecund, to placate Crocodile and Hippopotamus, to prevent Crocodile and Hippopotamus from sucking the Inundation down their nostrils."

"I am as aware of that as you are, Cha'em!" said Cleopatra tartly. "Why do you bother telling me things you drummed into me when I was a girl? I worry about it night and day! But what can I do about it? My brother-husband is a boy and he prefers his full sister to me. My blood is polluted by the Mithridatidae, I have not enough Ptolemy in me."

"You must find another husband, Goddess on Earth."

"There is no one. No one! Believe me, Cha'em, I'd murder that little viper in a moment if I could! And his younger brother! And Arsinoë! We're famous for murdering each other! But the line of the Ptolemies has shrunk to the four of us, two girls, two boys. There are no other males to whom I might give my maidenhead, and I will not couple in Egypt's name with any but a God!" She ground her teeth, an unpleasant sound. "My sister Berenice tried! But the Roman Aulus Gabinius foiled her, preferred to reinstate my father. Berenice died at Father's hand. And if I'm not careful, I'll die."

A thin ray of light came through an aperture in the wall, dust motes dancing in it. Cha'em spread his long, thin brown hands out, fingers splayed, to make a shadow on the tiled floor. He put one hand over the other and made a rayed sun. Then he removed one hand and made the other into the shape of the *uraeus,* the sacred serpent. "The omens have been strange and insistent," he said dreamily. "Again and again they speak of a God coming out of the West . . . a God coming out of the West. A fit husband for Pharaoh."

Pharaoh tensed, shook. "The West?" she asked in tones of wonder. "The Realm of the Dead? You mean he is Osiris returned from the Realm of the Dead to quicken Isis?"

"And make a male child," said Tach'a. "Horus. Haroeris."

"But how can that be?" the woman, not Pharaoh, asked.

"It will come to pass," said Cha'em. He rose to his feet the long way, by first prostrating himself. "In the meantime, O Queen of Queens, we must see to the purchase of a good army."

For two months Cleopatra traveled greater Syria, enlisting mercenaries. All the kingdoms of old Syria had made a profitable industry out of producing mercenaries who were universally deemed the world's best hired troops. Idumaeans, Nabataeans. But the best mercenaries of all were Jewish. Cleopatra hied herself to Jerusalem. There at last she met the famous Antipater—and liked him. With him was his second son, Herod;

of that arrogant, ugly young man she wasn't so sure. Save that the pair of them were extremely intelligent and extremely rapacious. Her gold, they inferred, could buy their services as well as soldiers.

"You see," said Antipater, intrigued by the fact that this wispy scion of a degenerate house spoke impeccable Aramaic, "I am having grave doubts about Pompeius Magnus's chances of defeating the mysterious man out of the West, Gaius Julius Caesar."

"Man out of the West?" asked Cleopatra idly, biting into a delicious pomegranate.

"Yes, that's what Herod and I call him. His conquests have been in the West. Now we shall see how he fares in the East."

"Gaius Julius Caesar . . . I know little about him except that he sold my father Friend and Ally status and confirmed his tenure of the throne. For a price. Tell me who this Caesar is."

"Who is Caesar?" Antipater leaned aside to wash his hands in a golden basin. "In any other place than Rome he'd be a king, great Queen. His family is ancient and august. He is, they say, descended from Aphrodite and Ares through Aeneas and Romulus."

The large and beautiful eyes, leonine, looked startled; down came long lashes to veil them. "Then he is a god."

"Not to anyone Judaic like us, but yes, he might claim a degree of godhead, I suppose," said Herod lazily, browsing through a bowl of nuts with pudgy, hennaed fingers.

How conceited these peoples of the minor Syrian kingdoms are! thought Cleopatra. They act as if the world's navel were here in Jerusalem or Petra or Tyre. But it isn't. The navel of the world is in Rome. I wish it were in Memphis! Or even Alexandria.

Her army of twenty thousand men plumped out by volunteers from the Land of Onias, the Queen of Alexandria and Egypt marched down the shore road from Raphia between the great salt marsh of Lake Sirbonis and the sea, then dug herself in on the Syrian flank of Mount Casius, a sandhill just ten miles from Pelusium. Here was the proper place to decide who would sit on the Egyptian throne. She had pure water and a viable supply line into Syria, where Antipater and son Herod were buying in foodstuffs and taking a nice big commission she didn't grudge them in the least.

Achillas and the army of Egypt moved to contain her; midway through September he arrived on the Pelusiac side of Mount Casius and dug himself in. A careful soldier, Achillas wanted to wear Cleopatra down before he struck. At midsummer, when the heat was fierce and her mercenaries would think of cool homes versus the sweat of battle. That was the time to crush her.

Midsummer! The next Inundation! Cleopatra prowled her mud-brick house and itched to get the business over and done with. The world was falling apart! *The man out of the West had defeated Gnaeus Pompeius Magnus at Pharsalus!* But how, sitting here at Mount Casius, was she ever going to persuade him to visit Egypt? To do that she would need to occupy her throne securely and issue an invitation to pay a State visit. The Romans loved touring Egypt, demanded to see the crocodiles and at least one hippopotamus, wanted to be dazzled by gold and jewels, devastated by mighty temples. The tears coursing down her pinched face, Cleopatra reconciled herself to a third Inundation in the Cubits of Death. The omens were always right when Cha'em selected for purity. Gaius Julius Caesar, the God out of the West, would surely come. But not before midsummer.

Pompey arrived in the roads off Pelusium in the morning two days before his fifty-eighth birthday to find that old, neglected harbor choked with Egyptian war galleys and troop transports. No hope of easing inshore, even to anchor off some muddy beach. He and Sextus leaned on the ship's rail and stared at the pandemonium in fascination.

"There *must* be a civil war," said Sextus.

"Well, it's certainly not for my benefit," said his father with a grin. "We'd better send someone to scout for us, then we'll decide what to do."

"Sail on to Alexandria, you mean?"

"We might, but my three captains tell me we're low on food as well as water, so we'll have to stay here long enough to victual."

"I'll go," Sextus offered.

"No, I'll send Philip."

Sextus looked offended; his father punched him lightly on the shoulder.

"Serves you right, Sextus, you should have done your Greek homework years ago. I'm sending Philip because he's a Syrian Greek, he'll be able to communicate. If it isn't Attic, you're stuck."

Gnaeus Pompeius Philip, one of Pompey's own freedmen, came to receive his instructions. A big, fair man, he listened intently, nodded without questioning, and climbed over the trireme's side into its dinghy.

"There's a battle in the offing, Gnaeus Pompeius," he said when he returned two hours later. "Half of Egypt is somewhere in this vicinity. The Queen's army is camped on the far side of Mount Casius, the King's army is camped on this side. Talk in Pelusium is that they'll come to grips within days."

"How does Pelusium know when they'll fight?" asked Pompey.

"The little King has arrived here—a very rare event. He's too young to be war leader—someone called Achillas is that—but apparently the battle won't be official if he's not present."

Pompey sat down and wrote a letter to King Ptolemy asking for an audience immediately.

The rest of the day went by without an answer, which gave Pompey fresh things to consider. Two years ago that letter would have acted like a prod up the *podex* from a spear were it addressed to the rulers of Mount Olympus. Now a child king felt himself at liberty to answer it in his own good time.

"I wonder how long it would have taken for Caesar to get a reply?" Pompey asked Cornelia Metella, a little bitterly.

She patted his hand. "Magnus, it's not worth fretting about. These are strange people; their customs must be strange too. Besides, no one here might know about Pharsalus yet."

"That I don't believe, Cornelia. I think by now even the King of the Parthians knows about Pharsalus."

"Come to bed and sleep. The answer will arrive tomorrow."

Delivered by Philip to the merest clerk, Pompey's letter took some hours to ascend the ladder of the paper-pushing hierarchy; Egypt, so the saying went, could give lessons in bureaucracy to the Greeks of Asia. Shortly before sunset it reached the secretary to the secretary of Potheinus, the Lord High Chamberlain. He examined its seal curiously, then stiffened. A lion's head and the letters CN POMP MAG around its mane? "Serapis! *Serapis!*" He fled to Potheinus's secretary, who fled to Potheinus.

"Lord High Chamberlain!" the man gasped, holding out the little scroll. "A letter from Gnaeus Pompeius Magnus!"

Clad in a gauzy purple linen reclining robe because he had done with business for the day, Potheinus uncoiled from his couch in a single movement, snatched the scroll and stared at its seal incredulously. It was! It had to be!

"Send for Theodotus and Achillas," he said curtly, sat down at his desk and snapped the bright red wax. Hands trembling, he unfurled the single sheet of Fannian paper and began to try to decipher its sprawling, spidery Greek.

By the time Theodotus and Achillas came, he had finished and was sitting staring out the window, which faced west and the harbor of Pelusium, still aswarm with activity. He was looking at three trim triremes at anchor in the sea lanes.

"What is it?" asked Achillas, a hybrid Macedonian-Egyptian with the size of his Macedonian forebears and the darkness of his Egyptian ones. A lithe man in his middle thirties and a professional soldier all his life, he was well aware that he had to defeat the Queen sooner or later; if he did not, he faced exile and ruin.

"See those three ships?" asked Potheinus, pointing.

"Built in Pamphylia, from the look of the prows."

"Do you know who's on board one of them?"

"No idea at all."

"Gnaeus Pompeius Magnus."

Theodotus squawked, sat down on a chair limply.

Achillas flexed the muscles in his bare forearms, put his hands against the chest of his hard leather cuirass. "Serapis!"

"Indeed," said the Lord High Chamberlain.

"What does he want?"

"An audience with the King and safe passage to Alexandria."

"We should have the King here," said Theodotus, stumbling to his feet. "I'll get him."

Neither Potheinus nor Achillas protested; whatever was going to be done would be done in the name of the King, who was entitled to listen to his advisers in council. He wouldn't have a say, of course. But he was entitled to listen.

The thirteenth Ptolemy had stuffed himself with sweetmeats and was feeling rather sick; when he was informed who was on board one of those three triremes, his queasiness disappeared instantly, was replaced by eager interest.

"Oh! Will I get to see him, Theodotus?"

"That remains to be seen," said his tutor. "Now sit down, listen carefully, and don't interrupt . . . great King," he added as an afterthought.

Potheinus took the chair and nodded at Achillas. "Your opinion first, Achillas. What do we do with Gnaeus Pompeius?"

"Well, his letter doesn't tell us much, just asks for an audience and safe passage to Alexandria. He's got three warships, no doubt a handful of troops too. But nothing to be worried about. It's my opinion," said Achillas, "that we should grant him his audience and send him on to Alexandria. He'll be heading for his friends in Africa, I imagine."

"But in the meantime," said Theodotus, agitated, "it will become known that he sought assistance here, was received here, saw the King here. He didn't win Pharsalus—he *lost* Pharsalus! Can we afford to offend his conqueror, the mighty Gaius Caesar?"

Handsome face impassive, Potheinus paid as much attention to Theodotus as he had to Achillas. "So far," he said, "Theodotus makes a better case. What do you think, great King?"

The twelve-year-old King of Egypt frowned solemnly. "I agree with you, Potheinus."

"Good, good! Theodotus, continue."

"Consider, please! Pompeius Magnus has lost the struggle to maintain his supremacy in Rome, the most powerful nation west of the Kingdom of the Parthians. The will of the late King Ptolemy Alexander, which was given to the Roman Dictator Sulla, bequeathed Egypt to Rome. We in Alexandria subverted that will, found our present king's father to put on the throne. Marcus Crassus tried to annex Egypt. We evaded that and then bribed this same Gaius Caesar to confirm Auletes in his tenure of the throne." The thin, painted, febrile face twisted up in anxiety. "But now this Gaius Caesar is, one might say with truth, the ruler of the world. How can we afford to offend him? With one snap of his fingers he can take away what he gave—an independent Egypt. Our own destiny. Keeping possession of our treasures and our way of life. We walk the edge of a razor! We cannot afford to offend Rome in the person of Gaius Caesar."

"You're right, Theodotus," said Achillas abruptly. He put his knuckles to his mouth and bit them. "We're having our own war here—a *secret* war! We daren't draw Rome's attention to it—what if Rome should decide we're incapable of managing our own affairs? That old will still exists. It's still in Rome. I say that we send a message to Gnaeus Pompeius Magnus at dawn tomorrow and tell him to take himself off. Give him nothing."

"What do you think, great King?" asked Potheinus.

"Achillas is right!" cried the thirteenth Ptolemy, then heaved a sigh. "Oh, but I would have liked to see him!"

"Theodotus, you have more to say?"

"I do, Potheinus." The tutor got up from his chair and went around the table to stand behind the little King, his hands fondling the boy's thick, dark gold hair, sliding to the smooth young neck. "I don't think what Achillas suggests is strong enough. Naturally the mighty Caesar won't come chasing after Pompeius himself—the ruler of the world has fleets and legions for that, legates by the hundreds to depute. As we know, at the moment he is touring the Roman province of Asia like a king. Where might he be now? They say he is in his own ancestral home, Ilium, Troy of old."

The little King's eyes closed; he leaned against Theodotus and drowsed off to sleep.

"Why," asked Theodotus, carmined lips straining, "don't we send the mighty Gaius Caesar a gift in the name of the King of Egypt? Why don't we send the mighty Caesar the head of his enemy?" He fluttered his darkened lashes. "Dead men, they say, do not bite."

A silence fell.

Potheinus linked his hands on the table in front of him and stared down at them reflectively. Then he looked up, his fine grey eyes wide open, still. "Quite so, Theodotus. Dead men do not bite. We will ship the head of his enemy to Gaius Caesar."

"But how do we accomplish the deed itself?" asked Theodotus, delighted that his was the mind thought of it.

"Leave that to me," said Achillas crisply. "Potheinus, write a letter to Pompeius Magnus in the King's name, granting him an audience. I'll take it to him myself and lure him ashore."

"He mightn't want to come without a bodyguard," said Potheinus.

"He will. You see, I happen to know a man—a Roman man—whose face Pompeius will recognize. A man Pompeius trusts."

* * *

Dawn came. Pompey, Sextus and Cornelia ate stale bread with the lack of enthusiasm a monotonous diet makes inevitable, drank of water which tasted faintly brackish.

"Let us hope," said Cornelia, "that we can at least provision our ships in Pelusium."

Philip the freedman appeared, beaming. "Gnaeus Pompeius, a letter from the King of Egypt! *Beautiful* paper!"

The seal broken, the single sheet of—yes, beautiful paper indeed!—expensive papyrus spread open, Pompey mumbled his way through the short Greek text and looked up.

"Well, I'm to have my audience. A boat will pick me up in an hour's time." He looked startled. "Ye Gods, I need a shave and my *toga praetexta*! Philip, send my man to me, please."

He stood, properly robed as proconsul of the Senate and People of Rome, Cornelia Metella and Sextus one on either side of him, waiting for some gorgeous gilded barge with purple sail to swan out from the shore.

"Sextus," he said suddenly.

"Yes, Father?"

"How about finding something to do for a few moments?"

"Eh?"

"Go and piss over the other side, Sextus! Or pick your nose! Anything which might give me a little time alone with your stepmother!"

"Oh!" said Sextus, grinning. "Yes, Father. Of course, Father."

"He's a good lad," said Pompey, "just a little thick."

Three months ago Cornelia Metella would have found that whole exchange puerile; today she laughed.

"You made me a very happy man last night, Cornelia," Pompey said, moving close enough to touch her side.

"You made me a very happy woman, Magnus."

"Maybe, my love, we should take more long sea voyages together. I don't know what I would have done without you since Mitylene."

"And Sextus," she said quickly. "He's wonderful."

"More your age than I am! I'll be fifty-eight tomorrow."

"I love him dearly, but Sextus is a boy. I like elderly men. In fact, I've come to the conclusion that you're exactly the right age for me."

"Serica is going to be marvelous!"

"So I think."

They leaned together companionably until Sextus came back, frowning. "The hour's gone by and more, Father, but no royal barge do I see. Just that dinghy."

"It's coming our way," said Cornelia Metella.

"Perhaps that's it, then," said Pompey.

"For *you*?" his wife asked, tone freezing. "No, never!"

"You must remember that I'm not the First Man in Rome anymore. Just a tired old Roman proconsul."

"Not to me!" said Sextus through his teeth.

By this time the rowboat, actually somewhat larger than a dinghy, was alongside; the cuirassed man in the stern tilted his head up.

"I'm looking for Gnaeus Pompeius Magnus!" he called.

"Who wants him?" asked Sextus.

"General Achillas, commander-in-chief of the King's army."

"Come aboard!" cried Pompey, indicating the rope ladder.

Both Cornelia Metella's hands were fastened about Pompey's right forearm. He looked down at her, surprised. "What is it?"

"Magnus, I don't like it! Whatever that man wants, send him away! Please, let's up anchor and leave! I'd rather live on stale bread all the way to Utica than stay here!"

"Shhh, it's all right," said Pompey, disengaging her hands as Achillas climbed easily over the rail. He walked forward with a smile. "Welcome, General Achillas. I'm Gnaeus Pompeius Magnus."

"So I see. A face everyone recognizes. Your statues and busts are all over the world! Even in Ecbatana, so rumor has it."

"Not for much longer. They'll be tearing me down and putting Caesar up, I daresay."

"Not in Egypt, Gnaeus Pompeius. You're our little king's hero, he follows your exploits avidly. He's so excited at the prospect of meeting you that he didn't sleep last night."

"Couldn't he do better than a dinghy?" snarled Sextus.

"Ah, that's due to the chaos in the harbor," said Achillas nicely. "There are warships everywhere. One of them ran into the King's barge by accident and holed it, alas. The result? This."

"Won't get my toga wet, will I? Can't meet the King of Egypt looking bedraggled," said Pompey jovially.

"Dry as an old bone," said Achillas.

"Magnus, *please* don't!" Cornelia Metella whispered.

"I agree, Father. Don't go in this insult!" said Sextus.

"Truly," said Achillas, smiling to reveal that he had lost two of his front teeth, "circumstances have dictated the conveyance, nothing else. Why, I even brought along a familiar face to calm any fears you might have had. See the fellow in centurion's dress?"

Pompey's eyes were not the best these days, but he had learned that if he screwed one of them three-quarters shut, the other one snapped into focus. He did his trick and let out a huge Picentine whoop of joy—Gallic, Caesar would have called it. "Oh, I don't believe it!" He turned to Sextus and Cornelia Metella, face alight. "Do you know who that is down there in my ship of state? Lucius Septimius! A Fimbriani *primus pilus* from the old days in Pontus and Armenia! I decorated him several times, then he and I almost walked to the Caspian Sea. Except that we turned back because we didn't like the crawlies. Well! Lucius Septimius!"

After that it seemed a shame to crush his joy. Cornelia Metella contented herself with an admonition to be careful, while Sextus had a word with the two centurions from the First Legion who had insisted on coming along when they found Pompey in Paphos.

"Keep an eye on him," Sextus muttered.

"Come on, Philip, hurry up!" said Pompey, climbing the rail without fuss despite the purple-bordered toga.

Achillas, who had gone down the side first, ushered Pompey to the single seat in the bow. "The driest spot," he said.

"Septimius, you rogue, sit here right behind me!" said Pompey, disposing himself tidily. "Oh, what a pleasure to see you! But what are you doing in Pelusium?"

Philip and his slave servant sat amidships between two of the six oarsmen, with Pompey's two centurions behind them and Achillas in the stern.

"Retired here after Aulus Gabinius left a garrison behind in Alexandria," said Septimius, a very grizzled veteran blinded in one eye. "All went to pieces after a little scrap with the sons of Bibulus—well, you'd know about that. The rankers got sent back to Antioch and the ringleaders were executed. But yon General Achillas had a fancy to keep the centurions. So here I am, *primus pilus* in a legion full of Jews."

Pompey chatted for a while, but the trip was very slow and he worried a little about his speech; composing a flowery speech in Greek to deliver to a twelve-year-old boy had been difficult. He turned on his seat in the bow and called back to Philip.

"Pass me my speech, would you?"

Philip passed him the speech. He unrolled it, hunched his shoulders and began to go through it again.

The beach came up quite suddenly; he had become absorbed.

"Hope we run this thing up far enough not to muddy my shoes!" he laughed to Septimius, bracing himself for the jar.

The oarsmen did well, the boat coasted up the dirty, muddy beach beyond the waterline, and came to rest level.

"Up!" he said to himself, curiously happy. The night with Cornelia had been a lusty one, more lusty nights would come, and he had Serica to look forward to, a new life where an old soldier might teach exotic people Roman tricks. They said there were men out there whose heads grew out of their chests—men with two heads—men with one eye—sea serpents—oh, what mightn't he find beyond the rising sun?

You can keep the West, Caesar! I'm going East! Serica and freedom! What do the Sericans know or care about Picenum, what do they know or care about Rome? The Sericans will deem a Picentine upstart like me the equal of any Julian or Cornelian!

Something tore, crunched and broke. His body already half out of the boat, Pompey turned his head to see Lucius Septimius right behind him.

Warm liquid gushed down his legs; for a moment he thought he must have urinated, then the unmistakable smell rose to his nostrils. Blood. *His?* But there was no pain! His legs gave way, he fell full length in the dirty dry mud. *What is it? What is happening to me?* He felt rather than saw Septimius flip him over, sensed a sword looming above his chest.

I am a Roman nobleman. They must not see my face as I die, they must not see that part of me which makes me a man. I must die like a Roman nobleman! Pompey made a last, convulsive effort. One hand yanked his toga decently down over his thighs, the other pulled a fold over his face. The sword point entered his chest with skill and power. He moved no more.

Achillas had stabbed both the centurions in the back, but to kill two men at once is difficult. A fight broke out; the rear oarsmen turned to help. Still glued to their seat, Philip and the slave suddenly realized that they were going to die. They leaped to their feet, out of the boat, and were away.

"I'll go after them," said Septimius, grunting.

"Two silly Greeks?" asked Achillas. "What can they do?"

A small party of slaves waited nearby, a big earthen crock at their feet. Achillas lifted his hand; they picked up the crock—it seemed very heavy—and approached.

In the meantime Septimius had pulled the toga away from Pompey's face to reveal its contours: peaceful, unmarred. He put the tip of his bloodied sword under the neck of the tunic with the broad purple stripe on its right shoulder and ripped it down to the waist. The second blow had been true; the wound lay over the heart.

"It's a bit hard," said Septimius, "to cut a head off with the body like this. Someone find me a block of wood."

The block of wood was found. Septimius draped Pompey's neck across it, lifted his sword and chopped down. Neat and clean. The head rolled a little way; the body subsided to the mud.

"Never thought I'd be the one to kill him. Funny, that . . . A good general as generals go . . . Still, him alive is no use to me. Want the head in that jar?"

Achillas nodded, more moved than this Roman centurion. As Septimius lifted the head up by its luxuriant silver hair, Achillas found his eyes going to it. Dreaming . . . but what of?

The crock was full almost to the brim with natron, the liquid in which the embalmers soaked an eviscerated body for months as part of the mummification process. One of the slaves lifted its wooden plug; Septimius dropped the head in and stepped back quickly to avoid the sudden overflow.

Achillas nodded. The slaves picked the jar up on its rope handles and carried it ahead of their master. The oarsmen had pushed the dinghy off and were busy rowing it away; Lucius Septimius plunged his sword into the dry mud to clean it, shoved it back into its scabbard and strolled off in the wake of the others.

Hours later Philip and the slave crept to the place where Pompey's headless body lay on the deserted beach, its toga a browning crimson as the blood grew old yet still seeped through the porous woolen fibers.

"We're stranded in Egypt," said the slave.

Worn out from weeping, Philip looked up from the body of Pompey apathetically. "Stranded?"

"Yes, stranded. They sailed, our ships. I saw them."

"Then there is no one save us to attend to him." Philip gazed about, nodded. "At least there's driftwood. No wonder they came in here; it's so lonely."

The two men toiled until they had built a pyre six feet high; getting the body onto it wasn't easy, but they managed.

"We don't have fire," said the slave.

"Then go and ask someone."

Darkness was falling when the slave returned carrying a small metal bucket puffing smoke.

"They didn't want to give me the bucket," said the slave, "but I told them we wanted to burn Gnaeus Pompeius Magnus. So then they said I could have the bucket."

Philip scattered the glowing coals through the open network of sea-silvered branches, made sure the toga was well tucked in, and stood back with the slave to see if the wood caught.

It took a little time, but when it did catch the driftwood blazed fiercely enough to dry the fresh spate of Philip's tears.

Exhausted, they lay down some distance away to sleep; in that languorous air a fire was too warm. And at dawn, finding the pyre reduced to blackened debris, they used the metal bucket to cool it from the sea, then sifted through it for Pompey's ashes.

"I can't tell what's him and what's wood," said the slave.

"There's a difference," said Philip patiently. "Wood crumbles. Bones don't. Ask me if you're not sure."

They put what they found in the metal bucket.

"What do we do now?" asked the slave, a poor creature whose job was to wash and scrub.

"We walk to Alexandria," said Philip.

"Got no money," said the slave.

"I carry Gnaeus Pompeius's purse for him. We'll eat."

Philip picked up the bucket, took the slave by one limp hand, and walked off down the beach, away from stirring Pelusium.

FINIS

AUTHOR'S AFTERWORD

Having arrived at the years which are very well documented in the ancient sources, in order to keep my wordage within limits my publishers find acceptable, I have had to pick and choose rather than retell every aspect. The addition of Caesar's *Commentaries,* both on Gaul and on the civil war against Pompey the Great, enriches the ancient sources enormously.

I don't think there is much doubt that Caesar's *Commentaries* on the war in Gallia Comata are his senatorial dispatches, and so have made them; the modern debate occurs more about whether Caesar published these dispatches in one lump at the beginning of 51 B.C., or whether he published them over the years one at a time. I have chosen to have him publish the first seven books as one volume around the beginning of 51 B.C.

For my comments on the codex as used by Caesar, see the Glossary entry under **codex**.

The amount of detail in Caesar's Gallic War *Commentaries* is daunting, so also the number of names which come and go, never to be mentioned again. Therefore I have adopted a policy which curtails the mention of names never heard again. Quintus Cicero in winter camp along the Mosa had military tribunes under his command, for example, but I have elected not to mention them. The same can be said for Sabinus and Cotta. Caesar always cared more for his centurions than his military tribunes, and I have followed his example in places where a plethora of aristocratic new names would serve only to confuse the reader.

In some other ways I have "tampered" with the Gallic War *Commentaries,* one quite major. This major one concerns Quintus Cicero at the end of 53 B.C., when he undergoes an ordeal quite remarkably similar to his ordeal in winter camp at the beginning of that year. Again he is besieged in a camp, this time the *oppidum* of Atuatuca, from whence Sabinus and Cotta had fled. In the interests of brevity I have changed this incident to an encounter with the Sugambri on the march; I have also changed the number of his legion from the Fourteenth to the Fifteenth, as it is difficult later to know exactly which legion Caesar led in such a hurry from Placentia to Agedincum. Caesar's penetration of the Cebenna in winter has also been modified in the interests of brevity.

Other, more minor departures stem out of Caesar's own inaccuracies. His estimates of mileage, for example, are shaky. So too, sometimes, his descriptions of what is going on. The duel between the centurions Pullo and Vorenus has been simplified.

One of the great mysteries about the Gallic War concerns the small number of his Atrebates whom King Commius was able to bring to the relief of Alesia. I couldn't find a battle wherein they had perished en masse; until Labienus's little plot, Commius and his Atrebates were on Caesar's side. The only thing I could think was that they had marched en masse to the assistance of the Parisii, the Aulerci and the Bellovaci when Titus Labienus slaughtered those tribes along the Sequana (Seine) while Caesar was engaged in the campaigns around Gergovia and Noviodunum Nevirnum. Perhaps we should read "Atrebates" for "Bellovaci," as the Bellovaci did remain alive in sufficient numbers to be a great nuisance later on.

Again in the interests of simplicity, I have not done much with specific septs of the great Gallic confederations: Treveri (Mediomatrices and other septs), Aedui (Ambarri, Segusiavi), and Armorici (many septs from Esubii to Veneti to Venelli).

Some years after Caesar's death, a man from Gallia Comata turned up in Rome, claiming to be Caesar's son. According to the ancient sources, he resembled Caesar physically. Out of this I have concocted the story of Rhiannon and her son. The concoction serves a twofold purpose: the first, to reinforce my contention that Caesar was *not* incapable of siring children, rather that he was hardly in anyone's bed for long enough to do so; and the second, that it permits a more intimate look at the lives and customs of the Celtic Gauls. Though a late source, Ammianus is most informative.

There have been many papers written by modern scholars as to why Titus Labienus did not side with Caesar after he crossed the Rubicon, why Labienus sided instead with Pompey the Great. Much is made of the fact that Labienus was in Pompey's clientele because he was a Picentine from Camerinum and served as Pompey's tame tribune of the plebs in 63 B.C. However, the fact remains that Labienus worked far more for Caesar than he did for Pompey, even during his tribunate of the plebs. Also, Labienus stood to gain more from allying himself with Caesar than with Pompey. The assumption is always that it was Labienus who said no to Caesar; but why, I wondered, could it not have been Caesar who said no to Labienus? There is a logical answer supporting this in the Eighth Book of the Gallic War *Commentaries*. The Eighth Book was not written by Caesar, but by his fanatically loyal adherent Aulus Hirtius. At one stage Hirtius waxes indignant over the fact that Caesar had refused to record Labienus's plot against King Commius in his Seventh Book; it is up to him, says Hirtius, to record what was, as readers of this novel will have seen, a shabby and dishonorable affair. Not, I would have thought, anything Caesar would have approved of. Caesar's action at Uxellodunum, a horrific business, was nonetheless done right up front and publicly. As Caesar seems to have conducted himself. Whereas Labienus was sneaky and underhanded. To me, the evidence seems to say that Caesar tolerated Labienus in Gaul because of his brilliance in the field, but that he would not have wanted Labienus in his camp after crossing the Rubicon; to Caesar, a political alliance with Labienus might have been a bit like marrying a cobra.

Evidence favors Plutarch rather than Suetonius in the matter of what Caesar actually said when he crossed the Rubicon. Pollio, who was there, says that Caesar quoted some of a couplet from the New Comedy poet and playwright Menander, and quoted it *in Greek,* not in Latin. "Let the dice fly high!" *Not* "The die is cast." To me, very believable. "The die is cast" is gloomy and fatalistic. "Let the dice fly high!" is a shrug, an admission that anything can happen. Caesar was not fatalistic. He was a risk taker.

The *Commentaries* on the Civil War required far less adjustment than the Gallic War ones. On only one occasion have I altered the sequence of events, by having Afranius and Petreius return to Pompey earlier than it seems they did. My reason: to keep them in the minds of my non-scholar readers more comfortably.

Now to the maps. Most are self-explanatory. Only Avaricum and Alesia need some words of explanation.

What we know about these immortal situations is mostly based upon nineteenth-century maps and models done around the time Napoleon III was immersed in his *Life of Caesar,* and had Colonel Stoffel digging up France to look at Caesar's camp and battle sites.

I have departed from these maps and models in certain ways.

In the case of Alesia, where the excavations proved that Caesar didn't lie about what he accomplished, I differ from Stoffel in two ways (which do not contradict Caesar's reportage, I add). First, Caesar's cavalry camps. These, shown as free-floating and waterless, had to have been connected to Caesar's fortifications. They also had to have incorporated a part of a natural stream at a place the Gauls would find difficult to divert. Riverbeds shift with the millennia, so we have no real idea whereabouts precisely the streams ran at Alesia two thousand years ago. Aerial surveys have revealed that the Roman fortifications at Alesia were as straight and/or regular as was general Roman military custom. I have therefore partially "squared" the cavalry camps, which Stoffel draws most irregularly. Second, I believe that the camp of Rebilus and Antistius formed the closure of Caesar's ring, and have drawn it thus. In Stoffel's maps it "floats," and suggests that Caesar's ring was never closed at all. I can't see Caesar making that kind of mistake. To use the vulnerable camp as his closure, given that he couldn't take the circumvallation up and over the mountain, is good sense. He had two legions there to man the lines along his great weakness.

As for Avaricum, I depart from the models in four ways. First, that I can see no reason not to make the wall connecting Caesar's two flank walls as high as his flank walls. To have it the same height creates a proper fighting platform fed by troops from everywhere at once. Second, I fail to see why defense towers would have been erected on Avaricum's walls right where the gangplanks of Caesar's towers would have thumped down. In a famously iron-rich tribe like the Bituriges, surely iron shields were more likely opposite Caesar's towers; the Avarican towers would have been more useful elsewhere. Third, I have halved the number of mantlets these models have put outside the flanking walls and going nowhere of much help in getting troops on top of the assault platform. I believe these particular mantlets sheltered the Roman sappers. Fourth, I have not drawn in any shelter sheds or a palisade on top of the assault platform; not because they weren't there, but rather to show what the platform itself looked like.

The drawings.

Not so many in this book. The likeness of Caesar is authentic. So too is the likeness of Titus Labienus, which was drawn from a polished marble bust in the museum at Cremona. Very difficult to capture in reflected light. Ahenobarbus is reputed to be authentic. Quintus Cicero's likeness is drawn from a bust said to be of his famous brother, but examination of this bust says it is *not* Marcus Cicero. The skull shape is completely wrong, and the subject much balder than Cicero is ever depicted. There is, however, a pronounced resemblance to Cicero. Could this not, I asked, be a bust of little brother Quintus?

Vercingetorix is taken from a coin profile.

The drawings of Metellus Scipio and Curio are not authenticated likenesses, but taken from portrait busts of the first century B.C.

This drawing of Pompey the Great is taken from the famous bust in Copenhagen.

* * *

I do all the research myself, but there are a number of people to thank for their unflagging help. My classical editor, Professor Alanna Nobbs of Macquarie University in Sydney, and her colleagues; my loyal little band of secretaries, housekeepers, and men-of-all-work; Joe Nobbs; Frank Esposito; Fred Mason; and my husband, Ric Robinson.

The next book will be called *The October Horse*.

GLOSSARY

ABSOLVO The term employed by a court jury when voting for the acquittal of the accused.

aedile There were four Roman magistrates called aediles; two were plebeian aediles, two were curule aediles. Their duties were confined to the city of Rome. The plebeian aediles were created first (493 B.C.) to assist the tribunes of the plebs in their duties, but, more particularly, to guard the right of the Plebs to its headquarters, located in the temple of Ceres. Soon the plebeian aediles inherited supervision of the city's buildings, both public and private, as well as archival custody of all plebiscites passed in the Plebeian Assembly, together with any senatorial decrees (*consulta*) directing the enactment of plebiscites. They were elected by the Plebeian Assembly, and did not have the right to sit in the curule chair; nor were they entitled to lictors. Then in 367 B.C. two curule aediles were created to give the patricians a share in custody of the city's buildings and archives. They were elected by the Popular Assembly, which comprised the whole people, patrician and plebeian, and therefore had the right to sit in the curule chair and be preceded by two lictors. Very soon, however, the curule aediles were as likely to be plebeians as patricians. From the third century B.C. downward, all four were responsible for the care of Rome's streets, water supply, drains and sewers, traffic, public buildings, building standards and regulations for private buildings, public monuments and facilities, markets, weights and measures (standard sets of these were housed in the basement of the temple of Castor and Pollux), games, and the public grain supply. They had the power to fine citizens and non-citizens alike for infringements of any regulation appertaining to any of the above, and deposited the moneys in their coffers to help fund the games. Aedile—curule or plebeian—was not a magistracy of the *cursus honorum* (see **magistrates**), but because of its association with the games was a valuable magistracy for a man to hold just before he stood for office as praetor.

Agedincum An *oppidum* belonging to the Senones. Modern Sens.

agora The open space, usually surrounded by colonnades or some kind of public buildings, which served any Greek or Hellenic city as its public meeting place and civic center. The Roman equivalent was a forum.

ague The old name for the rigors of malaria.

Alba Helviorum The main town of the Helvii. Near modern Le Teil.

Albis River The Elbe.

Alesia An *oppidum* of the Mandubii. Modern Alise-Ste.-Reine.

Alexander the Great King of Macedonia, and eventually of most of the known world. Born in 356 B.C., he was the son of Philip II and one Olympias of Epirus. His tutor was Aristotle. At the age of twenty, he acceded to the throne upon his father's assassination. Regarding Asia Minor as in his purlieus, he determined to invade it. He first crushed all opposition in Macedonia and Greece, then in 334 B.C. led an army of forty thousand men into Anatolia. Having liberated all the Greek city-states therein from Persian rule, he proceeded to subdue all resistance in Syria and Egypt, where he is said to have consulted the oracle of Amon at modern Siwah. The year 331 B.C. saw him marching for Mesopotamia to meet the Persian King, Darius. Darius was defeated at Gaugamela; Alexander went on to conquer the empire of the Persians (Media, Susiana, Persia), accumulating fabulous booty. From the Caspian Sea he continued east to conquer Bactria and Sogdiana, reaching the Hindu Kush after a three-year campaign which cost him dearly. To ensure his treaties he married the Sogdian princess Roxane, then set out for India. Resistance in the Punjab ceased upon the defeat of King Porus on the Hyphasis River, from whence he marched down the Indus River to the sea. In the end his own troops curtailed Alexander's plans by refusing to accompany him eastward to the Ganges. He turned west again, dividing his army; half marched with him overland and half sailed with his marshal Nearchos. The fleet was delayed by monsoons, and Alexander's own progress through Gedrosia was a frightful ordeal. Eventually what was left of the army reunited in Mesopotamia; Alexander settled down in Babylon. There he contracted a fever and died in 323 B.C. at the age of thirty-two, leaving his marshals to divide his empire amid war and dissent. His son by Roxane, born posthumously, never lived to inherit. The indications are that Alexander wished to be worshiped as a god.

Ambrussum A town in the Roman Gallic Province on the Via Domitia to Narbo and Spain. It was near Lunel.

Anatolia Roughly, modern Turkey. It incorporated Bithynia, Mysia, the Roman Asian Province, Lycia, Pisidia, Phrygia, Paphlagonia, Pontus,

Galatia, Lacaonia, Pamphylia, Cilicia, Cappadocia and Armenia Parva (Little Armenia).

animus *The Oxford Latin Dictionary* has the best definition, so I will quote it: "The mind as opposed to the body, the mind or soul as constituting with the body the whole person." One must be careful, however, not to attribute belief in the immortality of the soul to Romans.

Aous River The Vijosë River, in modern Albania.

Apollonia The southern terminus of the Via Egnatia, the road which traveled from Byzantium and the Hellespont to the Adriatic Sea. Apollonia lay near the mouth of the Aous (Vijosë) River.

Apsus River The Seman River, in modern Albania. In Caesar's time it appears to have served as the boundary between Epirus to its south and western Macedonia to its north.

Aquae Sextiae A town in the Roman Gallic Province near which Gaius Marius won a huge victory against the Teutonic Germans in 102 B.C. The modern name is Aix-en-Provence.

Aquilifer The soldier who bore a legion's silver Eagle.

Aquitania The lands between the Garumna River (the Garonne) and the Pyrenees.

Arar River The Saône River.

Arausio Orange.

Arduenna The Ardennes Forest.

Arelate Arles.

Ariminum Rimini.

armillae The wide bracelets, of gold or silver, awarded as prizes for valor to Roman legionaries, centurions, cadets and military tribunes of more junior rank.

Arnus River The Arno River. It served as the boundary between Italian Gaul and Italia proper on the western side of the Apennine watershed.

Assembly (*comitium, comitia*) Any gathering of the Roman People convoked to deal with governmental, legislative, judicial, or electoral matters. In the time of Caesar there were three true Assemblies: the Centuries, the People, and the Plebs.

The Centuriate Assembly (*comitia centuriata*) marshaled the People, patrician and plebeian, in their Classes, which were filled by a means test and were economic in nature. As this was originally a military assemblage of cavalry knights, each Class gathered outside the sacred city boundary on the Campus Martius at a place called the Saepta. Except for the senior eighteen Centuries, kept to one hundred members, many more than one hundred men were lumped into one Century by Caesar's time. The Centuriate Assembly met to elect consuls, praetors and (every five years) censors. It also met to hear major charges of treason (*perduellio*) and could pass laws. Under ordinary circumstances it was not convoked to pass laws or hear trials.

The Assembly of the People or Popular Assembly (*comitia populi tributa*) allowed the full participation of patricians and was tribal in nature, convoked in the thirty-five tribes into which all Roman citizens were placed. Called into session by a consul or praetor, it normally met in the well of the Comitia, in the lower Forum Romanum. It elected the curule aediles, the quaestors, and the tribunes of the soldiers. Until Sulla established the standing courts it conducted trials; in the time of Caesar it met to formulate and pass laws as well as hold elections.

The Plebeian Assembly (*comitia plebis tributa* or *concilium plebis*) was also a tribal assembly, but it did not allow participation of patricians. The only magistrate empowered to convoke it was a tribune of the plebs. It had the right to enact laws (called plebiscites) and conduct trials, though trials were few after Sulla established standing courts. Its members elected the plebeian aediles and the tribunes of the plebs. It usually met in the well of the Comitia. See also **tribe** and **voting**.

atrium The main reception room of a Roman *domus*, or private house. It generally contained an opening in the roof (*compluvium*) above a pool (*impluvium*) originally intended as a reservoir for domestic use. By Caesar's time, the pool had become ornamental only.

auctoritas A very difficult Latin term to translate, as it meant far more than the English word "authority" implies. It carried nuances of pre-eminence, clout, public importance and—above all—the ability to influence events through sheer public reputation. All the magistracies possessed *auctoritas* as an intrinsic part of their nature, but *auctoritas* was not confined to those who held magistracies. The Princeps Senatus, Pontifex Maximus, other priests and augurs, consulars and even some private citizens outside the ranks of the Senate owned *auctoritas*. Though the plutocrat Titus Pomponius Atticus was never a senator, his *auctoritas* was formidable.

augur A priest whose duties concerned divination. He and his fellow augurs constituted the College of Augurs, an official State body which numbered twelve members (six patricians and six plebeians) until in 81 B.C. Sulla increased its membership to fifteen, always thereafter intended to contain one more plebeian than patrician. Originally augurs were co-opted by the College of Augurs, but in 104 B.C. Gnaeus Domitius Ahenobarbus brought in a law compelling election of future augurs by an assembly of seventeen tribes chosen from the thirty-five by lot. Sulla in 81 B.C. removed election, going back to co-optation, but after his death election was reestablished. The augur did not predict the future, nor did he pursue his auguries at his own whim; he inspected the proper objects or signs to ascertain whether or not the undertaking in question met with the approval of the Gods, be the undertaking a *contio*, a war, legislation, or any other State business, including elections. There was a standard manual of interpretation to which the augur referred; augurs "went by the book." The augur wore the purple-and-scarlet-striped *toga trabea* and carried a curved, curlicued staff, the *lituus.*

aurochs The progenitor of modern cattle, now extinct. In Caesar's time this huge wild ox still roamed the impenetrable forests of Germania, though it had disappeared from the Ardennes.

Auser River The Serchio River in Italy.

Avaricum The largest *oppidum* of the Bituriges, and said to be the most beautiful *oppidum* in Gallia Comata. It is now the city of Bourges.

ave Hello in Latin.

Axona River The Aisne River.

ballista In Republican times, a piece of artillery designed to hurl stones and boulders. The missile was placed in a spoon-shaped arm which was put under extreme tension by means of a rope spring wound up very tightly; when the spring was released, the arm shot into the air and came to rest against a thick pad, propelling the missile a considerable distance depending upon the size of the missile and the size of the machine itself.

barbarian Derived from a Greek word having strong onomatopoeic overtones. On first hearing certain peoples speak, the Greeks heard it as "bar-bar," like animals barking. "Barbarian" was not a word applied to any people settled around the Mediterranean Sea or in Asia Minor, but referred to peoples and nations deemed uncivilized, lacking in any desirable or admirable culture. Gauls, Germans, Scythians, Sarmatians, Massagetae and other peoples of the steppes and forests were barbarians.

battlement The parapet along the top of a fortified wall at its full (that is, above head level) height. The battlement afforded shelter for those not engaged in the actual fighting.

Belgae, Belgica The Belgae were those tribes of Gauls who were a hybrid mixture of Celt and German. Their religion was Druidic, but they often preferred cremation to inhumation. Some, like the Treveri, had progressed to the stage of electing annual magistrates called vergobrets, but most still subscribed to the rule of kings; the title of king was not hereditary, but attained through combat or other trials of strength. The Belgae lived in that part of Gallia Comata called Belgica, which may be thought of as north of the Sequana (Seine) River and extending east to the Rhenus (Rhine) River north of the lands of the Mandubii.

Beroea Veroia, in Greece.

Bibracte An *oppidum* of the Aedui, now Mont Beuvray.

Bibrax An *oppidum* of the Remi. Near Laon.

bireme A galley constructed for use in naval warfare, and intended to be rowed rather than sailed, though it was equipped with a mast and sail (usually left ashore if action was likely). Some biremes were decked or partially decked, but most were open. It seems that the oarsmen did sit on two levels at two separate banks of oars, the upper bank accommodated in an outrigger, and the lower bank's oars poking through leather-valved ports in the ship's sides. Built of fir or some other lightweight pine, the bireme could be manned only in fair weather, and fight battles only in very calm seas. Like all warships, it was not left in the water, but stored in shipsheds. It was much longer than it was wide in the beam (the ratio was about 7:1), and probably measured about 100 feet (30 meters) in length. There were upward of one hundred oarsmen. A bronze-reinforced beak of oak projected forward of the bow just below the waterline, and was used for ramming and sinking other galleys. The bireme was not designed to carry marines or artillery, or grapple to engage other vessels in land-style combat. Throughout Greek and Roman Republican times the ship was rowed by professional oarsmen, never by slaves. Slaves sent to the galleys were a feature of Christian times.

breastworks The parapet along the top of a fortified wall contained breast-high sections designed to enable the defenders to fight over their tops. These were the breastworks.

Brundisium Modern Brindisi.

Burdigala An *oppidum* of the Aquitanian Bituriges near the mouth of the Garumna (Garonne) River. Modern Bordeaux.

Cabillonum An *oppidum* of the Aedui upon the Arar (Saône) River. Modern Chalon-sur-Saône.

cacat! Shit!

Calabria Confusing for modern Italians! Nowadays Calabria is the toe of the boot, but in Roman times it was the heel. Brundisium and Tarentum were the important cities. Its people were the Illyrian Messapii.

Campus Martius The Field of Mars. Situated north of the Servian Walls, it was bounded by the Capitol on its south and the Pincian Hill on its east; the rest of it was enclosed by a huge bend in the Tiber River. In Republican times it was not inhabited as a suburb, but was the place where triumphing armies bivouacked, the young were trained in military exercises, horses engaged in chariot racing were stabled and trained, the Centuriate Assembly met, and market gardening vied with public parklands. At the apex of the river bend lay the public swimming holes known as the Trigarium, and just to the north of the Trigarium were medicinal hot springs called the Tarentum. The Via Lata (Via Flaminia) crossed the Campus Martius on its way to the Mulvian Bridge; the Via Recta bisected the Via Lata at right angles.

Capena Gate The Porta Capena. One of the two most important gates in Rome's Servian Walls (the other was the Porta Collina, the Colline Gate). It lay beyond the Circus Maximus, and outside it was the common highway which branched into the Via Appia and the Via Latina about half a mile beyond it.

capite censi Literally, the Head Count. Also known as *proletarii.* They were the lowly of Rome, and were called the Head Count because at a census all the censors did was to "count heads." Too poor to belong to a Class, the urban Head Count usually belonged to one of the four urban tribes, and therefore owned no worthwhile votes. This rendered them politically useless, though the ruling class was very careful to ensure that they were fed at public expense and given plenty of free entertainment. It is significant that during the centuries when Rome owned the world, the Head Count never rose against their betters. Rural Head Count, though owning a valuable rural tribal vote, could rarely afford to come to Rome at election time. I have sedulously avoided terms like "the masses" or "the proletariat" because of post-Marxist preconceptions not applicable to the ancient lowly.

Carantomagus An *oppidum* belonging to the Ruteni. Near modern Villefranche.

Carcasso A stronghold in the Roman Gallic Province on the Atax River not far from Narbo. Modern Carcassonne.

Carinae One of Rome's most exclusive addresses. Incorporating the Fagutal, the Carinae was the northern tip of the Oppian Mount on its western side; it extended from the Velia to the Clivus Pullius. Its outlook was southwestern, toward the Aventine.

Caris River The Cher River.

carpentum A four-wheeled, closed carriage drawn by six to eight mules.

cartouche The personal hieroglyphs peculiar to each individual Egyptian pharaoh, enclosed within an oval (or rectangular with rounded corners) framing line. The practice continued through until the last pharaoh of all, Cleopatra VII.

cataphract A cavalryman clad in chain mail from the top of his head to his toes; his horse was also clad in chain mail. Cataphracts were peculiar to Armenia and to the Kingdom of the Parthians at this period in time, though they were the ancestors of the medieval knight. Because of the weight of their armor, their horses were very large and bred in Media.

catapulta In Republican times, a piece of artillery designed to shoot bolts (wooden missiles rather like very large arrows). The principle governing their mechanics was akin to that of the crossbow. Caesar's *Commentaries* inform us that they were accurate and deadly.

Cebenna The Massif Central, the Cévennes.

Celtae The pure Celtic peoples of Gallia Comata. They occupied the country south of the Sequana River and were twice as numerous as the Belgae (four million against two million). Their religious practices were Druidic; they did not practise cremation, but elected to be inhumed. Those Celtic tribes occupying modern Brittany were much smaller and darker than other Celts, as were many Aquitanian tribes. Some Celts adhered to kings, who were elected by councils, but most tribes preferred to elect a pair of vergobrets on an annual basis.

Cenabum The main *oppidum* of the Carnutes, on the Liger (Loire) River. Modern Orléans.

censor The censor was the most august of all Roman magistrates, though he lacked imperium and therefore was not entitled to be escorted by lictors. Two censors were elected by the Centuriate Assembly to serve for a period of five years (termed a *lustrum*). Censorial activity was, however, mostly limited to the first eighteen months of the *lustrum*. No man could stand for censor until he had been consul; usually only those consulars of notable *auctoritas* and *dignitas* bothered to run. The censors inspected and regulated membership in the Senate and in the Ordo Equester (the knights), and conducted a general census of all Roman citizens throughout the world. They had the power to transfer a citizen from one tribe to another as well as from one Class to another. They applied the means test. The letting of State contracts for everything from the farming of taxes to public works was also their responsibility.
Centuriate Assembly See **Assembly**.
centurion He was the regular professional officer of the Roman legion. It is a mistake to equate him with the modern non-commissioned officer; centurions enjoyed a relatively exalted status uncomplicated by social distinctions. A Roman general hardly turned a hair if he lost even senior military tribunes, but was devastated if he lost centurions. Centurion rank was graduated in a manner so tortuous that no modern scholar has worked out how many grades there were, nor how they progressed. The ordinary centurion commanded the century, composed of eighty legionaries and twenty noncombatant servants (see **noncombatants**). Each cohort in a legion had six centuries and six centurions, with the senior man, the *pilus prior,* commanding the senior century as well as the entire cohort. The ten men commanding the ten cohorts which made up a legion were also ranked in seniority, with the legion's most senior centurion, the *primus pilus* (reduced by Caesar to *primipilus*), answering only to his legion's commander (either one of the elected tribunes of the soldiers or one of the general's legates). During Republican times promotion was up from the ranks. The centurion had certain easily recognizable badges of office: alone among Roman military men, he wore greaves covering his shins; he also wore a shirt of scales rather than chain links; his helmet crest was stiff and projected sideways rather than back-to-front; and he carried a stout knobkerrie of vine wood. He always wore many decorations.
century Any grouping of one hundred men.
Cherusci A tribe of Germans occupying the lands around the sources of those German rivers emptying into the North Sea.
chlamys The cloaklike outer garment worn by Greek men.
Cimbri A Germanic people who originally inhabited the northern half of the Jutland Peninsula (modern Denmark). Strabo says that a sea flood drove them out in search of a new homeland around 120 B.C. In combination with the Teutones and a mixed group of Germans and Celts (the Marcomanni-Cherusci-Tigurini), they wandered around Europe in

search of this homeland until they ran afoul of Rome. In 102 and 101 B.C., Gaius Marius utterly defeated them; the migration disintegrated. Some six thousand Cimbri, however, returned to their kinfolk the Atuatuci in modern Belgium.

Cimbric Chersonnese The Jutland Peninsula, modern Denmark.

Circus Flaminius The circus situated on the Campus Martius not far from the Tiber and the Forum Holitorium. It was built in 221 B.C. to hold about fifty thousand spectators, and was sometimes used for meetings of the various Assemblies.

Circus Maximus The old circus built by King Tarquinius Priscus before the Republic began. It filled the whole of the Vallis Murcia, a declivity between the Palatine and Aventine mounts. Even though it could hold over 150,000 spectators, there is ample evidence during Republican times that freedmen citizens were excluded from the games held there because of lack of room. Women were permitted to sit with men.

citrus wood The most prized cabinet wood of the ancient world. It was cut from vast galls on the root system of a cypresslike tree, *Callitris quadrivavis vent.*, which grew in the highlands of North Africa all the way from the Oasis of Ammonium in Egypt to the far Atlas Mountains of Mauretania. Though termed citrus, the tree was not botanically related to orange or lemon.

Classes These were five in number, and represented the economic divisions of property-owning or steady-income-earning Roman citizens. The members of the First Class were the richest; the members of the Fifth Class were the poorest. Those Roman citizens who belonged to the *capite censi* or Head Count did not qualify for a Class status, and so could not vote in the Centuriate Assembly. In actual fact, if the bulk of the First and Second Class Centuries voted the same way, even the Third Class was not called upon to vote.

client-king A foreign monarch might pledge himself as a client in the service of Rome as his patron, thereby entitling his kingdom to be known as Friend and Ally of the Roman People. Sometimes, however, a foreign monarch pledged himself as the client of a Roman individual. Lucullus and Pompey both owned client-kings.

codex Basically, a book rather than a scroll. Evidence indicates that the codex of Caesar's day was a clumsy affair made of wooden leaves with holes punched in their left-hand sides through which thongs of leather bound them together. However, the sheer length of Caesar's senatorial dispatches negates the use of wooden leaves. I believe Caesar's codex was made of sheets of paper sewn together along the left-hand margin. The chief reason for my assuming this is that his codex leaf was described as being divided into three columns for easier reading—not possible on a wooden leaf of a size enabling the codex to be read comfortably.

cognomen The last name of a Roman male anxious to distinguish himself from all his fellows possessed of identical first (*praenomen*) and family (*nomen*) names. He might adopt a cognomen for himself, as did Pompey with the cognomen Magnus, or simply continue to bear a cognomen which had been in the family for generations, as did the Julians cognominated Caesar. In some families it became necessary to have more than one cognomen; the best example of this is Quintus Caecilius Metellus Pius Scipio Nasica, a Cornelius Scipio Nasica adopted into the Caecilii Metelli. He was generally known as Metellus Scipio for short.

The cognomen often pointed up some physical characteristic or idiosyncrasy—jug ears, flat feet, humpback, swollen legs—or else commemorated some great feat—as in the Caecilii Metelli who were cognominated Dalmaticus, Balearicus, Macedonicus, and Numidicus, these being related to a country each man had conquered. The most delicious cognomens were heavily sarcastic—Lepidus, meaning a thoroughly nice fellow, attached to a right bastard—or extremely witty—as with the already multiply cognominated Gaius Julius Caesar Strabo Vopiscus (Strabo, meaning he had cross-eyes, and Vopiscus, meaning he was the surviving one of twins). He earned the additional name of Sesquiculus, meaning he was more than just an arsehole, he was an arsehole and a half.

cohort The tactical unit of the legion. It comprised six centuries; each legion owned ten cohorts. When discussing troop movements, it was more customary for the general to speak of his army in terms of cohorts rather than legions, which perhaps indicates that, at least until Caesar's time, the general deployed or peeled off cohorts rather than legions. Caesar seems to have preferred to general legions than cohorts, though Pompey at Pharsalus had eighteen cohorts which had not been organized into legions.

college A body or society of men having something in common. Rome owned priestly colleges (such as the College of Pontifices), political colleges (the College of Tribunes of the Plebs), civil servant colleges (the College of Lictors), and trade colleges (the Guild of Undertakers, for example). Certain groups of men from all walks of life, including slaves, banded together in what were called crossroads colleges to look after the city of Rome's major crossroads and conduct the annual feast of the crossroads, the Compitalia.

comata Long-haired.

comitium, comitia See **Assembly.**

CONDEMNO The word employed by a court jury when delivering a verdict of guilty.

Conscript Fathers When it was established as an advisory body by the Kings of Rome (traditionally by Romulus himself), the Senate consisted of one hundred patricians entitled *patres*—fathers. Then when plebeian senators were added during the first years of the Republic, they were said to be *conscripti*—chosen without a choice. Together, the patrician and plebeian senators were said to be *patres et conscripti;* gradually the once-distinguishing terms were run together. All members of the Senate were Conscript Fathers.

consul The consul was the most senior Roman magistrate owning imperium, and the consulship (modern scholars do not refer to it as the "consulate" because a consulate is a modern diplomatic institution) was the top rung on the *cursus honorum.* Two consuls were elected each year by the Centuriate Assembly, and served for one year. They entered office on New Year's Day (January 1). The one who had polled the requisite number of Centuries first was called the senior consul; the other was the junior consul. The senior consul held the ***fasces*** for the month of January, which meant his junior colleague looked on. In February the *fasces* passed to the junior consul, and alternated thus throughout the year. Both consuls were escorted by twelve lictors, but only the consul holding the *fasces* for that month had his lictors bear them. By the last century of the Republic, both consuls could be plebeians, but both consuls could not be patricians. The proper age for a consul was forty-two, twelve years after entering the Senate at thirty, though there is convincing evidence that Sulla in 81 B.C. accorded patrician senators the privilege of standing for consul (and praetor) two years before any plebeian; this meant a patrician could be consul at forty. A consul's imperium knew no bounds; it operated not only in Rome and Italia, but throughout the provinces as well, and overrode the imperium of a proconsular governor unless he had *imperium maius,* an honor accorded to Pompey regularly, but to few others. The consul could command any army.

consular The name given to a man after he stepped down from office as consul. He was then held in special esteem by the rest of the Senate. Until Sulla became Dictator, the consular was always asked to speak or give his opinion in the House ahead of all others. Sulla changed that, preferring to exalt magistrates in office and those elected to coming office. The consular, however, might at any time be sent to govern a province should the Senate require this duty of him. He might also be asked to take on other tasks, such as caring for the grain supply.

consultum, consulta The proper terms for a senatorial decree or decrees, though the full title is *senatus consultum.* These decrees did not have the force of law; they were merely recommendations to the Assemblies to pass laws. Whichever Assembly a *consultum* was sent to was not obliged to enact what it directed. Certain *consulta* were regarded as law by all of Rome, though never sent to any Assembly; these were matters mostly to do with foreign affairs and war. In 81 B.C. Sulla gave these latter *consulta* the formal status of laws.

contio, contiones A *contio* was a preliminary meeting of a comitial Assembly in order to discuss promulgation of a proposed law, or any other comitial business. All three Assemblies were required to debate a measure in *contio,* which, though no actual voting took place, was nonetheless a formal meeting convoked only by a magistrate empowered to do so.

contubernalis A military cadet, usually from a good family. He was the subaltern of lowest rank and age in the Roman military officers' hierarchy, but he was not training to be a centurion. Centurions were never cadets; they had to be experienced soldiers from the ranks with a genuine gift for command. Being relatively highborn, the *contubernalis* was attached to legatal staff and not required to do much actual fighting unless he chose to.

Cora River The Cure River.

Corcyra Island Modern Corfu or Kerkira Island.

Corduba Spanish Córdoba.

corona civica Rome's second-highest military decoration. A chaplet made of oak leaves, it was awarded to a man who saved the lives of fellow soldiers and held the ground on which he did this until the battle was over. It could not be awarded unless the saved soldiers swore an oath before their general that they were speaking the truth about the circumstances. L. R. Taylor argues that among Sulla's constitutional reforms was one pertaining to the winners of major military crowns: that, following the precedent of Marcus Fabius Buteo, he promoted these men to membership in the Senate no matter what their ages or their social backgrounds. Dr. Taylor's contention answers the vexed question as to when exactly Caesar entered the Senate, which she hypothesizes as aged twenty, after winning the *corona civica* at Mitylene. The great Matthias Gelzer agreed with her—but, alas, only in a footnote.

cubit A Greek and/or Asian measurement of length not popular among Romans. The cubit was normally held as the distance between a man's elbow and his clenched fist, and was probably about 15 inches (375mm).

cuirass Armor encasing the upper body without having the form of a shirt. It consisted of two plates of bronze, steel, or hardened leather, the front one protecting thorax and abdomen, the other a man's back from shoulders to lumbar spine. The plates were held together by straps or hinges at the shoulders and along each side under the arms. Some cuirasses were exquisitely tailored to the contours of an individual's torso, while others fitted any man of a particular size and physique. The men of highest rank—generals and legates—owned parade cuirasses tooled in high relief and silver-plated (sometimes, though rarely, gold-plated). As an indication of his imperium, the general and his most senior legates wore a thin red sash around the cuirass about halfway between the nipples and waist; the sash was ritually knotted and looped.

cultarius H. H. Scullard's spelling: *The Oxford Latin Dictionary* prefers ***cultrarius***. He was a public servant attached to religious duties, and his only job appears to have been that of cutting the sacrificial victim's throat. He may also have helped tidy up afterward.

cunnus, cunni A very choice Latin obscenity: cunt, cunts.

Curia Hostilia The Senate House. It was thought to have been built by the shadowy third King of Rome, Tullus Hostilius, hence its name: "the meeting-house of Hostilius." It burned down in January of 52 B.C. when the mob cremated Publius Clodius, and was not rebuilt until Caesar became Dictator.

Curicta Island Krk Island, off the Liburnian coast of Yugoslavia.

curule, curule chair The *sella curulis* was the ivory chair reserved exclusively for magistrates owning imperium. Consuls, praetors and curule aediles sat in it; I have gone back to thinking that plebeian aediles did not, as they were not elected by the whole Roman People, therefore could not have owned imperium. Beautifully carved in ivory, the chair itself had curved legs crossing in a broad X, so that it could be folded up. It was equipped with arms, but had no back. Possibly once a man had been consul, as a consular he had the right to retain his curule chair and sit in it. Knowing Rome, I believe it didn't belong to the State, if the State could insist those entitled to sit in the curule chair had to commission and pay for it themselves.

Dagda The principal God of Druidism. His elemental nature was water, and he husbanded the Great Goddess, Dann.

Dann The principal Goddess of Druidism. Her elemental nature was earth and she was wife to Dagda, though not, it would seem, his inferior. She headed a pantheon of Goddesses who included Epona, Sulis and Bodb.

Danubius River The Danube, Donau or Dunarea River. The Romans knew its sources better than its outflow into the Euxine (Black) Sea; the Greeks knew its outflow better, and called it the river Ister.

Decetia An *oppidum* of the Aedui situated on the Liger (Loire) River. Modern Decize.

decury To the Romans, any group of ten men, be they senators or soldiers or lictors.

demagogue Originally a Greek concept, the demagogue of ancient times was a politician whose chief appeal was to the crowds. The Roman demagogue (almost inevitably a tribune of the plebs) preferred the arena of the well of the Comitia to the Senate House, but it was not part of his policy to "liberate the masses." Nor were those who flocked to hear him made up of the very lowly. The term simply indicated a man of radical as opposed to conservative bent.

denarius, denarii Save for a very rare issue or two of gold coins, the denarius was the largest denomination of coin under the Republic. Of pure silver, it contained about 3.5 grams of the metal, and was about the size of a dime—very small. There were 6,250 denarii to 1 silver talent. Of actual coins in circulation, there were probably more denarii than sesterces, but accounts were always expressed in sesterces, not denarii.

diadem This was neither crown nor tiara. It was a thick white ribbon about 1 inch (25mm) wide, each end embroidered and often finished with a fringe. It was the symbol of the Hellenic sovereign; only the king and/or queen could wear it. The coins show that it was generally worn across the forehead, but could be (as in the case of Cleopatra VII) worn behind the hairline. It was knotted at the back below the occiput, and the two ends trailed down onto the shoulders.

dignitas To the Romans this word had connotations not conveyed by the English word derived from it, "dignity." *Dignitas* was a man's right and entitlement to public honor through personal endeavor. It gave the sum total of his integrity, pride, family and ancestors, word, intelligence, deeds, ability, knowledge, and worth as a man. Of all the assets a Roman nobleman possessed, *dignitas* was likely to be the one he was most touchy about and most protective of.

domine My lord. Vocative case.

Domus Publica The official State residence of the Pontifex Maximus and, in Republican times, also the residence of the six Vestal Virgins, who were in the hand of the Pontifex Maximus. It was located in the Forum Romanum at about the middle latitude.

Druid A priest of the Druidic religion, which dominated spiritual (and often earthly) thought among the Gauls, be they Celts or Belgae. It took twenty years to train a Druid, who was required to memorize every aspect of his calling from lays to rituals to laws. Nothing was written down. Druids once consecrated as Druids held the position for life. They were permitted to marry. As directors of thought, they paid no taxes or tithes, did not do military service, and were fed and housed at the expense of the tribe. They provided the priests, lawyers and doctors.

dug-mullets A kind of fish which lived in sandy or muddy bottoms around river estuaries. I imagine they were flounders.

Durocortorum The principal *oppidum* of the Remi. Modern Reims.

duumviri The two men, elected annually, who headed the municipal governing body or the town governing body.

Dyrrachium Modern Durrës in Albania.

Eagle Among the army reforms instituted by Gaius Marius was one which gifted each legion with a silver eagle set upon a long pole pointed at its nether end so it could be driven into the ground. The Eagle was the legion's rallying point and its most venerated standard.

Edepol! A very benign and socially unexceptionable expletive, akin to our "Oh, darn!" *Edepol* was reserved for men. Women said, *"Ecastor!"*

Elaver River The Allier River.

Elysian Fields A very special place in the afterlife for very few people. Whereas ordinary shades or spirits were thought to be mindless, twittering, flitting denizens of an underworld both cheerless and drab, some men's shades were treated differently. Tartarus was that part of Hades where men of great evil like Ixion and Sisyphus were doomed to toil literally eternally at some task perpetually unraveled or undone. The Elysian Fields or Elysium were a part of Hades akin to what might be called Paradise, Nirvana. Interestingly, entrance to either Tartarus or Elysium was reserved for men who in some way had connections to the Gods. Those doomed to Tartarus had offended the Gods, not man. And those transported to the Elysian Fields were either the sons of Gods, married to Gods, or married to human children of the Gods. This may account for the driving wish of some men and women to be worshiped as Gods while still living, or made into Gods after death. Alexander the Great wanted to be declared a God. So, some maintain, did Caesar.

Epicurean Pertaining to the philosophical system of the Greek Epicurus. Originally Epicurus had advocated a kind of hedonism so exquisitely refined that it approached asceticism on its left hand, so to speak; a man's pleasures were best sampled one at a time and strung out with such relish that any excess defeated the exercise. Public life or any other stressful work was taboo. However, these tenets underwent considerable modification in Rome. A Roman nobleman could call himself an Epicurean yet still espouse his public career. By the late Republic, the chief pleasures of an Epicurean were food and wine.

Epirus That part of the Grecian/Macedonian west adjacent to the Adriatic Sea which extended from the Apsus (Seman) River in the north to the Gulf of Ambracia in the south, and inland to the high mountains. Modern Albania is perhaps not the right description; it goes too far north and not far enough south to be aligned with ancient Epirus.

Equites, equestrian, Ordo Equester See **knights.**

Esus The Druidic God of war. His elemental nature was air.

ethnarch The general Greek word for a city or town magistrate. There were other and more specific names in use, but I do not think it necessary to compound confusion in my readers by employing a more varied terminology.

Euxine Sea The modern Black Sea.

fasces These were bundles of birch rods ritually tied together into a cylinder by crisscrossed red leather thongs. Originally an emblem of the Etruscan kings, they passed into the customs and traditions of the emerging Rome, persisting in Roman life throughout the Republic and on into the Empire. Carried by men called lictors (see **lictor**), they preceded the curule magistrate or promagistrate as the outward indication of his imperium. There were thirty rods for the thirty curiae or original tribal divisions of Roman men under the kings. Within the *pomerium* of Rome only the rods went into the *fasces,* to indicate that the curule magistrate had the power to chastise, but not to execute; outside the *pomerium* two axes were inserted into the *fasces* to indicate that the curule magistrate had the power to execute. The only man who could bring *fasces* holding the axes inside the sacred boundary of Rome was the dictator. The number of *fasces* (and lictors) told the degree of imperium: a dictator had twenty-four, a consul and proconsul twelve, a praetor and propraetor six, and a curule aedile two.

fasti The *fasti* were originally days on which business could be transacted, but came to mean other things as well: the calendar, lists relating to holidays and festivals, and the list of consuls (this last probably because Romans preferred to reckon up their years by remembering who had been the consuls in any given year). For a fuller explanation, see ***fasti*** in the Glossary to *The First Man in Rome.*

fellatrix, fellatrices A woman or women who sucked a man's penis.

filibuster A modern term for a political practice as old as the concept of a parliament. It consisted, then as now, of "talking a motion out."

flamen A special priest dedicated to one particular Roman God. They were the oldest in time of Rome's priests. Caesar had been *flamen Dialis,* the special priest of Jupiter (Marius had him so consecrated at thirteen years of age); Sulla stripped him of it.

forum The public meeting place of any Roman town or city. It was surrounded by public buildings and arcades housing shops or offices.

Forum Boarium The meat markets, situated at the starting-post end of the Circus Maximus, below the Germalus of the Palatine. The Great Altar of Hercules and several different temples of Hercules lay therein.

freedman A manumitted slave. Though technically a free man (and, if his former master was a Roman citizen, himself also a Roman citizen), the freedman remained in the patronage of his former master, who had first call on his time and services.

free man A man born free and never sold into slavery.

Gades Modern Cádiz.

Gallia Gaul. Commonly regarded as the area of modern France and Belgium. There were four Gauls: the Roman Gallic Province (always called, simply, the Province), which encompassed the coastline of the Mediterranean Sea between Niceia (modern Nice) and the Pyrenees and included a tongue which went from the Cebenna (the Cévennes) to the Alps as far up as Lugdunum (modern Lyon); the lands of the Belgae, which lay to the north of the Sequana River (the Seine) from the Atlantic to the Rhenus (Rhine); the lands of the Celtae, which lay south of the Sequana and to the north of the Garumna (Garonne); and the lands collectively called Aquitania, which lay between the Garumna and the Pyrenees. The latter three Gauls together constituted Gallia Comata.

Gallia Comata Gaul of the Long-hairs. That is, un-Romanized Gaul.

games In Latin, *ludi*. Public entertainments put on by certain magistrates of the year, and held in one of the two circuses (usually the Circus Maximus), or both circuses. Games consisted of chariot races (the most popular events), athletic contests and theatrical performances put on in temporary wooden theaters. The Republican games did *not* include gladiatorial combat, which was confined to funeral games put on by private individuals in the Forum Romanum. Free Roman men and women were permitted to attend the games, but not freedmen or freedwomen; the circuses could not accommodate all the free, let alone the freed.

garum A noisome concentrate made from fish which was used as a basis for many sauces. It was highly prized by gourmets.

Garumna River The Garonne River.

Gaul, Gauls For French Gaul, see **Gallia**. "Gaul" was what Romans called a man of Celtic or Belgic race, no matter which part of the world he inhabited. Thus there were Gauls not only in modern France, but also in Italian Gaul, Switzerland, Hungary, Czechoslovakia and that part of modern Turkey around Ankara.

Genava Modern Genève, Geneva.

gens humana The human family of peoples.

Genusus River The Shkumbin River in modern Albania.

Gergovia The principal *oppidum* of a very powerful Gallic tribe, the Arverni. It was near modern Clermont-Ferrand.

German Ocean Basically, the North Sea and the Baltic Sea.

Gerrae! Rubbish! Nonsense!

gladiator During Republican times there were only two kinds of gladiator, the Thracian and the Gaul. These were styles of combat, not nationalities. Republican gladiators did not fight to the death, because they were expensive investments owned privately by individuals; purchasing, training, feeding and housing a gladiator was costly. Few of them were slaves. Most were deserters from the Roman army, offered a choice between disenfranchisement and a term as a gladiator. The gladiator fought for a total of six years or thirty bouts (he had around five bouts per year), after which he was free to do as he pleased. The best gladiators were heroes to the people of Italia and Italian Gaul.

gladius The Roman sword. It was short, the blade being about 2 feet (600mm) long and sharp on both edges. It ended in a point. The handle was made of wood in the case of an ordinary soldier; those higher than a ranker who could afford it preferred a handle made of ivory carved in the shape of an eagle.

Gorgobina The principal *oppidum* of the Boii. Modern St.-Parize-le-Chatel.

Head Count See ***capite censi***.

Hellenic, Hellenized These are terms relating to the spread of Greek culture and customs after the time of Alexander the Great. Life style, architecture, dress, industry, government, commerce and the Greek language were all part of it.

Heracleia Near modern Bitola, in Makedonia.

Hierosolyma The other, Hellenic name for Jerusalem.

horse See **October Horse** and **Public Horse**.

hostis The term used when the Senate and People of Rome declared a man an outlaw, a public enemy.
Iberus River The Ebro River.
Icauna River The Yonne River.
Ides The third of the three named days of the month which represented the fixed points of the month. Dates were reckoned backward from each of these points—Kalends, Nones and Ides. The Ides occurred on the fifteenth day of the long months (March, May, July and October) and on the thirteenth day of the other months.
Ilium The Roman name for Troy.
Illerda Modern Lérida in Spain.
Illyricum The wild and mountainous lands bordering the Adriatic on its eastern side. The native peoples belonged to an Indo-European race called Illyrians, were tribalized, and detested first Greek and then Roman coastal incursions. By the time of Caesar, Illyricum was an unofficial province governed in conjunction with Italian Gaul. That Caesar's long years as governor were good for Illyricum is evidenced by the fact that Illyricum remained loyal to him during his civil wars.
imperium Imperium was the degree of authority vested in a curule magistrate or promagistrate. It meant that a man owned the authority of his office, and could not be gainsaid provided he was acting within the limits of his particular level of imperium and within the laws dictating his conduct. Imperium was conferred by a *lex curiata* and lasted for one year only. Extensions for prorogued governors had to be ratified by the Senate and/or People of Rome. Lictors shouldering the *fasces* indicated a man's imperium: the more lictors, the higher the imperium.
imperium maius Unlimited imperium, which outranked the imperium of the consuls of the year. The main benefactor of *imperium maius* was Pompey the Great.
in absentia Described a candidacy for public office approved of by the Senate (and the People, if necessary) and an election conducted in the absence of the candidate himself. He may have been waiting on the Campus Martius because imperium prevented his crossing the *pomerium* to register as a cadidate and fight the election in person. Cicero when consul in 63 B.C. enacted a law prohibiting *in absentia* candidacy; Pompey reinforced this during his consulship without a colleague in 52 B.C.
in suo anno Literally, "in his year." The phrase was used to describe men who attained curule office at the exact age the law and custom prescribed for a man holding that office. To be praetor and consul *in suo anno* was a great distinction, as it meant that a man had gained office at his first attempt.
intercalaris Because the Roman year was only 355 days long, some 20 days extra were inserted after the month of February every two years—or ought to have been. Very often this was not done, with the result that the calendar galloped ahead of the seasons. By the time Caesar

rectified the calendar in 46 B.C., the seasons were lagging 100 days behind the calendar, so few intercalations had been made. It was the duty of the Colleges of Pontifices and Augurs to intercalate; while Caesar, Pontifex Maximus from 63 B.C., was in Rome these intercalations were made, but when he went to Gaul in 58 B.C. the practice ceased, with one or two exceptions.

interrex It meant "between the kings." When Rome had no consuls to go into office on New Year's Day, the Senate appointed a patrician senator, leader of his decury, to assume office as the *interrex*. He served for five days, then a second *interrex* was appointed to hold elections. Sometimes public violence prevented the second *interrex* from this duty, with the result that a further series of *interreges* served until elections could be held.

Italia The Italian Peninsula. The boundary between Italia proper and Italian Gaul consisted of two rivers, the Arnus on the western side of the Apennines, and the Rubicon on the eastern side.

Italian Gaul In Latin, Gallia Cisalpina, meaning "Gaul on this side of the Alps." The peoples of Italian Gaul, which lay to the north of the rivers Arnus and Rubicon, and between the town of Ocelum in the west and Aquileia in the east, were held to be Gauls descended from the Gallic tribes which invaded Italy in 390 B.C., and therefore to the more conservative Roman mind not worthy to hold the full Roman citizenship. This became the sorest point in the minds of the Italian Gauls, particularly for those on the far (north) side of the Padus River (the Po); Pompey the Great's father, Pompey Strabo, legislated the full citizenship for those living south of the Padus in 89 B.C., while those living to the north continued as non-citizens or the second-class citizens who held the Latin Rights. Caesar was the great champion of full enfranchisement for all of Italian Gaul, and made it the first thing he legislated when appointed Dictator at the end of 49 B.C. It was, however, still governed as a province of Rome rather than as a part of Italia proper.

iugerum, iugera The Roman unit of land measurement. In modern terms the *iugerum* consisted of 0.623 (five-eighths) of an acre, or 0.252 (one-quarter) of a hectare. The modern reader used to acres will get close enough by dividing *iugera* by 2; for metric readers, divide by 4 to get the number of hectares.

Kalends The first of the three named days of each month which represented the fixed points of the month. The Kalends always occurred on the first day of the month. Originally they had been timed to coincide with the appearance of the New Moon.

knights The *equites,* the members of what Gaius Gracchus named the Ordo Equester or Equestrian Order. Under the kings of Rome, the *equites* had formed the cavalry segment of the Roman army; at this time horses were both scarce and expensive, with the result that the eighteen original Centuries comprising the knights were dowered with the Public Horse by the State. As the Republic came into being and grew, the importance of Roman knight cavalry waned. Yet the number of knight Centuries in the Classes kept increasing. By the second century B.C. Rome no longer fielded horse of her own, preferring to use Gauls as auxiliaries. The knights became a social and economic group having little to do with military matters. They were now defined by the censors in economic terms alone, though the State continued to provide a Public Horse for each of the eighteen hundred most senior *equites,* called the Eighteen. These original eighteen Centuries were kept at one hundred members each, but the rest of the knights' Centuries (between seventy-one and seventy-five) swelled within themselves to contain many more than one hundred men apiece.

Until 123 B.C. all senators were knights as well, but in that year Gaius Gracchus split the Senate off as a separate body of three hundred men. It was at best an artificial process; all nonsenatorial members of a senator's family were still classified as knights and the senators were not put into three senators-only Centuries for voting purposes, but left in whichever Centuries they had always occupied. Nor, it appears, were senators stripped of their Public Horses if they belonged in the ranks of the Eighteen.

Economically the full member of the First Class had to possess an income of 400,000 sesterces per annum; those knights whose income lay between 300,000 and 400,000 sesterces per annum were probably the *tribuni aerarii.* Senators were supposed to have an annual income of one million sesterces, but this was entirely unofficial; some censors were lenient about it, others strict.

The real difference between senators and knights lay in the kinds of activities they might pursue to earn income. Senators were forbidden to indulge in any form of commerce not pertaining to the ownership of land, whereas knights could.

latus clavus The broad purple stripe which adorned the right shoulder of a senator's tunic. He alone was entitled to wear it. The knight wore a narrow purple stripe, the *angustus clavus,* and those below the status of knights wore no stripe at all.

lectus imus, lectus medius, locus consularis A *lectus* was a couch, mostly used for dining (the *lectus funebris* was the funerary bier). Couches were arranged in threes to form a U; if one stood in the doorway of a dining room (the *triclinium*) looking into the U, the couch on the right was the *lectus imus,* the couch in the middle forming the bottom of the U was the *lectus medius,* and the couch on the left was the *lectus summus.* Socially the most desirable couch was the *lectus medius.* Positions on the couches were also socially graded, with the head of the household located at the left end of the *lectus medius.* The spot for the guest of honor, the *locus consularis,* was at the right end of the *lectus medius.* A continuous U of table at a little below couch height stood just in front of the couches.

During the Republic couches were reserved for men; women sat on chairs placed inside the U on the opposite side of the tables from the couches.

legate *Legatus*. The most senior members of a general's staff were his legates. To qualify to serve as a legate, a man had to be a member of the Senate. He answered only to the general, and was senior to all types of military tribune. Not every legate was a young man, however. Some were consulars who apparently volunteered for some interesting war because they hankered after a spell of military life, or were friends and/or relatives of the general—or were in need of some extra money from spoils.

legion *Legio*. Though it was rarely called upon to do so, the legion was the smallest unit of a Roman army capable of fighting a war on its own. In terms of manpower, equipment and warmaking facilities it was complete within itself. Between two and six legions clubbed together constituted an army; the times when an army contained more than six legions were unusual.

A legion comprised some 4,280 ranker soldiers, 60 centurions, 1,600 noncombatant servants, perhaps 300 artillerymen and 100 skilled artificers. The internal organization of a legion consisted of ten cohorts of six centuries each. In Caesar's time cavalry units were not grafted onto a legion, but constituted a separate force. Each legion appears to have had about thirty pieces of artillery, more catapultae than ballistae, before Caesar; he introduced the use of artillery into battle as a technique of softening up the enemy, and increased the number of pieces to fifty. The legion was commanded by a legate or an elected tribune of the soldiers if it belonged to the consuls of the year. Its officers were the centurions.

Though the troops belonging to a legion went into the same camp, they did not live together en masse in dormitory style; they were divided into units of eight soldiers and two noncombatants who tented and messed together. Reading the horrors of the American Civil War, one is impressed with the Roman arrangement. Roman soldiers ate fresh food because they ground their own wheat and made their own bread, porridge and other staples and were provided with well-salted or smoked bacon or pork for flavoring, and also ate dried fruit. Sanitary facilities within a camp predicated against enteric fevers and polluted water. An army not only marches on its stomach, it is also enabled to march when it is free from disease. Few Roman generals cared to command more than six legions because of the difficulties in supply; reading Caesar's *Commentaries* makes one understand how important a place Caesar gave to supply, as he mostly commanded between nine and eleven legions.

legionary This is the correct English word to call an ordinary Roman soldier (*miles gregarius*). "Legionnaire," which I have seen used by lesser scholars, is more properly applied to a soldier in the French Foreign Legion, or to a veteran of the American Legion.

lex, leges A law or laws. The word *lex* also came to be used of plebiscites, the laws passed in the Plebeian Assembly. A *lex* was not considered valid until it had been inscribed on stone or bronze and deposited in the vaults below the temple of Saturn. However, residence therein must have been brief, as space was limited and the temple of Saturn also housed the Treasury. After Sulla's Tabularium was finished, laws came to rest permanently therein. A law was named after the man or men who promulgated it and succeeded in having it ratified, but always (since *lex* is feminine gender) with the feminine ending to the name or names. This was followed by a brief description as to what the law was about. Laws could be—and sometimes were—repealed at some later date.

lex curiata A law endowing a curule magistrate or promagistrate with his imperium. It was passed by the thirty lictors who represented the thirty original Roman tribes. A *lex curiata* was also necessary before a patrician could be adopted by a plebeian.

lex data A law promulgated by a magistrate which had to be accompanied by a senatorial decree. It was not open to change by whichever Assembly the magistrate chose to present it to.

lex Julia Marcia Passed by the consuls Lucius Julius Caesar and Gaius Marcius Figulus in 64 B.C., it outlawed all but a few of the many different kinds of colleges, sodalities and clubs which proliferated throughout every stratum of Roman life. Its chief object was the crossroads college, which was seen as potentially dangerous politically. Publius Clodius was to prove this true after he, as tribune of the plebs, reinstated crossroads colleges in 58 B.C.

lex Plautia de vi Passed by a Plautius during the seventies B.C. and having to do with violence in public meetings.

lex Pompeia de iure magistratuum The infamous law Pompey passed while consul without a colleague in 52 B.C. It obliged all seekers of curule office to register their candidacy in person inside the sacred boundary of Rome; when reminded by Caesar's faction that the Law of the Ten Tribunes of the Plebs made it possible for Caesar to stand for consul the second time *in absentia,* Pompey said oops and tacked a codicil onto its end exempting Caesar. This codicil, however, was not inscribed on the bronze tablet bearing the law, and therefore had no validity at law.

lex Pompeia de vi Passed when Pompey was consul without a colleague in 52 B.C., and designed to reinforce the *lex Plautia.*

lex Pompeia Licinia de provincia Caesaris The law passed by Pompey and Crassus during their second consulships in 55 B.C. It gave Caesar all his provinces for a further five years, and forbade any discussion in the Senate about who would get his provinces afterward until March of 50 B.C.

lex Trebonia de provinciis consularibus Passed by Gaius Trebonius as a tribune of the plebs in 55 B.C. It gave Pompey and Crassus the provinces of Syria and both the Spains for a period of five years.

lex Villia annalis Passed in 180 B.C. by the tribune of the plebs Lucius Villius. It stipulated certain minimum ages at which the curule magistracies could be held and apparently also stipulated that two years must elapse between a man's holding the praetorship and the consulship. It is also generally accepted as stipulating that ten years must go by between a man's being consul for the first time and running for a second term as consul.

lictor The man who formally attended a curule magistrate as he went about his business. The lictor preceded the magistrate to clear him a way through the crowds, and was on hand to obey the magistrate in matters of custody, restraint or chastisement. The lictor had to be a Roman citizen and was a State employee; he was not of high social status, and probably depended upon largesse from his magistrate to eke out a poor wage. On his left shoulder he bore the bundle of rods called the ***fasces***. Within the city of Rome he wore a plain white toga, changing to a black toga for funerals; outside Rome he wore a scarlet tunic cinched at the waist by a broad black leather belt bossed in brass. Outside Rome he inserted the axes into his *fasces*.

There was a College of Lictors, though its site is not known. I have placed it behind the temple of the Lares Praestites on the eastern side of the Forum Romanum (behind the great inn on the corner of the Clivus Orbius), but there is no factual basis for this.

Within the College, which must have numbered some hundreds, the lictors were grouped in decuries of ten men, each headed by a prefect; the decuries were collectively supervised by several College presidents.

Liger River The Loire River.

Lissus Modern Lezhë in Albania.

litter A covered cubicle equipped with four legs upon which it rested when lowered to the ground. A horizontal pole on each corner projected forward and behind the conveyance; it was carried by four to eight men who picked it up by means of these poles. The litter was a slow form of transport, but it was by far the most comfortable known in the ancient world. Litters belonging to the richest persons were commodious enough to hold two people and a servant to wait on them.

Lugdunum Modern Lyon.

Lusitani The peoples of far western and northwestern Spain. Less exposed to Hellenic and Roman culture than the Celtiberians, the Lusitani were probably somewhat less Celtic than Iberian in racial content, though the two strains were mixed in them. Their organization was tribal, and they seem to have farmed and mined as well as grazed.

Lutetia An island in the Sequana (Seine) River which served as the principal *oppidum* of a Celtic tribe called the Parisii. Modern Paris.

magistrates The elected executives of the Senate and People of Rome. With the exception of the tribunes of the soldiers, they all belonged automatically to the Senate in Caesar's day. The diagram on page 642 clearly shows the nature of each magistracy, its seniority, who did the electing, and whether a magistrate owned imperium. The *cursus honorum* pro-

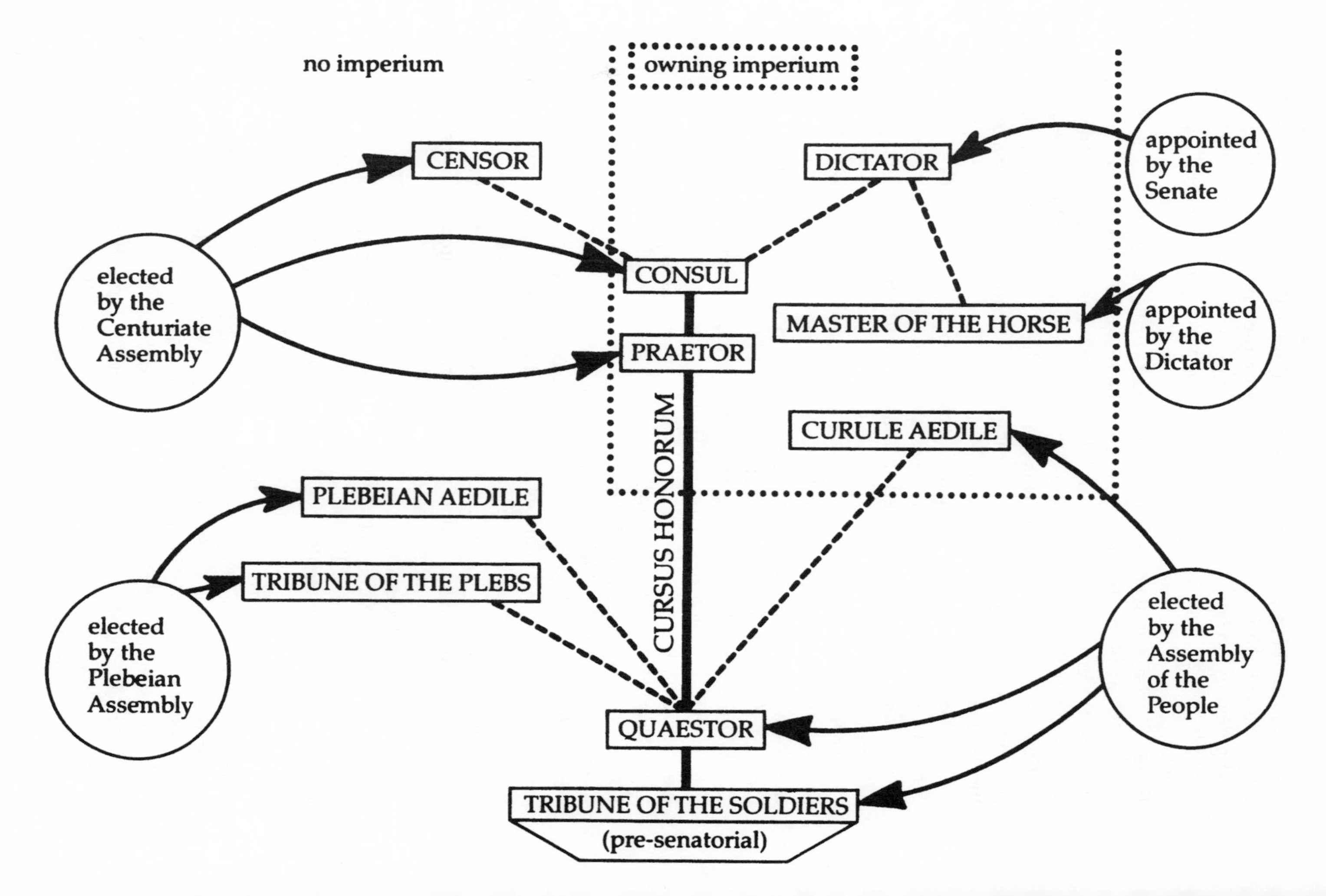

Roman Magistrates

ceeded in a straight line from quaestor through praetor to consul; censor, both kinds of aedile and the tribunate of the plebs were not magistracies attached to the *cursus honorum*. Save for the censor, all magistrates served for one year only. The dictator was a special case.

maiestas Treason.

malaria This pestilential disease, caused by four varieties of *Plasmodium* and vectored by the female *Anopheles* mosquito, was endemic throughout Italy. The Romans divided it into three kinds of ague: quartan (rigors occurring every four days), tertian (rigors occurring every three days) and a more malignant form wherein the rigors had no pattern. The Romans also knew the ague was more prevalent wherever there was swampy ground, hence their fear of the Pomptine Marshes and the Fucine Lake. What they didn't know was that the vector was a mosquito.

mantlet The shelter shed, usually roofed and walled with hides, which shielded Roman troops from enemy missiles.

marca Gallic for horse. Gallic was very akin to Latin and was quite easy for Romans to learn to speak; often we have no idea whether the Gallic word is actually a Latin word shifted into Gallic, or a Gallic word shifted into Latin.

Marsi One of the most important non-Roman Italian peoples. They lived around the shores of the Fucine Lake, which belonged to them, and their territory extended into the high Apennines. It bordered the lands of the Paeligni. Until the Italian War of 91–88 B.C., they had always been loyal to Rome. They worshiped snakes and were renowned snake charmers.

Massilia Modern Marseilles.

Mater Latin for mother.

Matisco One of the *oppida* belonging to a sept of the Aedui known as the Ambarri. It lay on the Arar (Saône) River. Modern Mâcon.

mentula, mentulae A very choice Latin obscenity meaning prick, pricks.

Mercedonius The name given to the twenty extra days inserted into the Roman calendar after the month of February to bring the calendar into line with the seasons.

Metiosedum The principal *oppidum* of a sept of the Parisii called the Meldi. It was an island in the Sequana (Seine) River. Modern Melun.

meum mel A Latin endearment. Literally, "my honey."

Mons Fiscellus The Gran Sasso d'Italia: Italy's highest mountain.

Mosa River The Maas in Belgium, the Meuse in France.

Mosella River The Moselle River.

mos maiorum The established order of things, used to encompass the customs, traditions and habits of Roman government and public institutions. It served as Rome's unwritten constitution. *Mos* meant established custom; in this context *maiores* meant ancestors or forebears. To sum up, the *mos maiorum* was how things had always been done—and how they should be done in the future too!

murus Gallicus The way Gauls built their *oppidum* walls. It consisted of very long, large wooden beams interspersed between stones, and was relatively impervious to the battering ram because the stones lent it great thickness, and the logs a tensile strength stone walls alone do not possess.

Narbo Modern Narbonne.

Nemausus Modern Nîmes.

nemer In Latin it could mean simply wood, but in Gallic seems to have referred specifically to the oak.

Nemetocenna An *oppidum* belonging to the Belgic Atrebates. Modern Arras.

nemeton The sacred oak grove of the Druids.

noncombatants There were sixteen hundred of these military servants in a legion. They were not slaves; they were free men of mostly Roman citizenship. It would seem likely that serving as a noncombatant acquitted a Roman citizen of his obligatory military duty if perhaps he felt himself ill equipped to be a soldier. One imagines they had to be fit men rather than physically handicapped, as they were required to keep up with the soldiers on the march and could (sometimes actually did) take up a sword and shield and fight. They seem to have been rural people in origin.

Nones The second of the three named days of the month which represented the fixed points of the month. The Nones occurred on the seventh day of the long months (March, May, July and October), and on the fifth day of the other months.

Noviodunum of the Bituriges An *oppidum* belonging to the Bituriges. Modern Neuvy.

Noviodunum Nevirnum An *oppidum* which seems to have belonged to the Aedui, though it bordered the lands of the Senones. It lay at the confluence of the Liger (Loire) and Elaver (Allier) rivers. Modern Nevers.

Novum Comum A full Roman citizen colony established by Caesar at the western tip of Lake Larius (now Lake Como); whether its inhabitants were citizens was moot, as magistrates like the senior Gaius Claudius Marcellus felt free to flog a citizen of Novum Comum. Modern Como.

nundinus, nundinae, nundinum The *nundinus* was the market day which came around every eight days, though it was almost always referred to in the plural, *nundinae*. The eight days which constituted the Roman week were called the *nundinum*.

October Horse On the Ides of October (which was the time the old campaigning season finished), the best warhorses of that year were picked out and harnessed in pairs to chariots. They then raced not in the Circus but on the sward of the Campus Martius. The right-hand horse of the winning team became the October Horse. It was sacrificed to Mars on a specially erected altar adjacent to the course of the race. The animal was ritually killed with a spear, after which its head was severed and piled over with little cakes, the *mola salsa,* while its tail and genitalia were rushed to the Regia in the Forum Romanum, and the blood dripped onto the altar within. The tail and genitalia were then given to the Vestal Virgins, who dripped some blood on Vesta's altar before mincing everything up and burning it; the ashes were then reserved for another annual festival, the Parilia.

The head of the horse was tossed into a crowd composed of two competing peoples, the residents of the Subura and of the Sacra Via. The crowd then fought for possession of the head. If the Sacra Via people won, the head was nailed to the outside of the Regia; if the Subura people won, the head was nailed to the Turris Mamilia, the highest building in the Subura.

What reason lay behind this very ancient rite is not known, even perhaps to the Romans of the late Republic themselves, save that it was in some way connected to the close of the campaigning season. We do not know if the competing horses were Public Horses, but might be pardoned for presuming they were.

Octodurum Modern Martigny in Switzerland.

Oltis River The Lot River.

oppidum, oppida The *oppidum* was the Gallic stronghold. With few exceptions it was not designed to be lived in, so was not a town. It contained the tribe's treasures and stockpiled foods in granaries and warehouses, also a meeting hall. Some *oppida* accommodated the king or chief thane. A few, like Avaricum, were real cities.

Oricum Modern Oriku in Albania.

Padus River The Po River.

palisade The fortified section of a wall above the level of the fighting platform inside it. It was usually divided into breastworks for fighting over and battlements for dodging behind.

paludamentum The bright scarlet cloak worn by a full general.

paterfamilias The head of a Roman family unit. His right to do as he pleased with the various members of his family was rigidly protected at law.

patrician, Patriciate The Patriciate was the original Roman aristocracy. To an ancestor-revering, birth-conscious people like the Romans, the importance of belonging to patrician stock can hardly be overestimated. The older among the patrician families were aristocrats before Rome existed, the youngest among them (the Claudii) apparently emerging at the very beginning of the Republic. All through the Republic they kept the title of patrician, as well as a degree of prestige unattainable by any plebeian, no matter how noble and august his line. However, by the last century of the Republic a patrician owned little special distinction apart from his blood; the wealth and energy of the great plebeian families had steadily eroded away patrician rights. Even in the late Republic, the importance of patrician blood can hardly be exaggerated, which is why men like Sulla and Caesar, of the oldest, most patrician blood, were seen as potentially able to make themselves King of Rome, whereas men like Gaius Marius and Pompey the Great, heroes supreme though they were, could not even dream of making themselves King of Rome. Blood was all.

During the last century of the Republic the following patrician families were still producing senators, and some praetors and consuls: Aemilius, Claudius, Cornelius, Fabius (but through adoption only), Julius, Manlius, Pinarius, Postumius, Sergius, Servilius, Sulpicius and Valerius.

pedarii See **Senate**.

People of Rome This term embraced every single Roman citizen who was not a member of the Senate; it applied to patricians as well as to plebeians, and to the *capite censi* as much as to the knights of the Eighteen.

peristyle Most affluent Roman houses, be they city or country, were built around an interior open court called the peristyle. It varied considerably in size, and usually contained a pool and fountain. For those who can get there, I strongly urge that they visit what will now be the old Getty Museum at Malibu, California; it is a replica of the villa at Herculaneum owned by Caesar's father-in-law, Lucius Calpurnius Piso. I can never go to California without once again visiting it. Now *there's* a peristyle!

phalerae These were round, chased, ornamented gold or silver discs about 3 to 4 inches (75 to 100mm) in diameter. Originally they were worn as insignia by Roman knights, and formed a major part of their horses' decorations. Gradually *phalerae* came to be military decorations awarded for exceptional bravery in battle. Normally they were given in sets of nine (three rows of three each) upon a decorated leather harness of straps designed to be worn over the mail shirt or cuirass. Centurions almost inevitably wore *phalerae*.

Picenum The calf of the Italian leg. Its western boundary formed the crest of the Apennines; Umbria lay to the north, and Samnium to the south; the eastern boundary was the Adriatic Sea. The original inhabitants were of Italiote or Illyrian stock, but there was a tradition that Sabines had migrated east of the Apennine crest and settled in Picenum, bringing with them as their tutelary god Picus, the woodpecker, from which the region got its name. A tribe of Gauls, the Senones, also settled in the area at the time Italy was invaded by the first King Brennus of the Gauls in 390 B.C. Politically Picenum fell into two parts: northern Picenum was closely allied to southern Umbria and was under the sway of the great family Pompeius, whereas Picenum south of the Flosis or Flussor River was under the sway of peoples committed to the Samnites.

pilum, pila The Roman infantry spear, especially as modified by Gaius Marius. It had a very small, wickedly barbed head of iron and an upper shaft of iron; this was joined to a shaped wooden stem which fitted the hand comfortably. Marius modified it by introducing a weakness into the junction between iron and wooden sections, so that when the *pilum* lodged in an enemy shield or body, it broke apart, and thus was rendered useless to the enemy as a missile. After a battle all the broken *pila* were collected from the field; they were easily mended by the legion's artificers.

pilus prior See **centurion.**

Pindenissus The whereabouts of this town have defeated me. Look though I will, I cannot find Pindenissus. Cicero informs us that it was in Cappadocia, and also that it took him *fifty-seven* days to besiege and take it. Which I interpret as a measure of the military ability of Cicero and his legate Gaius Pomptinus, rather than a measure of its might and power. Otherwise it would surely be better known.

Placentia Modern Piacenza.

plebeian, Plebs All Roman citizens who were not patricians were plebeians; that is, they belonged to the Plebs (the *e* is short: "Plebs" rhymes with "webs," not "glebes"). At the beginning of the Republic no plebeian could be a priest, a magistrate, or even a senator. This situation lasted only a very short while; one by one the exclusively patrician institutions crumbled before the onslaught of the Plebs, who far outnumbered the patricians—and several times threatened to secede. By the late Republic there was very little advantage to being a patrician—except that everyone knew patrician was better.

Because a plebeian was not a patrician, the Plebs invented a new aristocracy which enabled them to call themselves noblemen *if* they possessed praetors or consuls in the family. This added an extra dimension to the concept of nobility in Rome.

Plebeian Assembly See **Assembly.**

podex An impolite word for the posterior fundamental orifice: an arsehole or asshole rather than an anus.

pomerium The sacred boundary enclosing the city of Rome. Marked by white stones called *cippi,* it was reputedly inaugurated by King Servius Tullus, and remained without change until Sulla's dictatorship. The *pomerium,* however, did not follow the line of Servius Tullus's walls, which indicates that he did not determine the sacred boundary. The whole of the ancient Palatine city of Romulus was inside the *pomerium,* whereas the Capitol and the Aventine were not. Custom and tradition permitted a man to extend the *pomerium,* but only if he had added significantly to Roman territory. In religious terms, Roma herself existed only within the *pomerium;* all outside it was merely Roman territory.

pontifex Many Latin etymologists think that in ancient times the pontifex was a maker of bridges (*pons* means bridge), and that this was regarded as a mystical art which put the maker in very close touch with the Gods. Be that as it may, by the time Rome of the kings came into being, the pontifex was definitely a priest. Incorporated into a special college, he served as an adviser to the magistrates and *comitia* in all religious matters—and would become a magistrate himself (election to the pontificate meant a man was capable of winning almost every public office). At first all the pontifices had to be patrician, but a *lex Ogulnia* of 300 B.C. stipulated that half the members of the College of Pontifices had to be plebeian. Until 104 B.C. new priests were co-opted by the College; in that year, however, Gnaeus Domitius Ahenobarbus brought in a law requiring all priests and augurs to be elected at an assembly comprising seventeen of the thirty-five tribes chosen by lot. Sulla tried to restore co-optation, but the process was returned to election in 63 B.C. Priests could be well below senatorial age when co-opted or elected. They served for life.

Pontifex Maximus The head of Rome's State-administered religion, and most senior of all priests. He had always been elected, though there is strong reason to believe that Quintus Caecilius Metellus Pius, the Pontifex Maximus before Caesar's election, was not elected. A passage in Pliny the Elder suggests he stammered—*not* desirable in a role which had to be word-perfect. The *lex Labiena* which returned the priestly and augural colleges to election in 63 B.C. was very convenient for Caesar if, as I believe, Pontifex Maximus too had been removed from election. He stood and won shortly after the *lex Labiena* came into force.

Pontifex Maximus was bestowed for life. At first he had to be a patrician, but soon could as easily be a plebeian. The State gave him its most imposing house as his residence, the Domus Publica in the middle of the Forum Romanum. In Republican times he shared the Domus Publica with the Vestal Virgins on a half-and-half basis. His official headquarters were inside the Regia, but this tiny archaic building held no space for offices, so he worked next door.

popa A public servant attached to religious duties. His only job appears to have been to wield the stunning hammer at sacrifices, but no doubt he helped clean and tidy afterward.

Portus Gesoriacus A village on the Fretum Britannicum (the Straits of Dover). Modern Boulogne.

Portus Itius A village on the Fretum Britannicum (the Straits of Dover) some miles to the north of Portus Gesoriacus. Both these villages lay in the territory of the Belgic Morini. It is still debated as to whether Portus Itius is now Wissant or Calais.

praefectus fabrum One of the most important men in a Roman army, though technically the *praefectus fabrum* was not a part of the army. He was a civilian appointed to the post by the general, and was responsible for equipping and supplying the army in all respects, from its animals and their fodder to its men and their food. Because he let out contracts to businessmen and manufacturers for equipment and supplies, he was a very powerful person—and unless he was a man of superior integrity, in a perfect position to enrich himself at the expense of the army. That men as powerful and important as Caesar's first *praefectus fabrum,* the banker Lucius Cornelius Balbus, were willing to accept the post was indication of its profitability. And he, like his successor Mamurra, seems not to have foisted inferior equipment and gear on Caesar's army.

praenomen A Roman man's first name. There were very few *praenomina* in use—perhaps twenty in all—and half of these were uncommon, or else confined to the men of one particular family, as with Mamercus, a *praenomen* of the Aemilii Lepidi only. Each *gens* or family or clan favored certain *praenomina,* usually two or three out of the twenty. A modern scholar can often tell from a man's *praenomen* whether he was a genuine member of the Famous Family whose gentilicial name he bore. The Julii, for example, favored Sextus, Gaius and Lucius only; therefore a man called Marcus Julius is almost certainly not a patrician Julian, but rather the descendant of a freed Julian slave. The Licinii favored Publius, Marcus and Lucius; the Cornelii favored Publius, Lucius and Gnaeus; the Servilii of the patrician family of Servilians favored Quintus and Gnaeus. Appius belonged exclusively to the Claudii Pulchri.

praetor This magistracy ranked second in seniority in the Roman magisterial hierarchy. At the very beginning of the Republic, the two highest magistrates of all were known as praetors. By the end of the fourth century B.C., however, the highest magistrates were being called consuls; praetors were relegated to second best. One praetor was the sole representative of this position for many decades thereafter; he was obviously the *praetor urbanus,* as his duties were confined to the city of Rome, thus freeing up the two consuls for duties as war leaders outside the city. In 242 B.C. a second praetor, the *praetor peregrinus,* was created to deal with matters relating to foreign nationals and Italia rather than Rome. As Rome acquired her overseas provinces, more praetors were created to govern them, going out to do so in their year of office rather than after their year of office as propraetors. By the last century B.C. most years saw six praetors elected, but sometimes eight; Sulla brought the number up to eight during his dictatorship, but limited praetorian duty during the year of office to presiding over his new standing courts. From this time on, praetors were judges.

praetor peregrinus I have chosen to translate this as the foreign praetor because he dealt with non-citizens. By the time of Sulla his duties were confined to litigation and the dispensation of legal decisions; he traveled all over Italia as well as hearing cases involving non-citizens within the city of Rome.

praetor urbanus The urban praetor. After Sulla, his duties were almost all to do with litigation, but civil rather than criminal. His imperium did not extend beyond the sixth milestone from Rome, and he was not allowed to leave Rome for more than ten days at a time. If both the consuls were absent from Rome, he became the city's chief magistrate.

He was empowered to summon the Senate, execute government policies, and could even marshal and organize the city's defenses under threat of attack.

Priapus Originally an important Greek fertility deity, in Rome he seems to have been a symbol of luck. Represented as an ugly and grotesque man, his emblem was his penis, which was always huge and erect; so much so, in fact, that quite often the phallus was bigger than Priapus himself. A very great many of the cheap little pottery lamps were made in the form of Priapus, with the flame emerging from the penis tip. I would interpret the Roman attitude to Priapus as more one of affection than veneration.

primipilus, primus pilus See **centurion.**

privatus A man who was a member of the Senate but not in office as a magistrate.

pro: proconsul, promagistrate, propraetor, proquaestor The prefix "pro" was an indication that a man filling the duties of a magistrate was not a magistrate actually in office. Normally the promagistrate had served his term in office already, and was sent to do some kind of duty—mostly provincial—on behalf of the consuls, praetors or quaestors of the year. He held imperium of the same degree as those in office.

proletarii People so poor that the only thing they could give Rome were children—*proles*. See ***capite censi.***

prorogue In the context used in these books, to prorogue was to extend a man's promagisterial position beyond its usual duration of one year.

proscription The Roman name for a practice not confined to Roman times: namely, the entering of a man's name on a list which stripped him of everything, often including his life. There was no process of law involved, nor did the proscribed man have the right to trial, presentation of exonerating evidence, or any kind of hearing to protest his innocence. Sulla first made proscription infamous when Dictator; he proscribed some forty senators and sixteen hundred senior knights, most of whom were killed, all of whom served to enrich an empty Treasury. After Sulla, the very mention of the word "proscription" in Rome created absolute panic.

pteryges A Greek word used to describe the arrangement of leather straps which composed a high-ranking Roman military man's kilt or skirt; the *pteryges* were arranged in two overlapping layers and afforded good protection for the loins.

publicani The tax-farmers. These were men organized into commercial companies which contracted to the Treasury to collect taxes and tithes in the provinces.

Public Horse A horse which belonged to the State—that is, to the Senate and People of Rome. During the time of the kings of Rome the practice of donating a warhorse to Rome's knight cavalry had begun; it continued right through the five hundred–odd years of the Republic. Public Horses were confined to the eighteen hundred men of the Eighteen, the senior Centuries of the First Class. Evidence suggests that many senators continued to use Public Horses after Gaius Gracchus split the Senate off from the Ordo Equester. To own a Public Horse was a mark of a man's importance.

quadrireme See **quinquereme**.

quaestor The lowest rung on the *cursus honorum* of Roman magistracies. Quaestor was always an elected office, but until Sulla laid down that the quaestorship would be the only way (aside from being elected a tribune of the plebs) a man could enter the Senate, it was not necessary for a man to be quaestor in order to be a senator; the censors had had the power to co-opt a man to the Senate. Sulla then increased the number of quaestors from twelve to twenty, and laid down that the minimum age for a man to hold the office of quaestor was thirty. The chief duties of a quaestor were fiscal, and determined by casting lots. He might be seconded to Treasury duty within Rome, or to collect customs duties, port dues and rents elsewhere in Italia, or serve as the manager of a provincial governor's moneys. A man going to govern a province could ask for a quaestor by name. The quaestor's year in office began on the fifth day of December.

Quinctilis Originally Quinctilis was the fifth month of the Roman year, which had begun in March. When the New Year was transferred to the first day of January, Quinctilis kept its name. It is now known as July; we know from the letters of Cicero that it acquired the name "Julius" during Caesar's lifetime.

quinquereme A very common and popular form of ancient war galley; also known as the "five." Like the bireme, trireme and quadrireme, it was much longer than it was broad in the beam, and was designed for no other purpose than to conduct war on the sea. It used to be thought that the quadrireme contained four banks of oars and the quinquereme five, but it is now almost universally agreed that no galley ever had more than three banks of oars, and more commonly only two. The quadrireme or "four" and the quinquereme or "five" most likely got their names from the number of men on each oar, or else this number was divided between the two banks of oars. If there were five men on an oar, only the man on the tip or end of the oar had to be highly skilled: he guided the oar and did the really hard work, while the other four provided little beyond muscle power. However, four or five men on one oar meant that at the commencement of the sweep the rowers had to stand, falling back onto their seat as they pulled. A "five" wherein the rowers could remain seated throughout the stroke would have needed three banks of oars, as in the trireme: two men on each of the two upper banks, and one man on the lowest bank.

It seems that all three kinds of quinquereme were used, each community or nation having its preference.

For the rest, the quinquereme was decked, the upper oars lay within an outrigger, and it had room on board for marines and some pieces of artillery. A mast and sail were still part of the design, though usually left ashore if battle was expected. The oarsmen numbered about 270, the sailors perhaps 30; about 120 marines could be accommodated. Like all war galleys of pre-Christian times, the quadrireme and quinquereme were rowed by professional oarsmen, never by slaves.

Quirites Roman citizens of civilian status.

redoubt A part of fortifications outside the main defensive wall, a little fort. It was usually square, sometimes polygonal.

Regia The tiny ancient building in the Forum Romanum thought to have been erected by the second King of Rome, Numa Pompilius. It was oddly shaped and oriented toward the north, and in Caesar's day had long served as the headquarters of the Pontifex Maximus, though it was not large enough to use as offices; these had been tacked onto it. It was an inaugurated temple and contained altars to some of Rome's oldest and most shadowy gods—Opsiconsiva, Vesta, Mars of the sacred shields and spears.

Republic The word was originally two words—*res publica*—meaning the thing which constitutes the people as a whole—that is, the government. Rome was a *true* Republic in that its executives or magistrates were elected rather than designated from within the legislature: American-style government rather than the Westminster System of British Commonwealth countries.

Rhenus River The river Rhine.

Rhodanus River The river Rhône.

right act A phrase used by those who subscribed to the doctrines of Stoicism. It meant that the act was good, proper, right.

rostra A *rostrum* (singular) was the reinforced oaken beak of a war galley, the part used to ram other ships. In 338 B.C. the consul Gaius Maenius attacked the Volscian fleet in Antium harbor and utterly defeated it. To commemorate the end of the Volsci as a rival power to Rome, Maenius removed the beaks of the ships he had sent to the bottom or captured, and fixed them to the Forum wall of the speaker's platform tucked into the side of the well of the Comitia. Ever after, the speaker's platform was known as the rostra—the ships' beaks. Other victorious admirals followed Maenius's example; when no more ship's beaks could be fixed to the rostra wall, they were fixed to tall columns erected in the area of the rostra.

Rubicon River More properly, Rubico River. There is still great debate about which of the rivers running from the Apennines into the Adriatic Sea is actually the Rubico, which Sulla fixed as the border between Italian Gaul and Italia proper. Most authorities seem to favor the modern Rubicone, but this is a short, very shallow stream which does not extend into the Apennines proper, and so comes nowhere near the sources of the Arnus River, which was the boundary on the western side of the Italian Peninsula. After much reading of Strabo and the other ancient sources describing this area, I have fixed upon the modern Savio River, which does have its sources in the high Apennines. Rivers forming boundaries were major streams, not minor ones. The Ronco River, north of the Savio, would be a contender were it not so close to Ravenna at its outflow. The main problem, it seems to me, is that we really have little idea of what the ancient river map was like; during the Middle Ages massive drainage works were carried out all around Ravenna, which means that the ancient rivers may have had a different course.

Sabis River The river Sambre.

sagum The Roman military cape. It was made on the principle of a Mexican poncho, cut on the circle with a hole in its middle through which the head was poked. It probably extended to the hips, leaving the hands free. It was made of untreated, very oily (and therefore water-repellent) Ligurian wool.

Sallust The English name given to the Roman historian Gaius Sallustius Crispus, who lived during Caesar's time. It is interesting that the two historians who knew Caesar personally were both favorable to Caesar in their writings; the other was Gaius Asinius Pollio. Sallust seems to have been a rather randy fellow; his earliest claim to fame is that Milo took a horsewhip to him for philandering with Fausta, Milo's wife. Sallust wrote two surviving works: a history of the war against Jugurtha of Numidia, and a history of the conspiracy of Lucius Sergius Catilina.

Salona Modern Split in Yugoslavia

Samara River The Somme River.

Samarobriva An *oppidum* belonging to the Belgic Ambiani, a tribe closely allied to the Atrebates. Modern Amiens.

Samnium That region of peninsular Italia lying between Latium, Campania, Apulia and Picenum. The area was mountainous and not remarkably fertile; Samnite towns tended to be small and poor, and included Caieta, Aeclanum and Bovianum. The two prosperous cities, Aesernia and Beneventum, were Latin Rights colonies seeded by Rome to keep an eye on things and form a nucleus of pro-Roman feeling. Samnium was inhabited by the true Samnites, but also by peoples called Frentani, Paeligni, Marrucini and Vestini; true Samnites also dominantly inhabited parts of southern Picenum and southern Campania.

Several times during Rome's history the Samnites inflicted hideous defeats upon Roman armies. They were still active in resistance to Rome in 82 B.C. when they contended with Sulla for possession of Rome in the battle at the Colline Gate. Sulla won.

Sampsiceramus The quintessential Eastern potentate, if one is to believe Cicero, who seems to have—typical wordsmith—fallen in love with the sound of "Sampsiceramus." He was King of Emesa in Syria, which does not indicate a great degree of power or even of wealth. What Sampsiceramus apparently did par excellence was to flaunt what wealth he had in the most exotic way. Once Pompey became fabled, Cicero called him Sampsiceramus whenever they fell out.

satrap Originally the title given by the kings of Persia to their provincial or territorial governors. Alexander the Great seized upon the term and employed it, as did the later Arsacid kings of the Parthians and the kings of Armenia. The region administered by a satrap was a satrapy.

Scaldis River The Schelde River in Belgium.

Scipio Aemilianus Publius Cornelius Scipio Aemilianus Africanus Numantinus was born in 185 B.C. He was not a Cornelian of the Scipio branch, but rather the son of the conqueror of Macedonia, Lucius Aemilius Paullus, who gave him in adoption to the elder son of Scipio Africanus. Scipio Aemilianus's mother was a Papiria, and his wife was the surviving daughter of Cornelia the Mother of the Gracchi, Sempronia; she was his close blood cousin.

After a distinguished military career during the Third Punic War in 149–148 B.C., Aemilianus was elected consul in 147 B.C. As he was not old enough for the consulship, his election was bitterly opposed by many members of the Senate. Sent to Africa to take charge of the Third Punic War, he displayed that relentless and painstaking thoroughness which was thereafter the cornerstone of his career; he built a mole to close the harbor of Carthage and blockaded the city by land. It fell in 146 B.C., after which he pulled it apart stone by stone. However, modern scholars discount the story that he ploughed salt into the soil to make sure Carthage never rose again; the Romans themselves believed the salt story. He was an ineffectual censor thanks to an inimical colleague in 142 B.C.; then in 140 B.C. he took ship for the East, accompanied by his two Greek friends, the historian Polybius and the philosopher Panaetius. In 134 B.C. he was elected consul for the second time, and commissioned to deal with the town of Numantia in Nearer Spain. This tiny place had defied and defeated a whole series of Roman armies and generals for fifty years when Scipio Aemilianus arrived before it. Once he got there, Numantia lasted eight months. After it fell he destroyed it down to the last stone and beam, and deported or executed its four thousand citizens.

News from Rome had informed him that his brother-in-law Tiberius Gracchus was undermining the *mos maiorum;* Aemilianus conspired with their mutual cousin Scipio Nasica to bring Tiberius Gracchus down. Though Tiberius Gracchus was already dead when Aemilianus returned to Rome in 132 B.C., he was commonly held responsible. Then in 129 B.C. Aemilianus died so suddenly and unexpectedly that it was ever afterward rumored that he had been murdered. The principal suspect was his wife, Sempronia, Tiberius Gracchus's sister; she loathed her husband, all Rome knew it.

By nature Scipio Aemilianus was a curious mixture. A great intellectual with an abiding love for things Greek, he stood at the center of a group of men who patronized and encouraged the likes of Polybius, Panaetius, and the Latin playwright Terence. As a friend, Aemilianus was everything a friend should be. As an enemy, he was cruel, coldblooded and utterly ruthless. A genius at organization, he could yet blunder as badly as he did in his opposition to Tiberius Gracchus. An extremely cultured and witty man of pronounced good taste, he was also morally and ethically ossified.

Senate Properly, *Senatus*. It came into being as a patricians-only body of one hundred men and served as an advisory council to the King of Rome. Not long into the Republic, it contained some three hundred senators, a great many of whom were plebeians. Because of its antiquity, the legal definitions of its rights, powers and duties were mostly nonexistent. Membership in the Senate was for life (unless a man was expelled by the censors for inappropriate behavior or impoverishment), which predisposed it toward the oligarchical form it acquired. Throughout its history its members fought strenuously to preserve their pre-eminence in government. Until Sulla stipulated that entry to the Senate was via the quaestorship, appointment was in the purlieus of the censors. The *lex Atinia* provided that tribunes of the plebs should automatically enter the Senate upon election. There was a means test of entirely unofficial nature: a senator was supposed to enjoy an income of a million sesterces per annum.

Senators alone were permitted to wear the *latus clavus* or broad purple stripe upon the right shoulder of the tunic; they wore closed shoes of maroon leather (the black-and-white senatorial shoe belonged to Imperial times) and a ring which had originally been made of iron, but later came to be gold. Only men who had held a curule magistracy wore the purple-bordered *toga praetexta;* ordinary senators wore plain white togas.

Meetings of the Senate had to be held in properly inaugurated premises. The Senate had its own meeting house or *curia,* the Curia Hostilia, but it was prone to meet elsewhere at the whim of the man convoking the meeting. Senatorial sessions could go on only between sunrise and sunset and could not take place on days when any of the Assemblies met, though they were permissible on comitial days if no Assembly meeting was scheduled.

No matter what the speaking order of the particular era, a patrician senator always preceded a plebeian senator of equal rank. Not all members of the House were accorded the privilege of speaking. The *senatores pedarii* (described in my books by the Westminster Parliamentary term "backbenchers") could vote, but could not open their mouths in debate. They sat behind the men permitted to speak, so "backbencher" is a reasonable English compromise. No restrictions were placed upon the time limit or content of a man's speech, so filibustering was common. If an issue was unimportant or everyone was obviously inclined one way, voting might be by a show of hands; a formal vote took place by a division of the House, meaning that the senators left their stations and grouped themselves to either side of the curule dais according to their yea or nay, and were then physically counted.

Always an advisory rather than a truly legislating body, the Senate issued its *consulta* or decrees as requests to the various Assemblies. If the issue was serious, a quorum had to be present before a vote could be taken, though we do not know what precise number constituted a quorum. Certainly most meetings were not heavily attended; there was no rule which said a man appointed to the Senate had to attend meetings of it, even on an irregular basis.

In some areas the Senate reigned supreme, despite its lack of formal legislating power: the *fiscus* was controlled by the Senate, as it controlled the Treasury; foreign affairs were left to the Senate; and the appointment of provincial governors, the regulation of provincial affairs and the conduct of wars were senatorial.

Senatus Consultum Ultimum Properly, *senatus consultum de re publica defendenda.* This was the Senate's ultimate decree and dated from 121 B.C., when Gaius Gracchus resorted to violence to prevent the overthrow of his laws. Rather than appoint a dictator to deal with the violence, the ultimate decree came into being. Basically it was a declaration of martial law, though its restrictions on civilian movement were often clearly defined in the terms of its issuance. A Senatus Consultum Ultimum overrode all other governmental bodies and persons.

Sequana River The Seine River.

Serapis A hybrid chief deity for the more Hellenized parts of Egypt, especially Alexandria. Invented, it seems, during the reign of the first Ptolemy, an ex-marshal of Alexander the Great's, Serapis was a peculiar fusion of Zeus with Osiris and the tutelary deity of the Apis bull—Osirapis. Statues of Serapis were rendered in the Greek manner and displayed a bearded man wearing a huge basket crown.

Serica The mysterious land we know as China. In Caesar's day the Silk Route had not come into being; "silk" was a floss obtained from a moth native to the Aegean island of Cos.

sestertius, sesterces Roman accounting practices were established in sesterces, though the denarius, more valuable, was apparently a commoner coin in circulation. In Latin writing, "sesterces" was abbreviated as *HS.* A very small silver coin, the sestertius was worth one quarter of a denarius.

Sextilis Originally the sixth month of the Roman year when it began in March; its original name was retained even after the New Year shifted to January 1. During the principate of Augustus it acquired its modern name—August.

Sicoris River The river Segre in Spain.

Sol Indiges One of the most ancient Italian Gods. As the Sun, Sol

Indiges was the husband of the Earth, Tellus. He was enormously reverenced. Oaths sworn by him were very serious affairs.

sow A smelted lump of metal. Iron, copper, silver, gold and some other metals were kept as sows of various weight. Both silver and gold sows were smoother and more regular in shape because these were precious metals and quite soft. Base metal sows perhaps had a piggy shape, rounded on the underside, nipply on the upper side.

stadia A Greek measure of distance. The *stadium* (singular) was about a furlong in length, and is easiest reckoned at eight *stadia* to the Roman mile.

Stoic One who subscribed to the system of philosophical thought founded by the Phoenician Zeno. Though Zeno's system was a complete one, it is best summed up as holding that virtue is the only real good, and immorality or unethicality the only real evil. He taught that natural travails, from pain and death to poverty, are not important; a good man is a moral and ethical one, and a good man must always be a happy man. Called after the Stoa Poikile in Athens where Zeno taught, Stoicism eventually arrived in Rome. It was never very popular among such a pragmatic and commonsensible people, but it did have its Roman adherents. The most famous one was Cato Uticensis, Caesar's bitterest enemy.

Subura The poorest and most densely populated part of the city of Rome. It lay to the east of the Forum Romanum in the declivity between the Oppian spur of the Esquiline Mount and the Viminal Hill. Its people were notoriously polyglot and independent of mind; many Jews lived in the Subura, which in Caesar's time contained Rome's only synagogue. Suetonius says that Caesar was brought up in the Subura.

Suebi A Germanic people who inhabited the wilder and more forested regions of Germania from south of the Rhenus's (Rhine's) confluence with the Mosella (Moselle) to the Vosegus (Vosges), the Jura and the approaches to the lands of the Helvetii (Switzerland). The name means wanderers.

Suessionum The main *oppidum* of the Belgic Suessiones. Modern Soissons.

Sugambri A Germanic people who inhabited the lands adjacent to the Rhenus (Rhine) from its confluence with the Luppia almost to its confluence with the Mosella (Moselle). They were numerous and had broken the soil to farm.

sui iuris The term which indicated that a person of either sex was not under the authority of a *paterfamilias* figure. Such people were their own masters; they had complete control of their lives.

Sulla Lucius Cornelius Sulla Felix, whose remarkable career is detailed in the first three books in this series: *The First Man in Rome, The Grass Crown,* and *Fortune's Favorites.*

Superstes Means survivor.

talent This was the load a man could carry. Bullion and very large amounts of money were expressed in talents, but the term was not confined to precious metals and money. In modern mensuration, the talent weighed between 50 and 55 pounds (25 kilograms). A talent of gold weighed the same as a talent of silver, but was far more valuable, of course.
Tamesa River The river Thames.
Taprobane Modern Ceylon, Sri Lanka.
Taranis The Druidic God of thunder and lightning. His elemental nature was fire.
Tarnis River The river Tarn.
Tarpeian Rock Its precise location is still hotly debated, but we do know that it was quite visible from the lower Forum Romanum, as people being thrown off it could be seen from the rostra. Presumably it was an overhang at the top of the Capitoline cliffs, but since the drop was not much more than 80 feet (24.5 meters), the Tarpeian Rock must have been located directly over some sort of jagged outcrop—we have no evidence that anyone ever survived the fall. It was the traditional way to execute Roman citizen traitors and murderers, who were either thrown from it or forced to jump. The tribunes of the plebs were particularly fond of threatening to throw obstructive senators from the Tarpeian Rock. I have located it on a line from the temple of Ops.
tata The Latin diminutive for "father," akin to our "daddy." I have, by the way, elected to use the almost universal "mama" as the diminutive for "mother," but the actual Latin was *mamma.*
Tellus The Roman earth Goddess, of Italian origin. After the navel stone of Magna Mater was imported from Pessinus in 205 B.C., worship of Tellus became neglected inside the city of Rome, though she never fell out of favor with Italians. Tellus had a big temple on the Carinae, in earlier days imposing; by the last century B.C. it was dilapidated. Quintus Cicero is said to have restored it.
Tergeste Modern Trieste.
Teutones See **Cimbri.**
Thessalonica Modern Thessaloníki.
toga praetexta The purple-bordered toga which was reserved for curule magistrates. Children of both sexes wore the *toga praetexta* until they were registered as adults at about the age of sixteen.
togate The proper term to indicate a man wearing a toga.
Tolosa Modern Toulouse.
torc A thick round necklace or collar, usually of gold. It did not quite form a full circle, as it was interrupted by a gap about an inch (25mm) wide. This gap was worn to the front; the ends of the torc on either side of the gap were always larger and more ornamented, forming knobs or animal heads or other objects. The torc was the mark of a Gaul, either Celtic or Belgic, though some Germans wore it also. Miniature versions

of the torc, made of gold or silver, were awarded as military decorations for valor in the Roman army. They were worn on the shoulders of the shirt or cuirass.

Treves Modern Trier in Germany.

tribe *Tribus*. By the beginning of the Republic, *tribus* to a Roman was not an ethnic grouping of his people, but a political grouping of service only to the State. There were thirty-five tribes altogether; thirty-one of these were rural, only four were urban. The sixteen oldest tribes bore the names of the various original patrician clans, indicating that the citizens who belonged to these tribes were either members of the patrician families, or had once lived on land owned by these patrician families, or, after the Italian War of 91–88 B.C., had been put into these tribes by the censors. When Roman-owned territory in the Italian Peninsula began to expand during the early and middle Republic, tribes were added to accommodate the new Roman citizens within the Roman body politic. Full Roman citizen colonies also became the nuclei of fresh tribes. The four urban tribes were said to have been founded by King Servius Tullus, though they probably emerged somewhat later. The last tribe, the thirty-fifth, was created in 241 B.C. Every member of a tribe was entitled to register one vote in a tribal Assembly, but his vote counted only in helping to determine which way the tribe as a whole voted, for a tribe delivered just one vote, that of the majority of its members. This meant that in no tribal Assembly could the huge number of citizens enrolled in the four urban tribes sway the vote, as their four votes constituted only one-ninth of the full vote. Members of rural tribes were not disbarred from living in Rome, nor were their progeny made to register in an urban tribe. Most senators and knights of the First and Second Classes belonged to rural tribes. It was a mark of distinction to belong to a rural tribe.

tribune, military Those on the general's staff who were not elected tribunes of the soldiers but who ranked above cadets and below legates were called military tribunes. There were very many military tribunes in an army; they might but usually did not command legions, whereas they always acted as cavalry officers. They also did staff duties for the general.

tribune of the plebs This magistracy came into being early in the history of the Republic, when the Plebs was at complete loggerheads with the Patriciate. Elected by the tribal body of plebeians formed as the Plebeian Assembly, the tribunes of the plebs took an oath to defend the lives and property of members of the Plebs, and to rescue a member of the Plebs from the clutches of a patrician magistrate. By 450 B.C. there were ten tribunes of the plebs. A *lex Atinia de tribunis plebis in senatum legendis* in 149 B.C. provided that a man elected to the tribunate of the plebs automatically entered the Senate. Because they were not elected by the whole People (that is, by the patricians as well as the plebeians), they had no power under Rome's unwritten constitution and were not magistrates in the same way as tribunes of the soldiers, quaestors, curule aediles, praetors, consuls and censors; their magistracies were of the Plebs and their power in office rested in the oath the whole Plebs took to defend the sacrosanctity—the inviolability—of its elected tribunes. The power of the office also lay in the right of its magistrates to interpose a veto against almost any aspect of government: one single tribune of the plebs could veto the actions or laws of his nine fellow tribunes, or any—or all!—other magistrates, including consuls and censors; he could veto the holding of an election; he could veto the passing of any law; and he could veto decrees of the Senate, even those dealing with war and foreign affairs. Only a dictator (and perhaps an *interrex*) was not subject to the tribunician veto. Within his own Plebeian Assembly, the tribune of the plebs could even exercise the death penalty without trial if his right to proceed about his duties was denied him.

The tribune of the plebs had no imperium, and the authority vested in the office did not extend beyond the first milestone outside the city of Rome. Custom dictated that a man should serve only one term as a tribune of the plebs, but Gaius Gracchus put an end to that; even so, it was not usual for a man to stand more than once. The term of office was one year, and the tribunician year commenced on the tenth day of December. Headquarters were in the Basilica Porcia.

As the real power of the office was vested in negative action—the veto (it was called *intercessio*)—tribunician contribution to government tended to be more obstructive than constructive. The conservative elements in the Senate loathed the tribunes of the plebs—unless they owned them. A very few tribunes of the plebs were real social engineers. Tiberius and Gaius Sempronius Gracchus, Gaius Marius, Lucius Appuleius Saturninus, Publius Sulpicius Rufus, Aulus Gabinius, Titus Labienus, Publius Clodius, Publius Vatinius, Gaius Trebonius, Gaius Scribonius Curio and Marcus Antonius all defied the Senate; some of them died for it.

tribunus aerarius, tribuni aerarii These were men of knight's status whose 300,000-sestertius income made them junior to knights of the 400,000-sestertius census. See **knights** for further information.

trireme With the bireme, the commonest and most favored of all the ancient war galleys. By definition a trireme had three banks of oars, and with the advent of the trireme about 600 B.C. came the invention of the projecting box above the gunwale called an outrigger (later galleys, even biremes, were fitted with outriggers). In a trireme every oar was much the same length at about 15 feet (5 meters), this being relatively short. The average trireme was about 130 feet (40 meters) long, and the beam was no wider than 13 feet (4 meters) excluding the outrigger. The ratio was therefore about 10:1.

Only one rower manned an oar. The rower in the lowest bank the Greeks called a thalamite; he worked his oar through a port so close to the waterline that it was fitted with a leather cuff to keep the sea out. There were about 27 thalamites per side, giving a total of 54 thalamite oars. The rower in the middle bank was called a zygite; he worked his oar through a port just below the gunwale. Zygites equaled thalamites in number. The outrigger rower was called a thranite; he sat above and outboard of the zygite on a special bench within the outrigger housing. His oar projected from a gap in the bottom of the outrigger about 2 feet (600mm) beyond the ship's side. Because the outrigger could maintain its projection width when the hull narrowed fore and aft, there were 31 thranite rowers per side. A trireme was therefore powered by about 170 oars; the thranites in the outriggers had to work the hardest due to the fact that their oars hit the water at a sharper angle than the oars of zygites and thalamites.

With the trireme there had arrived a vessel absolutely suited for ramming. Rams now became two-pronged, bigger, heavier, and better armored. By 100 B.C. the genuine ship of the line in a war fleet was the trireme, as it combined speed, power, and splendid maneuverability. Most triremes were decked and could carry a complement of up to 50 marines. Mainly built from fir or some other lightweight pine, the trireme was light enough to be dragged out of the water at night; it could also be portaged on rollers for quite long distances. Because these light and porous ships became quickly waterlogged, they were routinely hauled out of the water each night.

If a ship of the line was well looked after, its seafaring life lasted a minimum of twenty years. A city or community (Rhodes, for instance) maintaining a standing navy always provided shipsheds for out-of-the-water storage of the fleet. It is the dimensions of these shipsheds as investigated by archaeologists which have confirmed that, no matter how many the oars or oarsmen, a war galley never grew to be much larger than 195 feet (60 meters) in length and 20 feet (6 meters) in the beam.

trophy This was a piece of captured enemy gear of sufficiently imposing appearance or repute to impress the civilian populace of the victorious side. If he won a significant battle or series of battles, it was the custom for a Roman general to set up trophies (usually suits of armor or standards). He might choose to do so on the actual battlefield as a memorial, or (as Pompey did) at the crest of a mountain pass, or inside a temple he vowed and built in Rome (the preferred alternative).

Tuatha The Druidic pantheon of Gods.

tumultus In the context used in this book, a state of civil war.

tunic The ubiquitous article of clothing for all the Mediterranean peoples of the ancient world, including the Greeks and Romans. A Roman tunic tended to be rather loose and shapeless, made without darts (the Greeks put in darts to give their tunics a waisted look); it covered the body from the shoulders and upper arms to the knees. Sleeves were probably set in (the ancients knew how to cut cloth, sew, and make clothing comfortable) and could be long. The Roman tunic was usually belted with a cord or with buckled leather, and was worn 3 inches (75mm) longer at the front of the knees than at the back. Upper-class Roman men were probably togate if outside the doors of their own homes, but there is little doubt that men of the lower classes wore their togas only on special occasions, such as the games, elections or a census. If the weather was wet and/or cold, some sort of *sagum* or cloak was preferred to a toga. The customary fabric for a tunic was wool and the customary color an oatmeal, but there is little doubt that a man could wear whatever color he wanted (other than purple, always the target of sumptuary laws); the ancients dyed beautifully and in many colors.

Ubii A German people who were in contact with the Rhenus (Rhine) River around its confluence with the Mosella (Moselle) and spread inland for a very considerable distance. They were famous cavalrymen.

Uxellodunum The main *oppidum* of the Cardurci. It is thought to be modern Puy d'Issolu.

vale Goodbye, farewell.

Valentia Modern Valence.

Varus River Now the Var River.

Vellaunodunum An *oppidum* belonging to the Senones. Modern Triguères.

Venus Erucina That aspect of Venus which ruled the act of love, particularly in its freest and least moral sense. On the feast of Venus Erucina prostitutes offered to her, as she was the protector of prostitutes. The temple of Venus Erucina outside the Colline Gate of Rome received a great deal of money in gifts from grateful prostitutes.

Venus Libitina That aspect of Venus (who was the Goddess of the life force) which ruled the extinction of the life force. A chthonic (underworld) deity of great importance in Rome, she owned a temple sited beyond the Servian Walls, more or less at the central point of Rome's vast necropolis (cemetery) on the Campus Esquilinus. Its exact location is not known. The temple precinct was large and had a grove of trees, presumably cypresses, as they were associated with death. In this precinct Rome's undertakers and funeral directors had their headquarters, operating, it would seem likely, from stalls or booths. The temple itself contained a register of Roman citizen deaths and was rich thanks to the accumulation of the coins which had to be paid to register a death. Should Rome for whatever reason cease to have consuls in office, the *fasces* of the consuls were deposited on special couches within the temple; the axes which were inserted into the *fasces* only outside Rome were also kept in Venus Libitina. I imagine that Rome's burial clubs (societies which formed to ensure that each member could be buried with rites and dignity at the expense of the club's funds), of which there were many, were in some way connected with Venus Libitina.

vergobret A magistrate of the Gauls. Two vergobrets were elected by a tribe to serve as leaders for one year. The office was more popular among the Celtic than the Belgic tribes, though the Treveri, very Belgic, elected vergobrets.

verpa A choice Latin obscenity used more in verbal abuse than as a sign of contempt. It referred to the penis—apparently in the erect state only, when the foreskin is drawn back—and had a homosexual connotation.

Vesontio The chief *oppidum* of the Sequani. Modern Besançon.

Vestal Virgins Vesta was a very old and numinous Roman Goddess having no mythology and no image. She was the hearth, the center of family life—and Roman society was cemented in the family. Her official public cult was personally supervised by the Pontifex Maximus, but she was so important that she had her own pontifices, the six Vestal Virgins.

The Vestal Virgin was inducted at from six to eight years of age, took vows of complete chastity, and served for thirty years. After the thirty years were done, she was released from her vows and sent back into the general community still of an age to bear children. Few retired Vestals ever did marry; it was thought unlucky to do so.

The chastity of the Vestal Virgins was Rome's public luck: a chaste College of Vestals was favored by Fortuna. When a Vestal was accused of unchastity she was formally brought to trial in a specially convened court; her alleged lover or lovers were tried in a separate court. If convicted, she was cast into an underground chamber dug for the purpose and left there to die, sealed away from all contact with humanity. If her lover was convicted, he faced flogging and crucifixion upon an unlucky tree.

Despite the horrors attached to unchastity, the Vestals did not lead a completely sequestered life. Provided the Chief Vestal knew and consented—and perhaps the Pontifex Maximus on some occasions—a Vestal could even attend a private dinner party. The College of Vestals stood on equal terms with the male priestly colleges and attended all religious banquets.

During Republican times the Vestal Virgins shared the Domus Publica with the Pontifex Maximus, though quite removed from him and his family. The House of Vesta was near the Domus Publica, and was small, round, and very old. It was not an inaugurated temple. A fire burned permanently inside the House of Vesta to symbolize the hearth; it was tended by the Vestals, and could not be allowed to go out for any reason.

Vienne Modern Vienne. Its Latin name was actually Vienna, but contemporary scholars have given it its French spelling because of confusion with modern Vienna, capital of Austria.

Vigemna River The Vienne River.

villa The country or rural residence of a wealthy Roman.

vir militaris, viri militares The *vir militaris* was what might be called a career soldier. His whole life revolved around the army, and he continued to serve in the army (as a military tribune) after his obligatory number of years or campaigns had finished. If he wanted to command a legion he had to enter the Senate, and if he wanted to command an army he had to attain election as praetor.

Virodunum An *oppidum* belonging to a sept of the Treveri known as the Mediomatrices. Modern Verdun.

voting Roman voting was timocratic, in that the power of a man's vote was powerfully influenced by economic status, and in that voting was indirect. Whether an individual was voting in the Centuries or the tribes, his own personal vote could influence only the collective verdict of the Century or tribe in which he polled. Juridical voting was different. A juror's vote did have a direct bearing on the outcome of a trial, as the jury's verdict was reached by a majority, not, as now, complete unanimity. To be a juror, however, a man had to be at least a *tribunus aerarius*.

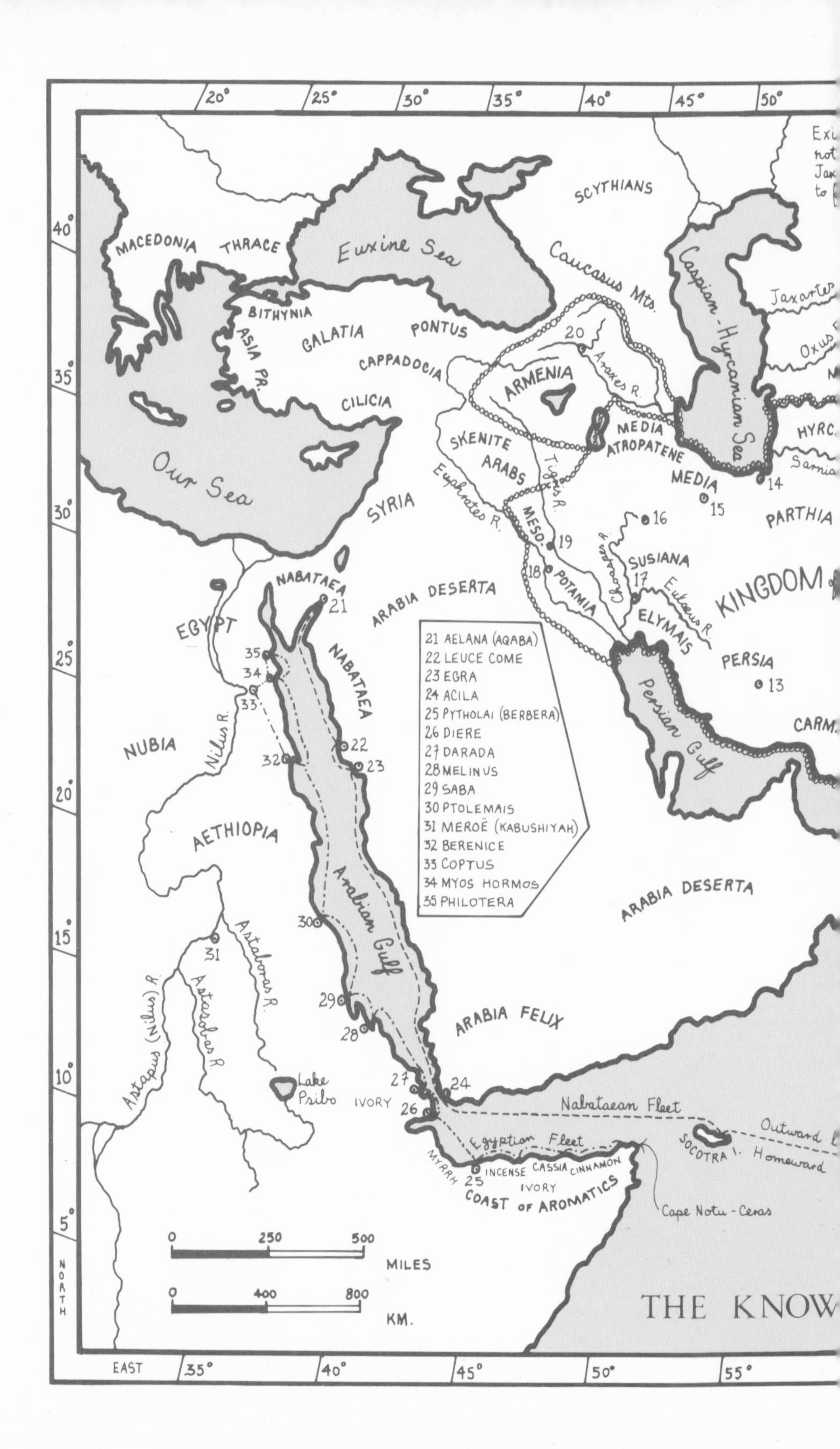

20°
25°
30°
35°
40°
45°
50°
SCYTHIANS
MACEDONIA
THRACE
Euxine Sea
Caucasus Mts.
Caspian-Hyrcanian Sea
BITHYNIA
ASIA PR.
GALATIA
PONTUS
CAPPADOCIA
CILICIA
ARMENIA
Araxes R.
MEDIA
ATROPATENE
SKENITE
ARABS
Tigris R.
Euphrates R.
Our Sea
SYRIA
MEDIA
PARTHIA
MESO.
POTAMIA
Choaspes R.
SUSIANA
Eulaeus R.
ELYMAIS
KINGDOM
PERSIA
Persian Gulf
NABATAEA
ARABIA DESERTA
EGYPT
NABATAEA
NUBIA
Nilus R.
AETHIOPIA
Arabian Gulf
ARABIA DESERTA
Astaboras R.
Astapus (Nilus) R.
Astasobas R.
Lake Psibo
IVORY
ARABIA FELIX
Nabataean Fleet
Egyptian Fleet
SOCOTRA I.
Homeward
MYRRH
INCENSE
CASSIA
CINNAMON
IVORY
COAST OF AROMATICS
Cape Notu-Ceras
21 AELANA (AQABA)
22 LEUCE COME
23 EGRA
24 ACILA
25 PYTHOLAI (BERBERA)
26 DIERE
27 DARADA
28 MELINUS
29 SABA
30 PTOLEMAIS
31 MEROË (KABUSHIYAH)
32 BERENICE
33 COPTUS
34 MYOS HORMOS
35 PHILOTERA
0 250 500
MILES
0 400 800
KM.
THE
NORTH
EAST
35°
40°
45°
50°
55°
40°
35°
30°
25°
20°
15°
10°
5°